D0193042

Sister Beneath the Sheet

By the same author

A Healthy Body
Murder Makes Tracks
A Whiff of Sulphur
Unknown Hand
Murder, I Presume

SISTER BENEATH THE SHEET

GILLIAN LINSCOTT

St. Martin's Press
New York

SISTER BENEATH THE SHEET. Copyright © 1991 by Gillian Linscott. All rights reserved. Printed in the United States of America. No part of this book may be used or reproduced in any manner whatsoever without written permission except in the case of brief quotations embodied in critical articles or reviews. For information, address St. Martin's Press, 175 Fifth Avenue, New York, N.Y. 10010.

Library of Congress Cataloging-in-Publication Data

Linscott, Gillian.
Sister beneath the sheet / Gillian Linscott.
p. cm.
ISBN 0-312-06464-0
I. Title.
PR6062.I54S58 1991
823'.914—dc20 91-20537
CIP

First published in Great Britain by Scribners, a division of Macdonald & Co. (Publishers) Limited.

First U.S. Edition: September 1991
10 9 8 7 6 5 4 3 2 1

Sister Beneath the Sheet

ONE

THE STORY BEGAN FOR ME in the middle of April, only nine days after I was let out of Holloway. I'd been relaxing at my home in Hampstead, enjoying being able to take baths when I wanted to and getting to know my cats again, until a cab drew up outside and Emmeline Pankhurst stepped out of it.

'Nell, my dear, I want you to go to Biarritz at once.'

'Oh,' I said, 'I'm not really so bad. Two days at Cookham will do very well.'

I can never resist teasing Emmeline a little. She has many strengths, but a sense of humour is not one of them.

'It's a delicate situation. A woman has died there, in distressing circumstances, and left us a great deal of money.'

'How much?'

'Possibly as much as fifty thousand pounds.'

'Wonderful. That would mean we could support fifty suffrage candidates at the next election. Who was she?'

For once Emmeline seemed at a loss for words.

'It's not easy for me to tell you, Nell.'

'Surely we know her name.'

'Apparently she was a Miss Brown.'

I waited.

'She had a *nom de guerre*, so to speak. Topaz.'

I waited again.

'She was a . . . a . . .'

I took pity.

'If she was the Topaz Brown I've heard of, she was a highly successful prostitute.'

Emmeline nodded, colouring up like a débutante.

'She's dead?'

'It seems she killed herself. Worn out, I suppose, by her degraded way of life.'

'And left us all her money. Was she one of us?'

'I don't see how she could have been. The question is, should we take it?'

'Fifty thousand pounds? Of course we should take it.'

I knew the state of our finances better than Emmeline did.

'I thought that would be your attitude. It makes you the most appropriate person to go to Biarritz and look after our interests. You even speak French.'

I didn't relish the prospect of weeks of French and English lawyers and probably litigious relatives, but fifty thousand is fifty thousand. Also, curiosity is one of my favourite vices and I was already very curious about the legacy of Topaz Brown.

'How did we hear about this?'

Emmeline looked grim. 'I received a long telegraph message yesterday from Roberta Fieldfare. It seems she's staying in Biarritz. Goodness knows why.'

'Bobbie? I shared a cell with her mother, Lady Fieldfare.'

She was serving three months for throwing horse dung at a cabinet minister. Her sister Maud, who's sixty-nine years old but has a sounder aim, actually hit the target and got four months. The Fieldfares, aunt, mother and daughter, are as enthusiastic as they come in our cause of votes for women, but all of them as wild as hares. They are not Emmeline's favourite allies.

'I'll call on young Bobbie as soon as I get there. Did she say where she was staying?'

'I should prefer that you didn't, Nell. In fact, I think it would be best if you keep your activities as discreet as possible while you do what has to be done in Biarritz.'

In other words, ease the legacy quietly into the bank account of the Women's Social and Political Union without creating any additional gossip about its source.

I promised to do my best, made arrangements with my neighbour to take care of my long-suffering cats and looked up timetables. I left Charing Cross at ten o'clock on Monday morning. At seven twenty-seven on Tuesday morning I stepped on to the sunlit platform of Biarritz station after travelling through the night from Paris. It was six days since Topaz had been found dead. I'd consulted my *Baedeker* on the journey and found a reasonably priced pension, the St Julien, listed in the Avenue Carnot, away from the sea but not far from the town centre. I took a cab there, secured a room, deposited my suitcase then breakfasted off coffee and croissants in the café next door. As I ate and drank I considered what I should do first.

One of the few things I'd been able to find out before leaving London was that Topaz Brown was found dead in her rooms at the Hôtel des Empereurs. I decided to take a stroll and look at the place. I'd never been to Biarritz before and, although I knew the King's visits had helped to make it fashionable, I was struck by the luxury and gaiety of it, especially after the greyness of prison life. Most of the grand hotels were clustered around the casino and main bathing establishment, behind a rocky headland called the Atalaye. Long sandy beaches stretched away to the north, more beaches southward to the Spanish border. The waves thumped in with shattering force against the headland and a stiff Atlantic breeze blew, but the early strollers parading in front of the hotels looked as if they'd come straight from Mayfair. Manservants pushed elderly invalids along in bath chairs, women struggled to hold on to hats with decorations of bird wings and silk streamers that seemed designed to make them take flight, uniformed nursemaids clung to the hands of children in sailors' suits. In another few years, probably, the fashionable world would move on and Biarritz would be left to the waves and the fishermen. Meanwhile the grand hotels towered along the parade like a line of great ships at anchor.

The Hôtel des Empereurs was easy to find, one of the largest and newest in the resort. It was built in a modern baroque style with wrought iron balconies bulging out from every floor, its frontage a surge of garlands, gymnastic nymphs and sea horses in terracotta. Two caryatids stood left and right of the front steps, stretching to the first floor and supporting a balcony on their heads. At either end, seven or eight floors up, were round turrets roofed with copper domes, the shape of inverted egg cups. There were rooms in each turret with windows facing north, south and out to sea. In the one on the right the blinds were down. I stood for a while, watching people going in and out of the hotel, wondering what it would feel like to be so tired of it, or so disgusted with it all that extinction would seem preferable. I was as eager as anybody to take Topaz's money, but thought I owed it to her to find out something more about her.

'Speaking for myself . . .' the solicitor said. He got up from his desk, fidgeted with a pile of papers, walked over to the window, as if reluctant to commit himself. 'Speaking for myself, I can only say that I found Miss Brown a very affable and businesslike woman. In fact, until this business of the will, we found her the ideal client.'

Topaz's lawyer had turned out to be English, and to have an office in the same building as the consulate. Apparently with so many rich and influential English people spending several weeks of the year in Biarritz, their professional advisers migrated with them.

'She'd been a client of yours for some time, then?'

'For some weeks. We were engaged in a property transaction on her behalf.'

He was being rather more forthcoming than I'd expected. There'd been just the suspicion of a wince when I introduced myself to him, but lawyers tend to be cautious when faced with people who've served prison sentences for throwing bricks through the window of 10 Downing Street.

'Was her will drawn up recently?'

He looked surprised, suspicious even.

'You haven't been told?'

'We know none of the details.'

'Last Wednesday afternoon.'

He said the three words very quickly and turned away to the window, as if disclaiming any responsibility for them.

'But . . . I thought . . . didn't she?'

'Miss Brown was found dead by her maid on Thursday morning.'

'So she made the will only half a day before she died? Did you see her? Did you have any idea . . .?'

The lawyer walked heavily back to his desk. He was quite a young man, but bald, and the sun glinted on his pink head.

'Miss Bray, I am in an awkward position. You may not know that Miss Brown's brother is challenging the will on the grounds that she could not have been of sound mind when she made it. I assume that your organisation may find itself contesting this in court. You will therefore appreciate that, in the circumstances, there's nothing more I can say to you.'

I did appreciate it. I thanked him for his politeness and told him that he'd be hearing officially from the Women's Social and Political Union in due course. As he showed me out I said: 'You mentioned a maid. I suppose there'd be no objection to my speaking to her.'

'None that I can see. You may find her a little . . . er . . . embattled. She was very loyal to Miss Brown.'

'Do you know her name, or where I can find her?'

'Tansy Mills. She's still at Miss Brown's suite at the Hôtel des Empereurs. Miss Brown had paid for the suite till the end of the month, and somebody must pack her things.'

'When is the funeral?'

'That is yet to be arranged.'

From the way he said it, I gathered there were difficulties there, but he wouldn't be the one to tell me about them. It was mid-morning by then. I made my way back to the Hôtel des Empereurs and, at the reception desk, asked for Topaz Brown's maid.

I got some curious looks, but a boy in a pill-box hat and gold-braided uniform took me up in the lift from the back of the foyer. The gates opened at the seventh floor. He led me along a crimson-carpeted corridor, and knocked at a pair of double doors painted in white and gold.

'Who's there? Who is it?'

The voice, speaking English with traces of an East London accent, came sharply from inside. The boy shrugged and walked away.

'My name's Nell Bray. Are you Tansy Mills?'

'Yes. What is it?'

'I'd like to talk to you about Miss Brown.'

'Did the lawyer send you?'

'Yes.'

It wasn't far from the truth and seemed to be the only way I'd get in.

'Wait a minute.'

There was a pause, the sound of a key turning, then one of the doors opened. The woman on the other side of it couldn't have been much more than five foot two in height, but broad shouldered and with a sense of pugnacity about her. Her nose was long, her eyes brown and angry. She was wearing a plain black dress and her hair, already showing signs of grey, was pulled back into a tight pleat. She looked a most respectable little body.

'You're English? Thank goodness for that. I'm tired to the bone with all of them jabbering away in French to me, except that lawyer, and he's not much better even if it is in English. And none of them listening to a word I say.'

She'd closed the door behind me and we were standing in a wide entrance hall, with doors leading off it, in the centre and to the right. To the left I noticed a small lift cage.

'Well, what do you want to know? Are you going to listen, or do you just want to jabber like the rest of them?'

'I want to listen.'

She looked at me and pushed open the door in front of us.

'You'd better come in and sit down, though it's all a muddle. I've been trying to pack up her things. Mr Jules is helping, but the more you pack the more there is.'

It was an enormous round room, with windows looking out over the promenade and up and down the coast. I realised that I was inside one of the two towers I'd looked at early that morning, the left-hand one. Islands of good furniture were scattered round it, armchairs and chaise longues with small tables beside them. Almost every available surface was heaped with gleaming piles of dresses, cloaks and shawls, or piled with papers, envelopes and leather cases. Tansy swept an armful off a chair for me.

'I suppose you want a cup of tea.'

'Yes please.'

As she took a spirit lamp from a cupboard, I tried to explain myself.

'Miss Brown left our organisation a very large sum of money. We know almost nothing about her.'

She put down a small tea kettle and stared at me, fists on hips.

'You're the ones who've been causing all the trouble over votes?'

'Yes.'

Feeling the anger radiating out of her, I decided not to add to it.

She walked across the room, trying to stamp her feet, hindered by the thickness of the carpet.

'Of all the silly things she ever did . . . Still, it was no use arguing with her once she'd made up her mind.'

She filled the kettle, with much clashing of metal and china. It was obvious that if Topaz Brown had been an unlikely convert to our cause, she'd had no success in convincing her maid.

Once the kettle was on, Tansy plonked herself down opposite me, sitting on the edge of a chair crowded with guides and railway timetables.

'What do you expect me to tell you, then?'

'All you can remember about the day before she died.'

It was clearly no use beating about the bush with Tansy, and it looked as if our claim to that fifty thousand pounds would hinge on Topaz's behaviour on that last day. To my surprise, Tansy seemed almost pleased.

'I'll do that. I'd tell anybody, only they won't listen.'

'I'm listening.'

She took a deep breath. 'The whole day before? Well, it was ten o'clock on the Thursday morning when I found her. If you go back a day from that, that's ten o'clock on the Wednesday. I'd taken her breakfast on a tray as usual, jug of chocolate, thick and creamy, those little twisty

French rolls she liked. I tapped on the door and said, "Your breakfast ma'am." I always started the day formal.'

'In this room?'

'No, in her bedroom, of course. Where else would she be?'

'On her own?'

The question had to be asked, but it annoyed Tansy.

'Of course she was on her own. I wouldn't have disturbed her otherwise, would I?'

'I suppose not. How did she seem?'

'Just like she always seemed in the mornings, curled up in the sheets like a big sleepy cat. Naturally lovely, she was, and don't let that woman on the other side or anybody else tell you different. Like that, only better.'

She pointed to a picture on the wall. I hadn't noticed it when I came in because the light wasn't on it, but when I looked at it, it seemed to glow with its own light. It was done in pastels, in tones of tawny, gold and apricot and showed a woman lying back, hair loose, among gold draperies and smiling a kind of lazy, satisfied smile. A replete cat rather than a predatory one.

'That was done by one of her artists. She liked being painted. You asked me what she was like that last morning, and it was just like that. Anyway, I put the tray down on the table by her bed and drew back the curtains to let the sun in, like I always did, and she asked me if the post had come.'

'Did she seem anxious about anything in the post?'

Again, she seemed aggrieved at the suggestion.

'No, she did not, and I'll tell you how I know. I'd got the post ready on the table outside the door, so I brought it in to her. It was much the same as it always is, all those square stiff envelopes with the crests on them and the foreign gentlemen's smells . . .'

'Smells?'

'You know, the oil they put on their hair and their beards and so on. She just glanced at them, put them to one side without even looking at them properly and said to me, "Have you heard from your little sister?" That's the kind of lady she was. A handful of European nobility and she puts them aside to ask after my sister, a ten-bob-a-week seamstress in a sweat shop off the Mile End Road.'

She glared at me as if challenging me to contradict her. I kept quiet, realising that I must let her get on with it in her own way.

'So I said no, I hadn't heard anything from Rose, and she said, "Do you think she'll come?" You see, two weeks before she'd caught me looking down in the mouth and got it out of me that I was worrying about Rose. Even then, though, I only told her the half of it, that Rose wasn't strong, not a work-pony like me, and I was worried about her working all hours, lodging in a fleapit of a place. Topaz said, without even stopping to think about it, "Well, you must write to her and tell her to come over here. I'll pay her to keep my underwear in good order." I thought she was joking, but there was no satisfying her until I'd written a letter to Rose and sent it off, with a ten pound note that Topaz had given me for her fare. And that last morning, she wasn't asking about Rose because she was worried about her ten pounds, don't think that.'

I said I was sure she wasn't. Tansy got up and poured a jet of boiling water into a silver teapot, swished it round, poured the water into a basin. She was angry with the world, with me, with everything including the tea kettle, but she still didn't forget to warm the pot. She was silent while she finished making the tea and I thought of what she'd told me so far. If Topaz had killed herself in a fit of madness or self-disgust, there'd apparently been no signs of it at the start of her last day. That is, if Tansy was to be believed. She poured the tea and put a white and gold cup on the table beside me, pushing papers away to make room for it.

'Anyway, when I told her I hadn't heard anything from Rose, I must have let too much of what I was thinking into my voice, because she put down her cup and said, "What's the matter, Tansy?" And, God forgive me, I went straight over to the bed and told her. "I'm afraid she's going to get herself into trouble with the police, ma'am."

' "What sort of trouble?"

'So I told her Rose wasn't bad in herself, only she'd been taking up with a bad set, giving her ideas she shouldn't have, wanting things she's got no business to want. She gave me one of her straight looks and said, "Are you trying to tell me your little sister's gone on the game?"

'Before I could think I blurted out, "No, ma'am, it's not that bad. At least . . ." Then she laughed and I felt myself going hot and knew my face was redder than a beet. I could have bitten my silly tongue out. But she only lay back there on her pillows and laughed, that deep laugh that a man who wrote a poem about her said was like a lioness purring.

' "Oh, my poor Tansy. There's a big difference between street corners in the East End and all this, now isn't there?"

'I nearly tripped over my silly tongue saying yes, of course there was. She gave that laugh again.

' "The difference is that this is so very much more comfortable. Now, what are these things your sister's got no business to want?"

'I blurted out: "Votes for women, ma'am."

'This time she laughed until I thought she'd never stop, and I stood there starting to get annoyed with her, as I did sometimes. At last she said, "Are you trying to tell me your little sister's a suffragette?"

' "That's about the size of it, ma'am." '

Tansy stopped for breath and took a gulp of tea. Her face, from embarrassment or indignation, was as red as she'd described it. In spite of the need not to annoy her, I couldn't let this pass.

'But why were you so concerned about it, Miss Mills? There are women from all walks of life in our movement. I've just been sharing a prison cell with a woman with a title.'

Tansy glared at me. 'It's all very well for the likes of them. They can afford to be political.'

'Afford?'

'If lady this or countess that hits a policeman and gets put in prison, it doesn't matter to her, does it? She doesn't have to worry about losing her job without a reference and ending up in the workhouse. Girls like my sister who've got precious little in the first place – they're the one's who can't afford to lose it.'

'Has Rose hit a policeman?'

'Not yet, as far as I know. But she's been on a big march to the Houses of Parliament, so it's only a matter of time.'

It was not the time or place to begin the political education of Tansy Mills. Instead, I asked how Topaz had reacted. Had Tansy, for instance, guessed her employer was interested in women's suffrage too?

'The papers were full of it before we left London, but that was two months ago, back in February. We always had more important things to talk about. Anyway, that last morning when I told her about Rose she just stretched her arms, in the way she had when she was waking up properly, and said: "It's all such nonsense." '

'She said votes for women was nonsense?'

'Votes for anybody. She said politics was half greed and half gossip. She said she'd known a fair number of politicians, and there wasn't one she'd vote for, not one.'

And yet, within hours of that conversation, Topaz had left us her fortune. If Tansy could be believed, it looked as if the brother would have a strong case in court. I wondered if he'd been in touch with Tansy already.

'What happened after that?'

'She finished her breakfast and opened her letters.'

'Was there anything unusual?'

For once, Tansy hesitated. 'Not really.'

'But there was something?'

'Nothing special. One of them was a big envelope with a little box inside it, and a card. She smiled to herself at what was on the card, then showed me what was in the box.'

'What was it?'

'Nothing special, as I said. Just a big fire opal in a pendant. It looked a bit old-fashioned to me and it was nothing to the things some of them gave her.'

'But she seemed pleased with it?'

'Quite pleased, yes. But it was nothing to get excited about.'

'What then?'

'Well, we got ready for her bath. I laid out her stockings

and the ivory silk chemise with the apricot ribbons and Chantilly lace. One of the ribbons was hanging by a few threads so I had to see to it, and she said that just showed we needed Rose over to help. She was always very fastidious about her lingerie. That was one of the things that shocked me when I found her.'

Her voice went cold and bleak. I think, while she'd been talking about Topaz, Tansy had almost forgotten that she was dead. Now she sat there, staring across her tea cup at the window. From the road below us the sound of hooters and carriage wheels reminded me that the town was going about its normal business of amusing itself.

I said, as gently as I could, 'From what you say, it was all very happy and normal that last morning, but that night, she killed herself. Can you . . .?'

She crashed her cup down and stood up. At five foot two she could hardly tower over me even when I was sitting down, but she did her best.

'You're as bad as the rest of them. Haven't you been listening to a word I've been telling you?'

'Of course I have. But if she killed herself . . .'

'She didn't kill herself. Topaz didn't kill herself. She had no reason to kill herself. She was murdered.'

Alarmed at the course her grief was taking, I stood up and put my arm round her stiff but unresisting shoulders.

'Miss Mills, I know you're upset, I know it must have been a shock for you, but . . .'

She glared at me from close quarters, dry eyed.

'She was murdered,' she repeated.

From outside in the hallway a bell rang.

'That will be Mr Jules. I'll have to go down and let him in.'

Efficient again, as if the word 'murdered' had never been spoken, she took a key from her pocket and hurried out. I heard a lift going down, then coming up again. Who Mr Jules was, beyond the man who was helping Tansy sort out Topaz's papers, I had no idea. I stood there with the luxurious detritus of Topaz Brown's career around me, wondering how much, if any, of this I should report to Emmeline.

TWO

WHEN JULES ESTEVAN WALKED IN and found me there, his look was unmistakably one of relief. I don't know what, if anything, Tansy had told him in the lift, but I think he was glad to see anybody who might share the burden of looking after Tansy. As for me, my impression was of a tall young man, in his early thirties, almost painfully thin, with the kind of face you see carved in marble on mediaeval tombs. To say he was well dressed would be like calling Leonardo da Vinci a man who sketched. His suit, hat and waistcoat were a harmony of greys and silvers. He wore pale lilac-coloured gloves and carried a black ebony cane, topped with silver.

'May I introduce myself? My name is Jules Estevan. I was a friend of Miss Brown.'

His voice was low and pleasant, with just a trace of accent to show that English was not his first language.

'He's the one who wrote the poem I told you about,' Tansy said.

I told him my name. 'You are a poet, Mr Estevan?'

He shrugged: 'I am a *flâneur*, Miss Bray.'

He said it as one would say lawyer or doctor. It struck me that I was probably meeting the first of Topaz's clients. He seemed to read my mind.

'You may be wondering about my relationship with Miss Brown. I can claim to be nothing other than a friend. We met here last season. I found her one of the least tedious people in the resort and she was good enough to return the compliment. Shall we sit down?'

Tansy didn't seem to resent Jules acting as host. She remained standing while I resumed my seat and Jules settled himself on a *chaise-longue*, moving aside a pile of lacy things.

I said, 'I represent the Women's Social and Political Union. I've been asking Miss Mills about the events leading up to Miss Brown's death.'

I didn't say suicide. I didn't want another outburst from Tansy. He nodded slightly. I had the impression that he already knew about the brother's challenge to the legacy. I don't know why, except Jules always contrived to give the impression of knowing about everything and being bored by most of it.

'I've told her she was murdered,' Tansy said.

'I'm sure you have. What exactly did you want to know, Miss Bray?'

'I want to understand more about her state of mind when she made her will.'

He smiled a little. 'I think we can help with that, can't we Tansy?'

She'd left the room for a minute and returned with a glass and an opened half bottle on a tray.

'Today,' he said, 'you'll only find this vintage in three places: the Royal cellars in Budapest, the Vatican – and Topaz's little store here in Biarritz. She and I usually shared a half bottle at this time of day. Will you join me in drinking to her memory now?'

It would have been ill-mannered to refuse. Tansy, her face impassive, went to fetch another glass and Jules poured for both of us.

'To Topaz.'

'To Topaz.'

We drank. I said, 'You came to see her every day?'

'At noon, every day except Saturday and Sunday. It was a ritual. She always liked to know what everybody had been doing the night before. I was usually able to tell her a little. She laughed a lot. She enjoyed laughing.'

He said it like a man who rarely laughed himself.

'And that last day, the Wednesday, you came as usual?'

'Oh yes.'

'And what did you talk about?'

'People. About Lord Beverley and his father. About La

Pucelle. About a dozen things that probably wouldn't mean much to you. She'd always tell me what invitations had come in the morning post, and we'd discuss which would be amusing and which wouldn't.'

'Was there anything else about the post?'

'She showed me a pendant that had been sent to her and wanted me to guess who it was from. I made a guess or two, but she said none of them was right.'

'A valuable pendant?'

He shook his head. 'Only opal.'

I could feel Tansy's eyes on me. She must have guessed I was testing the truth of what she'd told me.

'Did you talk about her work?'

I expected a cooling of the atmosphere. So far both Tansy and Jules Estevan had been talking as if Topaz Brown were any lady of leisure. I was almost falling into the trap of it, and thought it time to introduce a little reality. Jules seemed quite unconcerned.

'Well, Miss Bray, I suppose you'd have to class poor Lord Beverley as work.'

'You mean he was one of her clients? And why poor Lord Beverley?'

'Client. What a terrible word. It makes Topaz sound like a dentist. As for "poor", he's spent all his money and his father the Duke's arrived to take him home to England. That's what Topaz and I were talking about.'

'Was she disappointed at losing him?'

'Not in the least. I remember saying at the time that she seemed in no hurry to choose a replacement. I can see why now, of course.'

He sipped his wine, looking at me over the glass.

'And who is La Pucelle?'

'Oh dear, hasn't Tansy told you about La Pucelle yet? It's her favourite topic of conversation.'

From behind me, Tansy made a derisive noise. It struck me that the relationship between her and Jules was a strange one, demanding none of the respect usual between a rich man and a lady's maid.

'Well, since she hasn't, I should tell you that as far as Topaz Brown had a rival in Biarritz it was Marie de la

Tourelle, known amongst the vulgar as La Pucelle. I'm sure Tansy could tell you why.'

Tansy said, explosively, 'He says it's French for a girl who's still a virgin. Goodness knows why, because she's no girl and she certainly isn't the other thing either.'

Jules smiled. 'It was something of a tribute to her constant martyrdoms. One of the most interesting things to an onlooker about the rivalry between Topaz and Marie was the contrast between them. Topaz made no secret of enjoying her work, and liking men. Marie lets it be known that she is of the nobility, fallen into her profession through hard times. She, I think, prefers the company of women, except in the line of business, and often claims to regret the life she's forced to lead.'

Tansy said: 'There's always talk that she's going to join a convent and repent, but nothing seems to come of it.'

'Is she as beautiful as Topaz was?'

I couldn't help asking it. I was looking at Topaz's picture at the time.

'Yes,' said Jules.

'Not a bit of it,' said Tansy.

She glared at him, while he went on talking to me.

'Marie is tall and very slender, with the profile of a goddess and long, long hair as dark as the road to perdition. Put her next to Topaz – not that you'd often see them together – it was like the goddess of dawn next to the goddess of the shades.'

'But you said she was a rival to Topaz.'

'Some people, Miss Bray, prefer the shades. Two men have committed suicide over Marie, and two others are in prison for fighting a duel. For some men, that's part of the attraction. It's like taking death itself to bed and surviving.'

Tansy said: 'Nobody was ever the worse for taking up with Topaz.'

'That's probably quite true. I don't know quite how to describe it, Miss Bray, but there was always an abundance of life about Topaz. I think that was part of her success. Men thought, so to speak, that some of that vitality would rub off on them.'

He looked at me closely. I don't know if he expected to

see me blush, but if so, he was disappointed.

Tansy said: 'Lord Beverley soon found out which one of them he preferred.'

'Yes indeed. One of Topaz's little triumphs. In fact, I suppose one has to say her last triumph. She took Lord Beverley away from La Pucelle, apparently without even trying.'

'She wouldn't have to try. She could get more than Lord Beverley without trying.'

Tansy was blushing again, hot with indignation. Jules caught my eye and smiled. I thought he enjoyed teasing her, and it wasn't kind.

Tansy stalked over to the window, and stared out.

'I'll bet she's in there, watching us.'

'In where?'

'Marie lives in the other tower, the south one, just like this. She owns a villa just outside the town, but as soon as word got round that Topaz had rented this tower suite for the season, Marie had to have the other one at any price.'

There was an angry exclamation from Tansy.

'Just look at it.'

Then, as Jules and I crossed to the window. 'No, don't look. That's just what she wants.'

Too late, Jules and I were already beside her at the window, looking across to the opposite tower. All the blinds except one were down, but at that window I had a glimpse of a pale profile and a white hand.

'What's she looking at?'

Jules opened a door and stepped out on to the balcony. In spite of Tansy's protests, I followed. We looked down and there in front of the main doors was a florist's gig, drawn by two white ponies. You could only just see the gig and the ponies because it was packed from front to back with white lilies. Behind it two more gigs were drawn up, just as packed, and we could see lines of page boys staggering into reception with armfuls of lilies almost as large as themselves.

'Look at it,' said Jules. 'It's a positive wantonness of purity.'

'Are they all for Marie de la Tourelle?'

'Who else? It's probably the Archduke, apologising for laying lustful hands upon her.'

'He must have bought up every lily in Biarritz.'

Even high up on our balcony, you could smell them above the scent of the sea. The figure had gone from the window opposite, but as we watched lines of boys bearing lilies passed across it.

Jules said sadly, 'How Topaz would have laughed.'

We went back into the salon, where Tansy was busying herself ostentatiously with piles of clothes.

'I don't know how you can stand there and look at her, Mr Jules. If there were any rights in this country . . .'

He picked up his glass and said sharply: 'Tansy, please don't start that again.'

'Well, what am I supposed to do? Stand there and watch her queening it day after day and not say anything, after what she's done?'

She thumped a shawl into a small square, dropped it, had to pick it up and start again. From her voice, I think she was near to tears.

Jules said, sounding weary: 'Tansy thinks Marie murdered Topaz.'

'What!'

'Well, who else did if she didn't? That one hated her, grudged her every breath she took. Then in the end, when she couldn't get at her any other way, she just came and poisoned her.'

She picked up another shawl, took a corner of it in each hand then another corner of it in her teeth, pulled so hard that the delicate fabric tore.

'Now look what you made me do. All her nice things . . .'

She was really crying now. Jules put his arm round her, crouched down beside her.

'Tansy, you mustn't go round saying things like that. You could get yourself into serious trouble.'

'Why won't anyone believe me?'

Between us we managed to get her to sit down on the chaise longue, drink a little of the wine. She became calmer, but still insistent.

'They're all trying to make out she killed herself. She'd

never kill herself, not Topaz.'

I looked at Jules.

'Do you believe Topaz killed herself?'

'What else can I think? I certainly don't believe that Marie crept in unobserved and tipped half a bottle of laudanum into her wine.'

'It was laudanum that killed her?'

'Yes.'

'Did she take it habitually?'

Tansy said indignantly: 'She did not. She didn't have it in the place.'

Jules nodded. 'Topaz never had any trouble sleeping.'

'And yet on your evidence, up to and beyond midday on the Wednesday, Topaz was behaving quite normally. When did you leave her?'

'Just before one o'clock. I'd hoped to lunch with her, but she said no, there was something she wanted to discuss with Tansy. I said I'd meet her for a drive that afternoon, if she wasn't otherwise occupied, and left them to it.'

Tansy was calmer, staring at me.

'So Topaz had lunch here on her own?'

She shook her head. 'No, Topaz and me had lunch here together.'

I must have looked surprised.

'Don't think that was happening all the time, but we'd do it sometimes. On her birthday and mine, providing there weren't any other engagements, we'd sit down together and talk. Topaz wasn't ashamed of where she came from, not like that one over there. Anyway, that Wednesday, she said she had something to tell me and I should order lunch from the kitchens for both of us. Those little orange-coloured melons, a bit of lobster salad, raspberries and a bottle of her special Chablis. I said, a bit cheeky, "Whose birthday is it, then?" and she said I'd soon find out. I thought she probably wanted to tell me when we were going back to England. She liked to be back in good time for Ascot. Anyway, when we were well into the lobster salad, she sprang it on me.'

Jules was watching both of us like a man who'd heard it before.

'Sprang what?'

'She said she wasn't going back to England. "Not for Ascot?" I said.

' "Not for Ascot or anything else. I'm going to retire, Tansy." I didn't know what to say. There wasn't anybody in Europe who'd had more success than she had. So, as usual, I blurted out the wrong thing.

' "You're good for a few years yet. Your looks haven't even started to go."

'She took no offence.

' "Years ago, Tansy, before I knew you, I swore I'd give it up when I found my first grey hair. It's happened."

' "Where is it? I can't see it."

'I looked at her hair, still hanging down loose over her shoulders.

' "You look as if you wanted to swat it, Tansy, like a wasp. Who said it was on my head?"

'Then she laughed more, seeing me go red.

' "It's cruel, isn't it, Tansy? I do enjoy making you blush. That's probably why we get on so well. You do all my blushing for me."

'I said nothing, because it was still sinking in.

' "Oh, I know I could keep at it for another year or two, before my figure starts spreading and my complexion goes. But I'm thirty-one next birthday and I've been at it for thirteen years. I've made all the money I need for what I want to do."

'I asked her what that was, and she said she was going to buy a vineyard. She'd been looking round and she thought she'd found the right one. She said she was going to let herself get fat and her hair could go how it liked. She was going to drive herself around in a pony cart and shout at her workmen when they got lazy. She'd invite some men to visit her, but only the ones like Mr Jules or some of the others that made her laugh. She was excited as a girl about it, and I thought, well why shouldn't she, after all. So I raised a glass to her and her vineyard and wished her the very best of luck.'

I looked across at Jules.

'Did Topaz say anything to you about this?'

'Not at the time. I think she wanted to tell Tansy first.'

'But what other time was there?'

'You'll have to hear the rest of the story. Go on, Tansy.'

I noticed again that the anger seemed to drain away from Tansy when she was remembering Topaz. She was happy to talk about her.

'Well, the next thing she wanted was me to come with her to this vineyard, as housekeeper. I said she wouldn't really need me there and I'd miss England if I was away from it all the time, but I'd come and visit her. She said she'd miss me, and that we'd stay here in Biarritz for another month, to pack up and give Rose a bit of a holiday. Then she'd give me our fares back to London and a hundred pounds on top of my wages. She always was generous.'

Jules said: 'That's true. Topaz liked money, but she was always generous with it.'

'Anyway, I thanked her, and I only wish we'd left it there. But she has to start asking me what I'd do. She said she was getting what she wanted, and she wished I could have the same. "What would you do, Tansy, if you could have anything you wanted?"

'I closed my eyes and saw it developing like a photograph on a plate. It must have been the wine.

' "A cottage by the river. A vegetable garden. A few ducks. Enough for Rose and me to get by on without going out to service or factory work."

'I thought if Rose had somewhere comfortable like that to live, she wouldn't go worrying about votes. Anyway, for some reason, the idea of ducks really tickled Topaz.

' "Have you ever kept ducks, Tansy?"

' "No, it's just something I fancy."

'Then she came out with it, and I wish she hadn't.

' "Tell you what, Tansy, I'll leave you five hundred pounds in my will. Then if I die before you do, you'll get your ducks one day, even if you're an old lady."

' "In that case, I hope I'm as old as Methuselah."

'Then she said she was meeting her lawyer at the British Consulate after lunch to discuss transferring the money to buy her vineyard. She'd make her will at the same time, and I had to go along with her. Of course, by then I wished

I'd never opened my mouth, but off we went in her carriage with me sitting beside her in my best navy blue and all the gentlemen bowing and waving to her as we went along the promenade. We picked up Mr Jules on the way, and he can tell you the rest because I can't think about it without getting angry.'

'The making of the will,' said Jules. 'That's what you really want to know about, isn't it, Miss Bray?'

He was smiling, but I realised that I wasn't the only person in the room trying to find the answers to questions.

THREE

JULES LEANED FORWARD, SMILING a little, keeping his eyes on me.

'Topaz, I found out, had decided that I should be a witness. At first, Tansy and I had to sit there while she arranged the transfer of most of her money from England, in a most businesslike way. When that was done she said, "And I want to make a will."

'The lawyer was a little bald fellow. You could tell he was very much taken with Topaz, as most people were. He said if she'd let him know what she wanted, he'd make a note and send her a draft for her comments. But Topaz would never wait for anything. She said she wanted to do it there and then, and it wasn't complicated, so he had to give in, as people always did. So she just sat there and dictated. I can remember it word for word: "To my loyal maid and friend, Tansy Mills, I bequeath five hundred pounds for her to buy a cottage and some ducks. That's all."

'Of course, that was the first time I'd heard about the ducks, and I couldn't help laughing. The lawyer stared. "But your estate amounts to considerably more than five hundred pounds."

' "That's all right, then."

' "What is to happen to the residue? Normally it would go to your nearest surviving relative. Is that what you wish?"

'Topaz was furious. "No, it most certainly is not. The only relation I have is a brother, and I'm not leaving him or his family anything. Not a penny." '

Tansy interrupted: 'She told me about this brother. He ignored her for years, tried to borrow a lot of money off her when she started doing well, then said she'd burn in hell for her sinful life when she refused him.'

Jules said: 'The lawyer suggested she might leave the rest of her money to some good cause. But by then Topaz had had her joke and I think she was bored with it all. She said orphanages and old horses weren't very amusing. Then the idea seemed to hit her all of a sudden. She said: "I'll leave it to the suffragettes." '

He waited for a comment from me. I said nothing. I was already beginning to realise that Jules Estevan enjoyed experimenting with people.

'I said to her, "I didn't think you believed in them." She said, "I don't, but think how it would annoy my brother." She was insistent that we must get the name right and we had to hunt up an old copy of *The Times* in the lawyer's office to make sure of it. He drew up the will, Topaz signed it, a man from the consulate and I witnessed it. And that, Miss Bray, is how Topaz Brown came to leave her fortune to the Women's Social and Political Union.'

I said nothing. I was wondering what Emmeline would say when she heard, and reflecting that when this came out in court it would hardly help our case. It might be possible to argue that frivolity was no proof of an unsound mind, but it was hardly an attractive course.

Tansy said: 'I knew no good would come from making a mock of wills. I told her so at the time, but she wouldn't listen.'

I think Jules Estevan was disappointed at getting no obvious reaction from me. He asked:

'Is this money so important to your movement, Miss Bray?'

'It's vital. For the first time, the electorate is turning towards us. Last year our intervention decisively influenced the result of by-elections in Peckham, Mid Devon and Manchester North-West. The next general election will matter more to us than any in our history and we must have the money to support candidates who will vote for our cause in Parliament.'

'And you'd accept Topaz's money – after what you've heard?'

'I'd accept money from the devil himself, if it would help us.'

Tansy muttered something that I couldn't hear. I pushed my half-empty glass of wine aside. It was so good that I wanted to drink more, but the room was warm, my head was buzzing already and there was still a long way to go.

I asked Jules: 'What time was it when you left the lawyer's office?'

He looked at Tansy, questioningly.

'After four,' she said. 'I know that because by the time we got back here it was time for her tea.'

'What was Topaz's mood on the way back?'

'She kept laughing about the ducks and the suffragettes and her brother!'

'Hysterical laughter?'

'Normal laughter. She was like a child who'd been given some exceptionally amusing toy.'

'Did you go back to tea with her?'

'No. I had another engagement, so she dropped me outside one of the other hotels. That was the last I saw of her.'

'What was the last thing she said to you?'

'She waved to me as her carriage went off and said she'd see me at the usual time tomorrow.'

'As normal?'

'Exactly as normal.'

'You had no premonition then?'

'None.'

I turned to Tansy. 'Were there any guests at tea?'

'No. Tea was when she'd plan the serious part of the day. We'd see to it that this room and the bedroom were ready and the flowers arranged, with the bouquet from whoever she was entertaining that night given the best place. If she was going out to dinner or a reception, that was when she'd decide what dress to wear and what jewels to go with it. If she was entertaining here it would be a matter of ordering up supper from the hotel kitchens and choosing the wine from her special store. She might write a note or two, answering invitations. Then, if it suited her, she'd usually let me know who the guest was going to be. I'd guessed Lord Beverley, but she said nothing.'

'Did she write any notes that day?'

'A couple.'

'Who to?'

'I don't know. I just put them on the table outside and a boy comes up to collect them before dinner. I didn't look.'

'Long notes?'

'No. She didn't go in for long notes. Usually just a word or two.'

'What did she do after she'd written the notes?'

'She sat there drinking tea and looking at some more mail that had arrived while we were out.'

'Was there anything in it that disturbed her?'

'No.'

'No change from her usual routine?'

I expected another no, but this time it didn't come. There was a look of distress on Tansy's face and the fingers of her right hand were rubbing and twisting at a fold of her black dress.

'That was when she started acting . . . not like she usually did.'

It hurt her to admit it.

'In what way?'

'Well, when she'd been just sitting there for a bit, I thought I should remind her that time was getting on. After all, we hadn't retired just yet. I said, "Which is it tonight, out or at home?" She looked up from a letter. "Oh, at home."

' "His Lordship, is it?"

'I sensed that she was in an odd sort of mood, like the mood children get into when they're ready for more devilment. She said no, his father the Duke had arrived, so he couldn't come and see her, but she still didn't say who she was expecting instead. So I asked her if she'd decided what she wanted ordering for supper. Nothing, she said.

'I made myself busy collecting up the tea things, a bit annoyed with her. You may say I shouldn't have been, on account of the five hundred pounds, but that was hardly in my mind at all. I thought it was one of her jokes, a way of spicing up a boring afternoon at the lawyer's and that was that. After another few minutes, when she still hadn't said anything, I said: "What dress would you like me to put out then?"

' "The plain brown one, with the cream-coloured shawl and brown straw hat."

'I was flabbergasted. "But that's a day dress."

'It was the plainest one in her whole wardrobe.

' "I know it is. I'm going out to do some shopping."

'Well, that was unheard of. Ladies don't shop at nearly six o'clock in the evening, do they? That's only tradesmen's wives getting things for their supper. I said: "What in the world could you be wanting to buy at this hour?"

' "Oh, just a few things."

' "Well, tell me what they are, and I'll go out and get them for you." But no, she would insist on going herself. She changed into the brown dress, went out and came back less than an hour later. I was in the bedroom at the time, so I didn't see if she was carrying anything. When I came back into the salon she'd opened a window on to the balcony and was standing there, looking out. She said to me: "Tansy, how would you like this evening free?"

' "Free ma'am?"

'She said: "I shan't be needing you this evening. In fact, I don't want you to be here." '

Tansy's flow of words had stopped. She was staring at me as if waiting for me to register something – shock, disbelief, I don't know what. I was puzzled because it seemed to me quite an ordinary thing for a woman to say to her maid, especially a woman of Topaz Brown's kind. When she failed to get the right reaction from me, Tansy started talking again, not far from tears.

'I was cut to the heart. I never gossiped, Mr Jules will tell you. In six years with her, I'd been discretion itself. There wasn't the money in the world that would make me let down Topaz. She must have seen she'd hurt me, because she came over and put her arm round my shoulder.

' "Oh Tansy, I don't mean that. If I had all the royal princes in Europe in here at once, and the President of the United States as well, I wouldn't send you away. I trust you more than I trust myself."

' "I'd thought so, ma'am," I said.

' "You know so. Now, stop looking so tragic. I've booked you a nice little room for the night on the second floor and you can go and see that friend of yours down by the harbour this evening."

'She was practically pleading with me, like a mother trying to stop a child turning awkward.

' "Then in the morning you can bring me my breakfast as usual and perhaps I'll tell you all about it. But I want to be on my own tonight."

'I said, still hard: "You shouldn't have gone to so much trouble."

' "Tansy, it's nothing against you, I promise. It's only a kind of joke I'm planning." '

I couldn't help interrupting.

'She said that – a joke?'

'Yes. It made me feel better at the time. She loved practical jokes, didn't she, Mr Jules? She'd go to endless time and trouble planning them.'

Jules said: 'That's quite true. Topaz would do almost anything for a joke.'

'So you went?' I asked Tansy.

'I had no choice. She could hardly get me out of the way quick enough. She let me pour her bath and lay out her dressing gown, and that was it. The last thing I saw of her was her stepping into her bath, the scent of sandalwood all round her, and that smile on her face, like a child up to something.'

'And you did what she said, you didn't come back till morning?'

'No. I feel like choking when I think about it.'

'But if she'd told you not to . . .'

'I should have taken no notice of her. I should have known she wasn't safe on her own, with that one over there, biding her time.'

I'd already decided that Tansy was scarcely sane on the question of Topaz's rival. To change the subject, I asked her if she'd gone to see her friend.

'Yes. Janet her name is. I met her when we were over

here last year. She's Scottish but she went and married a French customs officer. As it happened, I stayed the night with her so I never used that room Topaz had booked for me. Her husband was away and one of the children was poorly, so by the time I'd got the other children to bed, cooked us some supper and had a good long talk with Janet it was after midnight. She didn't want me to walk back to the hotel on my own, and there were no cabs to be had down by the harbour at that hour, so I stayed and shared her bed.'

'What time did you get back in the morning?'

'I didn't hurry back. She never wanted her breakfast before ten. I got to the hotel just after nine and went in at the main entrance, instead of our side door, to see if there was a letter from Rose. When I got up to our suite her bedroom door was still closed, like it usually was, so I went to my room and tidied up a bit. Then the waiter came up with her breakfast tray as usual, and I went and tapped on her bedroom door, as usual.'

'And went in and found her . . .?'

'I thought she was just asleep at first, but she didn't move, didn't stir. I said, quite loud, "Your breakfast, ma'am," but there was something about my voice when I said it that sent the shivers through me. When she still didn't move I touched her on the shoulder, quite gently, and then of course I knew. Cold. But I still wouldn't let myself believe it. I pulled the sheets down, to feel for a heartbeat. I just couldn't believe what I was seeing.'

Jules was leaning forward intently, I thought almost ghoulishly.

'Now, this bit really is strange. Tell Miss Bray what you couldn't believe.'

I braced myself for some horror, and at first couldn't understand what Tansy was saying. The words tumbled out indignantly.

'You see, I knew how fastidious she was. The Empress of Russia herself couldn't have been more choosy about her lingerie, all hand stitched from the finest silk and satin that money could buy. But what she was wearing – cheap cotton knickers, clean enough, but the kind a shopgirl might wear on honeymoon at Southend, pink bows and a bit of machine-made broderie anglaise. And a petticoat down beside the bed, pink muslin with a net flounce and more scrappy little bows, common as they come. I couldn't help myself. I said: "Oh Topaz, what have you done to yourself? What have you done?" '

FOUR

TWO PAIRS OF EYES WERE on me, Tansy's tragic and resentful, Jules' with that experimenting look. I said slowly, trying not to make the question sound as ridiculous as I knew it would:

'You're saying when you found Topaz Brown dead, she was wearing lingerie she wouldn't usually wear?'

'She wouldn't have been seen d . . .'

Tansy stopped just before she went over the edge, and went red.

'That's how I knew, you see, right from the start, that she hadn't killed herself. Apart from everything else, I mean. Then there was that wine they took away.'

Jules explained: 'There were an empty glass and a half-full bottle of wine beside her. The police took them away, naturally. The laudanum had been in the glass of wine.'

'But she'd never drink wine like that. Even I knew that. You explain to Miss Bray, Jules.'

Jules sighed and shifted in his seat.

'The first thing to grasp is that Topaz was genuinely knowledgeable about wine and had laid up an excellent small cellar. People said she chose her lovers according to the quality of their vineyards. Like many things said about Topaz, that wasn't entirely true, but it wasn't so wide off the mark either.'

'I see, so I take it she drank the laudanum in a particularly good vintage of wine.'

'Quite the reverse. The bottle found at Topaz's bedside contained a villainously cheap wine, the kind of thing they serve in the worst sort of workmen's cafés. Tansy says

Topaz would never wear lingerie like that. I can say that never, in her right mind, would she have drunk a glass of wine from that bottle.'

'In her right mind.' I found that phrase depressing and Jules knew it.

I said: 'Perhaps if she were putting laudanum in it, she wouldn't want to spoil a good wine.'

Jules nodded. 'That's just possible.'

But would that be evidence for or against sound mind?

'Topaz, from what you both tell me, could be described as a person of expensive tastes.' Tansy and Jules both nodded. 'So why should she want to kill herself wearing cheap underwear and drinking cheap wine?'

A diagnosis of acute self-disgust might have covered it, but that hardly went with their description of Topaz's last day in the world.

Tansy said: 'It was done to shame her.'

Jules obviously knew what was coming. 'Tansy, if that means you think Marie came up here, persuaded Topaz to drink poison in a glass of wine that was practically poisonous anyway, then dressed her in awful underwear just to humiliate her, I can only say you're approaching a state of dangerous insanity.'

Tansy glared.

I said, more gently: 'From what you've told me, Topaz took great care to send you away for the night. Doesn't that look as if she'd made up her mind what she was going to do?'

'But she was happy, as happy as a sandboy, that day especially. You can't tell me somebody behaves like that then goes and poisons herself.'

Jules said: 'Tansy, I'm afraid several of my friends have killed themselves for various reasons. In every case, they were more cheerful just before they did it than for months past. I think it's because they've made up their minds.'

I said: 'Mr Estevan, do you believe Topaz Brown killed herself?'

'What else can I think?'

It must have been well past lunchtime by then. The sun had shifted over to the west and was shining in directly through the big windows. Jules had made no move to go, and neither did I. If, as seemed likely, our claim to Topaz's money hinged on her state of mind that day, we could afford no gaps.

'Miss Mills, you were under the impression that Topaz Brown was expecting a visitor that evening.'

'I supposed she must be. Why else would she stay in?'

'But you had no idea who it was?'

'No.'

'Have you any idea who might have visited her, Mr Estevan?'

'Half a dozen or so people might have. I don't know who did, if anybody.'

'Naturally, I'm wondering if there might have been a visitor who brought news so bad that she decided to kill herself.'

'Naturally.'

'I assume the police will have asked the hotel reception if there were any callers.'

'I doubt it. The police, like most other people, would know that very few of Topaz's visitors went through the hotel reception.'

'Why not?'

'Did you notice the small private lift off the hallway in this suite? There's a flight of stairs too. They go down to a little door in a side street. There's a similar arrangement in Marie's tower on the other side.'

'Very convenient.'

'Indeed. The local joke was that the architect was an *homme du monde* designing for *les femmes du demi-monde*. That's one of the reasons why these two tower suites command such very high rents.'

'And were Miss Brown's visitors' (I remembered not to say 'clients') 'issued with keys to this private door?'

'I believe not, though Tansy could tell you.'

She shook her head. 'There were only three keys. She had one, I had one and the other one was always kept locked up in the manager's office.'

'Did you have yours with you on Wednesday evening?'

'Yes. I let myself out of the side door and locked it

behind me as usual.'

Jules said: 'When the police called, after Tansy found Topaz's body, they naturally came through the main hotel entrance. But Tansy took it upon herself to check the side door, didn't you, Tansy?'

'It was locked.'

'Just as Tansy had left it?' I couldn't see what Jules was driving at.

'Yes, but there is a little mystery. Tansy can't find Topaz's own key. It seems to worry her for some reason.'

Tansy glared at him. 'She always kept it in the drawer of that little table. It wasn't there or anywhere else. I've looked.'

Jules was watching me, waiting for my reaction. I asked him what he deduced from that.

'Nothing whatsoever. Keys get lost all the time. But that's not the way Tansy sees it.'

Tansy said, as if there were no doubt about it: 'The person who killed her went out of that side door and took the key away with her.'

'Did you tell the police?'

'I tried to. They wouldn't listen.'

Jules shrugged. 'It was evident that Topaz killed herself. Why ask questions that would only embarrass people?'

We sat there for a while, then for no reason I could think of, I asked if I could see Topaz's bedroom. Tansy looked alarmed.

'I haven't been in there since they took her out.'

Jules said: 'You'll have to go in there some time, Tansy. Why not now?'

He stood up and led the way across the thick carpet to white and gold double doors, stretching the full height of the room. I was struck by Tansy's stubbornness and misery, staying there on her own in the luxurious suite, scared to open those doors. I followed Jules, with Tansy behind me.

The first impression when the doors were opened was of dimness and a fusty smell, reminiscent of something I preferred not to think about. Only the faintest sunlight filtered through the thick velvet curtains drawn across all the windows, enough to show a pale tent-like shape and scattered glints of gold. Jules was not, I think, reverent by nature but he moved across the room as slowly as a man in a ritual and drew back curtains to let the light in. It was a more ornate room than the salon, with a painting copied from Versailles on the ceiling and delicate chairs and tables that were either Louis Quatorze or good imitations. The bed was on a dais under a canopy of white damask, looped up with gold cords. The bedsheets, of dusky gold satin, were still disordered and Tansy's face crumpled when she looked at them.

I asked where the wine bottle had been. I couldn't help speaking in a whisper. Jules pointed to a small round table beside the dais, and the marks on it where a bottle and glass had stood. On the floor near the table was a pink petticoat, presumably the one that had offended Tansy. When I picked it up I smelt sandalwood, but I was still conscious of that other unidentified smell in the room.

I tried to disregard Tansy's disapproving eyes and went up the shallow steps of the dais to the bed. One of the gold pillows was still dented from her head. Thinking to spare Tansy that, at least, I lifted it to plump it up.

'Mr Estevan.'

My urgent whisper brought him across the room and up the step in two strides, Tansy jealously behind him.

'Didn't anybody see this?'

Where the pillow had been there was a sheet of white notepaper, folded double.

'Oh God. I thought it was strange that she hadn't left a note.'

He sounded shaken. I noticed that his right fist was tightly clenched. I think we neither of us wanted to pick it up.

'What is it?' Tansy's voice was sharp.

I picked up the paper and unfolded it. It was good quality notepaper with the name and crest of the Hôtel des Empereurs on the top of it. The note on it was a short one, oddly set out.

Too late.
8 p.m. Return of I.O.U. for one career.
Vin Poison.

Then a scrawled signature – Topaz Brown.

I showed it to Tansy.

'Is that her writing?'

'Yes. But what's it supposed to mean?' She was pale and her mouth was trembling.

I said, as gently as I could: 'I think it means she didn't want to go on any more with the life she was living . . . with her career as she saw it.'

'But she wasn't. I told you, she was going to retire.'

'She says "Too late." '

'And I.O.U. – that's when you owe people money.'

'Perhaps she felt she owed the world some kind of debt.'

'Topaz didn't owe anybody anything,' said Tansy flatly.

Jules read the note again, looking over her shoulder.

'I don't understand why she wrote that line about the wine and poison. She must have known the police would discover that in any case.'

'And took the trouble to write it in French. Did she know much French?'

'She could speak it a little, in fact she was picking it up quite quickly. But as for reading and writing it, no more than she needed to find her way round a menu or a couturier's bill.'

Tansy handed the note back to me, as if she wanted nothing to do with it.

I said: 'I suppose the police should see it.'

Jules seemed unconcerned. 'They know it's suicide anyway.'

I suggested that since I was going to see Topaz's solicitor again I should give the note to him. It seemed to me more likely to advance our case than otherwise. Tansy, after a last look at the disordered bed, went back to the salon and we followed.

She walked round fidgeting at piles of notes and papers, those stiff square envelopes with the foreign gentlemen's smells.

'I'll have to do something with all this.'

Jules said: 'Leave it for the solicitors, Tansy.'

'She wouldn't want that. Do you know, that solicitor had the nerve to send a man up on the Friday, just the day after she died, wanting to take her papers away. I sent him packing. Her not even in her grave, and they want to come poking round, disturbing all her things. I wasn't having that.'

She turned away from us, sounding near to tears. Jules and I exchanged looks. At some time, presumably, somebody would have to prise Tansy away from her guardianship of Topaz's treasures, but it wasn't our responsibility. Jules apparently guessed what I was thinking.

'I suppose, Miss Bray, all this may legally belong to you, or rather to your organisation.'

His smile seemed malicious, to have in it that taint of male superiority that says "enemy".

I looked round at the pictures and ornaments, the piles of gauzy scarves and stoles.

'I can't think what we should do with it.'

'Indeed, it's the money that matters, isn't it? It's a pity that wasn't what she wanted. I expect you'd like to believe that she entertained her visitors with your colours pinned secretly over her heart – or elsewhere.'

I glared at him, but was saved the trouble of replying when somebody knocked on the door into the salon from the landing. Tansy went to open it.

'Oh, it's you, is it?'

The words were practically hissed, but she opened the door and one of the most beautiful women I've ever seen swept in. She was as slim as a foxglove and tall, with pale creamy skin and enormous dark eyes. She wore an afternoon gown of light coffee-coloured silk with real white rosebuds tucked into the belt, and an expression of pure tragedy. Jules went to meet her, still with that malicious smile on his face.

'Miss Bray, may I introduce you to Mademoiselle Marie de la Tourelle. Marie, Miss Bray of the Women's Social and Political Union.'

A hand as light as a bird's wing fluttered briefly against mine, then she stepped wordlessly past me and collapsed on to a chaise longue like a shot swan.

'How dreadful . . . such despair . . . I blame myself.'

Tansy stood staring down at her with a look of total

disgust, and it was left to Jules to fetch another glass and pour the last of the Tokay. Marie sipped weakly then put a hand to her forehead, palm outwards, in a pose I'd never seen before except in Royal Academy paintings. There was a great bracelet of pearls and diamonds on her fragile wrist.

'Why do you blame yourself?' I asked.

'It is a very dreadful thing – jealousy.'

Her English was good, but with a drawling accent.

'Jealousy of whom?' asked Jules.

At least his urge to experiment was consistent, rather than just directed against me. I'd noticed that when he'd brought the wine glass he'd caught Tansy's eye and given her a look that practically dared her to make trouble. So far she'd stood mute but mutinous, watching Marie's every move.

Marie looked at Jules, hurt. 'Of me, of course. Who else?'

'Why?'

She sighed. 'Because of Lord Beverley.'

Tansy burst out: 'He'd left you and come to her. It was you who was jealous.'

The contrast between the angry little woman in her serviceable black and Marie, long and silky on the couch, was almost laughable. If looks could have killed, Tansy would have been beside her mistress in the morgue, but after that one look Marie ignored her and spoke to Jules.

'Lord Beverley found Topaz *vulgaire*. He told me so, poor boy, when he was begging me to take him back.'

'Sez you,' said Tansy. Marie ignored her.

'He is so very repentant. All those lilies. You saw them.'

Tansy said: 'Those lilies came from the old goat of an Archduke. Everybody knows about him.'

'Then on Wednesday afternoon, I was with Lord Beverley in his motor-car when Topaz went past in her carriage. I think it must have been then she decided to do this terrible thing.'

Tansy said: 'Didn't you see him giving her a wink? If you want to know what she thought about it, she was laughing herself sick.'

'Hiding her heartache,' Marie said to Jules, placing her hand over her heart with another flash of diamonds. 'So you see, I blame myself for bringing this terrible despair on her, that drove her to do this thing.'

She closed her eyes and lay back. Tansy advanced and stood over her.

'She didn't care a fiddlestick for you or Lord Beverley or any of the rest of it. She'd decided to give it up.'

Jules repeated what Topaz had said to Tansy about the first grey hair. I could see Tansy wished he hadn't. Marie opened her tragic eyes.

'You see, she knew she was growing old and it was all over for her. It will come to all of us in time, even to me, and if you have no faith to support you, what is there but to despair?'

'You'll never see thirty again either,' Tansy said.

I had the impression she was beginning to enjoy herself. It must have been difficult for Marie to go on ignoring her, but she managed it.

'I have come because I think it is my duty to see she is buried in holy ground, in spite of her sin.'

'Any sins she committed you've done too, only not as well.'

Jules cut in: 'I think Marie is talking about the sin of suicide.'

'But of course. The only sin for which there is no time to repent.'

Tansy said: 'It wasn't suicide,' but saw Jules' eye on her and turned away with an expression of disgust.

Later, when Marie and Jules were discussing arrangements for the funeral, he asked Tansy if there were any relatives who should be involved.

'The man from the consulate says the brother won't do anything. Anyway, she hated him like . . .'

She went red again and hurried away, probably to her bedroom. I think she couldn't trust herself to stay in the same room as Marie.

I left Marie and Jules in the process of deciding that Topaz, for all anyone knew to the contrary, might once have been a Roman Catholic and Marie saying she would speak to Father Benedict. When he saw I was going, Jules came to the door with me.

'I wonder whether I might call on you tomorrow, Mr Estevan. There are still some things I'd like to ask you.'

He bowed ironically and gave me his card.

I went back to my pension and spent most of the afternoon making notes of what I'd been told by the lawyer, Tansy and Jules Estevan. Then, drowsy from sitting up all night in the train, I decided I'd catnap for half an hour before going out to find dinner. I must have been more tired than I realised because I missed dinner altogether and slept the evening and night through on the pension's narrow white bed.

FIVE

MOST OF THE NEXT MORNING was taken up with composing a telegraph message for Emmeline Pankhurst, more remarkable for what it left out than what it told her. She'd been reluctant enough to take Topaz's bequest in the first place, and I didn't want to discourage her any further. I walked to the post office in the Rue Gambetta to send it, then decided to stroll back along the parade beside the sea in front of the grand hotels. It was just after lunch by then and I watched the visitors spilling decorously out for their afternoon of sea air, children bound for the beach under the care of starched white nursemaids, invalids in bath chairs drawn by donkeys, men's top hats and women's parasols turning unruly in the breeze from the sea. For some reason I stopped opposite the Hôtel d'Angleterre, rather less ornate than the one where Topaz had lived, slightly old fashioned. With my mind more than half on other things I watched a carriage with a plump woman sitting in it under a grey sunshade, with two little girls of about eight and six years old, smartly dressed but with faces dull as muffins. As I watched they were joined by a tall man in a grey suit and top hat. He was in his early forties, brown hair just flecked with grey, a square, lined forehead and a jutting chin ending in a sharp ledge of beard, like a cow-catcher on the front of an American railway engine. His eyes were grey and hard. Of course I couldn't see his eyes from the other side of the parade, but I didn't need to. I remembered them all too well from when he was making the speech for the prosecution that sent me to Holloway. Mr David Chester MP, barrister at law, on holiday with his family.

He didn't notice me, which was just as well, seeing that he'd described me as a vengeful virago and managed to convert my half brick into an assault on the fabric of society. That was quite mild by his standards. He was, you may remember, the man who said in the Commons that Christabel Pankhurst was 'a woman barren of everything except bitterness and anarchy' and that he'd as soon see his daughters scrubbing floors as going into a polling booth. As I watched him settling into the carriage I found my throwing arm twitching and had to remind myself that on my present mission I was supposed to be unobtrusive. I looked away from the family group and found myself staring, over a distance of a few feet, into a pair of eyes that mirrored so exactly what I was feeling that I thought at first I'd conjured them up.

They were brown eyes and they belonged to a young woman in her twenties with an oval face, serious and pale as if she spent too much time indoors. She was small and quite thin, but there was a determined set to her neck and shoulders, a forcefulness about the curve of the eyebrows and lips, that said the world wouldn't elbow her aside. She was wearing a skirt and jacket of brown serge, too heavy for Biarritz in the spring, and a plain straw boater with a brown ribbon round it.

She said, and it sounded like an accusation: 'You're Nell Bray.'

'I am. I see you recognise David Chester.'

'I recognise him.'

She stood there looking at me, making no move.

I said: 'Would I be wrong in thinking you're one of us?'

She nodded. 'That's how I knew you. I heard you speaking in Trafalgar Square.'

I was puzzled. From her voice, she wasn't the kind of girl who could afford holidays in Biarritz or, from her manner, one who'd enjoy them. But she didn't look or sound like a servant.

'Does Bobbie know you're here?'

That, at least, answered one of my questions. I knew that Bobbie was there and obviously she'd brought a friend with her. There was an obvious gulf in social class between them, but a movement like ours breaks down barriers.

'Bobbie Fieldfare doesn't know I'm here. I was sent by Mrs Pankhurst.'

That seemed to alarm her. She was on the point of saying something, but stopped herself.

I said: 'It's a coincidence, isn't it, that David Chester should be here too?'

'Yes.' Then, abruptly: 'Can I talk to you?'

I'd been instructed to keep clear of Bobbie and all her works, but I couldn't walk away from this girl. There was something like panic in those few words.

'Of course. Let's walk on the beach, shall we?'

I made for a stretch of open sand, well away from the family parties. Now that she had my company, the urge to talk seemed to have gone. I asked her how she'd met Bobbie.

'She pulled me out from under the hooves of a police horse in Parliament Square. She could have been killed.'

'And you've been friends ever since?'

'Well, we met a couple of times after that when she came down to meetings in the East End.'

'And she suggested you should come to Biarritz with her?'

'I think that was because of my sister.'

'Your sister?'

'She worked as a maid to a rich woman who was living here. Bobbie said it would be useful . . .'

Light dawned. 'Good heavens, you're Rose Mills, Tansy's sister.'

She stopped and stared at me, eyes furious.

'Has Bobbie been telling you about that?'

'I've had nothing to do with Bobbie. Tansy's been talking about you. I hadn't realised you were here.'

'Tansy doesn't know I'm here.'

'But she wrote, asking you to come. Topaz Brown wanted you to come.'

'That . . . that woman wanted me to come here?'

'Yes. Tansy had told her that you were in the WSPU. Topaz suggested she should invite you over here.'

'But . . . but she was a woman who . . . who sold herself.'

Her eyes were both defiant and miserable, blaming me, blaming anybody.

'Didn't you get Tansy's letters?'

She shook her head. 'I moved lodgings.'

Several things had fallen into place. It had seemed to me strange from the start that a firebrand like Bobbie had chosen to go on a seaside holiday, too much of a coincidence that two pairs of hostile eyes should be observing David Chester.

I said: 'How did Bobbie know that David Chester was coming here?'

'It was in one of the society papers. One of his children has been ill.'

'Why Mr Chester, particularly? Aren't there enough people to demonstrate against back in England?'

'He sent Bobbie's mother to prison, and her aunt.'

That would have been motive enough for Bobbie. The Fieldfares tend to take their politics personally.

'And you're keeping him under observation to pick the best time to act. I hope you've considered that the French police may be even rougher than the English.'

'Yes.'

We started walking again, slowly because our boots sank into the dry sand. I believed at that point that what Bobbie had in mind was the kind of demonstration we staged against politicians in Britain, throwing paint or dung, perhaps, among the more militant members, attempting a public horse-whipping. It seemed to me to be squandering energy and money to go all the way to France to do it, but then Bobbie Fieldfare had plenty of both.

Rose said: 'You seem to take it very lightly.'

I started to say that I was hardly likely to get excited about a little dung-spreading on foreign soil, then I saw her face.

'What exactly is Bobbie planning to do?'

'I don't know. I thought you did.'

'I've got nothing to do with whatever she's planning.'

'But I thought Mrs Pankhurst sent you.'

'She sent me because of Topaz Brown's money. I've orders to keep well clear of Bobbie.'

Rose stopped again and groaned like a child, weary and in deep trouble.

'You shouldn't have let me think that . . . I shouldn't have told you . . . what am I going to do?'

She was a strong-minded girl, but very near the end of her tether. I put my arm round her shoulders and made her sit down on the sand beside me.

'Rose, you can't betray Bobbie by talking to me. If you're worried about what's going to happen, then you must tell me.'

She took her time to think about it. I could practically feel the wrenching of loyalties in her head, like a tree branch before it gives way. Then she started to talk, quietly, looking out to sea.

'On the way out we stayed overnight in Paris. We wanted to save money so we found a cheap hotel near the station, only it turned out to be a rough area and there were two men banging on our door, trying to get in. We pushed the chest of drawers up against the door, but Bobbie thought I was still nervous . . .'

'You had a right to be.'

'. . . and she said I shouldn't be because she had her father's pistol with her and if the worst . . .'

'Bobbie Fieldfare brought a pistol with her?'

'In her carpet bag, wrapped in a scarf. She said she'd been practising with it.'

I'd always known that Bobbie was one of our wilder sisters, but this was beyond everything.

Rose said: 'She hasn't taken it out of the bag since we've been here. She leaves it in our room when she goes out.'

'Does she go out a lot?'

'Yes, especially in the evenings. She knows a lot of people here, her sort, from society. She's trying to find out what he does, where he goes.'

'And you take your turn in the day.'

'Sometimes.'

'Why haven't you been to see your sister? She's worried about you.'

'I don't want to bring her into it.'

'But Bobbie does. Isn't that why you're here?'

I thought I could guess why. When there'd been an assassination attempt, successful or bungled, Tansy's part would have been to hide or disguise them, for love of her sister, until they could get across the border into Spain.

'I don't know. She asked a lot about Tansy at first, not so much after we heard about that woman killing herself.'

That made sense. Once the attention of the police had been drawn to Topaz's household, for whatever reason, Bobbie would have to look elsewhere for her refuge. Which left Rose high, dry and in danger.

'You should go to your sister. She's alone. She needs somebody with her.'

She shook her head.

'I'm staying with Bobbie, whatever happens.'

'At least come and see Tansy. You owe her that much.'

I hoped that once I'd got them together, Rose would agree to stay.

'Where is she?'

'At Topaz Brown's hotel. I'll come with you.'

On the way Rose asked: 'Why did she leave us her money?'

'It's an odd story. I'll tell you later.'

I didn't want to tell her at all.

No sooner had Rose walked through the door of the suite than Tansy was clasped round her, hugging her ferociously.

'Rose. At last.'

She stood back and checked her sister's appearance like a cat with a newly-recovered kitten. Then:

'But it's too late, Rose. She's dead. Topaz is dead.'

I was angry with myself for not going ahead to prepare the way. Tansy naturally thought her sister had only just arrived in Biarritz.

'Look at you, you must have been travelling for days. You can't have got the letter telling you to come until . . .'

'I didn't get the letter.'

'The one telling you to hurry up and come out here because she wanted you. After I sent the one with her ten pounds in . . .'

Rose said slowly: 'Why did Topaz Brown want me?'

'I'd told her all about you and what you were up to, and nothing would satisfy her but I should write and tell you to come.'

Rose looked at me. I'd expected confusion, but there was something like triumph in her eyes. I saw what was coming, but too late. Again, I blamed myself for not being more explicit, but really, how could I have known?

Rose said: 'You mean because of what I told you in my letters, Topaz Brown wanted me to come and tell her about our fight for the vote?'

'Talk to Topaz about votes? Why in the world would she want you to do that? No, she wanted you to mend the ribbons on her underthings.'

If Rose had suddenly been dropped five floors in the lift, she could not have looked more astounded. Tansy had no idea that she was being cruel but, although unintentional, it brought cruelty back on her.

After a moment's humming silence Rose said: 'You were going to bring me here to sew ribbons on a harlot's knickers?'

Tansy darted at her and slapped her face, hard and sharp. Rose stared at her, then went out without another word. The door slammed, and Tansy and I looked at each other as we heard feet running along the corridor.

'Oh,' said Tansy, 'I could kill that Mrs Pankhurst.'

I'd have laughed, if I hadn't been aching with regret for both of them. In her grief, Tansy had forgotten who I was, or didn't care. She went on for minutes on end, as fluent as any speaker I've ever heard, about the wickedness of the suffragettes in breaking up families and making girls discontented. The most bitter of our male opponents couldn't have equalled Tansy in full flight. All the time half my mind was with Rose, but I knew it would have been no help trying to follow her, even if I had been quicker off the mark. With some justice she might blame me for her humiliation, although it had been the last thing I wanted.

After some considerable time Tansy simply ran out of breath, although not of aggression, and stood there glaring at me. I said the first thing that had come into my mind.

'Don't you think that you and I should go shopping?'

SIX

ONCE TANSY HAD GRASPED what I meant to do – and it didn't take her long – her anger faded to a grim satisfaction.

'We're going to do what she did?'

'If we can.'

I arranged to call back at the hotel for her just before six, about the time that Topaz had left on her shopping trip the week before. When I arrived, she was ready with her hat and coat on.

'That means you believe me. You don't think she killed herself either.'

'Don't take it that I agree with you. I'm puzzled, that's all. I like to be clear about things.'

At the very least, it was a missing piece of jigsaw.

We hesitated in front of the hotel.

I said: 'That evening, did Topaz go down by your private lift, or out at the front?'

'She used our lift.'

That meant she'd have come out by the side door. Tansy led me round the side of the hotel to that private entrance, an unobtrusive door with a small porch and its own bell button. I tried to imagine Topaz standing there.

'Which way would you go to get to the shops from here?'

'If it was the posh shops, back to the terrace, then turn right.'

'But it wasn't the posh shops, was it? She was wearing her plainest dress.'

'The other ones are back this way.'

We walked away from the hotel, along a side street at right angles to the sea. There were children playing in gutters and open-fronted shops with counters of bright vegetables and fruit. We went round a corner with a café on it and men playing cards on a table outside, into a square with more small shops. We'd been walking for twelve minutes. Topaz, I remembered, had been away for under an hour on her shopping trip, say twenty-four minutes there and back, with only half an hour for purchases.

'What about this one, Tansy?' I'd given up calling her Miss Mills.

Next to the pork butcher's shop was a lighted window full of dispirited-looking hats and bonnets, the sort women would buy for necessity rather than frivolity.

'I go there for my sewing things,' Tansy said.

'Does it sell underclothes?'

'Yes.'

'Tansy, did you think of doing this yourself?'

'I can't speak the language. When I go shopping, I just point.'

I hastily reviewed my own vocabulary, hoping it was adequate.

'Tansy, tell me again, what did the knickers look like?'

She told me. I took a deep breath, walked into the narrow shop with Tansy close behind and told my needs to the rock-faced woman behind the counter.

The apparition of a middle-aged English woman demanding white knickers with pink bows and a pink muslin petticoat produced from her an indrawn hissing sound, between teeth clenched so tightly that you'd have thought we were infecting the air. She regretted – in a tone implying relief rather than regret – that she dealt in nothing of that kind. When I persisted, asking what kind of underwear she could show me, she produced boxes from beneath the counter and began thumping out the kind of garments that might have been useful to Florence Nightingale in the Crimea, corsets as severe as strait-jackets, bloomers that would have enveloped me from rib to knee.

'Not those,' said Tansy scornfully, from behind me.

Cowed by the woman's expression, I bought a plain

camisole and several metres of elastic strong enough to moor ships with. Tansy picked up the parcel and we retreated in more or less good order.

'What did you want to go and buy that for?'

I said something apologetically about not wasting people's time and looked at my watch. The transaction had taken ten minutes.

'There's the other one,' Tansy said.

She led the way across the square into a side street, and I had to stride out to keep up with her.

'There it is.'

This shop too had hats in its window, but of a more frivolous design, running to artificial roses and violets and the occasional feather. I glanced inside and saw that the woman at the counter looked reassuringly young and good natured. We marched in and again I opened negotiations. The assistant hardly blinked. But of course. The counter became a froth of white and pastel as she rifled box after box, spilling their contents in front of us. I caught a glimpse of pink and intercepted it.

'Tansy?'

She caught her breath. 'Just like it.'

I told the assistant I'd take the petticoat and began looking through piles of knickers. When I found a likely pair I'd show it to Tansy, and I could see the assistant was beginning to look puzzled, wondering why I should consult my maid on such an intimate matter.

'What about these?'

'No, they had broderie anglaise round the legs, not lace.'

'These?'

'That's more like it, only the ribbons are the wrong colour. They were pink.'

I asked the assistant if they had the same style with pink ribbons, to match the petticoat. She replied that they had stocked some with pink, but sold the last of them a week ago.

I asked, trying to sound casual, if those had been sold to an Englishwoman too. She seemed surprised at the question, but not suspicious. Certainly they were sold to a foreign lady who spoke very little French. They'd laughed a lot, she and the lady, trying to convey in sign language what was wanted, but she'd been in a hurry and made up her mind quickly. A beautiful foreign lady, I asked? The direction of the question, though not its details, must have been clear to Tansy. I felt her tugging at my elbow and drew it away, annoyed. What was this foreign lady wearing? Could it have been a plain brown dress with a cream-coloured shawl? Yes. Tansy pulled at my elbow again.

'Show her this.'

It was a postcard-sized photograph of Topaz Brown, *en fête* with shoulders bare and a diamond choker round her neck, diamond bracelets, more jewels with a feather plume in her hair. The assistant took it and gave me a surprised glance.

'*Oui, c'etait madame. Mais c'est Topaz Brown.*'

I hadn't realised until then quite what a celebrity Topaz had been. To this girl, dreaming over her flowered hats and cheap underwear, she seemed to be as well known as royalty and, judging by her expression, every bit as enviable. Her first reaction was simple pride that the likes of Topaz should have patronised her shop. Then puzzlement.

'*Mais on m'a dit qu'elle est morte.*'

She looked from me to Tansy and back again, face full of questions. I said that, unhappily, that was true. I had the impression of having stepped too hastily, of things moving too fast. To avoid more questions, I said I'd take the knickers with the blue ribbons too and made a performance of finding the right money. After all that, I'd have left the parcel on the counter if Tansy hadn't remembered to snatch it up.

When we were back in the square, Tansy said: 'So she bought them herself.'

'Evidently.' I hoped that would put paid to any absurd ideas about Marie.

'Well, that proves it, doesn't it?'

'Proves what?'

'That she didn't kill herself.'

'I'm sorry, Tansy, but it proves nothing of the kind. All

that this proves is that whatever happened, Topaz planned it herself.'

I knew too that I'd just spent some pounds of the organisation's money damaging our case. If a court heard that a woman as rich as Topaz had spent some of the last hours of her life buying cheap underwear, it would come near to proving an unbalanced state of mind.

'But it must have been for a joke, don't you see that? She wouldn't have gone to all this trouble if she was just going to kill herself.'

I tried hard to think myself into Topaz's state of mind, suddenly disgusted with herself to the point of suicide, planning a bitter farewell to the world. But if that had been the case, wouldn't she have gone to one extreme or the other, either dressed herself up in all her dearly-bought finery or worn the simplest thing in her wardrobe as a gesture of contempt for it all? Instead, she'd taken pains to fall between the two extremes. She'd died in glamour of a kind, but cheap glamour. Even allowing for the fact that Topaz's mind was not mine, I couldn't see the point of it.

A joke, on the other hand, made more sense. Somebody pays for a night with one of the most expensive women in Europe and arrives to find her dressed like – well, like the kind of woman you could probably buy for a sovereign back in London. That might appeal to a sense of humour of a certain kind. Then if the joke went horribly wrong and the client, instead of being amused . . . No, that made no sense either. They kept no laudanum in the suite, or so Tansy had said. That meant that the murderer . . . I caught myself up. It was the first time I'd used the word, even in my head.

We were standing outside the café, with Tansy looking up at me as if to ask what we did next.

'The wine, I suppose,' I said. 'Can you remember what the bottle looked like?'

'An old fat man and bunches of grapes.'

We'd passed a small provision shop on the other side of the square. I led the way back there, following the smell of cheese and garlic. It was scarcely more than a dimly lit cave, hung about with swathes of dried herbs and stalactites of sausages. We squeezed in behind a fat woman who was taking her time about buying a few grammes of anchovies. I touched Tansy's arm and pointed to a row of bottles on a shelf. Even in the dim light, Bacchus and his bunches of grapes looked as garish as a bank holiday fairground.

'Yes. That was it.'

The sharp face of the woman behind the counter showed no expression when I paid my few francs for a bottle of wine, or when I produced Tansy's picture of Topaz. She mumbled that she had so many customers she could hardly be expected to remember all of them. It was patently untrue. Topaz, even in her plain brown dress, would have stood out in that cave like a lyre bird among sparrows. From the way she looked at me, I knew she was lying by custom and instinct. The world outside her cave was hostile and she wanted nothing to do with it.

'What does she say?' Tansy asked from behind me.

'She says she can't remember, but I think she's lying.'

'Of course she is, silly old cow.'

Tansy gave the woman a withering look, took the bottle of wine from me and marched out of the shop.

'That's what I don't like about living in foreign places. You never know what they're saying about you, and you can bet . . . oops, sorry, *pardon, mademoiselle*.'

Loaded with parcels, her attention distracted, she'd almost bumped into a depressed looking woman clustered with young children. The woman was carrying a baby in a shawl and an untidy parcel wrapped in newspaper. The impact of Tansy rocked both of them and I went to help, holding the parcel while the woman settled the baby. It left grease traces on my gloves and an oddly familiar smell. The woman thanked me and murmured something about going out to get their dinner. In Biarritz it seemed, just as in London, there were families so poor that they had no stoves of their own, and must fetch cooked food from the shops. I said I hoped her family would enjoy their fish. As I spoke the word *poisson* something fell into place so fast that it felt like a physical blow. I asked the woman where she'd bought it. She was incredulous at first, then pointed up a side street. I went like a dog on the scent, Tansy with her parcels protesting behind me.

'You don't want that. You know what their kitchens are like.'

The smell of fish led me on to an open-fronted shop consisting of no more than a wooden counter with a great stove and a man in a white apron behind it.

I ordered fish, and he slapped a large fillet into a pan on the top of the stove. His eyes were bright and amused.

'Madame is English?'

'Yes.'

'I work in London for two years at the Bayswater Caprice Hotel. You know it?'

I regretted that I didn't.

He grinned. 'I think you English ladies like my fish.'

'Why? Have there been other English ladies?'

'Just last week, last Wednesday evening. She knew the Bayswater Caprice Hotel, that lady. She said my fish reminded her of London.'

Again I produced Tansy's postcard.

'That lady?'

'Yes, that same lady. She was very, very beautiful. She is your friend?'

I nodded. If he'd recognised her as Topaz Brown, he gave no sign of it.

'Did she buy a lot of fish?'

'Enough for two. I lent her a little dish to take it away. Will you please give your friend my regards and say it doesn't matter about the little dish until next time she comes. Tell her, when she comes to see me again, I give her fish free.'

He flipped my portion of fish out of the pan, wrapped it in newspaper and handed it to Tansy. She propped it under her chin, on top of the wine bottle and the two parcels of underwear.

We got back to the side entrance of the hotel an hour and twenty minutes after we'd left it. Topaz had been quicker, but then she'd known exactly where to go for what she wanted. In the salon, Tansy put the wine and underwear on a chair, but handed me the parcel of fish.

'Are you eating it here or taking it out with you?'

She went towards a window with the intention, I think, of opening it to get rid of the smell, then found it was open already.

'That's funny, I could have sworn I shut the windows before we went out. I hope that maid hasn't been in again.'

She seemed put out by it, but I didn't pay much attention. She'd given me another idea.

'Tansy, you remember how you described seeing Topaz when she got back from the shopping trip. She had the window to the balcony open and was standing by it.'

'Yes.'

'Why?'

'How should I know why?'

'Could she have been putting something out on the balcony, like a parcel of fish, so that you wouldn't smell it and ask questions?'

'Why should she want to do that?'

'Why would she want to buy fish in the first place?'

'That's what I can't understand. She could have any fish she wanted sent up from the kitchens here.'

'Yes, but that would be expensive fish. Cheap underwear, cheap wine – and now, cheap fish.'

Tansy was looking as if I were out of my mind. I walked up and down the room, trying to think.

'It was on a plate, but she'd need to heat it up again. There's the spirit lamp . . .'

Tansy said, grudgingly: 'That was left out, after the police had been, but I was in such a taking then, I didn't think anything about it.'

'Then she took it to the bedroom, that was where the smell was, with the wine. What happened to it?'

Would anybody have thought about a plate of cooked fish, when there was a bottle of poisoned wine to analyse? The police might have cleared it away when they took the wine.

Tansy said: 'I can't see why you're making such a fuss about a piece of fish.'

I had to tell somebody my theory. Rightly or wrongly, I told Tansy.

'If I'm right, that plate of fish may prove that Topaz didn't kill herself after all.'

She was unimpressed. 'That's what I've been saying all along. But it wasn't the fish that had the poison in it, it was the wine.'

'It all hinges on that note she left.' I took it out of my bag and unfolded it.

Too late.
8 p.m. Return of I.O.U. for one career.
Vin Poison

'We took it for a suicide note. It wasn't that at all. It's an invitation. She's inviting somebody to come at 8 p.m. and offering him wine and fish. But she got one letter wrong and put "poison" instead of "*poisson*".'

Tansy still refused to be excited. 'But what's all that about I.O.U.?'

'I don't know. It must have been part of the joke.'

'You didn't believe me when I said it was a joke.'

'Tansy, I thought you wanted to prove she didn't kill herself.'

'What I want to see is whoever did it pays for it.'

I was still pacing up and down, full of triumph and excitement. At the time, I wasn't even thinking that a verdict of murder rather than suicide would help our case. I was not even concerned about justice. It was the excitement of the hunt, pure and primitive, and I'm afraid I started giving orders to poor Tansy as if she were a hunt servant.

'Tansy, I want you to sit down and write me a list of all Topaz's clients – or visitors, if you prefer – that you can remember. Start with this year in Biarritz, then last year, then all of them you can remember over the time you've been with her. Then if . . .' I paused in mid-flow. I'd caught sight of her face.

'No.'

'No what?'

'I've never gossiped about that while she was alive and I'm not going to do it after she's dead. She could trust me. She knew that.'

'Tansy, it isn't gossip. It's investigation.'

'It doesn't matter what you call it.'

I've sometimes been called stubborn, but my stubbornness was no match for Tansy's. She just stood there with her arms folded, as unmoved by my arguments as a granite rock in a whirlpool. She'd never talked about Topaz's business affairs, never would, and that was that.

'Not even to catch her murderer?'

'It wasn't one of them that killed her.'

'Tansy, you can't know that.'

'I know.'

In the end, I had to admit defeat.

'Very well then, I shall just have to find out from other sources.'

'That's up to you.'

Once I'd conceded defeat, a kind of peace was restored and she made tea for us. When we were sitting down drinking it she suddenly started chuckling to herself.

'What's funny?'

'I was thinking, it was a caution you going off after that fish. Took Mr Shadow by surprise too.'

'Mr Shadow? What are you talking about, Tansy?'

She grinned, enjoying her triumph in being more observant than I was.

'Didn't you notice him? I picked him out almost as soon as we started. Then when we came out of the second place where you bought the underthings, there he was on the other side of the road. He was the man from the solicitor's.'

'What man from what solicitor's?'

'The one I told you about who came round on Friday wanting to go through her papers.'

'Why didn't you say something?'

'I didn't want anything to do with him.'

'What does he look like?'

She considered. 'Quite tall, a bit on the plump side. Red-faced and clean-shaven. Forty or older, I'd say. Black coat and hat, respectable enough but not what you'd call a gentleman.'

'French or English?'

'English.'

'And you think he was following us?'

'I don't think, I know.'

I didn't suspect Tansy of making it up entirely, but I thought she might have exaggerated a chance reappearance of the man into the belief that she was being followed. I was beginning to recognise, under her no-nonsense manners, a strong taste for the dramatic. I told her to let me know if she saw the man again, finished my tea and got up to go.

'Mr Jules said he'll come tomorrow to let me know about her funeral. Will you be going?'

I said I would, and that I'd call on Jules Estevan in the morning. Tansy came down in the lift to the side door to let me out. She insisted I took the fish away with me, so I donated it to a deserving cat beside the hotel dustbins. In itself, it hardly counted as evidence.

SEVEN

I WALKED ROUND TO THE front of the hotel, intending to find my way back from there to my own part of the town and buy myself dinner. It was just after eight o'clock and there was a long line of carriages by the steps, bringing people to dine at the hotel. I stood watching idly, watching beaded dresses and jewels flashing in the electric light from the foyer, feather fans waving in the sea air. The simplest of those gowns would amount to six months' wages for the likes of Rose and Tansy.

No sooner had I let myself be lulled into this reflective state of mind than two things happened to throw me out of it. The first was seeing David Chester for the second time that day. He and his plump wife, unwisely dressed in green satin, were in an open carriage with another couple in evening dress, waiting until the press of traffic allowed them to drive the extra few yards to the hotel entrance. Finding my throwing arm twitching again, I was about to walk out of the way of temptation until something, I don't know what, made me look up at the front of the hotel.

There were lights among the garlands and nymphs, and the first thing I was aware of was a shadow moving near the head of the caryatid on the right. I thought at first it had been made by a roosting pigeon, but the thing that cast it was too large for that. Then it moved again and revealed itself as a young man in tweed jacket and breeches. If he lost his footing from the ledge beside the caryatid's head, he'd fall forty feet or so on to the flagstones below, yet he moved lightly. He took a step towards one of the lights and I had a better view of him. He was hatless, his dark hair curly and artistically long.

He'd been looking down at the carriages by the steps then, just for a second, he raised his head and stared straight out to sea. In that second I recognised him. It wasn't a man at all. I'd have bet all the money in Biarritz that I was looking at Bobbie Fieldfare. And, forty feet below her, about to be drawn into pistol range, David Chester said something to his friend and turned to face the hotel, his white shirt front presenting as prominent a target as an inexperienced assassin could wish.

I had a second to think, and for half of that second my hatred of David Chester said yes, let her do it. Then I thought of the certainty that it would set our cause back for years, perhaps for ever. I shouted: 'Look. *Regardez,*' and pointed at the caryatid. There were shouts and gasps as other people saw what I was pointing at. The doormen ran down the steps to look, and people in open carriages stood up for a better view. Then the horror turned to laughter.

'A drop too much of the bubbly,' an English voice said.

Apparently young men swarming round the outside of hotels were part of the natural fauna of Biarritz. As for the tweed-jacketed figure, when the laughter broke out it stood there quite still, looking down. I wanted to shout to Bobbie to run for it, but was afraid of making her lose her balance. Already a doorman had said something to a porter and I was sure staff were rushing to the first floor to deal with the nuisance. I thought, if they arrest Bobbie I must introduce myself at once as a friend of the family and try to pass it off as a harmless prank.

The figure stood, toes on the narrow ledge, one arm hooked around the head-dress of the statue. Then, to gasps, it let go and stood unsupported, advancing even closer to the edge. I thought, 'Oh, God, she's going to jump.' I was biting my knuckles, trying not to scream. Bobbie – by then I was sure of it – stared down at us. Then, very slowly, she bent forwards like a person about to dive. More gasps, a woman's scream. It seemed an eternity that the figure stayed there, bent in the light. Then, just as slowly, it straightened up, stepped back and waved its hand to the crowd, having accomplished the slowest and most courtly of bows. There was a gust of relieved laughter, even a scattering of applause.

'Drunk as an archbishop,' said the English voice that did not sound notably sober itself. 'Positively pie-eyed.'

By now several members of the hotel staff were on first floor balconies, yelling at the figure to come in. Bobbie looked at them, shook her head solemnly, then, with a speed that seemed all the greater for her previous deliberate slowness, walked along the ledge to a drainpipe at the corner of the building and began shinning down. She jumped the last ten feet or so, fell, picked herself up and sprinted off across the road and along the parade. Picking up my skirts, envying her the advantage of breeches, I followed. Behind us came the cries of the hotel staff, shouting to her to stop.

We must have been one of the oddest sights of the season as we scudded along the parade, Bobbie in sporting costume and hatless, me with the turn of speed you learn if you are trying to evade the close attentions of the Metropolitan Police. A few people called to us, asking what was going on. Some citizen tried to stand in Bobbie's path, but she dodged aside, and I saw the surprised expression on the man's face as I flew past in my turn. We'd gone about half a mile, easily outdistancing the hotel people, past the fashionable hotels and towards the fishing harbour. Bobbie was gaining ground all the time. I count myself a reasonable athlete, but I am ten years older than Bobbie, and I suppose prison takes its toll. I should never have caught her if she hadn't made the mistake of dashing into the path of a rag and bone cart on its evening duties as she rounded the corner of the home straight.

Bobbie was up at once and I could see she wasn't much hurt, but the cart owner's language was forceful. He grabbed her by the arm and wouldn't let go. She made a desperate effort to pull away as she saw me running up, then, as I got within a few steps of her, shouted out with relief.

'Nell Bray, always there when you're needed. What's this man yelling about?'

'He seems to think you've damaged his horse.'

Bobbie snorted, much like a horse herself.

'Of course I haven't. With the legs on that animal it would take a charging elephant to damage it. Look.'

The man had released her arm. She bent down and ran an expert hand over the horse's knees and thick fetlocks. 'Sound as a bell.'

I pushed a handful of coins into the man's fist and dragged her into a shop doorway. She was panting as I was, but grinning like a schoolgirl playing truant.

'Was it you chasing me all the time? I thought it was the gendarmerie.'

I said: 'You'd better give me the pistol in case the gendarmerie catch up with you after all.'

Her eyes opened wide. 'But I haven't got it with me. It's back in my room.'

She didn't seem in the least bothered that I knew about it.

'What were you doing up there?'

A wry look, as if I were a tiresome school prefect.

'Waiting.'

'For David Chester?'

'Yes.'

'I want to talk to you about that. Over here.'

She came with me, unprotesting, towards a line of black fishing boats moored against the harbour wall and we sat on two coils of rope among tar-smelling lobster pots.

'Nobody authorised this,' I said.

She shrugged.

'You think that doesn't matter? If you're part of a movement, you have to accept its discipline.'

'Discipline is a useful excuse for moral cowardice.'

'Are all the rest of us cowards, then?'

'I didn't mean you, Nell.'

'But it affects me. It affects all of us if what you do destroys everything we've worked for. Our cause depends on winning public opinion to our side. Desperate measures like yours . . .'

She interrupted: 'Don't they use desperate measures? Their prisons, their brutal police, corrupt lawyers, ignorant judges, lying newspapers. And we're supposed to sit there saying, "Please, kind gentlemen, give us the vote." '

'You don't have to make speeches at me. Even if you were successful, what difference would the absence of one man make?'

'It would be a warning to all the rest of the smug hypocrites.'

'Bobbie, I appeal to you not to go on with this.'

As a member of the committee of the Women's Social and Political Union, I suppose I could have ordered her, but orders don't go far with the Fieldfares, mother or daughter.

'And if I refuse, will you betray me to the French police?'

'Don't be ridiculous.'

'Well then.'

The implied question was what was I going to do about it.

'I shall have to make sure I'm always there to prevent it, as I was tonight.'

'It was you who shouted, was it?'

That at least seemed to disturb her. I didn't spoil the effect by telling her I was only on the scene by accident.

'Don't you think you should at least have been honest with Rose Mills about what you were dragging her into?'

'You've seen Rose?'

'This afternoon. And if you're wondering how much she told me, I guessed more than she told. She's a loyal girl.'

'If there's any risk, I'm taking it, not Rose. Besides, it wasn't a case of dragging. She's as convinced as any of us.'

'What about Rose's sister? She isn't one of us, yet you were quite prepared to involve her in it too.'

Bobbie was silent for a while, feeling guilty, I hoped. When she spoke, her voice was less certain.

'I'm not going to involve Rose's sister. Not now.'

'Yes, not now that it doesn't suit your plans. But you'd have used her if you could, wouldn't you?'

'Yes. Yes, I would.'

I let her think about it for a while.

'Bobbie, whatever you do, please send Rose back to England. It's not fair on her.'

'Shouldn't she decide that for herself?'

But the tone was thoughtful rather than aggressive. I thought I'd scored a few points and would get nowhere by pushing her any further. I couldn't see how, though, with my other duty in Biarritz, I could watch Bobbie every minute of the day.

It was late by then, and the cold and damp were settling round us. I offered to walk with Bobbie back to her lodgings, but she said she'd be all right. She still didn't move. She asked suddenly:

'Did you know Topaz Brown's being buried tomorrow evening?'

'No. How did you hear?'

'Everybody seems to know.'

I said: 'Did you ever meet her?'

'No, never. I heard about her.'

It was too dark to see her expression but I could detect no strain in her voice.

'And yet you heard about her legacy to us. You must have telegraphed Emmeline soon after she died.'

'Everybody knew about that too.'

Even allowing for society's specialised use of 'everybody', meaning, in my experience, a few dozen, this surprised me.

'Nell, why did she kill herself?'

'I don't know.'

We both of us stood up together. I put my hand on her arm and could feel the tension humming through it.

'Bobbie, go home. There's plenty of work to do there. Forget this.'

She shook her head slowly and turned away. Once we reached the main road we went our separate ways.

EIGHT

I'D TOLD TANSY THAT I'D find my list of Topaz's lovers from sources other than her, but it was something of an empty boast. I've become reasonably thick-skinned and resourceful, but even I could hardly tour Europe's capitals and watering places asking men if they'd ever paid for the services of Topaz Brown. So at ten o'clock the next morning I was on the doorstep of Jules Estevan. He lived in a tall white-painted house to the south of the town, with a vine putting out its shoots around a wrought-iron verandah. The door was opened by an elderly woman in black, presumably the housekeeper, who said Mr Estevan was at breakfast.

'Please tell him Nell Bray would like to speak to him.'

She gave me a resentful look, but returned a few minutes later to show me upstairs.

'I was wondering when you'd call, Miss Bray.'

He was wearing a dressing gown of black silk with purple facings, drinking chocolate from a white porcelain cup. The room was so large that it must have run the length and width of the house, and was unlike anything I'd seen before. Apart from a huge square couch upholstered in white and a pair of carved and gilded pews it contained none of the things that most people find necessary for living, no small tables, no ornaments, no comfortable chairs. A huge mural of a rising sun with various horned and antlered creatures stretching out to it covered the wall opposite the windows. An ivory pillar carved for the whole of its length with skulls supported an opera cape and a top hat. A tailor's dummy stood in the middle of the room swathed in an oriental ballet costume, topped with a life-sized china head. The floor was of plain polished wood with islands of Bokhara carpets. Jules invited me to sit down, and I chose one of the pews.

'Have you heard, Topaz is being buried at six o'clock tonight in the cemetery outside the town? It was the best Marie and Father Benedict could do.'

I said I'd be there. 'There was something else too, Mr Estevan.'

'I hope I can be of service, Miss Bray.'

He sat on the edge of the white couch, quite unembarrassed by his state of undress or his calves and bare feet showing beneath the dressing gown. I'd never seen a man's feet so well-shaped.

I said: 'I want a list of Topaz Brown's lovers.'

He whistled and almost slopped his chocolate. I think it was a defeat for him to show surprise at anything, because after that first reaction he reverted to his usual attitude of amused cynicism, but sharper than before.

'Are you writing her biography, Miss Bray, or should I say hagiography? Is she to be numbered among the patron saints of your movement?'

'I'll leave that to the poets like you, Mr Estevan. I have a practical reason for asking.'

He looked at me, smiling but eyes shrewd. I knew he was longing to ask what my reason was, but wouldn't condescend to simple curiosity.

'I'm not sure that I'm your best authority. Wouldn't the maid help?'

'I tried. Apparently it offended her sense of professional discretion.'

He laughed. 'Poor Tansy. She is so desperately respectable.'

I waited.

'So you had to come to me. You realise that I'd only known Topaz for fourteen months or so, and that mostly here in Biarritz. We were together briefly in Paris last autumn, then met again when she came back here in February.

'But you talked to her every day. She must have said something about her . . .'

'Clients? Yes indeed. She was very candid.'

'Well, let's start with the men you know about in Biarritz this season.'

He put his cup down on the floor and sat up straight. 'I think you've gathered that the Englishman, Lord Beverley, was the current favourite, but that was only for the past week or so. There was a German baron for most of February, but his health broke down a couple of weeks ago, so he took himself off to Baden Baden. There was a man from the circus the baron didn't know about, but he doesn't count because he wasn't paying. Between you and me and the rest of Biarritz, the baron wanted her more for show than for anything, so naturally Topaz took her entertainment elsewhere.'

'What would have happened if the baron found out?'

'I don't know, because he never did. The latest news from Baden Baden is that the poor old devil is just about able to totter to the pump house.'

'Who else?'

'In between the baron and Lord Beverley there was an Italian, ugly as sin, but owned half Piedmont, who whisked her off to Paris for a few days, mainly to annoy his wife who was having a blatant affair with a Russian violinist.'

'And that's all?'

'You're implying that Topaz was hardly over-working? I defer to your knowledge of these matters. To be honest, the same thought had struck me. In the light of what we know now, I can understand why.'

'Do you mean her retirement or her suicide?'

He shrugged. I'd been wondering all the way there whether I should tell him about the underwear and the fish and admit that I didn't now believe it was suicide. I still wondered.

'If any of Topaz's former clients knew she was going to retire, would they have been worried that she might become indiscreet?'

He laughed. 'That's Tansy's influence showing. What do you mean by indiscreet?'

'Well, that she might do damage by talking about who her lovers had been . . .'

'My dear Miss Bray, if Topaz published advertisements in the newspapers, she could hardly tell the world anything it didn't know already. What you don't understand is that a man who becomes the lover of a woman as well known as Topaz is virtually taking up a public position. Isn't that the whole purpose of it?'

'Purpose?'

'To show he can afford her, to show he has the confidence to live at her level. It's not like some father of a family, good bourgeois church-goer in Paris or London, giving a handful of silver to a slut for ten minutes he hopes nobody will ever know about. What would be the point of paying a small fortune to women like Topaz or Marie if nobody knew about it?'

'I see.' I sat there, watching the sun bringing out the colours of the carpets, trying to adjust to this scheme of things. 'But didn't Lord Beverley have to stop seeing her when his father arrived?'

'His father, yes – although I'm sure the old boy's heard about it by now. But you may be sure young Beverley will be the hero of his clubs when he gets back. Worth losing a fortune for.'

'Has he lost a fortune?'

'So they say.'

'What about last year? Who were her lovers then?'

He put his hands to his temples, feigning weariness.

'Oh my dear Miss Bray, you are a hard taskmistress. Last year is a world away, further than the fall of Rome. If you insist, I shall try to make you out a list, but it will take some time.'

I left it at that for a while, and began to work my way round to another question, that had been worrying me since my conversation with Bobbie Fieldfare.

'You were there last Wednesday afternoon when Topaz made her will. In fact, you witnessed it. I don't want to imply that you would betray a confidence, but I wonder if it's possible that you mentioned it to anybody at all afterwards.'

I tried to be tactful, because I expected him to be mortally offended. All I got was another of his twisted smiles, as if he was amused against his will.

'Mentioned it? Only to about half of Biarritz by dinner time.'

I must have looked disapproving.

'You are about to tell me, Miss Bray, that a will is confidential. If I'd thought she intended it as her real will, I don't suppose I should have told a soul.'

'You didn't think it was meant as a real will?'

'Of course not. It was simply a good story, and Topaz would have been highly disappointed in me if I hadn't passed it on to as many people as possible.'

Again, my expression must have spoken for me.

'You see, some of us write poems or paint pictures. Topaz delighted in doing unexpected or amusing things and having them talked about. If every dinner table that mattered that evening had not been talking about Topaz Brown leaving all her money to the suffragettes, I should have been failing in my duty.'

'I see.'

We were silent for a while. I think he was interested to see that the idea hurt me. After a while I said I'd taken up enough of his time, and should see him at the funeral. He told me that he'd promised to escort Tansy Mills. I wondered whether that was because he thought it amusing to be seen in the company of the maid, or whether there was a touch of kindness in him.

'Marie will be there?'

'Of course. It will be a chance for her to practise her attitudes.'

'Attitudes?'

'Didn't you know she's to embark on a stage career? There's an American impresario who thinks she'll be the new Bernhardt – as long as she's not required to speak.'

I stood up. I'd still said nothing to him about my investigations.

'One thing I haven't asked, you've told me you and Topaz liked jokes. Were you planning a joke that last night?'

'No.'

'Is it possible that she was?'

He gave me a quick look: 'The underwear and the wine, you mean?'

'Can you think of any explanation for them?'

'No. Can you?'

'Topaz was . . . expensive, wasn't she? If somebody paid a good deal for a night with her and arrived to find her looking like, well . . .'

'Like any cheap tart?'

'Thank you. And the kind of food and wine that would cost a few francs in a back street café. Would that be Topaz's idea of a joke?'

He shook his head.

'Women don't make as much money as Topaz did without being serious about their work.'

'But did it matter to her any more? Suppose she decided to finish her career by making some kind of derisive gesture at the life she'd been living.'

'She wouldn't do that. It would be like a painter deliberately choosing the wrong colour, or a musician playing a wrong note.'

It seemed to matter to him that I should understand. I wasn't sure that I did.

'Suppose it had been somebody she'd hated for a long time, but had to tolerate because he was paying her.'

'Topaz didn't hate people. Besides, she could pick and choose. She once turned down two thousand pounds to spend a night with a man because she didn't like the shape of his beard.'

'I thought you said she took her work seriously.'

'She did. He went straight off to the barber's and sent her the beard in a parcel, along with a bank draft for three thousand pounds. He told everybody it was worth every whisker.'

As he showed me downstairs, I said I hoped Tansy would not make trouble with Marie at the funeral. His shrug was not reassuring. I think he saw life as a theatre-goer, a connoisseur of scenes. Perhaps that was why he'd decided to go to the funeral with Tansy. Perhaps that too was the reason for his sudden invitation to me, for a very different event.

'I wonder if you happen to be free tomorrow evening. Marie is giving a *Soirée Ancienne*.'

'What's that?'

'It's by way of being a preview of her stage performance, for an invited audience. Great ladies of the ancient world. All the guests are to wear classical costumes too. There's hardly a sandal or a laurel leaf left in Biarritz.'

'Alas, I've left my toga at home.'

'You could go as a Maenad. I'm sure they were continually throwing bricks.'

'I'm sorry to disappoint you, but I don't make a social habit of it. Is that why you wanted to take me there?'

He opened the front door, winced away from the rush of sunlight and sea air, recovered quickly.

'No. I thought you might appreciate the chance to keep at least one of your suspects under observation. I'll see you at the funeral, Miss Bray.'

I was angry with myself for underestimating Jules. It occurred to me too late that Tansy might have told him every detail of our shopping trip, including my guess about the suicide note. I couldn't trust either of them, and yet they were my two main sources of information. It was this annoyance at being trapped within Topaz's circle that led to my next move. I wanted some scientific facts instead of this web of personalities and values only partly understood.

I went to the consulate and asked them to recommend a good doctor. They assured me that everybody – meaning everybody from English society – went to Dr Campbell. They spoke highly of his friendliness and good manners and, as an afterthought, his professional skills. He lived and practised at a house in the Avenue de Bayonne, in the new quarter of the town north of the Grande Plage. There are medicinal baths there, fed by warm saline springs, and the numbers of fine new mansions and doctors' plates prove their popularity among fashionable invalids. I took the tramline – paying ten sous and saving on the cab fare – and found Dr Campbell's plate outside one of the most attractive of the mansions. After a short wait, a woman in an elegant grey dress showed me into a consulting room that looked more like a salon.

The man facing me was younger than I expected, but with a touch of grey in his square-cut beard, setting off an aquiline nose and intelligent, assessing eyes. There was an air of self-satisfaction about him as he invited me to take a seat, so I decided to waste no time tip-toeing around the point.

'Dr Campbell,' I said, 'how long would a fatal dose of laudanum take to work?'

'Why do you ask, Miss Bray?'

'Because I've become involved in the legal affairs of somebody who died from an overdose of laudanum.'

'Are we by any chance talking about the late Miss Topaz Brown?'

'We are.'

The fashionable doctor to the English community would naturally hear all the gossip. It was part of his work. He leaned back in his chair, gazing over my shoulder at a picture on the wall. It was a nocturne by Whistler, evidence of both fashionable taste and fashionable fees.

'It would depend on many things – the general health of the subject, body weight, whether the subject had taken alcohol . . .'

'There's evidence that she drank it in wine.'

'That might delay the onset of symptoms. But you could take it that the person would be overcome by a feeling of intense sleepiness within an hour. Soon after that she would lapse into sleep, then unconsciousness, then a state of deep coma. If no preventive action were taken, one would expect her to be dead within twelve hours of taking the dose.'

Topaz had invited her visitor to call at eight. She was dead and cold when Tansy found her at about ten o'clock the following morning. That would suggest the poison had been taken soon after her visitor's arrival.

Dr Campbell got up and moved over to the window. Yellow curtains framed a garden of daphnes and mimosa trees, the scent drifting in. He was proud of his position and his possessions.

'Was Miss Brown a patient of yours?'

'She never consulted me.'

He sounded disappointed. There were invitation cards and calling cards arranged along his mantelpiece, apparently casually but giving no doubt of his social success. Lord something would welcome his company at dinner. Sir John so and so requested the pleasure of calling at four.

'You said, doctor, "if no preventive action were taken". Do you mean her life might have been saved?'

'Indeed. Poisoning by laudanum, or other opium derivatives, is a comparatively gradual process. It's not like strychnine or cyanide. If the patient is reached in time, the prognosis may be hopeful.'

'There's an antidote?'

'The antidote is, in layman's terms, simply keeping the patient awake. Copious quantities of black coffee, walking her up and down, fighting off by any means the onset of unconsciousness may be effective.'

'What if somebody had found Miss Brown unconscious? Could she have been revived?'

'There would be a point when the coma became irreversible, but within limits, yes.'

'What limits? An hour after she'd taken it? Two hours? More?'

'It's almost impossible to answer that with any accuracy.'

'An informed guess, then. Suppose somebody had found Miss Brown three hours after she'd drunk the laudanum.'

'I should not wish to give this as evidence in a court of law, and it would depend on the dosage. But I should hazard a guess that if Miss Brown had been found up to three hours after losing consciousness, her life might have been saved.'

'And beyond that?'

'Beyond that, I should refuse even to guess.'

He picked up an invitation card from the display on his mantelpiece and turned it over and back, letting the sun glint off its gilt edge. I tried to adjust my view of Topaz's death to what he'd just told me. I'd assumed that the poisoning would be a quick process, that the murderer – if there had been a murderer – could kill her and go. But that wasn't the case at all. He, or she, couldn't be sure that nobody would find Topaz in those three hours, and if Topaz had been revived, surely her first words would accuse whoever had given her the wine. He, or she, would have to sit beside the sleeping woman for three hours or perhaps longer, until sleep became irreversible. I looked up and found the doctor's eyes on me.

'How much would it take to kill her?'

'That would depend on many things. If the person had been accustomed to using laudanum, then it would take quite a large amount. Laudanum contains only one per cent morphine. I've even heard of some nurse-maids giving a drop of it to children on a sugar lump to send them to sleep, not that that's a practice I'd recommend. An addict might drink it by the glassful and survive. Another person – a child or an adult in poor health – might be killed by a coffeespoonful.'

'So two or three teaspoons in a glass of wine . . .?'

'Might kill a person unaccustomed to laudanum, yes.'

'And yet I could walk out of here and buy as many bottles as I liked at any chemist's.'

'Indeed. But then I daresay you've taken Dover's Powders from time to time.'

'Occasionally for a stomach upset, when travelling.'

'And yet those powders, too, contain opium, Miss Bray. Should they be locked in a poison cabinet?'

I thanked Dr Campbell and said he must send me his bill.

'I believe you know my aunt, Lady Fieldfare,' he said.

'Indeed I do. We spent a lot of time together quite recently.'

He looked gratified, but a little embarrassed. 'Or my aunt by marriage, I should say. My mother's brother married her younger sister.'

He'd been helpful, and if he chose to take out some of his fee in harmless snobbery, I didn't resent it.

'Did you know that Lady Fieldfare's daughter Roberta is here in Biarritz? A charming young lady. I hope she is sleeping better.'

'Bobbie came to you with sleeping problems?'

'I hope you don't think I would betray my patients' confidence, Miss Bray. It was nothing at all serious, I assure you. As I told Miss Fieldfare, travelling often causes some disruption in ladies' sleeping habits.'

I'd got up to go, but this struck me stock-still, on the way to the door. Travelling might disrupt some women's sleep, but I was prepared to bet that Bobbie would not be one of them. The doctor was staring at me, and I did my best to sound unconcerned.

'I'm sure you were able to prescribe something helpful for her, doctor.'

But professional discretion had reasserted itself. He smiled, held the door for me and hoped I'd call on him again if he could do anything to help. His receptionist was standing at her desk, fiddling with a pot of mimosa.

'Mrs David Chester and her little girl will be here in five minutes,' he said to her. 'Show them in straightaway.'

He said it, I'm sure, only for the pleasure of using the MP's name, but it was an uncomfortable moment. I thought I'd rather not meet her and hurried down the path, hoping to be well out of the way by the time she arrived.

But Mrs Chester was early. I'd only just closed the gate behind me when a cab drew up, and the plump woman I'd last seen beside David Chester climbed out clumsily, her face full of worries. Everything about her was rounded, her calves exposed in clambering down, her eyes, her flushed cheeks, but it was a heavy rather than a comfortable roundness, as if her own body were one of her many burdens.

She didn't see me at first and turned back inside the cab, making plaintive noises. The driver showed no signs of helping her and sat there flicking at the reins, so that just as a child was stepping down the horse lurched forward and she came tumbling down the step, missed her mother's arms and landed on her knee in the gutter. It would have taken a harder woman than I am to resist the child's bawling and the mother's distress. I picked up the girl, no light weight, and set her down on the path.

'There, let's have a look at you.'

The child went on yelling. A smudge of red was appearing on the knee of her white stocking.

'Oh dear, oh dear,' said Mrs Chester. 'I knew something was going to happen.'

'It's all right,' I told her. 'It's only grazed.'

In an attempt to stop the bawling, I tried on the child a formula that worked very well with my nephews.

'Come along, dry your tears and be a brave little soldier.'

The child stopped bawling just long enough to give me a look that reminded me disconcertingly of her father in court.

'Girls can't be soldiers,' she said. Then she started yelling again.

I suggested to Mrs Chester that we should get the child into the house and let the doctor have a look at her.

'Don't like the doctor. Don't want to see the doctor.'

Her mother gave me a despairing look.

'She won't go in, not when she's in that mood, and Louisa must see him.'

'Mummy, what's happening, Mummy?'

Another child's voice, older but plaintive, came from inside the cab. A pale round face looked out.

'Wait a minute, Louisa. Your sister's . . . Oh Naomi, please stop crying . . . oh dear . . .'

The sight of the woman's complete helplessness gave me my idea. She was, in spite of her plumpness, a feather for any wind. Fate had shown me, in this yelling infant, a means of spoiling Bobbie's plans, and I was not going to neglect it.

I said to Mrs Chester: 'Would you like me to look after little Naomi in the garden, while you go in and see the doctor?'

'Oh dear . . . oh would you . . .? I'm sorry to be such a nuisance, only . . .'

I led Naomi firmly to a little gazebo in front of the house, sat her on the bench and tied up the knee with my handkerchief.

'You see, we're quite all right here, aren't we, Naomi?'

With many backward glances and nervous waves, Mrs Chester made for the doctor's front door, the older pale child trailing behind her. Naomi went on snivelling for a while after the door had closed behind them, until she realised that I was not a sympathetic audience.

'It hurts.'

'Try counting up to fifty and see if it still hurts.'

She got as far as fifteen then: 'Are you a governess?'

'Why do you ask?'

'You sound like a governess.'

I didn't contradict her. It was as good an identity as any.

'Do you like being here at the seaside?'

'No. I hate the seaside. We're here because of Louisa's lungs.' She said it as if she disliked her sister's lungs intensely.

'What's wrong with Louisa's lungs?'

'She coughs a lot, especially at nights.'

'That's a pity.'

'Yes, it is, because it wakes me up. Anyway, it used to wake me up, only now I sleep in the same room as Mummy, and the nurse sleeps with Louisa. Well, she did, until Mummy gave her notice.'

'Oh dear. What for?'

'Mummy said she'd been disrespectful to Daddy. Mummy says foreigners are disrespectful and dirty most of the time, especially the women.'

'Doesn't your mummy like foreign countries?'

'No, Mummy wants to go home to London. Daddy will have to go home soon anyway. Mummy says he's a very important man and the King can't do without him.'

Can't do without him, I thought, for sending my friends to Holloway. Still, what the horrible child was telling me was good news. It sounded as if it would take very little to detach the family from Biarritz.

'My daddy's in Parliament.'

'Is he? Are you going to be in Parliament when you grow up?' I thought I'd try a seed or two, even in this unlikely ground.

Again, that look of her father's. 'Ladies can't be in Parliament. I'm going to marry the Prime Minister and have lots of dresses with long trains and go to tea with the Queen.'

Gradually, she forgot about the graze on her knee and

chattered on as if she'd known me for years. They had a parrot at home in Knightsbridge that she was anxious to see again, and a little dog belonging to her mother. Louisa had to take nasty medicines, but always got the second helping at meals because of building her up. Daddy liked Louisa best because she was the eldest, but her hair was nowhere near as long as Naomi's. Most of this passed me by like the buzzing of the early bees in the garden, then the door opened and Mrs Chester came out, holding Louisa by the hand and looking a little less worried.

Now that she'd had time to collect her wits she seemed to notice me properly for the first time, but to my relief there was no sign of recognition. She would leave anything to do with politics or the law courts to her husband.

'Have you been good, Naomi? I'm so grateful to you, Miss . . .'

'Miss Jones,' I said. 'Jane Jones.'

'She's a governess,' Naomi piped up. I didn't contradict her. We walked together to the cab, Naomi holding my hand in her hot, plump paw.

'May we drop you anywhere, Miss Jones?'

'That's very kind.'

I named a hotel at some distance from my own and asked how the consultation with the doctor had gone.

'He was quite pleased with her, wasn't he, Louisa. He says she's got to keep on taking the medicine, and make sure she gets her sleep in the afternoons.'

Louisa made a face. I was sure there was nothing seriously wrong with her that looser clothes and a run along the sands wouldn't cure, but Dr Campbell couldn't buy Whistler paintings on that kind of prescription.

I said earnestly: 'And I'm sure she'll be a lot better when you can get her away from Biarritz.'

'What?'

Mrs Chester's jaw dropped, and her mouth went as wide as her eyes.

I chattered on: 'Such an unhealthy spot for children, but of course there's no help for it if your husband has to be here and I'm sure Louisa will pick up wonderfully when you go home.'

'But . . . but . . . everybody said it was such a healthy place.'

I dropped my voice. 'Well, it would just suit the French to say that, wouldn't it?'

'But the King comes here.'

It was a wail of appeal to the highest authority.

'Yes, but he's not looking very well either, is he, poor man? And I happen to know . . .' I dropped my voice even lower, as if imparting state secrets. 'I happen to know that he almost didn't come here last year because of a cholera scare. Of course, they pretended that they'd done something to improve the drains and it was all hushed up, but . . .'

'The drains. Oh dear, oh dear.'

She stared at me, then, to my alarm, large tears ran slowly down her cheeks.

'Oh dear, what will my husband say?'

'Your husband can hardly blame you for the state of the municipal drains.'

I'm afraid I spoke more sharply than a governess should, but luckily she didn't notice.

'He didn't want to come here at all. He's such a busy man. Only he'd do anything for Louisa so when the doctor in London recommended here, I persuaded him and . . . oh dear.'

Both the girls were quite impassive, as if it was normal to see their mother in tears. I'd have accused myself of cruelty, except that I was trying to avoid a worse cause for tears. Although, when I saw what the man had done to his wife and daughters, I was half inclined to let Bobbie shoot him after all.

I persevered. 'And then there are the other things.'

'Other things?'

Her eyes darted round the cab, as if expecting to see plague germs made visible.

'The things we mustn't talk about in front of the little ones.' Naomi began to pay attention, face avid. 'Some of the people who come here, walking up and down the parade as bold as brass. You simply wouldn't believe . . .'

I saw from her face that she had caught my meaning,

would have been half eager for me to go on, if the children hadn't been there.

'Altogether,' I said, 'if the choice were mine, I'd be on my way back to England tomorrow.'

Short of throwing train timetables at her, I thought I could hardly do more. With luck, the Chester family would be on its way home within days. Even if Bobbie followed them, her opportunities would be fewer in London and the rest of the organisation would be there to restrain her.

I got down from the cab at the hotel I'd named with the sense of a piece of work well done. For the while at least I'd done what I could about one of my problems, and could turn my mind to the other. As a small experiment, I found a chemist's shop and asked for a bottle of laudanum. The apothecary took my money, wrapped up a bottle in blue paper and handed it over, hardly looking at me. It was as simple as that.

NINE

TOPAZ BROWN WAS BURIED THAT evening in a churchyard on a cliff top. I arrived early, while two labourers were still digging the grave, and took my stand among the tombs. I watched as the hearse rumbled up the steep road drawn by two black horses with nodding plumes, two carriages behind it. A trim little priest got out of the first one, followed by a woman in a black cloak and a very elegant hat, heavily veiled, carrying sprays of mauve and white lilac. As they came nearer, I realised it must be Marie de la Tourelle.

The second carriage contained Tansy, Jules Estevan and the bald solicitor. Tansy and Jules made an odd pair as they stepped carefully among the graves, he tall and well-tailored, she clinging to his arm in her thick black coat, looking smaller than ever. Then, some way behind, there was a motor-car. I saw the first five arrivals looking at it and was near enough to hear a gasp from Marie when a man got out. He was dressed strangely for a funeral in full evening dress with cloak and top hat. But it was, all things considered, very civil of Lord Beverley to find time to pay his last respects to Topaz. They arranged themselves round the open grave after the hired pall-bearers had manoeuvred the coffin into place, the priest at one side, Marie close to him, Tansy as far away from Marie as she could get, with Jules beside her and the solicitor hovering in between. Lord Beverley, after looking around with a lost air as if wondering when the next race was due to start, stood beside Tansy.

I'd begun to hope that the occasion would pass off without the official presence of the Women's Social and

Political Union when the churchyard gate creaked open and the largest wreath I'd ever seen walked in. That, at least, was the first impression because I couldn't see Bobbie and Rose behind it. The outside of the wreath was laurel, the inner part a mass of white flowers with a bullseye of purple violets in the centre. A ribbon lashed across it read 'Votes for Women'. The assemblage halted not far from Tansy. She gave one glance towards Rose, then looked away. Caught between the wreath and Marie with her lilacs she looked red with anger, and I was relieved when the priest began reading.

During the service I had the unmistakable feeling of being watched. It was not by any of the group at the graveside. They were too intent on the priest or each other. Eventually I let my eyes follow the feeling. Not twenty yards away from me was a plump, clean-shaven man in a black coat and hat, standing very still, looking very carefully. He seemed to be doing as I was, attending the funeral but keeping far enough away from it to avoid contact with the other mourners. In fact, from the way he had tucked himself in beside a stone angel, you might almost have said that he was hiding. Tansy's Mr Shadow, beyond a doubt. The man who'd followed us on our shopping trip. The man from the solicitor's who said he wanted to see Topaz's papers. Well, Tansy might have believed that, but I didn't. To my eyes, the man had plain-clothes police officer written all over him. It was typical, I thought, of police tactics against us that they should find out about Topaz's legacy even before we did and send somebody to snoop round and do his best to discredit us.

I was so annoyed at first that I intended, as soon as the funeral was over, to go and have it out with him. I'd come to France with no dangerous intent, and it was bitter to find myself trailed like a criminal. Then I saw Bobbie glance at him from behind her wreath and knew what a waste it would be to drive him away. Nothing would be more likely to cramp the style of a prospective assassin than finding Scotland Yard or its French equivalent dogging her steps. The only problem would be to get him to transfer his attentions from myself to Bobbie, but unless I was greatly mistaken, she was likely to attend to that herself soon enough.

At the graveside, Jules and Marie were joining the priest in prayer. Tansy was crying into a large white handkerchief provided by Jules. The priest finished his prayer and rained down a handful of earth. As it pattered on the coffin lid, Marie stepped forward like an actress on cue.

'Farewell,' she said, flung the lilacs on top of the coffin, crossed herself then stood with head bent, as still as a statue. But the effect was spoiled by Bobbie, who could also recognise a cue. She left Rose staggering under the weight of the giant wreath, took a step back from the graveside and let fly.

'We have come here to pay tribute to our sister, Topaz Brown.' Her beautiful voice, deep but clear, rang out over the darkening graveyard. I heard a gasp of protest from somebody.

'Yes, our sister. However degraded a life she may have led, however tarnished in the eyes of the world, our sister Topaz Brown kept alive in her heart and in her mind one great hope, the hope that one day women would rise up and claim . . .'

There was a babble. Marie the statue had come alive and uttered cries of protest when Bobbie talked about Topaz's degraded life. Jules Estevan moved towards her, taking his attention away from Tansy. So when Bobbie got to women rising up, Tansy called out:

'That's rubbish.'

Jules lunged away from Marie back towards Tansy, without being able to stop either of them shouting. The priest was making shushing sounds at Marie and the solicitor at Bobbie, without any effect on either. Bobbie, who was used to worse interruptions than this, pressed on.

'. . . would rise up and claim their rights. Topaz Brown, alas, did not live to see that new dawn. She died a victim of the world that men have imposed upon women. Although her death may have been, in one sense, by her own hand . . .'

Marie shouted out something in French. The priest raised his voice in protest. The solicitor laid a hand on Bobbie's arm and was shaken off. But all these things were nothing in comparison with what Tansy did. She took a step towards Bobbie and yelled at the very top of her voice:

'It wasn't by her own hand. She was murdered, and the person who did it is standing here.'

And that was almost the end of Topaz Brown's funeral. Bobbie went on with her speech, but most of the audience faded away. Jules got his arm round Tansy, half support and half restraint, and led her off sobbing towards the gate, the solicitor following. The priest nudged Marie, who had reverted to her mourning statue pose, and led her in the same direction, but with more dignity, and only after we had heard Jules' carriage driving away. That left just three of them at the graveside: Bobbie still talking about the wrongs of women to the flying clouds, Rose staring after her sister and Lord Beverley with the air of somebody who was finding events more interesting than he'd expected.

'Topaz Brown, we honour you,' Bobbie concluded.

She and Rose laid down the wreath.

'Jolly well done,' said Lord Beverley.

Bobbie glared at him, took Rose's arm and they moved off together. I looked towards the stone angel where the plump man had been standing, but there was no sign of him. He could easily have slipped away while everybody was arguing.

That left only Lord Beverley. He jumped when I walked over and introduced myself.

'I've heard about you. You're the woman who throws bricks and things.'

'Only in a good cause.'

'Quite,' he said. 'Oh quite.'

He was perhaps twenty-seven or twenty-eight, tall and fair haired, with an aquiline nose and well-shaped lips.

'Got a lot of sympathy for you myself,' he said. 'Very plucky women.'

'I'd like to talk to you.'

He shied away. 'Not very political, I'm afraid.'

'It's not about politics. It's about Topaz Brown.'

I'd half expected him to walk away, but he looked mildly interested.

'That's it, is it? What about coming back to town with me in my motor?'

As we walked away, the labourers moved in and began shovelling the banked earth into the grave. Lord Beverley helped me up into the passenger seat and began the long business of starting the motor. Then, suddenly:

'Well I'll be . . . What's going on there?'

He was looking back towards the site of the grave. Perched up as we were, we could see it well, and the two labourers leaning on their shovels. But there was something else, and when I saw it I couldn't help gasping, hit by the superstition that will never leave even the most rational of us in graveyards. Topaz Brown's grave had suddenly acquired its own statue, an equestrian statue, of marble so white that it seemed to generate a light of its own in the dusk, with the black form of a rider just visible on its back. Lord Beverley let the engine die and we stared, transfixed. Then, as we watched, the marble horse moved, extended a foreleg, bowed down its head in a long gesture of respect and grief. It held the pose for what seemed like minutes but were probably only seconds, then raised its head and moved away quite collectedly, like any horse of flesh and blood, away from the grave, picking its way through the tombs, out of our sight.

'Well,' Lord Beverley said. 'Well.'

He started the motor again, and talk was impossible on the journey back to town because of the noise. When we got back to the promenade he stopped the car and a merciful silence fell. It was dark by now, except for strings of coloured lights, with the sea thumping at the beach a few yards away.

'Who was the chap on the horse?'

'I don't know. Do you?'

'Whoever he was, I wouldn't mind his stable. She knew a lot of people, of course, foreign royalty and so on.'

He sounded almost cheerful again. I think the horse incident had shaken him as it had shaken me, but he was not a man who pondered things for long. If anything, the idea of some exotic prince riding up to pay a last farewell to Topaz seemed to please him. There was still, ten years after Eton or Harrow, something of the schoolboy about Lord Beverley.

I said: 'You know Topaz Brown left our movement a great deal of money?'

'Bit of a surprise, what?'

'Indeed. Is it true you'd left Topaz and gone back to the woman they called La Pucelle?'

He gave a little 'phew' of surprise, but I saw no reason for beating about the bush.

'It was the other way about. I, um, started with Marie, so to speak, and moved on to Topaz.'

Once he'd got over his surprise he seemed quite happy to talk about it, but then a man might be complacent to have two of the best-known courtesans in Europe competing for his custom.

'Marie seemed to think you'd changed your mind again. She said you found Topaz *vulgaire*.'

'Did she indeed? Well, if it means she liked to enjoy herself and didn't mind who knew it, then I suppose Topaz was vulgar. But in the best possible way, if you see what I mean. After La Pucelle, she came as rather a relief.'

'Marie was temperamental?'

'Marie likes to play the goddess.'

'And since you were footing the bill, you didn't see why you should provide the worship as well?'

He whistled. 'You're remarkably straight talking, Miss Bray.'

It was just as well I hadn't bruised his aristocratic ears with some of the things I heard in Holloway.

'Anyway,' he said, 'I have the impression that Marie, um, prefers women. When she's not on duty, so to speak.'

It was too dark to see, but I believe he was blushing.

'Lord Beverley, would I be right in thinking that this kind of thing is all rather new to you?'

'Oh dash it. Come off it. I mean naturally a fellow's been around a bit . . .'

'I mean the likes of Marie and Topaz.'

'You're wondering how a chap like me can compete, you mean? You haven't heard about my stroke of luck?'

I said I'd only recently arrived in Biarritz.

'But it was all over London as well. I won ten thousand pounds in one afternoon at the Cheltenham spring meeting and I thought well, I'll jolly well spend it. I mean, I'm getting married next month so I shan't have many other chances, shall I? Nearly all gone now, worse luck, and the guv'nor's arrived to read the riot act. *Les jeux sont faits*, so to speak. And now Topaz is dead as well.'

He sounded quite sad about it. We listened to the waves for a while, then he said: 'I was probably the last man, um, with her, so to speak.'

'When?'

'The night before she killed herself. Tuesday night.'

'Did she seem unhappy?'

'No, merry as a grig. One of the best times I ever had.'

'And you had no appointment to see her on the Wednesday evening?'

'We'd planned a motor trip along the coast but I had to call it off. I heard the guv'nor was on his way, prodigal son's presence required in sackcloth and ashes.'

'When did you call it off?'

'I sent a note round to her hotel early on the Wednesday morning.'

So Topaz had been left with Wednesday evening unexpectedly free. Whatever she had planned for it must have been decided at short notice.

'Miss Bray, may I ask you something? Her maid, that outburst about Topaz being, um, murdered. Was there anything in that?'

'Tansy is upset. She thinks Marie poisoned Topaz.'

'But why, for goodness' sake?'

'Jealousy. Over you.'

He groaned. 'I hope that one doesn't get to the guv'nor. Wild oats is one thing, but being mixed up in this sort of thing – well, that would be a bit over the odds.'

'You don't believe it?'

'It's insane. You must stop the woman saying things like that.'

I said I'd do what I could. I still needed his co-operation.

'Lord Beverley, I'd be grateful if you could tell me something about the procedure when you visited Topaz.'

'Ye gods, Miss Bray . . .'

I think he was on the point of jumping out of his

motor-car and bolting.

'For instance, I suppose you used her private door at the side of the hotel. Did she give you a key to it?'

'Oh no. You rang a bell and the maid came down and let you in. Then you went up in the lift while the maid waited downstairs. I suppose she came back up later.'

'Did you ever go through the main hotel entrance instead?'

'No, you didn't do that.'

He was beginning to relax again, although he was obviously puzzled.

'One more thing, when you sent Topaz a note to say you wouldn't be seeing her on Wednesday, did you send anything else with it?'

'No.'

'Did you ever send her a fire opal pendant?'

'No, nothing in the way of jewellery. A flower or two, but apart from that she made it pretty clear she preferred the money direct. Saved a great deal of messing about.'

'When you were with Topaz on Tuesday, did she say anything about a practical joke she was planning?'

'No, no particular joke that I can think of. We laughed a lot, though. You did, with Topaz.'

He sighed. I said I must let him go to his dinner.

'Can't say I'm looking forward to it very much. Lecture from the guv'nor, probably, on being a good husband and father. By George, Miss Bray, you women keep on about not having opportunities, but we men lead a dog's life too sometimes, you know.'

I said he must tell the House of Lords about it in due course.

'You will stop that maid of hers going around talking nonsense, won't you? Apart from anything else, Marie couldn't have killed her on Wednesday night. She has a whatjumacallit . . . an alibi.'

'Has she?'

'She was in the hotel dining room having supper until after midnight. I noticed because I was afraid she'd come across and say something while I was with the guv'nor, but luckily she didn't.'

'Who was with her?'

'Plump little Yankee fellow. Seems he's a theatre producer and he's going to put her on the stage as Mary Stuart or Cleopatra or somebody like that. Anyway, there they were with their heads together, so it's all nonsense about her and Topaz.'

He helped me out then roared off along the promenade, steering with one hand, raising his top hat to me with the other.

I walked until I'd found what I wanted. It didn't take long. The posters were all over the town and I'd noticed them with half an eye, not thinking there was anything significant about them because one circus poster looks much like another. Until, that is, you look at one of them closely in the light from a hotel foyer and see a white horse standing on its hind legs and a masked rider, cloak billowing out, plumed hat flourished in his left hand. El Cid and his wonderful white horses, said the poster. There were performances daily at 5 p.m. and 8 p.m. When I'd told Lord Beverley that I didn't know who the rider of the white horse could be, I'd spoken the truth. But I'd had my suspicions and didn't share his romantic notion of a farewell from anonymous royalty.

El Cid, though, would have to wait till morning. I spent the next few hours in a shop doorway, watching the rooms above a grocer's in an unfashionable street where, as Rose had told me, she and Bobbie were lodging. Rose returned alone soon after I took up my position. Her shoulders were slumped and she was walking slowly, looking depressed. More than an hour later Bobbie arrived, also alone, striding along as purposefully as usual. I waited, alert for a young man in sporting dress, but by midnight neither of them had reappeared. By then I judged that David Chester should be safe in his bed and I could go to mine. I wondered whether Lord Beverley had enjoyed his evening with his father, and whether anybody could possibly be as innocent as that young man appeared to be.

TEN

NEXT MORNING I WALKED TO the Champ de Pioche, an open space about a mile outside the town where the circus had its camp. I arrived, judging by the noise and the smells, just as they were mucking out the animals. Nobody seemed to notice me as I wandered past the big top into the village of caravans, huts and cages that made up the living quarters. Eventually I stopped a red-haired lad in an overcoat several sizes too large for him and asked him in French where I could find El Cid. He replied, in fluent Liverpudlian, that I'd find him at the stables. Straight on past the llamas and turn left at the camels. The stables turned out to be remarkably solid structures for a travelling circus, made mostly of wood with canvas roofs. A row of shining, shifting haunches was visible over the half doors, there was a smell of good hay and the sound of champing from inside the boxes. I saw a man shovelling dung into a basket and again asked for El Cid. He grinned, dumped a shovelful and yelled cheerfully:

'Sid, lady wants you.'

The face that appeared from the end box was as brown and creased as a sailor's, with bright dark eyes under a helmet of black hair. The man called Sid looked at me then walked out to meet me, taking his time, wiping his hands on his breeches. He was smaller than I am, jockey-sized, but with shoulders as broad as a prize-fighter's under a grey jersey. His legs were bowed from much riding, and he must have been forty or more, but he walked as if he were pleased with himself. A cock on a dung-heap, if ever there was one. I thought of Lord Beverley and his European royalty, and couldn't help smiling. The little man smiled back, like a child letting another child in on a joke.

'What can I do for you, lady?'

The voice could have come from any street market in London.

I said: 'I believe you knew Topaz Brown.'

He nodded, quite at ease.

'My name's Nell Bray. I wonder if I could have a word with you.'

'Sidney Greenbow at your service, otherwise known as El Cid. I'm giving Grandee his grooming. If you'd like to step in with me we could have our chat while I'm getting on with it.'

The other man had stopped shovelling dung and was grinning at me, curious, I think, to see if I'd accept the invitation. Sid Greenbow swung back the half door and I followed him into the dim light of the box. Clean golden straw came almost up to my knees. A gleaming white horse stopped eating from the manger and swung his head towards me, whickering a little. I stroked his muzzle and found it as soft as a cat's fur.

'Was it Grandee you took to Topaz Brown's funeral last night?'

'Of course. Nothing but the best for Topaz.'

The horse turned back to his feed and Sidney picked up a body brush and curry comb and began smoothing his flank in long, arching strokes. At every third stroke he ran the brush over the teeth of the curry comb with a shimmering, rasping sound, hissing gently through his teeth all the time. He showed no curiosity at all about why I was there and for the first few minutes I just watched him at work, lulled by the dim light and the soft regular sounds.

At last I said: 'Had you known her long?'

He was brushing the horse's belly by then, and didn't look up or break the rhythm of his brushing.

'Twelve years or more. When I first met her, she was on the halls. I had an act myself, "Cuthbert the Calculating Horse", pot-bellied skewbald with a liking for mint pastilles, so naturally we'd find ourselves on the same bill from time to time.'

'I didn't know Topaz was on the halls. What did she do?'

'Precious little. She was part of a novelty singing act called the Chanson Sisters, though they weren't any more sisters than I am. The other one did most of the singing and Topaz did the good looks, only she wasn't called Topaz then. She took that up after she went into her present line of work – or her past line of work I should say.'

He sounded regretful, but not grief stricken, though perhaps it's hard to sound grief stricken when you're gently brushing round a horse's most intimate parts. The animal fidgeted, but calmed down at once when he murmured a few words to it.

'How long ago was that?'

'About ten years. For a while she kept up both lines and went on doing a bit on the halls, then she was doing so well on the other thing she gave it up.'

'But you kept on seeing her?'

I knew, from a sociological study I'd read on the subject, that most prostitutes had a man as a kind of manager and guardian who took much of their profits. I thought that might have been Sidney Greenbow's rôle in Topaz's life.

'No, not kept on. I'd just see her from time to time, and we'd have a drink together and tell each other how we were doing. The thing about Topaz, however famous she was, she never went standoffish. I remember one night I saw her coming out of the Empire on the arm of some toff and I'd just come straight from doing my act so was in my diddicoy gear. I yelled out "How'y doing, Topaz?" not thinking. And she turned round and smiled at me and called out, "Not so bad, Sid. Are you going to tell my fortune for me?" You should have seen the toff's face, but the crowd loved it. She'd do anything for a laugh, would Topaz.'

'What about when she started travelling? Did you go with her?'

'Of course not. I had my act, didn't I? By then I'd got together with an Irishman and we'd worked up a comic cossack turn and were doing the circuses. But now and then it would happen that I'd be somewhere and she'd be somewhere, and we'd meet each other again, and so it would go.'

He moved sideways and started working on the horse's near hind quarter. I was relieved to find him so willing to talk, but worried about what would happen when we came to his more recent relationship with Topaz. From what Jules had said, there was considerably more to it than meeting for an occasional drink.

'Did you know she was going to be here in Biarritz?'

'Oh yes. I tried to work it so I'd be here at the same time as she would. I wanted her to see the Dons working; after all she was a shareholder, wasn't she?'

'Shareholder? In what?'

'In this.' He tapped the body brush gently on the horse's haunch. 'Grandee and the rest of the Dons. She gave me the money for them.'

'The Dons.'

'The horses. That's my name for them, on account of them being high bred Spaniards. I told Topaz, "You and I might have come out of the gutter, but we own six horses with better pedigrees than half the royalty in Europe." She liked that.'

'Were they very expensive?'

He whistled. 'You can say they were. A thousand for Grandee here, he's the stallion, five hundred for the two geldings, then another two thousand for the three mares. I'll show you them later. We have to keep them over the other side of the ground because of Grandee.'

That made, according to my calculations, three thousand five hundred pounds' worth of horseflesh.

'And she paid for all that?'

'All but a few hundred I'd managed to save. What happened, I met her in Paris three years ago, a bit down on my luck because the circus I'd been with had gone bankrupt. Anyway, we had a drink as usual, and I told her about these horses I'd heard of for sale in Barcelona. The owner had died and the whole circus world knew these were class horses. Anyway, not thinking anything, I talked about it to Topaz and said what an act I could get up with horses like that. I knew there was no more chance of me having them than getting the Archangel Gabriel to come down and sit in a canary cage. And she said, cool as you please: "Well, why don't we buy them?"

'Of course, I didn't believe her at first, but she said she had a bit of money to spare, and nothing would content her but we should both go off to Barcelona as soon as she was free and buy them. Which was just what we did.'

'You said she was a shareholder?'

'That's right. We had a regular business proposition. I had the right to work them for three years, building up the act. After that I'd start paying back the money, until in the end I'd paid her back the original capital, plus five hundred interest, and the Dons would be mine outright.'

'It would take you a long time to pay back that sort of money, wouldn't it?'

'Not as long as you might think. We're doing very nicely now, me and the Dons. After Biarritz it's Nice, then the summer in Paris, then back to London for Christmas. Anyway, it wouldn't have mattered with Topaz. She'd never have pressed me for money I hadn't got.'

'And what happens now she's dead?'

For the first time he stopped his brushing and looked at me directly.

'What do you mean, what happens?'

'About the horses?'

'Well, they're my horses. That's what she wanted.'

He went on brushing, carefully moving the thick tail aside from the horse's hocks. I wondered if he was as blind as he seemed to be to the legal complexities, and whether there'd been anything in writing. I already knew enough about Topaz to doubt that. I moved on to equally sensitive ground.

'You'd been seeing quite a lot of Topaz while you were here in Biarritz, hadn't you?'

'Who told you that? Tansy, I suppose.' He sounded amused rather than annoyed.

'No, not Tansy.'

'I know who it is then.' Again, no annoyance. He'd moved over to the offside leg, so now I could see his face as he worked. 'If you're asking were Topaz and I keeping company, well, yes we were for a while.'

I was struck by that 'keeping company', the homely old-fashioned phrase that might go with a country courtship and sounded so oddly here.

'While she was earning her money from the baron?'

He laughed. 'Yes, I do know who you've been talking to.'

He glanced up at me, as if it had struck him for the first time that I was there for some reason other than idle curiosity. But his tone didn't change.

'Yes, it would happen from time to time. Topaz was a girl who needed her exercise, and not every man who paid through the nose for her company knew what to do with it when he got it. Topaz said the baron was a nice enough old gent and of course she did what she could for him, which with Topaz would be something like his money's worth, but there wasn't much steam left in the boiler. So I'd go round to see her now and then and we'd . . .'

He whistled two chirpy notes.

'At her hotel?'

'Yes. That's why I thought you'd heard about me from Tansy. Tansy didn't approve of me one little bit, what with being from the circus and not paying for it. She'd come down to let me in with a face on her that said if it was left to her she'd kick me straight out again.'

'You didn't have a key to that side door?'

'Of course not. Topaz didn't give people keys. You can see why not. I mean, supposing I was to walk in while the baron was there doing his best?'

I said, feeling thankful that I didn't blush easily: 'Would Topaz wear anything special for you?'

I had in mind, of course, the shop-girl's honeymoon underwear and whether it would appeal to Sid. I stared straight down into his face, expecting anger or ridicule. What I did not expect was the expression on it of sudden tenderness, an expression reminding me that this little man had ridden a valuable horse a long way in the dusk, to make one sorrowing gesture at Topaz's grave.

'It was always special with her. Silk so fine you could see her skin through it. Satin you'd think would purr when you stroked it. Nothing flashy though, never flashy. Taste she had, better than a lot of women who were born to it. I'd open the bedroom door and she'd be lying there: "What do you think of this then, Sid?" And I'd tell her what I thought of it. In my own way I'd tell her.'

He'd put the body brush down, and while he was talking he'd been stroking the horse's gleaming haunch with his hand, long, lingering strokes. He went on stroking when he finished talking, staring at nothing.

I said: 'You'd have a glass of wine?'

'Oh yes.' He smiled, but it was a sad smile. 'She was trying to educate me, you see. She'd get them to send up a bottle from her stock along with a little something from the kitchens, and I had to guess what it was and when it was grown. She said we owed it to ourselves and where we'd come from to get the best there was and know when we'd got it.'

If Sid was speaking the truth, nothing in all this went with cheap underwear and cheap wine. And yet they sounded so much like a parody of what Sid had described that I was sure there must be a connection.

'Did she ever play jokes on you? Dress up as somebody else, for instance?'

'No, not with me. I'd be in, sometimes, on jokes she played on other people.'

'What sort of jokes?'

He picked up the body brush and started work again.

'Well, last year there was that time she pretended to be a Red Indian princess. I found her the ponies, of course, and two or three of the lads done up in grease paint and feathers. You should have seen the faces when they all turned up outside the hotel just at lunch time and asked for buffalo steaks.'

'Was she planning any sort of joke last week?'

He shook his head. 'Not that I'd heard of. She'd usually be in touch with me when she was planning something elaborate. But I hadn't seen her for a week or ten days because she was spending a lot of time with that young toff who won the fortune at Cheltenham.'

He sounded bitter about Lord Beverley, but perhaps

that wasn't surprising. As for the joke, Topaz wouldn't have needed circus ponies or grease paint for what she'd been planning on Wednesday night.

'How did she get in touch with you when she wanted to see you?'

'She'd send somebody down with a note.'

'Did she send a note asking to see you at eight o'clock on Wednesday night?'

'No, she didn't. She didn't send for me at all, but if she had it wouldn't have been for eight o'clock. She knew I'd be in the ring at eight o'clock. It was always later when I went to her, after the second show.' He was beginning to sound annoyed, and I could hardly blame him. He went on with his grooming for a few minutes, then: 'So they think she was killed at eight o'clock, do they?'

'Killed?'

'Yes. Isn't that what it's all about?'

'You know the verdict was suicide?'

The sound he made brought the horse's head swinging round to know what the trouble was.

'Topaz would never kill herself.' He said it with total certainty.

'But if you thought she'd been murdered, why didn't you do something about it?'

He shrugged. 'It wouldn't have brought her back, would it? Anyway, if you go making trouble for the authorities, they don't forget it, no matter what the reason might be.'

'Who do you think killed her?'

Another shrug. 'It could have been anybody. She was in a dangerous trade. She knew that.'

I'd been so well-schooled by Jules and Tansy in the gulf between Topaz and the street corner prostitute that this almost shocked me.

'You're talking as if she was operating up alleyways in Whitechapel.'

'It doesn't matter if the trapeze bar's solid gold. Make a mistake on it, and you're just as dead.'

'You think Topaz was killed by a client?'

He, at least, didn't object to that word.

'Yes, I do think that. What else is there to think?'

'And you haven't told anybody, haven't tried to get the police to investigate?'

'What would be the use? The kind of clients she had, they'd only hush it up.'

'Did she have any enemies you knew of?'

'Topaz didn't go in for enemies.'

He'd worked his way round to the stallion's head and was brushing, with great gentleness, between the wide brown eyes. When he'd finished he ran the brush down the curry comb for one last time, took something out of his pocket and fed it to the animal.

'There, that'll do him for now. Come and look at the mares.'

Various eyes followed us as we walked across the field, but without much curiosity. A woman was exercising a troupe of jet black greyhounds. A girl was hanging coloured tights to dry outside a brightly painted caravan. The three white mares shared their stable block with a group of Shetland ponies. We leaned over the half doors, looking in.

Sid said: 'I haven't asked you what your interest is.'

It was fair enough.

'I'm a member of the Women's Social and Political Union. Suffragettes, if you like. Topaz left all her money to us. You'd heard about that, I suppose.'

He nodded.

'Were you surprised?'

'It's her money.'

He didn't sound resentful.

'Did you think she might have left some to you?'

'Why should she? We didn't think about dying, either of us. If it happens, it happens.'

'Did she tell you she was going to retire this year and buy a vineyard?'

'Not this year, no. But I knew she was thinking of it. Does it make any difference to getting the money, finding out who murdered her?'

'It shouldn't.'

I didn't want to go into the legal implications.

'Well then?'

'I suppose . . . I suppose it seems unfair to take Topaz's money without trying to get . . . justice for her.'

It surprised me as I said it, but I realised I meant it. Sid gave me one of his twisted smiles. His hand was stroking a rug flung over the stable door. It seemed that he always needed to be stroking something.

'Will it do her any good?'

We stood leaning on the door for a while, so close together that I could feel the steady rhythm of his breathing. After a while I said I must go and he said he'd walk back with me to the gate. When we were almost there he said:

'Did you ever meet her?'

'No.'

'You're like her in some ways. No, I don't mean in looks. It was the way that when she wanted something, she'd go all out for it, no matter what.'

I took it as a compliment. But on the way back to town that phrase from Topaz's last note was going round and round in my mind. *I.O.U. for one career*. I'd taken it that she meant her own career, but supposing the I.O.U. was in the other direction? By Sid's own account, when Topaz had helped him he'd been half a comic cossack act, down on his luck. Now he was El Cid, proprietor of six of the finest horses I was ever likely to see. Everybody talked about Topaz's generosity, but surely it had its limits. Perhaps, needing money for her vineyard, she'd decided to call in an I.O.U. I thought of Sid stroking the stallion's white haunch and talking about satin underwear. I stopped beside one of the circus posters and there was El Cid, masked and cloaked on his rearing white horse. Performances 5 p.m. and 8 p.m. 'She knew I'd be in the ring at eight o'clock.' But one man, masked and cloaked on horseback, looks very much like another and Sidney Greenbow would hardly be the only rider in the circus. *I.O.U. for one career*.

ELEVEN

IT WAS NEARLY MIDDAY WHEN I found myself back at Topaz's hotel, outside her private door. The sun was warm, and I stood there in a daze, trying to calculate. Her note had said 8 p.m. If her guest were punctual, and if Topaz drank the poisoned wine almost at once, she would be deeply asleep by nine, or say nine thirty at the latest. But if the doctor's guess was right, her coma would not have become irreversible until well after midnight. I assumed that the murderer would have done some research into the effects of laudanum and would know that it would be unsafe to leave until, say, one o'clock in the morning. Alternatively, if the guest left as soon as Topaz became unconscious, he or she would have to return at some time after one, to make sure that everything had gone as intended. It would be safer, from every point of view, to stay. Then I thought of the steady ruthlessness it would take to sit for four hours or so, watching over the sleep of a woman you were killing, and felt cold in spite of the sun. Either way, stay or return, the murderer would surely have to leave Topaz's suite at some time between one o'clock and daylight.

I stared at the door. There was no light over it, and the nearest street lamp was a good thirty yards away on the corner. Even at midday there were few people coming and going in the street. As safe an escape route as any murderer could expect. As I stood there thinking, I'd been half conscious of a voice near me, piping away in French. I'd assumed it was a child's and it came as a shock when I turned round and saw a figure with an adult's lined face and a stocky body no more than four and a half feet tall.

He was dressed in grey flannel trousers and a tweed sporting jacket that came down to his knees. The piping words were a request, insistent but civil, for a few sous. I found some coins and gave them to him, surprised by the formality of his thanks. I expected him to go away when he had the money, but he didn't. I asked him what his name was.

'Demi-tasse. Demi to my friends.'

He spoke French with a strong Basque accent.

'Where do you live, Demi?'

He smiled and pointed towards the back of the hotel, where the kitchen doors and the dustbins were.

'I saw you giving fish to the cats. You keep it for me next time?'

I began to wonder how many people had been watching me on that shopping trip; first Mr Shadow, now Demi-tasse. Still, he was something of a godsend.

'Do you spend all your time in this street?'

'I used to.'

'Used to?'

He glanced up towards Topaz's tower.

'Yes, because of her.'

'The English lady?'

'Yes, the one who is dead.'

I'm afraid my first idea was that this little man had cherished a hopeless passion for Topaz Brown. I should have known France better.

'Men were always pleased with themselves after her. I'd ask for sous, and they'd give me more, sometimes much more.'

'But you're still waiting here?'

'Perhaps I must move to the other side. I am sorry about that.'

'Demi-tasse, would you like to have lunch?'

His eyes went bright. I took him to the café on the corner of the square that I'd noticed when shopping with Tansy. The pair of us got some odd looks as I ordered *boeuf en daube* for two.

'The wine here is also very good,' he mentioned.

His self possession was almost complete, but the looks he

was giving other people's food had them edging their plates away. With some misgiving, I ordered a half carafe of red wine. It would not suit my purpose to get him drunk. But in all humanity I waited until he finished his casserole before I started questioning him.

'You used to watch for men coming out of Topaz's special door?'

He nodded.

'Do you remember that last night, the night before she was found dead?'

'Yes, I do.'

'Where were you?'

'In the street outside her door.'

'When?'

'As usual, from when I finish helping with the potatoes in the kitchen. That is, about seven.'

'You have a watch?'

'No. I hear the church clock striking.'

'So you were watching Topaz's door from soon after seven o'clock. Did you see anybody go in?'

'No. I saw somebody coming out.'

'Who?'

'The other English woman, her maid I think.'

'Did you speak to her?'

'No. She never gives me anything. She is always angry.'

'When did she come out?'

'After seven, before eight.'

'Did you see anybody go in before eight?'

'Nobody.'

'You're quite sure about that?'

'Nobody.'

'What did you do then?'

'I waited, as usual. Then I needed a *pipi*. I went round the corner. That's how I came to miss the gentleman.'

My hand jerked so that I almost spilled my wine.

'What gentleman?'

'I came back round the corner, and there was a gentleman at the door.'

'Going in?'

'No, coming out. He was locking the door behind him. I

heard the key turning in the lock.'

Both Tansy and Sid had said that Topaz would never give a key to anybody.

'You're quite certain that nobody went in that door between the time that the maid left and when you saw this gentleman coming out?'

'Certain.'

'What time was it when you saw him?'

'After nine. About halfway between nine and ten.'

'Did you recognise him?'

'No. It was dark.'

'Didn't you follow him to ask him for money?'

'I do not run after people in the streets. That is only for children.'

It was a dignified rebuke. I apologised.

'But this is very important, Demi. Where did the gentleman go?'

'Towards the sea.'

'How was he dressed? Was he tall, short, fat, thin?'

'As far as I could tell he was dressed like any gentleman, black coat, black top hat. I do not know if he was fat or thin because of the coat. Tall?' He shrugged. 'Like anybody.'

To Demi, almost anybody would look tall.

I felt both gratified and scared, like somebody who rubs a lamp and meets a genie. I'd deduced a visitor leaving Topaz at some time after nine, but hardly expected him to become real. True, it was a shadowy reality, this gentleman who might have been fat or thin, tall or short, but for all that I had the feeling of cold again. I refilled our glasses, ordered another half carafe and Camembert for us both.

'What did you do then?'

'Waited.'

'But the gentleman had left.'

'I waited. What else should I do?'

'Did you see anybody else?'

'Yes. After ten o'clock there was the other gentleman. The nervous gentleman.'

'Did he go in?'

'No. That was why I called him the nervous gentleman to myself. He kept walking up and down, up and down, on the pavement opposite her door. I thought, He's wondering whether he dare ring her bell.'

'Did you go over and speak to him?'

'No, I kept in the shadows on my side. If he'd seen me, he might have gone away.'

He probably knew from experience that nervous suitors brought no sous.

'Was it the same gentleman you saw coming out?'

He shook his head, concentrating on an advancing wedge of Camembert.

'Why are you so sure of that? You didn't know what the other man looked like.'

'The second one wasn't in evening dress and he walked differently. The first gentleman walked like that.' His fingers on either side of the plate tapped out a deliberate, heavy beat. 'The other one walked like this.' The beat was lighter and quicker. 'He'd walk up and down, then he'd stop for a while, then walk again. He was there for a long time.'

'How long?'

'It was after midnight when he went.'

'Went where?'

'Just walked away towards the parade, like the other one.'

'Without going in?'

'Without going in. I felt sorry for him.'

I was reluctant to ask the next question, but there was no avoiding it.

'What did the second one look like? You were watching him for more than an hour and a half. You must have some idea.'

He cut a small piece of Camembert and ate it, savouring, considering.

'There's a gas lamp on the corner with the promenade. It's a long way from her door.'

'Yes, I noticed.'

'When he was walking up and down, he'd sometimes come near the lamp. I could see a little more clearly, but not very clearly because he was some way away then.'

'Yes, so what did he look like?'

I don't think Demi was making me wait deliberately, but the effect was the same. He swallowed his cheese and spoke slowly, screwing up his eyes to think.

'He was not fat. Quite young. He was wearing jacket and breeches and a cap. Once he took his cap off. His hair was dark.'

'Straight or curly?'

'I think not very straight. I'm not sure.'

I waited, but there was no more. The footsteps though, beaten out by Demi's short fingers, were enough to trouble me.

'And this young man was walking up and down opposite Topaz's door from some time after ten until after midnight?'

'Yes.'

'Did he come back?'

'No. Nobody came.'

'You were watching all night?'

'No. A man must sleep.'

He said it as if he had a four-poster bed and a valet waiting to turn back the covers.

'When did you leave?'

'When the clock struck two, as usual. By that time, the staff in the kitchen have finished clearing up the supper things. A sous-chef is my friend. If there is a slice of meat left on a plate, a glass of wine in a bottle, he keeps them for me. Afterwards, I sleep on the steps near the boilers. In the mornings, I help them unload the vegetables and they give me a bowl of coffee and bread.'

'I suppose the boilers are round at the back near the dustbins.'

'Yes.'

So after two o'clock he would have heard and seen nothing. He was staring at me, not defensively and yet not quite trusting. He hadn't asked me why I wanted to know all this. He survived in the world simply by being there, not by questioning it. We finished the cheese and wine and walked back to the hotel together, Demi thanking me for his lunch with fine formality. Opposite Topaz's door he wished me good afternoon.

'If you need to speak to me again, you know where to find me. Either here or on the other side.'

I walked on towards the parade, so deep in thought that I almost bumped into Jules Estevan, by the very lamppost Demi and I had been talking about.

'Good afternoon, Miss Bray. Have you been having a pleasant conversation with Demi?'

I was beginning to think I couldn't move without somebody watching me.

'You know him?'

'Everybody knows Demi. He's an institution.'

I should have liked to ask him how far anyone could rely on Demi, but then I wanted to ask the same question about Jules Estevan. I sensed that he knew a lot more than he admitted about what I was doing.

'I've been looking for you all morning, Miss Bray. Where have you been.'

'At the circus.'

I watched to see how he reacted, but his expression didn't change.

'Did you find it entertaining?'

'Instructive, at any rate. I had a long conversation with El Cid.'

He raised his hat half an inch, mockingly.

'Your hunting instincts are infallible.'

'Far from it. I wonder why you didn't tell me who Topaz's circus lover was in the first place.'

'I'd no idea it was important to your investigations. Did El Cid cast any light on Topaz's . . . suicide?'

There was the faintest of pauses before the last word.

'He's convinced she didn't kill herself.'

Almost without realising it, we'd strolled round the corner and joined the fashionable throng taking its afternoon stroll by the sea. Jules said, 'Really', as if I'd told him that it looked like rain. I wondered if anything would shake his affectation of calm.

'Why were you looking for me this morning?'

'To make arrangements to take you to Marie's *Soirée Ancienne*. You remember you accepted yesterday.'

'I did nothing of the kind.'

My evening would be spent like the previous one, trying to keep an eye on Bobbie.

'I think you'd find it interesting.'

'Frankly, I doubt it. I've had a fair sample of Marie's histrionic talents already.'

'There'll be at least one other friend of yours there.'

'Who?'

'Miss Fieldfare.'

I stopped walking, and the couple behind almost cannoned into us.

'Bobbie's going to Marie's soirée?'

'She told me so herself this morning.'

The idea of Bobbie doing anything half so frivolous amazed me. Unless . . .

'Excuse me, Mr Estevan, I've just seen somebody I simply must talk to.'

We'd drawn level with the hotel where David Chester and his family were staying and I could see three unmistakable figures crossing the road to the beach, a plump woman with a sunshade and two small girls in shiny boots and pink frills. A maid, loaded with bags, trailed behind them. Jules looked from them to me and, for once, registered mild surprise.

'Your circle of acquaintances amazes me. I shall call for you at your hotel at seven thirty this evening.'

I caught up with Mrs Chester as she was trying to choose the least germ-laden patch of the beach. Her pleasure at seeing me was touching and might have made me guilty about my duplicity, except that it was in a good cause – if preserving the life of David Chester could be described as that.

'Miss . . . Oh, I am glad to see you. I've been feeling guilty all day for not thanking you properly for looking after Naomi yesterday.'

Her manner, from MP's wife to supposed governess, would have been almost too friendly. But I was English among foreigners, had shown kindness to one of her daughters and that was enough for her. I chose a defensible patch of territory for them and helped the maid with cushions, lemonade bottles and the sunshade. Mrs

Chester settled herself and I stood and watched the two girls as they began, dutifully, to scrape at the sand with wooden spades.

'Be careful, Louisa. Don't do too much.'

The child had hardly moved a muscle. I restrained myself from saying that half an hour of solid digging would do her all the good in the world.

'Doesn't your husband come to the beach?'

'Oh no. He's brought so much work with him.'

That was a relief. If he saw a vengeful virago like me in his wife's company he'd probably have called the gendarmes out. His wife, clearly had no suspicions, and for the first time in my life I was grateful for political ignorance in a woman.

'Still, I expect you get out in the evenings together.'

In her place, I'd have regarded that as impertinent, but I couldn't waste time.

'Oh no, there's Louisa to think of. We shall have company tonight though. Mr and Mrs Prendergast are coming to dine with us. Do you know them?'

Relieved, I said I didn't.

'His brother's a bishop. We're going to play bridge in our suite after dinner. Mrs Prendergast was ladies' bridge champion of Somerset last year.'

She said it with timid gloom. I could imagine Mrs Prendergast's cold eyes, poor Mrs Chester's apologetic fumblings, her husband's relentless post mortem. And, in the next room, the over-protected child coughing and fretful. All the pleasures of matrimony and motherhood.

'That will be nice,' I said.

'Yes, very nice.' She sighed. 'I suppose you're engaged.'

'What?'

For a moment I'd forgotten my rôle of governess.

'Engaged for the season, I mean. You're with a family?'

'Oh, yes.'

Another sigh. 'I'd been hoping . . . My husband won't have another foreign girl, and since the last one left we've had so much to do looking after Louisa, and with all his work as well it's not fair on him . . .'

She'd been on the point of offering me a post.

'But you'll be going back to England soon, won't you?'

'On Tuesday. My husband and I had a talk after I saw you yesterday and we agreed it wasn't doing Louisa as much good as we hoped. We've paid till the end of the week, and he won't travel on a Sunday, and . . .'

I let her run on about travel arrangements, working out that there were four days left in which I'd have to keep Bobbie away from David Chester. That was longer than I'd hoped, but at least there was no need to worry about that evening, if Jules was right.

I wished Mrs Chester good luck with the bridge and took my leave. There were two things I had to do before keeping my appointment with Jules, and the first of them was something I wasn't looking forward to in the least. But with shifting sands all round me I needed to know that at least one person had been telling me the truth. I went towards the harbour and, in a world drowsy with siesta, asked among officials until I found one who could give me the address of a Scottish girl called Janet who'd married a French customs officer.

It turned out to be a white-painted house clinging to the harbour edge like a house martin's nest. I heard a child's laughter through the open window and a Scots voice chanting 'This little piggy went to market'. There was some delay when I knocked at the door, then a dark-haired young woman appeared, rather harassed, with a baby in her arms.

'My name's Nell Bray. I'm a friend of Tansy Mills.'

She looked surprised, a little suspicious, but was too polite to shut the door on me.

'Tansy knew I was coming down to the harbour. I said I'd look in and see if your child was better.'

'Danielle. Yes, much better, thank you. Will you come in?'

Her accent was from the Highlands, her face square and likeable, with determined eyebrows and direct eyes. She showed me into the sunny living room, where two more children were playing with toys on the floor, and invited me to sit down.

'Will you have some coffee? How is Tansy? I thought

when I heard about it I should go to her, then I didn't know whether she'd want it or not.'

It was clear from her blushing that she knew how Tansy's employer had made her living.

'I didn't want her to think I was keeping away, only with the bairns . . .'

'I'm sure she doesn't think that. You know it was when she went back from you that she found her?'

She glanced at the children, but they were absorbed in their game.

'Yes . . . yes, I thought it must have been.' Her voice was a whisper. 'When I heard, I wondered perhaps, if Tansy had got back earlier, if I hadn't persuaded her to stay the night . . .'

'It would have made no difference. She'd have been away for the night in any case. Topaz Brown had booked her a room in another part of the hotel.'

'Yes, she said that. She was grieved about it.'

I tried a wild chance. 'Did she say anything about any visitors Topaz Brown was expecting that night?'

'No, no she wouldn't. We never talked about that.'

What did they talk about, I wondered? Husbands and babies, sisters and cottages with ducks? I already had what I needed from Janet. Without prompting, she'd confirmed Tansy's story of staying the night with her, and Janet did not strike me as a skilled liar. I exchanged a few civilities, talked about the children and her husband's work, then said I must go because I had an appointment. As she opened the door for me, she said: 'Please tell Tansy that she's always welcome here, and she's to send me a note if there's anything I can do.'

I promised. As I walked away from the harbour I looked at my watch. Just in time for the first performance of the circus, if I hurried.

I arrived at the ground to find the big top already alive with noise and expectation and paid for one of the expensive seats, insisting that I wanted to be as close to the ring as possible. I'd just settled in my place when the trumpets blew and the march struck up for the grand parade. The performers came out from the arch facing me, under the orchestra stand, first the ringmaster, then a masked man in a gold-embroidered doublet, flowing cloak and black-plumed hat in the cavalier style, riding a white horse so fine that even this matinée audience of parents and children caught its collective breath. The rider made the horse rear up a little as they came through the arch and hold the position for a second, swept off his hat and bowed low over the horse's shoulder, acknowledging the applause. I found it hard to believe that the dung-hill cock of the morning had been transformed into this magnificence. Even the horse looked larger, gleaming with a silvery whiteness. The other five Dons followed more sedately, their riders also masked and cloaked, but with less in the way of plumes and embroidery.

Their appearance in the grand parade was only by way of an introduction. I had to sit through dogs, clowns, camels and trapeze artists until they galloped on again as the climax of the entire circus. They had the crowd roaring with enthusiasm at a mock battle with much flashing of swords and flying of banners, designed to show off the paces of the six horses, of Grandee and El Cid above all. It was, as far as I could tell, a fast variation on *haute école* movements, done with enough panache to please the crowd, and yet with a respect for the dignity of the six white horses. As I watched El Cid and Grandee leap off a ramp through the window of a mock fort, white mane flying, plumed hat waving, it struck me that Topaz had been wise in her investment.

The act ended with a hand gallop round the ring, band playing triumphant music, to acknowledge the applause. As they came towards me I stared at the leading rider. Would I know one rider from another under that mask, if I had no reason to be suspicious? El Cid was bowing to the crowd and as he came towards me, for a moment our eyes met. I was instantly certain that he'd recognised me and that was confirmed when, as he passed, he made Grandee turn sideways a little and perform that arrested movement of pawing the air, as he'd done at their first entrance. It took so short a time that I doubt the rest of the audience were even conscious of it, though they may have noticed the bow, a little deeper than the rest, towards where I was sitting. Almost before it had happened, Grandee and the others had galloped out of the ring and the clowns were tumbling in for the piece of slapstick that would send the audience away laughing.

A courteous gesture from El Cid? A mocking gesture from Sidney Greenbow? Or something more than that? There had been a combination of the powerful and the sinister about the white horse and the black-masked figure that might, equally well, have been a warning. As I went out with the rest of the audience I wondered about that, and the question that had brought me there and still wasn't entirely answered. The man who played El Cid would have to be a very good rider, but I wasn't sure that only one man could do it. After all, there were at least five competent riders in Sidney's team and any of them in the appropriate costume would have looked much like his leader. It was the horses rather than the riders that the audience noticed. As I walked back to town, I decided that my experiment had not been conclusive. I'd only learned one thing for the price of my ticket – that a man who loved horses would surely rather do anything than be parted from six such as those.

I got back to my hotel rushed and sticky, with hardly enough time to wash and change before Jules arrived. So I'm afraid that when the proprietor came bustling out of her room as I was halfway upstairs, I didn't give her my whole attention.

'The Englishwoman has gone. She waited for you, but you didn't come so she went.'

'What was she like?'

'Small and not well-mannered.'

Tansy.

My immediate thought, a guilty one, was that while I'd been at the circus Tansy had somehow found out about my visit to Janet and resented it, but I had no time to worry about it then. I added Tansy's anger to the list of things I'd have to deal with in the morning and hurried on upstairs.

TWELVE

MY HASTY PACKING IN LONDON had included a dictionary of French legal terms and quantities of note books, but no costume suitable for an evening with the demi-monde. The best I could manage was my Liberty silk dress with the fern print, a new pair of white silk stockings unearthed from the bottom of my case and my straw sun hat with a green ribbon. When I came down the proprietor gave me an odd look and said the gentleman was waiting for me outside. Jules was in the driving seat of a smart gig drawn by a fidgety bay mare. He was wearing a white tunic with a purple cloak thrown over it and had a wreath of bay leaves in his hair.

'I am determined to resist the motor-car. A chariot would have been better, but this must serve.'

We turned into the Avenue du Bois de Boulogne which runs southwards from the town, parallel to the long line of cliffs above the second bathing beach, the Plage des Basques. Jules, entering into the charioteer spirit, drove standing up and the mare went along at a spanking trot. It was a magnificent evening, with the sun setting over the Atlantic in scarlet rags of cloud and the scent of thyme blowing off the land.

I enjoyed the drive more than I had any right to and couldn't help thinking about what Emmeline would say if she could see her emissary racing along with one of the most handsome men in Biarritz, his purple cloak flying out in the warm wind like Lord Byron's in a painting, my hair past praying for. Jules took my laughter for encouragement to go faster. There were other carriages on the road and some motor-cars and we went spinning past them, their drivers shouting insults at Jules in a variety of languages. One open brougham contained a Roman legionnaire complete with plumed helmet and three girls in what looked like ballet costume, possibly dryads. A motor-car had come to a halt at the side of the road, with a chauffeur peering into its entrails and an enormously fat woman in a red wig and golden robes shouting at him in French from the passenger's seat to hurry up. After about a mile we turned off into a side road and a series of bends forced even Jules to go at a more considered pace. Somewhere along our journey I'd made up my mind.

'Mr Estevan, did you know a man left Topaz's rooms between nine and ten o'clock on the night she died?'

He was concentrating on the reins and didn't turn round.

'No, I didn't know. Is that what Demi told you?'

'And others.'

I didn't want to put the little man in danger.

'Do you know who the man was?'

'No. All I know is that she'd invited somebody to visit her at eight o'clock.'

He turned round briefly, frowning.

'Eight o'clock. But that was the time on her note.'

'The . . . suicide note, you mean?'

I paused before 'suicide', as he'd paused earlier.

'Meaning that you believe Topaz was murdered?'

This time he didn't even turn round. He might have been talking to the mare.

'You must have suspected it yourself.'

He negotiated another bend. By this time we'd slowed down so much that a queue of other vehicles was forming behind us. He didn't speak until we'd joined the tail end of another queue, waiting to turn in at the gates of Marie's villa. Then he turned round to me, holding the reins in the crook of his elbow.

'Well, Miss Bray?'

'Well what, Mr Estevan?'

'Aren't you going to ask me what I was doing between eight and ten o'clock last Wednesday night?'

'I'd like to ask a lot of people that.'

'Who, for instance?'

Sidney Greenbow, I thought. Also Lord Beverley. Marie de la Tourelle. Bobbie Fieldfare and Rose Mills. And, yes, Jules Estevan.

'Very well, you for instance.'

'This is a new experience. I have never been asked to supply an alibi before. I must admit that I find it banal.'

'Banal?'

'To have so little that's interesting to offer.' He raised his right hand. 'I, Jules Estevan, do solemnly swear that I spent the hours between seven o'clock and midnight last Wednesday insulting a friend about his poetry and drinking too much absinthe.'

'That's a very long insult, Mr Estevan.'

'They were very bad poems, Miss Bray.'

Since we'd begun on this, I was determined to go through with it, although Jules had made no attempt to lower his voice and we were attracting curious looks from carriages in front and behind.

'I suppose your friend could confirm that?'

'I very much doubt it. His memory is poor at the best of times, and he drank much more than I did. You should have given me some notice and I'd have worked out a much more interesting alibi for you.'

I should, I suppose, have asked for the friend's name and address, but knew it would be pointless. One drunken poet hardly amounted to a convincing alibi, and Jules had not intended that it should. The carriage in front of us moved forward and at last we turned in at the Villa des Lilas.

Up until then, I'd only seen Marie at her working address, the Hôtel des Empereurs, and although that had seemed luxurious to me it was nothing in comparison with the villa. Villa, in any case, was a deceptive word. I'd imagined a modest little place on the shore. This was a three-storey house on the cliff top, with a columned porch and a terrace looking out to sea with rows of statues, orange trees in pots and banks of white lilies that must have been nursed into flower in hothouses, attracting clouds of moths. The whole thing was lit by flaring torches positioned at intervals along the terrace, and by each torch a boy crouched, dressed in turban, loin cloth and bolero, waiting to renew it when it burned down. More torches on either side of the porch lit the wide gravel sweep where the guests were descending from carriages in costumes that suggested fashionable Biarritz took a liberal view of the ancient world. Noise and music from inside the house showed that the party was already in progress. A groom dressed as an ancient Gaul took charge of our gig, and I let Jules guide me towards the steps, wondering more and more what I was doing there. The moment we were inside the hall a Greek slave stepped forward with what turned out to be glasses of excellent champagne and, without reception or introduction, we were part of the throng.

I took a grateful gulp of the champagne and looked round. On my right, a Pharaoh was chatting to a plump man I recognised as a leading French statesman, quite soberly dressed in a toga and laurel wreath. On my left, a vestal virgin who'd taken possession of a whole bottle of champagne was having a violent argument in Spanish with a man who could only be Nero. Around the room I saw at least six other men who could only be Nero, several with violins. I mentioned this to Jules.

'That's the beauty of the classics,' he said. 'There are sufficient rôles for men who are fat and ugly, whereas all the women are beautiful. For Marie's line, nothing could be more suitable.'

The reminder of the source of all this splendour came as a jolt to me. In spite of Topaz's fortune, I hadn't realised how profitable her way of life could be.

'And all this is Marie's?'

He nodded. 'Given to her, so the story goes, in return for one night of her company by a man from Chicago who made his fortune in pork pies.'

I looked at the marble columns, the silk hangings, the pictures on the walls.

'Just one night?'

'So it's said.'

'Would a night with Marie be so very different from a night with any other woman?'

I'd asked in a simple spirit of inquiry, but Jules' rare

shout of laughter brought heads turning towards us.

'Really, Miss Bray, blasphemy in the temple. Ask questions like that, and what would become of it all?'

'Vanish, like a castle in a fairy tale?'

'Something like it. Don't you see, every man who goes to bed with Marie is going to bed with that story? If he hears that somebody else has paid so much, then naturally the thing paid for must be desirable, and with every fortune spent on her, the more desirable she becomes.'

'I see that my studies in economics have been sadly lacking.'

'Then I'm glad to be able to contribute to them.'

But his attention had begun to wander round the room. There were other young men there, good-looking and dressed very much like Jules in tunics, rich-coloured cloaks and sandals laced to the knee. One of them caught Jules' eye and smiled.

I said: 'I'm monopolising you. You must want to talk to your friends. Besides, I must find Mademoiselle de la Tourelle and thank her for letting me come.'

I can see now that this was an outbreak of London manners, quite unsuited to the party.

Jules smiled. 'She's over there.'

A little dais had been built in one corner of the room, surrounded by flowers with shallow steps leading up to it. An ivory-coloured divan was set on the dais with huge ivory and gold cushions round it and on the divan Marie was holding court in best classical style, with favoured guests on the cushions around her. As I came nearer I was taken aback, as I'd been at our first meeting, by the sheer beauty of the woman. In the vortex of other people's bright colours, she was dressed very simply in a white, high-waisted gown in the new style, not a jewel about her, long hair coiled up in a simple chignon, her feet bare. She was saying little, listening to the people on the cushions, smiling occasionally. I stopped at the foot of the steps, knowing I'd be quite out of place if I went further. I'd as soon as exchanged social platitudes with the goddess Athene. I had a crazy vision of sitting down on one of the huge cushions, asking her if she'd be kind enough to tell me what she was doing between eight o'clock and one o'clock on Wednesday night. She'd had supper with her impresario, that much I knew from Lord Beverley, but supper doesn't take all night. Then I thought of the knight of the pork pies and reflected that it might after all.

I was glad none of the people sitting respectfully around her could read my mind. There was the designer, Poiret, on one of the cushions, an Italian tenor on another, but to my surprise there were as many women around her as men. One girl, with a bright, malicious face and a tangle of brown curls was telling a story in French, with much gesticulating and laughter. Among the listeners I was caught by one young man in a saffron-coloured tunic with a wreath tilted over his forehead. All the time the story was going on, he didn't take his eyes off Marie, watching for her reaction, laughing when she laughed.

When the story was finished Marie put a question to him, asking him in French if he thought her performance would be a success in London. He blushed and stumbled in replying and she shrugged apologetically and repeated the question in English. The voice that answered her confirmed the suspicions that had been forming in my mind for the last few minutes.

'The English are a very unoriginal people. They like to know that something is approved of everywhere else, before . . .'

She couldn't help making a public speech of it. Bobbie Fieldfare.

I'd known she'd be at the party, but the surprise was to find her already one of Marie's inner circle. I remembered what Lord Beverley had said about Marie's personal preferences and felt suddenly angry. Bobbie's extreme views might be an embarrassment to the suffrage movement, but at least I'd given her credit for being totally committed to it. Now I began to suspect that she was a mere sensation seeker who'd take up any cause for the novelty and self-dramatisation of it. It was a disappointment and another worry too, because although Bobbie Fieldfare's private life was no concern of mine, I owed it to her mother to protect her from unnecessary scandal. But in one sense at least it made my work easier. Bobbie occupied with Marie's little circle would have less time and energy for stalking David Chester with the Fieldfare family pistol.

I turned away before Marie or Bobbie noticed me, making for the terrace and fresh air. On my way out I noticed for the first time among the crowd the man I came to think of as the baggy satyr.

In general, there were enough satyrs at the party to equip a fair sized forest, most of them lissom young men in masks and clinging tights with goatskins belted across their chests. My satyr was not at all lissom and his face under the half mask looked hot and heavy, his neck red. His legs were covered in shaggy pantaloons that might have come from the bottom half of a pantomime bear and a kind of Russian blouse enveloped his chest. The first time I noticed him I thought of him only as a curiosity, wondering if one of the guests had had the wit to come as a satyr in middle age.

It was cool on the terrace, and quiet enough to hear the waves thudding on to the Plage des Basques a long way below. I had it to myself except for the boys with the torches and a giggling couple at the far end where it shaded away into darkness. I sat on a stone bench by an orange tree, trying to get my ideas in order.

'Miss Bray. Miss Bray, may I talk to you?'

I nearly jumped out of my skin. The voice had come whispering up at me from the darkness below the terrace.

'Who's that?'

'Rose Mills.'

I stretched out a hand to help her climb up. When she came into the torchlight it was a relief to see that Rose at least was conventionally dressed in blouse, jacket and skirt.

'What's happening? Is Bobbie here?'

She was panting from the scramble and from nervousness.

'At present, she's dressed up as Alcibiades, having a cosy talk with La Pucelle.'

It was cruel to take my annoyance out on Rose. I knew that as soon as I saw the look on her face.

'Oh,' she said, as if I'd touched a bruise. Then, hesitantly: 'It's a funny sort of party, isn't it?'

'It is. Come and sit down. You look tired.'

Her skirt was covered in dust and the toes of her boots were scuffed.

'Have you walked up from the town?'

'Yes.'

She plumped down on the bench beside me. Her tiredness and confusion were something else to be charged to Bobbie's account, when I eventually told that young woman what I thought of her.

'Did you want to see Bobbie?'

'Yes. I knew she was coming here, then I thought . . .'

I waited for her to go on, but she didn't.

'You thought she might be having another try at David Chester?' She nodded. 'Well, you needn't worry. He's playing bridge back at his hotel.'

'Then what's Bobbie doing here?'

'I wish I knew. Listen, why don't you let me take you back to your lodgings? You can talk to her in the morning.'

I thought if necessary I'd commandeer Jules' gig. But Rose shook her head.

'Very well then, I'll try to bring her out to you later.'

The idea of Rose in her scuffed boots hunting Bobbie through that butterfly crowd was too pathetic to be borne. We sat there for a while among the moths and the scent of lilies.

'Rose, this matter of Topaz Brown's legacy to us. Bobbie must have telegraphed Emmeline Pankhurst quite soon after she died.'

'Oh yes. Bobbie knew it was important. She said we must do it before the family arrived.'

'That was sensible. But how did Bobbie know about it?'

She stared. 'Didn't everyone know?'

'When did Bobbie first tell you about the legacy?'

'As soon as she heard she was dead.'

'After she was dead? You're quite sure about that?'

'Of course.'

'Did you have the impression that Bobbie might have known about it while Topaz was still alive?'

'How could she?'

Rose had no contact with fashionable society in Biarritz that, by Jules' account, was talking about Topaz's will almost before the ink was dry on it. On the other hand, Lady Fieldfare's daughter could dodge in and out of it as she pleased. I thought Rose was telling me the truth as far as she knew it.

'You share a room with Bobbie, don't you? Has she been sleeping badly?'

I could feel Rose's tension increasing.

'Why?'

'I was speaking to a Dr Campbell. He happened to mention that Bobbie had been to him complaining of sleeplessness.'

'I don't think so.'

'Don't think she has trouble sleeping, you mean?'

'I . . . I don't know. She goes out a lot at nights.'

'Without you?'

'Yes.'

'In men's clothes?'

She said nothing, biting the knuckle of her glove.

'I know she does,' I said. 'I've seen her.'

'She . . . she says men can go into places that women can't.'

'I don't doubt it. Does she ever tell you where she's been?'

'I don't ask. She's collecting information.'

'What for?'

No answer. Her lips were pressed hard together.

'Rose, I know what she's planning. I've told her what I think about it.'

'Why do you ask me, then?'

It was a groan of confusion and suppressed anger. I wondered whether I should tell her that I knew Bobbie had been walking up and down outside Topaz's door on the night she died, and decided against it.

'Rose, leave her to it. Stay with Tansy, she needs you. Take her back to England. I'll look after Bobbie.'

One way or the other, I thought.

'No.'

I could recognise determination when I saw it, however misplaced. It was one thing she had in common with her sister.

'Upon your own head be it.'

A torch flared and guttered. A boy moved to replace it.

Rose said, as if most of our conversation hadn't happened: 'So will you tell her I'm here?'

I sighed. 'If I can. We'd better find somewhere else for you to wait. That looks like a summerhouse down there.'

As I walked with her down the steps into the dark garden she stopped suddenly, like a horse shying.

'What was that?'

'Where?'

'By the bush.'

I looked where she was pointing just in time to see a figure coming out of a bush and into a circle of torchlight. It stood for a moment, masked face questing, saw us and knew that it had been seen, scurried up the steps and away.

'What on earth was that?'

'Only a satyr. You see a lot of them round here.'

But not many with baggy legs and floppy Russian blouses, not many of such stolidity.

Rose said: 'It really is a very strange party.'

I left her on a seat in the summerhouse, went up the steps to the terrace and plunged back into it.

THIRTEEN

THE PARTY HAD MOVED TO a new phase while I'd been away. Marie's dais was untenanted and her guests were drifting through to an inner room, a columned salon with gilt chairs arranged in rows and a gold-curtained platform at the end. Jules appeared and took my arm.

'I've kept two seats for us near the front.'

'Where's Bobbie Fieldfare?'

'Gone to change, I suppose.'

'Change?'

'Didn't you know she was taking part?'

I thought with fury of poor Rose waiting outside in the dark, but short of pulling Bobbie out from behind the scenes, there was nothing for it but to wait.

'When will it start?'

'Soon.'

There were sounds of furniture being moved behind the curtains, but the audience was still chatting loudly and more champagne was circulating.

I said: 'What's Marie doing with Bobbie?'

'I thought you might be able to tell me that. Besides, isn't it a case of what Miss Fieldfare's doing with Marie?'

'Is that why you brought me here, to ask that?'

'It did occur to me that she might be trying to convert Marie to your cause. It could become a regular source of income for you. All over Europe *les grandes horizontales* rise up and pay for votes.'

Before I could reply to that, there was a hush in the audience and a grave, portly man stepped out between the curtains. Marie's American impresario.

'Ladies and gentlemen, we are privileged to present

Marie de la Tourelle in a series of classical interludes.'

He repeated it in French, there was a scattering of applause and a group of musicians struck up on flutes and Spanish guitars. The curtains swung back to reveal Marie in a glistening silver robe and an expression suggesting the onset of migraine. One of the turbanned boys ran on and crouched at the side of the platform, carrying a placard helpfully inscribed: *Antigone*.

Anybody who has ever been trapped in the kind of country house weekend where charades are performed would have found the next hour or so all too familiar, except you're allowed to laugh at charades. For Marie's classical interludes a silence descended, in spite of the fancy dress and the amount of champagne consumed, that showed we were in the presence of Art. The French, in any case, tend to take mime rather seriously. After Antigone had emoted over her brothers' bodies and taken part in a wordless confrontation with Creon – played by an imported professional actor – she departed decorously to hang herself off-stage, despair denoted by a lowering of silver-painted lids over huge dark eyes and back of wrist pressed to temples, palm outwards. She'd given me a preview of that particular gesture while mourning Topaz's death. The curtains swung together for another bout of furniture carrying, Attic slaves appeared to refill glasses and conversation revived.

'What's your opinion?' Jules asked me.

'Given audiences with a smattering of classical education and absolutely no sense of the ridiculous, she may escape lynching.'

'My dear, it will make her another fortune.'

'I hardly see how.'

'In Paris, they'll go to see her just because she is Marie. They would pay simply to see her walk across the stage. Then she goes on to St Petersburg, where they will naturally worship anything that's been a success in Paris. In New York and Chicago they'll flock to see the scandalous Frenchwoman who captivated the Czar of Russia . . .'

'Whether she did or not?'

'The Czar will hardly deny it. As for London, if she goes there, she simply needs to start a rumour that her performance is likely to be banned by the Lord Chamberlain, and success is assured.'

The next interlude was the assassination of Julius Caesar which, in this interpretation, seemed to have been inspired and led by Brutus' wife, Portia, played by Marie in a toga of purest white silk that clung to her breasts and swung apart when she moved to reveal a flash of long white thigh and calves laced with gold sandal straps. There was a rustle of a sigh from the audience and I began to revise my opinion of her likely commercial success. The professional mime artist as Caesar was duly stabbed, after waiting with stoic patience for Portia to finish a series of attitudes with her dagger that showed her bare arms to great advantage. A group of subordinate assassins who'd been loitering in the background surged forwards to join in.

'For heaven's sake.'

Several people looked at me reproachfully, but I couldn't help it. The sight of Bobbie Fieldfare, in toga and laurel wreath as one of the assassins, had been too much. The interlude ended and Jules laughed at the expression on my face.

'Your young friend seems to have a talent for the work. She killed him most convincingly.'

'She's making a fool of herself. I wish I could get her to come away.'

'But there's still Cleopatra to come.'

The next scene was, I think, something to do with Roxane and Alexander the Great, the main historical point being that it gave Marie the chance to appear in bare feet, harem trousers and jewel-studded bolero. I was too worried to notice much more about it, although I was aware of a longer interval than usual between that and the next scene. When Jules told me that Cleopatra would be the finale, I was relieved that the performance at least had an end to it.

A burst of applause, fuelled by goodwill and champagne, greeted the appearance of Marie on the Nile. She was lying on a golden barge with a backcloth of pyramids and palm trees, two Indian boys wafting peacock feather fans and a white greyhound with a collar of emeralds and rubies at her side. Her costume was mainly gauze and jewels. If audiences would be paying to see Marie de la Tourelle, this was where she'd be giving them value for their money. The actor who'd played Creon, Caesar and Alexander entered as Mark Anthony and departed after a lingering mimed farewell. Marie again performed her mime for despair, signifying presumably the lapse of time and a battle lost, and Bobbie Fieldfare entered in striped robes and a red fez, bearing a snake in a basket.

Although my knowledge of Egyptology is patchy, I'm reasonably certain that Cleopatra did not commit suicide by means of a small reticulated python. Still, even in Biarritz asps are presumably hard to come by and the audience was in no mood to be critical. There were gasps as Marie took the snake from the basket and draped it carefully round her neck, keeping a firm grip behind its head. Even Jules gasped. But his gasp came a second later than the rest. It wasn't the snake that had surprised him.

'That opal on her wrist.'

Either the surprise was genuine, or Jules was a better actor than any I'd seen on stage.

'Which wrist?'

She was smothered in amazing jewels. I couldn't see that one was any more remarkable than the others.

'The one holding the snake's head. That's why I noticed.'

'Noticed what?'

'I'll tell you afterwards.'

He was tense with excitement, sitting forward on the edge of his seat. Anybody watching would have thought he was carried away by Marie's performance. I could see the jewel he meant, a fire opal in a rather heavy setting, but still couldn't understand why it was anything to cause excitement. The audience held its breath. Marie, clasping the python's head to her breast, gave a little shudder and fell elegantly on her couch, body arched, head thrown back white throat extended. The curtains closed and the audience burst into applause and cheers.

Jules turned to me.
'You saw it?'
'Yes, but . . .'
'I've seen it before, ten days ago. You know where.'
Marie, *sans* python, was taking a curtain call. Around us, people were shouting and blowing kisses.
'It's the one Topaz showed me.'
I stared at him, trying to make sense of it.
'Surely you're mistaken. It must have been one that looked like it.'
'I don't think so. I looked at it quite carefully at the time because Topaz was making mysteries about who sent it.'
I remembered that Tansy had said something about a pendant and Topaz being quite excited about it.
'Is it very valuable?'
'No, that was the puzzle. By Topaz's standards, or Marie's, it's hardly more than a trinket and the setting's old-fashioned.'
'Then perhaps Topaz passed it on to Marie.'
'Topaz wouldn't have given as much as a fingernail clipping to Marie. In any case, Marie would never have taken a present from Topaz.'
The audience was beginning to turn itself back into a party. Marie had stepped off the platform and into the salon and people were clustering round her, offering congratulations. I saw Bobbie's red fez among the crowd.
Jules was looking at me, waiting for me to make the next move. I remembered again how insistent he'd been on bringing me there and wondered if I could trust him at all.
'But why should Marie . . .?'
Why should Marie, who wore a fortune in jewels, take a trinket from her rival?
Jules said, guessing what I was thinking: 'Unless it mattered very much who sent it.'
'I want a closer look.'
I didn't know what game Jules was playing, but if I memorised exactly what the jewel looked like I could ask Tansy if it was the one she'd told me about. I began to push my way through the crowd towards Marie, Jules at my heels. When I got near her, I had to take my place in a

queue for a chance of a few words with her.

'We met in less happy circumstances a few days ago. May I say that your performance tonight was quite unlike anything I've ever seen before.'

I spoke in French, because I find it easier to be hypocritical in a foreign language, also because I was aware of Bobbie's cool eyes on me from behind Marie's shoulder. Marie extended her hand graciously, inclined her head, thanked me. I should have resigned my place to the next person in the queue, but decided that English eccentricity would have to account for my lack of manners. I held her hand for a second longer than politeness allowed, pretending to notice the opal for the first time.

'What a very curious and beautiful stone. So appropriate for Cleopatra.'

This, of course, was quite unpardonable, more like the behaviour of a huckster than a guest. I could see Marie's eyes going round the crowd, wondering who'd invited me. Luckily, she decided to be amused.

'You admire it? Just a small thing.'

She uncoiled the chain from her wrist and dropped the pendant into my hand.

'Have a look at it.'

Somebody giggled. Bobbie's eyes were cold but I took my time, turning it round in my hand, trying to remember every detail of the jewel and setting for Tansy. When I handed it back to Marie at last she shook her head and smiled.

'No, you must keep it as a souvenir of this evening.'

Open laughter. It was a magnanimous gesture and by tomorrow would undoubtedly be all round the town, how Marie had given a jewel worth several hundred pounds to an odd Englishwoman, for a souvenir. I was going to insist that she should take it back, then remembered that I couldn't let myself be so scrupulous. As I thanked her, Marie looked over her shoulder at Bobbie and gave a little shrug, sharing the joke with her. But Bobbie didn't seem to find it in the least funny. For heaven's sake, did she think I was setting up as a rival for Marie's attention? I left her glaring and withdrew from the group, to find Jules waiting for me.

We walked back through the hall, now empty except for tired waiters and empty bottles.

'If this really is Topaz's pendant, how does Marie come to be in possession of it?'

'It is not I who am the detective, Miss Bray.'

'And yet you made sure I should know about it.'

'I was surprised.'

'It's surely inconceivable . . .'

'. . . that Marie should poison Topaz for that jewel you're holding?'

'Isn't it? And she knows there's some connection between Topaz and myself. She saw me in Topaz's rooms and at Topaz's funeral. Either it makes no sense at all or . . .'

'Or what?'

'Or Marie is an exceptionally cool and determined woman.'

I thought of that surprisingly capable grip behind the python's head.

'She's that in any case,' Jules said.

When we came out to the porch the baggy satyr was waiting, propped up against a pillar behind a tub of lilies. He straightened up when he saw us, but pretended not to be watching.

I said to Jules: 'Could that be something to do with you?'

Jules apparently noticed him for the first time.

'Good heavens no. Do you suppose it's somebody's pet?'

'Hound more like.'

'You're fond of animals, aren't you? Why don't you wait here and make friends with it while I go and find our gig?'

It was only at that point I remembered Rose, presumably still waiting patiently in the summerhouse.'

'Mr Estevan, I'm sorry, there's something I must do here before we go. If you'd be kind enough to wait for ten minutes or so, there's somebody who might be grateful for a seat in the gig.'

'Any friend of yours, Miss Bray . . .'

'But if I'm not back in ten minutes, please go on and don't wait for me. I'll make my own way back.'

My idea was to persuade Rose to come away without waiting to see Bobbie, but she might prove stubborn.

'And if you can do something to distract that satyr while I'm going, I should be very grateful.'

'What a complicated life you lead. I'll do my best to keep the creature in conversation, if it talks, that is.'

'I think you may find it talks English.'

I ran across the terrace and down the steps to the garden. It was a fine night, but moonless, and it took me some time to find the summerhouse again.

'Rose?'

There was a stirring inside and a dark shape came out to meet me. When I put a hand on Rose's arm I could feel her muscles stiff, through cold or anxiety.

'What's happening? Where's Bobbie?'

'Still inside, rather occupied. Why not come back with me? You'll see her tomorrow.'

'No, I want to see her tonight.'

'Can't I take a message to her?'

The friendship between Marie and Bobbie, the matter of the pendant, made me determined to keep Rose away from them if possible.

'No.'

The refusal was flat to the point of rudeness.

'Rose, whatever you're doing, I don't advise doing it here. That man you saw in the bushes in fancy dress – I've reason to think he's a secret policeman.'

She jumped. 'Where is he?'

'A few minutes ago he was waiting by the front door. You won't get in to see Bobbie without passing him and she can't get out.'

She was standing only a few feet away from me, and I could feel her tension and suspicion.

'There must be a back door.'

'With servants all over the place.' I put my hand on her arm again, tried gently to push her towards the terrace. 'Jules will drive us back to town, then we'll both go and see Bobbie in the morning.'

'No!'

She pulled away from me and went running off through

the dark towards the side of the house. I was about to follow her until I heard a thud and a cracking of twigs, followed by heavier steps running in the direction that Rose had gone. The silly girl had managed to get the baggy satyr on her track. I'm afraid my reaction was purely instinctive. If one of your colleagues is being pursued by a policeman, in whatever disguise and for whatever reason, then naturally you do all in your power to obstruct him.

I shouted, 'Here,' and began running as noisily as I could in the direction at right angles to the one Rose had taken, away from the house and towards the cliff. My footsteps made a satisfactory crunch on a gravel path and I was aware at once that the satyr's footsteps had halted. I imagined the shaggy beast confused, not knowing which of us to chase. I shouted again to encourage him and the footsteps began again, this time crunching in my direction. I needed to keep the chase going long enough for Rose to get wherever she was going, so I doubled and twisted among the flower beds, falling once in an explosion of scent among lavender bushes, getting up and running on. I was too clever, perhaps, in my twistings and turnings since the pursuer took a slower but straighter line directly over the flower beds. When I could hear his panting breath as well as the heavy feet I knew I'd let him get too close.

Nymphs, when pursued by satyrs, have saved themselves by turning into trees. I did the next best thing and climbed one, a spreading magnolia in fine white bloom, just before he arrived on the scene. A rustic bench surrounding it gave me the foothold I needed to get up into its branches and I sat there hidden among the blossoms while the baulked beast quested in the flower beds. He was panting heavily by then, and sighing to himself, and I think his heart wasn't in it. After a while he shambled away and, quite comfortable on my branch, I decided to stay there for half an hour or so until he was well away, then find my way back to town by some means and show Tansy the opal pendant. When I climbed the magnolia I'd hung it round my neck for safety. I let it stay there and passed the time composing mentally the letter I'd never have the heart to send to Mrs Pankhurst:

Dear Emmeline,

In pursuance of your instructions to avoid scandal, I should mention that I have just been pursued by a satyr through a garden owned by a wealthy courtesan, who appears to be much attracted towards one of the young enthusiasts of our cause. I have achieved nothing so far towards ensuring the smooth transition to us of Topaz Brown's legacy, but I have acquired a pendant with a large opal, a set of underwear with ribbon and net trims and a kilo of cooked fish, since disposed of. This afternoon I visited the circus. It is now midnight and I am sitting in a magnolia tree. Hoping this finds you as it leaves me.

Yours,
Nell Bray

FOURTEEN

I'D BEEN IN THE TREE for nearly half an hour and the night was turning too cold for comfort when I heard more steps coming down the gravel path. They weren't heavy enough for the satyr so I thought it might be Rose coming back to look for me and was about to call out. Then I saw a glow of light and heard a voice I recognised, pitched quietly but quite clear.

'Won't they wonder where you are?'

I couldn't hear the reply. It was another woman's voice, but not Rose's. The light came nearer and I saw it was one of the torches that had been used to light the terrace, guttering towards its end now, but still enough to show Bobbie's face above it and the other woman walking beside her. It was Marie, in a cloak of black sable that glistened in the torchlight, high collar turned up at the back to frame her white face. Bobbie too had wrapped herself in a black cloak, though not of fur, and had at least discarded the fez. They came on down the path, in no hurry.

'Yes, a magnolia. There's a seat round it. Shall we sit down?'

They settled themselves directly underneath me and Bobbie wedged the torch into the ground. If she'd shined it upwards into the branches they could hardly have failed to see me and the explanation would have been complicated. Luckily, they were absorbed in something else.

'You are quite determined on this?' Marie's voice.

'Quite. You too?'

'I've given you my word.'

'Seriously though, not acting? Not a gesture?'

'You think I only make gestures?'

'I think you take decisions impulsively.' That from Bobbie, of all people.

'Why not, if the impulse is the right one?'

'It is.'

'Well then.'

Silence for a while. The torch died down to no more than a glow and I could only see them in outline. I was becoming cramped on my branch but daren't move a muscle. Then Bobbie's voice again:

'It's desperately important that you shouldn't change your mind at the last minute. I've risked more than I should have done in telling you about it.'

'You think you could have done it if I didn't know about it?'

'Without your knowing beforehand, yes. But it's easier this way.'

'And better?'

'I hope so.'

I could have groaned from annoyance and disappointment. I'd hoped at least that Bobbie's sudden interest in Marie would distract her from plotting assassination. It looked as if the reverse had happened and she'd drawn Marie into the plot, though surely even Bobbie could see what a disastrous ally she'd make.

'But it will be difficult for you,' Marie said.

'I've been practising at home.'

She had too. That was what she said to Rose when she first produced the pistol.

'It's surely a job for a professional.'

'Not if you choose your position carefully and your hand is steady. Besides, I could hardly hire a professional, could I?'

'That's true.'

'We must work out the distance in advance, then I shall be relying on you to keep him still when it matters.'

'There are times when a man stays still,' said Marie.

After this pronouncement there was another silence, then Marie, in spite of her sables, said she was cold.

'Do you want to go back to the house?'

'Yes. Most of them will have gone now.'

'And I must go soon.'

They stood up and Bobbie took the stub of the torch. It threw a red glow round their silhouettes as they walked away. I heard Bobbie say:

'Why did you give the pendant to Nell Bray?'

'An impulse. You don't mind?'

'I wish you hadn't, but it's done now.'

'She's an important woman in your cause, isn't she? Does she know what you're planning?'

'She disapproves.'

I couldn't hear if Marie said anything to that, because they were too far away. I had to suppress the urge to jump down, run after them and argue some sense into them. They were beyond rational argument. How and when Bobbie had won Marie to the cause of women's suffrage I'd have liked to discover. Or perhaps Marie simply saw it as an extension of her classical attitudes, heroic assassination followed by consequences no more serious than the lowering of the curtain and roars of applause. She'd probably ask Poiret to design her something to wear to the guillotine. I gave them a quarter of an hour's start, then got down and spent a little time looking for Rose. I wasted no time going towards the cliff top, because there was no reason why she should be there, and kept to the paths between the magnolia tree and the terrace. There was no sign of her or of anybody else, so after a while I decided that she must have despaired of trying to speak to Bobbie and gone back down to Biarritz. It was time for me to do the same, and with all the cars and carriages long gone there was nothing for it but to walk.

The trek down the empty road with nothing but the sound of the sea for company seemed the most peaceful time I'd had for days and should have been a chance to sort out my ideas. I found, though, that they defied sorting. According to Jules, all the people who mattered in Biarritz had known about Topaz's will within hours of her making it. Bobbie, with her connections, would be well placed to hear gossip. Rose, as Tansy's sister, would also have been well placed to find out the details of Topaz's ménage. Since Topaz's death, Bobbie seemed to have distanced herself from Rose, and Rose was half distracted with worry. It began to cohere into a picture that my mind was very reluctant to develop.

But then my hand went to the pendant round my neck, and that started me on another track. Why should such an unimportant jewel be first in Topaz's hands, then on the wrist of her greatest rival? Surely nobody would kill Topaz for the possession of it. But then, that brought me back to the question of who had sent it to Topaz in the first place. As for Marie, I'd just seen her sitting in her furs under her magnolia tree, talking calmly about a man's death as if it were a piece of stage management. Then again, there was the matter of Topaz's wine and fish invitation, and the cheap new underwear. I couldn't see how any plot of Bobbie's or Marie's could have included those. They seemed rather to point towards Topaz's apprentice days, her music hall past, Sidney Greenbow and his horses. Or to Jules Estevan, her ally in practical jokes. Jules had been intent on taking me to Marie's soirée, and I still didn't know why.

By two o'clock in the morning I was back in the town. It was as quiet as a deserted stage setting, too early for even the earliest workers to be about their business, too late for the most determined pleasure-seeker. Only here and there, as I walked past the seafront hotels, I could see the occasional lighted window. There's something about one lighted window in an otherwise dark building that teases the imagination. I pictured nocturnal gamblers crouching over their cards, sleepless lovers writing letters, nurses sitting by the beds of invalids. Behind one of the windows Mrs Chester, her head swimming from the bridge game, was probably watching over the sleep of her daughter.

It was no more than three hours to dawn, and though I was physically tired I knew that my brain wasn't ready for sleep. I found myself walking down the side road by Topaz's hotel, past the lamp on the corner along to her dark private doorway. There was nobody to hear me. At this hour, even Demi would be curled up on the steps of the boiler room, half an ear open for the sound of the early vegetable carts rumbling in from the country. I turned and walked back to the front of the hotel, looking up from force of habit to Topaz's tower. To my surprise I saw a light, glowing through the curtains of the room I thought was her salon. Until then, I'd forgotten Tansy's appearance at my hotel. It struck me that if she was awake too then I might as well go up then and let her rage at me. The doors of the hotel were closed but the night porter appeared as soon as I rang the bell. It took some persuasion and quite a large tip to convince him that my friend Tansy would be glad to see me at that hour in the morning and I felt his eyes on my back as I walked towards the lift. I turned round.

'What time at night do you lock the doors?'

'One o'clock, madam, until six in the morning.'

So if the other night porters were as vigilant as this one, nobody could have gone up to or down from Topaz's room by the hotel foyer between one and six in the morning without being observed.

I got out of the lift into the carpeted, softly lighted corridor that led to Topaz's suite. On the way up it had occurred to me that I might find Rose there, and that was why the lights were still on. Puzzled by Bobbie's behaviour, scared by the satyr, perhaps from old habit she'd run to her elder sister. I hoped so at least. I knocked softly on the door.

'Who's there?'

Tansy's voice, sharp and aggressive.

'Nell Bray. May I come in?'

'You'll have to wait.'

I waited for several minutes. From inside came the swishing sound of furniture being dragged over carpet, then at last the door opened a few inches and Tansy's face appeared, pale and drawn from lack of sleep.

'I'm sorry you've had to wait, but you can't blame me, not after what's been going on.'

She was fully dressed in her black. A chest of drawers that had evidently been pushed up against the door had been dragged back just enough to let me in and, incongruously, a rolled-up parasol with an ebony handle was propped against the wall.

'What's this for, Tansy?'

'It was the nearest thing I could find to a weapon.'

'Weapon? Is Rose with you?'

She shook her head.

'What did you want a weapon for?'

'After what happened this afternoon. I went to your hotel to try and tell you, but you weren't there and I couldn't make that Frenchwoman understand anything. I didn't know what to do.'

I took her gently by the arm and guided her over to a chair.

'Tansy, get your breath and tell me what happened.'

Her hands were locked together in her lap, her eyes fixed on me in a glare that I was coming to realise had more to do with anxiety than hostility.

'What was it that happened this afternoon?'

'Somebody tried to come up in the lift.'

Her voice was a creaking whisper and her eyes tried to hypnotise me into sharing her fear. At first I didn't understand. It was a hotel after all. People were coming and going all the time. Then the significance of it hit me.

'Topaz's own lift, you mean? The private lift?'

'That's right.' A grim nod from Tansy. She was satisfied now.

'But there's only one way into that lift, isn't there?'

'That's right. The side door. And the side door was locked.'

I wouldn't give in to her fear without a struggle.

'Are you quite sure of that, Tansy? You might have left it unlocked accidentally.'

'No. It was locked and before you ask, my key's been in my pocket the whole time.'

'Then how could anybody get into the lift?'

'The one with the key could.'

'Which one with the key?'

'The one that took her key away after they killed her.'

'That's nonsense, Tansy. Even if somebody killed her and took the key, why should he risk coming back more than a week later?'

'Well, if it's nonsense, you tell me who it was in the lift and how they got there.'

There was a kind of grim triumph about her. I asked her to tell me exactly what had happened.

'It was just after two o'clock. I was in this room, putting some of her hats away in their boxes.'

'On your own?'

'Of course I was. I was standing just there, near where you're sitting, then I heard it, that grinding noise it makes when it's coming up. Then it stopped on the landing out there as usual and I heard somebody open the gates.'

'What did you do?'

'At first I was too flabbergasted to do anything. Then I thought . . . you know what silly ideas you get sometimes, when somebody's . . .' She looked away.

I said: 'You mean, you imagined it might be Topaz Brown coming back?'

She nodded, shame-faced. 'Then I thought, still silly-like, well, it wouldn't be her, she'd have let me know. Then I started thinking properly again and knew it wasn't her out there, it was the other one.'

'Other one?'

'The one with the key. The one that killed her.'

I was sure that, as usual, she meant Marie, but wouldn't risk another argument with me by saying the name. I asked her what she did next.

'I knew the door to this room was locked from the inside. I went over to it and I said, "Who's that?" I could hear somebody breathing on the other side, but there was no answer. I said, "Who's that?" again, quite sharp. Then I heard some steps on the carpet outside, then the lift going down. I went running down the stairs after it, but by the time I got to the bottom whoever it was had gone and the door was locked again. I'd still got my key in my pocket, so I unlocked it and looked out in the street, but there wasn't anybody there.'

I said nothing for a while, thinking of Tansy, all seven stone or so of her, flinging herself downstairs ready to tackle a murderer. That is, if I believed her story. Something had happened, there was no doubt of that.

Tansy wouldn't barricade herself in for nothing.

'So I thought I'd tell you about it. I went to your hotel and waited, but of course you didn't come.'

'I'm sorry. Did you tell anybody else, the police, the hotel management?'

She shook her head. 'What good would they do?'

She sat there for a while, staring into space, then asked me if I'd like some tea. I said I would. It seemed a good idea to give her something to do and champagne and tiredness had given me a sour thirst. While she busied herself with kettle and spirit lamp I tried to fit this latest news into the scrappy picture and failed. If there was something so damaging among Topaz's possessions, why hadn't the murderer come for it a week ago, instead of waiting until the rooms had been searched by the police and anybody else interested? The pendant round my neck only complicated things. I didn't believe that even Bobbie would have committed burglary to set the finishing touch to Marie's Cleopatra costume.

But when we'd drunk the first cup of tea I took the pendant out from under my dress and showed it to Tansy.

'Do you recognise this?'

Her mouth fell open, and she looked at me as if I'd hit her.

'It's hers. The one that was lost.'

'Whose?'

'Topaz's, of course. The one I told you about. You remember, that last day. I told you she showed it to me and wouldn't say who it came from.'

I handed it to her. She seemed reluctant to touch it at first.

'You're quite sure it's the same one?'

'Of course I'm sure. I remember that flame-coloured streak through it, and that scratch on the side of the mount. I couldn't understand why she was so fascinated with it. She had better stones on the back of her hairbrush.'

'She was fascinated with it?'

'Well, amused more like.'

'But pleased?'

'I'd say so.'

She sat there for a while, staring at the pendant, then looked at me sharply.

'How did you come by it?'

'I can't tell you that, Tansy.'

If I'd admitted it had been round Marie's wrist, Tansy would have rushed straight out to attack her with her bare hands.

'Why not? Why are you keeping things from me?'

'I can't tell you at the moment. In time I hope to be able to, but not now.'

'It's not yours. It's staying here with all her other things.'

It was a questionable point whether it was mine or not.

'It's evidence, Tansy. I'll keep it safe, I promise you.'

'Evidence of what?'

'I'm not sure yet.'

I took it from her gently. When it left her hands, her face crumpled and she started crying.

'All her nice things. They'll take away all her nice things and there's nothing I can do about it.'

I crouched down beside her and put my arm round her rigid shoulders. Tansy was lonely and confused. Somewhere out there Rose too was lonely and confused, perhaps worse. The two sisters had never needed each other more but weren't even on speaking terms. I told Tansy that she must keep her spirits up, that Rose might be needing her. She shook her head.

'She's got her other friends. She doesn't need me any more.'

'Those friends might not be good for her.'

'Of course they're no good for her. I knew that. It was you that encouraged her.'

'Tansy, don't let's argue about that. Just promise me that if Rose comes to you for help, you won't turn her away.'

'She won't come to me.'

She was as stubborn in her grief as in everything else. I tried to calm her, made more tea. I suggested that if she was nervous about being in Topaz's suite on her own after the latest events she should go and stay with her friend Janet for a few days. She wouldn't consider it. She was the guardian of Topaz's things and was no more to be moved than a dog from its master's grave.

It was getting light outside by the time I left. I walked back to my hotel, where I found the proprietress up and about, inclined to be censorious of my return at daylight, still in my best party dress. I slept for a couple of hours, then revived myself with a cold splash in the hip bath, a pot of piping hot coffee and some croissants and considered what to do next. I decided to give myself one more day. If, by evening, things looked as black against Bobbie as they did at the moment, I had no right to delay any longer.

By nine o'clock I was back in Jules Estevan's living room. I was glad to find him up so early, and told him so.

'I didn't go to bed. Sleep is simply another addiction.'

He looked pale, but then he always did. He was wearing his black dressing gown again. The china head on the tailor's dummy had gained a bay wreath since I last saw it.

'You found your way back safely last night, Miss Bray? I waited for a while, then decided you'd made other arrangements.'

'Mr Estevan, why did you take me to Marie's party?'

'Did you dislike it so very much? I thought you might enjoy it.'

'That's beside the point. You wanted me to see something, didn't you? Was it Bobbie and Marie together, or was it Marie with Topaz's pendant?'

'I assure you, that pendant was as much of a surprise to me as it was to you. Have you shown it to Tansy?'

'Yes. She identifies it. So if it wasn't the pendant, you wanted to make sure I knew about Bobbie and Marie. Do you know what those two are planning?'

He leaned back on his white couch, blowing out the smoke from a long black cigarette.

'Do you know what they're planning, Miss Bray?'

'I'm afraid so. I knew what Bobbie was trying to do, then I heard her and Marie talking in the garden last night.'

'How careless of them. So what's your opinion of their plan?'

'I'm entirely against it. I dislike the man, but politically it would be quite disastrous for us. I've told Bobbie so. The question is, how can I stop it without getting her arrested?'

'Have you thought of warning the man in question?'

'I'm trying to do something about that, obliquely, but I'm not sure I can manage it in time. Anything more direct would bring Bobbie under suspicion. You know the secret police are following us?'

'Your sylvan friend last night, I suppose.'

He was looking thoughtful. I wondered if he guessed that I had by now even worse fears about Bobbie. I thought he probably did, but hoped that he'd do nothing about it, from indolence if not from discretion.

I said: 'What I can't understand is how Marie can be so suicidally foolish. With Bobbie – well, she comes from a wild family, and at least there's real conviction there, however misdirected, but how in the world can a woman like Marie let herself be involved in this?'

'I suppose it's all good for her legend.'

'Legend!'

'She enjoys grand gestures. You've seen that for yourself.'

I hadn't realised it, but while we'd been talking I'd been walking up and down on the polished floor. I became conscious of it when I saw the quizzical expression on his face.

'Some kind of ceremony, Miss Bray?'

'Ceremony?'

'Ten steps one way, ten steps another.'

'Oh dear. A recent bad habit, I'm afraid.'

'A prison cell habit?'

I nodded.

'Has your mind been on prisons over the last few days? Prisons and law courts?'

I made myself sit down on the pew facing him.

'Why do you say that?'

'It's obvious that something has happened. At first you thought Topaz had killed herself. Then you began wondering if she might have been murdered. Now I think you're sure of it.'

I waited, watching him. When I didn't rise to that bait, he said:

'The question is, do you think you know who killed her? Do you?'

'Know, or think I know?'

I had a feeling that he was closing in, that he, like me, had been piecing together some of Bobbie's activities. That worried me, because I didn't want the initiative to pass to Jules Estevan. I tried to set him off down another trail.

'Topaz had invited somebody that night, I know that. She'd invited him for eight o'clock. An hour before that, she went out on her own for the underwear, the wine and some fish.'

'From which you deduce that the note we found was the invitation itself. I've been thinking about that. I'm sorry, but there are two objections.'

'What?'

'Firstly, what was the note doing under her pillow? Whoever she'd invited wouldn't need to bring it with him.'

'I'd thought of that. He might have regarded it as the I.O.U. that he had to return to her.'

'But which way was the debt? Did she owe somebody for her career, or somebody owe her for his?'

'I'd thought at first that she must be the one in debt. I doubt it now.'

'I doubt it too. But there's a more serious objection than that, you know. Have you got her note here?'

It was still in my bag. I handed it to him.

He read: '*Too late. 8 p.m. Return of I.O.U. for one career.* It's ingenious of you to make out that's an invitation, but why the "Too late"? Is that something one puts on an invitation?'

I hadn't quite forgotten those first two words, but I had pushed them to the back of my mind. Without them, my theory worked so well.

'No, but how do you explain them?'

He shrugged. 'Our first theory. Suicide.'

'But the underwear, the fish?'

'Suicides do strange things.'

He gave the note back to me.

I said: 'I don't believe Topaz killed herself.' I was beginning to sound as stubborn as Tansy.

'In which case, we come back to my question. Who was it, Miss Bray?'

I said I didn't know, that I'd taken up too much of his time. He was as courteous as ever when he showed me out, but since the night's events I'd had the feeling of a threat gathering, and I sensed that Jules might be part of that. He knew as much as I knew, perhaps more.

I wanted very much to believe in the mysterious, probably male, visitor at eight o'clock, so much so that I'd let myself forget one of the facts, and I wasn't grateful to Jules for reminding me of it. 'Too late.' Not too late though to use my brain on it. Assuming that the words didn't mean suicide, taking them at their face value, what had been too late? Then, as I walked along beside the sea, I thought that they might be no more than a reply to another note. Supposing the unknown had tried to fix his own time to see her, but the time had been too late and Topaz had named one more suitable. That would make perfect sense of the note. But if that were the case, then another note must have existed, a first note from the unknown visitor asking to see her at the later time. And if it did exist, then it might still be there among the haphazard piles of correspondence lying around Topaz's hotel suite. When I thought of that, Tansy's story of the person who'd tried to get in took on a new significance. I'd have gone back there and then to search, risking her anger, only there was an engagement I had to keep first. A routine one, I thought. But, as it turned out, what happened there drove the hypothetical note out of my mind. Too late.

FIFTEEN

SEVERAL DAYS BEFORE, WHEN I'D just arrived and was still giving my mind to the business that had brought me to Biarritz in the first place, I'd made an appointment that morning for another talk with Topaz's solicitor. Although I now had serious doubts that we'd ever be able to claim Topaz's legacy, I kept the appointment and tried to talk as if nothing had changed. I asked if he'd had any response to a telegraph message I'd sent to our office in London.

'Yes, Miss Bray. We heard from your organisation's solicitor this morning. I've already drafted a letter informing him that it may be some time before Miss Brown's estate is settled. Quite informally, I can tell you that the family are contesting her will.'

'The brother?'

'Quite so. He is alleging that Miss Brown could not have been of sound mind when the will was drawn up, in view of the ... um, eccentricity of her bequest to your organisation, and her subsequent suicide.'

He was friendly still but guarded, and I could understand why. If it came to court, as seemed likely, his assessment of Topaz's state of mind would be important evidence.

I said, advancing a cautious foot on to thin ice: 'I suppose the examining magistrate had no doubt that it was suicide.'

'There was no reasonable doubt, was there, even in the absence of a note?'

Topaz's note was still in my bag. Once I'd intended to hand it over to him, but now that seemed a long time ago.

I said: 'Can you tell me if you sent anybody to Topaz

Brown's suite the day after she was found dead, asking to go through her papers?'

'No. It will have to be done at some time, of course, but we've taken no steps so far. Why do you ask?'

'A man went to her suite claiming to come from the solicitor's. Middle-aged, thick-set, wearing a black coat and hat.'

He frowned. 'That doesn't sound like anybody we know.'

I think he'd have asked me more about it, but at that point his clerk looked round the door.

'They want you at the consulate, Mr Smith. There's an Englishman drowned and they don't know who it is.'

The solicitor winced at the lack of ceremony.

'I'm in a meeting. I hardly see what I can do that the consul can't. Tell them I'll come down later.'

The youth persisted. 'They want to know if you know whether there were any English visitors holding a fancy dress party last night.'

I felt the air go out of my lungs.

'Fancy dress party?'

Both of them stared at me. I think the clerk hadn't noticed I was there.

The solicitor said: 'Why Miss Bray? Do you know of one?'

I said reluctantly, wishing I'd kept my mouth shut: 'I was a guest at a fancy dress party last night, outside the town. But it wasn't an English party. Anyway, what's that to do with the man who drowned?'

The clerk said: 'Apparently he was wearing some kind of fancy dress.'

The solicitor was giving me a sideways look.

'Where was your party, Miss Bray?'

'At the Villa des Lilas.'

The clerk whistled. 'That's La Pucelle's place.'

He got a withering look from the solicitor, but I could see they were both wondering what I was doing there, and I didn't blame them.

The solicitor said: 'I don't suppose there's any connection, but they might be grateful for a word with you downstairs at the consulate – if you have time, that is.'

I could hardly refuse. The two of us went downstairs and

across a hallway into a large room with several desks in it. The consul raised his eyebrows when I was introduced to him, and I braced myself for yet another remark about bricks. He restrained himself and listened to the solicitor explaining why I was there.

'This party of yours, Miss Bray, was it any particular kind of fancy dress?'

'Yes, classical. Mainly togas and Greek tunics and things of that kind.'

He smiled and relaxed, glancing down at a paper on his desk. 'In that case, we seem to be taking up your time unnecessarily. It looks as if the deceased attended a different party.'

'Why?'

'He was found dressed as some kind of animal.'

The relief I'd felt drained away.

'What kind of animal?'

'It's not entirely clear, but he was probably supposed to be a bear.'

'Oh no.'

I heard the consul shouting to somebody to bring brandy. From tiredness and shock I must have staggered where I was standing. I accepted a chair and asked for a glass of water instead of the brandy, trying to gain time.

The consul said, too gently: 'Did you know somebody dressed as a bear?'

Think, I told myself, think. Don't tell them any more than you need. I spoke slowly, hoping they'd put it down to shock.

'There was a man I noticed. I didn't speak to him, so I don't know if he was English or not. I think he was meant to be a satyr, but he was wearing baggy trousers that looked like a bear's legs.'

The consul glanced down again at his paper.

'What did he look like?'

'He was wearing a half mask, so I couldn't see his face. I noticed he was quite thick-set and didn't move like a young man. He had a plump red neck.'

The consul sat with his elbows on his desk, head between the palms of his hands, looking at me.

'Would you be prepared to come with me to the police station? It may help us to identify him.'

Though it was the last thing I wanted, I could hardly refuse. Nor could I refuse when, after an interview at the police station with the consul present, I was politely asked if I would be kind enough to go to the morgue. In the closed vehicle on the way there I asked the consul:

'Why do they think he was English?'

'There was a label inside his vest.'

'A satyr in a vest, poor man.'

The morgue was a square grey building on the outskirts of the town, a mile and a world away from the grand hotels. I thought that ten days ago Topaz's body would have been driven from the Hôtel des Empereurs to this same building. An *agent de police* led the way along a tiled corridor with the consul on one side of me and the solicitor on the other. It felt horribly like being back in prison. They'd put the corpse in a side room on its own. When the *agent de police* pulled the sheet back I was conscious of a smell of disinfectant and seawater, of a gaping mouth and round open eyes. He'd lost his mask and the plump face was much as I remembered it from when I'd seen him standing beside the stone angel at Topaz's funeral. He was still wearing the Russian tunic, but they kept the sheet over his legs so I couldn't see if they'd taken off the bear-like trousers.

'When I saw him at the party he was wearing a half mask, and I wasn't close to him. But yes, I believe it's the same man.'

Death has its own claims. I could not then, however much I wanted to, walk away from it. I spent more time at the police station, giving a carefully edited account of my dealings with the man. I said simply that I'd seen him a couple of times at the party, and my last sight of him had been in the garden of the Villa des Lilas a little before midnight. I said nothing about the chase through the garden, or of having seen him on any occasion before the party. I told them truthfully that I hadn't exchanged as much as a word with him, and had no idea what his name was or where he came from. It was late afternoon before we'd got through all that, and the consul insisted on delivering me back to my hotel afterwards. He sat on the seat of the fiacre opposite me, staring at me rather apprehensively.

I said: 'I think Scotland Yard may be able to help you identify him.'

'I'm sure the French police will forward a description to them in due course. They'll check the list of missing persons and . . .'

'I think it's closer to home than that. I think he was working for Scotland Yard.'

'What?'

'I've reason to believe that man was keeping me under observation for most of my time in Biarritz. I have a certain reputation for my political activities, and I believe Scotland Yard arranged to have me followed.'

That, at least, kept us clear of any reference to Bobbie and Rose.

The consul shifted unhappily in his seat. 'Miss Bray, our police don't work like that. They're not spies.'

I said nothing, but he saw the expression on my face.

'If they suspected you or anybody else of illegal activities on foreign soil, they would properly take the precaution of warning the authorities of that country. They would hardly send a man to follow you across Europe. England has no equivalent of the Czar's secret police, Miss Bray.'

It was a waste of breath to argue. It was his duty to say that, but I sensed his uneasiness.

'All the same, I advise you to send your own description of him to Scotland Yard as soon as possible. It's only fair to his family. Wasn't he carrying anything to identify him?'

'No. But then if a man goes out for the evening dressed in half a bear skin, he could hardly carry a wallet of cards with him.'

'He'd have to carry something, wouldn't he? He'd need his cab fare home if nothing else.'

'Perhaps he lost it when he fell in the sea.'

The French police had established that there was a depressed skull fracture at the back of the man's head, suggesting that he'd fallen and knocked himself unconscious on a rock, though death had been due to drowning.

He'd been discovered by fishermen on the Plage des Basques about half way between the Villa des Lilas and the town.

Our fiacre jogged slowly along, slowed by the press of horse and motor traffic taking people back to their hotels for the evening.

'Miss Bray . . .'

He stopped, red in the face.

'Yes?'

'It . . . occurs to me that if you believed the man to be following you, however mistakenly, you might have . . .'

'Might have what?'

I knew very well what was coming.

'You might have indulged in some kind of . . . altercation with him.'

'Meaning that I might have hit him on the head with a brick,' (he winced a little at the word), 'and thrown him in the sea? It's possible that I might have, but I can assure you I did nothing of the kind. I was so anxious to avoid any altercation, as you call it, that I actually climbed a tree to avoid him.'

He closed his eyes, looking pained.

'I'm not sure that we shouldn't have told the French police about this.'

'I should wait until you've consulted Scotland Yard. After all, you don't want a diplomatic incident on your hands, do you?'

I could tell, from the way he looked at me, that I'd won my point. He dropped me at my hotel with undisguised relief.

The moment I arrived the proprietress handed me a note with Bobbie's decisive writing on the envelope. The message said simply: *I must speak to you. Can you meet me at 8 p.m. where we talked the other night?*

I was on the quay by the lobster pots well before that time, watching the fishermen working in the dusk, tidying their boats ready for the morning sailing. Eight o'clock came, then half past. It grew dark, the fishermen went away and there was still no sign of Bobbie.

At a quarter to nine I jumped up, cursed myself for my idiocy and ran full pelt away from the harbour to the main road. I virtually commandeered a cab and told him to drive to the Hôtel d'Angleterre as fast as he could. At the hotel I thrust coins at him, didn't wait for change and rushed up the steps into the foyer, more than half expecting to see police and a stretcher party. Everything looked quite normal, with the sounds of an orchestra playing waltzes in the salon, people in evening dress coming and going, pages standing by the doors. It surely wouldn't have been so calm if somebody had attempted to kill one of their guests.

I went over to the reception desk and asked if Mr Chester was in. The reception clerk consulted a colleague. Yes, he was in the dining room with his wife. Would I care to send in a message? I said I must speak to Mrs Chester and it was urgent. By that point I was so worried that I'd have faced the man himself if need be, but I still hoped to deliver a warning in a way that would not lead back to Bobbie. I'd tell Mrs Chester point blank that there was a threat to her husband's life and she must make him go away at once, at all costs. A page boy departed with a note that I'd scrawled on the hotel paper. I stood with the curious eyes of the reception clerk on me, scrutinising every young man in evening dress in case he turned out to be Bobbie in disguise. Another thought struck me.

'Is Mademoiselle de la Tourelle dining here tonight?'

The clerk regretted that she was not, looking at me even more curiously.

A plump figure in a dress of olive green silk came towards me from the dining room, walking so quickly that she skidded and slithered in her evening slippers on the marble floor.

'Oh, thank goodness it's you. I've been wanting to talk to you, but I forgot to ask your name again, so I . . .'

'My name doesn't matter. It's about your husband. I'm afraid he's in danger, very great danger. You must make him go away at once.'

'Oh I know, I know. This dreadful place. You were quite right about it. I wish we'd never come here. Louisa is no better, no better at all, and now this. I simply do not know where to turn.'

'You knew?'

I was thunderstruck, marvelling at the disorder of her brain, that she could mention an assassination threat to her husband and a child's minor illness in the same breath.

'Yes, I read the letter. But how do you know about it? Are they all talking about it?'

By now some of her confusion was spreading to me. I suggested we should sit down and guided her to a sofa beside a potted palm. Waltz music drifted round us.

'Where's your husband?'

'In the dining room.'

'You say you saw a letter. What letter?'

'From that awful woman. I'd heard about women like her, but I didn't know they allowed them here, or I'd never have come. She's writing to David, actually writing. I can't believe anybody would be so brazen about it.'

If Bobbie had sent David Chester a letter saying she intended to kill him, I thought brazen was a mild word for it.

'She signed it?'

'Quite openly. Marie de la Tourelle, just as if she were respectable.'

'Marie . . . Your husband had a letter from Marie de la Tourelle?'

She nodded, eyes full of tears.

'And you saw the letter?'

'I was waiting for a note from the doctor about Louisa's medicine for the journey back. I opened it and . . . oh dear.'

'What exactly did it say?'

'I can't tell you. Read it for yourself.'

She produced a small square envelope, I assume from the front of her corset. It was perfumed with a scent I remembered from the soirée. Trust Marie to send a perfumed murder threat. The writing was in a delicate italic hand.

Dear Mr Chester,

I am an admirer of yours and should very much like to meet you. I should be charmed if you could visit me at home at the Villa des Lilas tomorrow evening.

Marie

I stared from Mrs Chester to the note and back again, wondering which of us was going mad.

'But it's just an invitation.'

'Anybody would know what an invitation meant from a woman like that. To send it quite openly to my husband, and for a Sunday evening of all times. If he'd seen it, he'd have been so angry. It was my fault we came . . .'

'If he'd seen it. You mean he hasn't seen it?'

'Would you put a note like that into your husband's hands? He'd be so angry, so disgusted.'

I felt like laughing out loud from relief. I wondered, light-headedly, if Mrs Chester would be reassured if I told her that the note was simply an attempt on her husband's life rather than his virtue. I could have laughed, too, at the simplicity of the plot. Marie – no doubt suitably rehearsed as Delilah – was to entice the victim to her perfumed garden, then Bobbie would leap out from behind the oleanders with the family pistol. Then the urge to laugh dried up and all my anger against Bobbie returned. But at least I knew now that David Chester was safe for the night.

I said: 'I'd like to keep this letter.'

Her eyes had never left it. It had a fascination for her.

'I could show it to somebody in authority. I'm sure they wouldn't like to think that distinguished visitors were being subjected to this kind of thing.'

Since that kind of thing was precisely what some of the distinguished visitors came for, I wondered if even Mrs Chester would swallow so blatant a lie.

She looked anxious. 'I wouldn't want his name brought into it. Some people might think . . .'

'Of course not. But you do agree that this woman should be stopped?'

She agreed.

'And perhaps you should say nothing about this to your husband. If you think he might be angry, it would be best not to.'

She shook her head and dabbed at her eyes with a handkerchief, the large handkerchief, lace-edged but serviceable, of the anxious mother.

'Will he wonder what you've been doing out here?'

'I'll say it was the man with Louisa's medicine.'

I watched her pattering back to the dining room and put the letter away in my bag, hardly believing my luck at how Bobbie and Marie had played into my hands. I walked to my pension. There was a figure standing just outside the door, waiting for me.

'Nell Bray, I need to speak to you.'

'Bobbie, what are you doing here? I was waiting for you by the harbour.'

She was at least wearing women's clothes this time. Her face looked older, white and strained.

'I was looking for Rose. That's what I wanted to speak to you about. Since last night, I can't find Rose anywhere.'

'You mean since last night at the villa?'

'No, Rose didn't go to the villa.'

'Yes she did. She was there in the garden, looking for you. I talked to her.'

'She wasn't supposed to be there. What was she doing there?'

I'd never heard Bobbie so anxious.

'She said she had something to give you. She was upset, puzzled. You must expect that if you take up people and drop them.'

'I haven't dropped Rose. She knows that.'

'She didn't seem to know it last night.'

'Where did she go? You surely didn't just leave her there?'

I took a deep breath. 'The last I saw of Rose she was being followed by a secret policeman dressed as a satyr. I managed to draw him off, but I don't know what happened to her after that.'

Bobbie groaned. She looked more tired than I was, but I had no pity for her.

'As I said, I don't know what became of Rose after that, but I do know what became of the secret policeman. He was found knocked on the head and drowned. I saw his body in the morgue.'

I pushed past her into the pension and left her standing there, speechless for once in her life.

SIXTEEN

I WOKE AS IT WAS getting light, knowing that what mattered above all was to find Rose. I knew that she hadn't intended to kill the baggy satyr. He must have followed her down the garden to the cliff top, or somehow persuaded her to go there, and tried to question her about Bobbie or me. I could imagine her fear and anger, the desperate push that sent him staggering backwards over the cliff, her panic when he fell. Whoever's fault it was, it wasn't poor Rose's and she must not suffer for it.

I dressed hurriedly, let myself out and walked the streets and the seafront, trying to think of the places where a poor and frightened girl might take refuge in a rich holiday town. There was nobody but a snoring drunk in the seafront shelters, nobody on the sands apart from two fishermen down by the tideline, digging for bait against a pearl-coloured sky. It was a Sunday morning and soon the bells started to ring for early mass and men and women, respectably dressed in black, emerged from the fishermen's cottages by the harbour. It was still too early for the hotel guests to be up and about. I went inland, around the streets and the square where Tansy and I had gone shopping. The café was open and brown-faced working men sat over bowls of milky coffee and glasses of *marc*, but there was no sign of Rose.

I drank my breakfast coffee at the station buffet as soon as it opened, watched the first train pull out, then went round questioning ticket collectors and porters. I described Rose and asked if they could remember a girl like that leaving on the early train the morning before. The first train to Paris left at six fifty-two and I hoped she might have had the sense to take it and go straight back to England. No, nobody had seen her, either on the early train or later. In any case, I thought, she probably didn't have the four pounds she'd have needed for her ticket. As I was going round the station I kept an eye out for Bobbie in case she'd had the same idea. I was relieved not to see her. I had an account to settle, but that would have to wait until its due time in the evening, and I wanted to find Rose before she did.

Soon after ten o'clock I gave up the station and went to the Hôtel des Empereurs. The staff knew me by then and the man at the reception desk said good morning and nodded me towards the public lift in the foyer. I knocked on the door of Topaz's suite and Tansy's voice, sharper than ever, called: 'Who is it?'

'It's all right. Nell Bray.'

'What do you want this time?'

She was getting worse. She hadn't even opened the door to me.

'Can I have a word with you?'

'What about?'

'Tansy, don't be silly. It won't do any harm to let me in, will it?'

The door opened grudgingly. Tansy's eyes were red-rimmed, and it looked as if she'd slept in her black dress.

'Tansy, have you seen Rose?'

She plumped herself down in a chair, lips pressed together, and turned her head from side to side.

'She's in trouble, isn't she?'

She asked it flatly, as if she'd always known it would happen. I didn't answer.

'And it's all because of you, all the ideas you've been putting into her head. Isn't it enough for you, you've got Topaz's money and all her nice things? You want Rose as well.'

I said, as gently as I could: 'If she comes here, you will get a message to me, won't you? It's important.'

'Why should she come here? You've turned her against me.'

I didn't try to answer that. I stood by the door and she sat there, making no pretence of civility, waiting for me to go. The silence went on for minutes and she didn't move a muscle, then she said: 'Well, what else do you want?'

'I've been thinking about the day before yesterday, when you heard somebody in the lift.'

'Oh yes.'

'Do you think anybody could have been in here before? You remember when we went shopping, you came back and found the window open.'

'I must have just left it open and forgotten about it.'

'You didn't think so at the time.'

She burst out: 'Stop going on at me. What else am I supposed to do for you? All the time you've been nagging at me with questions, not helping me. I'm sick and fed up with it. Get out.'

'Tansy . . .'

I went over and laid what was meant to be a calming hand on her shoulder. She shook it off and drew herself up to her full five foot two, face red and eyes bright.

'Get out. What right have you got to come in here asking me questions? I told you, get out, get out, get out.'

She was shouting and actually pushing at me. It must have looked like an angry bantam trying to see off a heron. I tried to reason with her, but without success. In the end, I walked to the door and left her there in the middle of the room railing at me. As I closed the door behind me I heard her yell: 'And don't come back.'

By early afternoon, with no sign of Rose, I decided reluctantly that it was time to visit the consul again. For all I knew, Rose might already be in a prison cell. I could hardly ask the consul about that outright, but if it had happened I should surely hear something from him. On a Sunday I could not expect to find him at his desk, but my luck was in. As I got to the consulate he was just coming out of the front door with hat and walking cane, set on an afternoon stroll. He invited me to take a turn with him round the garden.

'I was intending to get in touch with you tomorrow, Miss Bray. We had a long telegraph message from Scotland

Yard last night about this man of yours.'

'Not my man. Did they know anything about him?'

'Nothing whatsoever. I hope it's not too serious a blow to your self-esteem, but he wasn't following you.'

'I'm quite certain that he was.'

'Not on behalf of Scotland Yard, in any case. They inform me that none of their men is currently in France and they have no interest whatsoever in your movements, provided you keep away from the Prime Minister's windows. In fact, the commissioner hopes you are enjoying your holiday.'

It was precisely the tone of joking superiority that most annoyed me, but I couldn't afford to be annoyed.

'The description you sent meant nothing to them?'

'Nothing. It fits nobody on their staff, or on their list of missing persons. It seems they are quite unable to help us.'

And yet there was an air of satisfaction about him that hadn't been present the day before. I feared for Rose.

'What about the French police? Have they found out anything more?'

He smiled. 'A little. In fact, they're following up what seems to be quite a promising line of inquiry.'

'What's that?' I tried to sound casual.

'They've found out where his costume came from, or part of it at least. You remember that he was wearing baggy trousers like a bear's legs? When the police dried them out and took a proper look at them, there was a name-tape stitched inside in indelible ink.'

'His name?'

'No, the circus's.'

I stared. 'Circus's?'

'Yes, there's a circus on a field just outside the town. I dare say they belonged to one of the clowns. So this morning the police chief came back to me and asked if I knew of any British subjects working with the circus.'

'And did you?'

I was still trying to sound no more than politely interested, but my mind leapt at once to Sidney Greenbow.

'As I told him, circus folk are hardly the kind who come and sign the book at the consulate. Still, it answers the question of what he was doing at Mademoiselle Marie's party.'

'Does it?'

'I expect the poor beggar decided to go and mingle and see what he could pick up. I dare say he was behaving shiftily and you jumped to the conclusion that he was following you.'

'Have you asked the people at the circus if they knew him?'

'We leave that kind of thing to the police. I suppose I shall have to see to conveying the remains home sooner or later, if there's anybody at home who wants the poor beggar, that is.'

Remembering what I'd come for, until this latest news had blown me off course, I sympathised with the difficulties of his post and said I was sure he must be kept very busy.

'Up to a point, though to be honest with you there hasn't been a lot happening with us lately. In fact, poor old bear's legs is the most exciting thing we've had for weeks.'

He surely wouldn't be talking so lightly if the police were holding a British girl on a murder charge.

'Have the police any more idea about how it happened?'

'I shouldn't think so. It seemed to be pretty much an open and shut case of accidental death, apart from the problem of identifying him. Perhaps he'd managed to get hold of a glass of champagne or two and that made him unsteady on his hooves, or paws, or whatever. There was plenty of it around, by most accounts.'

He sounded regretful at not having been invited. Deciding there was no more to be learned from him, I left him to his stroll and, as soon as I'd made sure he wasn't watching me, turned down the road that led to the Champ de Pioche.

It was all I could do to stop myself breaking into a run. I'd been so sure that there were political reasons for following us that I hadn't thought about any others. If I could be wrong about that, then I could be wrong about other things too. It was that hope that sent me hurtling in search of Sidney Greenbow, with no very clear idea of what I'd say when I found him.

The circus field was busier and more purposeful than on

my first visit because it was mid-afternoon when I got there, and the first performance began at five. In a far corner I saw four of Sid's white horses trotting round in a circle, their riders in ordinary shirts and breeches. Nobody challenged me as I walked towards them. Sid, on foot in the middle of the circle, didn't notice me at first, intent on the horses and riders.

'Keep his head up. No, don't jerk at his mouth. He's not a bloody seaside donkey. Use your bloody wrists, man.'

I moved closer. He saw me and gestured to me to stay where I was. After a few minutes he sent two of the horses and riders away and made the other two practise part of the sabre fight routine from their finale. Stripped of its brassy music and costumes it was, if anything, even more impressive, as carefully worked out as a ballet. He made them do the same movements several times over, cursing the men when they got it wrong, but never the horses. In the end, grudgingly satisfied, he let them go and walked over to me, wiping his hands on his breeches.

I said: 'Did you know that man who was drowned?'

'Bobsworth? The one the police were asking about this morning?'

'His name was Bobsworth?'

'I don't know what his proper name was. Bobsworth was what our English lads called him.'

I was watching his face carefully and could read nothing on it, not even curiosity. He was polite enough, but his manner would have been the same if I'd been asking about the price of hay.

I asked: 'Was he a friend of yours?'

'No. He was just a hanger-on. You get them with circuses.'

'One of your team?'

'Not likely. I wouldn't let just anyone touch the Dons. No, he helped with the tent and the cart driving and so on, a bit of ticket selling. He joined us in Paris in the winter and moved on with us when we came down here.'

I looked hard at him and he stared back, hands on hips, head on one side.

'What's your interest in Bobsworth?'

'He was spying on me. Before that, he might have been spying on Topaz. Do you know anything about that?'

He shook his head. Behind him the two white horses were being led up and down. He turned to call an order to the men with them, and I had the feeling that at least half his attention had been on them all the time.

'You're sure?'

His eyes came back to me. 'Of course I'm sure. You're not accusing me of anything, are you?'

At least I'd stirred up some reaction. 'It's a coincidence, isn't it? You were a friend of Topaz. You work with this man. He spies first on her, then on me.'

'I told you, I never worked with him. He was just one of the rag tag and bobtail. Besides, why should I want anybody to spy on Topaz, or you either, come to that?'

I said: 'Was there anybody here who knew him well?'

'Nobody seemed to like him that much. I suppose Joe was the nearest thing he had to a friend, and even Joe wasn't what you'd call close to him.'

'Could I speak to Joe?'

'He'll be over in the men's van. I'll take you over there, then I'll have to go and get ready.'

He walked with me across the field to a pair of old green-painted railway carriages under a tree in the far corner.

'The police kept him talking half the morning, so he's probably fed up with it all by now. Anyway, he won't be able to talk long because he's got to change for his act.'

There was a babble of voices in several languages inside the first van. Sidney beat on the door with the flat of his hand and yelled for Joe.

'He'll be out in a minute,' he said. 'I'll leave you here. I've got to go and see to Grandee.'

He loped off across the grass, leaving me standing beside the steps to the van. After a few minutes the door opened and a young, lugubrious face looked out. It had red-brown curls, a wide mouth and the expression of a man who hopes for the best but expects the worst.

'Are you Joe?'

'Yes. Who wants me?'

'My name's Nell. I wonder if you can tell me anything about the man they call Bobsworth.'

He blinked several times, very quickly.

'Are you his wife?'

I couldn't help laughing. 'Certainly not. Did he have a wife?'

'I don't know.'

Joe emerged cautiously and shut the door behind him. As he stood at the top of the steps his feet were at the same level as my eyes. He was wearing green socks, with the big toes sticking out. Above them were a pair of moleskin trousers and a Russian tunic, much like the one the baggy satyr had been wearing. He sat down on the steps, curling his feet out of sight behind them.

I said: 'I think I might have known him. I'm not sure.'

He shook his head slowly, apparently bewildered.

'What do you want to know?'

'Whatever you can tell me. For instance, what was he doing before he joined the circus?'

'I don't know. I never asked him. In January, when we were in Paris, one of our men broke a leg. I met Bobsworth in a bar and got talking, the way you do when you meet somebody who speaks English, and it turned out he was down on his luck, so I said why didn't he see if he could pick up a bit of work with us, so he did.'

'Did he talk about his life, where he came from?'

'He didn't talk about anything much, not even when we'd had a drink or two. The more he drank, the quieter he got.'

'Did he have any other friends?'

'Not what you'd call friends. He had this manner, as if he was a bit above the rest of us, if you see what I mean. The lads don't like that.'

'Did he have any friends outside the circus?'

'I don't know. He'd go off by himself sometimes. That was one of the things the lads didn't like about him, going off by himself.'

'When did you last see him?'

Joe said, very promptly: 'Round about midday, last Thursday week.'

'You're sure of that?'

The day Topaz was found dead.

'Yes, I had to work it out for the police this morning. I knew it was a Thursday because that's the day the hay wagons come. We're all supposed to be there to unload them, and he wasn't, then about midday up he comes and says will I see they send on his pay to him, because he's leaving.'

'Did he say where he was going?'

'I didn't ask. We were all annoyed with him over not helping with the hay, and I thought good riddance. He was pleased with himself, though. He said something had come up, all important and mysterious like, and he was wearing a coat and hat I hadn't seen him in before. Anyway, I said I'd see about sending his pay on, then the shout went up that the soup was ready, so I went off and left him to it.'

'And you didn't see him again?'

'No.'

'Did he take the bear's legs with him when he went?'

'He might have, I suppose. They were kept in a trunk in our van, along with a lot of other things, but we didn't notice they'd gone because we hadn't used them in the act since Christmas. Seems a funny thing to take.'

'Were they yours?'

'Yes. I was the bear. I'm not what you'd call a proper clown, you see. Haven't got the training for it. I run round a bit in various costumes and fall over when they hit me.'

Somebody shouted from inside the van. Joe uncurled his feet and stood up.

'I've got to go and finish getting dressed. I'm sorry I couldn't help you more, Miss, but nobody knew much about Bobsworth.'

'You've been very helpful. Just one more thing: you said he wanted you to have his pay sent on. Where were you supposed to send it?'

The surprise on his face showed the French police hadn't asked him that question. Perhaps they'd been handicapped by having to talk through an interpreter.

'He gave me this piece of paper. To be honest with you,

I'd forgotten all about it till you asked. I meant to do something about it, only . . .'

'Have you still got it?'

'Wait there.'

He bolted back into the van and emerged clutching a grey, much-folded piece of paper.

'May I keep this?'

'If you want to. He won't be needing his pay where he's gone, poor blighter.'

I thanked him. He wished me good afternoon and shot back up the steps. From the laughter as he closed the door behind him I guessed that poor Joe was being teased about his assignation with an older woman. I unfolded the paper. The writing on it, in block capitals, was surprisingly neat and even for a circus labourer:

MR ROBERT WORTH
C/O HOTEL COQ D'OR,
RUE DES NAUFRAGES, BIARRITZ.

I managed to seize a cab just outside the circus field, as it was delivering a group of children and their parents. Rue des Naufrages, I told the driver, and as quickly as possible.

The Hôtel Coq d'Or turned out to be a mean little hostel in a street not far from the old harbour. Paint was flaking from door and window frames, cracked glass in an upstairs window was held together with paste and brown paper. On the way, I'd prepared a story about being related to Mr Worth, but I could have saved my time. All the drunken proprietor wanted was money. I passed over a fistful of coins and received a mumbled word, '*Huit,*' and a key attached to a block of wood by a dirty string. His lack of curiosity showed that the police had not been there before me.

Number eight was on the second floor, near the top of the stairs. I put the key in the lock and hesitated, remembering suddenly that it had last been turned by a man who was now lying in the morgue. I told myself not to be a fool, turned the key and pushed the door open.

The blind was up, so he'd left by daylight. The sun came in weakly through a dirty window but the room itself was surprisingly tidy. I thought at first that I was too late and that somebody had already come in to clear it, but it was simply that Robert Worth had been an orderly man. The bed, with its yellowed sheet and thin grey blanket, was as neatly made as one in a hospital, or a prison. A tweed jacket, old but well brushed, hung across the back of the room's one chair. Apart from that and the bed, the only furniture was a cupboard in the corner. I opened it and found a shirt, crumpled but clean, a pair of polished brown boots and a cheap canvas-covered suitcase with a strap round it.

I picked up the case, light to lift, and put it on the bed. When I'd unbuckled the strap I discovered that the two clasps were locked and I could see no sign of a key. Luckily the locks were as cheap as the rest of the case and a little implement from my manicure set made short work of them. My aunt had given it to me on my sixteenth birthday, saying a lady should always carry a manicure set because she never knew when she might need it. This was the only time I could remember my aunt being right about anything.

I lifted the lid and found a checked waistcoat, a clean, clumsily darned set of vest and combinations, a sponge bag containing soap and shaving kit. Apart from that, only a notebook covered in red cloth and a large brown envelope. I opened the notebook first.

Tall woman and short woman leave hotel 6.04 p.m.

TW and SW enter hat shop.

T & S enter 2nd hat shop . . .

And so on for two neat pages, a carefully itemized account of our eccentric shopping trip. I turned the page and found a new entry, with *Apr. 22* at the top, the date of Topaz's funeral. *TW arrives early. SW with foreign gent. 2 YW with wreath. One makes speech.*

Robert Worth clearly knew none of our names, yet he'd been providing a most detailed observation service for somebody. I rifled through the rest of the notebook, finding nothing but blank pages, then opened the brown envelope. It contained four English five-pound notes, looking quite new, and one letter in an unsealed white envelope, with no address. The letter inside was on the notepaper of a solicitor in Gray's Inn Road, London, dated November 1901 and headed, To Whom it may Concern. A reference.

> Mr Robert Worth has been employed by us for six years, in the capacity of clerk. We have found him honest, sober and industrious and can recommend his employment in any similar capacity.

So, eight years ago, the plump man had been honest, sober and industrious. From the evidence of the notebook, industrious he'd remained to the end. Sobriety, judging by his complexion as I remembered it, probably hadn't lasted so well. As for honesty, there must be some reason why a solicitor's clerk falls to working as a circus hand. Possibly somewhere between 1901 and the present, Bobsworth had been caught with his hand in the cash box. But there was something pathetic in the thought that he'd carried with him to his death this thin testimonial to his employable qualities. I replaced it carefully in the case with the rest of his things, did up the strap and returned it to the cupboard as neatly as he'd left it, apart from the broken locks. Downstairs the proprietor was asleep over his counter, mouth open. I put the key to room eight down beside him, and let myself out.

SEVENTEEN

I'D ASKED THE CAB TO wait for me. It was past six o'clock by then, only just enough time to do what was needed before eight.

Within a quarter of an hour I was in Jules Estevan's studio.

'Mr Estevan,' I said, 'I need a man.'

'I admire your directness, Miss Bray, but doubt my capability.'

'You'll do perfectly well. In fact, practically any presentable man would do.'

It struck me that he looked a little alarmed. I tried to reassure him.

'It won't take long, perhaps no more than two hours of your time. And there's no need to change, you could just put on an overcoat.'

'Miss Bray, perhaps you'd be good enough to let me know exactly what it is you have in mind.'

'Bobbie Fieldfare and Marie de la Tourelle are about to do something extremely stupid. I want to be there, to show them how ridiculous the whole thing is.'

He blew out his cheeks and sat down heavily on the couch. He seemed to be losing some of his poise.

'Miss Bray, I understand your concern about this. If you think Miss Fieldfare and Marie are bad influences on each other, I might even agree with you. But in matters like this, surely it's anybody's right to go to the devil in his or her own way.'

I knew it was his affectation never to be excited about anything, but this was going too far.

'I'm afraid I can't take such an Olympian view of attempted murder.'

He sat up. 'Murder?'

'From the way you were talking, I thought you knew about it.'

'Of course not. I've no idea what you're talking about.'

'Then what did you think I meant?'

He hesitated, then smiled. 'I'm afraid I'd assumed that it was your intention to surprise them in . . . so to speak, Sapphic dalliance.'

'Good heavens, no. I can assure you I've far more serious things to worry about than that.'

Jules started laughing and I couldn't help joining in, both of us, I think, more than a touch hysterical. Our laughter resounded off the polished floor, the painted pagan figures on the wall, the tailor's dummy with its china head, until it scared me. I wondered whether I'd chosen the right ally, but as I'd told Jules, I needed a man, and my choice was limited. When we'd sobered down I told him as much as I intended to. Bobbie and Marie, I said, were plotting to assassinate somebody for political reasons. I preferred not to tell him the name of the victim. The point was to break up their plot in a way that gave me enough hold over Bobbie to hustle her straight back to England. At first he was incredulous.

'Even Marie wouldn't be such an idiot.'

'I'm sure Bobbie's been playing on her over-developed sense of drama. And Marie wouldn't be the one who actually fired the pistol.'

'Pistol, is it?'

'I'm afraid so. But it's all right. The man they're expecting won't be there. The letter inviting him was intercepted, only Bobbie and Marie don't know that.'

'So who exactly will Bobbie be firing the pistol at?'

'Well, you in theory, only . . .'

'I see. And do I only get shot in theory?'

'It won't come to that.'

'I wish I shared your confidence.'

'All I need you to do is to act as a guide. You see, Marie will have told her servants that she's expecting a male visitor at eight o'clock but I doubt very much if she'll have told them his name. If you arrive at eight, the servants will assume you're the man she's expecting, and they'll show you to the room where she is. Bobbie will already be hiding somewhere in the room. I follow you, catch Bobbie red-handed with the pistol and bundle her off by the next train.'

'There seems to me to be one small flaw in all this. Supposing the enterprising Miss Fieldfare takes a shot at me as soon as I walk in the room.'

'That's not their idea at all. The plan is that Marie decoys the victim into a position that will give Bobbie plenty of time to take aim. I'll be through the door long before that.'

'Can you give me one good reason, Miss Bray, why I should do this?'

I considered pointing out that Marie was a friend of his, but suspected he'd find that banal.

'It will at least be a new experience, Mr Estevan.'

'Here lies a martyr to experience.'

He collapsed flat on his back on the couch, then got up, left the room and re-appeared in white gloves and an opera cloak, carrying a top hat.

'Where is the tumbril?'

'I've a cab waiting outside.'

Horse cabs in Biarritz cost two francs an hour, so I'd already spent three shillings of the Union's money, but that was the least of my worries. I'd more than half expected Jules to refuse, but he'd agreed so I was committed. I wished I could understand Bobbie Fieldfare. Jules, silent on the seat opposite me as the cab lurched its way uphill, must have been thinking much the same thing. He said suddenly:

'A vote must be very important to Miss Fieldfare.'

'It is to us all.'

'Not to me. If one knows the majority of the population is invariably wrong about anything, how can one accept a political system that assumes it's always right?'

'What's your preferred system?'

'To avoid systems. The point is, Bobbie Fieldfare is, by your own admission, a determined young woman who would kill if she thought it would help get her this precious vote. Has she done it already?'

It was almost dark in the cab but I think he sensed, if not saw, the way my muscles tensed.

'What do you mean?'

'I've suddenly understood the point of one of your questions to me. You wanted to know if Bobbie could have known about Topaz's legacy while Topaz was still alive.'

I said nothing.

'And the answer was that she could have known – could very well have known.'

He waited. 'Well, Miss Bray, did she poison poor Topaz?'

'Even if she knew, that's no proof against her.'

'And that's no answer. I sense there are some things you haven't told me.'

That was all too true: Bobbie's visit to the doctor complaining of sleeplessness, Bobbie in men's clothes walking up and down in the street outside Topaz's door.

'And then,' Jules said, 'we have this strange business of the opal pendant.'

It was as if he'd been reading my mind. He sat back in the seat, but didn't relax.

'I can see why you're so anxious to get her out of the country.'

The cab slowed down as the road climbed. I looked out of the window and saw we were negotiating one of the sharp bends not far from the Villa des Lilas. It was dusk already, with the sunset no more than a long golden smudge over violet-coloured sea.

Jules said: 'Does the fact that you've recruited me mean I'm not under suspicion any more?'

I could see no point in lying to him.

'No, not entirely. But something I found out today makes you less likely.'

'What was that?'

'There's been a man spying on me and Bobbie. Before that, I think he was spying on Topaz. He was an Englishman, and I think he'd been paid in English money.'

'Was?'

'He's dead.'

A silence.

'So how does that make me less likely?'

'You're at home in France. If you needed a man as a spy you'd probably choose a Frenchman and pay him in French currency.'

'Not necessarily. If I needed a really efficient spy I'd choose you and pay you in my unwanted votes.'

I said I was flattered.

We were rounding the last bend and, in the dusk, I could see the high garden wall of the Villa des Lilas ahead. It was about a quarter to eight. The difficult point, I knew, would be finding out where Jules was taken after he'd been let in by one of the servants. I suggested that he should ask where Marie was, then pretend he'd left something in the cab and come out and tell me. The likelihood was, I thought, that she'd be in the salon where her performance had been staged, or her bedroom. Jules disagreed.

'No, they'll be in the temple. Much more convenient for an assignation, or an assassination.'

'Temple?'

'Marie's Temple of Venus. It's a pavilion in the garden. If I'm right, we'll see the lights as soon as we're inside the gate.'

The cab turned through the gateway and into Marie's gravel drive. In contrast to the night of the party, house and garden were silent and apparently deserted, although there were lights on in some of the downstairs rooms. As the cab came to a halt Jules touched my arm and pointed.

'Look.'

I could see a lighted window glowing about a hundred yards away, from a white building on a little hill surrounded by bushes.

'That's where they are.'

Close enough, I thought, for them to hear the wheels of the vehicle on the gravel and believe David Chester was driving into their trap. I wondered how Bobbie felt and imagined her giving a last check to the pistol. Marie would be striking some appropriate attitude.

I whispered to Jules: 'You go to the house and let the servants know you're here. I'll go straight down there and wait outside.'

We both got out. I told the cab driver to wait and watched Jules as he went up to the house. When I heard him ringing the bell I walked down some steps on to the sloping lawn and cut across it towards the pavilion.

The ground was soft and I made no sound. The building was sideways on to me, the light coming from a small semi-circular window near the top of the wall. As I came closer I could smell woodsmoke. I pushed my way through harsh-leaved bushes as carefully as I could, freezing when I disturbed a roosted bird and sent it clattering away. There was no sound from inside. I waited for a minute, then moved on. It was completely dark by now and I had to feel my way carefully up the slope. When I came alongside the wall I found that the bottom course of stones projected out further than the rest. It gave me the foothold I needed to pull myself up and look in at the window.

The room inside was like a stage set, a white rectangle dimly lighted, with a fire burning in a wide marble fireplace, an armchair covered in apple green velvet, modern tapestries on the walls showing gods and goddesses in athletic poses. The centre piece was an enormous couch covered in tawny furs. Marie was on the couch wearing a pale-coloured dress that poured itself over her like a jug full of cream. For once, though, she wasn't posing. She was sitting there like a schoolgirl at a dormitory feast, bare feet burrowed into the furs, knees drawn up under her chin with an arm clasped round them. Her long dark hair was hanging loose and she was eating something, a plum I think. Bobbie was perched on the edge of the couch. Unlike Marie she looked worried and kept glancing towards the door. She was wearing an ordinary jacket and skirt and I could see no sign of the pistol. I guessed it might be behind the great bank of ferns and lilies in pots at the end of the room facing me. As a floral arrangement, it was overpoweringly large for the room. As a screen for an assassin it would probably do very well.

I waited, my fingers hooked on the windowsill, toes braced against the wall. If Bobbie had looked up she'd have seen me, but she was intent on Marie. I think, though, that she heard Jules' steps on the path almost as soon as I did. The servant was guiding him along the gravel path parallel to the wall, carrying an oil lamp. The first part of my plan had worked, with apparently nobody questioning that Jules was the visitor Marie expected. Bobbie said something to Marie and at once the plum was skimmed into the fire and Marie's bare feet wriggled out from the comfort of the furs. She crossed her ankles and leaned back, resting on one elbow and facing the door. Two practised flicks of the hand sent her heavy hair into obedient rivers on either side of her, framing her from pale forehead to white feet. Bobbie meanwhile had disappeared behind the ferns and lilies as smartly as a rabbit into its burrow. By now Jules and the servant were level with me, down on the path to my right. I saw Jules' face in the lamplight. He looked worried and I wished there was some way of signalling to him that I was so close. The servant stopped, pointed to the door and said something to Jules, then went back along the path, taking the lamp with him. I willed Jules to go on. He hesitated for a moment, then I heard his footsteps on the gravel and a firm knock on the door. From inside, Marie called to him in English to come in. When I heard him push the door open I jumped off my ledge and hurled myself down the slope towards the sheet of light coming through the open door. I got there in time to hear Marie's exclamation of surprise and anger.

'Jules, what are you doing here? Go away.'

Then there was a second's silence, followed by a flash as bright as lightning, a sharp crack, a man cursing in French and the sound of a heavy body falling into foliage. Marie screamed. From up the path the servant shouted something and came running back. Cursing myself for my idiocy I ran through the open doorway and saw Jules' elegantly trousered legs threshing among shattered ferns and lilies in what I took to be his death throes, and Bobbie shouting, whacking a stick up and down on his shoulders like a boy killing a rat. I flung myself at her, conscious as I dived through the air of Marie's screams and the scent of lilies combined with a hot metallic smell, struck her with all my weight and knelt on her, wrenching the stick away from her. Its end was a mass of splinters. I was shouting at Bobbie, calling her a fool and a murderer, as if one were as bad as the other, and all the time I could feel Jules' body twitching beside me. She was yelling back at me, but I couldn't hear what she was saying for the noise Marie was making. When Bobbie went on struggling I pushed her head against the floor, wincing at the crack it made. It didn't knock her unconscious, but at least it quietened her enough to let me get at Jules. I picked a hart's tongue fern off the back of his neck and turned him over as gently as I could on to his torn cloak. His face was set in a painful rictus, his chest heaving as he fought for breath. I put my arm round his shoulders and let his head rest against me.

'Jules, I'm sorry, I'd no idea . . .'

He struggled to say something.

'. . . wrong, you were wrong.'

'Yes, I was wrong. But that's not what matters now. The thing is to get a doctor for you and . . .'

The servant was standing there, staring down at us.

'. . . don't need a doctor.'

Jules managed to force the words out. His breathing was becoming less laboured, but that might not be a good sign.

'. . . wrong . . . not a pistol at all . . . a camera . . . oh gods.'

He took a gulp of air and sat up and before his words hit me I realised what was wrong with him. It was nothing but laughter, a shaken, hysterical laughter that wasn't far away from pain.

'A camera?'

I repeated the words, still not understanding them. I looked at the splintered stick Bobbie had used to hit Jules and slowly recognised it for what it was: the broken leg of a camera tripod. The other two legs and a splintered stump were there in the wreckage of the ferns, scorched by the remains of the magnesium flare. Behind them was the camera itself. Bobbie had pulled herself into a sitting position and was staring at it, as if wondering how it and she had got there. She looked at me and said, quite quietly:

'You didn't have to do that, Nell. Even if you disapproved, you didn't have to do that.'

I stood up. My legs felt weak, so I sat down beside Marie on the fur-covered couch. She'd stopped screaming and begun glaring at me instead. The servant picked up Jules and helped him to the armchair. Bobbie, still looking dazed, began to disentangle herself from the foliage.

I said: 'Of all the half-witted ideas I've ever encountered, this was one of the worst.'

Bobbie's head must have been aching, but there was still fight in her. 'It would have worked perfectly well if you hadn't interfered. It might even work now if you'll only go away.'

'No it won't. The camera's broken and Mr Chester won't be coming. Your invitation to him was intercepted.'

'By you?'

I said nothing.

'It was you, wasn't it, Nell? You've been spying on me. I know we have our differences, but you might have gone on doing things your way and left me to do mine.'

'Including blackmail? What would you have done with your compromising photograph if you'd got it?'

'Sent copies to every newspaper editor, every bishop and every High Court judge.'

Marie told the servant to go away. It struck me as the first sensible thing she'd done for days. He left without a word or a backward glance, making me wonder if this kind of thing was routine in Marie's household.

'Even if it had worked,' I said, 'it would have been a squalid way of fighting.'

'Unladylike?'

'Ungentlemanly.'

She stalked over to the fireplace, beating her clenched fist against her thigh.

'Nell, I can't tell you how much you annoy me. You think if we go on fighting by their rules, they'll invite us in the end to join their nice cosy gentleman's club and we'll all be happy. They won't. They'll hold that door shut with all the brute strength, all the dirty tricks, they can manage. The only way we'll ever get in is by battering it down.'

'And this was the best battering ram you could use? For goodness sake, what made you think David Chester would walk into this in the first place? I dislike the man every bit as much as you do, but as far as his private life goes, he's a model of domestic duty.'

'There's no such thing.'

Marie said: 'He'd have come to me. If he'd received the letter, he would have come.'

She was warming her feet at the fire and putting her hair up, as efficiently as a musician putting away his instrument when a concert has been cancelled.

'Why?'

'Because they always do.'

Jules said, from the armchair: 'You both have a touching faith in male lust.'

'No,' Marie said. 'In male vanity.'

Bobbie said: 'It was a question of finding the right bait.'

Marie winced, but Bobbie was too angry with me to notice.

'You've studied the subject, have you?' I said.

'You know very well what I've done. It was probably you interfering the first time. In fact, I'm sure it was.'

It was the first I'd heard of another attempt, but I didn't admit that.

'I thought at first it was assassination you had in mind.'

She snorted. 'I wish it had been. It would have been over and done with by now.'

'It is over and done with. The best thing you can do now is take the next train back to England. I've a cab waiting. You've done enough harm.'

'I'm not going without Rose.'

'That's the harm I'm talking about. You must go without her.'

'You know where she is, don't you? You're hiding her from me.'

I didn't reply. At that moment, there was nothing I wanted to share with Bobbie.

'You tricked her into telling you all about this, didn't you? You accuse me of squalid behaviour, but you've been using your position in the movement to bully poor Rose.'

'There's no question of bullying. You've brought Rose into very deep trouble. The best thing you can do now is go away and leave me to deal with it.'

Bobbie turned her back on me, staring into the fire.

Jules said to her back, in a quiet conversational tone: 'Miss Fieldfare, did you kill Topaz Brown?'

Bobbie turned round to him, her face blank with shock.

'What did you say?'

'Did you kill Topaz Brown?'

We were all frozen, Marie with her arms behind her head, putting a pin in her hair, Bobbie like a statue beside the fireplace, myself staring at her, feeling as if I'd laid a gunpowder trail and Jules had chosen to put a match to it. In the silence you could hear the logs crackling and the earth trickling from the pot of an overturned fern.

'Why should I kill Topaz Brown?'

The words, when they came at last, were as quiet as Jules' question. His reply was equally calm.

'For her money. Not for yourself, naturally; for votes.'

'How could I?'

I said: 'Did you know before Topaz Brown died that she'd left her money to us?'

She nodded. She seemed relieved to have a question she could answer.

'Yes, the evening before. It was all round town. Everybody knew.'

'The night Topaz Brown died, there was a young man walking up and down outside her private hotel entrance from ten o'clock until after midnight. That young man was you.'

Only Jules' sudden movement in the chair showed his surprise. Marie gasped. The blank expression on Bobbie's face had given way to anger, a cold determined anger.

'Yes, he was.'

Marie began to say something. Jules put up a hand to stop her.

'Your witness, Miss Bray.'

I said: 'There was fire opal pendant. It was seen in Topaz's possession the day before her death. Later, it was in Marie's possession. I believe you gave it to her.'

'Yes, yes, she did.'

At last Marie had been given a cue she recognised. She registered horror with all the force of her great dark eyes, hand flying to her throat, released hair cascading down her back. With the other hand she pointed at Bobbie, an unnecessary action since she was only a matter of yards away.

'She gave it to me. She told me it had been sent by somebody who admired me. She is a murderer. She betrayed me. She murdered my friend . . .'

Jules stood up, grabbed the long rope of her hair and gently but firmly wrapped it round her protesting mouth. She tried to bite him, but he was clearly stronger than he looked. Then he sat himself down beside her, right arm round her shoulders, left hand holding the hair tight against her cheek. From the back, they might have been a close pair of lovers looking into the fire. He soothed her with his voice, the way Sidney Greenbow might have calmed a nervous horse.

'Marie, *ma mignonnette*, save it for the ticket holders. Sit and listen.'

Bobbie hadn't moved.

I said: 'Then there was your visit to Dr Campbell. He wouldn't tell me what he prescribed for your sleeplessness. Was it laudanum?'

I could see Jules' arm tightening on Marie's shoulders. Bobbie looked puzzled, then angry. I sensed a change of balance, as if in the last question I'd somehow blundered, giving her back the initiative, although I couldn't see how.

'Laudanum? No. Besides, I wouldn't have taken it. There was nothing wrong with me.'

'Of course not. So why did you go to see the doctor?'

I waited for her answer, and as I waited she began to smile, first to herself, then a wide, mocking grin. She looked me in the eye.

'Oh, Nell Bray, you're a fool after all, and I was almost a worse one. You don't know after all, do you? You were bluffing.'

'It isn't a bluff. Did you kill Topaz Brown?'

'No,' she said. She began to walk towards the door. 'I

didn't. I don't know who did, if anyone did.'

Jules let go of Marie and stood up. We both moved towards Bobbie.

'Are you going to stop me? Are you arresting me for the murder of Topaz Brown?'

She took another step, daring me to come between her and the door. I could have stopped her, but what would I have done after that? I let her pass. In the doorway, she raised a hand to us all.

'I'm sorry, Marie. It wasn't my fault. Happy hunting, Nell Bray.'

We heard her footsteps going away up the path, jaunty footsteps. Then Jules and I had to turn our attention to Marie. She'd decided that it was the opportunity to register rage and betrayal, modelled loosely on Queen Dido of Carthage. It took some time.

EIGHTEEN

IT WAS ALMOST MIDNIGHT BEFORE we were able to hand Marie over to the care of her Spanish maid to be put to bed. By then Jules and I were almost too tired to speak. The manservant showed us out to the porch – and we discovered that Bobbie had taken our cab. I suppose I should have expected that. Contemplating the walk back to town, I wondered if my boots would stand the strain. Jules, who seemed to be developing a taste for decisiveness, simply informed the servant that we'd be staying the night. The man didn't seem in the least put out, not even when Jules informed him that we'd also be needing some supper.

'Are you sure Marie won't mind?' I said to Jules.

'Why should she? Anyway, it's her own fault.'

We followed the man back inside and were shown into an intimate dining room with pale green walls and curtains the colour of seashells. I thought I was too tired to be hungry but changed my mind when supper arrived, cold chicken in mayonnaise and aspic, decorated with slivers of black truffle. A green salad came with it, glossy with olive oil, and the man brought champagne as a matter of routine, but Jules told him to take it away and bring Muscadet instead. Jules pulled out a chair for me, sat down and helped us to chicken and wine.

'I'm afraid Marie's cellar is undistinguished. In that respect, Topaz won easily.'

I thought of Marie upstairs, with her maid brushing her long hair, then of the bowing white horse in the churchyard. The chicken was good, and I found myself eating hungrily. Jules poured more wine.

'Was Miss Fieldfare telling the truth?'

'About not killing Topaz? Yes.'

'You seem certain.'

'I don't think she'd lie to me.'

'But you believed her capable of murder.'

'Oh yes, capable. Bobbie Fieldfare is capable of anything, but I don't think she murdered Topaz. There's something I've missed, though, and I can't think what it is.'

'Her plan to discredit this politician you dislike so much, would it have achieved anything?'

I took another piece of chicken from the plate he was holding and thought about it.

'If he'd have been the kind of man who'd have walked into a trap like that, if she'd taken her precious photograph and used it as she intended to, yes it might. But Bobbie got one important thing wrong.'

'What was that?'

'She has very romantic ideas about sexual attraction. She over estimates its force. For a young woman, she has some rather old-fashioned notions.'

Jules choked on his wine. 'Old-fashioned?'

'Yes. She's inexperienced. She thinks it's some great wild force like classical legends or the Old Testament, Mars and Venus, Salome and King Herod. She imagined that all she had to do was expose him to this force, and the job was done.'

Jules was looking at me in a way I found disturbing.

'What about you, Miss Bray? You don't see it as a great wild force?'

'I'm afraid the great forces aren't wild at all; they're all too tame. Vanity and ignorance, mostly.'

'You said Miss Fieldfare was inexperienced, implying that you . . .'

'Implying nothing whatsoever, Mr Estevan.'

I should have been annoyed, but I found myself laughing. It was late, very late, and I'd drunk my second glass of wine.

'I think you're a wild woman, Miss Bray.'

'Then you're a wild man. Whatever possessed you to take a leap at Bobbie like that?'

'I saw something move, and instinct took over. It's unspeakably commonplace to follow one's instincts. I should be ashamed of myself.'

But he didn't sound ashamed.

The manservant came in, cleared the empty plates and brought a great bowlful of pears and hothouse peaches. Jules peeled a peach carefully, drawing off the skin in long regular strips.

'So Bobbie Fieldfare, you say, did not kill Topaz. Do you still believe that Topaz was killed?'

My mouth was full of pear. I nodded.

'Then who did?'

I swallowed and said tentatively: 'Have you wondered about Sidney Greenbow?'

'El Cid? He was one of her oldest friends. Why should he kill her?'

'The horses, his Dons. Did you know she lent him a lot of money to buy them? Suppose she was pressing him to pay it back because she needed it for her vineyard.'

Jules looked doubtful.

'That wouldn't have been like Topaz. I never heard of her pressing anybody for a debt. Is that the only reason?'

'No. I told you that somebody had been spying on Topaz, then on Bobbie and me. He was an Englishman who worked for the circus.'

'And you say he's dead.'

'You remember the baggy satyr at Marie's party? That was the man. He was found drowned the next day.'

I'd no intention of telling Jules about Rose. I was already feeling guilty for taking my ease there when I should have been down in the town, looking for her.

'And you think El Cid paid this man?'

'I can't prove it, but he certainly knew him.'

Jules suddenly looked tired and miserable.

I said: 'That bothers you, doesn't it? Is Sidney Greenbow a friend of yours?'

'Not particularly. I met him a few times in Topaz's company and found him amusing, in his way. Only . . .'

'Only what?'

'I suppose I don't want to think of anybody murdering

her. When we know who it was, if we ever do, she'll seem so finally dead. It will be like killing her again.'

I shivered. I felt as tired as he looked.

'Time for bed.'

Jules pressed an electric bell by the fireplace and the man came back to show us upstairs. At my doorway, Jules said goodnight with a formal little bow. I supposed it was meant ironically but I was too weary to care. I undressed completely and slid between sheets of finest satin, smooth as diving into a dream. Topaz would have slept like that many nights of her life. I fell asleep wishing that, just once, I could have talked to her.

Next morning Jules was deeply unhappy.

'It really is the worst of feelings. My whole skin is trying to crawl away from it.'

He'd woken up to realise that he had no clean shirt.

'And I didn't change before you carried me off yesterday evening. Do you realise that means I've been wearing the same shirt for twenty hours?'

He seemed to blame me for it, and yet he hadn't been in the least angry when he thought I was close to getting him killed. I mentioned unsympathetically that in Holloway they allowed us one change of blouse a week and he closed his eyes and shuddered. The camaraderie of the night before seemed to have ebbed away, or perhaps it was simply Jules retreating to his usual distance from the rest of the world. He only permitted us one quick cup of coffee before hurrying out to the porch where Marie's coachman was waiting for us, with two grey ponies harnessed to a light barouche.

'Shouldn't we wait to say thank you to Marie?'

'Good heavens, no. She won't be up before midday.'

As we bowled along the Avenue du Bois de Boulogne at a brisk trot, Jules sat miserably in the corner of the seat, shoulders hunched as if he were trying to keep as much distance as possible between himself and his shirt. Pitying him, I suggested that we should ask the driver to put him down at his home first, then take me on to the town centre. He made no serious objection to that, and hurried inside with only the briefest of goodbyes. I imagined him tearing the offensive garment off as soon as the door closed behind him.

The driver asked me where I wanted to go and I said anywhere on the promenade. It seemed high time to get on with the search for Rose, though I had no idea where to start. Then, on the steps outside a hotel, I saw a dumpy woman with two children waving at me, almost jumping up and down in her eagerness to attract my attention. My heart sank. Mrs Chester. I neither wanted nor needed to talk to her any more, but it would have been a snub to trot on past her. I looked quickly round to make sure her husband was nowhere in sight, then told the driver I would get down there. She came bustling across the pavement towards me, her two little girls trailing behind. She was, as usual, so absorbed in her family worries that she didn't seem to find it surprising that a supposed governess should step out of one of the smartest carriages in Biarritz.

'Oh my dear, I'm so glad to have seen you. You know we're going away tomorrow? I did want to see you and say goodbye.'

Marie's carriage turned and drove away. I tried to look interested in what Mrs Chester was telling me, but now I knew that her husband had never been in danger from Bobbie's pistol it was no concern of mine whether they stayed or went. I pretended a decent interest in the health of the coughing child, Louisa.

'Oh, she's glad to be going home too, aren't you, dear? Poor David was up with her nearly all night again. I'd stayed with her the night before and he insisted I must get my sleep.'

The two girls, taking no interest in what their mother was saying, were edging her to the kerb.

'Mama, can we look at the boats?'

Abstractedly, still talking at me, she let them take her across the road to a telescope mounted on the promenade railing, fumbling in her bag for coins. I was impatient to break away, but the stream of domestic inanities went running on and she seemed determined not to let me go. When the two girls were safely occupied, quarrelling over the telescope, I understood why. Her voice sank to a whisper.

'That awful woman, the letter, did you do anything?'

'I can assure you, Mrs Chester, that the woman involved now very much regrets sending it. I'm sure your husband won't be troubled by a repetition of anything from that quarter.'

'Oh. Oh, I'm so grateful.'

Standing there among the strolling people she grabbed my hand and pressed it between both of hers. There were tears in her eyes.

'So grateful. He's so good and thoughtful, it makes me miserable when anything upsets him. We women can't understand the burdens on a man in public life like him. All we can do is try . . .'

This was altogether too much. I drew my hand away.

'I assure you, Mrs Chester, you have nothing to thank me for. Now I see somebody I must speak to over there. I hope you have a pleasant journey home.'

I left her with her mouth open at the abruptness of my going, telling myself not to feel guilty. It was a pitifully small world of hers, and I'd done what I could to make it safer for her. When I'd pretended to see an acquaintance over the road it had been a lie to get away from her, but it turned into truth before I was halfway across. On the hotel forecourt was Lord Beverley, in motoring coat and cap, standing beside his motor-car. He recognised me and waved.

'Good morning, Miss Bray. We're going off this morning, back home.'

The fashionable world was gathering for its migration from the shore of the Atlantic back to the parks of London and Paris, driven by instincts as mysterious and reliable as those of the swallows. Trunks and suitcases were piled outside the hotel doorway. The engine of Lord Beverley's motor-car was open and he was holding a spanner.

'Doing a few adjustments. The guv'nor thinks she won't make it. He's promised if I get us back to London in her, he'll buy her from me.'

I asked him what he thought the chances were and he

said about five to one, given reasonable going. He began to explain to me in great detail what he was doing to the vehicle. The whole world seemed to be in a conspiracy to waste my time that morning. He insisted that I should look into the engine to see something called a fuel feed. When our heads were almost touching over pipes and cylinders, in a haze of petrol fumes, it became clear what he really wanted. He whispered to me:

'Any news about poor Topaz?'

'What sort of news?'

'You seemed to think somebody might have murdered her. Has all that blown over?'

'Nothing else has happened.'

That was true in the sense that nothing had happened to bring me closer to finding Topaz's murderer. I had no intention of telling him about Bobbie or the baggy satyr. Lord Beverley blew a great sigh of relief into the motorcar's giblets.

'Suicide after all, then?'

'That's still the official verdict, yes.'

'Thank the Lord for that. I've had enough trouble calming down the guv'nor as it was. If he thought I'd been mixed up in a murder case . . .'

A gruff, bad-tempered voice yelled from the hotel steps: 'Charles, the man says we didn't order a picnic hamper. I told you to be sure to order a hamper.'

Lord Beverley sighed, stood up and put down his spanner.

'The guv'nor. Excuse me, Miss Bray, I'll have to go and see to him. I won't introduce you, if you don't mind. He's not one of your warmest supporters.'

I waited, leaning on the motor-car with my back to them, while father, son and hotel manager sorted out the question of the hamper. In a few minutes Lord Beverley returned.

'Sorry about that. So it's all over, suffragettes get her money and everybody satisfied. Pity though.'

He asked me if I'd be staying long. I'd just started to reply when the thing happened. Somebody gave a scream and a long black lash hissed out of nowhere like a snake's fangs and thudded against the shoulder of Lord Beverley's leather motoring coat.

A man shouted: 'That's for her, you bastard.'

I turned round and there a few yards away was Sidney Greenbow, standing quite at ease in boots, shirt and breeches, legs astride, coiling the slack of a long ringmaster's whip back into his left hand. All round him the people who'd been chatting in the sunshine had drawn back, thunderstruck.

For several seconds Lord Beverley just stood there, staring at Sidney. He put his hand to his shoulder where the whiplash had struck, looking not so much angry as puzzled. If he'd heard what Sidney had shouted it didn't seem to register with him. He said plaintively:

'What was that for?'

'You know damned well what it's for.'

Sidney drew back his right arm and this time there was a whole chorus of screams. I was standing a few feet from Lord Beverley but it didn't occur to me to move away. Like everybody else, I couldn't believe it was happening. The lash hissed out again, so close that I could feel the wind from it on my cheek, but this time Lord Beverley wasn't there when it landed. He yelled something incoherent and threw himself sideways, landed on his knees but was up in an instant, hurling himself at Sidney before he could coil up the whip for a third attack. The speed of it caught Sidney off balance. Lord Beverley was several inches taller and perhaps two stone heavier than he was. The two of them went thumping down on to the gravel of the forecourt, Sidney underneath still keeping tight hold of his whip, Lord Beverley kneeling on him and trying to pull it away from him. But Lord Beverley's advantages of height and weight weren't much use against Sidney's circus muscles. After some panting and heaving the positions were reversed, with Lord Beverley's head on the ground and Sidney's knee braced against his chest. Lord Beverley could hardly speak, but had just enough breath left to ask Sidney what he was supposed to have done. Sidney kept repeating: 'You know, you bastard, you know.'

One of the worst things about it was that nobody did anything to stop them until I walked over to them.

'Sidney, what do you think you're doing? That's Lord Beverley.'

'Hello, Miss Bray. Yes, I know damned well who he is, and I don't care if he's Lord Muck. The police might not be able to touch him, but there's nothing to say that I can't.'

'Let him up. You're hurting him.'

'I'll let him up if he promises to make a proper fight of it. I don't want him running off to his daddy.'

Lord Beverley, thinking Sidney's attention was distracted, made another attempt to throw him off. After more grunting and writhing they ended up much as they'd been before. But by then somebody had sent for help. It arrived in the shape of four burly hotel porters and Lord Beverley's father, the Duke. When he saw what was happening his face went red and he shouted:

'Charles, what the hell are you up to this time?'

Lord Beverley had just enough breath left to say it wasn't his fault.

'Well, what are you all standing there for? Get that man off him.'

The porters closed in. Sidney looked up at them and rose slowly to his feet, taking his time about it. Lord Beverley followed his example, rather shakily, but seemed more concerned with his father's reaction than anything else.

'I promise you, guv'nor, I've no idea what it's all about. This man just came up and started laying about me with a damned great horsewhip.'

'Horsewhip? Why were you trying to horsewhip my son?'

One of the porters had picked up the whip. Sidney just stood there, arms folded. The Duke looked round the faces in the crowd, trying to make sense of it, then, unluckily, noticed me. I saw recognition dawning and his face went an even more alarming shade of red.

'I know that woman. She's one of those damned suffragettes. Good God, it's not enough for them now attacking people on the streets of London. They come out here and lie in wait for you while you're on holiday.'

I tried to protest that the attack had been nothing to do with me.

'She was talking to the man with the whip,' somebody from the crowd said. 'Urging him on. She organised it all.'

Lord Beverley tried to help.

'I don't think it was Miss Bray's fault, guv'nor. She was just standing there talking to me when this maniac arrived. Nothing to do with her.'

'Distracting you, that was what she was doing, while he crept up on you. Part of the plot. You're my son and that's enough for them. Nothing they won't stoop to. Prison's too good for them.'

Sidney tried to say something and the Duke told him to keep quiet. The woman who'd said I was urging Sidney on suggested we should call the police. Lord Beverley looked thoroughly miserable. I said to him:

'I promise you, I had nothing to do with this.'

'She didn't, nothing to do with it,' said Sidney.

I hope Lord Beverley believed me. At any rate, there must have been enough doubt in his mind on my side to make him do what he did. He said: 'I don't think that's a very good idea, guv'nor. The gendarmerie, I mean.'

'Why not?'

The Duke's respect for his son seemed to have increased now he thought he'd been the victim of a suffragette outrage.

'We'd be held up here for days talking to the police, then a court case. Not worth it. Besides, I gave the man a good thrashing for his pains.'

That was not strictly true, but in the circumstances I didn't blame him.

'What about her? We can't let her off scot free.'

'I honestly don't think Miss Bray had anything to do with it, guv'nor.'

The Duke snorted. 'Of course she did,' but the argument about a French court case clearly weighed heavily with him. He was the sort of man who'd regard anything foreign as sinister. He turned to me, cheeks bulging, chewing his rage like underdone beef.

'Let me tell you and all those other unnatural harpies of yours, you can do what you like, you can break every window in Downing Street and attack us with bricks or horsewhips or anything else you can lay your filthy talons on, but we're not going to give in. As long as there's a man left in England who's worth the name, we'll never give in.'

I said nothing. He wasn't worth it. He glared at me for a while, then turned away and put his arm round his son's shoulders.

'Come on, Charles. Somebody go and get him a brandy.'

As they went, Lord Beverley looked back at me over his father's shoulder. It was a look that mingled apology and puzzlement.

I watched as father and son went inside, then turned my attention to Sidney Greenbow. He was still surrounded by porters. Two of them had grabbed him none too gently by the arms as he tried to follow Lord Beverley, another was still holding the whip.

'You can let him go,' I said. 'He can't do anything now.'

It would confirm my status as Sidney's accomplice in crime, but I could hardly leave him there. I think the porters were quite glad to let him go. He held out his hand for the whip, but the man holding it shook his head and put it behind his back.

'Come on,' I said. 'You can't blame them.'

He came reluctantly, grumbling that the whip had cost five pounds. The crowd drew back to let us go, muttering and looking askance. I could see no sign of Mrs Chester and hoped for her sake that she'd been safely on the beach when it happened. As soon as we were away from the fashionable area, I steered Sidney into a café and ordered coffees. He was surprisingly biddable, in the state of reaction, I think, that comes after you've screwed yourself up to some violent deed. I knew what it felt like.

I said: 'Why are you so convinced that Lord Beverley killed Topaz?'

He stared at me. 'He was the last one, wasn't he?'

'That's the only reason, because you thought he was her last lover?'

He leaned towards me, shirt-sleeved elbows on the metal-topped table. I could smell the perspiration on him, and the sweet hay from the stables.

'Look, Miss Bray, I told you a girl in Topaz's line of business takes risks, whether she's doing it up back alleys or where she'd got to. One of the risks is that someone will expect to be given it for nothing and he'll kill her if she doesn't give it to him.'

'But Lord Beverley didn't expect to be given it for nothing, as you put it. He'd spent a lot of money on her.'

Sidney nodded. 'All of it. The last of the money he won, he spent on her. That's when it happens. They come up the stairs one night, kidding themselves the girl loves them for their own sakes because they've bedded her a few times. She tells them it's no ticket, no show, they get annoyed and that's it.'

It was a horrible enough summary, but its naïvety surprised me. I'd taken Sidney Greenbow for a quick-witted man. If, on the other hand, a quick-witted man wanted to turn suspicion from himself, the morning's little display might have done very nicely. The coffees arrived.

I said: 'I don't think Lord Beverley would feel like that. He was quite matter of fact about having no money left. That was why he came here – to spend it all.'

'But he'd fallen for her.'

'I don't think he had. He liked her, yes, but that was all. Anyway, if you really think he murdered her, why don't you go to the police?'

He made a derisive noise. 'What would they do, me against him? Anyway, I can't prove it. But I owed her something, and that was it.'

He drank his coffee thirstily, hot as it was. I wondered whether to show some of my cards and decided I had nothing to lose by it.

'What makes you so certain that Lord Beverley was the last one?'

'I asked around. I know a few people.'

He had a trick of looking into your eyes, very directly. I gave him back stare for stare. 'Yes, you know a few people, and you had some paid help as well, didn't you?'

He blinked. 'What do you mean?'

'The man they called Bobsworth, Robert Worth. Somebody paid him to keep a watch on Topaz. Then, after she was dead, he started following me and some people connected with me. I think the person who hired Bobsworth was you, Mr Greenbow.'

He shook his head. 'Not me. If I'd ever wanted a spy I'd have done better than Bobsworth. But I didn't.'

'Robert Worth was quite an educated man. He hadn't always been a circus hand.'

'Oh, they'll all tell you that. We've got two college professors and a prince of the blood putting up that circus tent, if you listened to their stories.'

'He wasn't so ambitious. But he had worked in a solicitor's office up to eight years ago.'

'Did he tell you that?'

'I never spoke to him.'

'How do you know then?'

I said nothing. For some reason the information seemed to interest him more than anything I'd said so far, but I couldn't understand why. For the next couple of minutes he said nothing at all, and when he broke his silence at last the question was unexpected.

'London was it, where he worked?'

'Yes.'

'Eight years ago?'

'It was eight years ago he left his job. He must have been working for the firm for some years before that. They gave him a reference.'

A long silence again, then he said: 'I wonder . . .'

'Wonder what?'

'If I tell you what I'm thinking, I suppose you'll say I'm jumping to conclusions.'

'You jumped to conclusions when you tried to horsewhip Lord Beverley.'

'Yes.' This time he wasn't looking me in the eye. 'What you've just said makes me wonder if I might have been wrong about that.'

'What I said about Bobsworth?'

'It's a long shot.'

'Long shot or not, you'd better tell me.'

So he did, sitting forward with his elbows on the table, eyes back on my face to see how I was reacting.

'We have to go back ten or eleven years, while Topaz was still on the Halls, but starting to do all right with her business on the side. I saw her now and then, when we happened to be on the same bill, and she told me about this man she had who was something in the legal business.'

'A client?'

'No, that was the point. This time the boot was on the other foot. He was working to pass some kind of examination, but he didn't have enough money to live on and Topaz was looking after him.'

'Why?'

'Because she liked him, I suppose. It was putting on side a bit too, showing she could afford a man for herself. Him being in the legal business was a kind of step up for her. Of course, later on she could have had all the judges in the High Court if she'd fancied them, but that was how it was at the time.'

I could see where this was leading, but wanted to make him say it.

'What has this got to do with Bobsworth?'

'Well, when you talked about him spying on her, then said he'd worked in a lawyer's office, I started putting two and two together.'

I was putting two and two together as well, with a speed and exhilaration that left me breathless, like walking in the wind: seeing the young clerk of ten years ago, poor but ambitious, working his way as he saw it from clerk's stool to solicitor's desk. Then the same man sinking in his world as Topaz rose in hers, stealing from his employers to try to impress her, falling to utter ruin. Then years later, by a cruel coincidence, finding himself a hired hand living with apprentice clowns in a circus wagon, while she slept on gold sheets in the same town. *I.O.U. for one career*. I could see from the brightness in Sidney's eyes that he sensed my excitement.

'Supposing it was Bobsworth,' he said, as softly as an endearment.

I thought of Bobsworth asking for a meeting with Topaz late at night after his circus work was finished – and Topaz replying with the note that began *Too late*. Too late for Bobsworth, altogether too late. I tried to fight the current.

'Wouldn't he have been working at the circus that evening?'

Sidney smiled. 'It wouldn't have been any novelty to anyone if Bobsworth had gone bunking off again.'

The waiter had brought more coffee. Sidney drank his slowly this time, like a satisfied cat.

'And Bobsworth's dead?'

'Drowned. I've seen his body.'

We sat for a while, not talking, as the café began to fill up with people coming in for an early lunch. Sidney sorted out a franc and some centimes and piled them on the tablecloth.

'So that's it then.'

His jauntiness seemed quite restored. We went out into the sunshine together.

'I suppose I took my whip to the wrong one then?'

'Yes.'

'Serves me right, losing it.'

He wished me good morning and walked away, swinging along past the strolling holidaymakers with the air of a sailor among landlubbers. So that was it, then.

NINETEEN

I NEEDED CALM. I WALKED up and down along the parade with the great sweep of the Atlantic beside me, but for all I saw of it I might as well have been back in a prison cell. If Sidney had been speaking the truth, I knew the name of Topaz's murderer. If, on the other hand, Sidney had not been speaking the truth I surely still knew another name for Topaz's murderer, because what other reason could he have for inventing this legal lover? Every wave that broke repeated, 'Bobsworth, Bobsworth, Bobsworth,' thumping in on the 'Bob' and hissing out on the 'sworth'.

There was an irritation that came with it like grains of sand, a thoroughly unworthy irritation, but there it was. If Bobsworth killed Topaz, then Bobbie Fieldfare was a much better detective than I was. Almost from the time Topaz died she must have suspected the man. Take, for example, the matter of the fire opal pendant. On Tansy's evidence, it arrived with a card on the morning before Topaz's death. She seemed pleased and amused by it, quite likely reactions if it had come out of the blue from a lover of ten years ago. The card might have carried Worth's plea for a meeting with her late at night, after his circus work was over. How a poor circus hand would acquire an opal didn't need much explaining on the assumption that he'd committed theft to impress Topaz at least once before in his career. The only mystery was how Bobbie had managed to guess the significance of the pendant and get it into her possession. Then, having got it, she passed it to Marie, apparently on a whim. That needed explaining too, unless for some reason it had ceased to matter.

I walked along the road beside the Grande Plage,

towards Cap St Martin and its lighthouse. Perhaps the pendant had ceased to matter because Bobbie knew there was stronger evidence against Worth, the card in his handwriting, re-introducing himself to Topaz, asking her to see him. Suppose Bobbie, or possibly Rose, had somehow managed to get into Topaz's suite and taken both pendant and card. Suppose, further, that Bobsworth had found out they had evidence that could send him to the guillotine. That might be why he had followed Bobbie to the party in his hastily assembled satyr's outfit, to try to get it back. Then, failing to corner Bobbie on her own, he might have turned his attention to the two people he'd seen with her, myself and Rose. When I thought of that I wanted even more to find Rose, to apologise to her for not understanding soon enough and protecting her. If Rose had killed the man in her panic, it was my fault, and Bobbie's.

Bobbie had been clever, cleverer than I was, and yet neither of us had been clever enough. I'd gone to Biarritz to claim Topaz's fifty thousand pounds for our cause. If we could prove murder rather than suicide, that would strengthen the claim that Topaz was of sound mind when her will was made. But with Bobsworth dead, we were in no position to prove his guilt without incriminating Rose.

By the time I'd come that far, the very cries of the seagulls sounded derisive. I sat down on an upturned rowing boat. All this assumed that Sidney was telling the truth, that there really had been a lover with legal ambitions about ten years ago who might have been Worth. There was only one person I knew of in Biarritz who might help me, and that was Tansy. The legal lover would have been before her time, but she'd been Topaz's confidante. It was likely that at some time, in those woman-to-woman sessions that Topaz seemed to enjoy with her maid, the existence of the man had been mentioned. I needed to talk to Tansy. The difficulty was that the last time we'd met she'd ordered me out of the room. Well, if she wouldn't let me in we'd have to speak outside. Surely at some time of the day she'd venture out of the hotel for fresh air.

I waited in the side street outside Topaz's private entrance from mid-afternoon until after six o'clock. I collected some suspicious looks from cab drivers and once Demi-tasse sauntered past and wished me a polite good afternoon. The sun was low down over the sea, sending a wash of gold light up the street and setting the pigeons cooing on the hotel ledges, when the side door opened and Tansy walked out, carrying a shopping bag. She locked the door and walked quickly down the street away from the seafront, the way we'd gone together on our hunt for underwear. She hadn't seen me so I walked some way behind her, not wanting to scare her into bolting back inside. When she came to the small square with its shops she made a beeline for the grocer's. I crossed over and stood outside the shop and when she came out ten minutes or so later, shopping bag bulging, she nearly bumped into me.

'Oh, Miss Bray, you did give me a fright. What are you doing here?'

She was nervy, but less angry than she'd been in the hotel suite.

'Strolling around. I see you've been shopping.'

She clutched the bag to her as if I had designs on it.

'More than I wanted. They don't understand when you ask for a pound.'

I fell into step beside her. 'I'm sorry if I annoyed you the other day.'

'I'm sorry if I was snappy, only they fray at your nerves, all those questions.'

We walked on in silence and she stopped when we came to the side door.

'I'll be saying goodbye to you then, Miss Bray. I suppose you'll be leaving soon, like all the others.'

For all the world as if I'd been on holiday. I hadn't wanted to show my hand so soon, but there was nothing else for it.

'May I come up for a minute please, Tansy. There's something I think you'll want to hear.'

She hesitated. 'What's that?'

'I think I may know who killed Topaz Brown.'

Her face was blank. 'Who?'

'It's a long story. I think we should go upstairs.'

She turned the key in the lock, didn't hold the door for me but made no protest when I walked in behind her. We went up in the lift together, still in silence. Only when we were standing outside the door of Topaz's suite she began complaining loudly.

'I'm not asking much, just a bit of peace and quiet to get her things in order. That's all I'm asking from you, Miss Bray, just a bit of peace and quiet.'

Since I was standing behind her, she hurled the words at the closed door and made a great business of finding her key, asking herself out loud what she'd done with it, then clattering it into the lock as if it had done her an injury. The big salon looked untidy. In the twelve days since Topaz's death it had taken on the air of a luxurious waiting room, impersonal and unrestful. A tray of used tea things stood on a small table near the spirit lamp. Tansy dumped her bag down.

'Well?'

'Well what?'

'Who was it then?'

'Tansy, I'm not going to tell you just like that. Take your coat off and sit down.'

I sat down myself on an armchair. After a second or two she followed my example, but still as tense as a spring.

'Who was it?'

'I'm afraid there's one more question first. I hope it will be the last one.'

'I thought you were going to tell me something for a change.'

'Yes, I am. But please, Tansy, answer this question first. It's desperately important.'

'They're all supposed to be important.'

But she waited, hands locked tight in her lap, feet pressed together in her dusty, sensible boots.

'Did Topaz ever talk to you about the men she knew before you came to work for her?'

She glared. 'I told you. I never gossiped about her business, and I'm not going to start now.'

'It wasn't business, Tansy. It was a man she was fond of and trying to help in his career. This man had something to do with the legal profession. She knew him about ten years ago.'

'That was three years before my time.'

'Did she ever talk about anybody like that?'

She was silent. At first I thought it was the old stubborn silence, but then I saw that the expression on her face was not stubbornness but misery and her locked hands were gripping each other so tightly that the bones showed white. A fight was going on between her loyalty and the need to know what I could tell her. I tried to make it easier.

'It's all right, Tansy, you don't even have to tell me his name. I know that already. But there was a man, wasn't there?'

The nod she gave was only the faintest movement. If I hadn't been watching her very closely I'd have missed it.

'She talked to you about him?'

Another nod.

'Often?'

'Once.'

The word came out like the creak of a hinge on a chest unopened for years.

'What did she say about him?'

'She'd helped him and he'd been ungrateful. It just came up one day when we were talking about men not being grateful.'

'Came up recently?'

'No, a year or two ago. Only I remembered it because she didn't usually criticise people. She'd liked him, you see, liked him quite a bit.'

She said 'liked' in the way most women would have said 'loved'. She sat there, eyes on my face.

'Well then, what have you got to tell me?'

I took a deep breath. 'I think he killed her, Tansy. He was here in Biarritz. He probably sent her that pendant asking her to see him again. She let him come to her. She even went out and bought cheap underwear and cheap wine to remind him of the time they'd spent together, before she had much money. And the fish – I expect they used to eat fish and chips together. She wanted to surprise him, and he killed her.'

I see,' she said. 'I see.'

We sat in silence, with no sound in the room but our breathing. The noise of the evening traffic, hooves and car horns, came up to us from a long way below. I remembered what Jules had said about feeling that Topaz would finally have died for him when he knew who killed her, and guessed that Tansy was feeling the same.

As we sat there I wondered if it would help her to know that Robert Worth was dead, and that her own sister had accidentally avenged Topaz. I decided that it wouldn't. The silence drew itself out for minutes on end and the light in the room changed from gold to copper red as the sun went down over the sea. I was tired, but I had to leave Tansy to her grief and go on looking for Rose. There was only one thing I could do for her before I left, pitiful enough but not to be neglected.

'I'll make us some tea, Tansy.'

I went over to the table with the unwashed cups and the spirit lamp.

'No, leave those alone. I don't want tea.'

Her cry came just too late to prevent me from seeing it. I went back to the door and switched the light on, revealing a tray with two used cups.

'A visitor, Tansy?'

'Yes, my friend Janet.'

But she wasn't a good liar. I remembered her haste to get me out of the suite on my last visit, the bulging food bag, the fumbling of her key in the lock. I walked over to the big double doors leading to the bedroom and opened them.

'I should come out, Rose,' I said.

TWENTY

SHE'D BEEN SITTING THERE IN the darkness, curtains drawn, on a chair beside Topaz's bed.

'You stay there, Rose. Don't take any notice of her.'

But Rose ignored her sister and came out, blinking in the light. She was wearing the same skirt as when I'd seen her in Marie's garden and one of her sister's striped blouses that was too small for her, straining across the bust, showing her wrists. Her face was pale and the skin below her eyes dark and sunken.

'Hello, Miss Bray. Don't worry, Tansy, it's probably just as well. I couldn't stay there forever.'

'Have you been here all the time?'

'Yes, I'm sorry. After what happened in the garden I was . . . I was scared and didn't know what to do. I came to Tansy.'

She sounded weary, defeated. The younger sister had gone to the older one like a child in trouble. I wondered whether she'd told Tansy about the death of Robert Worth and decided probably not.

'I didn't know what Bobbie was doing any more, what she wanted me to do.'

Her eyes were on me and there was an appeal in them. No, she hadn't told her sister.

She asked: 'Does Bobbie know I'm here too?'

I was about to say that she didn't when there was a thunderous knocking on the outside door of the suite and a familiar voice, breezy and sure of itself.

'Tansy, Tansy, have you got Rose in there? I want to speak to her.'

Tansy shouted back: 'She's not here. Go away.'

'I don't believe you, Tansy. I'm going to stay here until Rose comes out, even if it takes all night.'

There was a sliding sound and I imagined Bobbie taking up a sitting position, back against the door.

'She won't go away,' Rose said.

There was still a touch of pride in her voice. I knew she was right and that Bobbie would stay there if necessary until the cleaning maids came in the morning.

I said to Rose: 'If you don't want to see her you can go out by the side door. I'll give you the key to my hotel room.'

'No, I do want to see her. I want her to know I didn't just go away and leave her.'

Tansy said: 'I'm not letting another of them in here. One's more than enough.'

It took me a while to realise that she meant more than enough suffragettes.

I said: 'I think we might let her in, Tansy. She owes Rose an explanation.'

And me an explanation too, I thought. I was still smarting about Bobbie's superior detective powers and wondering how she'd found out about Worth so soon.

In the end, although Tansy refused to unlock the door herself, she made only a token objection when I said I'd do it.

'On your own head be it.'

It was a small, unworthy satisfaction to me when Bobbie fell into the room backwards when the door opened, but she rapidly recovered her dignity.

'I've been looking for you all over the place, Rose. We're leaving by the six fifty-two train tomorrow morning. I've got our tickets.'

From her manner, she might have been making the most routine holiday arrangements.

Tansy said: 'She's not coming with you.'

Bobbie ignored her and me and spoke to Rose. 'I was worried about you. I suppose I should have guessed that Nell Bray had kidnapped you. That's exactly her style.'

When I'd let Bobbie in I'd intended to be calm and reasonable, but as usual one minute of her company was enough to change that.

'Of course I didn't kidnap Rose. I've only just found her myself.'

Bobbie stopped short of calling me a liar, but she gave me a disbelieving look and plumped herself down on a sofa. In spite of the failure of her ambush, she still had the air of being pleased with herself. I hated to add to it, but I wanted to know how she'd guessed about Topaz and Bobsworth.

I said: 'I think I owe you an apology, Bobbie. In one respect at any rate you were ahead of me.'

She looked surprised, but took it as her due.

'I'm glad you see it that way, Nell.'

'Yes. I don't know how you immediately grasped the significance of that opal pendant.'

'Oh, that wasn't very difficult. In fact, it was the obvious thing to do.'

'What was the obvious thing to do?'

I was mystified, feeling as so often when dealing with Bobbie that things were slipping out of my control.

'Steal it back, of course. We needed it, didn't we, Rose?'

Rose said nothing. She was perched on the edge of a chair looking from one to the other of us like a spectator at a game of lawn tennis.

'Steal it back? What do you mean, steal it back?'

'It may have seemed disrespectful to do it so soon after she was dead, but it was no use to her and it wasn't as if I had pockets full of pendants. We had to have it to try again with the next one.'

Tansy said to me: 'What is she talking about?'

I was on the point of admitting that I had no idea, but I stopped myself. Bobbie was talking as if I knew all about it, and I wasn't going to disillusion her. I wished, though, that I had more time to think. It was like skidding down a mud slide, being carried faster than I wanted to go, but with no power to stop.

I said, struck by a moment of clarity: 'She's saying that it was her own pendant, that she sent it to Topaz herself.'

'It used to be my grandmother's. She left it to me. I'd heard men sent necklaces and such like to them when they wanted to spend the night with them, so I had to send something or I knew she wouldn't invite him.'

Tansy was still looking as if Bobbie were talking in a foreign language, but for me the moment of clarity had broadened into certainty. I remembered what Bobbie had said when I spoilt her plot with Marie: 'It was probably you interfering the first time.' The words made sense to me now. I didn't look at Bobbie, but explained it for Tansy's benefit as if I'd known all along.

'Bobbie had a wild idea that it would be to our advantage if we could put one of our political opponents into a compromising situation. Being in some respects an unworldly young woman . . .' (a gasp of protest from Bobbie) '. . . she decided to do it by arranging an assignation for him with a prostitute.' (Another sound of protest, this time from Tansy.) 'She made a few inquiries around the town, then she sent Topaz that opal pendant you saw, implying somehow that it had come from the man in question. The hope was that Topaz would invite him to come and see her, and that he'd be unable to resist.'

'Well, of all the wicked . . .'

I shushed Tansy. 'In the event, the plan failed. Whether Topaz would at some time have invited the man we shall never know. But we do know that she had other plans for that evening. Those other plans led to her death.'

I had to abandon the attractive idea that Bobsworth had stolen the pendant and sent it to her. His note, pleading for a meeting, must have come by the same post.

Bobbie, I was glad to see, was looking considerably less pleased with herself. Rose was biting her lip, staring out of the window at the darkening sky.

'Bobbie, of course, knew nothing about Topaz's other plans for the evening. In fact, she spent two hours walking up and down outside the side door, in the hope that the man she was trying to trap would come in or out. She didn't give up hope until after midnight.'

Rose looked across at Bobbie.

'When Bobbie heard that Topaz was dead, she decided to reclaim the pendant for use a second time – this time with Marie de la Tourelle as the bait in the trap. How she managed to steal it I don't know . . .'

Bobbie said: 'If you must know, I watched the two of

you go out, then I came up in the public lift and bribed the maid to let me in. I had to go out over the balcony when I heard you coming back. That's when you saw me mountaineering, Nell.'

Tansy said: 'Stealing from a dead woman.'

'I wasn't stealing it. It belonged to me.'

I said: 'I have to admit that there's still one thing in all this that puzzles me.'

'What can possibly puzzle Nell Bray?'

'I still can't understand why you made that visit to the doctor.'

Bobbie laughed. 'Oh that. Did she ask you about that, Rose?'

Rose said nothing.

'It was part of my reconnaissance. I needed to learn how things were done here, and everybody said the doctor was a gossip. A snob, too. Did you notice all those cards on his mantelpiece? I saw one I knew would come in useful, so I pocketed it while he wasn't looking. You can guess whose it was, Nell.'

'David Chester's. He wanted to see the doctor about his daughter.'

She nodded.

'So you sent his card to Topaz with the pendant. Did you use the card again for Marie too?'

'No. I couldn't find it. It wasn't with the pendant and you came back while I was still looking for it. I suppose it's in this room somewhere.'

Rose said something so quietly that I couldn't hear her at first. She repeated it.

'It's here. I found it this morning.'

Tansy fired up again. 'I told you not to touch her papers.'

'I couldn't help it. A pile of letters fell off that table over there and I was picking them up. I knew it would only cause trouble if anybody else saw it, so I took it.'

She slipped a hand into the pocket of her skirt and passed me a visiting card, crumpled by now, with the gloss rubbed off it. I didn't even look at it, too worried about Rose. She looked near to tears and I was afraid she'd break down and talk about Bobsworth in front of Bobbie and her sister.

I said quietly: 'That's the whole story then. You'd better go now, Bobbie. You'll have packing to do.'

To my surprise, she stood up.

'I suppose so. Shall we go, Rose?'

Rose got up and took a step towards her, looked at her sister, stopped.

'Come on, Rose,' Bobbie said. 'It's not the end of the world. There's plenty to do back at home.'

'She's not going,' Tansy said. 'She's had enough of it.'

Rose looked daggers at her, took another step, stopped again.

I said: 'You go on ahead, Bobbie. Rose will follow later if she wants to.'

Bobbie couldn't in any decency oppose that. She stood in the doorway looking at me, then suddenly smiled and raised her hand.

'Goodbye, Nell Bray. See you at the battle front.'

When the door closed behind her, Tansy let out an explosive sigh of relief. Rose stood halfway to the door, where her two steps had taken her.

I said: 'I want to talk to Rose on her own.'

I took her by the arm, guided her gently into Topaz's bedroom and closed the doors on Tansy's protests.

TWENTY-ONE

I SAT ROSE DOWN ON the chair beside the bed and switched on the lamp. The light reflected off the golden sheets making a warm cave round us with the rest of the room in darkness. I wondered if it had been like that on the evening Topaz entertained her last guest. There was no other chair, so I had to perch on the side of the bed, my feet on the step of the dais. This meant I was looking down at Rose's pale face and resentful eyes.

I said: 'Rose, you should know I don't blame you for what happened, and neither would any other fair-minded person.'

She sat stiff and upright: 'I'm not having that. It may have been Bobbie's idea, but I agreed with it. I'm not putting all the blame on her.'

'If you insist on sharing the responsibility for that idiotic plot, I shan't deprive you of it. I'm talking about something else, about what happened in the garden the night Marie gave her party.'

'Oh that.' She looked away from me. 'I was silly to be so upset about it. It caught me off balance, I suppose.'

Even though I believed she had no cause for guilt about Robert Worth's death, this seemed a little too casual.

'I thought it was the other party who was caught off balance.'

She disregarded that, which was probably just as well.

'I didn't know what was happening. I heard the man following you and I waited behind a shed at the side of the house. Then everything went quiet so I went to look for you. I couldn't find you.'

'I was up the magnolia tree.'

'I went right to the end of the garden. I could hear the waves and I guessed it was near the top of the cliffs. I still couldn't see anyone, but I heard him saying something.'

'Him? You mean the man who was following us?'

'Who else could it have been? He sounded angry and I thought he was talking to you. But he wasn't, it was another man.'

'You saw another man?'

'No. It was dark. I couldn't see either of them.'

'Heard another man, then?'

'No.'

'Then how did you know it was another man?'

'A woman's voice would have carried, especially your voice. They were having an argument about a key.'

'What did they say?'

'The one I could hear said if the other one wanted the key back he'd have to pay him a hundred quid. He kept repeating, "a hundred quid" and he said if he didn't get it he'd know what to do with the key.'

'An educated voice or a working man's voice?'

She hesitated. 'In between.'

There was silence inside our cave of light. Outside it I could hear Tansy moving things around in the other room to remind us she was there.

'Rose, you would tell me the truth, wouldn't you? Whatever happened, I can't help you unless I know about it.'

'Of course I'm telling you the truth. Why shouldn't I?' She seemed genuinely puzzled.

'All right. What happened then?'

'I went back towards the house. I wanted to find you or Bobbie.'

'You simply left them there?'

'Why not? Whatever they were arguing about, it had nothing to do with me.'

The picture of Rose frightened by Worth, pushing Worth, had been so clear in my mind that it took me some time to replace it with what Rose had told me.

'You didn't find me. Did you find Bobbie?'

Another hesitation. 'In a way.'

'What does that mean? Either you did or you didn't.'

'I saw her. I didn't speak to her.'

'Why not? You'd come all that way to find her.'

'She was with somebody.'

'Who?'

'Marie. They came out of the house together and stood on the terrace talking. Some of the torches were still burning so I could see them. Marie was wearing a long black fur cloak. Then Bobbie picked up a torch and they went down the garden.'

There was stark misery in her voice.

I said: 'Hadn't Bobbie told you what she was planning with Marie?'

She shook her head.

'After Topaz, she didn't tell me everything. She knew I'd talked to you.'

I owed Bobbie nothing, and I was beginning to believe that we both had debts to Rose. I told her about the trap and its ludicrous end. She listened without saying a word, then sighed: 'Poor Bobbie.'

'Nonsense. Let's come back to you. You saw her and Marie together and decided not to speak to them. What did you do then?'

'Came here.'

'Straight here to Tansy?'

'No, I walked around for a long time, trying to decide what to do. I didn't know what I was doing any more. You all had your plans, but nobody had told me.'

Her eyes were bright with hurt and anger.

'You did the right thing to come to your sister.'

'I don't think so. We argue all the time. She wants me to give up the movement, and I won't, whatever happens.'

I thought the poor girl was being torn apart and it was high time we took her away from the conflicting influences of Bobbie and Tansy. When all this was over I'd find her a place in a teachers' training college and persuade one of our richer supporters to pay for her keep. But there was something that must be settled first.

'Rose, will you swear to me that all you did was listen to that man's voice, then go away?'

'Yes. It's true. But why . . .?'

'You didn't speak to him?'

'Of course not. I didn't want him to know I was there.'

'You didn't go back there later to speak to him?'

'No. Why should I?'

I believed her. The account of Marie in her sable cloak and Bobbie with the torch compared exactly with what I'd seen. I said, as gently as I could:

'The man who was following us, the one you probably heard – he's dead.'

She stared blankly.

'He was found in the sea the next day. He'd been knocked unconscious and drowned.'

Her hands went to her mouth. Two scared eyes stared at me over her bitten nails. She lurched forward from the chair and I managed to catch her before she fell. The noise brought Tansy bursting in.

'What have you been doing to her? Can't you leave the poor girl alone?'

Rose was saying weakly that she was all right, that we mustn't bother.

I wanted her to lie down on Topaz's bed but Tansy, either from respect or superstition, pulled her away from it as if it were live coals.

'She wants to come and lie down in my room, don't you, Rosie? Don't worry, my love. Her and her questions. If she tries to ask you any more she'll have me to deal with.'

When I tried to help support Rose as far as the door, Tansy gave me a withering look.

'You stay here. We'll be better off on our own, Rosie and me, won't we, my duck?'

The look of appeal that Rose gave me over her sister's shoulder showed she had her doubts about that, but I was bone weary and knew when I was beaten. I sat in my chair, turning over in my hand the visiting card that had cost so much trouble. 'David Chester MP' embossed in copper plate. Then underneath, *May I call at 11 p.m.?* When I held it close to the light I could see that the 'p.m.', though cleverly forged, was in a slightly less glossy black ink than the rest. Bobbie's hand, of course. I was even angrier at the stupidity of her plot now I knew the harm it had done to Rose.

Then as I sat there, half dozing beside Topaz's bed, something connected in a way that would never have happened in my waking mind. I came bolt upright and awake, feeling as if some great catastrophe had happened. I went through to the salon for my bag – luckily Tansy was still occupied with Rose in her bedroom – brought it back to my chair beside Topaz's bed and rummaged for what I wanted. All the time I'd been carrying round with me Topaz's note: *Too late. 8 p.m. Return of I.O.U. for one career. Vin Poison.*' I held the visiting card in one hand and the note in the other, feeling as if each throbbed with an electric current and the consequences of completing the circuit by bringing them together were too dangerous to be faced. I must have sat there for a long time. I heard Tansy closing the door of her bedroom, coming back into the salon. She called through the door to me:

'Are you staying there all night? You can't sleep on her bed.'

I heard my own voice promising not to sleep on Topaz's bed, then Tansy moving around next door. I think she must have been making up a bed for herself on the chaise longue. Then she settled, switched off the light and the room fell quiet. I sat there, conscious of the sounds of a hotel also settling itself for the night, lifts ascending and descending with metallic creakings that I never noticed by day, pipes suddenly gurgling. I heard a clock outside striking midnight, then I must have dozed again because I was jerked back to consciousness by the sound of Tansy's voice whispering urgently from the other side of the door. My first thought was that she was checking to make sure I wasn't profaning Topaz's bed and I told her, rather impatiently, that she need not worry, it was all right.

'No, it isn't all right. I'm coming in.'

The light was still off in the salon. She closed the door behind her and came into my circle of lamplight. She was in stockinged feet, still wearing her black day dress.

'Somebody's coming up.'

Her voice was a scared whisper.

'What do you mean?'

'Coming up in her lift. Listen.'

When I listened I could hear the sound of the private lift on to the landing creaking up its shaft, but I still didn't grasp the significance of it.

Tansy said: 'Whoever it is must have her key. Nobody could use that side door otherwise.'

Then the fear in her voice ran into me and I felt icy cold. Only one person was likely to have Topaz's missing key. Topaz's last visitor.

The lift stopped on the landing. At first nothing happened. The silence stretched itself into ten, twenty heartbeats, then I heard the lift doors opening.

'Tansy, the man she said was ungrateful, you must . . .'

She shushed me. There was a metallic scraping sound at the outside door of the salon. I stood up and instinctively we moved closer together.

I mouthed at her: 'Is it locked?'

She nodded, but no more than a minute later there was a click and the sound of the door opening. Even grand hotels may be catchpenny in the matter of inside locks, and that one had put up little resistance. There was now only the width of the salon and one set of unlocked doors between us and whoever had broken his way in. We could hear him now moving round the salon. A thin beam of light from a hand lamp came through a crack in the door, went away, cut back from another angle. Tansy was so close to me that I could feel her heart thumping. I put my arm round her and she didn't resist. The soft steps moved closer to our door, then away again. Tansy's heart thumped harder. She mouthed at me: 'Rose.' I nodded. He couldn't be allowed to wake up Rose. I led Tansy firmly to the chair, made her sit down in it, then walked to the double doors between Topaz's bedroom and the salon. I waited for a second, feeling the porcelain doorknobs smooth under my hands, just as months before I'd been very conscious of the roughness of the half brick in the second before I threw it. Then I took a deep breath and pulled the doors open.

'You'd better come in,' I said.

TWENTY-TWO

I THINK HE WAS DAZZLED for a moment by the golden light pouring in from the bedroom because he stood there blank and staring, not focusing on me. When he moved it was not so much a conscious step as an overbalancing. He caught himself up in the doorway, inches away from me. I stood to one side and again invited him to come in, surprised to hear my own voice so level. He came, his eyes on me, not noticing Tansy in the chair. I shut the doors and leaned against them. I said to Tansy:

'That was the name you wouldn't tell me, wasn't it?'

She nodded, staring at him transfixed. When he saw there was somebody else in the room I thought he was going to turn and run. He looked at Tansy, then at the golden bed with its newly plumped pillows.

'Is this a trap of some kind?'

His voice was calm and low, but with a threat in it, just as I remembered from court.

I said: 'If it is a trap, you've taken some trouble to break into it.'

A barrister learns to control his expression. He gave me the same level stare he'd given me in the dock.

'I've come to recover a piece of my property which was stolen.'

The card and the note were on the floor by Tansy's feet. I'd dropped them when I fell asleep. I crossed the room, picked both of them up and handed him the card.

'This?'

That look again. 'May I ask how you came by it?'

'Do you confirm that it's your property?'

'It's a moot point whether a calling card left with one's doctor remains one's property, especially if it is subsequently stolen. I suppose that was your doing, Miss Bray.'

'Certainly not. Do you recognise it as your writing?'

'All except the last two letters, which are a palpable forgery. A forgery with malicious intent.'

He'd moved to a position in the middle of the room, trying to dominate it as if it were a court. I noticed that, after the first glance, he didn't look towards the bed.

I said: 'Exactly what malicious intent?'

'I'm sure that's clearer to you than to me, Miss Bray.'

'I doubt it, but let me summarise.'

Two could play at the court game. I stepped up to the dais round Topaz's bed, turned to face him from the foot of it. Tansy stayed in the chair. Her eyes hadn't moved from him since he came in.

I said: 'You've confirmed that this is your card, stolen from your doctor's consulting room. You left it to arrange an appointment for eleven o'clock, meaning of course eleven o'clock in the morning.'

He nodded. The stare wasn't quite so confident now he had to look at me across the bed.

'It was, as we've established, stolen. We've also established that it was subsequently amended.'

'By forgery.'

'Indeed. I can tell you that it was stolen by one of your political opponents – and believe me that gives a very wide field of suspects – who forged the letters "p.m." to make it appear that it was a request for an assignation late at night. It was then sent, along with an opal pendant, to Miss Topaz Brown.'

He winced a little. 'You accept, Miss Bray, that I knew nothing of this, and to put it in the mildest terms, would have protested most strongly if I had known.'

'I accept that.'

'Then do you accept that it was a wicked attempt to harm my reputation by implying an association between myself and a common prostitute?'

Tansy stirred in her chair. I gave her a glance.

'I should describe it as stupid rather than wicked. Apart from that, I accept what you say.'

Tansy muttered something.

'Very well then. You can hardly be surprised that I should wish to recover my card.'

'No indeed, I'm not surprised.'

He seemed taken aback by my reasonable tone. He slipped the card into the pocket of his evening jacket.

'In the circumstances, since it is to nobody's advantage that such a squalid attempt should be made public, I'll refrain from any immediate legal action against you or your misguided supporters. I need hardly say that if any of this should become public knowledge I should immediately take the most serious steps to defend my reputation.'

He gave me another stare, held it for a count of three seconds, then turned and stepped towards the door. I waited until his hand was on the knob, then I said:

'Are we also supposed to be quiet about what happened next?'

He turned. 'What are you talking about?'

I held out Topaz's note but didn't move from where I was standing. He stayed by the door.

'What is that?'

'A note of invitation from Miss Brown.'

'I hardly see how that can interest me.'

He should have opened the door and walked out. He didn't move a muscle.

'She sets an assignation for eight o'clock in the evening. The note begins *Too late*. What do you suppose that means?'

'I can hardly be expected to guess.'

'I think it has a very simple meaning – that eleven o'clock is too late and she regards eight o'clock as preferable. A reply to the message on your card, Mr Chester.'

'If so, a reply to a forged message which you have already admitted was part of a plot.'

But his voice wasn't as level as it had been. If I'd been a rival barrister, I'd have sensed that the scales were tipping my way.

'But Miss Brown believed the card and the pendant

came from you, so naturally the reply would be sent to you.'

'I received no such note.'

He took a step towards me.

'I believe that you did receive it, Mr Chester. And I believe that you brought it with you when you came to call on Miss Brown at eight o'clock that night to ask her what she meant by it, though I suspect you had a very good idea already.'

He wrapped his courtroom manner round him like a gown.

'In that case my behaviour surely would have been inexplicable. You are asking the . . .' (He almost said 'asking the court'.) '. . . You are claiming that I received out of the blue an invitation from a notorious prostitute to visit her and that I went in person to ask what she meant by it. Surely that would have been the action of a simpleton?'

'Indeed it would – if you'd never met Miss Brown in the past.'

'If you are implying, Miss Bray, that I'm in the habit of frequenting prostitutes, I can only say you have an even fouler mind than I should have expected from your activities.'

He was quite buoyed up by his indignation.

I said: 'I wasn't accusing you of that.'

'Then what were you implying?'

'I believe that a normal relationship between a man and a woman like Topaz Brown is that he pays her expenses. In your case, it was quite the reverse.'

I read from Topaz's note, although I knew it by heart: '*Return of I.O.U. for one career*. Your career, Mr Chester, your very successful career. And yet at the outset it depended on Topaz Brown's support and Topaz Brown's money.'

He made a pretence of turning away, but took only a token step to the door.

'Your brain's completely turned by your hatred of me.'

'There's a witness.' I gestured towards Tansy. 'This is Tansy Mills, Topaz Brown's maid. Tansy told me that

Topaz once spoke to her about a man in the legal profession whom she'd helped early in her career. She said he'd been ungrateful. Tansy refused to tell me the name of that man. I'll ask her again now.'

'Yes, it was him.'

Tansy's voice was no more than a croak.

'We'll do this properly, Tansy. What was the name of the man Topaz said had been ungrateful?'

Another croak. 'David Chester.'

He took two quick steps towards her, then stopped himself.

'You've coached her. She's one of yours.'

'Oh no. If there's one person on the face of the earth who's more opposed to women's suffrage than you are, it's Tansy Mills. If there's one person who dislikes me more than you do, that's Tansy too.'

'That's a fact,' Tansy croaked.

He looked from her to me, utterly at a loss.

I said: 'The person who set that stupid trap for you had no idea how deadly it was. I swear to you that neither she nor I knew that you'd had any connection with Topaz Brown.'

'I don't believe you.'

'You received this note.' I walked across the room, let him look at it but didn't put it in his hand. 'Poor Topaz Brown meant exactly what she said. She was touched by the pendant that she thought came from you. She was prepared to forgive your ingratitude, to write off all that you owed her. She'd prepared a little supper to remind you of the old days when you were both poor; fried fish and cheap wine. She'd even gone out and bought underclothes of the kind she used to wear before she could afford better.'

His eyes flickered at the mention of the underwear.

'But you'd been making your preparations too, hadn't you? Topaz bought wine, but you bought laudanum. You kept the appointment, poisoned Topaz and returned in time for a late supper with your wife and friends. You took the key to her private door away with you and used it at some time after two o'clock in the morning to make sure she was dead or dying.'

'Without my wife noticing my absence?'

He was trained to fight a hopeless case to the end.

'As far as your wife was concerned, you were sitting up with a sick daughter, with Louisa. You probably gave her a few drops of the laudanum on a sugar lump, to make sure she didn't wake up while you were away.'

He closed his eyes at the mention of his daughter's name. I think those few drops he gave his daughter caused him more guilt than the laudanum he'd poured into Topaz's wine glass.

I said: 'There was still a problem, though, wasn't there? When you met Topaz, she'd have thanked you for the pendant. You would naturally ask how she knew it came from you, and she told you your card was enclosed with it. The next morning it occurred to you that you couldn't afford to have your card discovered among her papers. You paid a man to try to get it back for you, first by impersonation. When that failed, you gave him the key and told him to steal it. That failed too. Worse, he kept the key and tried to blackmail you. And he knew quite a lot by then, because you were paying him to spy on us as well, in case we'd guessed anything.'

'Could you produce this alleged man to give evidence in court?'

'You know very well that I can't. He's lying in the morgue. I can tell you his name, though: Robert Worth. You'd met him in London more than ten years ago when he was working for a solicitor. You met him again here – probably when you took Naomi and Louisa to the circus.'

That had been a sudden guess of mine, but I knew from his face that I'd hit it. I'm sure it was my knowledge of his family affairs that broke him. He lurched towards me and I tensed myself for an attack, but he stumbled past me up the step to the dais and sat down heavily on Topaz's bed. For once Tansy made no protest at the desecration. He slumped there, head in his hands, long fingers pressed to his forehead. I remembered my hours in the dock and felt no pity – or only a very little.

'I'm sorry,' he said.

It seemed hopelessly inadequate as a confession, but

that wasn't what he was trying to say.

'I'm sorry, I need some air. Is there a balcony?'

I signed to Tansy to stay where she was, led him out like a blind man through the dark salon and opened the French windows on to the balcony. A rush of cool air hit us, and the sound of Atlantic waves pounding the beach a hundred feet below. It was quite dark. The promenade lights had been switched off long ago and we were too high up to see the windows of other hotels. He stepped out on to the balcony, taking deep breaths. I'd guessed he had something to say to me that he didn't want Tansy to hear. I followed him, feeling as if I were treading on the broken fragments of something valuable, trying to tell myself that it deserved breaking. He had his back to me, looking out to sea. I waited.

'What do you intend to do?'

He asked the question without turning, his voice level again. It was the question I'd intended to ask him.

'What do you expect me to do?'

My voice sounded as calm as his. We might have been two colleagues discussing a difficult case.

'To name your price.'

'Price . . .' I was beginning to be indignant, then I realised he wasn't talking about money. 'What price were you thinking of?'

'A vote?'

'Our vote?'

'My vote.'

He was still facing out to sea, and the words were so quiet I hardly heard them. I moved closer.

'Your vote in Parliament?'

'It's not without influence.'

To hear him I had to stand close enough to touch him, but he still hadn't looked at me.

'Do I understand that you're offering to vote on our side the next time the suffrage question comes up in Parliament?'

His 'Yes' hardly moved the air on the balcony, but the stir it would make in London would be our biggest step forward for years. And he was right about his influence.

He'd carry others with him, perhaps make the difference at last.

I said: 'And the price?'

I knew the price. To forget about Topaz, who'd never been a supporter of ours. To forget about Bobsworth, who'd been part of the world's small change.

He murmured something so quietly that I had to move closer to hear it, but as I moved something happened to my body. My ribs crushed in so that I could hardly breathe, the sky spun round and my back came up against something hard. It took a second of blackness and panic before my mind grasped what was happening, that he was trying to throw me over the balcony. But my body knew what to do and, even without instructions, was going into the routine for resisting attack. My feet kicked out, making contact with something solid, my left arm pulled itself free, grabbed for a handful of cloth. By the time my mind had caught up my fingers were locked on his lapel and I was trying desperately to pull myself up, to take the pressure of the stone balustrade off my back. I heard myself shouting something, I don't know what.

He'd stepped back a little when I kicked his shin and I almost managed to pull myself upright. His face was inches away from mine, intent, eyes no colder than they'd been in court. A man doing a necessary job. I pulled my other arm free, jabbed my nails into his eye. He grunted with pain and I felt flesh tearing, but he didn't let go and I was still off balance, bent backwards. I felt the balustrade under my back again, my kicking legs being levered off the ground. All I could see was night sky and a constellation whose name I couldn't remember. I wondered if it would come to me on the way down. One foot, one toe was in contact with the balcony, and that was sliding.

'Stop that.'

Tansy's voice. She might have been speaking to a dog stealing the remains of the joint. He hadn't expected it. There'd been nothing else in the universe for either of us. He hesitated just long enough for me to get one foot back on the ground, to throw my weight forward. At the same time, Tansy simply grabbed his ear and pulled.

I think it was the indignity of it as much as anything that distracted him. He gasped as his head twisted round and I pulled upright and away from him. It looked for a moment as if he was going to attack Tansy, but by then I was standing beside her. He stared at us, chest heaving, one hand automatically massaging his mistreated ear.

'There's no sense in going on like that,' Tansy said.

The rebuke was directed equally at both of us, but Tansy and I had him boxed in now at one end of the balcony.

I said to Tansy: 'I'll keep him here. You go and ring for somebody.'

Then he moved, but not towards us. For a moment he was a shape on the edge of the balcony, black against the sky, then there was just sky. He made no noise as he went. Then, after a gap of silence worse than any scream would have been, there was a sound from the pavement below like a heavy door closing a long way away. When Rose came into the salon, blinking from sleep, she found me and Tansy clinging together like Babes in the Wood.

TWENTY-THREE

IT WAS TWO MONTHS BEFORE I met Bobbie Fieldfare again. She and I found ourselves under arrest together in the same police vehicle, after the fracas in Parliament Square when Mrs Pankhurst was arrested for slapping a police inspector's face in the House of Commons. I was the first occupant and Bobbie landed on top of me, still shouting defiance at the two police constables who'd bundled her in.

'Oh it's you again, is it, Nell Bray?'

As the vehicle jogged along the familiar route to Bow Street police station she said:

'I suppose you're not going to tell me what really happened.'

'The verdict was suicide.'

'Like Topaz Brown?'

'Like Topaz Brown. There seems to have been quite an epidemic of it in Biarritz this year.'

'From her balcony?'

'He'd suffered a complete mental collapse from overwork.'

'That's what *The Times* said. If it was in *The Times*, it must be a lie.'

We slowed from a trot to a walk, caught in the queue of other police wagons heading for Bow Street with our supporters on board.

'You're protecting him, aren't you, Nell? Him of all people. Why?'

I said nothing. I could give no answer that would satisfy Bobbie. For a silly, plump woman who thought it was wicked to want votes, for a cold-eyed child who'd said ladies couldn't be in Parliament. For Tansy, who wanted

Topaz to rest in peace. Their worlds had been torn apart already. Should I shred them more to make a political point?

The crowd were shouting outside, but above the traffic I couldn't tell if it was support or insults.

I said: 'There's some good news about Topaz's will, anyway. It looks as if the brother may settle for half the money.'

'Half!'

'That still leaves us with twenty-five thousand. That's twenty-five candidates and a general election coming up any month now.'

An election that surely must make the difference at last, must give us what we deserved in justice and logic. And Topaz Brown, whether she'd supported us or not, deserved to be part of it too.

Bobbie said: 'Have you seen Rose Mills lately?'

She sounded a little less sure of herself.

'I rather think she may be in one of the police vans up in front. She was leading a detachment of garment workers who were trying to storm the Home Office.'

'That's good.'

For once I agreed with Bobbie. I was almost sure that I'd managed to secure Rose a place in the autumn at a teachers' training college that would not be shocked by a police record acquired in a good cause. Tansy might be pleased by that, and if Topaz's will were settled, she'd get her five hundred pounds for the cottage.

'And the ducks, of course.'

'I beg your pardon.'

Bobbie was staring at me. I must have spoken out loud.

'Cats, I mean. I was just thinking my neighbour will have to look after my cats again.'

The wagon had drawn to a halt. We could hear the heavy boots of a police constable stamping round to the back of the van to escort us up the steps to the police station. We both stood up at once, looked at each other, then laughed. Bobbie sat down again.

'After you, Nell Bray.'

It was as near as we'd ever get to a truce.

HB 7 W

EGYPT OF THE PHARAOHS

AN INTRODUCTION

PLATE I

THE MAJESTY OF EGYPT

Seated statuette of Ammenemēs III, broken from the waist downwards. Dark grey granite. Moscow Museum

EGYPT OF THE PHARAOHS

AN INTRODUCTION

BY

SIR ALAN GARDINER

OXFORD UNIVERSITY PRESS

LONDON OXFORD NEW YORK

RED ROCKS
COMMUNITY COLLEGE

57565 # 4761654
DT
83
G2
1964

OXFORD UNIVERSITY PRESS
Oxford London Glasgow
New York Toronto Melbourne Wellington
Nairobi Dar es Salaam Cape Town
Kuala Lumpur Singapore Jakarta Hong Kong Tokyo
Delhi Bombay Calcutta Madras Karachi

© Oxford University Press 1961
First published by the Clarendon Press, 1961
First issued as an Oxford University Press paperback, 1964

printing, last digit: 20 19 18 17 16 15

Printed in the United States of America

TO THE MEMORY OF

JAMES HENRY BREASTED

RED ROCKS
COMMUNITY COLLEGE

PREFACE

IN undertaking to introduce to a wider public the subject of my life-long studies I was responding to wishes often expressed by my colleagues. Breasted's great *History of Egypt*, they complained, was largely out of date, and H. R. Hall's *Ancient History of the Near East* they found too complex and covering too wide a field to suit the English-speaking persons who came to them for advice. These opinions, justified at the time when my project was first mooted, are no longer entirely so in view of several admirable works which have recently appeared in America, and which I should have no hesitation in recommending. Nevertheless, what I am now offering differs from these so widely in both intent and content that I hope to be in some degree supplying the want felt by my friends. At the outset I was less aware of a precise purpose than of two extremes which I wished to avoid. On the one hand mere popularization was definitely not my aim; readable descriptions of the wonderland of the Pharaohs abound, and I have no wish to decry them, but I repeat that my own aim has been different. On the other hand, to attempt to squeeze into five hundred pages an account of Ancient Egypt in all its aspects could only have resulted in something like an enlarged encyclopaedia article, and those who read such articles for pleasure are, I imagine, few and far between. In this situation I summoned up memories of my own aspirations as a boy nearing the end of his schooldays. I recalled that already at that age I was fired with the desire to become an Egyptologist, and my budding interest lay almost as much in the course and methods of discovery as in the things to be discovered. Like Neneferkaptaḥ in the demotic story my ambition was to read the hieroglyphic inscriptions and to capture the actual words of the ancient people. Art and archaeology were by no means wholly alien to my interest, but I confess that they there occupied only a secondary place. And so it has come about that my present book has been written from an avowedly philological point of view. Hence the many excerpts from the original texts, with which I have dealt somewhat more freely than if I had been catering for advanced students. The space available to me has rendered necessary restriction to what is euphemistically called Egyptian history. That I have devoted so much discussion to what survives of Manetho in the corrupt excerpts of later chronographers will need no excuse for those familiar with the evolution of our science; no Egyptologist has yet been able to free himself from the shackles imposed by the native annalist's thirty Dynasties, and these are likely always to remain the essential framework of our modern expositions. More justifiable criticism of my present effort might point to its obvious incompleteness, a defect admitted in my sub-title; it is no full-dress history that I am here presenting, only one which will, it is hoped, lure some readers to penetrate further into our captivating field of study. It is for such serious students that the many bibliographical references have been devised. My footnotes have been cut as short as possible to prevent them from sprawling all over my pages, and the complete titles of books or periodicals referred to will be easily found in the list of abbreviations at the beginning of the book or in the supplementary references at the ends of the chapters.

The problem how best to transcribe Proper Names is one that has often vexed even classical scholars; with Orientalists it is much more acute, and among the latter the Egyptologist is worse off than any. The hieroglyphs write no vowels and the correct supplying of these from Coptic or elsewhere is seldom possible; guesswork is therefore inevitable, but it is necessary because vowelless transcriptions would be an austerity which no ordinary reader could stomach. Furthermore, Egyptian consonants by no means all correspond to our own; the ancient writing shows two kinds of *h*, two of *k*, two of *kh*, two of *s*, and no less than four of *t* and *d*, besides possessing among other peculiarities an important guttural in common with Hebrew and Arabic, there called the *ʿayin*. In more than one publication I have explained what seems to me the most rational way of facing up to this difficulty, and it would be wearisome to go over the same ground again. For the present work it was decided, after much consideration, to retain all diacritical marks throughout, at all events in such Old Egyptian names as Ḥatḥōr, Amenḥotpe, Maʿkarēʿ; in Greek or graecized names a greater latitude seemed not merely permissible, but even advisable, so that inconsistencies like Horus, Typhōn, Coptos, Elephantinē, Thebes have been accepted without hesitation. After all, those students who find the diacritical marks too pedantic for their taste are at liberty to ignore them in their writings or their memories. One innovation which I have allowed myself will probably not find general favour: it being certain that the feminine ending *-et*, though shown in the writing, had disappeared from pronunciation as early as the Old Kingdom, Hebrew and Arabic presenting a like phenomenon, I have replaced the usual 'Punt', 'Wawat', and 'Ḥatshepsut' by 'Pwēne', 'Wawaĕ', and 'Ḥashepsowe'. Lastly, Arabic place-names: here I have felt unable to do better than to follow Baedeker, the admirable editor of which has been invariably right so far as I have been able to check him.

At the last moment it was decided to reject the relatively complete special indexes already made, and to substitute a single general one of limited scope. This decision was prompted by the realization that my original plan would add more than thirty pages to a greatly overloaded book without bringing compensating advantages to the particular readers for whom it was intended. The shorter selective index which has taken its place is not wholly satisfactory, but has at least the merit of occupying considerably less space. Critics may perhaps censure the omission of the Pharaohs themselves, but this seemed excusable since their complex names, together with the Manethonian corruptions of them, had been fully set forth in the king-lists of the Appendix.

It remains only to acknowledge the assistance which I have received from many quarters. My lesser debts have been so numerous that mention of them here could serve no useful purpose, and I trust that my oral thanks will have been deemed adequate. But there have been important cases where I felt the need of consulting recognized authorities, and great has been the benefit which I derived from their comments on pages submitted to them for criticism or approval; here I must particularly name

A. Andrewes, A. J. Arkell, R. Caminos, O. Gurney, W. C. Hayes, K. S. Sandford, and D. J. Wiseman. As regards my illustrations, these necessarily few in number, it proved no easy task to make a selection which would present the Egyptian achievement at its most typical, but here again the ready help given by a number of colleagues has been of the greatest value; in addition to the acknowledgements made in my list of Plates I must specially mention C. Aldred (XV), Nina Davies (II, XII), Dows Dunham (VI), Labib Habachi (IX, X, XIV, XX, XXI, XXII), J.-Ph. Lauer (IV), J. Sainte Fare Garnot (XIX), E. Scamuzzi (XVII), and W. D. van Wijngaarden (VIII); but I regard as my principal good fortune the securing for my Frontispiece of the wonderful statuette of King Ammenemēs III in the Moscow Museum, a privilege which I owe to the Director V. V. Pavlov and to the never-failing kindness of Madame M. Matthieu. Lastly, my indebtedness to those concerned with the production of my book in one way or another cannot be overestimated. The help received from Miss Barbara Sewell greatly exceeds that involved in the typing and indexing for which it was enlisted. The care and patience devoted at the Clarendon Press to my confessedly exacting demands have been beyond all praise. Two names call for special mention: it was K. Sisam, the former Secretary to the Delegates, who first urged this work upon me, and now his second successor C. H. Roberts has not only done the like, but also has met my every whim with the utmost indulgence. This being in all probability my swan-song, I can only hope that my colleagues' final performances may be made as happy as mine.

CONTENTS

BOOK III

BACK TO THE BEGINNING

LIST OF PLATES

LIST OF FIGURES IN THE TEXT

LIST OF MAPS

ABBREVIATIONS

Abh. Berlin	*Abhandlungen der Königlichen Preussischen Akademie der Wissenschaften*, Berlin.
Äg. Stud.	O. Firchow, *Ägyptologische Studien*, Berlin, 1955.
AJSL	*American Journal of Semitic Languages and Literatures.*
Am.	Cuneiform letter from El-ʿAmârna. *See* p. 211.
Amenemhet	Nina de G. Davies and A. H. Gardiner, *The Tomb of Amenemhet*, London, 1915.
ANET	*Ancient Near Eastern Texts relating to the Old Testament*, edited by J. B. Pritchard, Princeton, 1950.
Ann. Serv.	*Annales du Service des Antiquités de l'Égypte*, 56 vols., Cairo, 1900–59.
Anthes	R. Anthes, *Die Felseninschriften von Hatnub*, Leipzig, 1928.
Arab.	Arabic.
Baedeker	K. Baedeker, *Egypt and the Sûdân*, 8th edition, Leipzig, 1929.
Ball, *Contributions*	J. Ball, *Contributions to the Geography of Egypt*, Cairo, 1939.
B*AR*	J. H. Breasted, *Ancient Records of Egypt*, 5 vols., Chicago, 1906–7. *See* p. 69.
von Beckerath, *Tanis*	J. von Beckerath, *Tanis und Theben*, Glückstadt, 1951.
Beiträge	K. Sethe, *Beiträge zur ältesten Geschichte Ägyptens, See* p. 70, n. 1.
Bibl. Or.	*Bibliotheca Orientalis*, 17 vols., Leyden, 1944–60.
Borchardt, *Mittel*	L. Borchardt, *Die Mittel zur zeitlichen Festlegung von Punkten der ägyptischen Geschichte*, Cairo, 1935.
Borchardt, *Saḥurēʿ*	L. Borchardt, *Das Grabdenkmal des Königs Saḥurēʿ*, Leipzig, 1913.
Bull. Inst. fr.	*Bulletin de l'Institut français d'Archéologie orientale*, 57 vols., Cairo, 1901–60.
Bull. MMA	*Bulletin of the Metropolitan Museum of Art*, New York, 1915 ff.
Bull. soc. fr. d'Ég.	*Bulletin de la société française d'Égyptologie*, 29 nos., Paris, 1949–59.
c.	*circa*, about (with dates).
CAH	*The Cambridge Ancient History*, 6 vols., Cambridge, 1923–7.
Caminos, *Misc.*	R. A. Caminos, *Late-Egyptian Miscellanies*, London, 1954.
Chron. d'Ég.	*La Chronique d'Égypte*, 68 nos., Brussels, 1925–59.
Cl.–V.	J. J. Clère and J. Vandier, *Textes de la première période intermédiaire et de la XIme Dynastie*, I. Brussels, 1948.
CoA	(Various authors), *The City of Akhenaten*, 3 parts, London, Egypt Exploration Society, 1923–51.
Couyat	J. Couyat and P. Montet, *Les Inscriptions hiéroglyphiques et hiératiques du Ouâdi Hammâmât*, Cairo, 1912–13.
D. el B.	É. Naville, *The Temple of Deir el Bahari*, 6 vols., London, 1895–1908.

Daressy, *Cerc.*	G. Daressy, *Cercueils des cachettes royales*, Cairo, 1909.
Davies, *Am.*	N. de G. Davies, *The Rock Tombs of El Amarna*, 6 parts, London, 1903–8.
Davies, *Ramose*	N. de G. Davies, *The Tomb of the Vizier Ramose*, London, 1941.
Davies, *Rekh-mi-rēʿ*	N. de G. Davies, *The Tomb of Rekh-mi-rēʿ at Thebes*, 2 vols., New York, 1943.
Dyn., Dyns.	Dynasty, Dynasties, the lines or families of kings into which Manetho divided his history of Egypt. *See* pp. 46–47.
Edwards, *Pyramids*	I. E. S. Edwards, *The Pyramids of Egypt*, West Drayton, 1947.
Eg.	Egyptian.
Eg. Gr.	Alan H. Gardiner, *Egyptian Grammar*, 3rd edition, 1957.
Elliot Smith, *RM.*	G. Elliot Smith, *The Royal Mummies*, Cairo, 1912.
Emery, *GT*	W. B. Emery, *Great Tombs of the First Dynasty*, vol. i, Cairo, 1949; vol. ii, London, 1954; vol. iii, London, 1958.
Erman, *Lit.*	A. Erman, *The Literature of the Ancient Egyptians*, translated by A. M. Blackman, London, 1927.
Festival Hall	É. Naville, *The Festival-hall of Osorkon II in the Great Temple of Bubastis*, London, 1892.
fl.	*floruit*, flourished in or about the year named.
Frankfort	H. Frankfort, *The Mural Painting of El-ʿAmarneh*, London, 1929.
Gardiner, *Late-Egyptian Stories*	Alan H. Gardiner, *Late-Egyptian Stories*, Brussels, 1932.
Gardiner, *Mes*	Alan H. Gardiner, *The Inscription of Mes*, in K. Sethe, *Untersuchungen zur Geschichte und Altertumskunde Aegyptens*, iv, Leipzig, 1905.
Gauthier, *LR*	H. Gauthier, *Le Livre des rois d'Égypte*, 5 vols, Cairo, 1907–17.
Gk.	Greek.
Gurney	O. R. Gurney, *The Hittites*, Harmondsworth, 1952.
Hayes, *RS*	W. C. Hayes, *Royal Sarcophagi of the XVIII Dynasty*, Princeton, 1935.
Hayes, *Scepter*	W. C. Hayes, *The Scepter of Egypt*, 2 vols., Cambridge, Mass., 1953, 1959.
Hdt.	Herodotus.
Hist. Rec.	W. F. Edgerton and J. A. Wilson, *Historical Records of Ramses III*, Chicago, 1936.
Ḥuy	Nina de G. Davies and A. H. Gardiner, *The Tomb of Ḥuy*, London, 1926.
JAOS	*Journal of the American Oriental Society*, Baltimore.
JEA	*Journal of Egyptian Archaeology*, 45 vols., London, 1914–59.
Jéquier	G. Jéquier, *Le Monument funéraire de Pepi II*, 3 vols., Cairo, 1936–40.
JNES	*Journal of Near Eastern Studies*, 19 vols., Chicago, 1942–60.
Junker, *Turah*	H. Junker, *Bericht über die Grabungen . . . in Turah* in *Denkschriften der kaiserlichen Akademie der Wissenschaften in Wien*, vol. lvi, Vienna, 1912.

Kawa	M. F. Laming Macadam, *The Temples of Kawa*, 4 vols., Oxford, 1949, 1955.
Kêmi	(Periodical), 12 vols., Paris, 1928–52.
Kienitz	F. K. Kienitz, *Die politische Geschichte Ägyptens vom 7. bis zum 4. Jahrhundert vor der Zeitwende*, Berlin, 1953.
Kraeling	E. G. Kraeling, *The Brooklyn Museum Aramaic Papyri*, New Haven, 1953.
Kuentz	Ch. Kuentz, *La Bataille de Qadech*, Cairo, 1928.
Kush	(Periodical), 6 vols, Khartoum, 1953–8.
Lefebvre, *Grands prêtres*	G. Lefebvre, *Histoire des grands prêtres d'Amon de Karnak*, Paris, 1929.
Lefebvre, *Romans*	G. Lefebvre, *Romans et contes égyptiens*, Paris, 1949.
Leps., *Denkm.*	R. Lepsius, *Denkmäler aus Ägypten und Äthiopien*, 6 vols., Berlin, 1849–58.
Luckenbill	D. D. Luckenbill, *Ancient Records of Assyria and Babylonia*, 2 vols., Chicago, 1926–7.
Med. Habu	*Medinet Habu*, ed. J. H. Breasted and others, 5 vols., Chicago, 1930–57.
Mercer	S. A. B. Mercer, *The Tell el-Amarna Tablets*, 2 vols., Toronto, 1939.
Mes	*See above under* Gardiner, *Mes.*
Mitt. Kairo	*Mitteilungen des deutschen Instituts für ägyptische Altertumskunde in Kairo*, 15 vols., Augsburg and Wiesbaden, 1930–59.
Nachr. Göttingen	*Nachrichten von der Kgl. Gesellschaft der Wissenschaften zu Göttingen.*
OLZ	*Orientalistische Litteratur-Zeitung*, 53 vols., Berlin, 1898–1958.
Onom.	A. H. Gardiner, *Ancient Egyptian Onomastica*, 3 vols. Oxford, 1947.
PM	B. Porter and R. L. B. Moss, *Topographical Bibliography*. See p. 17.
Parker	R. A. Parker, *The Calendars of Ancient Egypt*, Chicago, 1950.
Peet, *Tomb-robberies*	T. E. Peet, *The Great Tomb-robberies of the Twentieth Egyptian Dynasty*, 2 vols., Oxford, 1930.
Petrie, *History*	*See* p. 68.
Petrie, *Royal Tombs*	W. M. F. Petrie, *The Royal Tombs of the First Dynasty*, 2 vols., London, 1900–1.
Petrie, *Scarabs*	W. M. F. Petrie, *Scarabs and Cylinders with Names*, London, 1917.
Posener	G. Posener, *La première domination Perse en Égypte*, Cairo, 1936.
PSBA	*Proceedings of the Society of Biblical Archaeology*, 40 vols., 1879–1918.
Psu.	P. Montet, *Les constructions et le tombeau de Psousennès à Tanis*, Paris, 1951.
RAD	Alan Gardiner, *Ramesside Administrative Documents*, London, 1948.
Rec. trav.	*Recueil de travaux relatifs à la philologie et à l'archéologie Égyptiennes et Assyriennes*, 40 vols., Paris, 1870–1923.

Rev. d'Ég.	*Revue d'Égyptologie*, 11 vols., Paris, 1933–57.
RT	*See above under* Petrie, *Royal Tombs.*
Rylands	*See under* F. Ll. Griffith, p. 383.
Sandman	M. Sandman, *Texts from the Time of Akhenaten*, Brussels, 1938.
Säve-Söderbergh	T. Säve-Söderbergh, *Ägypten und Nubien*, Lund, 1941.
Seele, *Coregency*	K. C. Seele, *The Coregency of Ramses II with Seti I*, Chicago, 1940.
Sethe, *HP*	K. Sethe, *Das Hatschepsut-Problem. See* p. 211.
Sinai	*See* p. 146.
Thuc.	Thucydides.
Untersuchungen	*See* p. 70, n. 1.
Urk.	*See* under Historical texts, etc., p. 69.
Vandier	*See* under É. Drioton and J. Vandier, p. 69.
Winlock, *Excavations*	H. Winlock, *Excavations at Deir el Bahri*, New York, 1942.
Winlock, *Rise*	H. Winlock, *The Rise and Fall of the Middle Kingdom in Thebes*, New York, 1947.
Wiseman	D. J. Wiseman, *Chronicles of Chaldaean Kings*, London, 1956.
Wreszinski	W. Wreszinksi, *Atlas zur altägyptischen Kulturgeschichte*, 2nd part, Leipzig, 1935.
WZKM	*Wiener Zeitschrift für die Kunde des Morgenlandes*, 56 vols., Vienna, 1886–1960.
ZÄS	*Zeitschrift für ägyptische Sprache und Altertumskunde*, 84 vols., Leipzig, 1863–1960.
ZDMG	*Zeitschrift der Deutschen Morgenländischen Gesellschaft.*
ZDPV	*Zeitschrift des Deutschen Palästina-Vereins.*

BOOK I

PRELIMINARY

I

EGYPTOLOGY ANCIENT AND MODERN

THE first writers to provide their fellow-countrymen with elaborate descriptions of Egypt and the Egyptians were two Greeks from cities on the western coast of Asia Minor. There, in the Ionia of the sixth century B.C., dwelt a race of men more hungry for knowledge than any people that had till then inhabited the earth. But there were special reasons why their curiosity should have been attracted towards Egypt in particular. Before the middle of the seventh century Ionians and Carians were serving as mercenaries in the army of the Saite king Psammētichus I, then striving to establish his mastery over the entire Nile Valley. Traders and ordinary travellers doubtless followed in the warriors' wake, and carried home many stories of the strange things they had seen and learned in a land so different from their own. They will have astonished their auditors by telling them of a country where rain only seldom fell, and where the fields were fertilized by the annual inundation of a great river. They had entered Egypt with the preconceived idea of finding there the counterparts of much that was familiar to them in their own native land, and many of the names they gave to places and things which they encountered have clung to them right down to the present day. Approaching from the sea they found themselves within a vast triangular area that reminded them of the fourth letter of their alphabet. On reaching the apex of the Delta they came upon the great city of Memphis, an alternative name of which—Ḥikuptaḥ,

'Mansion of the Soul of (the god) Ptaḥ'—may have furnished Homer with the word *Aigyptos* (Egypt), used by him to designate both the river Nile and the country which it watered. At Memphis the visitors were amazed at the gigantic structures that they jestingly called pyramids, i.e. 'wheaten cakes', while at near-by Hēliopolis their wonder was excited by those lofty monoliths of granite for which they could discover no more suitable a designation than obelisks, i.e. 'little spits'. Proceeding up the Nile, close to a canal leading to the Lake of Moeris, the modern Fayyûm, they were shown a great many-chambered building which they were told was built to serve as his tomb by a king Lamarēs or Labarēs, now known to us as Ammenemēs III of Dyn. XII; this building they concluded was a second Labyrinth, a duplicate of the maze-like edifice devised by the skill of Cretan Daedalus. Farther south they reached an important town, the Egyptian name of which vouched for its being the equivalent of Abydos in the Hellespont. Still farther upstream was a great city, whose many pylons proclaimed it to be none other than the poet of the Iliad's 'hundred-gated Thebes'. Just opposite, across the Nile on the fringe of the western desert, were seen temples the names of whose builders recalled, as in the case of a great temple at Abydos, the memory of the Ethiopian hero Memnōn slain by Achilles before the walls of Troy; obviously such buildings should all be described as Memnoneia. But the queerest fancy of the Ionian visitors was that the gods and goddesses worshipped by the Egyptians were none other than their own deities, Cronos, Zeus, Hēphaestos, Apollo, Aphroditē, and the rest. It was puzzling, however, to find Zeus, or Amūn (Ammōn) as the Egyptians called him, depicted as a ram, and Apollo, the Egyptian Horus (Ōros), wearing the head of a falcon. For such eccentricities there must be some profound mystical reason. The multitude of the wonders to be seen in Egypt, and their indisputable antiquity, cannot have failed to strike awe into the hearts of those travellers from across the Mediterranean; and thus was sown the seed of that legendary Wisdom of the Egyptians, belief in which remained almost uncontested for the next 2,000 years.

If, then, among these visitors there chanced to be any more observant and with greater descriptive powers than the rest, clearly they would find plenty to write about. Such were the two authors Herodotus and Hecataeus. The earlier of them, HECATAEUS of Miletus (*fl.* 510 B.C.), was apparently more concerned with the problems of the Nile flood, the formation of the Delta, and the fauna of the country than with its inhabitants and their history. The 'Survey of the Earth' in which he discussed all these things is lost and he calls for mention here only on account of his priority in point of time. It is difficult to imagine that had his book survived, its importance would not have been dwarfed by the work of HERODOTUS of Halicarnassus (*c.* 484–430 B.C.). To that great genius we owe the first comprehensive account of Egypt which has survived intact. His second book, called *Euterpē* after the Muse, is a discursive, anecdotal, and highly entertaining digression introduced into the tale of the epic struggle between Persians and Hellenes, and he excuses himself for the length of his narrative by reference to Egypt's 'wonders more in number than those of any other land, and works it has to show beyond expression great'. Herodotus had, soon after 450 B.C., travelled as a tourist as far as the First Cataract, but modern criticism believes that his voyage may have lasted no longer than three months. This might explain the absence of any extensive account of Thebes and its monuments, though other similar omissions, such as reference to the Sphinx, are perhaps to be attributed rather to his predilection for the marvellous and for the merely amusing, a characteristic which led him to recount at length the stories told him by the native interpreters and the temple underlings whom he mistook for priests. It is largely on account of Herodotus's description of Egypt that charges of mendacity have been levelled against him alike in antiquity and in modern times. In truth there is no reason to impugn his good faith. The student has rather to be on his guard against popular traditions that are offered as history, measurements that are inaccurately quoted, and assertions containing a kernel of truth but presented in exaggerated or distorted form. There are hardly any aspects of Egyptian life that did not excite Herodotus's interest. His account of the older Egyptian monarchy is deplorable, though he knew of Mīn (Mēnēs) as its initiator. Also he was able to give in only slightly distorted form the names of the builders of the Gîza pyramids, namely Cheops, Chephrēn, and Mycerīnos. Wildly wrong, however, was his placing before these, instead of after them, of a king Sesōstris who is a conflation of several rulers named Senwosre belonging to Manetho's Dyn. XII, and whose conquests, exaggerated out of all proportion, are represented as having extended as far as Scythia and Colchis at the eastern coast of the Black Sea. But Herodotus's treatment of the rulers of Egypt from Psammētichus I (664–610 B.C.) onwards is as trustworthy as could be expected from one who was after all, as Cicero called him, the Father of History and the first to distinguish that art from mere poetic romancing. As regards geography Herodotus gives some valuable information, but mainly concerning the Delta; south of the Fayyûm he mentions but few cities, in Egypt itself only Chemmis (Akhmîm), Thebes, Syēnē, Elephantinē, and a mysterious Neēpolis. Of the eighteen 'nomes' or provinces that he mentions about half are easily identifiable; however, his list contains some names unknown from other sources and possibly due to misapprehension of one kind or another. His account of Egyptian religion, though extended, is disappointing; he declares his intention to be reticent on this topic. Some of the divinities (Ammōn, Bubastis, Isis, Osiris, Ōros) he mentions by their Egyptian names, but as a rule he prefers Greek equivalents, being obsessed by the idea that the Hellenes derived from Egypt, not only many of their religious observances, but also the gods themselves. The descriptions of local festivals may well have preserved many true details. Indeed, his work is packed with all sorts of interesting statements that cannot be checked from other sources. Most remarkable, for instance, is the passage (ii. 35–36) where he enumerates the traits in which the Egyptians differed from all other peoples. Only rarely can he be convicted of definite error, as when he declares that there were no vineyards in Egypt (ii. 77), here actually contradicting himself (ii. 37, 39).

Of all that was written about Egypt in the following centuries only little has survived. No other author of note has to be recorded until the time of PLATO (428–347 B.C.), in whose works there occur occasional references not without value; he knows, for instance, the name of the goddess Nēith of Sais, and correctly defines the attributes of Thōth, the god of letters, science, and astronomy, as well as of the game of draughts. Being here concerned mainly with extant authors, we may pass over the scattered remarks in the scanty fragments of such fourth-century writers as Hecataeus of Abdera. After Alexander the Great, under the Ptolemies, Greek settlers swarmed into Egypt, too busy with their commerce and their agriculture to pay much heed to the alien habits of their native neighbours. From the time of Julius Caesar we have an account of Egypt slightly longer than that of Herodotus, though far less important. This is preserved in Book I of the *General History* of the Greek author DIODORUS SICULUS. He sojourned in Egypt for a brief space about 59 B.C., and once or twice quotes from his own experience; his main sources, however, were earlier writers like the afore-mentioned Hecataeus of Abdera (*fl.* 320 B.C.) and the geographer and historian Agatharchides of Cnidus (2nd cent. B.C.). He could not avoid using Herodotus extensively, though joining in the chorus of that author's critics. The topics treated by Herodotus and Diodorus are roughly identical, but each has much to tell that is omitted by the other. As regards literary ability they are poles apart. Diodorus has none of that power of rapid and highly individual characterization, none of that feeling for a good story, which make the work of Herodotus so precious a possession. The later writer is methodical, plodding, and prosy; consequently easy to analyse, but dull to read. A brief sketch of cosmic development leads up to a description of the Egyptian conception of this and its basis in the achievements of the gods; much space is devoted to the god Osiris, many authentic and valuable details concerning whom are unhappily supplemented by a singularly un-Egyptian narrative of his military campaigns. There follows a completely fictitious record of Egyptian colonies in Babylonia, Colchis, and Greece. Then comes a lengthy section on the land of Egypt, its river, flora, and fauna, concluding with an elaborate discussion of the causes of the inundation. Thence, after a short paragraph on the food of the Egyptians, Diodorus passes on to their history. Mēnās (Mēnēs) is acknowledged as the first king, but the reigns of fifty-two successors are dismissed as undistinguished by any occurrences of note. Next we are made acquainted with an unidentifiable Busiris, the mythical founder of Thebes, of which an extended description is given, culminating in an account, strikingly accurate by ancient standards, of that monument of Osymandyas (Ramessēs II) now known as the Ramesseum. In making the foundation of Memphis subsequent to that of Thebes and to the reign of Osymandyas Diodorus reverses the true order of facts, and indeed the rest of his long account of the early history, though recording with rough accuracy a number of names, is even more glaringly out of its real sequence than that of Herodotus. Disproportionate space is accorded to the exploits and fortunes of Sesoōsis (Sesōstris) of whom we have spoken above. Of great interest are the last thirty paragraphs of his first book, which deal with a variety of topics—the ritually regulated life of the kings, administration of the provinces and the caste system, justice and laws, education, medicine, animal worship, burial and cult of the dead, and finally the debt of the Greeks to Egypt. But it is only in Diodorus's account of the fifth and fourth centuries B.C. that his work becomes absolutely indispensable; here he stands side by side with Thucydides and Xenophon as an authoritative historian. For really ancient times much that is related by him cannot be controlled from any other source, and, the entire work being a compilation, it is naturally of very unequal value. Here, as in estimating all the classical writers, we are faced with a dilemma: wherever a detail is confirmed by trustworthy external evidence, that confirmation renders the statement in some degree superfluous; where such evidence does not exist, our confidence can seldom be sufficient to carry complete conviction.

A partial exception to this generalization must be made in the case of STRABO, a Greek-speaking native of Pontus who lived for some years at Alexandria and accompanied his friend the Roman prefect Aelius Gallus on an expedition as far as the First Cataract, probably in 25–24 B.C. Strabo's account of Egypt is a relatively short one incorporated in the seventeenth and last book of his *Geographica*, though some items of information concerning the same land are dispersed throughout other parts of the work. He begins with a brief discourse on the Nile, continuing with a long description of Alexandria and of the country to the east of it. His survey then proceeds in topographical order. The nomes and towns of the Delta are dealt with particularly fully, this emphasis upon Lower Egypt being the more welcome because here the native documents and monuments are scanty. Strabo's interests were by no means exclusively geographical, and in addition to a few historical digressions he never fails, when occasion offers, to give us interesting details concerning buildings, cults, and other topics of interest. An example of Strabo's accuracy is his account of the well of Abydos, 'which lies at a great depth, so that one descends to it down vaulted galleries made of monoliths of surpassing size and workmanship'; this obviously refers to the pool discovered by Naville[1] in the so-called Cenotaph of Sethōs I. Strabo is the first to refer to the Vocal Memnōn at Thebes, one of a pair of colossal seated statues still existing on the plain to the west of Luxor (Pl. XII) which at dawn emitted a sound heard by many distinguished Greek and Roman visitors.[2] Also he tells us about the Nilometer at Elephantinē, a particularly celebrated specimen of a type of stairway on the walls of which was annually recorded the height reached by the Nile flood. Strabo's remarks upon history and religious custom are naturally subject to the same critical caution as the earlier mentioned authors, but on the purely geographical side his book is thoroughly sound. Within the limits of present-day Egypt, i.e. as far as the Sûdân border some twenty miles north of Wâdy Ḥalfa, he mentions no less than ninety-nine towns and other settlements, most of which can be located with some degree of certainty. In conclusion, let it be noted that Strabo was a vivacious and by no means unskilful writer.

The encyclopaedic *Historia Naturalis* of PLINY THE ELDER (A.D. 23–79) is a vast compilation from the works of earlier authors treating of all material objects that are not the products of man's manufacture; but he incorporates many digressions on human inventions and institutions, and Egypt comes in for her fair share of attention. As an authority on Egyptian geography Pliny is important, though much less so than Strabo and CLAUDIUS PTOLEMAEUS, who produced his *Geography* about A.D. 150. The sections of Ptolemy dealing with Egypt and the adjoining districts

[1] *JEA* i. 159 ff.; also PM vi. 29. [2] PM ii. 160; Baedeker, 345 f.

are short and consist in the main of a bare list of nomes, each with its metropolis and sometimes a few other towns. It is the more unnecessary here to comment on the other sources for Egyptian geography in Graeco-Roman times, since an admirable book in English by the late Dr. J. Ball will provide the interested reader with all he may wish to know on the subject.

Nor need we pursue further our account of the information concerning aspects of Egyptian secular life and history to be gleaned from Greek and Roman authors. Premising that the all-important Manetho is reserved for later discussion we turn now to what the classical and later writers have to tell us about the Egyptian religion. As the Greek, and later the Roman, influence fastened its grip on the land of the Pharaohs, the traditional native lore was withdrawn more and more into the hands of the priesthood, in whose interest it lay to insist upon and to over-emphasize the profound wisdom and mysterious knowledge of their ancestors. It was all very well for scoffers like JUVENAL (A.D. 47–127)[1] to pour scorn on a people who worshipped cats and crocodiles, but many even of the ablest post-Augustan writers thought they knew better. With the decay of belief in the old gods of Olympus, the populations of Rome and the provinces fell easy victims to whatever Oriental faith was dangled before their eyes. The cult of Isis spread into every corner of the Empire, though even those who most greatly honoured the goddess were at a loss to know what to make of her. Deeply interesting as evidence of their perplexity is the treatise by PLUTARCH of Chaeronea (A.D. 50–120) entitled *De Iside et Osiride*. In some chapters not far from the beginning he narrates in simple language the story of Osiris, the good king who was treacherously murdered by his wicked brother Typhōn (Sēth) and subsequently avenged by his son Horus, who had been nurtured in secret seclusion by his mother Isis. The tale as Plutarch tells it, and as Diodorus had told it before him, agrees substantially with that which can be reconstructed from the Egyptian texts, though overlaid with many details of which some at least must be derived from lost native sources. It is when he embarks upon his explanations that Plutarch's

[1] The passages are collected in Th. Hopfner, *Fontes Historiae Religionis Aegyptiacae*, Bonn, 1923, pp. 281–4.

unconscious embarrassment becomes apparent. He insists that the legend is not to be taken literally; the many forms under which the truth may appear are likened to the many colours of the rainbow as a reflection of the sun. At one moment he equates Osiris with the Nile consorting with Isis as the Earth, but then overwhelmed by the sea (Typhōn). Or else Osiris is to be recognized in all germinative moisture and, Isis being the Earth, their son Horus is the seasonable atmospheric dampness of the Delta. Or again, Typhōn is the power of drought, while Horus is the rain victorious over it. But some have held that Typhōn is the pitiless sun, and Osiris the moist moonlight. And so the book goes on from page to page, one allegorical interpretation giving place to another. It cannot be affirmed with certainty that all these interpretations are un-Egyptian in origin, but taken as a whole they bear the unmistakable hallmark of Western speculative ingenuity.

With the spread of Christianity the pagan deities were gradually driven into banishment, Isis finding a last refuge on the island of Philae above the First Cataract, whence her cult disappeared only in the fifth century. But though the native religion of Egypt had perished, the belief in the profound esoteric knowledge of her ancient priests persisted, and was even encouraged by Biblical references to the 'Wisdom of Egypt' (1 Kings iv. 30) and to the wonderful performances of her magicians (Exod. vii. 11, 22). Credence was still given to the late tradition according to which early Greek philosophers like Thales and Pythagoras had sat as pupils at the feet of the Egyptian priests.[1] But perhaps the most powerful influence for perpetuating the same exaggerated views was the enigmatic appearance of the hieroglyphs. Surely these miniature pictures of men and animals, plants and celestial bodies, houses and furniture, must be symbols of deep mystical doctrines, especially since they were seen to cover all the walls of the great Egyptian temples. The older Greek authors were singularly silent concerning the nature of the hieroglyphs,[2] Diodorus (iii. 4) alone being explicit on this topic; and he affirmed that they were not phonetic in character, but

[1] Th. Hopfner, *Orient und griechische Philosophie*, Leipzig, 1925.

[2] The relevant passages in P. Marestaing, *Les Écritures égyptiennes et l'Antiquité classique*, Paris, 1913.

definitely allegorical. CHAERĒMŌN, the tutor of Nero, followed suit in a book of which only a brief excerpt has been preserved.[1] However, the greatest stumbling-block of the kind in the way of the later decipherers was the book on hieroglyphics by one HORAPOLLO, a particularly erudite Egyptian of the fifth century A.D. Here is a sample taken from one of his chapters:

HOW THEY INDICATE THE SOUL

Moreover, the Hawk is put for the soul, from the signification of its name; for among the Egyptians the hawk is called BAIĒTH and this name when decomposed signifies soul and heart, for the word BAI is the soul, and ĒTH the heart; and the heart, according to the Egyptians, is the encasement of the soul; so that in its composition the name signifies 'soul in heart'.

There are elements of truth in this account, for the Egyptian word for 'soul' was in fact written with a sign representing a bird; but the allegorical interpretation is utterly false, and misleading in the highest degree. A passage in the works of the learned presbyter CLEMENT OF ALEXANDRIA[2] (*c.* A.D. 150–215) might seem to imply a more correct appreciation of the nature of the hieroglyphs, but his expressions were too ambiguous to counteract the fantastic conceptions of the majority.

By the seventh century the Dark Ages had closed in upon Europe, and Egypt passed into the power of the Muhammedan invaders. It was not until after the Renaissance that interest in the antiquities of that country awoke from its slumber. Such travellers as ventured thither were mostly bound for the Holy Land, and few penetrated beyond Grand Cairo. With the more daring of them it became fashionable to push forward to Saḳḳâra and there bribe the natives to dig up a few mummies for their delectation. Only a few brought home new information of value. Perhaps the most important of these was the Jesuit CL. SICARD (1677–1726), the first relatively modern investigator to reach Aswân. He rediscovered the site of Thebes and claims to have visited twenty-four temples and more than fifty painted or sculptured rock-tombs; unhappily

[1] S. Birch in *Trans. Royal Soc. Literature*, iii (1850), ser. 2, vol. 3, 385 ff.

[2] *Rec. Trav.* xxxiii, 8 ff.

he published but little, and his chief contribution was the map subsequently utilized by D'ANVILLE for his own map of Egypt that appeared in 1766. Among the most distinguished travel books here to be recorded are those of the Dane FR. L. NORDEN (1708–42) and of our own RICHARD POCOCKE (1704–65) and JAMES BRUCE (1730–94); but long before their time a truly scientific monograph on the pyramids was issued, the Pyramidographia of the Oxford astronomer JOHN GREAVES (1646). The engravings contained in practically all these books were grossly inaccurate. Of great use to stay-at-home scholars were the Coptic manuscripts which began to be imported into Europe from the beginning of the seventeenth century onwards. Several of these that had been secured in Egypt by PIETRO DELLA VALLE came into the hands of the learned Jesuit ATHANASIUS KIRCHER,[1] whose book entitled *Lingua Aegyptiaca restituta* (1643) proved the real starting-point for the serious study of this latest phase of the old Egyptian language, written in the Greek alphabet with a few additional letters. Without a good knowledge of Coptic the later decipherment of the hieroglyphs would not have advanced so rapidly. It is to be regretted that the meritorious Kircher could not restrain himself from launching out on wildly fantastic interpretations of the hieroglyphs. To give an example, the name of the Pharaoh Apries, written on a Roman obelisk, signifies for Kircher[2] that 'the benefits of the divine Osiris are to be procured by means of sacred ceremonies and of the chain of the Genii, in order that the benefits of the Nile may be obtained'. At the same time this very able scholar, like the somewhat later P. E. JABLONSKI (1693–1757) and like G. ZOEGA at the end of the eighteenth century, gathered together in huge tomes all that his predecessors had said or thought about Egypt. Little further headway could be made until the country itself was opened up and until the key to the ancient scripts could be discovered.

Such, briefly and with many omissions, was the pre-Napoleonic Egyptology, if that term may be applied to a branch of learning as

[1] *Chron. d'Ég.*, no. 35, 240 ff.

[2] *Obelisci Aegyptiaci interpretatio*, Rome, 1666, p. 53.

yet wholly uncritical and unscientific. The new era began with Bonaparte's expedition to Egypt (1798) and the discovery of the trilingual Rosetta Stone in the following year. The latter was a decree promulgated by the assembled priesthoods of Egypt in honour of Ptolemy V Epiphanes in the year 196 B.C. The Greek and demotic texts were nearly complete, the hieroglyphic rather less so. It was quickly realized that this precious document afforded a better chance of decipherment than anything previously found. The story of the ultimate success has been often told. The first step was taken by the Swedish diplomat ÅKERBLAD, who concentrated his efforts on the cursive script immediately below the hieroglyphic, recognized that it was the demotic spoken of by Herodotus (ii. 36), and after determining from comparison with the Greek the place of the proper names, identified about half the letters of the alphabet and assured himself that the language used was that later surviving as Coptic. Åkerblad's essay was published as early as 1802, but it was not until 1814 that any further advance was made. This came from the celebrated THOMAS YOUNG, the author of the undulatory theory of light. A man of deep learning and wide interests, he was always ready to tackle any new puzzle. He quickly recognized that the demotic and hieroglyphic systems were intimately related, and, noticing that the Greek section of the Rosettana was full of words that repeated themselves, succeeded in dividing the demotic into eighty-six word-groups, most of them correct. For the hieroglyphic he took as his point of departure the fact, long before guessed by de Guignes and Zoega, that the 'cartouches' or 'royal rings' (Fig. 1) contained the names of kings and queens and (to quote the late Prof. Griffith) 'very ingeniously but rather luckily identified the cartouche of Berenice in addition to the known one of Ptolemy, and correctly suggested that another cartouche must be that of Manetho's Tuthmosis of Dyn. XVIII. He also pointed out in hieroglyphic the alphabetic characters for *f* and *t*, and the 'determinative' used in late texts for feminine names, and recognized from variants in the papyri

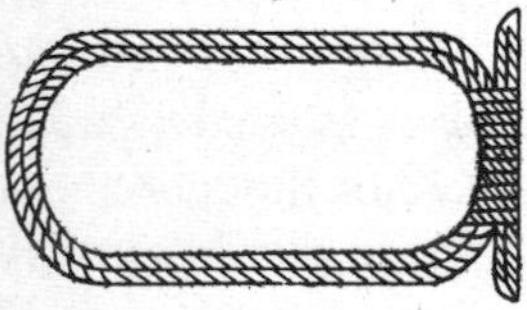

FIG. 1. An elaborate early cartouche.

that different characters could have the same powers—in short, the principle of homophony. All this was mixed up with many false conclusions, but the method pursued was infallibly leading to definite decipherment.'

At a loss to make further headway and absorbed in other work of many kinds, Young was content to leave the question of the hieroglyphs to a brilliant young schoolmaster from Grenoble. Believing from early youth that it was his destiny to solve the problem, Jean François Champollion (1790–1832) had prepared himself for the task by familiarizing himself with all the classical sources and by gaining a complete mastery of Coptic. For a long time the solution eluded him, and even within a year of his immortal discovery he was hesitating whether the hieroglyphs were not, after all, a purely symbolic script. Åkerblad had read the demotic name of Ptolemy alphabetically, and Champollion, in spite of his wavering, had proved by his identification of the demotic signs with those in the cartouche that the hieroglyphs also could, at least on occasion, be alphabetic. The decisive proof was afforded by an obelisk that had apparently stood on a base block covered with Greek inscriptions in honour of Ptolemy Physcon and the two Cleopatras. Both obelisk and base had been transported to England in 1819 to adorn Mr. W. J. Bankes's park at Kingston Lacy in Dorset. A lithograph of the Greek and hieroglyphic inscriptions was made for Bankes in 1821 and in January of the following year a copy fell into Champollion's hands. There he saw accompanying the cartouche of Ptolemy another which could not fail to be that of Cleopatra, since in both occurred the hieroglyphs for *P*, *O*, and *L* in just the positions where they were to be expected. It is true that the sign for *T* differed in the two cases, but this was easily explained by the theory of homophones. The two cartouches gave Champollion thirteen alphabetic characters for twelve sounds. Armed with these, he soon identified the hieroglyphically written names of Alexander, Berenice, Tiberius, Domitian, and Trajan, besides such imperial titles as Autocrator, Caesar, and Sebastos.

The problem was thus solved so far as the Graeco-Roman cartouches were concerned. But what of those belonging to the older times? On 14 September 1822 Champollion received from an architect copies of bas-reliefs in Egyptian temples which finally dispelled his doubts. At the end of one cartouche he found twice repeated the sign which he knew from his alphabet to represent *S*, and separated from them by an enigmatic hieroglyph was the circle of the 'sun', in Coptic *rē*. The royal name Ramessēs or Rameses flashed across his mind as he read *Re-?-s-s*. The possibility became a certainty a few minutes later when he came across another cartouche with the ibis Thōth at its head, and between this and an *s* the sign assumed by him to read *m*.[1] Surely this must be the name of the king Tuthmōsis (often wrongly given in old-fashioned books as Thothmes) of Manetho's Dyn. XVIII. Confirmation of the value of the enigmatic sign was found in the Rosetta Stone, where it formed part of the group corresponding to the Greek word for 'birthday', which at once suggested the Coptic *misi*, *mose*, 'give birth'.

FIG. 2. Cartouches used by Champollion in his decipherment. (1) Ptolemaeus, (2) Cleopatra, (3) Beloved of Amūn Ramessēs, (4) Tuthmōsis.

From that moment every day brought its new harvest. Realizing that there was no longer any reason for holding back his discoveries, on 29 September Champollion read at the Paris Academy his memorable *Lettre à M. Dacier*. In this letter he characteristically makes no reference to the names Ramessēs and Tuthmōsis, reserving his account of their decipherment for the marvellous *Précis du système hiéroglyphique*, which appeared in 1824. Prolonged visits to Turin and to Egypt filled no small part of the remainder of his short life. Before he died at the early age of 41 he was able to make out the general drift of most historical inscriptions. The miracle of Champollion's achievement lay less in the initial discovery than in the amazing use he was able to make of it.

[1] Champollion's reasoning was sound, but not quite correct: the 'enigmatic hieroglyph' reads *ms*, not simply *m*.

For the full utilization of the key thus provided the urgent need was for more material and better copies; and the enthusiasm engendered ensured that both should be forthcoming in plenty. Champollion himself led the way; his Egyptian voyage in company with the Italian Professor I. ROSELLINI resulted in a stately assemblage of drawings published in large folio volumes. A Prussian expedition under the great scholar RICHARD LEPSIUS (1810–84) outdid the preceding efforts with the twelve vast tomes of the *Denkmäler* (1849–59). Meanwhile Britain had not been idle; here the most important names are those of ROBERT HAY of Linplum, JAMES BURTON, and (Sir) JOHN GARDNER WILKINSON; these three, sometimes working together but sometimes in association with other partners, produced unrivalled collections of facsimiles of reliefs, paintings, and inscriptions of all the greater value today since many of the originals have perished or are seriously damaged; of this work, done in the twenties and thirties of the last century, only a small portion got published, though Wilkinson's copies provided the illustrations to his famous *Manners and Customs of the Ancient Egyptians* (1837). The same period saw the foundation of the great collections of Egyptian objects in the British Museum, the Louvre, and at Turin, Florence, Bologna, and Leyden, to mention only the most important; here the purveyors were the French, English, and Swedish Consuls-General, DROVETTI, SALT, and ANASTASI, but the excavations exploited or instigated by them were little better than lootings, though their authors should not be condemned for disregard of scientific standards not yet born. Digging on a larger scale and of a more systematic character was conducted from 1850 onwards by the Frenchman AUGUSTE MARIETTE (1821–81), to whose influence with the khedive Said Pacha was due the foundation of the Boulaq[1] Museum (1858), later to develop into the great Cairene treasure-house now the centre of attraction for every visitor to Egypt. Truly scientific excavation was, however, slow in starting; it was not until 1884 that FLINDERS PETRIE, perhaps the most successful of all diggers, introduced more rigorous methods and set a good example, unhappily too seldom followed, by rapid publication of his results. It would be tedious to

[1] Name of a suburb of Cairo.

the reader, and unfair to those left unmentioned, to record the chief excavators of more recent times; but it is impossible to pass over in silence the names of the Americans George Reisner and Herbert Winlock, and that of the discoverer of the tomb of Tutʿankhamūn, Dr. Howard Carter.

Candour obliges us to add that there has been, and still is, far too much excavation, especially when left unpublished or published badly, and that the growing science would have been better served if more attention had been paid to the eloquent appeal for more copying of the monuments above ground made in 1889 by that great scholar Francis Llewellyn Griffith (1862–1934). To his initiative is due the fact that the Egypt Exploration Fund (later Society) founded in 1882 divided its activities in Egypt pretty equally between those two functions. America was late in entering the field, but has more than made up for lost time. The splendid publications of Theban tombs by the Metropolitan Museum of Art in New York (largely due to the devotion of the Englishman N. de G. Davies) are being even surpassed by the work in the temples done by the Oriental Institute of the University of Chicago, that great archaeological organization which we owe to the far-sighted inspiration of James Henry Breasted (1865–1935) and to the munificence of John D. Rockefeller Jnr.

At home a number of able scholars continued the work which Champollion had begun. In an essay published in 1837 Richard Lepsius finally silenced the voices of those still sceptical of the genuineness of the decipherment. Early investigators in this domain were Samuel Birch (1813–85) and Edward Hincks (1792–1866); a little later came C. W. Goodwin in England, E. de Rougé, F. J. Chabas, and Th. Devéria in France, and, greatest of all, Heinrich Brugsch (1827–94) in Germany. The rivulet of Egyptological research was gradually swelling into the mighty stream which now makes it impossible for any student to keep abreast of all that is written save at the cost of abandoning all hope of personal contributions. Of later names it must suffice to mention that of Adolf Erman (1854–1937), who with his pupils, particularly Kurt Sethe, rightly distinguished the different phases of the language and laid the foundations of a scientific grammar of each, and that of the already mentioned F. Ll. Griffith, whose instinctive genius as a palaeographer enabled him to read varieties of hieratic and demotic writing that had defeated all his predecessors.

The universities were slow in honouring the new discipline. Champollion was the first occupant of the Chair at the Collège de France founded for him in 1831. Göttingen was perhaps the next centre of learning to acquire a Professor of Egyptology, its choice falling upon Brugsch (1868). England held back until 1894, when a bequest by the novelist Amelia B. Edwards provided Petrie with a Professorship at University College, London. Nowadays there is hardly a self-respecting University but has its Professor or Reader in the subject.

Our last pages have perforce been restricted mainly to a string of names. The rest of this book will be devoted to the knowledge recovered by the efforts of the owners of those names.

SELECT BIBLIOGRAPHY

So far as possible only works in English are here quoted; foreign books only when of exceptional importance. Invaluable for reference: B. Porter and R. L. B. Moss, *Topographical Bibliography of Ancient Egyptian Hieroglyphic Texts, Reliefs, and Paintings*, 7 vols. (vol. i in course of revision), Oxford, 1927–51; J. M. A. Janssen, *Annual Egyptological Bibliography*, 9 vols., Leiden, 1948–56; for finding writings by different scholars, I. A. Pratt, *Ancient Egypt*, New York Public Library, 1925, Supplement 1925–41.

Various aspects of Egyptology illustrated from Museum collections: with R. Engelbach as editor, *Introduction to Egyptian Archaeology with special reference to the Egyptian Museum, Cairo*, Cairo, 1946; W. S. Smith, *Ancient Egypt as represented in the Museum of Fine Arts*, Boston, 1942; W. C. Hayes, *The Scepter of Egypt*, Part I, New York, 1953, Part II, Harvard University Press, 1959.

Classical writers: original texts with English translations, Herodotus, Diodorus Siculus, Strabo, Pliny the Elder, Plutarch, all in the Loeb Classical Library, London and Cambridge, Mass.; see too W. G. Waddell, *Herodotus, Book II*, London, 1939. Horapollo, text and commentary, F. Sbordone, *Hori Apollinis Hieroglyphica*, Naples, 1940; French translation, *Chronique d'Égypte*, No. 35 (1943), pp. 39 ff.; 199 ff. For Manetho see below, pp. 46–47.

History of Egyptology: F. Ll. Griffith, *The Decipherment of the Hieroglyphs*, in *JEA* xxxvii. 38 ff. Short biographies, W. R. Dawson, *Who was who in Egyptology*, London, 1951.

Subjects not specially treated in the present book: (1) Egyptian Religion, brief introduction, J. Černý, *Ancient Egyptian Religion*, London, 1952; S. A. B. Mercer, *The Religion of Ancient Egypt*, London, 1949; Id., *The Pyramid Texts*, 4 vols., New York, 1952; E. A. Wallis Budge, *The Book of the Dead*, 3 vols., London, 1898; works in French by J. Vandier and J. Sainte Fare Garnot; in German by A. Erman, K. Sethe, and H. Kees. Very useful also is H. Bonnet, *Reallexikon der ägyptischen Religionsgeschichte*, Berlin, 1952.

(2) Art: W. Stevenson Smith, *The Art and Architecture of Ancient Egypt*, Pelican History of Art, Harmondsworth, 1958; C. Aldred, *Art in Ancient Egypt: Old Kingdom*, London, 1949; *Middle Kingdom*, 1950; *New Kingdom*, 1951; Nina M. Davies, *Ancient Egyptian Paintings*, 3 vols., Chicago, 1936.

(3) Building: S. Clarke and R. Engelbach, *Ancient Egyptian Masonry*, Oxford, 1930.

(4) Mummification and funerary rites: G. Elliot Smith and W. R. Dawson, *Egyptian Mummies*, London, 1924; E. A. Wallis Budge, *The Mummy*, 2nd ed., Cambridge, 1925; Nina de G. Davies and A. H. Gardiner, *The Tomb of Amenemhēt*, London, 1915.

(5) Antiquities: a long series of books illustrating different classes of objects in the Edwards collection, University of London, by W. M. Flinders Petrie.

For other works recommended see at the end of the following chapters; for Geography at the end of Chapter III.

II

THE EGYPTIAN LANGUAGE AND WRITING

MAN'S successive discoveries, at very great intervals, of the respective techniques of Speech and Writing, have been the two main stages passed by him on his long road to civilization. The use of articulate sounds enabled him to interchange thoughts, wishes, and questionings with his fellow men. Writing, building upon the same basis, substituted visible for audible signs, and so extended the range of his communications in both space and time. In our attempt to outline the history of one of the oldest, and certainly the most splendid, of all Eastern civilizations it is fitting to begin with some account of the impact upon it of these two techniques, so far as it can be known. Unfortunately the origin of the EGYPTIAN LANGUAGE lies so far back in the uncharted past that only little that is certain can be said about it. Since it is generally agreed that the oldest population of Egypt was of African race, it might be expected that their language should be African too. And in fact many affinities with Hamitic and in particular with Berber dialects have been found, not only in vocabulary, but also in verbal structure and the like. On the other hand, the relationship with Semitic (Hebrew, Arabic, &c.) is equally unmistakable, if indeed not greater. In this matter there have been wide differences of opinion among scholars, and even if some measure of agreement could be reached as to the place or places of origin, there would still remain the problems of date. We therefore turn without further delay to the consideration of the EGYPTIAN WRITING, the evolution of which can be witnessed in detail.

The decorations of vases and other objects of common use were a sort of visual communication, this growing even more obvious when the images of men, animals, ships, and so forth were introduced. Writing began when there were added visible signs which absolutely compelled translation into the sounds of Language. In Egypt this innovation becomes observable shortly before the advent of Mēnēs, when it is marked by the introduction of isolated miniature images clearly distinguishable from the surrounding purely pictorial representations. The images are the same in both cases, mirroring all kinds of material objects such as weapons, plants, animals, human beings, and even the gods themselves. The emergence of HIEROGLYPHS, as the miniature signs are called, was due to the fact that there was much which people wished to communicate that could not be exhibited visually, such as numbers, proper names, and mental phenomena. This supplementary character persisted, side by side with others, throughout the whole of Egyptian history, so that when, as often happened, the scenes in sculptural reliefs were furnished with explanatory hieroglyphic legends, the latter might be fairly said to illustrate the former rather than vice versa. There were, however, many important further developments which it will be our next business to explain, and there even came a time, not long before the Christian era, when three different kinds of Egyptian script were in simultaneous use for different purposes, while the Greeks, who by then had taken possession of the land, employed their own alphabet for all the main business of life.

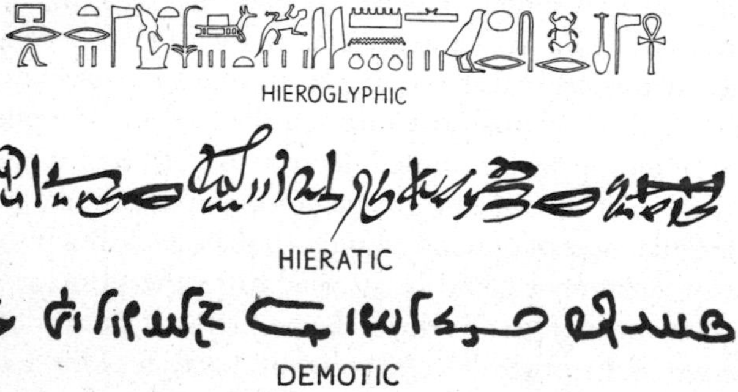

FIG. 3. The three main kinds of script.

The three kinds of script (Fig. 3) just mentioned are still called by the names given to them by Champollion and his contemporaries, though derived from different sources and strictly applicable only to the Graeco-Roman period. The term HIEROGLYPHIC used by Clement of Alexandria in a famous passage above alluded to (p. 10), means literally 'sacred carvings' and deserves its name solely because in the latest times it was almost exclusively employed for the inscriptions graven on temple walls. It is now applied, however, to all Egyptian writing which is still truly pictorial. ranging from the detailed, brightly coloured signs found adorning the tombs down to the abbreviated specimens written with a reed-pen in papyri[1] of religious content. Hieroglyphic is, of course, the original variety of writing out of which all the other kinds were evolved; sometimes it reads from top to bottom, sometimes from right to left, but sometimes also from left to right, this being the form adopted in our printed grammars; when the writing is from right to left the signs face towards the right.

The name HIERATIC, Clement tells us, was given to the style of writing employed by the priestly scribes for their religious books. This is a derivative of the abbreviated hieroglyphic mentioned in the last paragraph, but Egyptologists have extended the use of the term to several still more shortened varieties of script found in literary or business texts; ligatures, i.e. signs joined together, are frequent, and in the most cursive sort all but the initial signs are apt to be reduced to mere strokes. For scholarly convenience Hieratic is customarily transcribed into Hieroglyphic, though this practice becomes well-nigh impossible in extreme cursive specimens. The direction of writing is normally from right to left.

For the third kind of Egyptian writing, called Enchorial 'native' on the Rosetta Stone and Epistolographic 'letter-writing' by Clement, modern scholars have retained Herodotus's name DEMOTIC 'popular'. This was evolved out of Hieratic only about the time of the Ethiopian Dynasty, from *c.* 700 B.C. It presents many peculiarities and demands intensive specialist study. In the Ptolemaic and Roman ages it was the ordinary writing of daily life, and its range of employment is best described as non-religious.

Between the two extremes of Hieroglyphic and Demotic there are many intermediate varieties, the main motive discernible being the desire for increased speed. This could be achieved only by a gradual diminution of the pictorial character, with the result that the principles underlying the system at length faded out of sight.

[1] See below, pp. 38–39.

Another factor that assisted in the evolution was the writing surface involved. Hieroglyphic was essentially monumental, cut into stone with a chisel or painstakingly executed in ink or paint upon carefully prepared walls. Hieratic was practically as old as Hieroglyphic, but was employed like Demotic for writing on papyrus, on wooden boards covered with a stucco wash, on potsherds, or on fragments of limestone.

When Christianity began to supersede the Pharaonic paganism, a medium more easily intelligible became required for the translations of Biblical texts. That was the reason for the introduction of COPTIC, already mentioned (p. 11) as the latest phase of the Egyptian language. This was written in Greek characters with a few additional letters taken over from Demotic. The literature of Coptic is full of Greek words, and indeed the entire set-up proclaims it to be more of a semi-artificial jargon than a direct lineal descendant of the old language; for this state of affairs modern Palestinian Hebrew may be quoted as an analogy.

The serious student will not be content without some further account of the hieroglyphs, the more so since it is only through Champollion's discovery that an orderly and historically accurate picture of the ancient civilization has become possible. It has already been intimated that hieroglyphic writing was an offshoot of direct pictorial representation. In this respect it resembled the original Babylonian script, and indeed it is not improbable that there was actual relationship between them, though it may have amounted to no more than a hearsay knowledge that the sounds of language could be communicated by means of appropriately chosen pictures. The subsequent development, however, differed very considerably in the two cases. Babylonian writing, using cuneiform (wedge-shaped) characters, quickly ceased to be recognizable as pictures, whereas the Egyptian hieroglyphs retained their pictorial appearance throughout the centuries, only losing it, and then only partially, in their derivative hieratic and demotic forms. By virtue of this fact many signs continued to mean what they represented, though of course when the things in question were referred to in speech, they bore their Egyptian names: signs so used are called

Ideograms and examples are  *iaw* 'old man',  *rēʿ* 'sun'. However, many signs like  *pōr* 'house' (this is the ideographic use) could also be employed in words whose sound was similar, but whose signification had no connexion whatsoever with the object depicted; when so employed the hieroglyphs are termed Phonograms or Sound-signs; thus  is found in the hieroglyphic spelling of 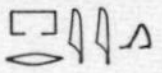 *pery* 'go forth',  *proyet* 'winter', 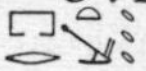 *peret* 'seed'. Egyptian writing, like Hebrew and Arabic, normally did not indicate the vowels, so that the pronunciations which for once we have supplied are not strictly justifiable, being merely a concession to those by whom the more scientific *pry*, *pr(y)t*, and *prt* would be found unpalatable. It will be seen that in our three examples  has the common consonantal value *p*+*r*, and is consequently a Biliteral sign. The underlying principle is that of the rebus or charade; one thing is shown, but another meant. By this method the Egyptians very early evolved a whole body of Uniliteral signs, in fact an alphabet of twenty-four letters; for example , depicting a mouth and when accompanied by a simple stroke  often conveying the word *rā* 'mouth', gave them their letter *r*; other alphabetic signs will be quoted further on. There were also Triliteral signs like  *nfr* and  *ḫpr*. Now one disadvantage of the hieroglyphic system of writing was that the miniature pictures which it used were apt to be ambiguous in both sound and meaning; thus the sign  depicting a scribe's palette, water-jar, and reed-case might represent not only that entire outfit, for which the word was *mnhḏ*, but also the activity of writing (*sš*), the professional writer or scribe, and other things besides. To ease this situation some other sign or signs were apt to be added; when pictorial, as in  *sš* 'scribe' the additional sign served as a Determinative, but when phonetic, as in  *nfr* (strictly *nfr*+*f*+*r*) 'good' 'beautiful' or as in  *ḫpr* (*ḫpr*+*r*) 'become' the additional sign or signs are known as Phonetic Complements. There are three kinds of Determinatives, (1) Specific, as in the word for 'scribe' just quoted, (2) Generic, when the sign indicates only the kind of notion that was meant, as , a striking man, employed not only in the word  *ḥwi* 'strike', but also in such words as 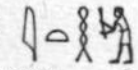 *itḥ* 'drag'; or again , 'the sun' as in  *hrw* 'day',  *wbn* 'shine forth', (3) Phonetic, a rarer variety, like the sign representing a kid in the verb *ỉbỉ* 'be thirsty' which inserts the entire word *ỉb* 'kid' in front of the generic determinatives for water and for actions performed by the mouth.

In sum, the hieroglyphic writing of the Egyptians was a mixed system comprising both sound-signs and sense-signs. The following short sentence accompanied by transliteration and translation will suggest that the analysis above is more or less exhaustive:

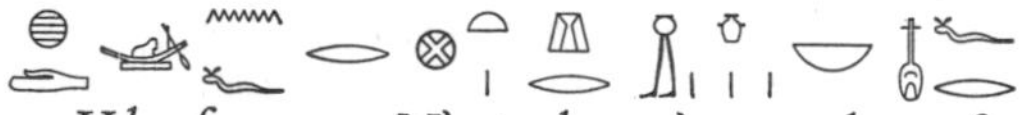

Ḥd·n·f *r* *Nỉwt* *ẖr* *ỉnw* *nb* *nfr*

Fared downstream he to (the) City with presents all (sorts of) goodly

Here , , , , and are the alphabetic signs for *f*, *n*, *r*, *ḥ*, *t*, and *d* respectively; , and are biliterals for *ỉn*, *nb* and *ẖr*, and a triliteral for *nfr*; the *r* after *ẖr* is a phonetic complement, and the *f*+*r* after *nfr* are two such; , , and are determinatives; lastly , depicting a village with intersecting streets, is an ideogram.

Students must not be deluded into thinking that hieroglyphic writing has anything particularly mysterious about it. It is a genuine script, containing many complexities it is true, but possessing the advantages of appealing to the eye as well as to the mind. Since the absence of written vowels makes it unpronounceable, some might conclude that it does not represent a language at all, or else that the language is one without grammar. Nothing could be more untrue, though it must be confessed that our ignorance of the underlying vocalization is a serious handicap. The subtleties of tense and mood can be deduced only from the context, or mostly so, since these nuances were conveyed more often by internal changes than by prefixes and affixes. To classical scholars accustomed to traditional vocabularies Egyptian is apt to be disconcerting. Coptic has proved less helpful than might have been hoped; but for establishing word-meanings, as well as for the division of one word from another, the determinatives have rendered important service. So too have the scenes which the accompanying legends were intended to explain. Most valuable of all, especially in historical texts and stories, is the logic of the situation. On the whole it may be said that the translations given in the following chapters possess a high degree of certainty, but it is only fair to warn the reader that we have dealt with them more freely than if this book had been intended for experienced scholars; notes of interrogation have been omitted, broken or obscure words supplied somewhat daringly, and on occasion whole clauses disregarded. This course seemed justifiable in view of the introductory character of what is here offered.

The latest extant example of Egyptian hieroglyphic writing has been found on the island of Philae above the First Cataract, and belongs to the year A.D. 394; here the priests of Isis, driven from other parts of the land, found their last refuge. From the same place there has survived a demotic graffito of A.D. 470. But there is also more than a likelihood that the hieroglyphs live on, though in transmuted form, within our own alphabet. In 1905 Flinders Petrie, excavating near the turquoise mines in the peninsula of Sinai, came across a number of much damaged inscriptions using signs obviously borrowed from the Egyptian hieroglyphs, but here serving to write some other language, probably Semitic. These picture-signs numbered thirty at most, and it is evident that the fewer different signs there are in a script, the greater its chance of being alphabetic. But the most remarkable fact about these signs was that at least six of them presented appearances corresponding to the meanings of letter-names belonging to the Hebrew and Greek alphabets; unmistakable, for example, was the bull's head , for *aleph* (Greek *alpha*) means 'bull' in Hebrew; a zigzag sign , closely resembling the Egyptian for 'water' must surely be an *m*, since *mēm* is the Hebrew letter-name meaning 'water', and both Phoenician and Greek give their *m* a very similar shape; the clear eye  of the Sinai script recalled the Hebrew letter-name *ʿayin* meaning 'eye', a signification easily recognizable in the circular O of the same two alphabets. Most convincing of all, however, was a several times repeated group of four letters 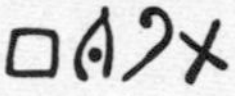 which on the same principle could be read as Baʿalat, and when it was realized that Baʿalat 'the Mistress', the female Baʿal, was the name always given by the Semites to the Egyptian goddess Ḥatḥōr, the very goddess worshipped at the place where Petrie's inscriptions were found, there seemed little doubt that the origin of our own alphabet had been discovered. Unhappily, however, the rest of the inscriptions proved recalcitrant to would-be translators. This may well be due in part to their much weathered condition, but until more evidence of a decisive kind comes to light there will always be sceptics or champions of some other less plausible theory.

SELECT BIBLIOGRAPHY

The Egyptian language: affinity with Hamitic, E. Zyhlarz, *Ursprung und Sprachcharakter des Altägyptischen*, Berlin, 1933; *Zeitschrift für Eingeborenensprachen*, Bd. 23 (1927), 25–45, 81–110, 161–94, 241–54; also his article *ZÄS* lxx. 107–22; with Semitic, T. W. Thacker, *The Relationship of the Semitic and Egyptian Verbal Systems*, Oxford, 1954.

1 Writing and grammar: A. H. Gardiner, *Egyptian Grammar*, 3rd ed., Oxford, 1957; G. Lefebvre, *Grammaire de l'Égyptien classique*, 2nd ed., Cairo, 1955.

Vocabulary: the commonest words, Gardiner, *Eg. Gr.*; all periods, of fundamental importance, A. Erman and H. Grapow, *Wörterbuch der ägyptischen Sprache*, Text, 5 vols.; references, 5 vols., Leipzig, 1926–53.

The different scripts: Hieroglyphic: N. M. Davies, *Picture Writing in Ancient Egypt*, Oxford, 1958. Hieratic: G. Möller, *Hieratische Paläographie*, 3 vols., Leipzig, 1909–12. Demotic: F. Ll. Griffith, *Demotic Papyri in the John Rylands Library*, 3 vols., Manchester, 1909; W. Erichsen, *Demotisches Glossar*, Copenhagen, 1954.

Other linguistic works: grammar of Old Egyptian, by E. Edel, Rome, 1955; of Late Egyptian, by A. Erman, 2nd ed., Leipzig, 1933; of Coptic, J. M. Plumley, London, 1948; the Sinai script, *The Legacy of Egypt*, Oxford, 1942, pp. 55 ff.

Literature: A. Erman (translated A. M. Blackman), *The Literature of the Ancient Egyptians*, London, 1927; G. Lefebvre, *Romans et Contes égyptiens de l'époque pharaonique*, Paris, 1949.

PLATE II

THE NILE OF UPPER EGYPT
Looking westward towards the Theban hills

III

THE LAND, ITS NEIGHBOURS, AND RESOURCES

THAT Egypt is the gift of the Nile is Herodotus's eloquent way of expressing a truth self-evident to those who know the country, but requiring some commentary for those who do not. As seen on the map (p. 29), Egypt resembles a lotus plant with the Nile Valley as the stalk, the Delta as the flower, and the depression of the Fayyûm as a bud. If our map were suitably coloured, the fields would be shown of a brilliant green, while the outlying desert would be tinted a golden brown. The old Egyptians themselves thought in terms corroborating the dictum of Herodotus, since they called Egypt  Kēme[1] 'the Black Land' in reference to the rich mud which countless inundations had spread over the country and to which this owed its unparalleled fertility; the desert they sometimes described as  Dashre 'the Red Land'. The contrast is indeed striking: you can stand with one foot on the gleaming sand and the other on the corn-carrying soil. In the midst flows the broad river, often dotted with white sails and reflecting the brilliant blue of the sky. On either hand the desert rises rapidly, frequently mounting, particularly on the east, to lofty cliffs that tower above the stream and leave no room for intervening cultivation. Where the mountains recede they shimmer forth with pinkish or opalescent hues in the early morning. It is a land of almost perpetual sunshine, with only scanty rainfall even near the Mediterranean, not more than an inch and a half at Cairo annually and practically none at far-away Aswân. Thus for its crops Egypt is entirely dependent upon the Nile flood resulting from the heavy rains of tropical regions lying far to the south; these pour down upon the Abyssinian table-land from June to September, causing the Blue Nile and the Atbara to rise rapidly. Aswân, at the north end of the First Cataract, notices the first traces of the rise in the

[1] So vocalized in Coptic.

fourth week of June; the full height is reached at Cairo towards the end of September. A fortnight later the inundation begins to subside, but it is not until April that the river sinks to its lowest level. There is considerable variation in both the dates and the quantity of the flood, and in the old days a low Nile might spell starvation for the teeming population. Any such disaster is now rendered impossible by the great dams erected by European engineers at Aswân, Esna, Asyûṭ, Cairo, and elsewhere, mostly within the last sixty years. By means of these dams perennial irrigation has been achieved, the water being held back and distributed into the canals whenever wanted. From the earliest times some degree of control had been practised, the river-banks being raised so as to limit the extent of flooding, and the dykes being cut at the appropriate moments. Nevertheless, it was common down to the latter part of the nineteenth century to see the entire Nile Valley converted into a wide lake, with palm-groves and villages rising out of the water like islands, only linked together by the roads raised above the inundation level.

The present dominion of Egypt is a rectangle larger than any European country except Russia, but with its 20 million inhabitants[1] crowded into the cultivated area of some 12,500 square miles. All the rest is desert, the western extension of this stretching out almost without a break towards the Atlantic. Of the Delta only about half can be sown, the other half being occupied by shallow lakes and marshes and low-lying salty ground not yet reclaimed. The seven Nile branches reported by Herodotus are now represented by only two, the western debouching at Rosetta and the rather longer eastern one at Damietta; but canals are seen everywhere. Of the 750 miles of the Nile's course downstream from Aswân to the Rosetta mouth, not far short of 600 belong to the Valley, the cultivable area of which, however, is only about the same as that of the Delta; this is because the breadth nowhere exceeds 13 miles. In so elongated a country it is natural that the temperature should vary considerably. In the Delta the weather is seldom, if ever, unbearably hot; at Aswân during the summer it is

[1] Perhaps four times the number living in the times with which we shall be mainly occupied. But this is the merest guess.

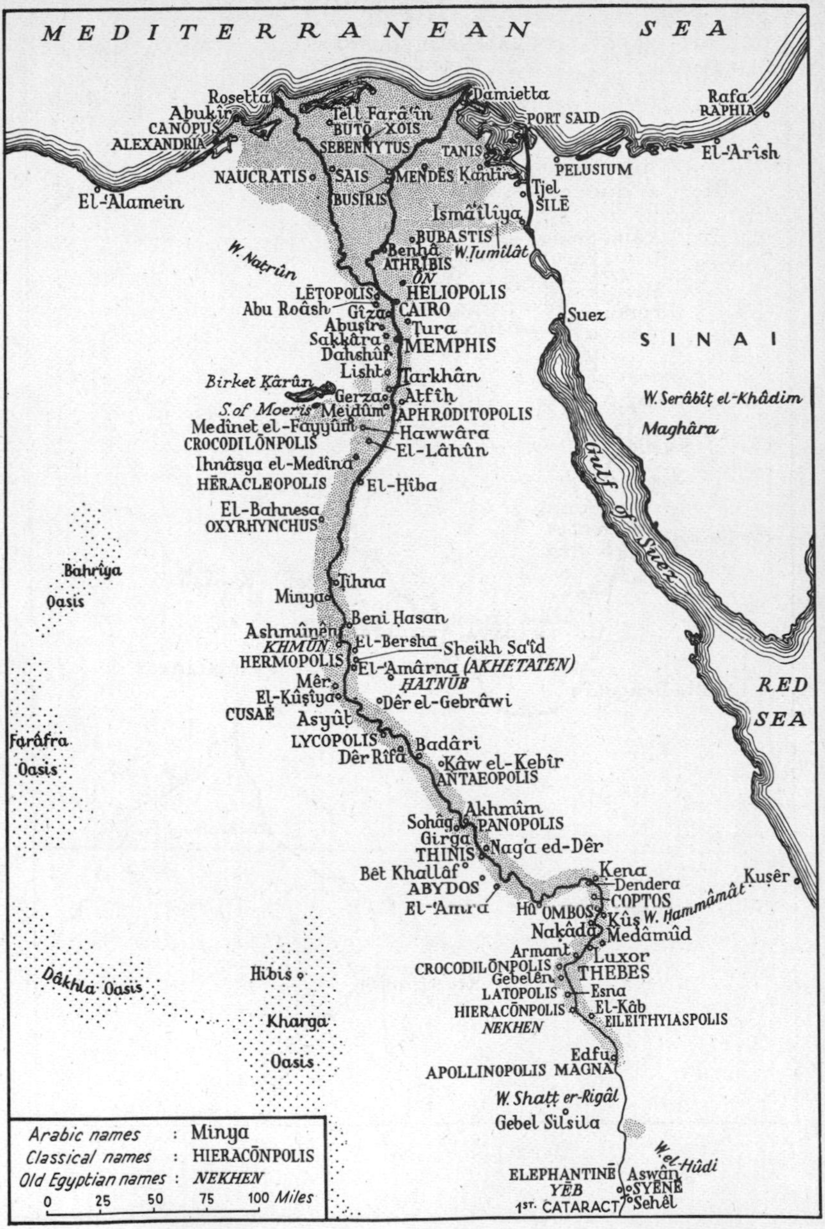
MEDITERRANEAN SEA
Rosetta
Abukîr
CANOPUS
ALEXANDRIA
El-'Alamein
Tell Fara'in
BUTO
XOIS
SEBENNYTUS
NAUCRATIS
SAIS
BUSIRIS
Damietta
PORT SAID
Rafa
RAPHIA
El-'Arîsh
TANIS
Kantir
MENDES
PELUSIUM
Tjel
SILE
Ismâ'iliya
BUBASTIS
W. Tumilât
Benhâ
ATHRIBIS
W. Natrûn
ON
HELIOPOLIS
LETOPOLIS
Abu Roâsh
Gîza
CAIRO
Abuşîr
Tura
Sakkâra
MEMPHIS
Dahshûr
Suez
SINAI
Lisht
Tarkhân
Birket Kârûn
Gerza
Atfîh
S. of Moeris
Meidûm
APHRODITOPOLIS
W. Serâbît el-Khâdim
Maghâra
Medînet el-Fayyûm
Hawwâra
CROCODILONPOLIS
El-Lâhûn
Ihnâsya el-Medîna
HERACLEOPOLIS
El-Hiba
Gulf of Suez
El-Bahnesa
OXYRHYNCHUS
Bahrîya
Oasis
Tihna
Minya
Beni Hasan
Ashmûnên
KHMUN
El-Bersha
Sheikh Sa'îd
HERMOPOLIS
El-'Amârna (AKHETATEN)
Mêr
HATNUB
El-Kûşîya
Dêr el-Gebrâwi
CUSAE
Asyût
RED
SEA
Farâfra
Oasis
LYCOPOLIS
Badâri
Dêr Rifa
Kâw el-Kebîr
ANTAEOPOLIS
Akhmîm
Sohâg
PANOPOLIS
Girga
THINIS
Nag'a ed-Dêr
Bêt Khallâf
ABYDOS
El-'Amra
Kena
Dendera
Kuşêr
COPTOS
Hû
OMBOS
Kûş
W. Hammâmât
Nakâda
Medâmûd
Armant
Luxor
CROCODILONPOLIS
THEBES
Gebelên
Dâkhla Oasis
Hibis
LATOPOLIS
Esna
HIERACONPOLIS
El-Kâb
NEKHEN
EILEITHYIASPOLIS
Kharga
Oasis
Edfu
APOLLINOPOLIS MAGNA
W. Shatt er-Rigâl
Gebel Silsila
W. el-Hûdi
Arabic names : Minya
Classical names : HIERACONPOLIS
Old Egyptian names : NEKHEN
0 25 50 75 100 Miles
ELEPHANTINE
YEB
Aswân
SYENE
1ST. CATARACT
Sehêl

MAP I. Egypt.

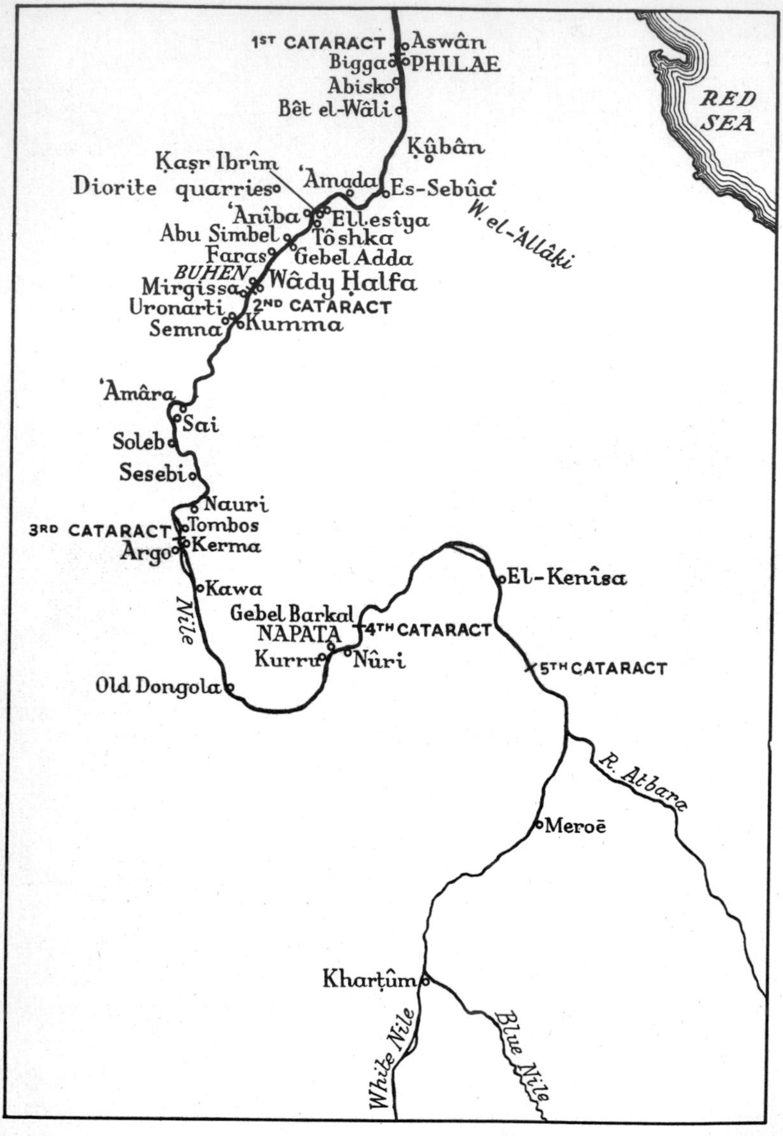

MAP II. Nubia and the Sûdân.

tolerable, if at all, only on account of the dryness of the air. At Luxor from December to the end of March the tourist may expect the equivalent of our best English months, though the thermometer falls steeply after sunset. The midday heat is usually tempered by what the ancient people spoke of as 'the sweet breath of the north wind'. From March to May, however, this is apt to give place to sand-laden winds from the south or south-west, the so-called Khamâsîn. That season of the year is relatively unhealthy, but not more so than the late autumn, when exhalations from the flood-soaked ground encourage dysentery and other diseases. Snakes and scorpions were greatly feared, the cobra (Gk. *ouraios*) and the horned viper (Gk. *kerastēs*) being the most dangerous of the former. Ophthalmia, propagated by the millions of flies, has always been the curse of Egypt. Otherwise the climate is singularly salubrious, and the natives have never ceased to extol the virtues of the Nile water; 'to drink water from the eddy of the river' is a wish often expressed in the inscriptions.

Isolated as Egypt was within almost limitless tracts of desert, for her means of livelihood she was largely dependent on her own resources. Intensive agriculture was the occupation of the great mass of the population, though during the months of the late summer the inundation put a temporary stop to this, and diverted the workers' activities in the direction of building and handicrafts. The rich Nile mud was extraordinarily fertile, but full benefit could be won from it only by the most strenuous and unremitting toil. As soon as the waters receded, ploughing and sowing commenced as a simultaneous operation—for the ploughing the same primitive wooden contrivance being employed as was still in use at the beginning of the present century. Elaborate precautions had to be taken both to prevent overflooding and to guide the water into runnels for distribution over land that would otherwise have remained barren, though for the latter purpose but little use appears to have been made of the simple water-hoist now familiar to every visitor to the Nile Valley under the name 'shadûf', which is only very rarely depicted in the wall-paintings. The dykes of course had to be kept in good repair, and canals to be dug. Harvest-time ushered in a period of renewed activity, and many are the pictures we possess of the reaping of the corn and the pulling up of the flax, the carrying of the crops on donkey-back to the threshing-floors, there to be trodden out by the oxen; finally, after the winnowing in which women played a large part, transport by road or river to the domed brick-built granaries, there to be stored until required for use. No small part of the local produce was exacted in taxation. A twofold harvest was the general aim, the summer crops demanding ever more strenuous labour as the level of the river grew lower.

Fig. 4. A typical Ushabti figure.

If agriculture was the common lot of the peasant, such employment could not fail to be abhorrent to the wealthy. The tombs of the well-to-do often yield hundreds of small statuettes mostly of faience or wood now generally known by their later name of Ushabti figures or 'answerers' (Fig. 4); the earlier writing Shawabti is of doubtful meaning. Here is a shortened translation of the magical spell usually inscribed upon them:[1]

O *ushabti*, if I am called upon, if I am appointed to do any work which is done in the necropolis ... even as a man is bounden, namely to cultivate the fields, to flood the river-banks or to carry the sand of the East to the West, then speak thou 'Here am I!'

Such figures are often depicted with hoe and basket indicating the kind of work from which the owner whom they portray hoped by their agency to escape. A common theme with the ancient scribes was that in which they extolled their own profession, and contrasted it with the miseries of other callings. This is the way in which the troubles of the small landowner are described:[2]

I am told you have abandoned writing and taken to sport, that you have set your face towards work in the fields and turned your back upon letters. Remember you not the condition of the cultivator faced with the registering of the harvest-tax, when the snake has carried off half the

[1] Chapter VI of the wrongly so called 'Book of the Dead'. [2] *JEA* xxvii. 19–20.

corn and the hippopotamus has devoured the rest? The mice abound in the fields. The locusts descend. The cattle devour. The sparrows bring disaster upon the cultivator. The remainder that is on the threshing-floor is at an end, it falls to the thieves. The yoke of oxen has died while threshing and ploughing. And now the scribe lands on the river-bank and is about to register the harvest-tax. The janitors carry staves and the Nubians rods of palm, and they say 'Hand over the corn' though there is none. The cultivator is beaten all over, he is bound and thrown into the well, soused and dipped head downwards. His wife has been bound in his presence, his children are in fetters. His neighbours abandon them and are fled. So their corn flies away. But the scribe is ahead of everyone. He who works in writing is not taxed, he has no dues to pay. Mark it well.

Looking now outside the boundaries of Egypt proper, we follow the ancient example and start with the south. Midway between Edfu and the narrows of Gebel Silsila, some 55 miles north of Aswân, the landscape changes completely. Here one passes from the limestone country which forms the bulk of Egypt into an inhospitable sandstone region extending southwards for 1,000 miles into the territory of the Sûdân. Only a short stretch intervenes before the First Cataract is reached just beyond the large island of Elephantinē. The Cataract consists of rapids caused by the intervention of great red or black granite masses barring the way. This provided Pharaonic Egypt with its natural frontier, though ethnically as well as physically the Nubian land may well have begun near Silsila. From the now submerged island of Philae to the longer and yet more beautiful Second Cataract above Wâdy Ḥalfa is the poverty-stricken tract of country known as Lower Nubia. This has been wittily described as a land 200 miles long and 5 yards broad: an exaggeration, of course, but one having thus much justification that the desert sands or commanding cliffs (the latter, for example, at Ḳaṣr Ibrîm on the east bank and at Abu Simbel on the west) often come right up to the riverside; scanty strips of cornland occur at intervals, or there may be plantations of palm-trees or of the Nile acacia (Arab. *ṣunṭ*) or dune-forming clumps of tamarisks. Lower Nubia now supports barely 120,000 inhabitants, nearly all of Berberine race and language, just as for the largest part of the early history, its people and those of the Sûdân, called  *Nḥsyw*, 'Neḥasyu' by the Egyptians, spoke a tongue that required the services of a dragoman for its interpretation. In some contexts the term Neḥasyu refers especially to the Nubians who lived along the river as contrasted with the  *Mḏ3yw* 'Medjayu', desert-dwellers of hardier stock who ultimately provided Egypt with her policemen.[1]

Beyond the Second Cataract the desolation is, if possible, even greater; villages are rare and cultivation mostly conspicuous by its absence. At one time in Egyptian history the boundary was set at Semna and Kumma, the two fortresses facing one another at the south end of the Cataract. There began the land of  *K3s*, later  *K3š*, the Cush of the Old Testament, where it has a very wide sense corresponding to the Greek Ethiopia. The original 'Cush' was a restricted area first heard of about 1970 B.C., but it was not long before it obtained an extended significance to embrace all the lands farther south, thus contrasting with the much older term  *W3w3t* Wawaĕ, this likewise at first a name of limited application, but subsequently covering the entire stretch between the First and Second Cataracts.[2] In course of time a whole cluster of colonies or outposts grew up southwards from the twin fortresses above mentioned, with their terminus at the mighty rock of the Gebel Barkal later to become the capital of an independent Ethiopian kingdom (*c.* 750 B.C.). Nor was this the extreme limit reached by a Pharaonic expedition; near el-Kenîsa, only 350 miles short of Kharṭûm, a conspicuous quartz boulder bears boundary-texts of those great warriors Tuthmōsis I and III (*c.* 1530–1440 B.C.).[3] The interests of Egyptology end at this point, and we need trace no further back the fortunes of the Nile in its journeyings from the source near Lake Tanganyika. Suffice it to say that after the confluence of the Blue and the White Niles at Kharṭûm and of the Atbara 200 miles to the north, the great river receives no other tributaries until it pours its waters into the Mediterranean 1,700 miles away.

The west flank of Egypt is now almost entirely desert, but one must reckon with considerable desiccation during the past 5,000

[1] *ZÄS* lxxxiii. 38 ff. [2] *Kush*, vi. 39 ff. [3] *JEA* xxxvi. 36.

years. Along the Mediterranean, at all events, there has always been a habitable region, partly pastureland and partly arable, the home of the white-skinned, red-haired, and blue-eyed people whom, following the example of the Greeks, we have come to know as Libyans. This name is, strictly speaking, both a misnomer and an anachronism, since the important tribe of the Libu[1] is first heard of in the reign of Merenptaḥ (*c.* 1220 B.C.), when they headed a coalition of invaders from much farther west. In earlier times two peoples are distinguished, the Tjeḥnyu[2] and the Tjemḥu,[3] of whom the former were perhaps originally identical in both race and culture with the Egyptians of the western Delta, though they were always definitely regarded as foreigners. They wore phallus-sheaths, had a large curl hanging from one side of their heads, and carried feathers in their hair. It is difficult to believe that they were ever very numerous, and it seems probable that it was they who peopled the oases,[4] those strange depressions, below sea-level and fed by springs, which occur at discreet distances from the Nile Valley. The names of these from north to south, are Sîwa, Baḥrîya, Farâfra, Dâkhla, and Khârga; but Sîwa is too far away to have been of interest to the Pharaohs until Saite times. The population of the five together is now little above 40,000. The Fayyûm is also in a certain sense one of the oases, but lies much closer to Egypt and was broken into by the Nile long before historic times. Thus was formed a great lake, of which the last remains are still to be seen in the Birket Ḳârûn, 144 feet below sea-level. According to the latest theory, which seeks to co-ordinate the data obtained by a large number of able geologists with the observations and traditions recorded by Herodotus, the original lake then sank to below sea-level through silting up of the channel until a king of Dyn. XII, by widening and deepening it, again brought the lake into equilibrium with the river. Thus was formed the famous Lake of Moeris, which, by functioning 'as a combined Nile flood-escape and reservoir, not only protected the lands of Lower Egypt from the destructive effects of excessive high floods,

[1] *Onom.*, i, pp. 121* ff. [2] Op. cit., i, pp. 116* ff. [3] Op. cit., i, pp. 114* ff.

[4] This Greek word is derived from Egyptian , old *Wḥȝt*. Coptic ⲟⲩⲁϩⲉ, meaning etymologically 'cauldron', see *ZÄS* lvi. 44 ff.

but also increased the supplies of water in the river after the flood-season had passed'.[1] According to the same theory, the level and consequent size of the lake were artificially reduced in early Ptolemaic times by the construction of two barrages, a portion of the submerged area being thus reclaimed. Evaporation has further reduced the Birket Ḳârûn to its present size, connexion with the Nile being maintained only by the sinuous Baḥr Yûsuf, which takes off from the river in the neighbourhood of Deirûṭ.

Concerning the Mediterranean, which forms the northern boundary, little need be said except that Egypt became vulnerable from this quarter only when sea-borne adventurers became more daring. There must early have been some contact with Crete, because the Minoan culture betrays unmistakable signs of Egyptian influence. But for direct maritime activity in that direction we have no evidence. On the contrary the Pharaonic ships appear to have preferred to hug the shore, since to large seafaring vessels, even if they plied on the Red Sea, was given the name *kebenwe*, that is to say 'Byblos ships', so called after the port of Gublu or Byblos at the foot of the Lebanon.

It was on the east that Egypt was most vulnerable, though only in one restricted area. The route to or from Palestine lay across the north of the peninsula of Sinai, a march of some 90 miles (from Ḳanṭara to El-ʿArîsh) over a sandy waterless waste.[2] But that distance was insufficient to deter those whom need or greed attracted towards the fleshpots of Egypt. If, as there seems good reason to think, the dynastic civilization owed much to Mesopotamian influence, it was probably that way that its originators came. It has been plausibly argued that they approached the Nile Valley from the north, since the Egypto-Semitic word for 'west' in Egyptian stands also for 'right hand'. The same road or that through Pelusium nearer the sea was taken by the conquering armies of Esarhaddon, of Cambyses, and of Alexander, as well as in the reverse direction by several of Egypt's own rulers. That there was danger to be feared from this quarter is indicated by the mention, about 1970 B.C., of the Walls of the Ruler 'made to repel the Setyu (Asiatics) and to crush the Sand-farers'.[3] But farther south Egypt

[1] J. Ball, *Contributions*, p. 199. [2] *JEA* vi. 99 ff. [3] *JEA* i. 105.

was perfectly safe from any chance of aggression, for there the Gulf of Suez and beyond this the Red Sea served as protection, both moreover separated from the Nile by peaks sometimes rising to well over 4,000 feet. On this flank there was no people powerful enough to force an entry. The Egyptians themselves, however, found a way from Coptos to the Red Sea harbour of Ḳuṣêr whence they could sail to  Pwēne,[1] probably the African coast opposite Aden, the land of spices, myrrh, and other much-prized products.

Taking all in all, Egypt in her early days was about as happily isolated as any continental country could be to develop her own highly individual culture. Nor did such fortunate circumstances lessen her good opinion of herself; the Egyptians were, they themselves considered, the only true 'men', the only people really entitled to bear the name *rōme*.[2] Normally she was contemptuous of her nearest neighbours, to whose chieftains she invariably applied the epithet 'vile'. Of the Nubians a Middle Kingdom scribe wrote:[3]

> When one rages against him he shows his back; when one retreats he starts to rage. They are not people worthy of respect; they are cowards, craven-hearted.

A somewhat earlier writer thus characterizes the Asiatics of southern Palestine:[4]

> The miserable ʿAam, it fares ill with the place wherein he is, troublesome in respect of water and difficult on account of the many trees, its roads toilsome by reason of the mountains. He dwells not in any single place, driven abroad by want and his feet always on the move. He has been fighting ever since the time of Horus, but he never conquers, nor is he ever conquered.

In spite of the self-confidence betrayed in these quotations, Egypt has been successfully invaded time and time again, and for the last 1,300 years her own ancient civilization has been completely overlaid

[1] In most Egyptological books the name is given as Punt, with a pronunciation that is certainly wrong; but that adopted here is also conjectural.

[2] The word *pirōmis*, i.e. *rōme* preceded by the definite article, was known to Herodotus (ii. 143), who attributed to it a sense approximating to that of our 'gentleman'.

[3] *Eg. Gr.*, p. 361.

[4] *JEA* i. 30.

by that of Islam. The truth is that though her agriculture has always exacted unremitting industry, the country's conditions have never been such as to develop great military prowess, and whenever faced by a hardier and more warlike race Egypt has invariably succumbed.

FIG. 5. Papyrus plants.

At the most flourishing moments of her history, Egypt's material resources were incomparably great. Except in the worst years she had cereals in abundance, the principal crops being barley and emmer, the latter a coarse kind of wheat. Of vegetables, there were lentils, beans, cucumbers, leeks, and onions; of fruits, dates, the sycamore-fig, and the ordinary fig, persea, and above all the heaven-sent blessing of the grape. The Egyptians were great lovers of flowers, and the wall-paintings of their tombs display great bouquets adorning the piled-up food tables; guests at banquets hold lotuses before their noses, while necklets of blossoms are fastened round their necks by maidservants. The sweet-smelling blue lotus (*Nymphaea caerulea*), which, like the white variety, grew so abundantly in swamps and backwaters, supplied a motif much in favour with architects and artists. Apart from the aesthetic enjoyment afforded by flowers, and their mystical significance as symbols of life, they were the source of the honey that compensated for absence of the sugar-cane. Flax was grown in great quantity, and furnished the thread which was woven into the finest linen tissues. A unique product of Egypt was the papyrus plant; this served for the making of ropes and mats, of boxes, sandals, and light skiffs, but above all its stalk, sliced into thin sections laid side by side and crosswise to be beaten into sun-dried sheets, provided the scribes with an unsurpassed writing-material, later inherited by the Greeks and the Romans; to us it has given the word 'paper'. An oil-producing tree called *baḳ* has been thought by some to have been the olive, but was more probably the moringa,[1] whence ben-oil is obtained. Concerning the scarcity of wood we shall speak later.

There were great stocks of domesticated animals, first and foremost several fine breeds of African cattle. The favourite meat was beef, and the ox was the principal sacrificial animal; in the fields it was used to draw the plough. Sheep, goats, and pigs are often seen in the tomb-paintings, and the dedicators of funerary stelae[2] boast of the number of these that they possessed. Goats, and more rarely, pigs were employed to tread in the seed, but must surely also have served as food, though there seems to have been a prejudice against speaking of them in that connexion. So too with fish, nor can the sheep have had any other purpose, since superstition prohibited the employment of their wool for clothing. There was in Pharaonic

[1] *Bull. Inst. fr.* xxxi. 130 ff.

[2] 'Stēlē', the Greek word for a pillar of stone, is used in Egyptian archaeology for the very common objects of the kind employed for funerary or commemorative scenes and inscriptions; they are often round-topped, see Fig. 6 below.

times, as nowadays, no more practically serviceable a quadruped than the donkey, whether for bringing in the harvest or for carrying human beings. The horse was not to make its appearance in Egypt until late Hyksōs times (*c.* 1600 B.C.), when it was introduced from Asia, mainly for use in chariots; the camel was a far later introduction.

FIG. 6. A small Middle Kingdom stela.

Large flocks of geese and ducks were to be found in the farms. But here we must break off our account of the living creatures which contributed to the amenities of Pharaonic life, and must direct our attention to the inanimate sources of Egyptian wealth. The magnificent limestone of Middle Egypt, and above all that from the quarries of Ṭura opposite the pyramids of Gîza, served for the construction of all the temples and tombs of early times, in so far as these were not extemporized out of sun-dried bricks or cut into the hillsides; and it is a matter of some surprise that the much less pleasing sandstone should have supplanted it from the New Kingdom (*c.* 1500 B.C.) onwards. Costlier and less easily worked stones were reserved for the great sarcophagi of kings and nobles, and for the gateways and columns of their sepulchres and sanctuaries. The most highly favoured of these was the showy red granite from the First Cataract, which also furnished another sort, grey-black and not much less appreciated. The value attached to the greywacke, vulgarly known as basalt, brought from the eastern desert at the level of Coptos, is attested by the rock-inscriptions of the Wâdy Ḥammâmât.[1] Farther north are several quarries whence was fetched the brilliantly translucent alabaster, even better esteemed for jars and vessels of all shapes and sizes than for building purposes. From the Gebel el-Aḥmar north-east of Cairo comes the reddish quartzite, the hardest and one of the most beautiful kinds of stone with which the Egyptians ever successfully dealt. Only comparatively recently was discovered some 40 miles north-west of Abu Simbel the source of the diorite of which the superb statue of Chephrēn in the Cairo Museum is made.[2] Other fine stones from the outskirts of Egypt are breccia, jasper, chert, and schist. Nowhere in the world have there ever been more skilful stoneworkers than the Egyptians, and the perfection of the innumerable vases, jars, plates, and so forth found in the Step Pyramid is as much a wonder as the Great Pyramid itself.

All the materials thus far mentioned come either from places within the Valley itself or from the desert not more than a couple of days' trek away. It was well within the power of so resourceful a people to drag even the largest blocks as far as the Nile, but then they might still be several hundred miles away from the site for which they were required. The most beneficent factor in the Egyptian economic structure was the river itself. All distant travel within the country was by boat, and the ancient people were as expert as ship-builders as they were in all other practical techniques. But for ship-building wood was a prime necessity, and the deficiency of this was notorious. Perhaps the position was not quite so bad as is sometimes represented, since though the climate in the Valley has not changed for 5,000 years, the degree of efficiency in the matter of irrigation has, and where there are now only fields there may once have been a good many more trees than can be seen at the present time. It was in the quality of the timber rather than in the quantity that the lack made itself felt. For example, the date-palm

[1] *Ann. Serv.* xxxviii. 127 ff. [2] PM vii. 274.

so common in Egypt at all periods was wellnigh useless for building other than roofing, and the very different wood of the dōm-palm was also not much in favour. Hence the importance of those constant journeys to Byblos which have already been mentioned. Our texts are full of references to the wood *ʿash* which was brought from the Lebanon. It has become the fashion to decry the translation of this word as 'cedar' and to substitute the rendering 'pine', but if the not quite unambiguous pronouncements of the latest experts may be trusted, we may perhaps content ourselves with being no more inaccurate than Pliny, and adhere to his use of the word 'cedrus' to cover the juniper and other conifers. To quote only one of the oldest mentions in our texts, forty seafaring vessels laden with *ʿash* were brought to Egypt in a single year of King Snofru of Dyn. IV (*c.* 2620 B.C.).[1] But we also read of ships of acacia wood being built in Lower Nubia to transport great quantities of granite through the First Cataract for use in the pyramid of King Merenrēʿ.[2] On one occasion too we are told of a ship being built on the Red Sea coast for an expedition to Pwēne.[3]

From time immemorial the possession of gold has been regarded as synonymous with wealth. In such possession Egypt far outstripped all her neighbours. So rich was the eastern desert in the precious metal, both as occurring in alluvial sands and gravels and as veins in quartz rock, that for long ages it was unnecessary to seek it farther south than the latitude of Coptos; only when the mines there began to be exhausted or too difficult to work were others established in Lower Nubia and beyond. A papyrus in the Turin Museum depicts the road to one of the gold-bearing regions and is surely the oldest map in the world.[4] The position as regards silver is less clear. Egypt has never, so far as is known, had either native silver or silver ores, though all Egyptian gold contains silver in various proportions. No method is on record, however, whereby the ancients could have extracted the silver from the gold, and it has been suggested that what in the earliest texts is called *ḥadj* 'white (gold)' was really a natural alloy so pale in colour as to have been regarded as a metal distinct from gold. The Greeks called such

[1] *BAR* i, § 146. [2] Op. cit. i, § 324. [3] Op. cit. i, § 360.
[4] *Ann. Serv.* xlix. 337 ff.

an alloy of gold and silver 'electrum', and Egyptologists often use that word to translate the hieroglyphic *djam* which, however, appears to be merely a more elegant term for 'gold' (Eg. *noub*). It is certain, however, that *ḥadj* later meant true silver, and from Dyn. XVIII on (16th cent. B.C.) it is constantly named as coming from Syria, Babylonia, and the Hittite country in Asia Minor. Perhaps, after all, it was imported even in the oldest times.

There is some mystery too about copper, which was fairly widely used even before the dynasties, and after Mēnēs was the indispensable metal employed for tools and weapons. Such copper ores as malachite and chrysocolla are found in the eastern desert, but not in sufficient quantity to supply any but the earliest needs. There are, however, vast workings in the Peninsula of Sinai, not far from the two sites (the Wâdy Maghâra and Serâbîṭ el-Khâdim) where many inscriptions record the visits of Egyptian expeditions in quest of turquoise. It is strange that only turquoise should be mentioned, but for many reasons the Egyptian word *mafke* can hardly have signified anything else. From Dyn. XVIII onward Syria is spoken of as sending tribute of copper, and some may have come from Cyprus and Cilicia as well.

Iron was certainly not used for tools until far on in the first millennium B.C., and the presence in the tomb of Tutʿankhamūn of a richly ornamented dagger with iron blade[1] indicates how much of a luxury that metal still was. Beads of meteoric origin were found in a predynastic tomb at Gerza, and sporadic occurrences of iron, meteoric or otherwise, have been noted later, though too rarely to be of interest to us here. Nor, in this necessarily incomplete sketch of the Egyptian wealth, need we discuss lead and tin, for which A. Lucas's authoritative treatise can be consulted.

Egypt had no precious stones in the sense in which we understand the term. For jewellery lapis lazuli, turquoise, amethyst, carnelian, and the like had to suffice, and the use made of these less spectacular, but not less attractive, stones was brilliant and skilful in the extreme. The art of producing glazed ware was acquired very early, and every collector knows how highly the blue and green faience of Egypt is to be prized. Glass was much less easily

[1] *JEA*, xxviii, Pl. I.

achieved, and specimens are far less common, though beautiful vases from Dyns. XVII and XVIII have found their way into our museums.

In a land where natural resources were so abundant, and where craftsmanship of so high an order was rapidly developed, it was natural that much should be available for barter with foreigners. Many pictures are to be found, especially in the tombs of the nobles at Thebes, of Syrians, Nubians, and even Cretans bringing exotic treasures for presentation to the king. These are always represented as tribute or gifts, but it is difficult to suppress a suspicion that payment in gold had usually to be made. Nubia had always been the source of ebony and ivory, besides leopard-skins, giraffe-tails, ostrich feathers, monkeys, and so forth. Pwēne, as we have seen, was the land of myrrh and spices. From Syria came fantastically shaped vases, swords, helmets, chariots, leather reins; many articles are obviously Minoan in origin, sometimes actually brought by Cretans with cunningly decorated skirts and comical little curls. A pathetic form of tribute consisted of the tiny children left behind as hostages. But besides such direct contributions from the peoples with whom the Egyptians came into actual contact there were substances from much farther afield. Scarabs[1] and other objects of lapis lazuli have frequently been found in excavations, and no semi-precious stone is more often mentioned in the inscriptions; yet for this no sources are known much nearer than Abyssinia and Afghanistan. What has been called amber may turn out to be worked resin, but the fine jet-black mineral called obsidian is a good example of what is here contended, rival theories maintaining that it came from Abyssinia or from Armenia. In periods behind historical recollection trade was wider flung than we are apt to imagine.

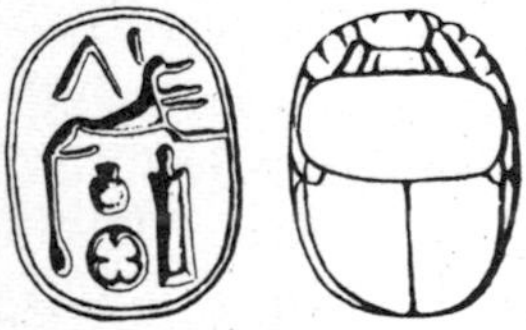

FIG. 7. A typical scarab.

[1] Scarabs (Fig. 7) are imitations in faience or some other hard material of the Egyptian beetle *Scarabaeus sacer*. Used as an amulet or as a seal. The flat lower surface may bear the name of a king or an official or else some decorative device. Symbolically the scarab (Egyptian name *kheprer*) represents 'growth' or 'becoming', and in company with the mummy represents the heart, the sentient organ of the body. See *Eg. Gr.*, pp. 268–9; the god Khepri symbolizes the rising sun.

SELECT BIBLIOGRAPHY

The land: K. Baedeker, *Egypt* (English), 8th ed., 1929, with valuable introductory articles; J. Ball, *Contributions to the Geography of Egypt*, Cairo, 1939; Id., *Egypt in the Classical Geographers*, Cairo, 1942.

Towns and other place-names, H. Gauthier, *Dictionnaire des noms géographiques*, 7 vols., Cairo, 1925–31; A. H. Gardiner, *Ancient Egyptian Onomastica*, 3 vols., Oxford, 1947.

Foreign peoples: Nubia and the Sûdân, T. Säve-Söderbergh, *Ägypten und Nubien*, Lund, 1941; Libya, W. Hölscher, *Libyer und Ägypter*, Glückstadt, 1937; Eastern neighbours, W. Max Müller, *Asien und Europa*, Leipzig, 1893, out of date, but still useful.

Resources of Egypt: A. Lucas, *Ancient Egyptian Materials and Industries*, 3rd ed., London, 1948.

IV

THE FOUNDATIONS AND NATURE OF EGYPTIAN HISTORY

THE first task which lay before the successors of Champollion was to establish the true order of the pre-Ptolemaic kings, and their decipherments quickly led to the rehabilitation, or at least the partial rehabilitation, of the Egyptian priest MANETHO. The respect felt to be due to Herodotus and Diodorus had hitherto thrown into the shade the far more trustworthy information afforded by that learned contemporary of the first two Ptolemies (323–245 B.C.). Manetho undertook a chronicle of the Egyptian kings of which, apart from some much edited extracts preserved by the Jewish historian JOSEPHUS (*fl.* A.D. 70), there remains only a garbled abridgement in the works of the Christian chronographers SEXTUS JULIUS AFRICANUS (early 3rd cent. A.D.) and EUSEBIUS (early 4th cent. A.D.), a much later compiler named George the Monk, known as Syncellus (*c.* A.D. 800), contributing greatly to the transmission. In Manetho's work the entire history of Egypt, after the reigns of the gods and demi-gods, was divided up into thirty-one dynasties of royal families beginning with Mēnēs and ending with Alexander the Great's conquest in 332 B.C. In spite of all defects this division into dynasties has taken so firm a root in the literature of Egyptology that there is but little chance of its ever being abandoned. In the forms in which the book has reached us there are inaccuracies of the most glaring kind, these finding their climax in Dyn. XVIII, where the names and true sequence are now known from indisputable monumental sources. Africanus and Eusebius often do not agree; for example Africanus assigns nine kings to Dyn. XXII, while Eusebius has only three. Sometimes all that is vouchsafed to us is the number of kings in a dynasty (so in Dyns. VII–X, XX) and their city of origin. The royal names are apt to be incredibly distorted, that of Senwosre I of Dyn. XII, for instance, being assimilated in the form Sesonchosis to that of the Shōshenḳ of a thousand years later. The lengths of reigns frequently differ in the two versions, as well as often showing wide departures from the definitely ascertained figures. When textual and other critics have done their best or worst, the reconstructed Manetho remains full of imperfections. What is even more serious, the story of Amenōphis and the lepers quoted from him by Josephus, as well as the fantastic happenings ascribed to some of the kings, shows that he made use, not only of authentic records, but also of popular romances devoid of historical value. None the less, his book still dominates our studies, and perhaps has further surprises in store for us, as when only a few years ago the name of an unknown king Nephercherēs, whom he placed in Dyn. XXI, was unexpectedly found on a small object from Tanis.[1]

In the vindication of Manetho Champollion himself led the way. The second edition of his famous *Précis*, published in 1828, announced the finding on various monuments of the cartouches of the Manethonian kings Achōris, Nepheritēs, Psammētichus, Osorchō, Sesōnchis, Ramessēs, Tuthmōsis (for the last two see above, p. 14), as well as of that Amenōphis whom the Greeks called Memnōn. With the help of the Egyptian historian all these could be assigned to their correct positions. Nor did Champollion's discoveries stop here. His many successes and few failures form a fascinating story, but one difficult to disentangle. With the mass of material now at our disposal there still remain many doubts with regard to the order of the different reigns, worst of all in what we shall come to know as the First and the Second Intermediate Periods, and then again between Dyns. XXI and XXIV. Help is sometimes afforded by inscriptions extending over several reigns, but the most valuable assistance has been offered by the king-lists of which some account must now be given.[2]

In the so-called TURIN CANON OF KINGS (Fig. 8) we have the remains of a genuine chronicle remarkably like the Manetho of Africanus and Eusebius. Tradition has it that this hieratic papyrus of about the reign of Ramessēs II (1290–1224 B.C.) was as good as perfect when Drovetti (p. 15) acquired it. When, however,

[1] P. Montet, *Tanis*, Paris (Payot), 1942, p. 164, with Fig. 43.

[2] See the bibliography below, p. 69.

Champollion started sifting the almost inexhaustible store of fragments that had passed into the possession of the Turin Museum, he found this most precious of all Egyptian documents represented only by some fifty pieces, in many cases very incomplete, yielding at most between eighty and ninety royal names. Two years later, in 1826, the German Gustav Seyffarth, a scholar sceptical of Champollion's results, set to work to collect afresh all the fragments and to join together such as could be joined. Working solely on the fibres and on the positions of the lines of writing on *recto* and *verso* he achieved remarkable results, which have, however, since been considerably improved. The chronicle started, like that of Manetho, with the gods and demi-gods, to whom reigns of fabulous length are attributed. It agrees with Manetho and the classical authors in making Mēnēs the founder of the Egyptian monarchy. The rest of the document is a mere list of royal names beginning with him, each name followed by indication of length of rule and life; the monotony is broken only by an occasional total serving the same purpose as Manetho's division into dynasties, though the points at which a fresh family is begun do not always coincide in the two authorities. The number of kings recorded is roughly the same in both; for the first six dynasties the Turin Canon had fifty-two names, Manetho forty-nine; for Dyn. XII both have seven names. After that dynasty comes a long enumeration of ephemeral kings not specified by Manetho. The following ever scantier fragments include a few of the foreign intruders known as the Hyksōs (below, p. 155), but also give some names of so fantastic an appearance that they are unlikely to have belonged to any real kings.

In course of time other king-lists emerged to supplement Manetho and the Turin Canon. The most important is the so-called TABLE OF ABYDOS (Fig. 8)[1] inscribed on the walls of that great temple which is among the most attractive sights in store for the visitor to Egypt. The scene displays the King Sethos I (1309–1291 B.C.) accompanied by his eldest son Ramessēs in the act of making offerings to no less than seventy-six of his ancestors, these not depicted in person, but represented by the cartouches containing their hieroglyphically written names; here again Mēnēs heads the

[1] PM vi. 25 (229)–(230).

A fragment of the Turin Canon of Kings.

Part of the Table of Abydos.

Part of the Table of Saḳḳâra.

FIG. 8. Samples of the three principal king-lists.

list. The Table of Saḳḳâra (Fig. 8),[1] found in 1861 in the Memphite tomb of an overseer of works named Tjuneroy, originally had the cartouches of fifty-seven earlier kings honoured by Ramessēs II, but damage to the wall had reduced the number to about fifty. The Table of Karnak,[2] inscribed in the great Theban temple of that name and dating from the reign of Tuthmōsis III (1490–1436 B.C.) had contained sixty-one names of which forty-eight were legible wholly or in part at the time of the discovery (1825), but this list, remarkable for mentioning a number of rulers omitted in the others, has the disadvantage of not giving its kings in their true consecutive order.

The purpose which these three lists were intended to serve imposed no obligation of completeness, and only such kings gained admission as were regarded as legitimate or deserving of honour. For that reason the Hyksōs rulers of Dyns. XV–XVII were excluded, as well as the heretic king Akhenaten and his three immediate successors. But there are peculiarities in the choice of names which defy explanation. It is comprehensible that the Karnak list should pay special attention to Dyn. XI and again to the predecessors of Amōsis (ʿAḥmose I), the expeller of the Hyksōs, since those monarchs sprang from Theban families. But why should the Table of Abydos name a number of petty kings of Dyn. VIII whom Manetho's excerptors deemed unworthy of mention, while the no more insignificant rulers of Dyns. XIII–XIV are passed over in silence? Nor is it clear why the Table of Saḳḳâra omits the first five kings of Dyn. I, starting its series with Miebis. It is particularly regrettable that there is no king-list later than Ramessēs II, the great son and successor of Sethōs I, since the end of Dyn. XIX presents serious problems, and Dyns. XXI–XXIII are still more intractable. The only really important equivalent of a king-list later than those already mentioned is the sequence of kings attached to the names of a long line of Memphite priests all claiming to have belonged to a single family; here the earliest king belongs to the end of Dyn. XI, the latest being a Shōshenḳ of Dyn. XXII.[3]

The identification of the names in the king-lists with those recorded by Manetho was at first often impeded by the fact, already

[1] PM iii. 192. [2] Op. cit. ii. 42. [3] Borchardt, *Mittel*, Pls. 2, 2A.

recognized by Champollion, that most kings possessed not merely one cartouche, but two; thus the Table of Abydos often quotes the religious or royal forename or Prenomen, while Manetho gave preference to the secular name or Nomen. This difficulty was gradually overcome by the finding of inscriptions in which both cartouches were linked together. In the high noontide of the Pharaonic civilization the full titulary of the kings was even more complex, comprising no less than five separate names.[1] A commemorative stela from the reign of Egypt's greatest conqueror is headed as follows:

> Life to the Horus 'Strong bull arisen in Thebes', the Two Ladies 'Enduring of kingship like Rēᶜ in heaven', the Horus of Gold, 'Powerful of strength, Holy of appearances', the King of Upper and Lower Egypt 'Menkheperrēᶜ', the Son of Rēᶜ 'Dḥutmōse ruler of truth', beloved of Amen-Rēᶜ who presides in Ipet-eswe (Karnak), may he live eternally. The king himself gave command, &c.

This seemingly unintelligible rigmarole loses something of its mystery for the modern reader when it is explained that the five elements preceding the individual names printed within quotation marks are titles or epithets common to every Pharaoh, and express, except in the fourth case, his relation to some deity or deities. Thus the expression 'Horus "Strong bull arisen in Thebes"' indicates that Tuthmōsis III—we usually refer to Dḥutmōse under this his Manethonian name—was the re-embodiment of the falcon-god Horus in the aspect indicated, and the words following the quaint epithet 'Two Ladies' (Eg. *nebty*, written in hieroglyphs 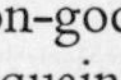) describe the particular quality entitling the holder of this second name to consider himself under the protection of Nekhbe and Edjō, the vulture and uraeus (cobra) patronesses of Upper and Lower Egypt respectively. The names 'Menkheperrēᶜ' and 'Dḥutmōse ruler of truth' are the only two of the five enclosed in cartouches, the former being what was above described as the Prenomen and the latter being the Nomen; the Prenomen is preceded by the hieroglyphs  given the pronunciation *insibya*[2] on a Babylonian tablet and accurately interpreted on the Rosetta Stone

[1] *Eg. Gr.*, pp. 71 ff. [2] *ZÄS* xlix. 17.

as 'King of the Upper and Lower Countries'; the Nomen introduced by 𓅭𓇳 proclaims the king to be 'the son of the sun-god', but retains the personal name which he bore before his accession to the throne.

A peculiarity of the Horus name is that it was very often written vertically in a rectangle with the recessed panelling characteristic of the earliest brick buildings; this design, known to the Egyptians as the *serekh*, evidently represents the façade of the palace occupied by the king as reincarnation of the falcon seen presiding over it (Fig. 9).

FIG. 9. *Serekh* of King Amōsis.

This opportunity may fitly be taken to deal with the term 'Pharaoh'. This has come to us from our Bible: the stories of Joseph and of Moses use it as a general term for the reigning Egyptian monarch; the Second Book of Kings describes a ruler of Dyn. XXVI as 'Pharaoh Nekō', adding the personal name as was sometimes done in the native literature from Dyn. XXII onwards. But as applied to any king earlier than Dyn. XVIII our English employment of the term is an anachronism, and there is no warrant for the plural 'Pharaohs' at all, though we shall not wish to abandon so convenient an appellation on that account and have actually used it in the title to this book. The Egyptian original Per-ʿo, written 𓉐𓉻, meant simply 'Great House' and was one of the many ways of referring to the royal palace. Then, in the reign of Tuthmōsis III, the term began to be used for the king himself, just as 'the Sublime Porte' formerly served to designate the Ottoman Government of the sultans in Constantinople. Hence the word 'Pharaoh' passed into the Hebrew scriptures, and out of these into our own vocabulary.

If the reader of this book has any previous knowledge of Egyptology he will doubtless be shocked, on perusing the lists of kings at the end of this book, to find the names of some of them rendered in a manner different from that to which he has become accustomed. The fact is regrettable, but at the same time necessary and, up to a point, even desirable. At all events it testifies to the progressive character of our science, and to its reluctance to acquiesce in transliterations demonstrably inaccurate. The familiar Thothmes, in place of our Tuthmōsis or Breasted's Thutmose, is a solecism which should be remorselessly banned. This is not the place to defend our own preferences. Suffice it to state the general principle, which is to employ forms consecrated by Manetho when these bear sufficient resemblance to what is given by the hieroglyphs, and when that criterion fails, to use spellings that take into due account the rules of vocalization and accent afforded by Coptic. But let it be clearly understood: only in the rarest possible cases—especially where a writing in Babylonian cuneiform has survived—can we know the true contemporary pronunciation.

Even when full use has been made of the king-lists and of such subsidiary sources as have survived, the indispensable dynastic framework of Egyptian history shows lamentable gaps and many a doubtful attribution. If this be true of the skeleton, how much more is it of the flesh and blood with which we could wish it covered. Historical inscriptions of any considerable length are as rare as the isolated islets in an imperfectly charted ocean. The importance of many of the kings can be guessed at merely from the number of stelae[1] or scarabs[2] that bear their names. It must never be forgotten that we are dealing with a civilization thousands of years old and one of which only tiny remnants have survived. What is proudly advertised as Egyptian history is merely a collection of rags and tatters. One reason for the paucity of genuine historical material needs to be specially emphasized. Nine-tenths of all Egyptian excavations have been conducted on the high desert, where the ancient people established their 'houses of eternity' and where the dry sand preserves even the most perishable objects. To this circumstance is due the overwhelmingly funerary character of most of the finds. The habitations of the living, purposely constructed of less durable materials, were located mainly in the midst of the cultivation. The towns and villages existing there today are built on the debris of former ages. As the mud-brick houses fell into decay they were replaced by others on top of them, the level

[1] Above, p. 39, n. 2. [2] Above, p. 44, n. 1.

of the ground rising ever higher out of range of the inundation. Hence the designations Kôm and Tell, both of them Arabic words signifying 'mound', which enter so often into the composition of present-day Egyptian place-names. It is awkward to dig among modern hovels and unprofitable to do so in damp soil or where water is quickly reached. Damp is, in fact, the main cause why documents on papyrus are so rare, and is, moreover, the greatest difficulty with which excavators have had to contend. Hence work in the Delta has not as a rule compensated for the expense involved, and the disparity of our information concerning the two halves of the country is a factor which should never be lost sight of. It is true, however, that this generalization is liable to exceptions. Bubastis and Tanis are great cities of the north which have yielded important results, though mostly only of stone monuments resistant to the action of water. So too in the south the superb temples of Luxor and Karnak stand on the cultivation within a stone's throw of the Nile, but at Karnak Legrain's great find of 1905, bringing to light many hundreds of splendid inscribed figures, was rendered possible only by a process wittily described by Maspero as 'Fishing for Statues'.

It would be good if the quantitative defects of our documentation were offset by its qualitative excellence. Unhappily it is not. In order, however, to forestall the criticism that the account about to be given is unduly pessimistic, let it at once be admitted that for vividness of expression and richness in human touches the Egyptian records vastly excel their counterparts from other ancient Oriental lands. All that will here be called in question is their adequacy from the strictly historical point of view. True history is unthinkable without knowledge of personal relationships, and in Egypt itself the chronicles of Arab times offer an almost continuous spectacle of bitter animosities, of family and sectarian feuds, of violence and of bloodshed, to mention only the more sombre aspects. In the Pharaonic age it cannot have been otherwise, or at all events we must largely discount the unruffled narratives of positive exploits which are so nearly invariable. It is more by inference than by explicit statement that we become aware of the conflict between Queen Ḥashepsowe and her youthful co-regent Tuthmōsis III and that we can trace the rise of the rulers, all of them military or at least militant, who inaugurated respectively Dyns. XII, XVIII, XIX, and XXII. Our knowledge of the conspiracies which ended the life of King Ammenemēs I and at least threatened that of Ramessēs III is owed in the former case to chance references in two separate literary compositions, and in the latter to the preservation of the actual document recording the fate of the culprits. In general it may be said that anything sinister or unsuccessful in the careers of the Pharaohs is carefully suppressed, thus depriving us of just that information which gives authentic history its colour and complexion. It is a piquant fact that while individual character and fortune were thus so carefully concealed, we still possess the mummified bodies of a number of the monarchs.[1] In one case only, that of Akhenaten towards the end of Dyn. XVIII, do the inscriptions and reliefs bring us face to face with a personality markedly different from that of all his predecessors, but the much varying estimates of this religious innovator only confirm the point which it is here sought to drive home, namely the essentially one-sided and unreal picture of the rulers which emerges from the records they have left behind them.

It is curious to observe how much our supply of historical texts depends on the degree of prosperity enjoyed by Egypt from time to time. There are two great Intermediate Periods separating the Old Kingdom (Dyns. IV–VI) from the Middle (Dyns. XI, XII), and the Middle from the New (Dyns. XVIII–XX), after which follow four centuries of foreign encroachment before the Renaissance of the rulers of Sais (Dyn. XXVI) sets in. For the three troubled ages just mentioned the monuments are sparse and singularly uninformative, and it is only when fresh families of strong monarchs climbed into power that narratives of events become at all frequent. In the Old Kingdom official records of Pharaonic achievement are completely absent; the kings were gods, too lofty and too powerful to care for recitals of their doings to be communicated to their subjects; their pyramids were sufficient testimony to their greatness. The same is true, only in a lesser degree, of the mighty Dyn. XII, which has left us, as almost its sole State

[1] For the great Dêr el-Baḥri find see below, pp. 319–20.

records, only the account of the building of a temple at Hēliopolis by Senwosre I[1] and the boundary stone from the region of the Second Cataract bearing the already cited (p. 37) contemptuous characterization of the Nubian enemy. The rulers of the XVIIIth and the two following dynasties were much less intolerant of self-glorification; this is doubtless because they were sprung from petty local princes, who, as we shall see, had from the start no dislike for perpetuating on stone the outstanding events of their careers. Commemorative stelae erected in the temples by royal command begin to be frequent only in the late Dyn. XVII and end at the close of the XXth. The range of subjects is very limited, the predominating topics being the building of some favoured deity's shrine or the quelling of rebellion in a neighbouring land. A suspect feature is the stereotyped setting in which the narrative is wont to be cast: the Pharaoh summons his courtiers and asks their advice; they reply with fulsome flattery or with counsel which their master is unable to accept; then he divulges his own wise plan. The approximate truth of what is thus recorded is seldom open to doubt, but there will certainly have been some distortion through the mode of presentation. Here we find exemplified one of the most characteristic traits of the Egyptian habit of mind, the extraordinary attachment to the traditional as opposed to the actual, in fact a conservatism of expression without parallel elsewhere in the world. No other people has ever shown a greater reverence for what was by them termed 'the time of the ancestors', 'the time of the god', or 'the first occasion'. Occasionally this love of the time-honoured and the typical led to downright falsification. Every Egyptian king was represented as a conqueror alike in the ancient writings and in the reliefs on the temple walls. The model often goes back to the earliest times. The Pharaoh grasping a group of foreigners by the forelock with the other arm upraised to batter their skulls to pieces has its prototype on the famous palette of Naʿrmer (Pl. XXI) belonging to the very beginning of Dyn. I, save that there a single prisoner is depicted instead of a multitude. Such a disregard of reality was sometimes carried to absurd lengths. Who is going to believe that the eighteen-year old Tutʿankhamūn ever drove his

[1] *Studia Aegyptiaca*, i, Rome, 1938, pp. 48 ff.

chariot straight into an alien host killing a score of foes with the arrows from his bow, or again that he slaughtered unaided a whole pride of lions? Yet such are the scenes depicted on the wonderful painted box from the famous tomb. An even more deceptive situation resulted from the combination of the above-mentioned trait with a lack of scrupulosity as regards ancestral property. Not only did certain kings ruthlessly quarry stone from the buildings of their predecessors, with the result that many valuable inscriptions and scenes remained hidden behind temple walls claimed by them as their own, but also they did not hesitate to ascribe to themselves deeds of heroism or piety in reality borrowed from others. The funerary temple of King Śaḥurēʿ of Dyn. V depicts a group of Libyan chieftains brought as prisoners and specifies the number of cattle taken as booty;[1] the identical scene is found depicted in the pyramid temple of Piopi II of Dyn. VI,[2] where the Libyan princes bear precisely the same names; so, too, for a third time in a far distant Nubian temple under the Ethiopian king Taharḳa (*c.* 690 B.C.).[3] From much later times some war-pictures of Ramessēs III at Karnak have been proved to be exact copies of earlier ones due to Ramessēs II,[4] just as the great calendar of offerings at Medînet Habu was a mere replica of that in the Ramesseum.[5] Nor is this kind of borrowing confined to the monuments of royalty. At Thebes the tombs of three distinct viziers contain precisely the same speech of exhortation addressed to them on the occasion of their appointment;[6] it need hardly be said that the chance of different Pharaohs having used identical words at even relatively short intervals is remote in the extreme.

In some ways the narratives found in the tombs of the nobility and men of lesser degree who had received exceptional promotion are less conventional and more illuminating than those reflecting the monarchical activities of the sovereign. But such texts are far from common; of the Old Kingdom mastabas[7] at Gîza and Saḳ-

[1] Borchardt, *Saḥurēʿ*, ii, Pl. 1. [2] Jéquier, ii, Pls. 8, 9, 11. [3] *Kawa*, ii, Pl. 9, *b*.
[4] *ZÄS* lxv. 26 ff. [5] *Med. Habu*, iii, p. ix. [6] Davies, *Rekh-mi-rēʿ*, i, pp. 84 ff.
[7] Maṣṭaba is the Arabic word for the benches of mud seen in the courtyards of modern native houses; then employed by the workmen at the excavations for the oblong tomb superstructures of similar appearance.

ḳâra and of Dyn. XVIII rock-tombs at Thebes not one in twenty recounts any incidents of its owner's career. On the other hand, long sequences of honorific titles are almost invariable; never was there a race of mortals so enamoured of outward recognition and so given to the flaunting of decorative epithets. It is, of course, not denied that many of the titles thus found refer to actual administrative functions. Where autobiographical inscriptions occur they mostly dwell on the performance of royal commands or upon the dignities conferred by successive monarchs: a recurrent phrase of early times reads

I acted so that His Majesty should praise me on account of it.

More frequent, however, are stereotyped phrases in which the virtues of a tomb-owner are proclaimed:

I gave bread to the hungry and clothes to the naked

or else

I was beloved of my father, praised by my mother, and kind to my brethren.

At a later date such professions assume a much more elaborate form, and breathe ideals of generosity and kindliness not substantially different from those of Christianity. The great man's fellow-citizens could look to him for justice and protection at all times, witness such a common assertion as

I rescued the poor man from him who was more powerful than he.

There is no reason to doubt that in the best of cases such claims corresponded closely to the reality; in the worst they testified to principles to which at least lip-service was done. But an additional motive for recordings of this kind was the often mentioned hope that passers-by, impressed by such evident merit, might be stirred to make some offering or at least to recite the habitual prayer. By way of illustrating the general tone and character of these semi-historical texts there is here translated a particularly interesting letter written by the youthful king Piopi II and inscribed upon a tomb-wall of the prince Ḥarkhuf at Aswân:[1]

Thou hast said in this thy letter that thou hast brought a Deng of the

[1] *BAR* i, § 351.

god's dances from the land of the Horizon-dwellers like to the Deng[1] brought by the god's seal-bearer Bawerded from Pwēne in the time of Izozi; and thou hast said to My Majesty that never had the like of him been brought back by any other who has visited Yam previously. Truly I know that thou doest what thy Lord loves and praises. Truly thou passest day and night taking thought for me. . . . My Majesty will perform thy many excellent requests so as to benefit the son of thy son eternally, and so that all people shall say when they hear what My Majesty did for thee: 'Is there the like of those things which were done for the Sole Companion Ḥarkhuf, when he returned from Yam, on account of the vigilance which he showed to do what his Lord loves and praises and commands?' Come north to the Residence at once. Hurry and bring with thee this Deng. . . . If he goes down with thee into the ship, get stalwart men who shall be around him on the deck, beware lest he fall into the water. Also get stalwart men to pass the night around him in his tent, and make inspection ten times in the night. My Majesty desires to see this Deng more than all the tribute of the Mine-land and of Pwēne. . . .

Combined or alternating with such narratives of personal experience, the walls of Old Kingdom tombs sometimes hurl imprecations against possible violators or else record testamentary dispositions assuring to the tomb-owner the funerary offerings necessary for his welfare after death. But signal examples of the royal favour are also a common theme. From these we incidentally learn that it was the king alone who had power to concede the granite and the fine white limestone required for the doorways of his nobles' mastabas, and occasionally there is question of food left over from the palace which was either distributed among the courtiers or handed over to the *ka*-priests ('soul-servants') to be placed upon the offering-tables of the deceased.[2] It is significant that the funerary formula repeated in almost every inscribed tomb begins with the words 𓇓𓊵𓂞 *ḥtp dì nzw* 'A boon which the king gives',[3] the same expression being applied, though less often, to royal favours granted while the recipient was still upon earth. Evidently the power of the Pharaoh was paramount in every province of Old Kingdom life. The reverence shown to his person was abject in the extreme.

[1] Undoubtedly a real pygmy from the heart of Africa, as the determinative shows; see *JEA* xxiv. 185 ff.

[2] *JEA* xxiv. 83 ff.

[3] *Amenemhet*, pp. 79 ff.

One priestly attendant tells how by accident the king's sceptre brushed against his foot and how great was his relief when his master refrained from striking him.[1] Other high officers of state boast that they were permitted to kiss their sovereign's foot instead of the ground in front of him.[2] Apart from the tomb-inscriptions the only other stone records of the period are those in the quarries and mine-workings, graffiti on the rocks on the way thither, and lastly some royal rescripts which were set up in temples like those of Coptos and Abydos exempting their priesthoods from taxation and from arbitrary removal from their posts. Of papyri only a very few have survived, mainly accounts and scraps of letters.[3] The annals of the Palermo Stone will be discussed later. For the rest our evidence for the Old Kingdom is purely archaeological. The absolute power of the Pharaoh is unmistakable. The size of the pyramids tells its own tale of overweening ostentation. In death as in life the king liked to gather his nobles around him, and the widespread streets of mastabas surrounding the royal sepulchres bear witness to the high degree of centralization in those times.

It is not without good reason that the above brief characterization of Egyptian history has drawn for its illustration so largely upon the Old Kingdom. For this is the age in which the distinctive features of the Pharaonic civilization are seen at their purest and best. The actual formative period lay in the preceding centuries, but these are inarticulate for lack of written material. In the Middle and New Kingdoms the general aspect of such records as may strictly be called historical remains the same; unchanged is the self-satisfaction of the writers, the obvious predilection for the picturesque, the suppression of everything except isolated incidents—all these things invariably accompanied by the stringing together of titles and laudatory epithets. But now all sorts of subsidiary material come to swell the sources at the historian's disposal, stories, moralizing tractates, judicial documents, letters, and accounts. This increase in our documentation is connected with the clearly observable fact that the older papyrus manuscripts and the like are, the less the chance of their survival; the few Old Kingdom papyri which we possess are remarkably fragile. As regards the content,

[1] *Urk.* i. 232. [2] *BAR* i, § 260. [3] See below, pp. 86–7.

the new experiences of civil war and foreign invasion had supervened to damp down the serene optimism pervading all the Old Kingdom records; more will be said on this subject in Chapter VI. If it be asked where our best historical material is to be found, our answer may seem to be almost a contradiction in terms; it is to be found in Egyptian fiction, where the authors were able to depict existing conditions and to vent their feelings with a freedom impossible when the predominant intention was that of boasting. It is needless here to quote examples substantiating what has just been said; they will encounter us as we proceed.

The rest of this chapter must be devoted to the difficult topic of chronology. If in dating their inscriptions and papyri the Egyptians had employed a consecutive era like our own or like that which the Muhammedans reckon from the Flight of the Prophet from Mecca to Medîna, no serious chronological problem would have arisen. Unfortunately for us from Dyn. XI onwards each king counted only by the years of his own reign, and for the earliest dynasties there are still further complications. These preferences of theirs would have mattered but little had we been lucky enough to know the precise order of all the Pharaohs and the highest year-date in every case, since the position of each monument relatively to our own mode of dating could then have been elicited by simple addition or, as it is called, by 'dead reckoning'. Clearly it was by this process that Manetho obtained his totals, since wherever he goes into the details of a dynasty he specifies the number of years belonging to each reign. In the earlier days of Egyptology its adepts accepted the evidence of Manetho with a childlike credulity which had as its only excuse the absence or shortage of more trustworthy information, and today there are still certain scholars not wholly innocent of this erroneous mode of calculation. It is useless here to repeat what has been stated above as to the untrustworthiness of Manetho, at least in the form in which he has come down to us, but the reader may be interested to compare his figures for the whole of Egyptian history with those now generally admitted. For the first eleven dynasties he gives 2,300 years, from Dyn. XII to Dyn. XIX 2,121 years, and 1,050 years from Dyn. XX to the death of that Darius who was conquered and replaced by Alexander the

Great. This makes in all just over 5,800 years from Mēnēs down to the birth of Christ, in glaring contrast to the maximum of 3,200 years which so sane a historian as Eduard Meyer was ready to admit for the same period.

Of far greater chronological value is the Turin Canon of Kings (above, pp. 47–8), or would be if it had extended further and had been better preserved. Here not only were the years of each reign recorded, but also the number of months and days above the full years completed. It is evident that the compiler had at his disposal sources of information not only relatively free from gaps, but also on the whole accurate and reliable. The figures for Dyn. XII have been shown to be pretty well in accord with what has been ascertained from the contemporary monuments. The few totals given were obviously obtained by dead reckoning, and use of them will be made for the guesses which are to form the conclusion to this chapter. Whether the compiler's sources were identical with the 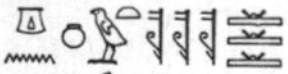 *gnwt* referred to in inscriptions of Dyn. XVIII onwards is uncertain; this word clearly indicated ancient historical records of one kind or another, and is habitually translated by scholars as 'annals'. But nothing of the kind had been recognized by Egyptologists until the beginning of the present century, when H. Schäfer, in collaboration with L. Borchardt and K. Sethe, acutely diagnosed the true nature of what has been alluded to already in passing under the name of the PALERMO STONE.

The main piece of this all-important document is named after the Sicilian capital where it is now preserved, and is an insignificant looking piece of diorite measuring no more than 17 inches in height and a foot in breadth. It is a mere fragment; other fragments, either belonging to the same monument or to one exactly resembling it in scale and arrangement, were later recovered and are for the most part in the Cairo Museum. The *recto* of the Palermo portion is reproduced here in Pl. III, which will help to make more comprehensible the description now to be given. The text of the *recto* was continued on the *verso*, and we must picture to ourselves the whole as a free-standing oblong stela erected in some temple so as to be visible alike at front and back. Both sides were divided horizontally into registers or rows, these again divided vertically into

THE PALERMO STONE, *recto*

THE STEP PYRAMID OF KING DJOŚER
Centre and left, part of the restored pyramid-enclosure

compartments each carrying its own hieroglyphic legend. The top row of the *recto* enumerated the bare names of predynastic rulers concerning whose lengths of reign and whose doings presumably nothing was known. In all the other rows each compartment was separated from that to its left, not by a straight line as in the first row, but by the symbol ʃ for 'year'. Between the rows there is always a horizontal band naming the king to whom belonged the compartments below, and his name is usually accompanied by that of his mother; and beneath each compartment is an indication of the height reached by the Nile inundation in that particular year. Thus it is plain that the monument, when complete, was a continuous year-by-year record of all the kings named on its two sides, the first (in row 2) having undoubtedly been Mēnēs, while the last, at the bottom of the *verso*, may well have been Niuśerrēʿ, the sixth king of Dyn. V, though the latest name preserved on the stone is that of the third earlier Neferirkarēʿ. The hieroglyphs within the compartments always record some outstanding event or events of the year in question—a thing or things which could serve to characterize it and by which it could be remembered. It will be observed that whereas from the second to the fifth row of the *recto* each compartment contains only a single crowded column of writing, in the sixth row the compartments are large enough to hold three or four such columns. On the *verso* the size of the compartments is even greater, with the consequence that the number of events recorded is much increased. For this there are two possible reasons: either the happenings of the more remote centuries had passed into oblivion or else they were deemed of little importance in comparison with the signal successes of recent times. However this may be, it is evident that had we been fortunate enough to possess the entire chronicle intact, its inscriptions would have taught us as much about the achievements of the past as the Pharaohs of Dyn. V wished posterity to learn. Their interests lay in religious festivals, the creation of statues of the gods, occasional victories over foreign tribes, expeditions in quest of minerals, and the building of temples and palaces. Our own concern in the present context is only with the chronological significance. How valuable this would have been to the historian if we had the stela complete can be easily realized. Assuming the ancient chronicler's knowledge to have been correct, we should have ascertained the exact sequence of all the kings from Mēnēs to Niuśerrēʿ, the exact number of years reigned by each of them, and above all a simple counting of the compartments would have put us in possession of the total of years covered by the first five dynasties. Even in its present fragmentary condition, the stone can to some extent be utilized for chronological purposes, as will be seen later. But it embraces only a small part of the entire history, just as the Turin Canon of Kings fails to reach even the great Tuthmōside period. From that point onwards we should be utterly at a loss to establish a sound chronology were it not for a wholly different method of reasoning which must now be explained.

It is curious to reflect that it is nothing but another defect which has come to our assistance. But this time the defect lies not in the imperfect condition of the historical documents at our disposal, but in an imperfection of the old Egyptian calendar itself. From time immemorial the civil year of the Egyptians had been one of 365 days, made up of three seasons[1] of four 30-day months each, to which five so-called 'epagomenal' days were added. But since the true astronomical year comprises a trifle more than 365¼ days, in the fifth year New Year's Day of the civil calendar would be a whole day ahead of whatever event marked the start of the astronomical year. In the absence of any such intercalation as we undertake in leap year, after about 120 years that calendar would be a whole month in advance of the astronomical year, and the discrepancy would grow worse and worse until the position described thus in a Ramesside papyrus would be reached:

> Winter is come in Summer, the months are reversed, the hours in confusion.

The trilingual Decree of Canopus (237 B.C.) affords good evidence that the Egyptians, with their inborn conservatism, never sought to remedy the position by intercalation, for in that decree Ptolemy III Euergetēs proclaimed the introduction of an extra

[1] Names of the seasons: Akhe 'Inundation', Prōye 'Winter', Shōmu 'Summer'. See *Eg. Gr.*, p. 203.

day of festival after the five epagomenal days in order to prevent that

the national feasts kept in winter should come to be kept in summer, the sun changing one day in every four years, and that other feasts now kept in summer should come to be kept in winter in future times, as has formerly happened.

Ptolemy's attempted reform proved abortive, and things went on as before until Augustus imposed on the Egyptians in 30 B.C. the Julian calendar of 365¼ days. Even then this 'Greek year', as it was called, was not used by the natives until after they had embraced Christianity.

It is obvious that the relation of the civil calendar and the astronomical year would right itself in $4 \times 365 = 1{,}460$ years, after any astronomical event had fallen in turn on every different day of the civil calendar. Various theories have been put forward to explain how the brilliant star Sirius (the dog star, equated by the Egyptians with their goddess Sopde, Greek equivalent Sōthis) began to be recognized as offering a sound basis for determining the most suitable date for New Year's Day. Perhaps it had been noted that the Nile began to rise with special rapidity about the same time when Sirius, after having been invisible for a prolonged period, was first again observed in the sky shortly before sunrise. At all events this latter event, described by modern astronomers as the heliacal rising of Sirius and by the Egyptians as 'the going up of Sōthis', came to be regarded as the true New Year's Day (𓄋𓆳 *wpt-rnpt*), the day with which 'first month of Inundation (the first season), day one' of the civil calendar ought always to have coincided. We have it on the authority of Censorinus that heliacal rising and civil New Year's Day did so coincide in A.D. 139, and thence it is calculated that similar coincidences had occurred in 1317 B.C. and 2773 B.C. In our hieroglyphic inscriptions two records of Sothic risings have been found, namely from an unspecified year of Tuthmōsis III (on xi. 28),[1] and from year 9 of Amenōphis I (xi. 9), and the like is determined for year 7 of Senwosre III (viii. 16) in a papyrus from the temple of El-Lâhûn in the Fayyûm. Combination of these dates

[1] For convenience we designate thus the 28th day of the eleventh month, i.e. of the third month of summer.

with those previously mentioned yields as the corresponding years 1469, 1536, and 1877 B.C. For technical reasons there are slight differences of opinion among scholars as to the exact figures, the most recent alternative given for the last of them being 1872 B.C. Otherwise there seems to be unanimity.

No attempt can here be made to describe the ways in which Egyptologists have set about determining the dates of Pharaohs subsequent to Dyn. XVIII, that to which both Amenōphis I and Tuthmōsis III belong. Suffice it to say that for most of those rulers agreement has been reached within fairly narrow limits. For the last thousand years there have been found occasional synchronisms with events in other Near Eastern lands, so that in connexion with them the researches of scholars in several different fields have to be taken into account. As regards the Second Intermediate Period, the dark age intervening between Dyns. XII and XVIII, for a host of different reasons scholars will now allow little more than a couple of centuries. Here, however, a formidable difficulty has always been felt, since the Turin Canon enumerates at this point well over a hundred kings, a very large number to crowd into a space of 200 years. However, the figure given for most of the reigns seldom exceeds three years, and since there is no trace of any total in the columns recording these, no insuperable objection stands in the way of the hypothesis that many of these kings were contemporary with one another and ruling in different parts of the country. The alternative is to throw back the Dyn. XII Sothic date an entire 1,460 years. This was the solution long advocated by Sir Flinders Petrie, but the dearth of monuments and various archaeological considerations militate strongly against this view, and it is obviously best to accept 1872 B.C. as the earliest relatively certain fixed date in Egyptian history.

Nevertheless, legitimate curiosity will not be satisfied without some attempt to estimate the probable date of Mēnēs. The arguments to be drawn from the Palermo Stone are too complicated for more than the briefest of statements. The evidence of the bottom registers of the *verso* makes it likely that the breadth of the original monument was about nine times that of the fragment still extant in the Palermo Museum, and when this conclusion is utilized for calculating the number of years comprised in registers 2–5 of the *recto*, that is to say the part occupied by the first two dynasties, that number works out at about 450 years. Students cannot be too often warned how precarious such calculations must necessarily be. We clutch at a straw, likewise, when we assume that the Turin Canon is to be implicitly trusted. On the other hand, its evidential value has often been under-estimated, for the sober figures which it offers should inspire confidence rather than the reverse, as we shall now attempt to show. The restoration of the broken total at the end of Dyn. VI has been disputed, but undoubtedly gave 955 years as the sum of years from Mēnēs down to that point in Pharaonic history. Then followed eighteen insignificant rulers of whom Achthōēs of Hēracleopolis (Dyn. IX) was the chief; their names are mostly lost, as well as the total of their reigns; here we may fairly choose between Ed. Meyer's estimate of 200 years and a lower one of, say, 100 years. Next comes Dyn. XI with six kings for whose last four reigns 49, 8, 51, and 12 years are preserved, making 120 years in all; since the kingship of the first two was certainly of short duration we must accept the recorded total of 143 years for the entire dynasty; there is a slight palaeographical difficulty, but this is disposed of by the above argument. As regards Dyn. XII we have already accepted 1872 B.C. for Senwosre III's seventh year, and indisputable monumental evidence for the interval fixes the accession of Ammenemēs I, the founder of the dynasty, to 1991 B.C. or thereabouts. Adding these figures, we obtain 1991 + 143 + 100 (or 200) + 955 = 3189 (or 3289) B.C. for Mēnēs and the beginning of Dyn. I, a date approximating closely to the 3197 B.C. finally admitted by Meyer.

Such doubt as subsists with regard to this calculation obviously centres in the Turin Canon's total of 955 years for Dyns. I–VI, making desirable a rather closer scrutiny. The 1,497 years given by Africanus can be rejected without further ado, the superior authority of the Ramesside papyrus being incontestable. For the Pharaohs of Dyns. I–VI there are 51 places occupied now or formerly, yielding an average of 18½ years for each reign. For Dyns. I and II excavations have disclosed the names of about 17 rulers, while the Canon has 18, the Abydos list 15, and Manetho again 17; if, as has been explained above, the Palermo Stone allotted 450 years to these dynasties, the average reign would be about 27 years, a rather high, but not impossible, figure. Of the 21 kings recorded by the Turin fragments for Dyns. III–V, the names of only 8 are preserved, but the lengths of reign are intact except in 4 lost instances and 2 more where what has been read as 10 may be either 20 or 30; the sum of the remaining 15 is 208 years or about 14 years apiece, but we are somewhat disconcerted at finding only 19 years allotted to Djośer, the builder of the Step Pyramid with its vast temple area, and only 23 years to Cheops who raised the greatest pyramid of all. Lastly, in Dyn. VI the nonagenarian Piopi II was followed by eight ephemeral rulers of whom the last four count only 5½ years between them; here the short reigns and the long one balance one another, making the preserved total of 181 years quite plausible for the 14 kings in question. The foregoing analysis will have been justified if it has demonstrated the inherent self-consistency and rationality of the Canon, at least for the period here under consideration. Caution demands, however, that we should not place unquestioning faith in a single papyrus from an uncritical age, and it is not surprising that many scholars should have expressed their scepticism. For our part we find it difficult to accept for the beginning of Dyn. I so low a date as 2850 B.C., that proposed by the late A. Scharff on the basis of the equally uncertain chronology of Babylonia. Our own preference is to take 3100 B.C. as the most probable date, and to allow a margin of 150 years in either direction as a safeguard; but perhaps even that precaution will some day prove to have been insufficient.

SELECT BIBLIOGRAPHY

Histories of Pharaonic Egypt: in English, J. H. Breasted, *A History of Egypt*, New York, 1905; abridged edition, London, 1911, admirable, though needing to be brought up to date; W. M. Flinders Petrie, *A History of Egypt*, vols. i, ii, iii, revised editions, London, 1924–5, especially valuable for the lists of monuments; vols. iv, v, vi deal with Ptolemaic, Roman, and Arab times; H. R. Hall, *The Ancient History of the Near East*, 7th ed., London, 1927, a work of great erudition covering a very wide field; chapters by the same author, by J. H. Breasted, and by T. Eric Peet in *Cambridge Ancient History*, vols. i, ii, iii, Cambridge, 1923–5; in French, E. Drioton and J. Vandier, *L'Égypte* (in the series Clio) 3rd ed., Paris, 1952, with admirable notes and discussions of debated points; A. Moret, *Histoire de l'Orient* (in *Histoire générale*, edited by G. Glotz) vols. i, ii, Paris, 1936; in German, Ed. Meyer, *Geschichte des Altertums*, vols. i (3rd ed.), ii (2nd ed.), Stuttgart, 1913, 1928, of fundamental importance; A. Scharff and A. Moortgat, *Ägypten und Vorderasien im Altertum*, Munich, 1950.

The king-lists: the contents of these are given fairly fully in the Appendix to the present work; the Abydos and Saḳḳâra lists, hieroglyphic text, Ed. Meyer, *Ägyptische Chronologie*, in *Abhandlungen* of Berlin Academy, 1904, Pl. 1; the Karnak list, K. Sethe, *Urkunden des ägyptischen Altertums*, Leipzig, iv, pp. 608–10; the Turin fragments: Alan H. Gardiner, *The Royal Canon of Turin*, Oxford, 1959; G. Farina, *Il Papiro dei Re*, Rome, 1938, is useful only for the photographic plates; Manetho: W. G. Waddell, *Manetho*, in the Loeb series, London, 1940. Comprehensive account for all periods, H. Gauthier, *Le livre des rois d'Égypte*, 5 vols., Cairo, 1907–17; index, *Bull. Inst. fr.* xv. 1–138; additions, *Rec. trav.* xl. 177–204.

Chronology: Ed. Meyer, *Ägyptische Chronologie*, see above; also *Die ältere Chronologie Babyloniens, Assyriens und Ägyptens*, Stuttgart, 1925; L. Borchardt, *Die Mittel zur zeitlichen Festlegung von Punkten der ägyptischen Geschichte*, Cairo, 1935; R. A. Parker, *The Calendars of Ancient Egypt*, Chicago, 1950; also *Rev. d'Ég.* xi. 85–107.

The Palermo Stone: H. Schäfer, *Ein Bruchstück altägyptischer Annalen* in *Abhandlungen* of Berlin Academy, 1902; text combined with that of the Cairo fragments, Sethe, *Urkunden* i. 235–49.

Historical texts, translations, and commentaries: J. H. Breasted, *Ancient Records of Egypt*, 5 vols., Chicago, 1906–7, indispensable for all serious students, though now partly out of date; excellent recent translations by J. A. Wilson in J. B. Pritchard, *Ancient Near Eastern Texts relating to the Old Testament*, Princeton, 1950. The original hieroglyphic texts are conveniently assembled in G. Steindorff's *Urkunden des ägyptischen Altertums*, vol. i: Old Kingdom edited by K. Sethe; vol. iii: Ethiopic period, by H. Schäfer; vol. iv: Dyn. XVIII by K. Sethe continued by W. Helck; this work is quoted as *Urk.* with number in the footnotes of the present book; texts of Dyn. XI edited by J. J. Clère and J. Vandier in *Bibliotheca Aegyptiaca X*, Brussels, 1948.

EXCURSUS

REGNAL YEARS AND METHOD OF DATING[1]

JUST half a century ago Kurt Sethe noticed that the group for 'year' in numbering the years of a Pharaoh's reign did not, as formerly supposed,

[1] See further *JEA* xxxi. 11–28.

employ the sign 𓇳 for 'sun' which was the usual determinative of words signifying time, but employed another sign 𓊗 which read *zp* (Coptic ⲥⲟⲡ) and was originally an independent word meaning 'occasion' or the like. The further study of inscriptions and especially of the Palermo Stone threw unexpected light on this expression for 'regnal year'.[1] Ivory tablets of Dyn. I revealed that in the beginning the years of a reign were not numbered, but were remembered, as in Babylonia, by some outstanding event that had occurred in them. By the middle of Dyn. II such an event was the counting of all the cattle of Egypt, and since this administrative measure took place in alternate years a number had to be used to indicate which particular count was to be understood in any given year. Thus under King Ninūtjer the eighth year of the reign was expressed on the Palermo Stone by the words 'Time (*zp*) 4 of the count'. Inscriptions of Dyns. IV–VI rendered the sense of such a dating in less laconic fashion. For example, under Neferirkarēʿ of Dyn. V a stela is headed by the words 'Year of time 14 of the count of all oxen and small animals', while in the reign of King Izozi towards the end of the same dynasty we find the date 'Year after time 4 of the count', &c., these datings obviously referring to the twenty-eighth and the ninth years of those respective reigns. Before long even the word 'count' was occasionally omitted, so that all that was now written was 'Year time *n*', and when this stage was reached nothing but the presence of contemporary examples using the words 'Year after' could prove that the count of cattle had not ceased to be biennial. Examples with 'after' occur until late in the reign of Piopi II, one of the last kings of Dyn. VI, and it must consequently be assumed that throughout the Old Kingdom whenever 'Year time 24' or the like is written, this denotes the forty-eighth year of the reign. From Dyn. XI onwards, however, it is quite certain that 𓆳𓏏𓊗 means no more than 'regnal year', and that the figure that follows names the actual year of the reign; if by this time there was still made any count of the cattle it must have become annual.

In this connexion the calendrical aspect of the king's accession is of importance. For the greater part of Egyptian history every regnal year started on New Year's Day, i.e. the first day of the first month of the Inundation season (above, p. 65). Since, however, the predecessor may have lived on for several months and days after the beginning of his last year, the first year of the successor may have consisted only of what remained over from the predecessor. Suppose, for example, that

[1] K. Sethe, *Beiträge zur ältesten Geschichte Ägyptens*, pp. 60–100, in *Untersuchungen zur Geschichte und Altertumskunde Ägyptens*, iii, Leipzig, 1905.

a Pharaoh died on the twenty-fifth day of the fourth month of summer in his thirty-second year, his son's first year will have embraced only the five days until the end of that month, *plus* the five epagomenal days, i.e. ten days in all. Another way of stating this position is to say that for the purposes of his dating each king annexed to himself all that there was of his predecessor's last year, and that for chronological purposes the king whom we have presupposed must be counted as having reigned thirty-one years. However, in the great Tuthmōside and Ramesside periods (Dyns. XVIII–XX) a change was made, each king dating his regnal year from the actual calendar date of his accession. The consequence of this innovation was remarkable: if, for example, an accession fell on iii. 25, then in the reign in question 'year 6, third month of Inundation, day 23' would fall 361 days later than 'year 6, third month of Inundation, day 27'. This paradoxical state of affairs could not fail to be awkward for a scribe seeking to place in proper sequence a series of dated documents, and is equally awkward for the modern historian attempting to reconstruct the events of a given year. It is, accordingly, desirable to determine the exact accession days of each separate New Kingdom king. Some time before the Saite period (Dyn. XXVI) the old method had been reverted to, so that once again regnal year and civil year were brought into harmony with one another.

BOOK II

FROM THE PYRAMID-BUILDERS TO ALEXANDER

V

THE OLD KINGDOM

THE generalities of the last chapter might well leave the novice's mind in a state of confusion were they not quickly followed by a more orderly account of the course of events. It will be necessary, however, to postpone until later any treatment of the Predynastic Period and the first two dynasties, since those remote ages raise problems too debatable for discussion at the present juncture. A beginning is here, therefore, made with the THIRD DYNASTY, which with the next three dynasties constitutes the Old Kingdom, characterized by the grand line of pyramids running along the western desert from near the level of modern Cairo. The first king of Dyn. III was the monarch whom later generations knew by the name of Djośer, and whose importance as the founder of a new epoch is marked in the Turin Canon by the exceptional use of red ink. Djośer's outstanding achievement was the Step Pyramid at Saḳḳâra overlooking the great city of Memphis. This is a massive structure rising in six unequal stages to a height of 204 feet (Pl. IV). Egypt has no more remarkable spectacle to offer than the comparatively recently excavated and restored complex of buildings of which that earliest of the pyramids forms the centre. The credit for this is, however, probably due less to Djośer himself than to his famous architect Imḥōtep (Gk. Imouthēs), whose later reputation as writer and healer ultimately led to his deification and identification with the Greek demigod Asclēpios. It is not without reason that Manetho ascribes to Imouthēs the invention of building in stone, since Djośer's great funerary monument was in fact the first to be constructed wholly in that material. The royal tombs of the previous dynasties had been mastabas of brick, with little employment of granite and limestone except for flooring and the like. The Step Pyramid too was originally conceived of as a mastaba, though square and not oblong, but later obtained its present unique appearance by successive changes of plan. Investigation of the maze of underground galleries revealed a few walls lined with blue faience tiles to imitate matting, and elsewhere thousands of splendidly shaped vases and dishes of alabaster, breccia, schist, and other fine stones were found strewn about. Some low reliefs depict the king in ceremonial poses, and their exquisite delicacy shows that the sculptors of the time had mastered this technique no less well than that of the noble seated statue of Djośer that was also among the finds. The vast area outside brought to light edifices of the most unexpected types. Apart from the temple chambers on the north side which were needed for the daily service of offerings and other ceremonial, as well as a row of shrines apparently for the celebration of the Sed-festival or royal Jubilee, various imposing structures were uncovered of which the purpose is unknown or only guessed. These everywhere employed small blocks of limestone contrasting markedly with the cyclopean masonry favoured by the next dynasty. Evidently the brick buildings of the foregoing age still largely influenced the architect's mind, the possibilities of stonework being as yet only dimly perceived. Particularly strange are the half-open stone doors copied from earlier ones of wood, and here for the first time are seen fluted or ribbed columns, some of them with pendent leaves apparently copied from a now extinct plant;[1] these columns are, however, still engaged in the adjacent walls as if lacking confidence in their own strength as supports. The entire site is enclosed within a magnificent panelled and bastioned wall of finest limestone no less than a third of a mile long from north to south and about half that length from east to west.

[1] *JEA* xxxv. 123 ff.

Passing over a mysterious building at the south-west corner of the enclosure the substructure of which looks for all the world like a second tomb of Djośer himself, only on a smaller scale, we now turn to the sepulchres of the other kings of Dyn. III. Much excitement has been caused by Zakaria Goneim's discovery since 1951 of a second very similar pyramid a little farther to the south-west. Here again there is a huge enclosure flanked by a stately wall of limestone displaying much the same features, but constructed with an eye to economy that proclaims it a copy of slightly later date. The same conclusion is suggested not only by the choice of a somewhat less advantageous site and the use of larger masonry, but also by the fact that unlike the Step Pyramid, the result of many hesitations and changes, Goneim's pyramid was obviously designed as such from the start. The excavation is still incomplete, and it remains to be seen whether after the disappointment of an empty sarcophagus any substantial part of a royal equipment will ultimately emerge. There are at least clear indications that the monument was not abandoned unused, and the sealings on some clay stoppers revealed the king who had been the owner to have borne the name 'the Horus Śekhemkhe'. This has been shown by Hayes to be the name to be read on a relief in the Wâdy Maghâra (Sinai) which had previously been attributed to Semempses of Dyn. I. It is a strong corroboration of his view that the relief in question is now seen to have been one of a group of records of expeditions in quest of turquoise all belonging to Dyn. III. Not only was Djośer represented in this group, but also a Pharaoh named Zanakht closely associated with Djośer at Bêt Khallâf in Upper Egypt, where the two kings appear to have possessed large brick mastabas (cenotaphs?) side by side.[1] The pyramid of Zanakht, if ever he had one, is unknown, and Lauer has suggested that he died young and that the mastaba out of which the Step Pyramid grew was originally meant for him. Yet another pyramid of what we are now entitled to call the Dyn. III type was discovered by Barsanti in 1900 at Zâwiyet el-ʿAryân a few miles south of Gîza, and is known as the Layer Pyramid.[2] This monument, so badly ruined that its nature has been seriously called in question, is attributed to an otherwise

[1] PM v. 37. [2] PM iii. 69, 70.

almost unknown Pharaoh, whose name Khaʿba was found on stone vessels in the vicinity. The last and the latest of the pyramids that can be placed in the same category is situated many miles south of Saḳḳâra at Meidûm, not far from the entrance to the Fayyûm. Stripped as this now is of all its outer coating it presents the appearance of a huge tower with sloping sides and two high steps near the top. Graffiti in the small and simple temple at its base show that in Dyn. XVIII it was believed to belong to Śnofru, the first king of Dyn. IV, but for reasons to be given later a different view is held by some.

If Dyn. III be taken as beginning with Djośer, it will have comprised only four, or at most five, rulers covering, according to the Turin Canon, a span of no more than fifty-five years. The nineteen years allotted to Djośer seem an absurdly short time for the completion of so stupendous a monument as his. The twenty-nine years given by Manetho might be accepted the more readily were it not that his Dyn. III counts nine kings, all of them except Tosorthros (Djośer) with unidentifiable names and having 214 years as the total of their reigns. The Abydos and Saḳḳâra king-lists support the Turin Canon's figure of four rulers, but there are disturbing discrepancies in the names that they give. In particular there is a doubt about the position of Nebkarēʿ,[1] whom the Saḳḳâra list places after Djośer's similarly named successor Djośer-teti, while the Abydos list substitutes the otherwise unknown Sedjes and Neferkarēʿ. The Turin Canon and the Saḳḳâra list agree in making Ḥuny the immediate predecessor of Śnofru, and this is confirmed by a well-known literary text.[2] A fact that may at first perplex the student is the absence from the king-lists of the Śekhemkhe, Khaʿba, and Zanakht mentioned above as the names of Dyn. III kings. The reason is that in their time preference was still given to the ancient habit of referring to kings by their Horus-names (above, p. 52) instead of by the Nomen, which occupied a less prominent position until the reign of Śnofru, and which was thenceforward enclosed in a cartouche. It is thus more than probable that the identity of the three kings in question is concealed in the cartouches of the king-lists. This is known to be the case with Djośer, who in the Step Pyramid

[1] Discussion, Vandier, p. 200.

[2] *JEA* xxxii, Pl. 14, l. 7.

and at Bêt Khallâf is always described as 'the Horus Netjrikhe'. The name Djośer is first recorded on an only slightly later ivory plaque where it appears as the king's *nebty*-name,[1] but definite proof of the identity of Netjrikhe with the Djośer of the hieroglyphs and the Tosorthros of Manetho is found no earlier than in a long rock-inscription of Ptolemaic date on the island of Sehêl in the First Cataract.[2] This inscription relates that King Netjrikhe Djośer, being in deep sorrow because of a seven-year famine that had afflicted the land, sought counsel from the wise Imḥōtep. Through him he learned that the Nile inundation was under the control of the ram-headed god Chnūm of Elephantinē, whom Djośer consequently appeased by the gift of the large tract of Lower Nubian country known in Greek times as the Dōdekaschoenos. The degree of historicity to be attributed to the contents of this late effusion has been much debated, but it seems improbable that this extensive stretch of land was at the disposal of the Pharaoh at so early a date.

Of contemporary remains of Dyn. III there remains nothing more to record save some blocks of a temple built by Djośer at Hēliopolis,[3] so that we may now pass to the period which marked the apogee of Egyptian history. If its five great pyramids were all that the FOURTH DYNASTY had to show by way of accomplishment, these would still have to be viewed as a manifestation of purposeful power and technical genius unsurpassed in any age or clime. The excavations of the last sixty years have brought about an important modification in our conception of a pyramid. So far from this being merely a self-sufficient geometrically shaped tumulus of masonry raised above a royal burial, or, to define it more exactly, a gigantic tomb having a square base and four equal triangular sides meeting at the apex, it now appears rather as the culminating point of a vast funerary area comprising, apart from the pyramid itself, three distinct parts.[4] First, near the desert edge and overlooking the cultivation so as to be accessible by boat in the Inundation season, there was regularly a Valley Chapel of modest,

[1] M. Z. Goneim, *Horus Sekhkem-khet,* Cairo, 1957, Pl. 65, *b.*

[2] P. Barguet, *La Stèle de la famine à Séhel,* Cairo, 1954.

[3] W. Stevenson Smith, *A History of Egyptian Sculpture and Painting in the Old Kingdom,* Boston, 1946, Figs. 48–53.

[4] See Pl. VII.

though none the less stately, proportions. Thence a walled-in Causeway often exceeding a quarter of a mile in length led upwards to the Funerary Temple proper, this abutting directly on to the east side of the pyramid, where a 'false door' or stela recessed so as to imitate a doorway enabled the deceased monarch to emerge in order to partake of the lavish fare from the many estates attached to the funerary foundation. The walls of all three elements were apt to be adorned with reliefs and inscriptions illustrating the various activities of the estates, the achievements of the Pharaoh, and the daily and festival ritual celebrated in his honour. Smaller pyramids close to his own were the burial-places of his wives and daughters. The pyramid shape was definitely the prerogative of royalty, both in size and in outward aspect contrasting vividly with the flat-topped mastabas of the related princes, courtiers, and officials which clustered around, and were apt to be laid out in orderly streets like those of a well-planned town. No visual symbol could have better conveyed the awe-inspiring relationship between an all-powerful monarch habitually described as 𓊹𓉻 *nṯr ꜥꜣ* 'the great god' or 𓊹𓄤 *nṯr nfr* 'the goodly god' and those who were at once his servants and his worshippers. A feature that has come into increasing prominence of late is the presence on several sides of the pyramid of a full-sized wooden boat lying within a special roofed-over trench of its own; examples of such boats have now been found as early as Dyn. I,[1] and they have often been supposed to enable the king to travel across the sky in the train of the sun-god, but since they are found facing towards all four points of the compass, it is probable that they were intended simply to enable the pyramid-owner to voyage wherever he desired, even as he did while living upon earth.[2]

Manetho's Dyn. IV starts with a king whose name is corruptly given as Sōris. By this must be meant Śnofru, already referred to as the successor of Ḥuny. Since his wife, of whom more hereafter, bore the title 'Daughter of the God' it has been supposed that Ḥuny was her father and that Śnofru owed his throne to this connexion. However that may be, the importance of what has survived of his activities, as well as the fact of his later deification at the turquoise

[1] Emery, *GT* iii, p. 42 and Pl. 44. [2] *JEA* xli. 75 ff.

mines of Sinai, makes it natural to think of him as the initiator of a new era. By a lucky chance the Palermo Stone together with the large Cairo fragment has preserved records of six of his twenty-four or more years of reign; besides the building of many ships and the making of doors and statues for his palace there are recalled a campaign against a Nubian land whence he is asserted to have brought back 7,000 captives and 200,000 head of cattle, and another campaign against the Tjeḥnyu Libyans which yielded very substantial, although smaller, booty. Even more interesting is the already mentioned arrival, doubtless from Byblos at the foot of the Lebanon, of forty vessels laden with cedar-wood. Any other achievements of the kind that there may have been would, however, doubtless pale against the mighty memorials of himself still to be seen at Dahshûr, 4 miles south of Saḳḳâra. It cannot but seem extraordinary that one and the same king should have built for himself two pyramids of vast dimensions at no great distance from one another, but the fact is vouched for by a decree of the time of Piopi I exempting their personnel from certain services to which less fortunate subjects of the Pharaoh were liable. The stela bearing this decree[1] was found in what may well have been the Valley Chapel of the Northern Stone Pyramid of Dahshûr, which therefore almost certainly belongs to Śnofru. Recent excavations have proved that the second stone pyramid 2 miles farther south likewise belonged to him, and since it is hard to imagine that he erected three pyramids, the one at Meidûm is now tentatively ascribed to Ḥuny, though Śnofru may have been responsible for its completion. The balance of evidence, however, seems to point to the unpalatable conclusion that Śnofru did possess three pyramids. The southern of the two Dahshûr pyramids is known as the Bent or Rhomboidal Pyramid on account of the conspicuously lower angle of its upper half. Its northern neighbour displays practically the same decrease throughout its whole slope, and consequently may be the later of the two. Both exceed 310 feet in height, and internally show the further resemblance of possessing very lofty corbelled burial-chambers. The excavations by Ahmed Fakhry[2] at the Bent Pyramid have brought to light in its Valley Chapel admirable

[1] *ZÄS* xlii. 1 ff. [2] *Ann. Serv.* li. 509 ff.; lii. 563 ff.

reliefs depicting female offering-bearers personifying Śnofru's funerary estates in the various nomes of Upper Egypt, these presented in the order that subsequently became stereotyped. There had also been a Lower Egyptian series, but of this only a tiny scrap has been preserved. These scenes are of great importance as showing that already at this early date there had come into existence the broad administrative pattern which was to survive right down into Graeco-Roman times.

Śnofru left behind him the reputation of an ideally beneficent and good-humoured monarch.[1] After him the line of pyramids moved north to Gîza almost opposite Cairo, thenceforward with only a single exception to move consistently southwards. To describe the Gîza pyramids as among the Seven Wonders of the World might even seem an understatement, since the Great Pyramid[2] surpasses in bulk every building known to have been raised by the enterprise of man, its height (481 ft.) being exceeded in monuments made entirely of stone only by the tower of Ulm Cathedral. As already mentioned, the names of the creators of the three architectural giants stretching diagonally across the desert plateau at Gîza (Pl. V) are given by Herodotus as Cheops, Chephrēn, and Mycerinus respectively, and though in these forms they are far from correct, their familiarity justifies their continued use. The Great Pyramid has been described elsewhere so fully and so well that no more need here be said than that its internal arrangements exhibit two complete changes of plan, the last of which involved the construction of the marvellous Grand Gallery slanting upwards to the actual burial-place, a stately hall of granite now known as the King's Chamber. Three small pyramids at the base of the eastern side were destined for the royal builder's wives, while large mastabas in front of these were reserved for his principal sons. The funerary temple is now completely destroyed, but some blocks with sculptured reliefs are believed to have come from the causeway.[3] Little is known of the author's career apart from this material testimony to his autocratic power; his cartouche, giving the name Khufwey or more fully Khnomkhufwey, is found in various

[1] G. Posener, *Littérature et Politique*, Paris, 1956, p. 32.
[2] PM iii. 5 f.
[3] W. Stevenson Smith, op. cit., p. 157, n. 1. But see *Ann. Serv.* xlix. 111 ff.

quarries, in the tombs of his kinsfolk and his nobles, and in certain writings of later date. But among these many mentions no contemporary record can claim genuine historical value except that connected with the burial of his mother Ḥetepḥraś. In February 1925 the Harvard expedition directed by Dr. Reisner was investigating the area immediately in front of the east side of the Great Pyramid when it hit upon the carefully concealed entrance to a tomb-shaft at the bottom of which was discovered the collapsed, but entire, burial outfit of this wife of Śnofru and mother of Khufwey.[1] The reconstitution of the furniture required many years of patient effort, but the result was the acquisition by the Cairo Museum of a collection of objects unrivalled for their chaste beauty and lovely proportions. This is not the place to expatiate upon the gold-cased and inlaid bed, carrying-chair, curtain box, and other treasures of this unique find, but we need to dwell a little upon the enigma which it presents. Though the wrapped viscera of the queen were found stored away in an alabaster box of the kind already at this period sometimes used for the purpose, not a trace of her mummified body was to be seen when the lid of the sarcophagus was raised. The dark romance reconstructed by Reisner to explain so strange a circumstance must be read in his own words; all that seems appropriate to be said in the present statement of facts being that there had clearly been a reburial carried out with the utmost secrecy and in such a way as to guard against any further molestation. It must be added that the family relationships of Khufwey's wives and children have been reconstructed by Reisner and his assistant Stevenson Smith with the utmost skill and ingenuity, but are too speculative to be discussed here. Nor is there any sound criterion upon which to base a decision as to Khufwey's length of reign. This the Turin Canon states as twenty-three years, while Manetho, perhaps only guessing, accords to him no less than sixty-three.

The like may well apply to the sixty-six years which Manetho allows to Khufwey's second successor, the builder of the Second Pyramid.[2] We have seen that the name given to him by Herodotus was Chephrēn. On the strength of this Egyptologists have been generally agreed to read his cartouche as Khaʿfrēʿ, but not long ago

[1] See below, p. 106. [2] PM iii. 6 f.

Ranke produced strong reasons for inverting the two elements of the compound name and for reading it as Raʿkhaʿef.[1] If this be correct, we must suppose that the true pronunciation was later forgotten and replaced by another reflecting the written order of the two elements. Since, however, Ranke's surmise has not yet received the hall-mark of Egyptological acceptance, it is best to adhere to the time-honoured appellation Chephrēn. The magnitude of Chephrēn's achievement as a pyramid-builder has been unduly overshadowed by that of his father Khufwey, since alike in area and in height there is no great difference between their two monuments, and owing to the Second Pyramid's position on higher ground it actually appears the larger. The broken sarcophagus of polished granite still stands in its place in the burial-chamber, but the robbers left no trace of its original occupant. Substantial remains of the three constituent parts of a normal pyramid establishment are still to be seen. The outstanding feature in Chephrēn's Funerary Temple is the immense size of the limestone blocks used in its construction, larger than any elsewhere known from Ancient Egypt. Whatever sculptured reliefs there may have been here and in the Causeway have perished, save perhaps one or two fragments; neither have any been found in the Valley Chapel, where such decoration could only have detracted from the beauty of the plain red granite walls. As it still survives, this Valley Chapel, formerly miscalled the Temple of the Sphinx, is among the most awe-inspiring sights of the Gîza area. The spacious halls with their austere square pillars reflect the simple, but for that reason all the more impressive, aesthetic standards of those early times. Here too, among other statues of Chephrēn, was found that marvellous diorite figure which is surely among the greatest masterpieces of statuary that have survived from antiquity.

Immediately to the north-east is the Sphinx,[2] in the popular fancy of all ages the embodiment of unsolved mystery and recondite truth. Now that this colossal image of a human-headed lion has been completely disengaged from the surrounding sand, much of its cryptic charm has disappeared. But the riddle of its origin remains. The most probable view seems to be that it was fashioned

[1] *JAOS* lxx. 65. [2] PM iii. 8.

by Chephrēn out of the knoll of rock close to his Causeway and so conveniently inviting portrayal of himself in the combined aspect of a man and a lion. The model doubtless did not start with him, and was fated to become a commonplace not only of Egyptian architectural adornment, but also as a decorative motif throughout the entire world. The Egyptians themselves were not interested in the historical origin of this particular specimen. For them the Gîza Sphinx was a god whom they named Ḥar-em-akhe 'Horus in the horizon', in Greek Harmachis. But it is certain that it was also regarded as a likeness of the king. There is much plausibility in the late Professor Gunn's suggestion that the word *Σφίγξ* is derived from  *šsp ʿnḫ* 'living image', a phrase properly requiring the addition 'of the Lord of the Universe' or 'of (the god) Atum' that is sometimes found. It is strange that Herodotus completely ignored the Sphinx, and that Pliny[1] was the only classical author to mention it.

Concerning the events of Chephrēn's reign there is no more to be told than in the case of Cheops. The tradition preserved by Herodotus (ii. 124, 128) that both these kings were cruel and impious tyrants was perhaps only a deduction from the immense labours that they imposed upon their unfortunate subjects. The lie is given to the charge of impiety by large granite blocks from Bubastis bearing their names and evidently belonging to a temple. The reigns of the two kings were separated from one another by that of Raʿdjedef, whose tenure of the throne lasted only eight years. For some mysterious reason he selected for his pyramid a site a few miles to the north-west of Gîza, and there, at Abu Roâsh, its unfinished remains have been excavated.[2] Another short reign or even two may have intervened between Chephrēn and Mycerinus, if the figure of 18 (or 28?) years in the Turin Canon is to be assigned to the latter. To Mycerinus or Menkaurēʿ, to give his name a pronunciation in better accord with the hieroglyphic writing, belongs the Third Pyramid at Gîza,[3] a much smaller structure which would have vied with its gigantic neighbours in magnificence if the plan of coating the whole of it in red granite could have been carried out. The work was, however, left unfinished, and the use of crude brick for much of the Causeway and the

[1] *Nat. Hist.* 36. 17. [2] PM iii. 1. [3] Op. cit. iii. 7 f.

THE PYRAMIDS OF GÎZA

View from the air, looking north-east: the Third Pyramid, of Mycerinus, in the foreground; the smaller pyramids probably those of his queens; beyond the Great Pyramid maṣṭabas of the nobles

MYCERINUS AND HIS QUEEN

Slate statue in the Boston Museum

Valley Chapel bears witness to its owner's unexpected demise. There is no means of telling how this came about, nor is it possible to say what credence should be given to Herodotus's statement that Mycerinus was a pious and beneficent king, in glaring contrast to his two great predecessors. The thoroughgoing investigation of his pyramid site by Reisner and his assistants was rewarded by the discovery of much splendid statuary; of this perhaps the finest piece is the life-size slate group of Mycerinus and his queen which is among the principal treasures of the Boston Museum (Pl. VI). There was also a series of much smaller slate triads representing Mycerinus between the goddess Ḥatḥōr and one or other of the deities of the nomes; of these there may originally have been as many as forty-two, but only four have survived intact.

After Mycerinus the fortunes of the dynasty rapidly fell to pieces. His pyramid was hastily completed and equipped by Shepśeśkaf, the only other king of Dyn. IV recognized as legitimate by contemporaries and the Table of Abydos, though the Saḳḳâra king-list added three more whose names are lost and consequently cannot be checked with those given by Manetho. That something went amiss about this time is suggested by the fact that Shepśeśkaf chose South Saḳḳâra as his burial-ground and caused to be built there for himself, not a pyramid, but a tomb shaped, except for its sloping walls, like a typical sarcophagus of the period with bevelled roof and straight upstanding ends.[1] This tomb, known to natives of the district as the Maṣṭabat el-Faraʿūn, was shortly afterwards imitated at Gîza in a monument sometimes called the Unfinished or Fourth Pyramid.[2] Excavations have shown that this monument between the causeways of Chephrēn and Mycerinus belonged to a King's Mother named Khantkawes whose cult was assiduously kept up throughout Dyn. V. Controversy has arisen over the inscription upon her huge false door, Junker believing it to show that she actually arrogated to herself the title 'King of Upper and Lower Egypt', a claim made by only three other women throughout the entire course of Egyptian history. There is, however, an alternative translation which is philologically tenable, and which describes her as the mother of two kings, not only of one.[3] In any case, it seems

[1] See below, p. 106. [2] *Mitt. Kairo* iii. 123 ff. [3] *Ann. Serv.* xxxviii. 209 ff.

agreed that Khantkawes was the ancestress of Dyn. V, though that opinion is in conflict with the tradition preserved in a story of the late Middle Kingdom, according to which the first three kings of Dyn. V were the triplet sons of the wife of a simple priest of Rēʿ in the Delta town of Sakhebu.[1]

Whatever the origin of the FIFTH DYNASTY, there can be no doubt as to its changed and highly individual character. According to the tale Reddjede's eldest son was foretold to become high-priest of the sun-god Rēʿ in Ōn, the great city known to the Greeks as Hēliopolis and now merely a northern suburb of Cairo. There is neither confirmation nor likelihood that Uśerkaf, the first king of the dynasty, ever exercised that office, but certain it is that under him the Hēliopolitan priesthood began to wield an unprecedented influence. The Palermo Stone has little to record except gifts of land and offerings to the sun-god Rēʿ, to his daughter Ḥatḥōr, and to the problematic beings called *B3w 'Iwnw* 'the Souls of Ōn'. It is important to realize, however, that this intensified solar cult was not exclusive like that of Akhenaten over a thousand years later, since among other deities the goddesses of Upper and Lower Egypt were also beneficiaries. The dominant position of the sun-god is reflected in a fresh development that now befell the royal titulary. Hitherto the name of Rēʿ had appeared only in the cartouches of Raʿdjedef, Chephrēn, and Mycerinus. In Dyn. V -rēʿ became a fairly regular element, as will be seen from the enumeration of its nine kings in their well authenticated sequence: Uśerkaf, Śaḥurēʿ, Neferirkarēʿ (Kakai), Shepśeśkarēʿ (Izi?), Raʿneferef, Niuśerrēʿ (In), Menkauḥōr, Djedkarēʿ (Izozi), Uniś. The names here added in brackets were alternative personal names, likewise enclosed in a cartouche and ultimately to become the king's Nomen, while the name with -rēʿ became the Prenomen. What is still more important, the epithet *z3 Rʿ* 'Son of Rēʿ', first found quite exceptionally with two of the three Dyn. IV Pharaohs above mentioned, now began to be a frequent concomitant either inside or outside the cartouche, in the end obtaining a fixed position between the Prenomen and the Nomen. The final pattern of a royal titulary has been illustrated and explained above on p. 51.

[1] Erman, *Lit.*, p. 43.

Far more striking, however, is the evidence from a new type of monument which, so far as is known, was the original invention of Dyn. V and was discontinued after its eighth reign. No doubt these new enthusiasts for the solar cult felt unequal to honouring their chosen god with the magnificence that the Dyn. IV rulers had bestowed upon the glorification of themselves, for they removed the scene of their building activities some miles to the south of Gîza, where invidious comparison would be less practicable. A site at Abu Gurâb which had long borne the name of the Pyramid of Righa proved, when cleared by the Deutsche Orientgesellschaft under the able direction of the architect L. Borchardt (1898–1901), to have concealed a great sun-temple plausibly supposed to have been copied from the temple of Rēʿ-Atum at Hēliopolis. The general lay-out resembled that of a normal pyramid complex, with an entrance building near the valley, a causeway leading to a higher level, and at the top the counterpart of pyramid and funerary main temple. The essential difference lay in the substitution for these latter of a rather squat obelisk perched on a square base like a truncated pyramid . The obelisk recalled a very ancient stone at Hēliopolis known as 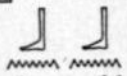 *bnbn*, etymologically perhaps 'the radiant one', which undoubtedly symbolized a ray or the rays of the sun. Six of the nine kings of Dyn. V are known to have built sun-temples of the kind, each with its own name like 'Pleasure of Rēʿ', 'Horizon of Rēʿ', 'Field of Rēʿ'. Of these temples only two have been actually located, that of Uśerkaf, apparently a poor affair in course of being excavated by Borchardt's former pupil H. Ricke, and that of Niuśerrēʿ, thoroughly investigated by Borchardt himself.[1] Here the sun-god was worshipped under the open sky, as befitted his nature. At the foot of the obelisk and its base is a great raised terrace with a large alabaster altar in its midst. North of the altar is an extensive area where oxen were slaughtered, and north of this again a row of magazines. The platform upon which the obelisk stood was approached by a long covered passage skirting the terrace on the south and adorned with exquisitely sculptured and painted scenes, some representing the seasons with the flora and fauna created by the sun-god, while others depicted the Sed-festival,

[1] See the bibliography below, p. 106.

which was a periodic renewal of the kingship when the gods of the two halves of the country assembled to do honour to the Pharaoh. Sensational must have been the moment in the ceremonies when the priests emerged from the relative darkness of the corridor into the brilliant sunshine spread abroad by their god. Serious problems are, however, raised by this strange category of monuments. That each king should have aspired to a magnificent sepulchre of his own is comprehensible, even if the modern mind cannot refrain from wondering at the over-ostentation displayed by the pyramids. But it is perplexing to find each successive ruler adding a separate sun-temple of similar dimensions in order to mark his filial relationship to the deity. The strain upon his resources must have been enormous, the more so since there is good evidence that the predecessors' foundations were not abandoned at their demise. It is not surprising that the cumulative responsibility proved too much for Izozi, in whose time such enterprises came to an end. Much careful thought has of late been devoted to this and other questions connected with the sun-temples,[1] but only with limited success through the lack of positive evidence.

Borchardt's exploration of Niuśerrēʿ's sun-temple was followed by his systematic unearthing of the Dyn. V pyramids clustered together at Abuṣîr about a mile farther to the south; but before discussing these it will be well to say something about the pyramids of three kings of the dynasty who elected to occupy sites still farther south at Saḳḳâra, close to the Step Pyramid. Uśerkaf's burial-place, unusual in several respects, was found completely ruined and used as both quarry and cemetery in Saite times. It had been furnished with splendid low reliefs, the most striking fragment being part of a fowling scene that may perhaps have served as model for similar representations in later tombs.[2] But the great prize was the head of a colossal red granite statue of the king now in the Cairo Museum; it is thought that the statue, if seated, will have exceeded 15 feet in height.[3] The two excavators of the pyramid of Djedkarēʿ Izozi, both prematurely defunct, unfortunately left no account of their work. This may well be the neighbourhood from which in 1893

[1] *Mitt. Kairo*, xiv. 104 ff.; *WZKM* liv. 222 ff.

[2] W. Stevenson Smith, op. cit., Pl. 52. [3] *Ann. Serv.* xxix. 64 ff., with Pl. 1.

PLATE VII

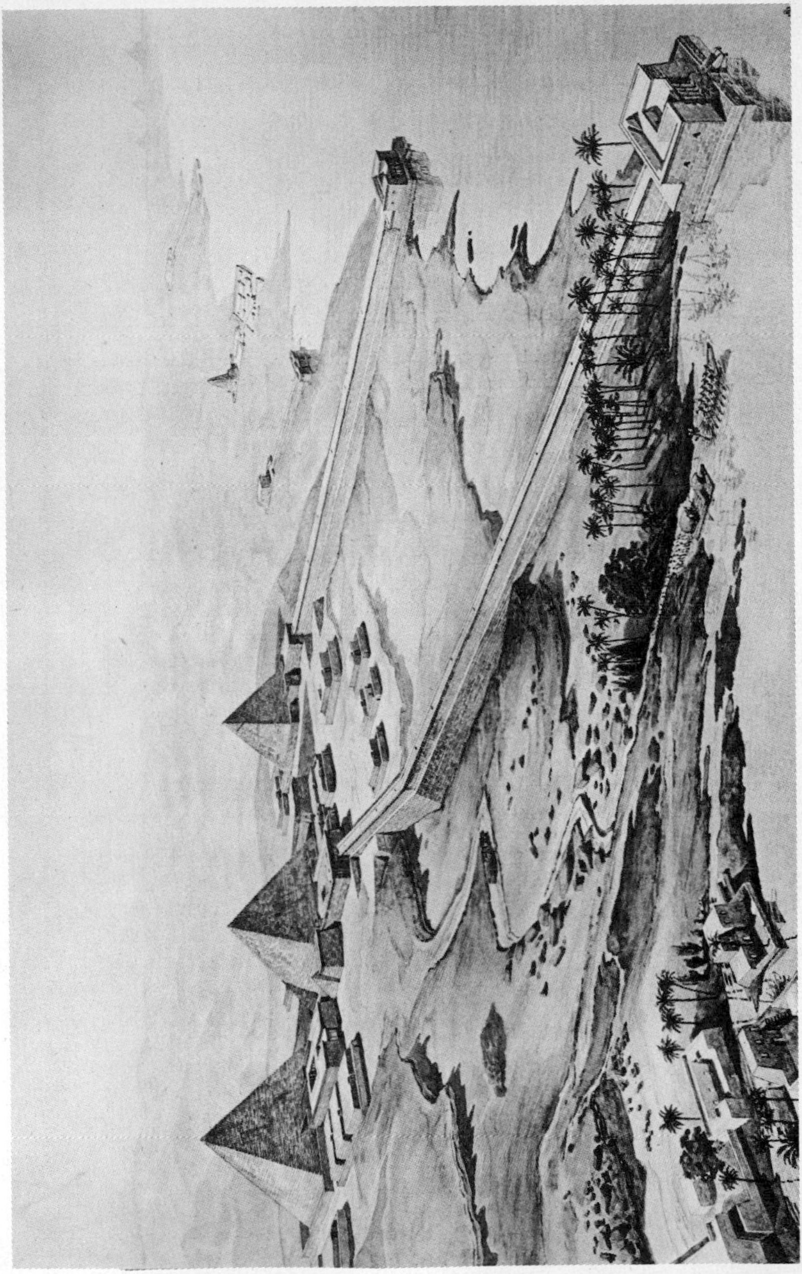

THE PYRAMIDS OF ABUṢÎR

PLATE VIII

PREPARATIONS FOR THE TOMB-OWNER'S FEAST

Limestone relief from a Dyn. V maṣṭaba. Leyden Museum

came a large number of papyrus fragments still unpublished and distributed among several museums. They are all dated in Izozi's reign, but relate to the funerary property and administration of the earlier king Neferirkarēʿ Kakai. Among the subjects are the daily payments made to the head priests or 'prophets'[1] and to the tenants of the sun-temple. Other things treated are the transfer of revenue to Kakai's pyramid estate, and the offerings made to his statues and to that of the Queen-mother Khantkawes. So rare are such documents at this period that these are of the utmost value, but intensive study will be required to decipher their difficult handwriting and to determine their exact contents. The pyramid of the last king Uniś, smaller than that of any of his predecessors, has been more fruitful in results of interest, the causeway, 730 yards long, being embellished with reliefs of the finest quality;[2] the subjects are very varied and unusual, illustrating, for example, the transport by ship from Aswân of the granite date-palm columns and architraves used in the construction of the funerary temple. There are also scenes of workmen engaged in various crafts, and strangest and least explicable of all, the emaciated figures of people evidently dying of hunger. The internal arrangements of the pyramid are likewise unusual, their main importance to Egyptologists lying in the fact that the walls of the vestibule and burial-chamber are covered with the oldest religious texts that have survived from Ancient Egypt, written in vertical columns of hieroglyphs. These texts, containing spells providing for the welfare of the king in the hereafter, are known as the Pyramid Texts, since they are found not only here but also in the pyramids of four kings of Dyn. VI and elsewhere.

To revert now to the pyramids excavated at Abuṣîr by Borchardt, they are those of Śaḥurēʿ, Neferirkarēʿ, and Niuśerrēʿ. Of these, the pyramid of Neferirkarēʿ was left unfinished and the lower half of its causeway was adapted by Niuśerrēʿ to his own purposes. In the absence of a full publication of the pyramid of Uniś, it is that of Śaḥurēʿ in which the characteristics of the funerary monuments

1 This is the name which the Greeks gave to the highest grade of Egyptian priests, in the native language called 'god's servants'; when so used it has no implication of power to foretell the future.

2 W. Stevenson Smith, *Art and Architecture*, Harmondsworth, 1958, pp. 75, 76, with p. 262, nn. 28, 29.

of Dyn. V can be best realized. In size greatly inferior to those of Cheops and Chephrēn, in beauty they are at least their equals. Massiveness and rugged simplicity here give place to elegance and artistic perfection; a development analogous to that in our own country from Norman architecture to Gothic. In Dyn. V plain rectangular pillars are superseded by columns representing papyrus stems bound together or with capitals delicately carved to imitate the leaves of the date-palm. The wealth of sculptured relief adorning all parts of the complex is amazing, in spite of the disappearance of a large portion through the depredations of later generations hungry for the fine limestone that could be used for their own buildings. The brilliance of the general appearance can be imagined from the fact that often the floors were of polished basalt, while the glittering white limestone sculptures rested on dados of red granite. A startling innovation in Śaḥurēʿ's pyramid complex was a copper drain-pipe that ran the whole length of the causeway, a distance of no less than 330 yards. The subjects of the reliefs are very varied, and if we possessed them in their entirety they would have illustrated the activities and aspirations of the king and his subjects more vividly than any possible written narrative. Among the less realistic representations there survives one showing the Pharaoh being welcomed by the god Chnūm and nursed at the breast of the vulture-goddess of Nekhen (Hieracōnpolis), and there are also seen fictitious offering-bearers personifying varying aspects of nature such as the sea and corn, or abstract notions such as joy. Strongly contrasted with such purely conceptual themes is a magnificent scene of hunting in the desert and the remains of another depicting the baiting of hippopotamuses in the river, though even here the subject may already have become conventional, and it is impossible to be sure that Śaḥurēʿ himself was endowed with these sporting proclivities. Reference has been made earlier (p. 57) to the campaign against the Libyans which resulted in so sensational a capture of booty and the submission of the foreign princes and their families. Even more attractive pictorially is a great scene of ships returning from Syria with sailors and Asiatics aboard, their arms uplifted in homage to the Pharaoh. The occasion may well have been an expedition to the Lebanon to fetch the highly prized wood of its forests; the excavations at Byblos by Montet and Dunand have yielded stone vessels bearing the names of many Old Kingdom kings, probably not excluding that of Śaḥurēʿ. It would be too much to describe Byblos as an Egyptian colony, but at least the Egyptian envoys were always welcome there and this coast-town had a temple of the goddess Ḥatḥōr identified with the native Semitic Astartē. This picture of ships reminds us that the sole references in the fragments of the Palermo Stone to any secular undertakings of the Dyn. V Pharaohs are two which record voyages to Sinai in quest of its turquoise and to Pwēne, the source of incense and various spices. Apart from the Libyan campaign above mentioned and the Asiatic war in which Weni (see below, pp. 95–6) was the commander-in-chief, all foreign ventures of the Old Kingdom appear to have been utilitarian in aim—journeys to procure to the sovereign the materials wherewith to sate his passion for building, to enhance the luxury of his Court, and to meet the requirements of the deities whom he worshipped.

The present tendency is to assign to Dyn. IV a duration of no more than 160 years and to Dyn. V no more than 140. These figures are small in view of the great works accomplished, but apparently will have to be still further reduced,[1] for there seems no reason to doubt the veracity of a courtier who claimed to have been honoured by six kings from Raʿdjedef to Śaḥurēʿ, or of a royal prince who enjoyed similar favour, but starting only with Raʿdjedef's successor Chephrēn.[2] Meanwhile, however, a striking change had come over the sources from which our knowledge of the period is drawn. The mute and uncommunicative character of the early mastabas had given place to an eagerness unparalleled in any other ancient land to depict and illustrate almost every aspect of daily life. It is not to be imagined, of course, that either the sculptors or their masters had posterity in mind. Apart from the urge to create beauty inherent in all artistic creation, here the incentive was the belief that such pictures could enable the tomb-owner to enjoy after death all the good things that had been his lot upon earth. The development must now be described in somewhat greater detail. In the early Dyn. IV the funerary rites had been performed in small brick

[1] A. Scharff, *Grundzüge der ägyptischen Vorgeschichte*, Leipzig, 1927, pp. 51 ff.

[2] *Ann. Serv.* xxv. 178 ff.

chapels leaned up against the north side of the mastaba, the sole testimony concerning the identity and aspirations of the tomb-owner being a stone stela showing him seated before an offering-table with hieroglyphic legends naming the kinds of food and drink of which he hoped to partake, the qualities of linen intended for his clothing and bedding, and the vessels and furniture needed for his household. But there are some exceptions to this reticence. At Meidûm there are tombs as early as Śnofru[1] with frescoes illustrating occupations on a great nobleman's estate, boat-making, fishing, snaring birds, ploughing, slaughtering oxen, and so forth. From about the same time are inscriptions recording the fortunes of a great Delta magnate named Metjen,[2] who informs us how, besides inheriting from his father, he bought much land, built himself a fine house with a large walled garden, and was appointed to many responsible posts. Other hieroglyphic narratives from the next generations deal with different subjects: the remuneration of 'soul-servants' for continued funerary service after the tomb-owner's death; a will for the distribution of his lands made by a son of Chephrēn;[3] grateful acknowledgement of the Pharaoh's interest in the building of a tomb.[4] Such texts can barely be described as historical, but they cast sidelights upon the civilization of those times. The point here emphasized, however, is that they are exceedingly rare. With the approach of Dyn. V such records, both pictorial and written, greatly increase in number, evidence it would seem of a growing realization that for all the Pharaoh's claims to be a divinity, he was in fact only a man not so far exalted above the heads of his nobles; the many gifts and concessions which had to be made in order to sustain the power of the ruler were already laying the foundations of a feudal state. Interior chambers began to be built within the body of the mastabas, assimilating them to the mansions of the wealthy; the famous tomb of Tjey,[5] for example, possessed two great columned halls, a fine corridor, a large store-chamber, and an impressive portico. A far greater variety of pursuits was now displayed in the reliefs, hardly any aspect of ordinary life being unrepresented; on the walls of the tombs one can accompany the

[1] PM iv. 90 ff. [2] *BAR* i, §§ 170 ff. [3] Op. cit. i, §§ 190 ff.
[4] *Ann. Serv.* li. 131 ff. [5] More familiar to the tourist under the name of Ti.

tomb-owner on his way to inspect bakers, brewers, vintners, cooks, sculptors, carpenters, goldsmiths, or can sit with him to enjoy music and dancing, or join him in a game of draughts. Little humorous details sometimes insinuate themselves into these pictures, such as a monkey ruffling the feathers of a crane or biting the leg of an attendant. And hieroglyphic legends eke out each episode with the snatches of conversation passing between the people engaged, in flat contradiction of the popular preconception which credits the Ancient Egyptians with no thoughts beyond death and mummification. The Egyptologist knows that never was there a race more fond of life, more light-hearted, or more gay. A lovable trait is the evident equality of the sexes: both in the reliefs and in the statues the wife is seen clasping her husband round the waist, and the little daughter is represented with the same tenderness as the little son.

After Uniś the Turin Canon inserted a total of all the years from the accession of Mēnēs down to that reign; the number is unfortunately lost, but the entry serves a useful purpose by showing that a great period was thought of as terminating here. Manetho is in agreement, starting his SIXTH DYNASTY of six Memphites at the same point, and naming as its first king an Othoēs who is obviously the Teti given as the successor of Uniś in the Abydos and Saḳḳâra king-lists. Manetho had curiously and doubtless inaccurately designated Elephantinē as Dyn. V's place of origin; he was correct, however, in describing the next dynasty as Memphite, since the pyramids of all its rulers are situated at Saḳḳâra within a few miles of one another; indeed it was the pyramid of its third king Piopi I, called 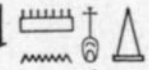 *Mn-nfr* '(Piopi is) established and goodly', that gave its name to the great city of Memphis in the midst of the Valley just opposite Saḳḳâra. It is unknown why Teti should have been regarded as the inaugurator of a new dynasty, but it is about this time that we first become fully aware of the momentous change that had come about in the character of the Egyptian realm. Past and gone was the extreme centralization of the previous periods, when it was every nobleman's highest ambition to be accorded a tomb beneath the shadow of the sovereign's pyramid. The generosity of the Pharaoh towards his favourites was now finding an unwelcome reward; not only was his own wealth becoming depleted, but that of his nobles was so greatly increased that they could almost vie with him in power and importance. Fine cemeteries had sprung up everywhere in the neighbourhood of the larger provincial towns, where not only the local princes but also the most prominent of their servants sought to invest their mastabas and rock-tombs with something of the splendour that had been achieved at the royal capital. Here we need only mention the tombs that have been excavated and copied at such sites as Zâwiyet el-Amwât, Mêr, Dêr el-Gebrâwi, Akhmîm, Dendera, Edfu, and Aswân;[1] even one or two at Thebes, though the pre-eminence of that place still lay very far ahead. Although thus a provincial aristocracy had already firmly taken root, it must not be imagined that the Pharaohs of Dyn. VI were by any means weaklings. On the contrary they included among their number some of the greatest names in all Egyptian history if one may judge by the ubiquity of their cartouches and the echoes of their energy and enterprise that have come down to us. It is true that their monuments cannot vie artistically with the achievements of previous generations, and have little to show in the way of originality. The workmanship of their pyramids is decidedly shoddy, so that most of them have collapsed into shapeless rubbish heaps. Gone also was the religious fervour which concentrated almost all the efforts of Dyn. V upon honouring the sun-god; instead of this, the Pyramid Texts which lined the walls of their burial chambers had the sole aim of promoting the welfare of the god Osiris, with whom, as we shall see later, the deceased king was actually identified. It may be objected, and perhaps not without some justice, that a development such as is here described must of necessity have been gradual, and that our judgement is apt to be warped by the paucity of the official records of Dyn. V in comparison with those of Dyn. VI; for instance, we possess from Abydos an isolated charter of immunity granted by Neferirkarēʿ to the priesthood of that place similar to many of later date.[2] Nevertheless, the general trend is unmistakable, though hand in hand with the appointment of prominent provincials to be great chieftains in their nomes, for example Ibi in the nome of Viper-mountain,[3] the Pharaoh will have wished to participate in the building

[1] See PM iv, v, under these headings. [2] PM v. 40. [3] *BAR* i, § 377.

of the local temples and the freeing of their dependants from irksome duties. Thus, to quote only a few examples, charters were given by Teti and Piopi II at Abydos[1] and Coptos respectively;[2] at Bubastis are the remains of a sanctuary erected by Piopi I,[3] who also undertook important building in Hēliopolis,[4] that city's god accordingly not being ignored, even if he was a little out of fashion. In Ptolemaic times the name of the same monarch was remembered in the temple of Dendera as that of its founder.[5] At Hieracōnpolis two copper statues of his were discovered, the finest specimens of metalwork that have survived from the Old Kingdom.[6] Even if under Dyn. VI the provinces came into ever greater prominence, there will have remained dignitaries enough whose duties dictated the acquisition of a tomb near the capital. The excavations by Loret, Quibell, and Firth around the pyramid of Teti have revealed many such.[7] His vizier Mereruka, who was also his son-in-law, was the owner of one of the finest of all mastabas.[8] A high-priest of Memphis named Śabu boasted of the protection which he afforded His Majesty when he went aboard his bark on ceremonial occasions,[9] and a second high-priest of the same name expresses his pride at his appointment.[10] Another official tells how he was sent to Ṭura to fetch limestone for some building operations.[11] The existence of two of Teti's spouses is recalled by the great Memphite mastaba of Khuye and the neighbouring pyramid of Ipwe;[12] the latter queen was the mother of Piopi I, who took steps to secure the unhindered administration of a cenotaph of hers at Coptos.[13] Of Teti's own doings nothing is known, and it is impossible to know whether there is any truth in Manetho's report that he was murdered by his bodyguard.

The reign of his successor Uśerkarēʿ was evidently ephemeral, since he is known only from the Abydos king-list and two cylinder-seals. The impression of greatness which the name of Meryrēʿ Piopi I evokes rests upon no imposing monument that has survived, but rather upon the superabundance and wide diffusion of the

[1] PM v. 40. [2] Op. cit. v. 126 f. [3] See below, p. 106. [4] *JEA* xxiv. 1 ff.
[5] Gauthier, *LR* i. 160. [6] PM v. 193. [7] Op. cit. iii. 131 ff.
[8] Op. cit. iii. 140 ff. [9] B*AR* i, § 286, but differently interpreted.
[10] Op. cit. i. § 288. [11] Op. cit. i. § 290. [12] PM iii. 84, 129. [13] Op. cit. v. 126.

inscriptions mentioning him. Further indications are the facts that, as already mentioned, Memphis was called after his pyramid and that he was remembered with veneration many centuries later. His reign was apparently a long one, Manetho, whose figures for this dynasty seem more trustworthy than elsewhere, crediting him with fifty-three years; an expedition to the alabaster quarry of Ḥatnūb[1] is dated in the year of the twenty-fifth cattle count, which being biennial at this period means his fiftieth regnal year. The same rock-inscription, as well as others in the Wâdy Ḥammâmât,[2] mentions the first occasion of his Sed-festival, which may have been celebrated in his thirtieth year; Piopi was proud of this event and commemorated it on alabaster vases now in the Louvre and elsewhere. No satisfactory explanation has been given of the well-attested change of his early Prenomen Neferzaḥōr into Meryrēʿ.[3] The Horus name Mery-towe 'Beloved of the Two Lands' may have expressed a reputation to which he really aspired. An unpretentious outlook seems indicated by his marriages, doubtless consecutively, to two daughters of a local hereditary prince named Khui, whose home appears to have been in Abydos;[4] both daughters were accorded the same name Meryrēʿ-ʿankh-naś, and if we may believe the inscription recording this fact, the one became the mother of Piopi I's successor Merenrēʿ and the other of his second successor Piopi II, their brother Djaʿu securing the high office of vizier. This connexion with the provinces seems quite in accordance with the spirit of the times.

In our last chapter we felt bound to stress the triviality, from the historical point of view, of most of the so-called autobiographical inscriptions belonging to the Old Kingdom. Here we are fortunate enough to be able to quote what is at least a partial exception. An insignificant looking slab of stone from a tomb at Abydos recounts the way in which Weni, a man of humble birth, rose to one of the most exalted positions in the land.[5] After serving as a minor official under Teti, he was made a 'Friend' ( *śmr*) or favoured courtier by Piopi I, this dignity being coupled with a priestly post in the pyramid-town. So quickly did he win the confidence of the king

[1] PM iv. 237. [2] Op. cit. vii. 329. [3] *ZÄS* xliv. 129; lix. 71.
[4] *BAR* i, §§ 344–9. [5] See the bibliography below, p. 106.

that he was next appointed a judge, in which capacity he was called upon, as sole assessor of the vizier, to hear cases of conspiracy that had arisen in the royal harem and the Six Great Houses. This important duty fulfilled he felt entitled to crave assistance for the adornment of his tomb, a request readily granted by the sovereign:

His Majesty caused a god's seal-bearer (𓊹𓋨𓀭 *śḏ3wtỉ nṯr*) to cross the Nile, with a company of sailors under him, to fetch me this sarcophagus from Ṭura. It returned with him in a great barge of the Court together with its lid, a doorway, lintel, two jambs, and a libation-table. Never had the like been done for any servant. . . .

The following paragraphs are of so great intrinsic interest and are expressed in so typically Egyptian a manner that they are here translated *in extenso*:

Whilst I was a (mere) magistrate, His Majesty made me a Sole Friend and Overseer of the tenants of the Palace, and I displaced four Overseers of the tenants of the Palace who were there, and I acted to His Majesty's satisfaction in giving escort, in preparing the king's path, and in taking up courtly positions, I doing all so that His Majesty praised me for it beyond anything.

When there was litigation in private in the king's harem against the Queen, His Majesty caused me to go to hear (the matter) alone, without there being any vizier or any official there, only myself alone, because of my excellence and of my being firmly planted in the heart of His Majesty, and because His Majesty had confidence in me. It was I who put it in writing alone with one magistrate, though my rank was that of an Overseer of the tenants of the Palace. Never before had the like of me heard a secret matter of the King's harem, but His Majesty caused me to hear it, because I was excellent in the heart of His Majesty beyond any official of his, beyond any noble of his, beyond any servant of his.

When His Majesty inflicted punishment upon the Asiatics and Sand-dwellers, His Majesty made an army of many tens of thousands from the entire (land of) Upper Egypt, from Elephantinē in the south to Medjneye[1] in the north, from Lower Egypt, from the Two Sides of the House[2] in their entirety, from Sedjer, from Khen-sedjru, from Irtje-Nubians, Medja-Nubians, Yam-Nubians, Wawaĕ-Nubians, Kaau-Nubians, and from the land of the Tjemḥu His Majesty sent me forth at

[1] Name of the XXII northernmost nome of Upper Egypt.

[2] Apparently a term for the two sides of the Delta.

the head of this army, there being counts, seal-bearers of the King of Lower Egypt, Sole Friends of the Palace, chieftains and heads of towns of Upper and Lower Egypt, overseers of dragomans,[1] overseers of prophets of Upper and Lower Egypt, and overseers of temple-dependencies at the head of the troops of Upper and Lower Egypt and the towns and villages which they ruled and the Nubians of these foreign lands. It was I who was in command of them, though my office was (merely) that of an Overseer of the tenants of the Palace, because I was well suited to prevent one from quarrelling with his fellow, to prevent any one of them from taking bread or sandals from a wayfarer, to prevent any one of them from taking a loin-cloth from any village, to prevent any one of them from taking any goat from any people. I dispatched them from Northern Isle, Gate of Imḥōtep, and Leg of Ḥōr-Nebmāʿe, though I was of this rank. . . . There was revealed to me the number of these troops, though it had never (before) been revealed to any servant.

At this point Weni breaks into poetry, a unique feature of this inscription:

This army returned in peace, it had harried the land of the Sand-dwellers.
This army returned in peace, it had razed the land of the Sand-dwellers.
This army returned in peace, it had overthrown its walled settlements.
This army returned in peace, it had cut down its figs and its vines.
This army returned in peace, it had cast fire into all its princely houses.
This army returned in peace, it had slain troops in it many tens of thousands.
This army returned in peace, it had carried away very many troops as prisoners.

And His Majesty praised me on account of it more than anything.

After this the narrative, continuing in prose, proceeds to tell how Weni was dispatched five times to deal with the rebellious Sand-dwellers. Then came the report of an insurrection at Nose of the Gazelle, a region that has been conjectured to be Mount Carmel. Crossing by ship with his troops to the back of the hill-country to the north of the land of the Sand-dwellers, while half of the army approached along the high desert road, Weni managed to catch and kill all the insurrectionists.

Weni's autobiography now switches to the reign of Merenrēʿ.

[1] Speakers of foreign tongues who acted as interpreters.

At this point a serious problem confronts us. It has been seen that Weni held a minor office already in the reign of Teti, and evidence utilized above seemed to demand for Piopi I a reign of over fifty years. On the assumption that Merenrēꜥ succeeded to the throne only after his father's death, Weni will have been well over 60 when he passed into the service of a new royal master. Under Merenrēꜥ, however, further strenuous tasks awaited him—tasks which it is hard to believe were imposed upon a man so advanced in age. This difficulty would be mitigated, even if not completely overcome, if it turned out that Piopi associated Merenrēꜥ with himself as king a number of years earlier, so that royal commands could be issued in either name, and for such an association definite, although somewhat slender, evidence has actually been discovered. At the beginning of Merenrēꜥ's reign Weni appears to have been merely a chamberlain and sandal-bearer, but it was not long before he was elevated to the post of Governor of Upper Egypt. As holder of this all-important administrative office in the southern half of Egypt he had to collect all the revenues due to the Residence and to exact all the labour involved. This he did twice over before being sent to a distant Nubian quarry to fetch the sarcophagus and a precious pyramidion for the king's pyramid, while at Elephantinē he secured doors of red granite and other parts for the same monument. All this he performed in one single expedition. Worn out as he may well have been, off he had to go to the alabaster quarry of Ḥatnūb, to cause to be hewn there a great offering-table the transport of which necessitated the building of a ship 60 cubits long and 30 broad. It was an astonishing feat to have acquitted himself of this formidable commission within three weeks of the third month of Summer, when the river was at its lowest. Yet another big task awaited him, the cutting of five navigable channels in the First Cataract, and the building of seven vessels of acacia wood contributed by the chieftains of various Nubian districts. After so long and meritorious a career it seems rather hard that Weni should have been constrained to attribute all his successes to the might and strength of purpose of his sovereign. But perhaps he would never have attained to such eminence without his character comprising an extra dose of obsequiousness.

From this narrative it emerges that Egypt had far greater difficulties to contend with on her north-eastern than on her southern front. Even if the enemy here are regularly referred to by the term  *ḥrìw-šʿ*, literally 'those upon the sand', it would be a mistake to imagine that only the poverty-stricken nomads of the Sinaitic peninsula were meant; to repel these no army of thousands would have been required. Unless the mention of figs and grapes in Weni's poem is to be dismissed as mere fancy, at least some considerable part of southern Palestine must have been involved, and probably the most plausible guess is that what was euphemistically described as rebellion was in reality the first wave of that Asiatic aggression which overwhelmed Egypt little more than 100 years later and was a recurrent menace throughout all her history.

It was but natural that relations with Nubia should have been more peaceful. Here the advantages to be gained from friendly intercourse were mutual. Nubia was the source of various prized commodities unobtainable elsewhere.[1] The Nubians for their part were very dependent upon their richer and more civilized neighbours, corn doubtless being their greatest need, though this is not mentioned in the sole record of what the Egyptians brought with them for purposes of barter and where the items named are 'oil, honey, clothing, faience, and all manner of things'.[2] Not until a much later date did the thought of colonizing Lower Nubia enter the Egyptians' minds; wisely they accepted Elephantinē as their southern frontier, realizing that the country beyond the First Cataract was undesirable as a possession and that their requirements could best be satisfied by special expeditions. Already in Dyn. IV Cheops was causing diorite to be fetched from a quarry to the north-west of Toshka[3] where the cartouches of several of his successors are also found, but the silence enveloping the details of all such enterprises remains unbroken until Dyn. VI. In the decree of Piopi I granting protection to the dependants of Śnofru's two pyramids,[4] several clauses forbid interference with them by 'peaceful Nubians', a term by which policemen like the Medjayu of later times have been thought to be meant. That Weni, as we have seen, was able to recruit for his Asiatic campaigns soldiers from various

[1] See above, p. 44. [2] *BAR* i, § 366. [3] PM vii. 275. [4] Above, p. 78, n. 1.

Nubian tribes shows how willingly these seized the opportunity of finding work in a land so much more agreeable than their own, a trait comparable to that of the Berberines of today, who are commonly employed in Egypt as cooks, valets, and so forth. In the first year of Merenrēʿ he visited the region of the First Cataract in person to receive the homage of the chieftains of Medja, Irtje, and Wawaĕ.[1] Apart from the facts just mentioned, little would be known about the dealings of the Egyptians of Dyn. VI with Nubia were it not for the inscriptions which several successive princes of Elephantinē caused to be carved upon the walls of their tombs opposite Aswân. These princes were probably themselves half-Nubian by race; at all events they were acquainted with the language or languages of the tribes which they were called upon to visit. They seem also to have been hardier and better adapted for foreign travel than most Egyptian nobles, since Pwēne and Byblos are mentioned as places to which one of their number was repeatedly sent,[2] while another[3] was dispatched to the 'country of the Asiatics', probably somewhere on the Red Sea, to retrieve the body of an Egyptian official slain together with all his company whilst building a ship for a journey to Pwēne. It is certain that in spite of the usual good relations serious troubles could also break out in Nubia, for the Pepinakht from whose tomb was learned the fact just mentioned had previously recorded as follows:

> The Majesty of my lord sent me to harry the lands of Wawaĕ and Irtje. I acted to the approval of my lord and slew a great number there, the children of the chieftain and doughty army-captains. And I brought thence to the Residence a large number of prisoners, I being at the head of many strong and bold soldiers.

Perhaps the most informative of these Aswân inscriptions is that from which was drawn the letter about the dancing pygmy translated above (pp. 58–59). It begins in the usual way with titles and epithets of the prince and overseer of dragomans Ḥarkhuf, and then continues as follows:[4]

> He said: The Majesty of Merenrēʿ my lord sent me together with my father the unique friend and lector-priest Iri to Yam to open up the way

[1] *BAR* i, § 317. [2] Op. cit., § 361. [3] Op. cit., § 360. [4] Op. cit., §§ 333–6.

to this country. I did it in seven months, and brought back from it all manner of goodly and rare presents, and was praised greatly on account of it. His Majesty sent me a second time alone. I set forth upon the Elephantinē road and returned from Irtje, Mekher, Tereros, and Irtjetj in the space of eight months. I returned and brought presents from this country in very great quantity, nor had ever the like been brought to this land before. I returned through the neighbourhood of the house of the chieftain of Zatu and Irtje. I had opened up these countries. Never had it been found done by any friend and overseer of dragomans who had gone forth to Yam before. His Majesty sent me a third time to Yam. I set forth from the Thinite nome upon the Oasis road, and found the chieftain of Yam gone to the Tjemeḥ-land to smite the Tjemeḥ to the western corner of heaven. I went forth in pursuit of him to the Tjemeḥ-land, and I satisfied him[1] so that he praised all the gods for the Sovereign. [I dispatched a messenger(?) . . . . .] Yam . . . . . to inform the Majesty of Merenrēʿ my lord [that I had gone to Tjemeḥ-land] and had satisfied that chieftain of Yam. [I returned(?) . . . . .] in the south end of Irtje and the north end of Zatu, and I found the chieftain of Irtje, Zatu and Wawaĕ, [these three countries?] united all in one, and I returned with three hundred asses laden with incense, ebony, *ḥknw*-oil, *śꜣt*, leopard-skins, elephant tusks, and boomerangs and all goodly products. Now when the chieftain of Irtje, Zatu and Wawaĕ saw how strong and numerous was the troop of Yam that returned with me to the Residence together with the soldiers who had been sent with me, then did this chieftain dispatch me and gave me oxen and goats and conducted me over the heights of Irtje by virtue of the vigilance which I had exercised beyond any friend and overseer of dragomans who had been sent to Yam before. Now when this humble servant fared downstream to the Residence, there was caused to come to me the unique friend and overseer of the double bathroom Khuni, meeting me with ships laden with date-wine, cake, bread, and beer. The prince, seal-bearer of the King of Lower Egypt, unique friend, lector-priest, god's seal-bearer, confidant of (royal) commands, Ḥarkhuf.

This narrative,[2] concluding with the titles and name of the tomb-owner, has been translated in full to give some further idea of the diction and the difficulties of a so-called autobiographical inscription of the Old Kingdom. The main problem resides in the identifica-

[1] i.e. paid him in full for the good things which he was going to receive.

[2] Latest discussion by E. Edel in *Äg. Stud.*, pp. 51 ff.

tion of the various Nubian districts involved. Where, above all, was Yam, the end-point of Ḥarkhuf's journeyings, situated? It appears to have been successfully argued that this district lay to the south of the Second Cataract, but it is impossible to believe in its equation with Kerma beyond the Third Cataract, which in Dyn. XII became an isolated garrison in the heart of the Sûdân. Of the other places, Wawaĕ extended southwards from the First Cataract for a considerable distance, Irtje has been definitely located near Tomâs half-way towards Wâdy Ḥalfa, and Medja, mentioned by Weni but not by Ḥarkhuf, in the near neighbourhood of the Second Cataract.

Merenrēʿ reigned little more than ten years before being succeeded by his half-brother Piopi II. The new king can only have been a boy at the time since the Turin Canon and Manetho agree in according him a reign of well over ninety years. At the start he seems to have been under the tutelage of his mother, since she is mentioned with him in the record of an expedition sent to Sinai in the fourth year.[1] Papyrus fragments of late date[2] relate how he was discovered paying long secret visits to one of his generals at dead of night, a story quite in the spirit of Herodotus. Some of the Nubian ventures alluded to in the last pages fell in his reign, of which in spite of its length little else is known. He had, at all events, plenty of time to devote to the building of his pyramid at South Saḳḳâra, which was larger than those of any of his immediate predecessors, and which, thanks to the admirable excavations of G. Jéquier, gives a better idea of the nature of an Old Kingdom pyramid-complex than any of its neighbours. Apart from this, we need recall only the decrees of immunity already mentioned and the 'autobiography' of a prince of the eighth and twelfth nomes of Upper Egypt named Djaʿu, in which he plumed himself on having given a fine burial to his father and upon having obtained the wherewithal from the king.[3] Poor material to sate the historian's appetite, but reading between the lines of all such inscriptions, we cannot fail to perceive the gradual decadence of the kingdom, due in part no doubt to the monarch's own failing strength. We have seen that the Turin Canon added eight successors before reaching

[1] PM vii. 342. [2] *Rev. d'Ég.* xi. 119 ff. [3] *BAR* i, §§ 380 ff.

the total of 181 years for the whole period from Teti onwards. Of these successors of Piopi II the names of only four are preserved, while the reign-lengths of five of the eight amount together to no more than ten years. It thus appears that Dyn. VI ended in a whole series of ephemeral kings all of whom might well have been taken as belonging to that dynasty had not Manetho preferred to end it with Nitōcris, a queen who, like Sebeknofru the last ruler of Dyn. XII, had contrived to wrest to herself the throne of the Pharaohs. Concerning this Nitōcris Manetho says that she was 'the noblest and loveliest of the women of her time', and to Herodotus (ii. 100) is owed the story of her suicide after taking vengeance on certain Egyptians who had slain her brother in order to put her in his place. In the Turin Canon Nitoḳerti—so her name is written there —was either the second or the third Pharaoh after Piopi II. Her historical existence can therefore not be doubted, but she can scarcely have been identical with the Queen Nēith whose pyramid Jéquier discovered at Saḳḳâra,[1] since that queen was the eldest daughter of Piopi I and can have become one of Piopi II's wives only at the beginning of the latter's long reign. Discussion of the remaining successors of Piopi II is reserved for the next chapter. All that need be said here about the close of Dyn. VI is that dynastic troubles clearly ensued immediately after the death of the aged king and that as in Dyn. XII a queen momentarily succeeded in taking advantage of the situation.

It is evident that without a strong and highly organized administration the vast architectural and artistic triumphs of the Old Kingdom could never have been achieved, but our materials for the reconstruction of a coherent picture are hopelessly inadequate. Valiant attempts have been made to infuse life and reality into the titularies of which the tombs are so lavish, but the highly precarious nature of the results has to be admitted. Here only the briefest sketch will be attempted, and it will be one which dwells rather upon the difficulties than upon the positive gains. A serious defect is that until Dyn. VI almost the sole source of our information is the Memphite area where the Court was situated, though from

[1] G. Jéquier, *Les Pyramides des reines Neit et Apouit*, Cairo, 1933.

that time onwards Upper Egypt begins to make valuable contributions. Throughout the best part of Egyptian history the Delta is uniformly silent. One important effect is that we are embarrassed to know the exact import of that duality of form apparent in such titles as 'Overseer of the two granaries', 'Overseer of the two chambers of the king's adornment'. The usual explanation is that these are survivals from the period immediately following the union of the kingdoms of Upper and Lower Egypt, though recently the novel theory has been spread abroad that there never was such a union, and that the duality in question was a figment of the Egyptians' imagination based on the very different conformation of the two halves of the country. It is our conviction that the former explanation is broadly true, but even so there would remain the question whether there were not throughout the Old Kingdom independent granary-departments for the Delta and for the Valley, whether indeed we have not to assume a thoroughgoing separation of the governments of Upper and Lower Egypt. It would seem at least that there can have been no exact parallelism, no strict uniformity in the two halves of the country; Upper Egypt was essentially agricultural, the Delta pastoral—there is evidence that the cattle were regularly driven to the meadows of Lower Egypt to be pastured. As an example of the differing magistracies of the Two Lands one may perhaps quote the title  *ỉmy-r Šmʿw* 'Governor of Upper Egypt', to which in the Old Kingdom at least no corresponding title is found in the Delta, though in the Middle Kingdom there are frequent occurrences of a  *ỉmy-r Tꜣ-mḥw* 'Governor of Lower Egypt', and we have to confess our ignorance of the period when this office originated. Concerning the title 'Governor of Upper Egypt' there are great difficulties. It has been argued, probably rightly, that the post was created in Dyn. V both to ensure the collection of taxes throughout the southern nomes and also to counteract the growing power of the provincial nobles; but it seems certain that towards the end of Dyn. VI this title was often conferred on those very nobles as a purely honorific one or else was claimed by them as a hereditary right. There has been much discussion as to which individual cases can be regarded as referring to actual administrative functions and those where the designation was no more than an ornamental epithet, but the judgements passed in this matter seem often to have been very arbitrary. A similar problem has arisen with regard to an even more important dignitary, no less a personage than the vizier himself. The bearer of the title  *ṯȝty*, appropriately translated 'vizier', was at all periods of Egyptian history the most powerful officer of state, in fact second only to Pharaoh himself. In Dyn. IV the vizier was regularly one of the royal princes, but later the office passed into the hands of some noble of outstanding ability, with whom it tended to become hereditary. Until half a century ago it was firmly believed that the vizierate was confined to one person at a time, but this belief was finally disposed of when a relief was found at Karnak dated to the reign of Tuthmōsis III (Dyn. XVIII) and depicting separate viziers for Upper and Lower Egypt. A generation later the funerary temple of Piopi II brought to light representations appearing to reveal the same state of affairs for the end of Dyn. VI, and further study has disclosed the existence of so many holders of the title that it is now assumed that besides the two viziers for Valley and Delta there were others who were given or assumed the title in a purely honorary capacity. The evidence is confusing, and the last word on this subject has not yet been said.

How many of the functions ascribed to the vizier in an elaborate enumeration found in several tombs of Dyn. XVIII apply to the Old Kingdom is uncertain, but no mention is there made of one title that occupies a prominent place in the titularies of all the early viziers, namely that of  *ỉmy-r kȝt nbt nt nsw* 'Superintendent of all the works of the King'. It is unlikely that many of the viziers were themselves skilled architects and sculptors like Imḥōtep, but at least it will have been their business to secure the most competent help available. That the vizier was the supreme judge was seen from the inscription of Weni, and is reflected in his frequent epithet 'prophet of Māʿe', i.e. of the goddess of Truth. He prided himself on being accessible to all petitioners, who it was recognized cared more about being allowed to vent their grievances than about having them redressed. All royal commands seem to have passed through the vizier's hands to be dealt with by the scribes of his bureau. It was he who dispatched the messengers carrying orders to the heads of distant towns and villages. The corvée and taxation were duties of all, except when the king granted exemption to some local priesthood. As regards the various departments of State we are very ill informed, but references to the *ḥwt-wrt 6* 'Six Great Houses' indicate that there was strict departmental differentiation.

Needless to say, the Court required a great variety of functionaries. Within the *šnyt* or courtiers 'surrounding' the Pharaoh the most favoured persons were called *śmrw* or 'Friends', and besides those who attained this rank without qualification there were others honoured with the epithet 'unique' or 'uniquely loved'. There is a doubt about the original meaning of the title *iry-ẖ nsw*, later interpreted as 'King's acquaintance', but the term seems to have been applied to relatives of Pharaoh who were not actually children of his. Among officials whose duty it was to look after the king's own person there were sandal-bearers, keepers of the robes and crowns, barbers, and physicians, the last sometimes highly specialized like oculists, stomach doctors, and the like. A host of servants were employed in kitchen and dining-room, and there were also domestics of a somewhat higher grade who kept order at the royal meals. What was left over from these was distributed by a special officer who bore the title *ḥry-wḏb* 'he who is over the reversion'.[1] And of course the sovereign had his own scribes to write his letters and commands, which were then sealed in his presence. The religious ceremonies of which the king was the centre had their own personnel, the *ẖry-ḥbt* 'lector-priest' being the only one who can here be mentioned.

What has been said about the tendency of the higher administrative posts to become hereditary is true also of men occupying more subordinate positions. It became one of the most ardent wishes of these to be able 'to hand over their offices to their children'. At all levels of the bureaucratic scale the greatest importance was attached to promotion, and from whatever source this might actually come it was always attributed to the king's favour. There are two books of worldly wisdom giving advice to budding bureaucrats, and from these much may be learnt concerning the qualities required

[1] See already above, p. 59, with n. 2.

for success in their careers. One is a mere fragment,[1] but the Maxims of the vizier Ptaḥḥotpe,[2] who lived under Izozi of Dyn. V, became justly celebrated. Obedience to a father and a superior were the prime virtues, the ability to keep silence in all circumstances, tact and good manners in social intercourse, faithfulness in delivering messages, a humility in fact little short of subservience. If indeed the civil servants of the Old Kingdom actually possessed these qualities, it would go far towards explaining the success of one of the best organized civilizations that the world has ever seen.

SELECT BIBLIOGRAPHY

I. E. S. Edwards, *The Pyramids of Egypt*, 2nd edition, London, 1961; J.-P. Lauer, *Le Problème des Pyramides d'Égypte*, Paris, 1948.

Third Dynasty: the Step Pyramid, Edwards, op. cit., ch. ii; É. Drioton and J.-P. Lauer, *Sakkarah, the Monuments of Zoser*, 2nd ed., Cairo, 1951; the south-west pyramid, M. Zakaria Goneim, *Horus Sekhem-khet*, Cairo, 1957; Zanakht, J. Garstang, *Mâhasna and Bêt Khallâf*, London, 1902; Zâwiyet el-ʿAryân, Edwards, op. cit., pp. 67–68.

Fourth Dynasty: the Great Pyramid, W. M. F. Petrie, *The Pyramids and Temples of Gizeh*, London, 1883; the tomb of Queen Ḥetepḥraś, G. A. Reisner, *A History of the Giza Necropolis*, vol. ii, Cambridge (Mass.), 1955; the Second Pyramid, U. Hölscher, *Das Grabdenkmal des Königs Chephren*, Leipzig, 1912; the Third Pyramid, G. A. Reisner, *Mycerinus*, Cambridge, Mass., 1931. See further G. Jéquier, *Le Mastabat Faraoun*, Cairo, 1928, p. 9, fig. 2.

Fifth Dynasty: the sun-temple of Niuśerrēʿ, F. W. von Bissing, *Das Re-Heiligtum des Königs Ne-woser-Re*, 3 vols., i, with L. Borchardt, Berlin, 1905; ii, iii, with H. Kees, Leipzig, 1923, 1928; also *Ann. Serv.* liii. 319 ff.; the sun-temple of Uśerkaf, *Ann. Serv.* liv. 75 ff., 305 ff.; lv. 73 ff.; the pyramids of Śaḥurēʿ, Neferirkarēʿ, and Niuśerrēʿ, by L. Borchardt, see PM iii. 73–78; the pyramid of Uniś, see above, p. 87, n. 2.

Sixth Dynasty: sanctuary of Piopi I at Bubastis, Labib Habachi, *Tell Basta*, Cairo, 1947, pp. 11 ff.; G. Jéquier, *Le Monument funéraire de Pepi II*, 3 vols., Cairo, 1936–40. The inscription of Weni, *BAR* i. §§ 291–4; 306–15; 319–24; latest translation of a part, *ANET*, pp. 227 f.

Art of the period: W. Stevenson Smith, *A History of Egyptian Sculpture and Painting in the Old Kingdom*, Oxford, 1946; also his Pelican volume, 1958.

Administration, &c.: W. Helck, *Untersuchungen zu den Beamtentiteln des ägyptischen alten Reiches*, Glückstadt, 1954; M. A. Murray, *Index of Names and Titles of the Old Kingdom*, London, 1908; R. Weill, *Les Décrets royaux de l'ancien empire égyptien*, Paris, 1912; the texts also *Urk.* i. 280 ff.

[1] *JEA* xxxii. 71 ff. [2] Erman, *Lit.*, pp. 54 ff.

VI

THE RISE AND FALL OF THE MIDDLE KINGDOM

IN the First Intermediate Period, as the age separating Dyns. VI and XII is called, Manetho—or rather the Manetho known to us from the chronicles of his excerptors—is seen at his worst. His SEVENTH DYNASTY consists of seventy kings of Memphis, who reigned for seventy days. His EIGHTH DYNASTY, likewise Memphite, comprises twenty-seven kings and 146 years of reign. Dyns. IX and X are both Hēracleopolitan, with nineteen kings apiece and a total duration of 594 years. Dyn. XI is of Diospolite or Theban origin, counting sixteen kings with the meagre allowance of forty-three years. Such is the account given by Africanus; the figures offered by Eusebius are somewhat less fantastic, but inspire confidence just as little. For all this stretch of time only one king is mentioned, namely Achthōēs, who is placed in Dyn. IX. Of him the authorities state that he was more cruel than all his predecessors, but in the end was smitten with madness and killed by a crocodile. This scrap of pseudo-history is obviously comparable to the already quoted legends concerning Cheops, Piopi II, and Nitōcris, but the existence of Achthōēs is not open to doubt. In spite of all defects, our Manetho does provide a framework into which the findings of research fit reasonably well, as will be seen from the enumeration of five overlapping stages hereafter to be discussed in some detail: (1) rapid disintegration of the old Memphite régime following upon the overlong reign of Piopi II; (2) bloodshed and anarchy resulting from the collapse of the monarchy and the rivalries of the provincial feudal lords or 'nomarchs', also possibly fomented by the infiltration of Asiatics into the Delta; (3) rise of a new line of Pharaohs with an Akhtoy (Manetho's Achthōēs) at the head and Hēracleopolis as their capital; (4) ever-growing importance of Thebes under a yet more energetic family of warrior princes of whom the first four bore the name of Inyōtef

(Antef in older histories of Egypt) and the remaining three the name of Menthotpe (Mentuhotep); (5) civil war with the Hēracleopolitans from which Menthotpe I emerged as victor, reuniting the Two Lands and paving the way for the Middle Kingdom—this ushered in by Ammenemēs I, one of the greatest of all Egyptian monarchs (Dyn. XII).

(1) Our last chapter dealt with the eight ephemeral successors of Piopi II who in the Turin Canon marked the close of Dyn. VI. The Abydos list replaces these eight by no less than eighteen kings prior to making its great leap to the last rulers of Dyn. XI. It is not easy to reconcile any of the Abydos names with the four which alone are preserved in the Canon, but it seems likely that the fourth cartouche from the end gave the Prenomen of that Ibi of the Turin fragments whose insignificant pyramid was discovered by Jéquier at Saḳḳâra.[1] The recurrence of the name Neferkarēʿ, which had been the Prenomen of Piopi II, as either whole or part in no less than six names of the Abydos series shows how great was still felt to be the solidarity of these petty rulers with the most venerable of the Pharaohs of Dyn. VI. But perhaps the most persuasive evidence of their short-lived domination is offered by some inscriptions discovered by Raymond Weill at Coptos in 1910–11.[2] Under the ruins of a structure of Roman date were found carefully stowed away a number of decrees carved in hieroglyphic on slabs of limestone, some dating from the reign of Piopi II, and most of them designed to protect the temple of Mīn and its priesthood from interference and the corvée. But among them as many as eight were apparently dispatched on the same day in the first year of a king Neferkauḥōr, the last king but one in the series of the Abydos list. The addressee was in each case the vizier Shemai and each royal command was concerned either with him or some member of his family. One of the decrees confirmed him in his vizierate in all the twenty-two nomes of Upper Egypt, while another recorded the appointment of his son Idi to the post of Governor of Upper Egypt in the seven southernmost nomes. A third decree grants precedence over all other women to Shemai's wife Nebye,[3] who is described

[1] *La Pyramide d'Aba*, Cairo, 1935.
[2] PM v. 126 f.
[3] See now *Ann. Serv.* lv. 170.

as a 'King's eldest daughter', and perhaps even more remarkable is a fourth making elaborate arrangements for the funerary cult of both husband and wife in all the temples of the land. There is no hint of unrest or political disturbance in any of these texts, though we may possibly read into them a desperate anxiety on the king's part to conciliate one specially powerful Upper Egyptian magnate.

(2) Thus the chances are that all the reigns corresponding to Manetho's Dyns. VII and VIII were compressed into a relatively short space of time, perhaps no more than a quarter of a century. At what precise moment serious disorders broke out it is impossible to say, but their reality is beyond a doubt, and there is reason to think that they persisted, whether continuously or intermittently, until well on into Dyn. XI. It is the picture of a real revolution that is painted in one of the most curious and important pieces of Egyptian literature that have survived the hazards of time. This extremely tattered papyrus in the Leyden collection dates from no earlier than Dyn. XIX, but the condition of the country which it discloses is one which cannot be ascribed to the imagination of a romancer, nor does it fit into any place of Egyptian history except that following the end of the Old Kingdom. The beginning is unfortunately lost, and with it the circumstances in which the speaker made his lengthy harangue. A long series of brief paragraphs first portrays the havoc into which the land has been thrown by the machinations of low-born adventurers and Asiatics pushing their way into the Delta. A few examples will suffice to illustrate the tone and substance of the narration:

The bowman is ready. The wrongdoer is everywhere. There is no man of yesterday. A man goes out to plough with his shield. A man smites his brother, his mother's son. Men sit in the bushes until the benighted traveller comes, in order to plunder his load. The robber is a possessor of riches. Boxes of ebony are broken up. Precious acacia-wood is cleft asunder.

The general upheaval has reversed the status of rich and poor:

He who possessed no property is now a man of wealth. The poor man is full of joy. Every town says: let us suppress the powerful among us. He who had no yoke of oxen is now possessor of a herd. The possessors of robes are now in rags. Gold and lapis lazuli, silver and turquoise are fastened on the necks of female slaves. All female slaves are free with their tongues. When their mistress speaks it is irksome to the servants. The children of princes are dashed against the walls.

These quotations, chosen at random, might, it is true, reflect the distorted vision of a die-hard aristocrat, but there are others describing the political confusion of the times, the dissolution of the laws, and the destruction of public offices and records which cannot well be so construed. Even the person of the king seems to have been subjected to violence, though the sentence where this appears to be stated is of not quite certain interpretation. Still more important are a few passages which affirm the part played by foreigners in the restriction of true Egyptian territory to Upper Egypt—Elephantinē and Thinis being towns specifically mentioned. The many pages of nostalgic lamentations are followed by adjurations to piety and religious observance, and it is these which justify the title 'Admonitions of an Egyptian Sage' by which the entire composition is known. Opinions have differed as to the way in which the remaining portions of the book are to be understood. Some have thought to find a reference to Piopi II dying in extreme old age and succeeded by a child too young to have any sense. But these events, if really alluded to, must have lain in the author's past and that king upon whom the wise Ipuwēr heaped reproaches for his weakness and indolence may well have been among the last of the Memphite line. However that may be, the trustworthiness of the Leyden papyrus as a depiction of Egypt in the First Intermediate Period is indisputable. And here for the first time Egyptian literature sounds that note of despairing pessimism which became a commonplace with the writers of the succeeding centuries even when no longer justified by prevailing conditions.

We have thus to picture to ourselves the Memphite kingdom as growing weaker and weaker until it failed any longer to command the allegiance of the nomarchs farther upstream. Direct information from the Delta now ceases entirely. Expeditions in quest of the turquoise of Sinai are at an end, not to be resumed until the approach of Dyn. XII. If a barbarous-looking cylinder with the cartouche of Khendy[1] and a scarab[2] with the name of Tereru really

[1] *JEA* xii. 92. [2] Petrie, *Scarabs*, Pl. 10, 7. 10.

belong to the kings so named in the Abydos list, this would be an indication that they had to look to Syrian skill for even such trumpery objects. It was perhaps in the extreme south that conditions became most gravely unsettled. The casual mention of a king Neferkarēʿ in a rock-tomb at Moʿalla, some 20 miles south of Luxor, places the inscriptions of its owner ʿAnkhtify among the earliest records of the age. This ʿAnkhtify was the 'great chieftain (or 'nomarch') of the nome of Nekhen', the third nome of Upper Egypt, that of which Hieracōnpolis opposite El-Kâb was the capital. He tells how Horus of Edfu, the god of the next nome to the south (No. II), had bidden him set it in order, with the result that he took over the chieftaincy, and tranquillized the region so thoroughly that a man would even embrace the slayer of his father or of his brother. Many are the incidents of ʿAnkhtify's prowess which he describes in laconic sentences interposed between epithets belauding his own virtues. For his main fighting force he had 'the valiant troop of Ḥefaĕ', a place which is either Moʿalla itself or a town not far distant. There is talk of conflicts between this force and Thebes and Coptos, whose combined soldiery had attacked the fortresses of Armant. ʿAnkhtify's references to his martial successes are of great obscurity, but if his account can be trusted he managed to cow the inhabitants to both the east and the west of Thebes, so that at all events we are here dealing with a time before the dynasty of the Inyōtefs had established for themselves an invincible supremacy. More significant than all these allusions to deeds of valour are the repeated mentions of years of famine in which ʿAnkhtify claims to have supplied other towns besides his own with gifts or loans of corn, this beneficent activity of his extending even as far north as Dendera. We need not take too seriously the statement that 'the entire south died of hunger, every man devouring his own children', but the inscriptions of other more or less contemporary princes constantly harp upon the lack of grain, a lack which we may surmise was due as much to the impossibility of undisturbed agriculture as to a succession of low Niles. It may here be noted that the deplorable state of Upper Egypt is clearly reflected in the clumsiness of its artistic efforts; evidently Egyptian civilization was at its lowest ebb.

(3) Concerning the rise of the 'House of Akhtoy' we are left almost completely in the dark. Hēracleopolis is the modern Ihnâsya el-Medîna, a town to the west of the river opposite Beni Suêf 55 miles south of Memphis. Not a shred of local evidence has survived to indicate its early importance, but Manetho's description of his NINTH and TENTH DYNASTIES as Hēracleopolitan is amply confirmed by testimony from elsewhere. As regards his Achthōēs it turns out that no less than three distinct kings chose to retain the name for their second cartouche. The king who without proof, but not without probability, is assumed to have been the first, adopted Meryibtowe ('Beloved of the heart of the Two Lands') as his Horus name, and by way of emphasizing his claim did not hesitate to equip himself with a full Pharaonic titulary. To have raised himself to such a height he must have possessed an exceptionally forceful character, but all that remains directly to authenticate his existence is a copper brazier in the Louvre, an ebony walking-stick from Mêr, and a few other equally insignificant objects.[1] A second Akhtoy whose Prenomen was Waḥkarēʿ is known only from a finely decorated coffin from El-Bersha, where his cartouches seem to have been inadvertently written in place of those of the real owner, the steward Nefri.[2] Yet a third king of the name, Akhtoy Nebkaurēʿ, is attested only by a weight from Petrie's excavations at Er-Reṭâba[3] and by a mention of him in one of the few Egyptian works of fiction that have survived in their entirety; this tells the story of a peasant from the outlying oasis of the Wâdy Naṭrûn who was robbed of his donkey and his merchandise on the way to Hēracleopolis, but poured out his complaints to the thief's liege-lord with such eloquence that he was detained in order that his supplications, reproaches, and invective might be written down for the sovereign's delectation. In the Turin Canon no less than eighteen kings belonging to the same royal line were originally recorded, and the name Akhtoy occurs twice, each time unexpectedly preceded by a Neferkarēʿ (see above), while all the adjoining names are damaged, unidentifiable, or lost. It is from some tombs at Asyûṭ that we obtain our most trustworthy glimpse of the Hēracleopolitan era.

[1] Gauthier, *LR* i. 204; *Ann. Serv.* x. 185; Hayes, *Scepter*, i. p. 143.

[2] *Rec. trav.* xxiv. 90–92.

[3] Op. cit., xl. 186.

The inscriptions in these three tombs are marred by the twin defects which are the bane of so much of our hieroglyphic evidence, namely extensive lacunae in the text and our still inadequate knowledge of the Egyptian language. Nevertheless the information that they afford is illuminating. The earliest of the three tomb-owners would hardly have retained his name Akhtoy had he not been a partisan of the Hēracleopolitan faction. Indeed, his youth seems to have been passed in a time of comparative calm. He tells how he was taught to swim together with the royal children, and was made a nomarch whilst still a babe of a cubit in height. Though he mentions that he recruited a regiment of soldiers, the achievements upon which he most prided himself were irrigation works and the encouragement of farming. He ends his main narrative with the words 'Hēracleopolis praised God for me', the Egyptian way of expressing gratitude. In the next oldest tomb Prince Tefibi plumes himself upon his impartial beneficence and the sense of security which his soldiers inspired:

When night came, he who slept upon the road praised me. He was like a man in his own house.

None the less the nomes of the south were on the move, probably under the command of one of the early Inyōtefs. Tefibi relates that he came into conflict with them, and we cannot doubt of his success, though the half-lines that told the sequel are among the obscurest of a narrative where everything is obscure. It is in the tomb of his son, again an Akhtoy, that the most explicit account of the civil war is to be found. A Hēracleopolitan king Merykarēʿ, of whom we shall hear more later, is named twice. Prince Akhtoy, for some unexplained reason addressed in the second person, is credited with having induced the sovereign himself to sail upstream:

... he cleared the sky, the entire land with him, the princes of Upper Egypt and the magnates of Hēracleopolis, the region of the Mistress of the Land being come to repel fighting, the earth trembling ... all people darting about, the towns ...ing, fear falling upon their limbs. The magistrates of the Great House are under the fear of, and the favourites under respect for, Hēracleopolis.

It appears that the king's fleet reached Shasḥōtp, a town a little to the south of Asyûṭ, before returning amid rejoicing to his capital. Doubtless out of thankfulness for so signal a success, King Merykarēʿ ordered extensive repairs to be made to the temple of Wepwawe, the jackal god of Asyûṭ.

If any part of Egypt was relatively peaceful in these troublous times, it was assuredly the portion midway between Memphis and Thebes. Many cemeteries of the central provinces, like those at Beni Ḥasan[1] and Akhmîm,[2] have yielded fairly rich funerary equipment. No finer sarcophagi of the period have been unearthed than those from El-Bersha,[3] at this time the burial-place of the 'great chieftains of the Hare Nome' (No. XV of Upper Egypt), whose seat of administration was Khmūn, the later Hermopolis and the modern El-Ashmûnên. A new family of princes had there come into power, replacing the Old Kingdom nomarchs whose tombs had been situated at Sheikh Saʿîd a little farther to the south. These places were well within the domain of the Hēracleopolite kingdom, but curious evidence has come to light showing that their rulers' loyalty to the northern cause was considerably less than wholehearted. The walls of the tombs are free from any compromising indications, but such abound at the alabaster quarries of Ḥatnūb, a little way out in the eastern desert. Here the lucky find of a large number of ink-written graffiti not only heaps flattering epithets upon the local nomarchs, but accompanies their names with wish-formulae such as 'may he live for ever' or 'the protection of life be around him like Rēʿ eternally', formulae both earlier and later elsewhere reserved exclusively for Pharaoh. Still more strange, these graffiti are dated in the regnal years, not of the contemporary king, but of the provincial princes themselves. Two of the earliest are credited with thirty and twenty years of rule respectively, a sure sign that they were less plagued by disturbances than the nomarchs farther to the south where the rival kingdoms were finally to meet in battle. Very incongruously these inscriptions express fidelity to 'the king's house', though the king's name is carefully suppressed, except once when an otherwise unknown Meryḥatḥōr is mentioned. It must not be imagined, however, that the laudatory phrases are completely without reference to rebellion and blood-

[1] PM iv. 141 ff. [2] Op. cit., v. 17 ff. [3] Op. cit., iv. 177 ff.

shed. One prince even seems to allude to a fight with his own fellow-citizens,[1] though as usual the expressions are so vague that we cannot be quite certain of their import. Also there are apparent contradictions which we are utterly at a loss to resolve, as when a ship's captain who lived under Prince Neḥeri tells us that in the king's business he travelled as far south as Elephantinē and as far north as the papyrus marshes of the Delta,[2] a feat surely impossible in the political conditions of the times.

It remains to characterize a literary composition which, had it been preserved in a less ragged and corrupt condition, might well have thrown more light on a particular phase of the Hēracleopolitan domination than all our other evidence put together. The text is contained in three papyri, one in Leningrad, another in Moscow, and the third in Copenhagen, all of them written no earlier than the end of Dyn. XVIII, and all riddled with lacunae and obscurities of every kind. It is a book of wise counsels addressed to the king Merykarēʿ with whom we became acquainted in the tombs of Asyûṭ. The name of the father is lost, but he may well have been an Akhtoy, though not the first of the name. Perhaps the earliest portion, had it been better preserved, might have been the most interesting of all, since it offers advice as to how unruly but popular vassals had best be dealt with. Stress is laid on ability to speak well and persuasively, and imitation of the ancient models is strongly recommended. Yet it is desirable to look to the future, a trait of character upon which nobles of the period particularly plumed themselves. It is wise to favour the rich, since they are less open to corruption than the poor. Justice and kindness to the oppressed are all the more essential since after death there comes a Day of Judgement when a man's deeds, however far back in the past they lie, will be requited as they deserve. The recruiting of young troops and the endowment of them with fields and cattle are obviously wise precautions. Yet nothing is more important than reverent service to the gods and the building of monuments in their honour. It is exasperating that just those sections which deal with concrete events are the most obscure of all, and the scholars who have used them with the greatest confidence have sometimes exceeded what

[1] No. 16. [2] No. 14.

is philologically permissible. Nevertheless, the claim of the royal counsel-giver to have taken Thinis 'like a cloud-burst' is unmistakably worded. In the same passage he seems, however, to have expressed regret for the devastation which he had caused in what was always the most sacred region in all Egypt. Still, this incursion of the Hēracleopolitans so far south seems to have brought about a temporary lull in the hostilities between the belligerents, since now 'thou standest well with the South; the bearers of loads come to thee with gifts . . . the red granite (of Aswân) comes to thee unhindered'. Far more perplexing are the paragraphs dealing with Merykarēʿ's relations with the Delta and with the Asiatic barbarians to the east. There is a reference to Djed-eswe,[1] the area around the pyramid of Teti at Saḳḳâra, and the actual mention on that site of many priests devoted to the funerary cult of this very Hēracleopolitan monarch proves that he must have been buried there, though his pyramid has never been found. A passage describing the nature of the Asiatics has been translated above (p. 37), and reveals at least that Merykarēʿ was in close contact with them. The book ends with exhortations to be industrious, with earnest emphasis upon the responsibilities of kingship, and with the warning that God, even if His power be hidden, nevertheless sways the fortunes of men, for He is the creator and arbiter of all. Last of all come the words 'Behold I have spoken to thee the best of my inner thoughts; set them steadfastly before thy face'.

(4) In the Old Kingdom Thebes, later to become the southern capital and second in importance among the cities of Egypt only to Memphis, was no more than an insignificant village stretching along the eastern bank of the Nile. Indeed, at that time it was perhaps the humblest of four small townships which lay within the confines of the fourth Upper Egyptian nome, the others being Ṭôd 20 miles to the south-east, Hermōnthis (Armant) opposite Ṭôd across the river, and Medâmûd to the north of Thebes near the eastern desert; all four observed the cult of the warlike falcon-headed god Montju (Mont), ultimately raising stately temples in his honour. It is unknown how Thebes or Wīse, to give the town its Egyptian name, came to outstrip its companions so vastly, but

[1] *JEA* i. 32, n.

the beauty of its situation may have been the decisive factor, for the entire land might be searched in vain for equal magnificence of scenery. The western desert, at no great distance beyond the fields, is dominated by the massive bluff of the Ḳurn, beneath whose lofty eminence smaller hills offer unrivalled opportunity for rock-tombs. To the north, almost facing the temple of Mont at Karnak, there winds into the mountain the long and narrow gorge of Bîbân el-Molûk 'the Tomb of the Kings', at the end of which the monarchs of the New Kingdom caused their mysterious sepulchres to be hewn. About a mile to the south and separating Ḳurna and Draʿ Abu'n-Naga the shorter and wider recess called Dêr el-Baḥri after the Coptic monastery which came to be placed there leads to a sheer cliff of indescribable grandeur (Pl. IX). On the east bank a large area of radiant fields discloses far away a line of hills behind which the sun rises in all its glory. For the modern tourist the attraction of Thebes is enhanced by the accessibility and good preservation of its many monuments, advantages which apart from the pyramids and their surrounding mastabas are sadly lacking in the neighbourhood of Memphis.

Among the multitude of tombs interspersed among the houses of the modern village of Ḳurna only three belong to the Old Kingdom, and of these only one belongs to a 'Great Chieftain of the nome', a small and mean affair suggesting that its owner was a personage of little consequence. The ease with which, as we have seen (p. 111), ʿAnkhtify of Moʿalla overran the region around and beyond Armant prompts the belief that it was not until a good deal later that the Theban territory began to take the lead among the provinces of the south. The initiative was undoubtedly due to a nobleman subsequently remembered as Inyōtef the great, born ot Iku, and on another stela described as 'hereditary prince'. He was evidently the founder of the line of monarchs classified by us as the ELEVENTH DYNASTY, and identical with the 'hereditary prince Inyōtef' included in the disorderly enumeration of kings of that name in the already mentioned (p. 50) Table of Karnak. There are three stelae which may fairly claim to be contemporary records of this prince, on two of which he or his homonym is described as 'Great Chieftain of Upper Egypt', while on the third he is 'Great

Chieftain of the Theban nome'. It seems simpler to presuppose only a single ancestor of the name, and at all events we are justified in picturing to ourselves an Inyōtef-ʿo ('Inyōtef the great') who subjugated parts of the south far beyond the territory of his own metropolis, yet did not dare to assume the predicates of royalty.

The first Inyōtef to have his name enclosed in a cartouche has left no contemporary monument, and apart from the rather doubtful mention in the Table of Karnak is known only from an all-important relief of the reign of Nebḥepetrēʿ Menthotpe discovered in the temple of Ṭôd.[1] Here that monarch is shown giving an offering to Mont, while behind him stands the local goddess Tjenenti. She is followed by three kings who must surely be Menthotpe's immediate predecessors in retrograde order; each of them bears within a cartouche the title and name 'Son of Rēʿ Inyōtef', but they are differentiated on a block above by the separate Horus names (3) lost, (2) Waḥ-ʿankh, and (1) Seher-towĕ. Thus Seher-towĕ 'Pacifier of the Two Lands' was the first royal Inyōtef and either a son or a descendant of the hereditary prince of the same name. Winlock[2] conjectured, possibly rightly, that he was the owner of the northernmost of three great tombs of a peculiar type excavated in the plain in a line between the temple of Mont at Karnak and the opening into the Valley of the Tombs of the Kings. These tombs are called *ṣaff* or 'row' because they have doorways which give them the appearance of being surrounded by porticoes on three sides. It seems probable that they were the burial-places of the first three Inyōtefs, since it is definitely known that one of them, perhaps that in the centre, belonged to the Horus Waḥ-ʿankh Inyōtef II. By a curious chance there is a reference to this in the papyrus of the reign of Ramessēs IX (*c.* 1115 B.C.) describing the official tour of inspection to examine the royal tombs which it was feared had been tampered with by the tomb-robbers.[3] Here we read:

The pyramid-tomb of King Si-rēʿ In-ʿo which is north of the House of Amenḥotpe of the Forecourt and whose pyramid is crushed down upon it; and its stela is set up in front of it and the image of the king

[1] *Bull. Inst. fr.* xxxvi. 101 ff.
[2] *AJSL* xxxii. 1 ff.; also Winlock, *Rise*, p. 11.
[3] See below, p. 300.

PLATE IX

DÊR EL-BAḤRI FROM THE AIR

The temple of Hashepsowe on the right, that of Menthotpe I on the left

PLATE X

SPEARMEN AND BOWMEN

Models of wood, painted, Dyn. XI. Cairo Museum

stands upon this stela with his hound named Beḥka between his feet. Examined this day; it was found intact.

Mariette found the lower part of this very stela in 1860, and depicted upon it were not merely one dog but five. Unfortunately it was left to be broken up by natives, but what remains of its inscriptions is of great interest. After telling how he built or restored a number of temples, Waḥ-ʿankh narrates that he established his northern boundary in the tenth or Aphroditopolite nome of Upper Egypt. Then he goes on to say that he captured the whole of the Abydos territory and opened up all its prisons. These extensions of his dominion are confirmed on the monuments of several of his officers of state, the finest of which belonged to a chancellor named Tjetji,[1] whose main pride, expressed in certainly exaggerated terms, was that he was put in control of the vast treasure brought to his lord not only from Upper and Lower Egypt, but also as tribute from the chieftains of the desert countries. From Waḥ-ʿankh's own sepulchral stela we learn that it was set up in his fiftieth year, this length of reign proving, like the similar indications in the inscriptions of the princes of the Hare nome at Ḥatnūb, that at least in the tract of land under his sway tranquil conditions prevailed. These would naturally be favourable to good craftsmanship, and it is interesting to see that the sculptors of reliefs at Thebes had by now developed a highly individual and not unpleasing style of their own, particularly in the forms of their hieroglyphs. This artistic skill, however, goes hand in hand with a great crudity on other stelae, showing that the reviving culture was not yet at all sure of itself.

Neither Waḥ-ʿankh himself nor his successors hesitate any longer to employ the proud title 'King of Upper and Lower Egypt', though a number of years had to elapse before it corresponded to the truth. The next king was another Si-Rēʿ Inyōtef, who adopted as his Horus name one which meant 'Strong, lord of a Good Start' (Nakht-neb-tep-nūfe).[2] It deserves to be mentioned here that such deliberately invented names often have a greater significance than is apt to be attributed to them; if they do not register historical facts, at least they may embody aspirations, and examples of both

[1] *JEA* xvii. 55 ff. [2] *Mitt. Kairo*, xiv. 44, 47.

possibilities will come to our notice before the end of this chapter. Inyōtef III was the last of his name for several centuries, and all that is known of his doings is that he restored the ruined tomb at Aswân of a deified prince named Ḥeḳayēb.

(5) Inyōtef III was followed by the first of several Pharaohs who exchanged the family name of Inyōtef for Menthọtpe, a name which signifies 'Mont is content'. And contented the local god had good reason to be, for Menthọtpe I's long reign of fifty-one years witnessed, after many years of conflict, the reunion of all Egypt under a single ruler. It is only comparatively recently that the personality of this great king has begun to emerge from the obscurity which previously surrounded him. We owe it to H. Stock to have recognized that three separate titularies, previously attributed to three distinct Pharaohs all bearing the name Menthọtpe, really belonged to one and the same sovereign, each titulary reflecting a different stage in his career.[1] Such a radical change of titulary is almost unique in the Pharaonic annals but is justified by the momentous events which it reflects. At the beginning of his reign Menthọtpe I, like the earlier rulers of his house, dispensed with a Prenomen, and was satisfied to be called the Horus Sʿankh-ib-towe 'He who makes to live the heart of the Two Lands', i.e. possibly who revives their hopes. A British Museum stela which is among the few monuments recording this phase notes that in his fourteenth year Thinis revolted, perhaps thereby giving the signal for the king's northward advance. In the next phase Menthọtpe often prefixed the Prenomen Nebḥepetrēʿ to his surname, at the same time using the Horus name Nebḥedje, which means 'Lord of the White Crown'; presumably this was intended to signify his now well-established suzerainty over Upper Egypt. Nothing dated has survived from this period, but the Horus name in question tells its own tale. From the thirty-ninth year onward, and probably a good deal earlier, the Horus name is metamorphosed into Sam-towĕ 'Uniter of the Two Lands', while the Prenomen, still to be read as Nebḥepetrēʿ, is strangely written with an oar  instead of with the indeterminate object having the form ; this latter fact led to the ultimate Prenomen being wrongly read as Nebkherurēʿ and

[1] Op. cit., xiv. 42 ff.

being attributed to a Menthotpe different from the two bearers of the Nomen already mentioned. Discarding this mistake, instead of the five distinct Menthotpes or Mentuhoteps counted by most historians in Dyn. XI, we shall here acknowledge only three.

Nothing very definite is known about the campaigns in which Menthotpe I regained the Double Crown, and so put an end to the internal anarchy which had finally given place to separate kingdoms in the north and the south. A tomb discovered by Winlock at Thebes contained the bodies of no less than sixty soldiers slain in battle doubtless at no great distance from the capital. Probably fighting was required upstream as well as downstream. There is an imposing rock-relief in the little valley of the Shaṭṭ er-Rigâl about 2 miles below Gebel Silsila showing Menthotpe I accompanied not only by his chancellor Akhtoy, but also by his mother Ioʿḥ and his father Inyōtef III; and close by are to be read the names of many of his courtiers. This visit, dated in the thirty-ninth year, may perhaps only have been an incident in a royal progress intended to display his power. At Abisko,[1] only a short distance above the First Cataract, a soldier has scratched upon a rock the information that he had accompanied his royal master on an expedition perhaps as far as Wâdy Ḥalfa. The role of Nubia throughout the foregoing period is very obscure. There is mention of a king Wadjkarēʿ who has been hesitatingly identified with one with the same Prenomen alluded to in a Coptos decree.[2] Then there are rather frequent occurrences of a Inyōtef who equipped himself with a full royal titulary,[3] yet cannot be fitted into Dyn. XI as we know it from Egypt itself. Difficult to account for is the model of a troop of Nubian recruits found in a tomb at Asyûṭ (Pl. X)[4] as well as the allusion at Ḥatnūb to men of Medja and Wawaĕ among the followers of a prince of the Hermopolitan nome;[5] from this it would seem that Nubian contingents were in the service of the Hēracleopolitan confederation.

To the soldier who commemorated his existence at Abisko is owed the further information that King Nebḥepetrēʿ, that is to say Menthotpe I in his third phase, 'captured the entire land and

[1] Säve-Söderbergh, p. 58. [2] Op. cit., p. 43. [3] Op. cit., p. 47.
[4] Op. cit., pp. 50 f. [5] Anthes, Nos. 16, 25.

proposed to slay the Asiatics of Djaty'. The pacification of the entire land must have been accomplished before the forty-sixth year, since a stela at Turin[1] of that date tells us that 'a good course was set by Mont's giving the Two Lands to the sovereign Nebḥepetrēʿ'. Before the end of the reign it had even become possible for a god's seal-bearer named Akhtoy to engage in extensive foreign travel and to bring back much valuable metal and precious stones of various sorts; but all this involved much successful conflict with the inhabitants.[2] So mighty a king could not rest content with a mere *ṣaff*-tomb like his ancestors. The site which he chose for his sepulchre was the cliff-bound inlet of Dêr el-Baḥri (Pl. IX), and it would be impossible to conceive of surroundings more impressive. Here, as so often in Egyptian history, there is evidence of changes of plan before the magnificent final funerary monument was decided upon and put into execution. Not the least mysterious feature is a tunnel-like cenotaph known as the Bâb el-Ḥoṣân,[3] which, when discovered by Howard Carter, contained an empty coffin, a box inscribed with the name of Menthotpe I, and a statue swathed in fine linen. Hardly less intriguing are six shrines of royal ladies, queens and concubines, later embodied in, and partly concealed by, the back wall of the ambulatory; each shrine had a shaft of its own leading to a chamber containing a finely decorated sarcophagus, and here were found elements of the titulary of Nebḥepetrēʿ in the form which, from the position of the find, was obviously the earlier. Of the temple which Menthotpe I's architects devised to perpetuate his fame and which was excavated by Naville and Hall, only little now remains to display its original grandeur. In it tradition and innovation were combined in the happiest fashion. As in the Old Kingdom pyramids a long causeway led up from the valley, but a new feature was the grove of tamarisks and sycamore-figs which bordered the inner end of a great court. A ramp intersecting a lower colonnade of square pillars that recalls a *ṣaff*-tomb gave access to a terrace with a similar colonnade at front and sides. A doorway led into a covered hypostyle hall at the back of which a solid podium supported a pyramid of very modest proportions.

[1] L. Klebs, *Die Reliefs und Malerei en des mittleren Reiches*, Heidelberg, 1922, p. 22, fig. 14. [2] *JEA* iv. 28 ff. [3] Plan, Winlock, op. cit., Pl. 34.

Westwards and penetrating into the mountain a narrower court ended in a second hypostyle hall and tiny sanctuary. The edifice thus created would have been absolutely unique were it not for the still more imposing structure which Queen Ḥashepsowe of Dyn. XVIII later placed alongside it, copying and developing many of its ideas. It was perhaps more on account of this visible token of his splendour than because of his victories that Nebḥepetrēʿ was revered centuries later as a patron of the Theban Necropolis, but he was also the first king since Dyn. VIII who was deemed worthy of a place in the Abydos and Saḳḳâra king-lists. The cliffs around his funerary temple are honeycombed with the tombs of his courtiers, systematically excavated by Winlock for the Metropolitan Museum of New York. Here, for example, were buried the vizier Ipi and the ubiquitous chancellor Akhtoy, but of more sensational interest was the discovery in one tomb of wonderful models displaying in the round such everyday occupations as weaving, brewing, and the census of cattle. In them the life of the period is exhibited with a vividness even surpassing the scenes in relief which bring the civilization of Ancient Egypt home to us with a realism unequalled in any other bygone age.

With Menthotpe I the First Intermediate Period may be deemed concluded. In treating of this as comprising five stages (pp. 107–8) care was taken to describe them as overlapping. It is to the unknown extent of this overlapping, as well as to the uncertain duration of the various stages, that the impossibility of obtaining a coherent picture is due. Many attempts have been made, but mostly go beyond what the evidence warrants. We do not know how soon after the last stragglers of the Memphite dynasties Hēracleopolis began to raise its head, or what was the exact date of ʿAnkhtify at Moʿalla. Equally obscure is the position of Merykarēʿ, though the 'Instruction' addressed to him links him with the civil war described at Asyûṭ. The statement of one Djari who lived under Waḥ-ʿankh Inyōtef II that he had 'fought with the House of Akhtoy on the west of Thinis' may seem to offer a bridge across three of the stages, but the conflict in question may not have been the same as that mentioned in the 'Instruction' and the expression 'House of Akhtoy' is highly ambiguous. The real crux of the matter is chronological, and if the most recent authorities agree in estimating the period from Nitōcris to the end of Menthotpe's reign at from 200 to 250 years, this is but little more than a guess.[1] The Turin Canon gives no help, since the total for the eighteen kings of the Hēracleopolitan dynasties and their successors is lost, and the possibility of an overlap with Dyn. XI appears to be ignored.

At the close of Menthotpe I's glorious reign nothing seemed to suggest that the power of his family was nearing its end. Yet so it was. The Turin Canon concedes to S'ankhkarē' Menthotpe II twelve years of rule, but makes him, though not quite accurately, the last king of Dyn. XI. Likewise in the Abydos and Saḳḳâra king-lists S'ankhkarē' is the immediate predecessor of Sḥetepibrē' Ammenemēs I, the founder of Dyn. XII and of what is known to us as the Middle Kingdom. Isolated inscribed blocks in many of the towns of Upper Egypt show that S'ankhkarē' was active as a builder of temples or chapels. A long inscription engraved in his eighth year upon the rocks of the Wâdy Ḥammâmât tells how his steward Ḥenu was sent thither to quarry stone for statues to be set up in these sacred buildings.[2] Ḥenu relates how he started out from Coptos with 3,000 well-equipped soldiers after a police force had cleared the road of rebels. On the way to the Red Sea he dug many wells. There had previously been mention of a fleet sent to fetch myrrh from Pwēne. It was on the return journey that the quarrying work was effected. The burial-place of S'ankhkarē' is something of a problem. Flanking Dêr el-Baḥri to the south is the broad and conspicuous hill of Sheikh 'Abd el-Ḳurna, and south of this is a bay roughly similar to that chosen by Menthotpe I for his tomb, but much less picturesque. Here traces of a great causeway may be seen, as well as the beginnings of a sloping passage. According to Winlock[3] the end of this passage was hastily widened into a burial chamber and then walled up. At all events S'ankhkarē' must have been interred somewhere in this neighbourhood, since high on the cliffs commanding both valleys are the graffiti of mortuary priests who served the cults of both these Menthotpe kings.

In the fragments of the Turin papyrus S'ankhkarē' is followed by the mention of seven kingless years. It is probable that these years

[1] See above, p. 67. [2] *BAR*, §§ 427 ff. [3] Winlock, op. cit., p. 52.

included a third Menthotpe subsequently not regarded as a legitimate Pharaoh. This Nebtowerēʿ Menthotpe III is known, apart from the fragment of a stone bowl found at Lisht,[1] only from two quarries to which he sent expeditions. Three graffiti of his first year and one of his second record an official's quest for amethyst in the Wâdy el-Ḥûdi,[2] some 17 miles to the south-east of Aswân. Much more interesting is a group of rock-inscriptions in the already often mentioned greywacke quarries of the Wâdy Ḥammâmât. Hither in Nebtowerēʿ's second year was sent his vizier Amenemḥē to fetch him a great sarcophagus.[3] It may well be doubted whether as many as 20,000 men really accompanied the expedition, but there is no need for scepticism as regards two miraculous happenings which attended their short stay. The graphic story is told of a gazelle advancing fearlessly in full sight of the workpeople to drop its young upon the very stone intended for the lid of the sarcophagus.[4] Eight days later there was a great rain-storm which disclosed a well 10 cubits by 10 across full of water to the brim.[5] To the prosaically minded historian the personality of the vizier Amenemḥē is of greater interest, for it seems well-nigh certain that he was none other than the future Ammenemēs I, to give his name the Manethonian form. We have to suppose that at a given moment he conspired against his royal master, and perhaps after some years of confusion mounted the throne in his place. A recent discovery lends colour to this hypothesis. A Dyn. XVIII inscription extracted from the third pylon at Karnak names after Nebḥepetrēʿ and Sʿankhkarēʿ a 'god's father' Senwosre who from his title can only have been the non-royal parent of Ammenemēs I.[6] The TWELFTH DYNASTY, dated from 1991 to 1786 B.C., was, as we shall see, composed of a number of kings whose surnames were either Amenemḥē or Senwosre, for the most part alternately.

Apart from the justified conjectures just mentioned, more personal details are known about the founder of the new dynasty than about any other Pharaoh. Characteristically the sources of our knowledge are works of fiction or semi-fiction rather than formal official records. There exists in the Museum of Leningrad a papyrus

[1] Hayes, *Scepter*, i, p. 167, fig. 102. [2] PM vii. 319. [3] *BAR* i, §§ 439 ff.
[4] Op. cit., §§ 436 ff. [5] Op. cit., §§ 450 f. [6] *Mitt. Kairo*, xiv. 46, n. 6.

of which the whole purpose is the glorification of this monarch and which must, accordingly, have been composed in his reign or not much later. It is there related that King Śnofru (p. 77), seeking amusement, called upon his courtiers to find some clever man who could supply the required diversion. A lector-priest from Bubastis named Neferti was recommended, who when Śnofru elected to hear about the future rather than the past, launched out upon a description of coming disaster vividly recalling the picture painted in the already mentioned 'Admonitions' (pp. 109–10). Salvation was, however, to arrive at last:

A king shall come belonging to the South, Ameny by name, the son of a woman of Ta-Sti, a child of Khen-nekhen. He shall receive the White Crown, he shall wear the Red Crown.... The people of his time shall rejoice, the son of Someone shall make his name for ever and ever.

Here the non-royal descent of Ammenemēs I is clearly enough indicated, for the phrase 'son of Someone' was a common way of designating a man of good, though not princely, birth. Ta-Sti is the name of the first nome of Upper Egypt, that of which Elephantinē was the capital, and where the population was no doubt partly of Nubian race. Ameny is a well-authenticated abbreviation of the name Amenemḥē, which, as already noted, Manetho graecized into Ammenemēs. Amenemḥē means 'Amūn is in front', and this mention of the god Amūn raises a problem the solution of which is still obscure. Up to then, as we have seen, the principal deity of the Theban nome had been the warlike falcon-god Mont, but with the advent of the new dynasty the human-headed Amūn quickly gained predominance over him, soon to be assimilated to the sun-god Rēʿ, and ultimately to become the principal national divinity under the name 'Amen-Rēʿ, King of the Gods'. According to a plausible theory propounded by Kurt Sethe, Amūn was an importation from Hermopolis, but he was also early identified with the ithyphallic nature-god Mīn worshipped in the neighbouring Coptite nome. There is some slight evidence that Amūn was known at Thebes before the middle of Dyn. XI, so that the possibility cannot be ruled out that the king who incorporated the god's name in his own was of Theban birth. Certain it is, at all events, that both he and his son Senwosre I continued to honour Thebes with their monuments,[1] though wisely adopting as their capital a site more central between the Delta and Upper Egypt. Here, at Lisht on the west bank, they raised their pyramids and surrounded them with the tombs of their courtiers. The scanty remains, after a first excavation by J.-E. Gautier and G. Jéquier, have been exhaustively investigated by the Metropolitan Museum of Art in New York. In the eyes of later generations It-towĕ 'Seizer of the Two Lands', to give the new capital its Egyptian name, became the typical royal residence, not merely that of Dyn. XII, though as a town it was of negligible importance after the close of the Middle Kingdom.

The attitude of the new dynasty towards the old was somewhat ambiguous. That Ammenemēs I thought of himself as inaugurating a new epoch is clear from his adoption as his Horus name of the epithet Weḥam-meswe 'Repeater of Births', a metaphor derived from the monthly rebirth of the moon. Yet we find Senwosre I dedicating a statue to that Inyōtef the great, born of Iku, who was the ancestor of Dyn. XI,[2] and an altar to the Sʿankhkarēʿ Menthotpe whom, as we have seen, the king-lists put at its close.[3] If Ammenemēs I had any quarrel with the Menthotpe family at all, it was only with the short-lived Nebtowerēʿ. Thus it is not wholly without reason that Manetho gave Ammenemēs a position midway between the two dynasties. On the other hand, the Turin Canon is decisive in starting a new section with the kings of It-towĕ. For Dyn. XII the Canon is remarkably trustworthy, even the lengths of reign being accurately stated. Nor at this point must a word of commendation be refused to Manetho for somewhat similar reasons. He is mistaken, however, in describing Dyn. XII as Diospolite (Theban), since perhaps its principal differentiating feature, apart from its interdependence as a single family, was its removal to a geographic position far away to the north.

Of the greatness of Sḥetepibrēʿ Amenemḥē (Ammenemēs I) there can be no doubt. Otherwise his son and descendants would have been unable to retain their sovereignty for two whole centuries. Monuments vastly increase in number and the individual reigns are almost all long, sure signs of the prosperity and stability

[1] PM ii. 19, 41, &c. [2] Winlock, op. cit., p. 5, n. 12. [3] Gauthier, *LR* i. 245.

of the country. Local temples built or added to by the kings of Dyn. XII abound, though as a rule only isolated blocks have survived, the remainder having been destroyed or removed to make way for later constructions. Private stelae are very numerous, particularly those found at Abydos, a resort of pilgrims as the reputed burial-place of the god Osiris. It is evident that the first Ammenemēs aimed at securing for himself an autocracy rivalling that of the Pharaohs of the Old Kingdom. A grave difference subsisted, however. As yet there could be no question of completely abolishing the power of the nomarchs. We must be on our guard against assuming identical conditions in all parts of Egypt, but the splendid wall-paintings in the rock-tombs of Beni Ḥasan display the Great Chieftains of the Oryx nome (No. XVI of Upper Egypt) as little potentates in their own right. Many officials are there depicted whose titles recall those of functionaries attached to the royal palace, stewards, a superintendent of the hall of justice, another of the storehouse and ergastulum, treasurers, and even a captain of the army. Nor indeed are there absent bearers of foreign tribute. The tomb of the nomarch Khnemḥotpe favoured by Ammenemēs I shows gaudily dressed and befeathered Libyans bringing flocks of goats, and Asiatics with presents of eye-paint are seen in the tomb of a grandson of the same name who never attained the nomarchy, but only authority over a more limited area. A long and important inscription in the last-named tomb yields explicit testimony to the hereditary character of these princely dignitaries and the origin of some of them in alliances with the daughters of rulers of adjacent nomes. And yet there is no attempt to disguise the dependence of all such tenures upon the will and condescension of the king. Of the first honour conferred by Ammenemēs I upon the original nomarch Khnemḥotpe I it is said[1] that he

> appointed him to be hereditary prince, count and governor of the eastern deserts in Menʿat-Khufwey. He fixed his southern boundary-stone and secured his northern one like heaven. He divided the great river over its back, its eastern half belonging to (the district) Horizon-of-Horus as far as the eastern desert, when His Majesty had come that he might crush iniquity, arisen as Atum himself, and that he might repair

[1] *BAR* i, § 625.

what he had found ruined, what one town had seized from another, and that he might cause town to know its boundary with town, their boundary-stones being secured like heaven and their waters being made known according to what was in the writings and verified according to what was in antiquity, through the greatness of his love of Right.

The great achievement of the founder of the dynasty thus lay in the complete reorganization of the country. For the splendour of his own household and the maintenance of his bureaucracy he needed ample resources; and Ameny, whom his son Senwosre I had appointed to the nomarchy as successor of Khnemḥotpe I, relates:[1]

I spent years as ruler in the Oryx nome, and all services to the King's House were effected by me. I gave staff-overseers to the farm-holdings of the Oryx nome, three thousand oxen as their contingents, and was praised on account of it in the King's House in every census year. I delivered all their produce to the King's House, and there was no shortage against me in any bureau of his.

Ameny goes on to say that in spite of all the exactions imposed by his loyalty he had ruled his province with unswerving justice, respecting the poor man's daughter and the widow, banishing poverty and tilling the land with such assiduity that in years of famine no one was hungry. Evidently a balance had been established between royal power and princely pride, and at this moment Egypt was a feudal state more completely than ever before or after. But, nevertheless, there are indications that for the retention of the Pharaoh's authority elaborate precautions needed to be taken. Probably Ammenemēs was approaching middle age when he came to the throne. In his twentieth year he associated with himself as king his eldest son Senwosre I, and both reigned together for ten years more. The practice thus initiated was followed throughout the entire dynasty. Perhaps even at the start it was not quite an innovation, for we found evidence that Piopi I of Dyn. VI may have adopted a similar course (p. 97). In less exalted circles, at all events, aged men of wealth and station had found it prudent to take to themselves a 'staff of old age', as the position was quaintly called. In the case of royalty, however, an embarrassing difficulty arose. If the usually accepted theory of Egyptian kingship is correct, the

[1] Op. cit., §§ 522 f.

divine nature of the falcon-god Horus descended from son to son, the dying monarch relinquishing that attribute in order to become an Osiris. An act of association which resulted in two Horuses functioning simultaneously made nonsense of this doctrine, but there is no hint that the Egyptians ever felt scruples on this score. In matters of religion logic played no great part, and the assimilation or duplication of deities doubtless added a mystic charm to their theology.

For the end of the reign two literary works combine to give a consistent and evidently trustworthy picture. Both compositions became great favourites in the Egyptian schools, and centuries later were copied and recopied, though with ever increasing inaccuracy. The death of Ammenemēs I is described in a dream where he revealed himself to his son and successor in order to give him wise counsels. Warning Senwosre against too great intimacy with his subjects, he reinforces his advice by recalling what happened to himself:

It was after supper when night was come, I took an hour of repose, lying upon my bed. I was tired and my heart began to follow sleep. Of a sudden weapons were brandished and there was talk concerning me, whilst I remained like a snake of the desert. I awoke to fight, being by myself. I found it was an attack by the guard. Had I hastened with weapons in my hand, I could have driven back the caitiffs. But there is none strong at night. None can fight alone. There is no successful issue without a protector.

This clearly refers to the conspiracy in which Ammenemēs lost his life, and a memory of it, though attributed to the wrong king, survives in Manetho's statement that Ammenemēs II was murdered by his eunuchs. The sequel is narrated in what is certainly the greatest glory of Egyptian literature, the celebrated Story of Sinūhe. The relevant passage is here translated in its entirety:

Year 30, third month of the Inundation season, day 7, the god mounted to his horizon, the King of Upper and Lower Egypt Sḥetepibrēʿ went aloft to heaven and became united with the sun's disk, the limb of the god being merged in him who made him; whilst the Residence was hushed, hearts were in mourning, the Great Gates were closed, the courtiers crouched head on lap, and the nobles grieved.

Now His Majesty had sent an army to the land of the Tjemeḥ (Libyans), his eldest son as the captain thereof, the goodly god Senwosre. He had been sent to smite the foreign countries, and to take prisoner the dwellers in the Tjeḥnu-land, and now indeed he was returning and had carried off living prisoners of the Tjeḥnu and all kinds of cattle limitless. And the Companions of the Palace sent to the western side to acquaint the king's son concerning the position that had arisen in the Royal Apartments, and the messengers found him upon the road, they reached him at time of night. Not a moment did he linger, the falcon flew off with his followers, not letting his army know. But the king's children who accompanied him in this army had been sent for and one of them had been summoned . . . .

Sinūhe, a youth who had been brought up at the court, chanced to be standing by when the State secret was being told, and was so much alarmed that he fled precipitately, not staying his flight until he found himself in Palestine, where he found favour with the prince of Upper Retjnu. Exciting as is the rest of the tale, we must refrain from following it up further, since the most that can be claimed for it is that it is 'founded upon fact'.

This, however, is a not unsuitable place in which to summarize the dealings of Egypt with its north-eastern neighbours throughout Dyn. XII. The Prophecy of Neferti (p. 126) had emphasized even more strongly than the similar compositions above quoted the incursions of Asiatics (ʿAamu) into the Delta, and had mentioned, like the story of Sinūhe, the 'Walls of the Ruler, made to repel the Setyu, and to crush the Sand-farers'.[1] Where exactly these walls built by Ammenemēs I were situated is not known, but their twofold mention suffices to stress the danger that could still be anticipated from that quarter. For the time, however, relations were generally amicable. Towards the end of the dynasty, under Ammenemēs III, the brother of the Prince of Retjnu was assisting the Egyptians in the turquoise-workings of Serâbîṭ el-Khâdim in the Peninsula of Sinai,[2] but these workings were certainly not in Retjnu itself. Upper Retjnu may have extended as far north as the level of Byblos. From the two pieces of evidence above mentioned one might possibly conclude that a single powerful ruler dominated almost the whole

[1] See above, p. 36. [2] *Sinai*, ii, p. 19.

of Palestine, but this is contradicted by other testimony. The Egyptians, particularly in early times, were apt to regard all foreigners as their natural enemies. Recent finds of great interest have brought to light the names of both persons and places scrawled in hieratic upon broken red potsherds or upon the limestone figures of local princes represented as prisoners with their arms tied behind their backs. Most of the place-names are unidentifiable, but among them Ashkelon and Shechem are probabilities. The Egyptians of the period certainly hoped that the magic inherent in these objects would dispose of their enemies without recourse to arms. The stela of Nesmont[1] dated in the joint reigns of Ammenemēs I and Senwosre I shows that this general had to take the field against the Asiatic nomads and destroy their strongholds, but it is not known how far into foreign territory his activities extended. Later, in the reign of Senwosre III, the king himself travelled north to overthrow the Asiatics, and reached the region of Sekmem, which is accepted by most scholars as Shechem in the hill-country of Samaria.[2] Here Sebekkhu, one of his warriors, performed notable exploits which he narrates on his stela. Other similar records are too vague to possess much historical value. The general impression left is that Palestine was at this time mainly occupied by small tribes or communities each ruled over by a petty prince of its own. Much farther north there is considerable evidence of Middle Egyptian penetration, and so experienced an archaeologist as Sir Leonard Woolley held that definite campaigns must be assumed to explain the number of Dyn. XII objects which have been found. Two kings of Byblos received valuable gifts from Ammenemēs III and IV respectively,[3] and at Ṭôd was discovered a rich treasure of gold, silver, and lapis lazuli objects clearly of Mesopotamian or Aegean workmanship and inscribed with the cartouches of Ammenemēs II;[4] these were presumably presents from the rulers of Byblos. At Ḳaṭna to the north of Ḥomṣ a sphinx bearing the name of a daughter of Ammenemēs II was unearthed,[5] and similar sphinxes, as well as the private statue of a vizier known also from other sources, have been found at Ugarit, near the later Laodicea.[6] The northernmost

[1] *BAR* i, §§ 469 ff. [2] Op. cit. i, §§ 676 ff. [3] PM vii. 386. [4] Vandier, p. 256. [5] PM vii. 392. [6] Op. cit., 393–4.

limit for such finds is Atchana[1] at no great distance from the mouth of the Orontes. In the absence of inscriptional testimony the exact import of these and other like discoveries is necessarily a matter of conjecture. In this connexion it should be noted, however, that on stelae and in papyri Asiatic slaves are increasingly often mentioned, though there is no means of telling whether they were prisoners of war or had infiltrated into Egypt of their own accord.[2]

The magical artifices adopted to counter the malignity of Egypt's north-eastern neighbours were utilized also against the south, but here again the tribal names are hopelessly obscure. On the other hand, the inscriptional and archaeological evidence for the relations of the Dyn. XII Pharaohs with Nubia and the Sûdân is considerably more abundant. Tantalizing fragments from the reign of Menthotpe I have already been mentioned, but there is one, even more defective than the rest, which appears to claim the annexation to Upper Egypt of Wawaĕ and the outlying oases.[3] With Ammenemēs I records of greater certainty begin. By this time a new occupying race known to archaeologists as the C-group had gained a foothold in Lower Nubia, but they were not negroes, whose contact with the Egyptians goes back no further than Dyn. XVIII.[4] The generic term for the population of Nubia remained as before Neḥasyu, a name familiar to us in the Phinehas ('the Nubian') of the Bible and surviving in the modern Jewish surname Pincus. Now, however, is found for the first time the geographical name Cush, which in the New Kingdom designated an administrative province distinct from Wawaĕ and lying to the south of the Second Cataract, while in the Old Testament it corresponds vaguely to Ethiopia.[5] At all periods the northern boundary of Wawaĕ was the First Cataract in the neighbourhood of Shellâl. The southern boundary in Dyn. XII is uncertain, but may as later have extended even as far as Wâdy Ḥalfa. We may certainly credit Ammenemēs I with the subjugation of Lower Nubia. An inscription of his twenty-ninth year at Korosko records his arrival 'to overthrow Wawaĕ'.[6]

[1] Op. cit. vii. 395.
[2] G. Posener in *Syria*, xxxiv. 145 ff.
[3] H. F. Lutz, *Egyptian Tomb Steles*, Leipzig, 1927, Pl. 34, No. 66.
[4] Säve-Söderbergh, pp. 39 ff.
[5] See already above, p. 34.
[6] *BAR* i, §§ 472 f.

Under his son and co-regent Senwosre I Wâdy Ḥalfa was firmly held and a garrison established there. A magnificent sandstone stela[1] erected by a general named Menthotpe depicts the god Mont of Thebes—be it noted, not as yet Amūn—presenting to Senwosre captives from a number of Sudanese lands, with Cush at their head. That it was not mere lust of conquest which was now the principal aim is clear from the narrative inscribed on the doorway of his tomb at Beni Ḥasan by the already mentioned Ameny, the nomarch of the Oryx nome.[2] He describes how, replacing his aged father, he sailed upstream and 'passed beyond Cush and reached the ends of the earth'. On this occasion Senwosre himself was at the head of the army, which returned from the campaign without suffering loss. Subsequently Ameny accompanied his namesake the king's eldest son, doubtless the later Ammenemēs II, to fetch treasures of gold for His Majesty, and having accomplished his mission successfully, won high praise at the royal palace. In the Old Kingdom gold from Nubia is never mentioned. Perhaps by Dyn. XII the workings to the east of Egypt were becoming exhausted or else the demands of the Pharaohs were increasing. Anyhow, from the Middle Kingdom onward Nubia was the gold-producing country *par excellence*. Nor was gold by any means the sole product sought in that direction; a number of other much-prized commodities from the Sûdân have been mentioned in Chapter III (p. 44). Most of these things were obtained by barter from the natives, the Medjayu from over the border at the Second Cataract being specially mentioned. It is clear, however, that invasion from the south was a perennial dread and that though expeditions to Lower Nubia and the neighbouring deserts now became frequent, they were always something of an adventure and there was little or no actual colonization. A papyrus[3] lists as many as thirteen fortresses between Elephantinē and Semna at the south end of the Second Cataract. Most of these have been identified and planned. Those to the north of Wâdy Ḥalfa are on the flat and were evidently intended to keep a vigilant watch upon the native population. No less than seven fortresses lie within the 40-mile stretch of the Second Cataract, mostly on eminences and several of them upon islands. These were

[1] Op. cit. i, §§ 510 ff. [2] Op. cit. i, §§ 519 f. [3] *Onom.* i, pp. 10* f.

obviously designed for defence, as indeed is shown by such names of theirs as 'Repelling the Tribes' and 'Curbing the Deserts'. They are vast structures of thick brick walls, enclosing sufficient space to house many officials and scribes as well as substantial garrisons. The exact dates at which these were built are mostly unknown, but there is no doubt that the Pharaoh who strove most energetically to promote his suzerainty in this direction was Senwosre III. It was he who gave his name 'Powerful is (King) Khaʿkaurēʿ' to the fortress of Semna at the southern end of the Second Cataract, just opposite to the fortress of Kumma on the east bank, the two combining to protect both the land and the river routes; and we have Senwosre III's own word for the fact that here was definitely fixed his southern boundary. On the great stela where he makes light of his apprehensions by the contemptuous description of the Nubians quoted above, p. 37, he concludes as follows:

> As for any son of mine who shall maintain this boundary which My Majesty has made, he is my son and was born to me . . . but he who shall destroy it and fail to fight for it, he is not my son and was not born to me.

In his eighth year when he sailed upstream 'to overthrow vile Cush' the same king had ordered a new channel to be dug near the island of Sehêl in the First Cataract to help his own ships,[1] but an inscription at Semna dated in the same year shows that the most stringent measures were taken to prevent the Nubians from intrusion in the opposite direction:[2]

> Southern boundary made in Year 8 . . . to prevent any Nubian from passing it downstream or overland or by boat, (also) any herds of Nubians, apart from any Nubian who shall come to trade in Iken[3] or upon any good business that may be done with them.

How strictly this policy was pursued is shown by dispatches of the early Dyn. XIII sent from Semna to the Theban capital, much tattered copies of which are preserved in a papyrus now in the British Museum.[4] These show that even the most trivial movements

[1] *BAR* i, §§ 642 ff.
[2] Op. cit. i, § 652.
[3] The fortress next to the south from Wâdy Ḥalfa.
[4] *JEA* xxxi. 3 ff.

of Medjayu people were reported, and the almost daily letters end with the stereotyped formula:

All the affairs of the King's Domain are safe and sound; all the affairs of the Master are safe and sound.

Centuries later Senwosre III was worshipped as a god throughout Nubia. In Manetho he is fused with his predecessor Senwosre II, both sharing the name Sesōstris. However great their foreign conquests may have been, it is hard to conceive how their combined victories can have been inflated into those of this world-conquering hero as described by Herodotus and Diodorus. But there was also another reason why most early Egyptologists refused to identify the semi-legendary Sesōstris with the fourth and fifth kings of Dyn. XII. In the hieroglyphs the Nomen or second cartouche of those kings appeared to show the reading Usertsen, which no amount of philological juggling could equate with the Manethonian Sesōstris. It was K. Sethe[1] who first proved that the Nomen involved the inversion of a divine name such as we have encountered earlier (pp. 80–1), and that consequently the true reading was Se-n-Wosre, meaning 'the man of Wosre, the powerful goddess'; the transition from Senwosre to Sesōstris was only a small one, and is not open to doubt.

Mention must, however, now be made of a discovery which can only with difficulty be reconciled with Sesōstris III's fixing of his southern boundary at Semna. At Kerma,[2] some little distance to the south of the Third Cataract and hence well over 100 miles upstream from the Second, the American excavator G. Reisner found a fort-like building and a cemetery which may have been occupied as early as the beginning of Dyn. XII. An inscription of Ammenemēs III which records the number of bricks required for the restoration of this outpost gives its name as 'Walls of Ammenemēs', and other finds point to the likelihood that the founder was none other than Ammenemēs I. There were even alabaster jars bearing the name of Piopi I (Dyn. VI), but these may have been imports brought much later for purposes of exchange. The cemeteries found here are utterly un-Egyptian in character, as also the

[1] *Untersuchungen*, ii. 1.

[2] PM vii. 175 ff.; Säve-Söderbergh, pp. 103 ff.

pottery, faience, bone inlays, and weapons discovered therein; the graves themselves are large circular tumuli completely different from the mastabas of contemporary Egypt. The dead lay upon their sides unmummified, and wives and attendants had been killed and buried with their master so as to serve him in the next world.[1] In one tumulus was found a magnificent statue of a Ḥapdjefai who may have been the governor, and another of his wife; this man is known from his tomb at Asyûṭ in the XIIIth nome of Upper Egypt to have lived under Senwosre I. Was then this a permanent trading and manufacturing station, and how can it have maintained itself if, as the line of fortresses in the Second Cataract seems to presuppose, all the territory further upstream was normally hostile?

The needs of architects, sculptors, and jewellers demanded ever more diligent exploitation of the deserts and countries surrounding Egypt, and wherever the necessary rocks afforded the opportunity, inscriptions record the names of the royal emissaries. The 'basalt' of the Wâdy Ḥammâmât, the alabaster of Ḥatnūb, and the diorite from the north-west of Abu Simbel were put under contribution as eagerly as ever, and the Wâdy el-Ḥûdi continued to supply its amethyst. In the peninsula of Sinai new workings on a grand scale were opened at Serâbîṭ el-Khâdim, where a temple was built to Ḥatḥōr, 'lady of the turquoise'. The relations with Palestine have already been discussed, but the even more problematical connexion with Crete cannot be ignored. In that great seat of the Minoan culture not many Egyptian objects have been found,[2] but in Egypt polychrome decorated pottery of undoubted Cretan manufacture has been forthcoming in Dyn. XII contexts at Hawwâra in the Fayyûm, and elsewhere; most striking of all is a magnificent bowl discovered by Garstang at Abydos and now in the Ashmolean Museum at Oxford. The vexed question whether Keftiu was the Egyptian name of Crete and is to be equated with the Biblical Caphtor is still hotly debated.[3] Far away to the south-east Egyptian expeditions were still busy with Pwēne and the Somali coast. From the Wâdy Gasûs some distance to the north of the Red Sea port of

[1] Dows Dunham, *Museum of Fine Arts, Boston: the Egyptian Department and its excavations*, Boston, 1958, pp. 82 ff. [2] PM vii. 405. [3] *Onom.* i, p. 203*.

Ḳuṣêr came a stela of the twenty-eighth year of Ammenemēs II recording such an expedition,[1] and another stela of the first year of the following reign doubtless refers to a similar undertaking with the words 'establishing his (the king's) monuments in the God's Land'. Curiously little consideration has been devoted to the question of what god is here meant; the expression 'the God's Land' is found not only here, but also in connexion with Asiatic expeditions, and since these were often headed by an official called a 'god's seal-bearer' or chancellor it seems likely that the deity in question was none other than the Pharaoh himself, so that the underlying notion would be his presumptuous claim to own the treasures of all foreign lands.

Though Ammenemēs I had chosen Lisht (It-towĕ) as the site for his pyramid, adjacent to which Senwosre I built his own, the remaining kings of Dyn. XII had other preferences. Ammenemēs II returned to Dahshûr and the neighbourhood of Śnofru's two vast edifices. The tumble-down ruins, investigated by J. de Morgan in 1894,[2] revealed nothing abnormal save in the method of construction, and it is only from the mastabas hard by that the name of the owner could be recovered. The reasons which prompted the next king Senwosre II to erect his pyramid over 30 miles to the south and a good 10 miles from the Nile can only be guessed. The chosen site of El-Lâhûn lies just north of the place where the important canal named the Baḥr Yûsuf turns westward to enter the oasis of the Fayyûm (p. 36). Senwosre I had given his special attention to that remarkably fertile province, placing at Ebgîg a cryptic monument nearly 50 feet high which has always been described as an obelisk, but which may have carried at its summit a statue of the king.[3] Whether it was he or one of his successors who instituted the irrigational improvements referred to by Herodotus and Strabo is unknown, but certain it is that from this time onwards the surroundings of the famous Lake of Moeris became a happy resort for the Pharaohs, who there indulged their passion for fishing and fowling.[4] The pyramid of Senwosre II[5] displays an innovation which

[1] PM vii. 338.
[2] Op. cit., iii. 234.
[3] Op. cit., iv. 99; *Ann. Serv.* xxvi. 105 ff.
[4] R. A. Caminos, *Literary Fragments*, Oxford, 1956, pp. 22 ff.
[5] PM iv. 107 ff.

was copied in two other pyramids of the dynasty. Experience had shown how rarely escape from robbery was possible so long as the entrance leading to the burial chamber occupied its normal position on the north side of the superstructure. Senwosre's architect therefore decided to place the entrance outside the pyramid itself.[1] This device, however, proved unavailing for the purpose for which it was intended, since when at last the burial chamber was reached it was found to have been remorselessly plundered; of the rich funerary equipment with which it had doubtless originally been filled all that remained was a magnificent red granite sarcophagus together with an alabaster table of offerings. Yet the architect had been at least so far successful that it cost Flinders Petrie months of tireless labour before he came upon the shaft which descended to the passage leading to the interior. A similar expenditure of time was exacted when five years later (1894) J. de Morgan investigated the pyramids of Senwosre III and Ammenemēs III at Dahshûr. Here again the robbers had got the better of the builders, at the same time frustrating any hope that modern archaeologists might have had of finding an intact Pharaonic burial. Consolation was, however, offered at both Dahshûr and El-Lâhûn (the latter in 1914) by the splendid jewellery discovered in the shaft-tombs of royal princesses within the pyramid enclosure walls. The pectorals, crowns, armlets, collars, &c., exhibiting craftsmanship of the highest order and mounting in gold many semi-precious stones such as lapis lazuli, amethyst, carnelian, and felspar, are among the greatest treasures of the Cairo and New York collections. If the designs no longer have the chaste simplicity of the rare examples from the Old Kingdom, they are nevertheless as yet free from the clumsiness seen in the jewels from the tomb of Tutʿankhamūn.

With Ammenemēs III we once again come across the strange phenomenon of a Pharaoh possessing more than a single pyramid. The monument which he caused to be raised in addition to that at Dahshûr was situated at Hawwâra, a few miles to the west of El-Lâhûn alongside a canal of Arab date. Here again elaborate steps had been taken to foil would-be plunderers, and Petrie's efforts to reach the actual place of burial (1886) were no less exacting than those at

[1] For all the following see Edwards, *Pyramids*, pp. 183 ff.

El-Lâhûn in the following season. It was the funerary temple of the Hawwâra pyramid which constituted the Labyrinth described in such detail by Herodotus, Diodorus Siculus, and Strabo. The site cursorily investigated by Petrie at the same time as the pyramid and then again in 1911, revealed itself as a vast area of limestone chips, with only scanty remains bearing the names of Ammenemēs III and the queen Sebeknofru of whom more will be heard later. The size of this area and its square shape preclude the idea that this funerary temple can have been one of the ordinary type. Indeed, it may be taken as certain that the accounts given by the classical writers were not far wide of the mark. Herodotus (ii. 148) speaks of the building as a wonder surpassing even the pyramids, and Strabo (xvii. 1. 37) describes it as containing a large number of courts interconnected by winding passages through which no stranger could find his way. How the Egyptian building came by the Anatolian name 'labyrinth' has been explained in our first chapter. Mention may here be made of the two 'pyramids' which Herodotus (ii. 149) claimed to have seen rising out of the Sea of Moeris. There can be no doubt that by this were meant the two colossal seated statues of Ammenemēs III which Petrie found looking out over the lake at Biyahmu;[1] these giants, including their pedestals, must have measured 60 feet in height, and it is supposed that they stood in a court very nearly on top of a reclaiming dike. No similar monument has been found in the whole of Egypt, unless the already mentioned obelisk of Ebgîg can be regarded as such.

It has been noticed that the great provincial tombs found at the beginning of the dynasty disappear after the reign of Senwosre III, and Ed. Meyer inferred with considerable probability that this monarch brought about, if not the suppression, at least a radical transformation, of the feudal state. At all events it is difficult to shut our eyes to the great enhancement of the royal power. Hymns of praise extol the virtues of both Senwosre III[2] and Ammenemēs III.[3] The latter king reigned upwards of forty-five years, and his successor Ammenemēs IV, according to the Turin Canon, nine years, three months, and twenty-seven days, though his sixth year is the

[1] PM. iv. 98. [2] Erman, *Lit.*, pp. 134 ff.
[3] Op. cit., pp. 84 f.; Wilson in *ANET*, p. 431.

latest date recorded at Sinai. The dynasty came to an end with Sebeknofru, whom Manetho possibly rightly gives as the sister of the last Ammenemēs; the Turin Canon assigns to her three years and ten months; and though she is ignored in the Abydos list, at Saḳḳâra she is mentioned by her Prenomen Sebekkarēʿ as the successor of Ammenemēs IV; a cylinder in the British Museum gives her an almost full royal titulary.[1] There is definite evidence that at one moment she was associated on the throne with Ammenemēs III, presumably her father, and even more decisive evidence that Ammenemēs III and Ammenemēs IV were for a time so associated, whereas there is no hint of a co-regency between Ammenemēs IV and Sebeknofru.[2] On such observations as these it is dangerous to base any positive conclusions, but there seems considerable likelihood of a family feud out of which Sebeknofru emerged the victor. It would be the second time in Egyptian history that a woman succeeded in establishing herself as 'King of Upper and Lower Egypt', but so abnormal a situation contained the seed of disaster. After Sebeknofru, as after Nitōcris, there followed a succession of kings none of whose reigns, so far as can be seen, exceeded three years. From whatever cause, the glorious Middle Kingdom had finally broken down.

Considering the large number of private stelae which can with confidence be assigned to Dyn. XII, it is disappointing that so few throw light upon individual events or prevailing conditions. Only a minority are dated, and most rest content with the stereotyped wish for 'all things good and pure on which the god lives' followed by the title and name of the owner and an enumeration of the members of his family. Laudatory epithets are not uncommon, but such claims as to have been 'truly loved of his lord' and 'cleaving to the path of him who adorned him' are often all that we are permitted to learn about the person in question. Is it illusion to suppose that the hand of the sovereign now weighed even heavier than of old upon his subservient subjects, and that under the new autocracy the cult of personality was deliberately discouraged? We must not exaggerate, however, and it seems appropriate here to mention a few sources that illumine different aspects of the life of

[1] Gauthier, *LR* i. 341. [2] *JEA* xxix. 74 f.

the period, though it will be left to those more adventurous to attempt to combine these into a comprehensive picture. Here again a work of fiction is the most colourful source. Nothing could be more picturesque than the account given of Sinūhe's return to Egypt. After a highly honoured life in Palestine, assailed by the longing to be buried in the land of his birth, he wrote a humble petition to Senwosre I, then occupying the throne of the Pharaohs. A free pardon having been granted for his precipitate flight many years before, he was met at the frontier by ships laden with good things. On arrival at It-towĕ he was at once conducted all dust-bespattered and unshorn into the royal presence, where the monarch welcomed him with a few kind words which his trepidation barely suffered him to understand.

The Royal Children were ushered in. Then His Majesty said to the Royal Consort: Behold Sinūhe, who is come as an ʿAam, an offspring of Setyu-folk. She gave a great cry and the Royal Children shrieked out all together. And they said to His Majesty: It is not really he, O Sovereign my lord! And His Majesty said: Yes, it is really he!

In this story we come closer to reality than perhaps in any other piece of ancient writing, but the rest of the tale must not be allowed to detain us. A glimpse of legalistic procedure may be seen in a long inscription carved upon the wall of Prince Ḥapdjefai's tomb at Asyûṭ. Here are set forth at length the paragraphs of contracts made with the priesthood of the local temple.[1] Ḥapdjefai had appointed a 'soul-servant' to attend to his funeral cult after his death, endowing him with land, serfs, and cattle as inducement for the loyal discharge of his duties. By a series of exchanges with the priests offerings to his statue were ensured throughout the year. One cannot read the elaborate stipulations of these contracts without realizing that strict rules of property lie behind them, for instance a distinction between what the prince owned by virtue of inheritance and what he owned by virtue of his office. Much information concerning the internal administration of the temples would, with closer study, be gathered from the mass of papyri discovered in a chamber of the pyramid-town of El-Lâhûn. As an example a docu-

[1] *JEA* v, 79 ff.

ment may be quoted where the daily payments to the various members of the temple staff are recorded,[1] the superintendent at their head receiving sixteen variously sized loaves of bread and eight jugs of beer. The staff payments[2] represented, however, only a sixth part of the daily revenue of the temple, the bulk being disposed of to 'soul-servants', but to whose we are not informed. Another papyrus fragment of administrative interest was found at Ḥaraga, a Dyn. XII site only a couple of miles away.[3] This is a memorandum of the days spent in measuring fields, assessing taxes, and reporting on the subject to the overseer of land of the Northern District. It would be quite in keeping with Egyptian habit if the statement of the duties of the vizier inscribed in several tombs of Dyn. XVIII[4] really referred to conditions four centuries earlier, but of this we cannot be sure, and the sparseness of our material and the stage thus far reached in our studies make any attempt at a synthesis very precarious.

The site of El-Lâhûn excavated by Petrie proved to be of exceptional interest, since it yielded the remains of a town all of one period, revealing an unexpected degree of town-planning and a mass of furniture, implements, and ornaments almost unique in the land of the Pharaohs. The houses of the wealthy, built of brick like those of the poor, all possessed an atrium bordered by columns and with a limestone tank in the centre. 'The roofing was usually of beams, overlaid with bundles of straw, and mud-plastered; but many arched roofs of brickwork remain, some entire, others with only the lower part. The doorways were always arched in brickwork, and we know now for certain that the arch was not only known, but was in constant use by the early Egyptians.'[5] A wall ran around three sides of the town, leaving it open to the Nile plain on the south. Within, a main street surrounded a main block of houses, minor streets running between the buildings. Besides the mass of temple accounts and correspondence later found in the temple itself, papyri dealing with various topics were gathered from many of the houses, the difficult task of their decipherment

[1] *JEA* xlii. 119. [2] *ZÄS* xl. 113 ff. [3] *JEA* xxvii. 74 ff.
[4] Davies, *Rekh-mi-rēʿ*, i, pp. 88 ff. See above, p. 104.
[5] Petrie, *Ten Years' Digging in Egypt*, London, 1893, p. 115.

being one of the outstanding achievements of that great scholar F. Ll. Griffith. One medical work deals with women's diseases, and a veterinary fragment with those of animals. Then there are wills from which we learn that a man was able to bequeath pretty well as he chose not only his house and chattels, but also such an office as that of director of a phylē of lay-priests. In another case a wife was left, among other things, four ʿAamu, Asiatic slaves. Such documents had to be formally witnessed, and deposited in the house of the Recorder. Censuses of households were taken and similarly registered. In a word, the busy life of this important local community was regulated by strict administrative measures, the extent and co-ordination of which can only be glimpsed from the surviving debris of manuscripts.

Elsewhere a tomb-wall or else a stela may illustrate some side of life not yet mentioned. One official tells how he was sent to the Oasis to round up some fugitives.[1] At Bersha a famous scene depicts the dragging of a colossal statue to its destination, not less than 172 young soldiers belonging to the Hare nome being engaged in the undertaking.[2] Soldiers of outstanding valour might receive valuable gifts from the king, perhaps a dagger and a bow chased in gold; the Sebekkhu who distinguished himself in Palestine (p. 132) was rewarded not only with these but with sixty serfs as well. Important missions might be entrusted to particularly esteemed officials. Thus Senwosre III sent his chief treasurer Ikhernofre to Abydos there to equip the temple of Osiris with splendid furniture encrusted with gold, silver, and lapis lazuli, and whilst on the spot he directed the dramatic ceremonies simulating the tragic life of the murdered god.[3] Before ending this chapter reference must be made to some of the more important monuments of the period which have escaped destruction. At Hēliopolis a solitary obelisk still stands a witness to the great temple which Senwosre I erected there,[4] as recorded also in a leather document already mentioned.[5] At Karnak gleaming limestone blocks later used in the construction of the Third Pylon have been reassembled into a small but beautiful jubilee chapel of the same king. It is possibly due to its remoteness that

[1] *ZÄS* lxv. 108 ff. [2] *BAR* i, §§ 694 ff. [3] Op. cit. i, §§ 661 ff. [4] PM iv. 60.
[5] See above, p. 56.

a modest temple excavated by the Italians at Medînet Mâḍî in the Fayyûm province is better preserved than other sanctuaries of the kind elsewhere. To characterize the art of Dyn. XII satisfactorily is hardly possible here, but at least it may be said that it displays differences from all that had gone before which even the unpractised eye can detect. The conventions are the same, the different models are the same, and yet there are palpable differences. In particular one may note the grimness and determination of the sculptured features of the Pharaoh, the supreme masterpieces being the obsidian head of Ammenemēs III formerly in the Macgregor collection[1] and the Moscow statuette of the same king which we have been privileged to reproduce as our Frontispiece.

SELECT BIBLIOGRAPHY

First Intermediate Period: H. Stock, *Die erste Zwischenzeit Ägyptens*, Rome, 1949, reviewed by G. Posener in *Bibl. Or.* viii. 165 ff. A. H. Gardiner, *The Admonitions of an Egyptian Sage*, Leipzig, 1909; latest translation by J. A. Wilson in *ANET*, pp. 441 ff. A. H. Gardiner, *The Story of the Eloquent Peasant*, in *JEA* ix. 5 ff. A. H. Gardiner, *The Instruction for King Merykarēʿ*, in *JEA* i. 20 ff.; latest translation by J. A. Wilson in *ANET*, pp. 414 ff. The Coptos decrees, listed with additions, W. C. Hayes in *JEA* xxxii. 3 ff. J. Vandier, *Moʿalla*, Cairo, 1950; also *La Famine dans l'Égypte ancienne*, Cairo, 1936, pp. 3–16. H. Brunner, *Die Texte aus den Gräbern der Herakleopolitenzeit von Siut*, Glückstadt, 1937. R. Anthes, *Die Felseninschriften von Hatnub*, Leipzig, 1928.

Eleventh Dynasty: H. E. Winlock, *The Rise and Fall of the Middle Kingdom in Thebes*, New York, 1947; also *Excavations at Deir el Bahri*, New York, 1942. J. J. Clère and J. Vandier, *Textes de la première période intermédiaire et de la XIIe Dynastie*, i, Brussels, 1948. J. Couyat and P. Montet, *Les Inscriptions hiéroglyphiques et hiératiques du Ouâdi Hammâmât*, Cairo, 1912–13; É. Naville, *The XIth Dynasty Temple at Deir el-Bahari*, 3 vols., London, 1907–13. H. E. Winlock, *Models of Daily Life in Ancient Egypt*, Cambridge, Mass., 1955.

Twelfth Dynasty: Lisht, PM iv. 77 ff.; El-Lâhûn, op. cit. iv. 107 ff.; Medînet Mâḍî, reports by A. Vogliano, Milan, 1936–7; Dahshûr, PM iii. 229 ff.; Fayyûm, op. cit. iv. 98 ff.; Beni Ḥasan, op. cit. iv. 141 ff.; Karnak, P. Lacau and H. Chevrier, *Une Chapelle de Sésostris I*, Paris, 1956.

Literature: G. Posener, *Littérature et politique dans l'Égypte de la XII dynastie*, Paris, 1956. The Prophecy of Neferti, A. H. Gardiner in *JEA* i. 100 ff.; latest

[1] *JEA* iv. 71.

translation by J. A. Wilson in *ANET*, pp. 444 ff. The Story of Sinūhe, A. H. Gardiner, *Notes on the Story of Sinuhe*, Paris, 1916; latest translation by J. A. Wilson in *ANET*, pp. 18 ff. The Instruction of Ammenemēs I, latest translation by J. A. Wilson in *ANET*, pp. 418 f.

Papyri from El-Lâhûn: F. Ll. Griffith, *The Petrie Papyri*, 2 vols., London, 1898; various articles by L. Borchardt in *ZÄS*; the letters, A. Scharff in *ZÄS* lix. 20 ff.

Relations with foreign places and peoples: Sinai, A. H. Gardiner and T. E. Peet, *The Inscriptions of Sinai*, 2nd ed. by J. Černý, 2 vols., London, 1952–5. The execration texts: K. Sethe, *Die Ächtung feindlicher Fürsten, Völker und Dinge*, in *Abh.* Berlin, 1926; G. Posener, *Princes et pays d'Asie et de Nubie*, Brussels, 1940. Nubia: T. Säve-Söderbergh, *Ägypten und Nubien*, Lund, 1941.

VII

FROM COLLAPSE TO RECOVERY

SINCE the passage of Time shows no break in continuity, naught but some momentous event or sequence of events can justify a particular reign being regarded as inaugurating an era. What caused Sebeknofru, or Sebeknofrurēʿ as later sources call her, to be taken as closing Dyn. XII will doubtless never be known, but the Turin Canon, the Saḳḳâra king-list, and Manetho are unanimous on the point, while the Abydos list jumps straight from Ammenemēs IV to the first king of Dyn. XVIII. The date of Amōsis I, the founder of Dyn. XVIII, being fixed with some accuracy, the interval from 1786 to 1575 B.C. must be accepted as the duration of the Second Intermediate Period, an age the problems of which are even more intractable than those of the First. Before entering upon details, it will be well to note that the general pattern of these two dark periods is roughly the same. Both begin with a chaotic series of insignificant native rulers; in both, intruders from Palestine cast their shadow over the Delta and even into the Valley; and in both relief comes at last from a hardy race of Theban princes, who after quelling internal dissension expel the foreigner and usher in a new epoch of immense power and prosperity.

Some account has already been given (p. 66) of the formidable difficulties here confronting us, but these must now be discussed at length. As usual we start with Manetho. The THIRTEENTH DYNASTY according to him, was Diospolite (Theban) and consisted of sixty kings who reigned for 453 years; the FOURTEENTH DYNASTY counted seventy-six kings from Xois, the modern Sakhâ in the central Delta, with a total of 184 or, as an alternative reading, 484 years. For Dyns. XV to XVII there is divergence between Africanus and Eusebius, while a much simpler account is preserved by the Jewish historian Josephus in what purports to be a verbatim extract from Manetho's own writing. For our present purpose the data supplied by Africanus must suffice. His FIFTEENTH DYNASTY consists of six foreign so-called 'Shepherd' or Hyksōs kings, whose domination lasted 284 years. The SIXTEENTH DYNASTY consisted of Shepherd kings again, thirty-two in number totalling 518 years. Lastly, in the SEVENTEENTH DYNASTY Shepherd kings and Theban kings reigned concurrently, forty-three of each line, altogether 151 years. Adding these figures, but adopting the lower number of years given for Dyn. XIV, we obtain 217 kings covering a stretch of 1590 years, over seven times the duration to which acceptance of the Sothic date in the El-Lâhûn papyrus (p. 66) has committed us. To abandon 1786 B.C. as the year when Dyn. XII ended[1] would be to cast adrift from our only firm anchor, a course that would have serious consequences for the history, not of Egypt alone, but of the entire Middle East.

Of the three monumental king-lists that of Karnak alone enumerates rulers of the period. In its undamaged state it may have mentioned as many as thirty, about half that number being authenticated by actual remains, building blocks, stelae, or the like, mostly from the Theban area. Unfortunately these names are interspersed among those of Old or Middle Kingdom kings in so disorderly a fashion that no trustworthy sequence is obtainable. The Turin Canon, despite its fragmentary condition, is a source of great value.[2] As remounted by Ibscher, the papyrus fragments distribute the kings from Dyn. XIII until far down in the direction of Dyn. XVIII over no less than six columns, each containing up to thirty entries. It would be unwise, however, to assume that the manuscript, when intact, named as many as 180 distinct kings, since columns 10 and 11 are somewhat doubtful quantities, and some of the names mentioned in them, as well as in column 9, have a very suspect appearance. Not more than about sixty names are still sufficiently well preserved to make their identity certain, only about a third of these being authenticated by external monuments. On the other hand, the monuments acquaint us with a considerable number of names which must belong to this period but for one reason or another—some no doubt on account of the Canon's defective condition—are not to be found in that document. Immense labour has been de-

[1] Parker, p. 69. [2] Translated in full at the end of this book.

voted to collecting this material, and to seeking to place the different reigns in correct chronological order. For this purpose the style of the scarabs found bearing royal cartouches, the appearance and structure of the names themselves, and other evidence equally tenuous, have all been employed; but when all is said and done the results have been of a hypothetical character ill calculated to commend itself to any but the most venturesome scholars. Here we shall content ourselves with little more than a scrutiny of the Turin Canon itself. Indubitably the Ramesside compiler believed himself able to present the hundred or so kings known to him in a single continuous series, with the exact length of each reign correctly stated. The number of years is preserved in some twenty-nine cases, these totalling in all 153 years without counting the odd months and days. Included in that total are six kings (mostly to be named hereafter) whose reign in each instance exceeds ten years, amounting together to 101 years, though the reading of the numerals is not always as certain as one could wish. This leaves for the remaining twenty-three kings a sum of no more than fifty-two years, an average of little more than two years apiece. It is conspicuous that in the rare occurrences of dated monuments the date is more often than not in the first, second, or third year. Remembering the contention of the last chapter that in Egypt prolonged length of reign is a sure indication of the country's prosperity, we can now maintain the converse and argue that during the period which in the Turin Canon corresponds to Manetho's Dyns. XIII and XIV the land was in a state of dire havoc and confusion, its rulers murdering and replacing one another with extreme rapidity. In two, if not three, cases[1] the Canon mentions a kingless interval, in one case of six years' duration. On four occasions[2] a formula is found which Ed. Meyer without solid ground interpreted as marking the advent of a new dynasty, but twice there occur words summing up a preceding one; of far greater interest than the isolated '[Total], five kings ....' in 11. 15 is an unnumbered fragment known already to Seyffarth and rediscovered by Botti, which Ibscher and Farina placed in the middle of column 10; immediately following a line which must be restored as '[Chieftain of a foreign country]

[1] Turin Canon 6. 6; 8. 12, 14. [2] Ibid. 6. 5; 7. 3; 8. 4, 20.

Khamudy' comes another giving '[Total, chieftains of] a foreign country, 6, making 108 years'. These are obviously the foreign usurpers referred to by Africanus in connexion with Manetho's Dyns. XV, XVI, and XVII. But of them later; here we are concerned only with chronology. The entry just quoted practically compels us to conclude that the Canon embraced contemporary dynasties ruling in different parts of Egypt, even if the compiler was unaware of the fact. For when 108 years are subtracted from the 211 which are all that can be allowed for the Second Intermediate Period, we find a hundred or more kings huddled into little more than a century, which is, of course, absurd and becomes still more so when account is taken of the above-mentioned 101 years assigned to six reigns. It follows that the 108 years of the Hyksōs rulers cannot be subtracted in this way, and must refer to domination somewhere in the Delta. The alternative, therefore, which all recent Egyptologists accept, is that the Canon's enumeration comprised many kings existing simultaneously, but presumably in widely distant parts of the country. Manetho, as may be seen from his reference to Xois, was not entirely unaware of the fact, though he too regarded his dynasties as consecutive. Unhappily it is only seldom that a king of the Turin list can be pinned down to a restricted area. Perhaps the dynast who took the Nomen of Mermeshaʿ 'the General' (6. 21) held sway only in the extreme north, since outside the Canon he is known only from two statues found at Tanis, and the like may be true of Neḥasy 'the Nubian' (8. 1) who despite his name seems to have belonged to the Delta. It is possibly significant that whereas nearly half of the kings of column 6 have left monuments or fragments in Upper Egypt, only very few have been found of the kings of the remaining columns. It will be seen how sadly, in discussing matters such as these, we are reduced to guessing.

Much ingenious argument has been used in the attempt to group the kings of the period differently from the way in which the Turin Canon presents them, and it would be unjust to dismiss all such hypotheses as failures. But nowhere apparently has its ordering of names been definitely proved at fault. In the observations that follow the sequence of the Canon is accepted only for the lack of one more solidly founded. There is no doubt, at all events, about the first two rulers of Dyn. XIII. They are respectively Sekhemrēʿ-khutowe and Sekhemkarēʿ, the last kings to be mentioned in the El-Lâhûn papyri, and the last in whose reigns levels of the Nile were recorded at Semna. Between them they ruled no more than ten years, after which came the already mentioned kingless gap of six years. That both exerted their authority over the entire land from the Fayyûm to the Second Cataract and beyond is clear, and the facts that the first of the two took the name Amenemḥē-Sebekḥotpe as his Nomen, and that the second may have adopted Amenemḥē-sonbef as his, show how desperately they clung to the hope of being recognized as legitimate successors of Dyn. XII. This hope is even more pathetically exhibited in the Nomen of Sʿankh-ibrēʿ, the sixth king of the dynasty, who could be satisfied with nothing less pompous than the name Ameny-Inyōtef-Amenemḥē. Immediately preceding him was an upstart with the very plebeian Prenomen Afnai ('He is mine') and half a dozen places later there occurs another ruler with the equally plebeian name Rensonb—he held the throne for no more than four months. It is remarkable that as many as six kings of the period chose for themselves the Nomen Sebekḥotpe 'Sobk is satisfied', with a reference to the crocodile-god of the Fayyûm first honoured in a cartouche by Queen Sebeknofru. Later on, in what we shall find convenient to describe as Dyn. XVII, kings and queens bearing the name of Sebekemsaf ('Sobk is his protection') show that the crocodile-god was still thought of as somehow connected with the monarchy. By that time, however, the link with the Fayyûm was broken, and we discern a tendency to associate the deity with another Crocodilōnpolis not more than 15 miles south of Thebes.[1] This continuity of nomenclature has sometimes been used, and probably rightly, as evidence of the shortness of the Second Intermediate Period, though other features like the trifling changes in art and material remains are equally cogent testimony.

At this point we will call a temporary halt to the dreary discussion of the period's ephemeral kings, and turn our attention to a document that transports us into the very midst of vital realities.

[1] Egyptian Smenu, now identified with Rizêḳât on the west bank.

This is a papyrus discovered at Dra' Abu 'n-Naga[1] a hundred years ago in the tomb of a scribe of the Royal Harem. It is nothing less than the accounts of the Theban court extending over twelve days in the third year of one of the Sebekḥotpe kings. Here the receipts and distribution of bread, beer, vegetables, and so forth are meticulously recorded from day to day. Two sources of revenue are distinguished. Firstly, there is the fixed income required for the sustenance of the king's womenfolk, officers of state, and so forth. This was supplied jointly by three departments (*wacre*), namely, the Department of the Head of the South, the Office of the People's Giving, and the Treasury, the first of the three contributing nearly twice as much as either of the other two. Secondly, there were very considerable additions called *inu*, a term elsewhere used for 'tribute' or 'complimentary gifts', which were utilized for exceptional purposes such as banquets for the chief dignitaries and the staff of what is curiously styled 'the House of the Nurses', or else as rewards for special services. The latter kind of income, for which the vizier or some other prominent functionary might be responsible, varied from almost as much as the former down to absolutely nil, so that no generalization can be given as to its amount; on the other hand, we learn that the daily needs of the royal household demanded nearly 2,000 loaves and different kinds of bread and between 60 and 300 jugs of beer; meat seems to have been reserved for special occasions. A surprising detail is that by the king's command the temple of Amūn had to supply 100 loaves *per diem*. The actual amounts distributed varied slightly according to the balance brought forward from the previous day. All manner of interesting information is obtainable from this fascinating text, or would be but for the usual obstacles of ragged condition and difficulties of decipherment. For instance, there extended over a fortnight the entertainment of a small body of Medja Nubians, including two chieftains later joined by a third, who had come to make their submission. These barbarians do not seem, however, to have been admitted to a great banquet in the columnar hall of the palace which counted as many

[1] For this site on the west of Thebes see above, p. 117. The papyrus is known as *P. Boulaq XVIII* after the Cairene suburb where Mariette established his museum in 1863. Full publication and discussion, *ZÄS* lvii. 51 ff.

as sixty participants, including the musicians. The queen and the king's sisters were not present on this occasion, which was the culmination of the festival of the god Mont of Medâmûd (p. 116), on the eve of the departure of his visiting statue from the capital. All the guests mentioned were males, with the vizier, the commander of the army, and the overseer of fields at their head. Elsewhere mention is made of the reception at the Court of the leading men of Hermōnthis and Cusae, the latter 25 miles north of Asyûṭ; it is important to note that by this time there is no longer mention of feudal princedoms or nomes, and that towns are referred to in their stead; hence the word *ḥaty-ʿo*, which earlier has been rightly rendered as 'prince' or 'count', is from now onward best translated as 'mayor'.

The vizier ʿAnkhu, who more than once heads the officials receiving gifts of food by the royal command, is known from several other sources. One is a papyrus in the Brooklyn Museum,[1] where a written command is addressed to him by a king who reigned at least five years. The same papyrus mentions another who is usually recognized as Sebekḥotpe III, and who has left more memorials of himself than most of the petty rulers of those troubled times; but the connexion between the two references is obscure. Our ʿAnkhu figures also on one of two stelae in the Louvre[2] recording the extensive restorations made in the temple of Abydos by a priestly personage of that neighbourhood named Amenysonb; this was in the reign of Khendjer, the bearer of a Nomen of outlandish appearance and possibly of foreign origin. Now Jéquier[3] in 1931 identified a small pyramid at Saḳḳâra as belonging to a king Khendjer, who unfortunately bore a Prenomen different from that on the Louvre stela. Were there then two Khendjers, one in the north and one in the south? It seems a more probable hypothesis that one and the same monarch vacillated as regards his Prenomen. The problem is typical of the difficulties presented by this period. The Saḳḳâra Khendjer is listed with certainty in the Turin Canon (6. 20) and if, as is believed, Sebekḥotpe III was intended by the entry four places

[1] W. C. Hayes, *A Papyrus of the Late Middle Kingdom*, Brooklyn, 1955. See too more recently Helck in *JNES* xvii. 263 ff.

[2] *BAR* i, §§ 781 ff.

[3] *Deux pyramides du Moyen Empire*, Cairo, 1933.

farther on (6. 24) we might have the strange phenomenon of a single vizier holding office during the reigns of five ephemeral and possibly hostile monarchs. W. C. Hayes has produced evidence[1] that throughout Dyn. XIII (roughly column 6 of the Canon) the Pharaonic capital was still at Lisht, though the Court sometimes moved to Thebes. The pyramid above mentioned and the fact that the vizier's son who assisted Amenysonb in his Abydos operations fared northwards when the work was finished certainly lend colour to this hypothesis.

According to the Canon Sebekḥotpe III was succeeded by a king Neferḥōtep (6. 25), who reigned eleven years. Memorials of him, like those of his predecessor, are relatively numerous. Many rock inscriptions at the First Cataract appear to attest a visit of his, and a steatite plaque found at Wâdy Ḥalfa at least suggests that his influence extended there. Even more interesting is a relief discovered at far-distant Byblos on the Syrian coast, and depicting the local prince doing homage to his person.[2] A portrait of him survives in a fine statuette in the Bologna Museum.[3] To the student of hieroglyphics, however, the most important relic of his reign is a great stela discovered by Mariette at Abydos, and left exposed on the spot on account of its much-damaged condition.[4] The general drift is still clear in spite of the defective copy alone available. It is the second oldest, and quite the most elaborate, example of a type of royal inscription referred to above, p. 56. The Pharaoh is represented as consulting with his courtiers, telling them that he wishes to fashion in their true forms statues of the god Osiris and his Ennead and asking them to arrange for his inspection of the ancient books wherein such things are recorded. The courtiers assent with characteristic obsequiousness. An official is sent to Abydos to prepare the way. He arranges for Osiris to appear in procession in his sacred boat, and then the king himself arrives, personally supervises the fabrication of the images, and takes part in the mimic destruction of the god's enemies. The rest of the text is devoted to pious adulation of the deity, and threats to future persons who may thwart the remembrance of so great a royal benefactor.

[1] *JEA* xxxiii. 10–11.
[2] PM vii. 389.
[3] Petrie, *History*, i. 221, fig. 127; 222, fig. 128.
[4] *BAR* i, §§ 753 ff.

This Neferḥōtep—there seems to have been a second of the name whom it is impossible to place—was followed by a Siḥatḥōr (6. 26) whose tenure of the throne was only three months. Then came a brother of Neferḥōtep by the same non-royal parents, a Khaᶜ-neferrēᶜ Sebekḥotpe reckoned as the fourth of the name (6. 27); the length of this king's reign is lost in a lacuna, but a stela of the eighth year is known,[1] and he too was evidently a powerful monarch to judge from the number of his surviving monuments; it is difficult to know what to make of a headless statue of him found at the Island of Argo[2] just south of Kerma, more especially since a damaged inscription in the British Museum alludes to hostilities in that direction.[3] Can the enterprise of this Dyn. XIII king have dispatched his agents or soldiers beyond the Third Cataract? A fifth Sebekḥotpe (7. 1) is accorded only four years by the Turin Canon, and he was succeeded by a Waḥibrēᶜ-Iaᶜyeb (7. 2) with ten years of reign and then by a Merneferrēᶜ (7. 3) with as many as twenty-three. Hardly anything, only a stela, a lintel, and some scarabs remain to commemorate these last two kings, but since they managed to hold the allegiance of their subjects for so long, they cannot have been insignificant. After a Merḥōtep with the Nomen Inai (7. 4) known elsewhere only from a stela and a single scarab, darkness descends upon the historical scene, leaving discernible in the twilight little beyond royal names for which the list of kings at the end of this work must be consulted. Our next concern here is with the momentous question of the rulers known as the Hyksōs.

Concerning these foreigners the Jewish historian Josephus, in his polemic *Against Apion*, claims to quote the actual words of Manetho:

Tutimaios. In his reign, for what cause I know not, a blast of God smote us; and unexpectedly from the regions of the East invaders of obscure race marched in confidence of victory against our land. By main force they easily seized it without striking a blow; and having overpowered the rulers of the land, they then burned our cities ruthlessly, razed to the ground the temples of the gods, and treated all the natives with a cruel hostility, massacring some and leading into slavery the

[1] Alliot, *Fouilles de Tell Edfou* (1933), Cairo, 1935, p. 33. [2] PM vii. 180.
[3] Säve-Söderbergh, pp. 119–20.

wives and children of others. Finally, they appointed as king one of their number whose name was Salitis. He had his seat at Memphis, levying tribute from Upper and Lower Egypt, and always leaving garrisons behind in the most advantageous places. . . . . In the Sethroite nome he found a city very favourably situated on the east of the Bubastite branch of the Nile, and called Avaris after an ancient religious tradition. This place he rebuilt and fortified with massive walls. . . . . After reigning for 19 years Salitis died; and a second king Bnōn succeeded and reigned for 44 years. Next to him came Apachnan, who ruled for 36 years and 7 months; then Apōphis for 61, and Iannas for 50 years and 1 month; then finally Assis for 49 years and 2 months. These six kings, their first rulers, were ever more and more eager to extirpate the Egyptian stock. Their race as a whole was called Hyksōs, that is 'king-shepherds'; for *hyk* in the sacred language means 'king' and *sōs* in common speech is 'shepherd'.

Josephus goes on to give from another manuscript a different derivation of the name Hyksōs, according to which it signifies 'captive-shepherds', the Egyptian *hyk* being a word for 'captive'. This etymology he prefers because he believed, as do many Egyptologists, that the Biblical story of the Israelite sojourn in Egypt and the subsequent Exodus had as its source the Hyksōs occupation and later expulsion.[1] In point of fact, although there are sound linguistic grounds for both etymologies, neither is the true one. The word Hyksōs undoubtedly derives from the expression *ḥik-khase* 'chieftain of a foreign hill-country' which from the Middle Kingdom onwards was used to designate Beduin sheikhs. Scarabs bearing this title, but with the word for 'countries' in the plural, are found with several undoubted Hyksōs kings and, as we have seen, the final proof is in the Turin Canon. It is important to observe, however, that the term refers to the rulers alone, and not, as Josephus thought, to the entire race. Modern scholars have often erred in this matter, some even implying that the Hyksōs were a particular race of invaders who after conquering Syria and Palestine ultimately forced their way into Egypt. Nothing justifies such a view, even though the actual words of Manetho might seem to

[1] For a very learned discussion of the Exodus problem, but rejecting the view held by the present writer, see H. H. Rowley, *From Joseph to Joshua*, London, 1950.

support it. It is true enough that for some centuries past there had been a growing pressure of alien peoples downwards into Syria, Hurrians from the Caspian region being among the first, these paving the way for the Hittites who followed from the north-west at the end of the sixteenth century. But of such movements there can have been no more than distant repercussions on the Egyptian border. The invasion of the Delta by a specific new race is out of the question; one must think rather of an infiltration by Palestinians glad to find refuge in a more peaceful and fertile environment. Some, if not most, of these Palestinians were Semites. Scarabs of the period mention chieftains with names like ʿAnat-her and Yaʿḳob-her, and whatever the meaning of the element *-her*, ʿAnat was a well-known Semitic goddess, and it is difficult to reject the accepted view that the patriarch Jacob is commemorated in the other name.[1] It is doubtless impossible to suppress the erroneous usage of the word Hyksōs as though it referred to a special race, but it should be borne in mind that the Egyptians themselves usually employed for those unwelcome intruders the term ʿAamu, which we translate with rough accuracy as 'Asiatics' and which had much earlier served to designate Palestinian captives or hirelings residing in Egypt as servants.

How much of the story told by Josephus can be accepted as historical? His very first word raises a problem, the name Tutimaios being merely a scholar's emendation, and even if it were correct, there are serious phonetic grounds for not identifying the bearer with a king Djedmose known to have belonged to this age. Of the six Hyksōs rulers named also by Africanus, but in slightly divergent form, Apōphis alone is recognizable with certainty in the hieroglyphs. Three separate kings having Apōpi as their Nomen are known, their respective Prenomens being ʿAḳenenrēʿ, ʿAweserrēʿ, and Nebkhepeshrēʿ; the last-named was presumably of less importance, since he is not accorded the full Pharaonic titulary enjoyed by the other two. Objects carrying the names of these kings are scanty, but suffice to show that at least ʿAḳenenrēʿ and ʿAweserrēʿ were regarded as true Egyptian sovereigns. A granite altar of ʿAḳenenrēʿ was dedicated 'as his monument to his father Sēth, lord of Avaris',

[1] *JEA* xxxvii. 62, n. 5.

and a statue of King Mermeshaʿ unearthed at Tanis was found to have been usurped by him. More about ʿAweserrēʿ will be learned later, but here already mention may be made of a palette presented by this his master to a scribe who responded with the grateful epithet 'the living image of Rēʿ upon earth'; and still more interesting is the fact that the great mathematical Rhind Papyrus in the British Museum is dated in his thirty-third year.

Less certain, but nevertheless probable, is the identification of Manetho's Iannas with a 'chieftain of foreign countries Khayan' so named on a number of scarabs, but sometimes described there as 'the son of Rēʿ Seweserenrēʿ'. Nomen and Prenomen are combined in a single cartouche on the lid of an alabaster bowl found by Evans in Cretan Cnossus, and the Prenomen Seweserenrēʿ occurs also on the breast of a small sphinx bought from a dealer in Baghdad. A Middle Kingdom statue discovered at Bubastis shows a usurpation by him similar to that by ʿAḳenenrēʿ at Tanis, and here he uses the Horus name 'Embracer of the Lands' and presumptuously declares himself 'beloved of his (own) ka' or 'soul'. A block bearing his name found at Gebelên will be mentioned again later. On this slender evidence some scholars have based the supposition that Khayan forged for himself a world-empire including all the above-named localities; this contention can be dismissed as fantastic, though it seems legitimate to think of him as at once a Palestinian local chief and an Egyptian Pharaoh. At all events he can claim a place among the six principal Hyksōs monarchs.

A very different view must be taken of some other claimants to sovereignty whose sole records are scarabs and cylinder seals emanating from regions as far apart as southern Palestine and the outpost of Kerma in the Sûdân. Their pretension to be Hyksōs kings rests in the case of one or two of them, like ʿAnat-her and Semḳen, on their use of the chieftain title, but others who, like Merwoser and Maʿayebrēʿ, enclose their names in cartouches, or who, like Yaʿmu and Sheshi, boast the proud attribute 'Son of Rēʿ', have no better right than is given by the style of the objects naming them. No monument or rock-inscription attests their rule, and the wide distribution of such easily portable and marketable objects as scarabs is worthless as evidence of its nature. It has recently become the fashion to distinguish two groups of Hyksōs, the one consisting of the six kings named by Manetho and the other comprising the nebulous personages here under discussion.[1] The latter group admittedly needs some explanation, and an attempt to give one will be made further on, but they certainly never obtained the Pharaonic status that has sometimes been attributed to them.

As already hinted, it seems inevitable to identify Manetho's six Hyksōs kings with the six 'chieftains of foreign countries' referred to in the all-important fragment of the Turin Canon. It has sometimes been maintained that two entries placed at the bottom of column 9 also named Hyksōs rulers, one of them being Manetho's Bnōn, but the hieratic has been faultily read and their possession of Prenomens enclosed in cartouches speaks decisively against this suggestion. The total offered by the compiler of the Canon (see p. 150) surely indicates that he knew of six Hyksōs and no more; he will have inserted them in his list of Egyptian kings only reluctantly and because they were too well known to be passed over in silence. It is our belief that there were only six real Hyksōs monarchs, and the 108 years allotted to them goes far to support this contention. It has been seen that the interval between the end of Dyn. XII and the accession of Amōsis, the founder of Dyn. XVIII and the expeller of the Hyksōs, was only 211 years. If we place the end of the foreign occupation in Amōsis's fourth year, and subtract the 108 years from the resultant 215, this leaves only 107 years for Manetho's Dyns. XIII and XIV, and a large overlap extending the occupation back into Dyn. XIV seems ruled out by the far-flung reign of Neferḥōtep, whose sway, as we have seen, reached northwards as far as Byblos. We conclude that there can hardly have been time for more than the six Hyksōs powerful enough to have usurped the throne of the Pharaohs, and in this case Manetho's description of them as 'their first rulers' was misleading, and his Dyns. XVI and XVII (in so far as the latter speaks of Shepherd kings) ought to disappear.

Another persuasive indication is given by the fact that Manetho's 'first rulers' included an Apōphis, for it will emerge that such was also the name of the Hyksōs against whom Amōsis's brother and

[1] Latest discussion by Säve-Söderbergh, *JEA* xxxvii. 62–63.

immediate predecessor Kamose fought, so that the six kings will have embraced not merely the beginning of the foreign domination but also its end. Not to be under-estimated is the testimony of an already mentioned (p. 50) stela of late date recording a long line of Memphite priests professing to have exercised sacerdotal functions from father to son until as far back as Dyn. XI. As so often happens in the case of genealogies, the information offered by this precious document is not wholly trustworthy, but at least no suspicion can be attached to the order of the kings there mentioned. Next before Amōsis I we find an Apōpi, who in his turn follows upon an otherwise unknown Sharek, undoubtedly one of the last of the Hyksōs. In the sixth place before Sharek there is an ʿAḳen given as the immediate successor of a king Ibi whose name proclaims him to have been a native-born Egyptian and who is probably the Pharaoh of that name recorded half-way down column 7 of the Turin Canon. A daring hypothesis might identify this ʿAḳen with the ʿAḳenenrēʿ Apōpi dealt with above, p. 157; but for that identification a piece of crude Egyptian humour would have to be assumed, since ʿAḳen as written on the stela signifies 'Strong Ass', whereas ʿAḳenenrēʿ means 'Great and strong is Rēʿ'! However this may be, the important point about this Memphite stela is that it covers the entire Hyksōs period and can accordingly have envisaged no more than six reigns provided that these were of normal length.

Little more headway can be made on the question of Manetho's reliability without giving some account of the Theban princes who at last ejected the foreign intruders. Since there is here much of interest to be told, we shall risk the charge of irrelevance and deal at some length with the sequence of monarchs who may well have spanned the entire latter half of the Second Intermediate Period. There are about a dozen kings to be considered, and it is characteristic of the influence exerted by Manetho that it is still solemnly debated how many and which of them should be allotted to Dyn. XVI and how many to Dyn. XVII. Only rarely is it possible to determine the precise sequence and it is impossible to point, as in Dyn. XI, to a common ancestor. We find it convenient to start with a king Raʿḥotpe who is mentioned in the Karnak king-list and possibly also in the Turin Canon (11. 1); on a broken stela from

Coptos[1] he is addressed by his courtiers with the usual flattery, and in an inscription from Abydos[2] an official of his speaks of repairs made to a wall in the temple of Osiris. This Raʿḥotpe is also mentioned in a story of much later date. It is possible that the next king in the Canon (11. 2), who is credited with sixteen years of reign, may have been the Sebekemsaf whose seventh year is named in a graffito seen by Lepsius in the Wâdy Ḥammâmât.[3] A little further on we read of a Nebirierau whose importance is due to the dating in his reign of a great stela[4] which, though dealing with the private concerns of two officials, this king commanded to be set up in the temple of Karnak as a permanent record. It appears that a certain Kebsi had incurred a large debt of sixty *deben* of gold, perhaps about £2,500 of our money, to a relative of high rank named Sebeknakhte, and having failed to pay it, agreed to transfer to his creditor the mayoralty of the important town of El-Kâb, together with its perquisites. The main narrative explains how Kebsi had come by that office, and there are all manner of details concerning the judicial proceedings involved, the court of the vizier, and the final oath sworn by the two parties. Certain obscurities remain, but do not prevent this document from being as illuminating a specimen of Egyptian administrative procedure as any that has survived from Pharaonic times.

It is from the hill-side of Draʿ Abu 'n-Naga on the west of Thebes that has come most of our knowledge of the following petty kings, and both for excavations on the site and for piecing together all the available information from other sources we are mainly indebted to the admirable researches of the American H. Winlock.[5] In the early part of the nineteenth century Arab plunderings had brought to light the tomb of a Pharaoh who had borrowed from Dyn. XI the time-honoured name Inyōtef, and whose gilded coffin ultimately passed into the British Museum; as with various other coffins of the period the image of the king here appears sheathed in a feathered garment. Two more Inyōtef kings of the period are known from similar *rishi* coffins which ultimately

[1] PM v. 129.
[2] British Museum, *Hieroglyphic Texts*, iv, Pl. 24.
[3] PM vii. 332.
[4] P. Lacau, *Une stèle juridique de Karnak*, Cairo, 1949.
[5] See particularly his article *JEA* x. 217 ff.

reached the Louvre; the owners were brothers, and the coffin of one of them had been given him by the other. There is reason to think that the Inyōtef whose coffin is in the London collection was the Nubkheperrēʿ known from inscriptions found at Abydos[1] and Coptos;[2] an unusual text discovered on the latter site is a royal decree depriving of his office a rebellious temple-official named Teti son of Minḥotpe and threatening with condign punishment any future king or other man in authority who should pardon him or any of his family or descendants. Now it so chances that the tomb of this Nubkheperrēʿ was one of a number inspected and found intact by a commission of officials appointed under Ramessēs IX some 500 years later to investigate charges of robbery brought by the mayor of Thebes Pesiūr to spite his colleague on the west bank.[3] Utilizing the information afforded by the famous Abbott papyrus in the British Museum, Winlock argued that not only had the commission proceeded from north to south in fulfilment of their task, but also that the tombs of the kings involved had been sited in the same direction. But if this was true, probably the sequence of several of these Pharaohs might be accurately determined. Researches on the spot have tended to confirm Winlock's argument, traces being found of a few insignificant looking pyramids of which that of Nubkheperrēʿ was the northernmost. The next royal tomb to the south may have belonged to one of the other two Inyōtefs. Beyond this we come to the sole pyramid which was admitted to have been despoiled, that of King Sekhemrēʿ-shedtowĕ Sebekemsaf. It is left to a footnote[4] to recount the romantic discovery of the missing half of the papyrus recording the trial of the

[1] PM v. 48. [2] Op. cit. 125; *BAR* i, §§ 773 ff.

[3] See below, p. 315, for bibliography of all the following.

[4] This manuscript, formerly known as the Amherst papyrus, when first published by Chabas in 1873 consisted of the lower halves of four admirably written pages of hieratic. In February 1936 J. Capart had occasion to examine some Egyptian antiquities brought back in 1854 by the then Duke of Brabant and now offered to the Brussels Museum. Putting his hand into the hollow interior of a wooden statuette Capart drew forth what proved to be the missing upper half of the roll; it was not an unusual habit of native finders of papyri to cut them in half on the principle that two manuscripts were saleable more profitably than one. When the halves had been joined for the purpose of a photographic publication they formed a document of a magnificence and dramatic interest equalled by only very few others.

thieves. Here the leader of the gang Amenpnūfe narrates how he and his accomplices forced their way into the tomb, and finding the coffins of the king and of his queen Nubkhaʿes stripped them of their gold, silver, and jewels, burning everything else. Doubts have been expressed as to the trustworthiness of this recital; at all events we can be sure that Amenpnūfe's confession did not assume the smooth graphic form given to it by the scribe, but was wrung from him gradually by a liberal application of the bastinado.[1] According to the Abbott papyrus the next two tombs to be visited belonged to two kings both of whom had borne the name Seḳenenrēʿ Taʿo. This is in the last degree improbable, and though the Nomen may in both cases have been Taʿo, it is only the second of them who will have had the Prenomen Seḳenenrēʿ.[2] With him we are well within hail of the end of Dyn. XVII and of the expulsion of the Hyksōs. A story[3] of which only the beginning has survived brings this Theban king and his Hyksōs contemporary into contact with one another, and though the theme of the whole is fantastic, the setting may well give a truthful picture. The opening paragraph reads as follows:

Now it befell that the land of Egypt was in dire affliction, and there was no Sovereign as king of the time. And it happened that King Seḳenenrēʿ was Ruler of the Southern City[4] . . . while the chieftain Apōphis was in Avaris and the entire land paid tribute to him in full, as well as with all good things of Timūris.[5] Then King Apōphis took Sutekh[6] to himself as lord, and served not any god which was in the entire land except Sutekh. And he built a temple of fair and everlasting work by the side of the house of King Apōphis, and he arose every day to make the daily sacrifice to Sutekh, and the officials of His Majesty bore garlands of flowers exactly as is done in the temple of Prēʿ-Ḥarakhti.

The story goes on to tell that the Hyksōs ruler wished to bring an accusation against Seḳenenrēʿ and trumped up the absurd charge that the hippopotamuses at Thebes were making such a din at night that he was unable to sleep. The sequel is lost, but we can be certain that the conflict ended in a victory for Seḳenenrēʿ, though not one

[1] *JEA* xxiv. 59 ff. [2] Op. cit. x. 243–4. [3] Op. cit. v. 40 ff.; Gardiner, *Late-Egyptian Stories*, 85 ff. [4] Thebes. [5] A name of Egypt.
[6] For this writing of the name of the god Sēth see pp. 164–5.

of a military kind. His adversary was presumably the same Apōphis who, as we shall see, became the enemy of his successor Kamose. As for himself, though his tomb has not been definitely located, Winlock was able, on the grounds stated, to indicate its approximative position. What is more interesting, we possess his actual corpse.[1] By the tenth year of King Siamūn of Dyn. XXI[2] the depredations in the Theban necropolis had assumed such proportions that all that could be collected in the way of royal coffins and their contents was transferred to the tomb of a Queen Inḥaʿpy near Dêr el-Baḥri, where they were discovered in 1881, an archaeological sensation unequalled even in the history of Egyptology where there have been so many.[3] For here were found, not only the coffins, but also the mummified corpses of many of the greatest Pharaohs of Dyns. XVIII to XX, though robbed of all the jewellery and precious metal which had once adorned them. The body of Seḳenenrēʿ, twisted as though in mortal agony, showed terrible wounds on head and neck. Some have supposed that he died in battle with the Hyksōs, but of this there is no proof; he cannot have attained much more than thirty years of age.

To return now to Josephus and his quotations from Manetho, it is clear that he was very well informed with regard to Avaris, the stronghold which the Hyksōs had from the start chosen for their base. According to the Jewish chronicler's account this was situated in that part of the eastern Delta known as the Sethroite nome. Opinions differ as to the actual location of Ḥawaʿre, to give Avaris its Egyptian name. The majority of scholars[4] believe that such was the earlier designation of what later became the great city of Tanis, though others[5] favour a site near Ḳantîr, some 11 miles to the south. At Avaris the Hyksōs worshipped the strange animal-god Sēth depicted as  in the temple reliefs and elsewhere. He has been mentioned already (p. 8) as the enemy and murderer of the good god Osiris, but the Hyksōs chose to ignore that regrettable aspect, as indeed had been done in this remote corner of the Delta from the earliest times.[6] Their version of Sēth, now written in Babylo-

[1] G. Elliot Smith, *RM*, pp. 1–4. [2] For the date see *JEA* xxxii. 24 ff.
[3] See further below, pp. 319–20, 350.
[4] *Onom.* ii, pp. 171* ff. [5] See further, p. 258. [6] *Ann. Serv.* xliv. 295 ff.

nian fashion as though pronounced as Sutekh, was certainly more Asiatic in character than the native original, bearing in his garment and head-dress a distinct resemblance to the Semitic Baʿal. There is abundant proof that the Hyksōs favoured him beyond all the other deities of Egypt, though there is no real justification for the further accusation that they despised and persecuted these latter. In connexion with the Hyksōs Sēth or Sutekh a remarkable stela discovered at Tanis by Mariette, then buried by him and later disinterred by P. Montet,[1] has probable chronological importance. The scene above the hieroglyphic text depicts Ramessēs II offering to the god, here described as Sēth Nubti, i.e. the Sēth of Onbo or Ombos, his original home in Upper Egypt. The text then relates how Ramessēs II's father Sety, later to become the Pharaoh Sethōs I, but at that time only a military commander and vizier, came in the four-hundredth year of the god to do him honour. It is argued with much likelihood that this inscription refers to the arrival of the Hyksōs at Avaris, and since the celebration in question will have taken place in the reign of Ḥaremḥab, approximately 1330 B.C., the first occupation of the place would be dated to about 1730 B.C., less than sixty years after the beginning of the Second Intermediate Period. Combining these figures with those already given, the Hyksōs might have held Avaris for more than fifty years before one of their number felt strong enough to pose as the legitimate Pharaoh. It is relevant to note that the date of the building of Tanis was long remembered: Num. xiii. 22 tells us that 'Hebron was built seven years before Zoan (Tanis) in Egypt', and this seems to confirm the identity of Tanis and Avaris; but the meaning of the assertion is much disputed.

No Egyptological discovery of recent years has caused more excitement among scholars than the unearthing at Karnak in 1954 of a great stela recounting at length the military measures taken by Seḳenenrēʿ's successor Kamose against the Hyksōs king ʿAweserrēʿ Apōpi.[2] Nearly fifty years earlier Lord Carnarvon's excavations had brought to light a tablet inscribed in hieratic narrating the early stages of the conflict.[3] At first some supposed this to be a mere

[1] *Kêmi* iv. 191 ff.; translated *ANET*, p. 253.
[2] *Ann. Serv.* liii. 195 ff.
[3] *JEA* iii. 95 ff.

literary essay, but in 1935 a few broken fragments were found at Karnak which proved that the Carnarvon Tablet was some scribe's copy of a genuine historical inscription erected in that temple.[1] Full publication of all three documents is still awaited from Labib Habachi, to whose efforts the finding of the practically complete stela was mainly due; but it is already evident that this was simply the continuation of the recital disclosed in the hieratic text. A shortened paraphrase of the gist follows here:

In Year 3 of the mighty king in Thebes, Kamose, whom Rēᶜ had appointed as the real king and had granted him power in very sooth. His Majesty spoke in his palace to the council of grandees who were in his suite: 'I should like to know what serves this strength of mine, when a chieftain is in Avaris, and another in Cush, and I sit united with an Asiatic and a Nubian, each man in possession of his slice of this Egypt, and I cannot pass by him as far as Memphis. See, he holds Khmūn,[2] and no man has respite from spoliation through servitude to the Setyu. I will grapple with him and slit open his belly. My desire is to deliver Egypt and to smite the Asiatics.' Then spoke the grandees of his council: 'See all are loyal to the Asiatics as far as Cusae.[3] We are tranquil in our part of Egypt. Elephantinē is strong, and the middle part is with us as far as Cusae. Men till for us the finest of their lands. Our cattle pasture in the papyrus marshes. Corn is sent for our swine. Our cattle are not taken away.'

The courtiers admit that under certain conditions it might be expedient to take the offensive, but Kamose expressed his displeasure at their cautious advice and declared his determination to regain the whole of Egypt. The narrative is then continued in the first person:

I fared downstream in might to overthrow the Asiatics by the command of Amūn, the just of counsels; my brave army in front of me like a breath of fire, troops of Medja-Nubians aloft upon our cabins to spy out the Setyu and to destroy their places. East and West were in possession of their fat and the army was supplied with things everywhere.

Kamose seems next to have detached a body of Medjayu to punish one Teti, the son of Pepi, apparently a prominent Egyptian

[1] *Ann. Serv.* xxxix. 245 ff.

[2] Hermopolis Magna, the modern Ashmûnên.

[3] Above, p. 153.

who had shut himself up in Nefrusy,[1] which he had made into a nest of Asiatics. The crushing of this enemy was, however, deferred until the morrow:

I spent the night in my ship, my heart happy. When the earth became light, I was upon him as it were a hawk. The time of perfuming the mouth[2] came, and I overthrew him, I razed his wall, I slew his people and I caused his wife to go down to the river-bank. My soldiers were like lions with their prey, with serfs, cattle, milk, fat, and honey, dividing up their possessions.

After a few more obscure sentences the hieratic text breaks off and, when the narrative is resumed at the beginning of the newly discovered stela, Kamose is near the fortress of Avaris, taunting his enemy with boastings and threats. The sequence of events is recorded at great length and in highly rhetorical language. Only a few salient passages can here be mentioned. Apōphis had evidently been driven from Middle Egypt, for among the words spoken by Kamose we find the claim

Your heart is undone, base Asiatic, who used to say 'I am lord, and there is none equal to me from Khmūn and Pi-Ḥatḥōr[3] down to Avaris'.

That the Theban warrior was by no means ashamed of his ruthlessness towards his own countrymen is clear from his own words:

I razed their towns and burned their places, they being made into red ruins for ever on account of the damage which they did within this Egypt, and they had made themselves serve the Asiatics and had forsaken Egypt their mistress.

There follows immediately an all-important passage:

I captured a messenger of his high up over the Oasis travelling southward to Cush for the sake of a written dispatch, and I found upon it this message in writing from the chieftain of Avaris: 'I, ʿAweserrēʿ, the son of Rēʿ, Apōpi greet my son the chieftain of Cush. Why have you arisen as chieftain without letting me know? Have you (not) beheld what Egypt has done against me, the chieftain who is in it, Kamose the Mighty, ousting me from my soil and I have not reached him—after the

[1] Near Khmūn, but a little farther to the north; *Onom.* ii, pp. 83*, 84*.

[2] The hour of the midday meal.

[3] This Pi-Ḥatḥōr must be the town near Gebelên, see *Onom.* ii, pp. 17* ff.

manner of all that he has done against you, he choosing the two lands to devastate them, my land and yours, and he has destroyed them. Come, fare north at once, do not be timid. See, he is here with me. . . . I will not let him go until you have arrived. Then we will divide the towns of this Egypt between us.'

The entirely unexpected fact which has emerged from this passage is that the Apōphis against whom Kamose fought was that very same ʿAweserrēʿ whose name, on a temple-wall at Gebelên together with that of Khayan,[1] constituted the main evidence that the Hyksōs had ever penetrated so far south. The whole tenor of the great inscription makes it clear that this Apōphis, presumably the last of his name, never extended his rule beyond Khmūn, except for a quite temporary occupation of Gebelên (Pi-Ḥatḥōr); and there is no real evidence that any other member of his race had ever done so either. The beginning of the Carnarvon Tablet had revealed the previously unknown existence of a separate Cushite kingdom, and that is here confirmed. Also there have recently come to light some stelae from Wâdy Ḥalfa dedicated by officers with Egyptian names who about this time were in the employ of the 'chieftain of Cush'.[2] But Kamose's courtiers in replying to him had maintained that Elephantinē was firmly held, and it is evident that he for the moment had no anxiety about his Nubian neighbours, nor indeed about any place north of the First Cataract as far as Khmūn; all his thoughts were concentrated upon the expulsion of the Asiatics. The conclusion of the newly found stela speaks of Kamose's triumphant return to his capital, where he was greeted by a populace hysterical with joy. Yet Fate had not decreed that he should be the final conqueror of the Hyksōs. That glorious achievement was reserved for his successor ʿAḥmose I (Amōsis in Manetho), whom later ages consequently honoured as the founder of the EIGHTEENTH DYNASTY. Details of the fall of Avaris are given in an inscription engraved on the wall of a tomb at El-Kâb belonging to a warrior named ʿAḥmose, son of Abana.[3] Early in life this man replaced his father Baba, who had served under Seḳenenrēʿ. His own long military career started under Amōsis, when the king sailed north

[1] PM v. 163.
[2] *JEA* xxxv. 50 ff.; *Kush* iv. 54 ff.
[3] *JEA* v. 48 ff.; Abana was his mother.

to attack the enemy. Promoted from one ship to another on account of his bravery, he fought on foot in the presence of his sovereign, and on several occasions received as a reward not only his male and female captives, but also the decoration known as the Gold of Valour. The siege of the Hyksōs fortress appears to have been no easy matter, and was followed by another siege, lasting no less than three years, at Sharūḥen, a place in the south-west of Palestine mentioned in the Book of Joshua (xix. 6). This appears to have been the limit of Amōsis's campaign in the Palestinian direction, for he had still to cope with the usurper in Nubia and with a couple of rebels who still remained on Upper Egyptian territory. His doughty henchman from El-Kâb accompanied him everywhere, and records a great slaughter in all the battles and further rewards to himself, including some fields in his own city. Similar feats of arms are recounted, though much more briefly, by a younger relative from the same place named ʿAḥmose Pennekheb, whose life as an active soldier and courtier extended over as many as five reigns.[1] There is evidence elsewhere that King Amōsis treated all his soldiers with great liberality, as indeed was their due. The twenty-five years given to this king by Manetho are clearly not far wide of the mark. His son and successor Amenōphis I (Amenḥotpe as written in the hieroglyphs) continued his father's policy, but with a difference. Hitherto the aim had been merely to restore Egypt within its legitimate borders, but now there sprang up the desire 'to extend the boundaries', a phrase commonly used henceforth, but previously hardly employed except once or twice in Dyn. XII. The preoccupation of Amenōphis was mainly with Nubia, in the campaign against which the two warriors from El-Kâb again took a distinguished part. The son of Abana claims to have convoyed the king upstream and later, after the capture of the enemy chieftain, to have brought his royal master back to Egypt in two days.[2] If this be true, the king himself cannot have ventured very far afield. But now it was definitely decided to colonize Nubia. In this reign we encounter for the first time the title ultimately to be crystallized in the form 'King's Son of Cush'. Already under Amōsis the future viceroy Turi is found as 'commandant of Buhen'

[1] *BAR* ii, §§ 17–25, 344. [2] Op. cit. ii, § 39.

(Wâdy Ḥalfa); under Amenōphis he is described as 'King's Son', an epithet to which was subsequently added 'overseer of southern lands'. Though his real name was ʿAḥmose and Turi only a sort of nickname, there is no reason to think that either he or any other holder of the title was really a son of the reigning Pharaoh. About this time there appears at El-Kâb, which as we have seen provided such brave soldiers, a mysterious title 'first King's Son of Nekhbe' (i.e. El-Kâb),[1] and it is difficult not to believe that this designation had something to do with that of the long succession of Nubian viceroys, the more so since two centuries later Nekhen, which is Hieracōnpolis just opposite El-Kâb, is named as the northern starting-point of their jurisdiction.[2]

Looking back over what the contemporary sources have revealed concerning the humiliating Hyksōs occupation we find Manetho's account as retailed by Josephus to contain truth and falsity in almost equal measure. R. Weill[3] was the first to insist on the distortion due to a type of literary fiction which became an established convention of Egyptian historical writing: a period of desolation and anarchy is painted in exaggeratedly lurid colours, usually for the glorification of a monarch to whom the salvation of the country is ascribed. Manetho's narrative represents the last stage of a process of falsification which started within a generation after the triumph of Amōsis. Not more than eighty years after the expulsion of the enemy Queen Ḥashepsowe[4] was characterizing their usurpation in much the same manner as is read in the story of Seḳenenrēʿ and Apōphis, and parallels are found later under Tutʿankhamūn, Merenptaḥ, and Ramessēs IV. It is not to be believed that a mighty host of Asiatic invaders descended upon the Delta like a whirlwind and, occupying Memphis, inflicted upon the natives every kind of cruelty. The rare remains of the Hyksōs kings point rather to an earnest endeavour to conciliate the inhabitants and to ape the attributes and the trappings of the weak Pharaohs whom they dislodged. Would they otherwise have adopted the hieroglyphic writing and have furnished themselves with names compounded with that of the sun-god Rēʿ? The

[1] *Ann. Serv.* x. 193 ff. [2] *Ḥuy*, p. 11. [3] In the book quoted on p. 175.
[4] *JEA* xxxii. 45, 47–48.

statement that they levied tribute from Upper as well as Lower Egypt must at least be doubted. As we have seen, the view that the Hyksōs rulers occupied the entire country is an illusion definitely disposed of by Kamose's great inscription, which clearly implies that the invaders never advanced beyond Gebelên, and suggests that a little later they were compelled to establish their southern boundary at Khmūn. Even before that discovery Säve-Söderbergh[1] had concluded from the words of the courtiers on the Carnarvon Tablet that a considerable part of the population had resigned themselves to the Asiatic occupation and had found it possible to treat with the invaders on mutually advantageous terms. The further information afforded by the complete stela strongly supports that view, and even suggests that the damage done by the strong man who arose in Thebes was greater than had ever been inflicted by the Hyksōs immigrants. Until further discoveries prove the contrary, we must think of the Theban princes as having always maintained their power in their own territory, even if for a short time they had been compelled to accept the position of unwilling vassals.

The Hyksōs episode was not without effecting certain changes in the material civilization of Egypt.[2] The most important of these was the introduction of the horse and of the horse-drawn chariot which played so large a part in the later history of the country. It is not proved that these importations contributed in any marked degree to the success of the Asiatics, but they certainly were of great assistance to the Egyptians themselves in their subsequent campaigns. New types of daggers and swords, weapons of bronze, and the strong compound Asiatic bow must also be counted among the benefits derived from what could otherwise be regarded only as a national disaster. In a confessedly philological rather than archaeological work such as this it would be out of place to dwell upon the new style of fortification which the enemy brought into the country, and as regards the Tell el-Yahûdîya ware often mentioned in this connexion, the reader must seek an opinion from those more competent to give it. Lastly, it remains to redeem our promise to make some suggestion with regard to the minor Hyksōs personages known only from scarabs and cylinder seals. It seems

[1] *JEA* xxxvii. 69–70. [2] Details, see op. cit., 57 ff.

possible that these were early aggressors who entertained the hope of sovereignty before the dynasty of Khayan and the Apōphis kings actually achieved that aim; but another possibility is that the objects in question were all of Palestinian origin and commemorated minor chieftains who assumed Pharaonic titles without any right whatsoever. These are, however, mere guesses. It must be repeated that Manetho's Dyn. XVI seems purely fictitious, and that his Dyn. XVII can be made serviceable only as a class-name for the Theban princes included in it.

The Theban saviours of Egypt were a closely knit family in which the women, whether on account of personal attractions or because they were the recognized transmitters of sovereignty, played an extraordinarily prominent part. The latter alternative is, however, ruled out in the case of Tetisheri, one of the earliest of these queens, since fragments of her mummy-cloth found in the great Dêr el-Baḥri *cache* inform us that she was the daughter of commoners.[1] Two statuettes of hers are known, both of which must have come from her Theban tomb. Concerning that tomb and concerning her relationships illuminating information is given by a stela discovered by Petrie at Abydos.[2] Here King Amōsis is described as sitting with his wife ʿAḥmose-Nofreteroi and pondering what benefits he could confer on his ancestors:

His sister[3] spoke and answered him: 'Why have these things been recalled? What has come into thy heart?' The King's own person said to her: 'I have recalled the mother of my mother and the mother of my father, king's great wife and king's mother, Tetisheri, deceased. A tomb-chamber and a sepulchre of hers are at this moment upon the soil of the Theban and Abydene nomes, but I have said this to thee because My Majesty has wished to make for her a pyramid and a chapel in the Sacred Land close to the monument of My Majesty.' . . . . His Majesty spoke thus, and these things were accomplished at once.

The important point here is that King Amōsis asserts his own parents to have been the children of the same mother and father, a classical example of brother and sister marriage. Now those

[1] *JEA* x. 246. [2] *BAR* ii, §§ 33–37. [3] Here, as often, with the meaning of 'wife'.

parents are known: the mother of Amōsis was ʿAḥḥotpe, and she was the wife of Seḳenenrēʿ Taʿo II. In all probability, therefore, Tetisheri was the consort of Taʿo I, whose tomb, like that of Taʿo II, had been inspected in the reign of Ramessēs IX and found intact. What subsequently happened to Taʿo II has already been told. About Taʿo I nothing further is known, but it is conjectured that his Prenomen was Senakhtenrēʿ.

ʿAḥḥotpe, Taʿo II's queen, attained to even greater celebrity than her mother. A great stela found at Karnak,[1] after heaping eulogies upon her son Amōsis I, its dedicator, goes on to exhort all his subjects to do her reverence. In this curious passage she is praised as having rallied the soldiery of Egypt, and as having put a stop to rebellion. Does this refer to a difficult moment after the death of Kamose, who is conjectured with plausibility to have been the short-lived elder brother of Amōsis? Kamose's tomb[2] was the last of the row inspected by the Ramesside officials, but later the mummy was removed in its coffin to a spot just south of the entrance of the wâdy leading to the Tombs of the Kings, where it was found by Mariette's workmen in 1857. The coffin was not gilded, but of the feathered *rishi* type employed for non-royal personages of the period. The badly mummified corpse crumbled to dust immediately after its discovery, but upon it, besides other jewels, was found a magnificent dagger now in Brussels.

Little more than a year later another gang of fellahîn, searching near the same place, came upon ʿAḥḥotpe's own coffin and mummy, bedecked with splendid ornaments which are among the greatest treasures of the Cairo Museum. Apart from a few things bearing the name of Kamose these had been the gift of her son Amōsis, whose cartouche they mostly show. She must have been an old woman of eighty or more when she was conferring rewards upon her steward Kares in the tenth year of Amenōphis I.[3] Long before this she had been obliged to surrender her position of special favour to Amōsis's wife ʿAḥmose-Nofreteroi. To judge from the number of inscriptions, contemporary and later, in which that

[1] *Urk*. iv. 14–24; partly translated B*AR* ii, §§ 29–32.

[2] For all the following see Winlock in *JEA* x. 252 ff.; 259 ff.

[3] B*AR* ii, §§ 49–53, unless she be that king's identically named wife.

young queen's name appears, she obtained a celebrity almost without parallel in the history of Egypt. Her titles of King's Daughter and King's Sister suggest that she may have been a daughter of Kamose, and consequently her husband's niece.[1] In an unspecified year of his reign Amōsis conferred upon her, or sold to her, the office of Second Prophet of Amūn at Karnak, to be hers and her descendants' to all eternity.[2] On stelae from the limestone quarries near Ṭura she is depicted behind her husband as he opens a new gallery in his twenty-second year;[3] the cattle dragging the sledge with the great block are said to have been captured in his Asiatic campaign. The site of his tomb is unknown, but his coffin and mummy came to light in the Dêr el-Baḥri find.[4] After his death ʿAḥmose-Nofreteroi was ever more closely associated with her son Amenōphis I, whose tomb was discovered high up on the hills south of the wâdy leading to the Tombs of the Kings;[5] possibly he shared it with her, as he did a funerary temple down in the valley immediately to the south.[6] The coffins of both, together with their mummies, though hers is somewhat doubtful, were among the discoveries of the great *cache*.[7]

The names ʿAḥmose and ʿAḥḥotpe so common at this period, not only for royalties but also for private persons, raise a problem that cannot be solved with certainty. These names mean 'The Moon is born', and 'The Moon is content' respectively, and presuppose a moon-cult in the locality whence the rulers of Dyn. XVII sprang. At Karnak the third member of the Theban triad was a moon-god named Chons, but the name Tuthmōsis (Eg. Dḥutmose) borne by several Pharaohs of the next generations shows that the lunar connexions of their ancestors were with Thōth rather than with Chons. There is no reason to think that the kings and queens whose names we are discussing had any connexion with Khmūn-Hermopolis, Thōth's main cult-centre, and for the present it can only be conjectured that their original home lay a little to the south of Medînet Habu on the west bank where there still exists a tiny temple of late Ptolemaic date dedicated to Thōth as the moon and

[1] Gauthier, *LR* ii. 159, n. 2; 183, n. 2. [2] *Bull. soc. fr. d'Ég.*, no. 12 (1953).
[3] B*AR* ii, §§ 26–28. [4] PM i. 173. [5] *JEA* iii. 147 ff. [6] PM ii. 147.
[7] PM i. 174.

known as the Kaṣr el-ʻAgûz.[1] In the not far distant village of Dêr el-Medîna, which some centuries later housed the workmen employed upon the royal tombs, the entire dynastic family beginning with the two Taʻos were worshipped as the 'Lords of the West'; many other princely names besides those already mentioned are found on the tomb-walls of these humble folk, with Menthotpe I of Dyn. XI as an exceptional case outside the ʻAḥmose clan. Special prominence was here given to Queen ʻAḥmose-Nofreteroi, depicted for some unaccountable reason with a black countenance, but also sometimes with a blue one; if she was a daughter of Kamose she will have had no black blood in her veins. An even more important role in the necropolis came to be played by Amenōphis I, to whom several separate chapels were dedicated differentiating him as 'Amenōphis of the Town', 'Amenōphis the darling of Amūn', and 'Amenōphis of the Forecourt'.[2] To one or other of these much loved deities prayers were addressed in time of trouble, or appeal was made to their oracles when need for litigation arose.

In an inscription in his Theban tomb an astronomer named Amenemḥē states that he lived twenty-one years under Amenōphis I,[3] and that may be accepted as only a few years short of the length of the reign, since it agrees approximately with the figure given by the excerptors of Manetho for an Amenōphthis of whom they make the third king of Dyn. XVIII instead of the second. About his tomb and his mummy we have already spoken.

SELECT BIBLIOGRAPHY

The kings of the Second Intermediate Period: H. Gauthier, *LR* ii. 1–153; R. Weill, *La Fin du moyen empire égyptien*, 2 vols., Paris, 1918; H. Stock, *Studien zur Geschichte und Archäologie der 13. bis 17. Dynastie Ägyptens*, Glückstadt-Hamburg, 1942; J. Vandier, *Clio*³, 313–17.

The Hyksōs: an excellent statement of the facts in Pahor Labib, *Die Herrschaft der Hyksos in Ägypten und ihr Sturz*, Glückstadt, 1937; Stock, op. cit. 63 ff.; see too Vandier, op. cit. 317–18.

[1] PM ii. 193–7.
[2] *Bull. Inst. fr.* xxvii. 159 ff.
[3] L. Borchardt, *Geschichte der Zeitmessung*, Berlin, 1920, Pl. 18.

The Theban rulers classed under Dyn. XVII: H. Winlock, *The Tombs of the Kings of the Seventeenth Dynasty at Thebes*, in *JEA* x. 217–77; Stock, op. cit. 75–81; Vandier, op. cit. 297–8; 318–21.

The King's Son of Cush: G. Reisner in *JEA* vi. 28 ff.; 73 ff.; supplement by H. Gauthier in *Rec. Trav.* xxxix. 182 ff.

The jewellery of Queen ʿAḥḥotpe: F. W. von Bissing, *Ein Thebanischer Grabfund aus dem Anfang des Neuen Reichs*, Beilin, 1900.

VIII

THE THEBAN SUPREMACY

AT the death of Amenōphis I (*c.* 1528 B.C.) the New Kingdom, or the Empire as it is sometimes called, was well set on its course, and there followed more than a century and a half of unbroken prosperity. Thebes was paramount among the cities of Egypt, and Amen-Rēʿ, the principal deity at Karnak, at last vindicated his right to the title 'King of the Gods' which he had borne for so long. Some distortion in our perspective is due to the paucity of monuments from Memphis, Hēliopolis, and the Delta, since military bases must clearly have been maintained in the north; none the less we can hardly be mistaken in stressing the Theban supremacy. The sculptures and inscriptions in the great temple of Karnak are a mine of information. On the west bank the main necropolis had moved southward, with a line of mortuary temples in honour of the Pharaohs and their patron deity at the edge of the cultivation, and the rock-tombs of the nobles describing a honeycomb pattern above in the hill of Sheikh ʿAbd el-Ḳurna (see Pls. XI, XII). Usually one wall in the outer chamber of these tombs is reserved to depict the activities of the owner, and sometimes another wall displays a stela giving a verbal account of his merits and exploits. Naturally other sites are not completely barren of material for the historian: the remains of provincial temples, graffiti on the rocks at the Cataracts, records of mining activities at Sinai and elsewhere, though writings on papyrus are of extreme rarity. But when all these scattered remains are bulked together, Thebes still retains its position as the main source of our knowledge.

Tuthmōsis I, the new king, was the son of a woman of non-royal blood named Senisonb. Probably his sole title to kingship was as husband of the princess ʿAḥmose, a lady evidently of very exalted parentage. Two sons are depicted in the tomb of Paḥeri, mayor of El-Kâb, where that noble's father is shown as their 'male nurse' or tutor.[1] Amenmose, perhaps the elder, is described, on a broken stela of year 4,[2] as hunting in the desert near the Great Sphinx and, if it be true that at that time he was already 'great army-commander of his father', the king's marriage must have taken place long before he ascended the throne. The other son Wadjmose is a mysterious and interesting character, since after his death the unusual honour was paid him of a tiny chapel erected just south of the Ramesseum.[3] A man named Amenḥotpe who had the rank of 'First King's Son of ʿAkheperkarēʿ' (this the Prenomen of Tuthmōsis I) was not a real son, because both his parents are named;[4] it is of interest to mention him here, since this instance illustrates the principal difficulty in dealing with Egyptian genealogical problems: one never knows whether terms like 'son', 'daughter', 'brother', 'sister', and so forth are to be understood literally or not.

The first official act of Tuthmōsis I was to send a rescript announcing his accession to Turi, who was still viceroy in Nubia; in this he set forth at length the titulary by which he wished to be known, and which was to be used in connexion with all offerings he might make to the gods, as well as in oaths to be sworn in his name.[5] One of the two copies which we have is said to have come from Wâdy Ḥalfa, but Tuthmōsis's ambition did not stop at that fortress-town. A great inscription of his second year is engraved on a rock opposite the island of Tombos above the Third Cataract,[6] but is richer in grandiloquent phrases than in solid information. A more sober account of the campaign is given by our friend ʿAḥmose of El-Kâb, who relates how he navigated the king's fleet over the rough Nile water when His Majesty, raging like a panther, transfixed the enemy chief's breast with his first arrow and carried him off to Thebes hung head downwards at the prow of the royal ship.[7] A greater feat of arms was the expedition which penetrated across the Euphrates into Nahrin,[8] the territory of the King of Mitanni, where a commemorative stela was set up.[9] A great slaughter was made and many prisoners taken. The two veterans from El-Kâb

[1] *Urk.* iv. 110. [2] Op. cit. iv. 91. [3] PM ii. 157–8. [4] *Urk.* iv. 105–6.
[5] *BAR* ii, §§ 54–60. [6] Op. cit. ii, §§ 67–73; PM vii. 174–5. [7] *BAR* ii, § 80.
[8] This Semitic name means 'the River-country', see *Onom.* i, pp. 171* ff.
[9] *BAR* ii, § 478.

again took part, each of them receiving a handsome reward in return for the horse and chariot which he had captured.[1] On the journey back the king celebrated his success with an elephant hunt in the swampy region of Niy, near the later Apamea in Syria.[2] Only once again for many centuries, namely under Tuthmōsis III, did an Egyptian army ever thrust so far to the north-east, and we shall hardly be mistaken in regarding Tuthmōsis I as no less of a military genius than his grandson.

It is not known how long the reign lasted, perhaps as little as ten years, the latest certain date recorded being the fourth year. A great stela[3] recounting his works in the temple of Osiris at Abydos has lost its date, if it ever had one. If the mummy found at Dêr el-Baḥri is really his, he may have been about fifty years old. In his funerary arrangements he followed Amenōphis I's innovation of making a spatial separation between mortuary temple and actual tomb, and this was copied by all his successors. The temple has not been actually found, unless it was incorporated in that of his daughter, concerning which we shall have much to tell later. The tomb is the oldest of those in the remote valley of the Bîbân el-Molûk ('Tombs of the Kings'), and consists of an entrance stairway leading steeply downwards, an ante-chamber and a sepulchral hall from which a small store-room branched off; a very modest affair compared with the great sepulchres which were to follow. The yellow quartzite sarcophagus found within and now in the Cairo Museum was apparently placed there later by his grandson Tuthmōsis III.[4] An important official named Ineni,[5] who had supervised the splendid buildings at Karnak, including the two obelisks of which one still stands erect, was entrusted with the quarrying of the tomb, his own words being

'I saw to the digging out of the hill-sepulchre of His Majesty privily, none seeing and hearing.'

We gather that the intention was so far as possible to place the king's mummy and rich equipment out of the reach of robbers, an abortive aspiration as it turned out. Ineni was rewarded with a gift

[1] *BAR* ii, §§ 81, 85.
[2] *Onom.* i, pp. 158* ff.
[3] *BAR* ii, §§ 90–98.
[4] Hayes, *RS*, pp. 138 ff.
[5] *BAR* ii, §§ 99–108.

of many serfs and daily rations of bread from the royal granary. Thereupon, he tells us,

the king went to his rest from life and ascended to heaven after he had completed his years in happiness.

The favours accorded to Ineni were continued and even increased by Tuthmōsis II, the son of Tuthmōsis I by a lesser queen named Mutnofre. The reign may have been brief, since Ineni declared himself to have been already old and yet was able to describe conditions under Tuthmōsis II's successor; but there is no valid reason for doubting the date of year 18 found upon a broken stela copied by Daressy[1] and now mislaid. The principal monument is a triumphal stela dated in year 1 and set up on the road between Aswân and Philae.[2] This tells with unusual wealth of detail how news was brought of an insurrection in Nubia:

One came to inform His Majesty that vile Cush had revolted and that those who were subjects of the Lord of the Two Lands had planned rebellion to plunder the people of Egypt and to steal cattle from those fortresses which King ʿAkheperkarēʿ had built in his victories in order to repel the revolted lands and the Nubian tribesmen of Khenthennūfe;[3] and now a chieftain in the north of vile Cush was falling into a season of disobedience together with two tribesmen of Ta-Sti, children of the chieftain of vile Cush who had fled before the Lord of the Two Lands on the day of the Goodly God's slaughtering, this land being divided into five pieces, each man being possessor of his portion.

On hearing this His Majesty raged like a panther, just as his father had done, and swore that he would not leave alive a single man among them. Thereupon his army overthrew those foreigners, sparing only one of the Nubian chieftain's children who was brought back to Thebes as a captive amid general rejoicing. About Tuthmōsis II's other doings little else is heard than that the younger ʿAḥmose of El-Kâb accompanied him to Palestine and took many prisoners:[4] also that he showed favour to a certain Nebamūn who was later to become a steward of Queen Nebtu as well as captain of the king's navy.[5]

[1] *Ann. Serv.* i. 99.
[5] B*AR* ii, §§ 119–22.
[3] An alternative name for Nubia.
[4] B*AR* ii, § 124.
[5] *Urk.* iv. 150–3.

The aged Ineni announces the death of Tuthmōsis II and the accession of his successor in the following words:[1]

Having ascended into heaven, he became united with the gods, and his son, being arisen in his place as king of the Two Lands, ruled upon the throne of his begetter, while his sister, the god's wife Ḥashepsowe governed the land and the Two Lands were under her control; people worked for her, and Egypt bowed the head.

Despite the terse way in which the fact is recorded, there is no reason to think that Tuthmōsis II died other than a normal death. An almost undecorated tomb at Bîbân el-Molûk[2] containing an uninscribed sarcophagus so closely resembles that of Tuthmōsis I that it is confidently ascribed to the son, and from its neglect one might conjecture that no one cared very much what was his fate; his funerary temple,[3] discovered by the French in 1926, is a paltry affair. A stela probably from Hēliopolis[4] depicts him accompanied by Queen ʿAḥmose, the widow of Tuthmōsis I, and by her daughter the 'king's great wife' Ḥashepsowe, so that the latter had certainly been married to Tuthmōsis II, and since her father was Tuthmōsis I her claim to the throne was a very strong one. Nevertheless, there was another formidable claimant in the person of a son of Tuthmōsis II by a concubine Ēse (Isis) who had to content herself with the title 'King's Mother'.[5] That there existed a powerful party which successfully asserted the rights of the youthful Tuthmōsis III is proved not only by Ineni's biography, but also by a later inscription at Karnak[6] telling in very flowery language the story of his elevation to the throne. It relates that he was a mere stripling serving in the temple of Amūn of Karnak and not yet promoted to the rank of 'prophet' ('god's servant'). One day, when the reigning king was sacrificing to Amūn, the god made the circuit of the colonnade seeking the young prince everywhere. As soon as he was found, Amūn halted before him and having raised him from his recumbent posture placed him in front of the king and made him stand in the place usually occupied by the sovereign. The pronouns

[1] *BAR* ii, § 341.
[2] Hayes, *RS*, pp. 7 ff.
[3] C. Robichon and A. Varille, *Le Temple du scribe royal Amenhotep*, i, Cairo, 1936, pp. 31 ff.
[4] Sethe, *HP*, p. 14, fig. 1; *JEA* xv. 60, n. 4.
[5] Sethe, op. cit., § 9.
[6] *BAR* ii, §§ 131–66.

used in this passage present some difficulty, but it seems clear that the intention was to present Tuthmōsis III as appointed king by divine oracle during the lifetime of his father. Since the inscription was probably written forty-two years later, its absolute truthfulness may be legitimately questioned. What, however, is certain is that he came to the throne under the tutelage of his father's wife Ḥashepsowe, who kept him well in the background for a number of years.

If disproportionate space seem here to have been devoted to a single dynastic problem, the excuse must be firstly the importance of the two great personages who now face one another in the centre of the stage and secondly the fact that no events in Egyptian history have given rise to such heated controversy. The aim of this book being not solely to revive the Egyptian past, but also to glance at the methods of Egyptologists, some reference to the arguments which have here played so large a part will not be out of place.[1] The Pharaohs had the unpleasant habit of causing to be destroyed the carved names of any hated predecessors, but those names were apt to be restored later or replaced by other names. Such was the enmity excited by Ḥashepsowe that her cartouche was systematically erased on many of her monuments and in later times was not admitted to any king-list. A frequent occurrence is that the name of Tuthmōsis I or Tuthmōsis II has taken the place of hers. Who was responsible for the erasures and who for these replacements? In an elaborate essay published in 1896 and remodelled and rewritten in 1932 Kurt Sethe argued that the restorations could only have been effected by the owners of the secondary cartouches, with the consequence that both these monarchs must have returned to the throne for a brief spell after Ḥashepsowe's original dictatorship; this, however, was not all, but along similar lines a novel and highly complicated theory was evolved of the entire Tuthmoside succession. In reply É. Naville, the excavator and editor of Ḥashepsowe's wonderful temple at Dêr el-Baḥri, maintained that the restorations were of Ramesside date. Both views were rejected by the historian Ed. Meyer and the archaeologist H. E. Winlock, these scholars reverting to the much simpler opinions that had prevailed

[1] For bibliographical references see below, p. 211.

before Sethe had embarked upon his venturesome hypotheses. In 1933 W. F. Edgerton, after a careful re-examination of all accessible cartouches, felt himself able to maintain that nearly all the erasures and restorations were due to Tuthmōsis III, whose aim was to vindicate his own dynastic claim, while Ḥashepsowe had the identical purpose in any cases where the names of Tuthmōsis I and Tuthmōsis II are original and intact upon monuments erected by her. Lastly, W. C. Hayes corroborated Edgerton's conclusions by a study of all the sarcophagi of the period. The reflection may here be hazarded that so great a diversity of opinion suggests the extremely precarious nature of this kind of testimony; conclusions derived from erasures and their replacements are best discounted so far as possible.

During the lifetime of Tuthmōsis II the full titles borne by Ḥashepsowe were 'king's daughter, king's sister, god's wife, and king's great wife'. She was still merely a principal queen like others before her, and there could be no thought of her receiving a tomb in the lonely and awe-inspiring spot then just beginning to be reserved for the Pharaohs. A tomb of her own dating from this period, with sarcophagus intact, was found at a dizzy height in a cliff a mile and a half southwards from Dêr el-Baḥri.[1] In the first years of her government she had to content herself with mere queenly status, and there even exists an inscription dated in her nephew's second year,[2] though this may not be a contemporary record. Later on he counted his reign, and she hers, from the very commencement of the partnership. Meanwhile, however, her ambition was by no means dormant, and not many years had passed before she had taken the momentous step of herself assuming the Double Crown. Twice before in Egypt's earlier history a queen had usurped the kingship, but it was a wholly new departure for a female to pose and dress as a man. The change did not come about without some hesitation, because there is at least one relief where she appears as King of Upper and Lower Egypt, and yet is clad in woman's attire.[3] But there are various places, particularly at Karnak,[4] where Ḥashepsowe is depicted in masculine guise and taking

[1] *JEA* iv. 114 ff. [2] *BAR* ii, § 169. [3] *Ann. Serv.* xxxiv, Pl. 4.
[4] Op. cit. xxiv, Pl. 3.

precedence of Tuthmōsis III, himself indeed shown as a king, but only as a co-regent. In many inscriptions she flaunts a full titulary, though both on her own monuments and on those of her nobles she is apt to be referred to by feminine pronouns or described by nouns with a feminine ending. A still unpublished inscription places her coronation as king as early as year 2,[1] and from that time onwards until year 20 there was no doubt as to who was the senior Pharaoh; in the latter year, however, the two are represented as on an equality.[2]

It is not to be imagined, however, that even a woman of the most virile character could have attained such a pinnacle of power without masculine support. The Theban necropolis still displays many splendid tombs of her officials, all speaking of her in terms of cringing deference. But among them one man stands out pre-eminent. Senenmūt seems to have been of undistinguished birth, for in the intact tomb of his parents discovered by Lansing and Hayes,[3] his father is given no title but the vague one of 'the Worthy', while his mother is merely 'Lady of a House'. Yet in the course of his own meteoric career, he secured at least twenty different offices, many of them no doubt highly lucrative. His principal title 'Steward of Amūn' may well have put at his command the vast wealth of the temple of Karnak. The great favour which he enjoyed with his royal mistress is attested by his tutelage over the princess Raʿnofru, the next heiress to the throne through her mother's marriage with Tuthmōsis II. No less than six of the ten or more statues which we have of Senenmūt[4] depict him holding the child in his arms or between his knees, but though she doubtless survived until long after Ḥashepsowe's magnificent temple at Dêr el-Baḥri had been begun, nothing more is heard of her after year 11.[5] If we may believe Senenmūt's claim on the statue from the temple of Mūt, it was he who was responsible for all the queen's many Theban buildings,[6] though the statement usually made that he was the actual architect lacks justification.

As mentioned earlier (pp. 122–3), Ḥashepsowe's funerary temple

[1] *Nachr. Göttingen*, 1955, p. 212
[2] *Sinai*, Pl. 57, No. 181.
[3] *Bull. MMA, Eg. Exped. 1935–1936*, pp. 5 ff.
[4] *AJSL* xliv. 49.
[5] *Sinai*, Pl. 58, No. 179.
[6] *BAR* ii, § 351.

at Dêr el-Baḥri situated within the grand semicircle of lofty cliffs, owes much of its inspiration to Menthotpe I's more modest monument lying alongside it to the south. Only traces remain of the causeway sloping gently upwards to the limestone enclosure wall. Here an entrance gives access to a vast court whence the approaching visitor sees in front of him portico above portico as he mounts by a central ramp to the top level. A colonnade of gleaming white limestone to the north of the middle court enables us to envisage the beauty of the structure before Time and human destructiveness had wrought the present ruin. Even now there is no nobler architectural achievement to be seen in the whole of Egypt. The sculptured reliefs behind the columns or pillars of the porticoes are of unique interest. In the bottommost portico is a splendid scene of ships bringing two great obelisks of red granite from Elephantinē to Karnak;[1] these are believed[2] to be those which Ḥashepsowe charged Senenmūt to erect outside the eastern girdle-wall and which have survived only in fragments; they are not to be confused with two others which she placed between the Fourth and Fifth Pylons in her sixteenth year and of which one, only a little short of 100 feet in height, is still standing. The portico in the next tier above has even more of interest to show: on the south side the famous expedition to Pwēne (p. 37) in year 9 and on the north the queen's miraculous conception and birth. In the former series of pictures[3] the ships of Queen Ḥashepsowe, by this time a king, are seen arriving at their destination near the Bâb el-Mandeb, and being greeted by the bearded chieftain and his hideously deformed wife. Less important chiefs prostrate themselves before the emblem of the queen.

They speak, praying for peace from Her Majesty: Hail to thee, king of Egypt, female Sun who shinest like the solar disk. . . .

The native inhabitants lived amid palms in round-domed huts the doors of which were reached by ladders. The Egyptian envoy pitched his tent near at hand and presented gifts of beer, wine, meat, and fruit by Ḥashepsowe's orders, but it is clear that her troops were to have the best of the exchange, for there are

[1] *D. el B.* [vi], Pl. 154. [2] *JNES* xvi. 88 ff. [3] *D. el B.* [iii], Pls. 69–76.

elaborate pictures of all sorts of valuables being carried to and loaded in the ships, among these products being myrrh trees, ebony, ivory, gold, baboons, and leopard-skins. In an upper register the fleet is displayed starting in the homeward direction, the necessary transportation across the desert to the Nile being ignored. The fanciful nature of these wonderful reliefs is, however, exceeded by those on the other side of the ramp.[1] Here, by a fiction of which traces have been found as early as Dyn. XII, the monarch is credited with a divine origin. The preliminaries to the act of procreation are discreetly indicated by the figure of the queen ʿAḥmose sitting on a couch opposite the god Amūn. The next episode shows the royal infant, accompanied by an indistinguishable counterpart which represents his *ka* or soul, being fashioned on a potter's wheel by the ram-headed god Chnūm. The pregnant queen-mother is now led to the actual birthplace, where many minor divinities are in attendance. Much of these scenes has been erased by the later malice of Tuthmōsis III. It is in keeping with the tortuous workings of the Egyptian mind that the boasted fatherhood of Amūn was not allowed to exclude that of Tuthmōsis I, for there is ample evidence of Ḥashepsowe's insistence on this human filiation. A long inscription at Dêr el-Baḥri[2] invents a formal assembling of the Court in which the old king announced his daughter's accession, and at Karnak a corresponding hieroglyphic record[3] thanks Amūn for having sanctioned the same auspicious occurrence. That these claims are fictitious is apparent both on account of the intervening reign of Tuthmōsis II and because in the early days of her rule Ḥashepsowe was still using only the title 'King's Great Wife'.

A nemesis overtook Senenmūt in the end. It was no unheard of thing for a Pharaoh to commemorate his leading officials on the walls of his funerary monument. Piopi II had done this at south Saḳḳâra and Ḥashepsowe did the same at Dêr el-Baḥri. But it was an unparalleled step for a court favourite, however powerful, to use his sovereign's temple for his own devotional purposes. In some of its chapels there are small niches or closets used for storing objects required in the ceremonies, and these niches had wooden doors

[1] *D. el B.* [ii], Pls. 47–51. [2] Op. cit. [iii], Pls. 60–63; *BAR* ii, §§ 232–9.
[3] *BAR* ii, §§ 243–5; PM ii. 57 (34).

which when opened concealed the sides behind them.[1] Here Senenmūt, hoping for his action to remain unobserved, even though he claimed to have had his royal mistress's permission,[2] caused to be carved images of himself praying for his royal mistress's wellbeing. Unhappily this artifice became known, and the reliefs were mercilessly hacked out, only four among them by chance remaining unscathed. A similar fate befell his sepulchral arrangements. Earlier in his career he had started upon a grandiose gallery tomb at Sheikh ʿAbd el-Ḳurna now almost totally ruined. But for safety's sake he planned to be buried in a small chamber near the northern edge of Ḥashepsowe's great court, reached by a descending stairway nearly 100 yards long.[3] This was discovered and entered by Winlock in 1927, when his portrait was found to have been mutilated everywhere, though the name of Ḥashepsowe was left untouched. Even greater rage was expended on the quartzite sarcophagus that had lain near his upper tomb, fragments being found scattered far and wide over a large area.

The last that we hear of Senenmūt is in year 16, but Ḥashepsowe herself certainly survived for five or six years more. Once she had proclaimed herself king there was no reason why she should not have a tomb at Bîbân el-Molûk, and this was excavated by Howard Carter in 1903.[4] It had apparently been meant to run it completely under the cliff so as to bring its sepulchral hall right under her temple, but the crumbly rock thwarted any such intention. Two sarcophagi were found, one altered as an afterthought to receive the body of Tuthmōsis I which she apparently planned to remove from his own tomb so that they might dwell together in the Netherworld.[5] It is uncertain whether this aim was ever achieved. How she met her death is unknown, but it was not long before Tuthmōsis III began to expunge her name wherever it could be found. She left many monuments behind her, but none in the north except at Sinai. According to a long inscription which she caused to be placed on the façade of the small provincial temple called Speos Artemidos[6] by the Greeks, her special pride lay in having restored

[1] Winlock, *Excavations*, pp. 105–6, with Pl. 45.
[2] *Mitt. Kairo*, xv. 80 ff.
[3] Winlock, op. cit., pp. 137 ff.
[4] PM i. 28, No. 20.
[5] Hayes, *RS*, pp. 2, 11–12.
[6] *JEA* xxxii. 43 ff.

the sanctuaries of Middle Egypt which had remained neglected ever since

> the Asiatics were in Avaris of the North Land, roving hordes in the midst of them overturning what had been made, and they ruled without Rēʿ, and he acted not with divine command down to the time of My Majesty.

Doubtless the claim is exaggerated and does scant justice to the merits of her predecessors.

Tuthmōsis III, now a full-grown man and having a free hand at last, clearly did not intend to be outdone by his defunct stepmother, whom he resembled in his determination to obtain full publicity for his achievements. Just as her own temple at Dêr el-Baḥri had offered its wall-space for the purpose, so he too utilized the steadily growing temple of Amen-Rēʿ at Karnak, this having the advantage that he could simultaneously express his gratitude to a deity who had by this time become the great national god. The sanctuary built by the first two kings of Dyn. XII had been a humble affair, but from the beginning of Dyn. XVIII much had been added, the contributions made by Amenōphis I, Tuthmōsis I, and Ḥashepsowe being very considerable. But still the Middle Kingdom edifice remained the limit in the eastward direction, while to the west the building along the main axis did not extend beyond what is now known as the Fourth Pylon. Centuries had to elapse before the vast complex of temples of which the ruins are seen today had come into being. The most conspicuous additions due to Tuthmōsis III were his fine Festival Hall to the east, and the Seventh Pylon to the south, but walls and doorways of his are everywhere, all of them covered with scenes and inscriptions testifying to his piety and his victories. In the Festival Hall he even caused to be depicted the strange plants with which he had become acquainted in Syria, though the identification of these would sorely puzzle a botanist. As usual we have to bemoan the disappearance of blocks which once completed his narrations, though enough is left to enable us to judge of their general trend and character. It is refreshing to find them more factual and less bombastic than the records of most other Pharaohs; here the information given can be accepted with considerable confidence. It must be noted, however, that most of the inscriptions are retrospective and were not composed until after year 40, when Tuthmōsis will have been past the age for strenuous military activity. In addition to the Karnak texts there are two stelae which summarize his physical prowess and deeds of valour, the larger and more important one having been erected in his far-off temple of Napata (Gebel Barkal) near the Fourth Cataract,[1] the other from Armant,[2] smaller and less complete, but covering much the same ground. The event to which Tuthmōsis harks back again and again and which he evidently regarded as the foundation of all his subsequent successes was his victory at Megiddo, a strongly fortified town overlooking the Plain of Esdraelon; this took place in his twenty-third year, the second of his independent reign, and the story is told on some unfortunately fragmentary walls in the very centre of the temple of Amen-Rēʿ.[3]

The reign of Ḥashepsowe had been barren of any military enterprise except an unimportant raid into Nubia,[4] with the result that the petty princes of Palestine and Syria saw an opportunity of throwing off the yoke imposed upon them by the first Tuthmōsis. At the head of the rebellion was the prince of Ḳadesh, a great city on the river Orontēs which owed its importance to its strategic position at the northern end of the so-called El-Biḳâʿ ('the Valley'), the defile lying between Lebanon and Anti-Lebanon.[5] Towards the end of the eighth month in his twenty-second year Tuthmōsis III marched out of his frontier fortress at Tjel[6] near the modern Ḳanṭara on the Suez Canal, his aim, as he tells us, being

> to overthrow that vile enemy and to extend the boundaries of Egypt in accordance with the command of his father Amen-Rēʿ.[7]

Ten days later found him at what subsequently became the Philistine city of Gaza, which he seized; this chanced to be on the anniversary of his accession, and the first day of his twenty-third year. Gaza he left on the morrow, to reach within ten days more a town named Yeḥem clearly at no great distance from the mountainous ridge which had to be crossed before he could come to grips

[1] *ZÄS* lxix. 24 ff. [2] Mond and Myers, *Temples of Armant*, London, 1940, Pl. 103.
[3] PM ii. 33 (37) ff.; 37 (73) ff. [4] *JNES* xvi. 99 ff. [5] *Onom.* i, pp. 137* ff.
[6] Op. cit. ii, pp. 202* ff. [7] The texts, *Urk.* iv. 647 ff.; translations etc., see p. 211.

with the enemy. Here he called a council of war and addressed his officers as follows:

That vile enemy of Ḳadesh has come and entered into Megiddo, and he is there at this moment. He has gathered to himself the princes of all lands who were loyal to Egypt, together with as far as Nahrin . . ., Syrians, Ḳode-people, their horses, their soldiers, and their people. And he says (so they say) 'I will stand to fight against His Majesty here in Megiddo'. Tell me what is in your hearts.

To this the officers reply:

How can one go upon this road which is so narrow? It is reported that the enemy stand outside, and have become numerous. Will not horse have to go behind horse, and soldiers and people likewise? Shall our own vanguard be fighting, while the rear stands here in ʿAruna and does not fight? Now there are two roads here. One road comes out at Taʿanach, and the other is towards the north side of Djefti, so that we would come out to the north of Megiddo. So let our mighty lord proceed upon whichever seems best to his heart. Let us not go upon that difficult road.

Fresh reports having been brought in by messengers, the king makes the following rejoinder:

As I live, as Rēʿ loves me, as my father Amūn favours me, and as I am rejuvenated with life and power, My Majesty will proceed along this ʿAruna road. Let him of you who wishes go upon those roads you speak of, and let him of you who wishes come in the train of My Majesty. Do not let these enemies whom Rēʿ abominates say 'Has His Majesty proceeded along another road because he has grown afraid of us?' For so they will say.

The officers reply humbly:

Thy father Amūn prosper thy counsel. Behold, we are in the train of Thy Majesty wherever Thy Majesty will go. The servant will follow his Master.

The above extracts will have given some idea of the style of this historic narrative, the earliest full description of any decisive battle; but without supplying missing words here and there even less could have been translated. From this point onwards the lacunae multiply, and in places it will be impossible to do more than indicate the general drift. Tuthmōsis having chosen the direct but more difficult road, swore that he would march at the head of his troops. After three days' rest at the village of ʿAruna he set forth northwards, carrying before him the image of Amūn to point the way. Arrived at the mouth of the wâdy he descried the south wing of the enemy forces at Taʿanach on the edge of the plain, while the north wing was deployed nearer Megiddo. Evidently it had been expected that he would take one of the two easier roads, and he recognized that owing to this mistake the confederates were as good as defeated already. Pharaoh's vanguard now spread out over the valley to the south of a brook called Ḳina, when the officers again addressed their sovereign:

> Behold, His Majesty has come forth together with his victorious army and they have filled the valley; let our victorious lord hearken to us this once, and let our lord await for us the rear of his army and his people. When the rear of the army has come right out to us, then we will fight against these Asiatics and we shall not have to trouble about the rear of our army.

Acting upon this advice the king halted his troops until noon when the sun's shadow turned. The entire army then advanced to the south of Megiddo along the bank of the brook Ḳina, by which time it was seven o'clock in the evening.

> Camp was pitched there for His Majesty and an order was given to the entire army saying 'Prepare yourselves, make ready your weapons, for one will engage with that vile foe in the morning'.

Rations were then served out and Tuthmōsis and his soldiers retired to rest, the king sleeping soundly in the royal tent. In the morning it was reported that the coast was clear and that both the southern and northern divisions of the army were in good shape. All this had occurred on the nineteenth day of the month and we are surprised to be told that the battle was fought only on the twenty-first; perhaps this was because the auspicious festival of the new moon had to be awaited. We next hear of the king's setting forth

> on a chariot of gold equipped with his panoply of arms like Horus Brandisher of Arm, Lord of Action, and like Mont the Theban.

For the last time the position of the forces is described, with the north wing to the north-west of Megiddo, the south wing on a hill to the south of the Ḳina brook, and the king in the middle between them. When the battle was engaged, Tuthmōsis displayed great personal valour. The rout of the enemy was complete, they fleeing headlong to Megiddo with frightened faces and leaving behind them their horses and their chariots of gold and silver. Then the gates of the town were closed and they were hoisted up into it by their garments. The compiler of this graphic story now allows himself a lament:

Would that the army of His Majesty had not set their hearts upon looting the chattels of those enemies, for they would have captured Megiddo at that moment, while the vile enemy of Ḳadesh and the vile enemy of this town were being hoisted up.

While the scattered Asiatics lay prostrate like fishes in a net the Egyptians divided up their possessions, giving thanks to Amūn. But ahead of them lay a long siege, which according to the Napata stela lasted seven months. How vital this operation was felt to be is shown by some words with which Tuthmōsis urged on his men to increased efforts:

All the princes of all the northern countries are cooped up within it. The capture of Megiddo is the capture of a thousand towns.

It cannot be denied that the description of the Megiddo battle, with its dialogues between king and courtiers, conforms to a common type, but it is none the less trustworthy on that account. The topographical facts have been verified on the spot by a highly competent scholar,[1] whose only adverse criticism was that the narrowness of the road chosen had been somewhat exaggerated. It is needless here to recount the details of the siege, which we are told were recorded on a leather roll deposited in the temple of Amūn.[2] A certain Tjenen who was 'scribe of the army' claims in his tomb[3] to have commemorated in writing the victories witnessed by himself, but since his soldierly career extended into the second reign after Tuthmōsis III, he can hardly have taken part in the latter's 'first campaign of victory'. The consequences of this did not lead as in

[1] H. H. Nelson, see below, p. 211. [2] *BAR* ii, § 433. [3] *Urk.* iv. 1004.

Nubia to the appointment of a viceroy, the conditions in Palestine and Syria being very different. The whole of that area was occupied by small townships or principalities apt to quarrel among themselves or to enter into new combinations, and their allegiance to the Egyptian conqueror was always being shaken by the imminence of the other great powers pressing downward from the north. The temple of Karnak possesses from this reign great scenes of subjugated localities each represented by a prisoner with his arms bound behind his back, and the chief list of Asiatics enumerates no less than 350 names;[1] and similarly the Napata stela mentions as many as 330 princes as having been engaged against the Egyptians in the Megiddo conflict. Little wonder that between year 23 and year 39 fourteen separate campaigns were needed in order to bring the entire north-eastern area into subjection. The Karnak records are more interested in the booty or tribute obtained than in the conduct of the military operations, but occasional entries throw light on the measures adopted and the policy pursued. From the start Tuthmōsis took the precaution of installing fresh princes of his own choosing and carrying off to Egypt their brothers or children as hostages.[2] While the fields around Megiddo were entrusted to Egyptian cultivators[3] and particularly fruitful districts provided the troops with welcome contributions to their rations,[4] there are also ominous references to the destruction of crops and orchards,[5] this doubtless as punishment of recalcitrant chieftains. A particularly noticeable feature is the supplying of the coastal harbours with provisions, suggesting that in the north at all events equipment and perhaps also men were seaborne in ships built at a great dockyard near Memphis.[6] All this successful organization cannot have failed to impress the rulers of the important states which might feel themselves to be threatened, and we read of gifts sent by the kings of Ashshur (Assyria),[7] of Sangar (Babylonia, the Biblical Shinʿār),[8] and even from the at this moment less dangerous Great Khatti (Hittites).[9]

[1] *Urk.* iv. 779–94. [2] *BAR* ii, § 467. [3] Op. cit. ii, § 437. [4] Op. cit. ii, § 461. [5] Op. cit. ii, §§ 461, 465.

[6] T. Säve-Söderbergh, *The Navy of the Eighteenth Egyptian Dynasty*, Uppsala, 1944, pp. 33 ff. [7] *BAR* ii, §§ 446–9; *Onom.* i, p. 191*.

[8] *BAR* ii, § 484; *Onom.* i, p. 209*. [9] *BAR* ii, § 485; *Onom.* i, p. 127*.

The real stumbling-block in the way of Tuthmōsis III's expansionist plans were, however, the forces of Nahrin, already mentioned in connexion with Tuthmōsis I (p. 178). The crossing of the Euphrates and the defeat of the King of Mitanni were the crowning achievement of the eighth campaign in year 33[1] (*c.* 1457 B.C.). A graphic account is given on the Napata stela:

> My Majesty crossed to the farthest limits of Asia. I caused to be built many boats of cedar on the hills of the God's Land in the neighbourhood of The-mistress-of-Byblos.[2] They were placed on chariots (i.e. wheeled wagons), oxen dragging them and they journeyed in front of My Majesty in order to cross that great river which flows between this country and Nahrin. Nay, but he is a king to be boasted of in proportion to the performance of his two arms in battle—one who crossed the Euphrates in pursuit of him who attacked him; first of his army in seeking that vile enemy over the mountains of Mitanni, while he fled through fear before His Majesty to another far distant land. Then My Majesty set up a stela on that mountain of Nahrin taken from the mountain on the west side of the Euphrates.

There are other descriptions of this expedition,[3] but none equally circumstantial. If the route from Byblos passed through Ḳaṭna, Tunip (near Aleppo), and Carchemish, the transportation of the boats will have covered well over 250 miles, and the use of four-wheeled ox-carts is a totally unexpected feature. But perhaps the victory was not so great as was painted, for two years later there was again fighting with the prince of Nahrin,[4] though not in that country itself. Certain incidents of the homeward journey deserve a mention. The recreations of the Pharaohs tended to be no less stereotyped than their art, and we need not be surprised that Tuthmōsis III, like his grandfather (p. 179), betook himself to Niy to hunt elephants.[5] Two distinct sources tell us that he there confronted a herd of no less than 120. On this occasion a doughty henchman of his named Amenemḥab descended into the water and cut off the trunk of the largest of these animals. The vividly written

[1] *BAR* ii, §§ 476 ff.; *JEA* xxxii. 39 ff.

[2] This epithet of the goddess Baʿalat or Ḥatḥōr here serves as name of the locality itself.

[3] For all the following see *Onom.* i, pp. 153* ff.

[4] *BAR* ii, §§ 498–9.

[5] Op. cit. ii, §§ 588 f.

autobiography in the same man's tomb recounts, among other incidents, a very unusual bit of strategy on the part of the prince of Ḳadesh: a mare which he let loose would have worked havoc among the steeds of the Egyptian chariots had not Amenemḥab run after it, dispatched it with his knife, and presented its tail to the Pharaoh. The town of Ḳadesh, which had been destroyed in the year 30, was then revisited and its new wall breached. Not even now was this neighbourhood completely subjected, for we read of three of its villages being plundered in year 42.[1]

To deal adequately with Tuthmōsis III's military successes would demand much more space than has here been devoted to them. Also we must pass over the far less interesting expeditions to Nubia, except to mention his capture there of a rhinoceros, a great rarity in Egyptian records.[2] Nor can any attempt here be made to deal at length with his building activities and with the festivals that he instituted in favour of the gods. It must suffice to say that few towns did not receive benefactions of his. The funerary temple[3] which he had built for himself on the edge of the western desert at Thebes is almost completely destroyed, but does not seem to have been particularly interesting, and his tomb in Bîbân el-Molûk differs but little from those of his predecessors.[4] In the tomb are mentioned the names, not only of his mother Ēse, but also of his chief wife Meryetrēʿ, who was a second Ḥashepsowe, and of two other wives.[5] Yet three more, with foreign names not improbably Asiatic, were found together with rich jewellery in a remote tomb which was doubtless intact until discovered and robbed by native Egyptians in 1916.[6] The king's coffin and mummy were discovered in the Dêr el-Baḥri *cache*,[7] and if Virchow was right in speaking of the king's almost youthful appearance, he can have been no more than a child when his stepmother took over the government in their joint names, seeing that he died in his fifty-fourth year.[8]

Among the noblemen of this reign none was greater than

[1] *BAR* ii, § 531 (for 'the cities' read 'three villages'); *Urk.* iv. 730.

[2] *ANET*, p. 244; *Urk.* iv. 1246, 1248. [3] PM ii. 148. [4] Hayes, *RS*, pp. 22 ff.

[5] P. Bucher, *Les textes des tombes de Thoutmosis III et d'Aménophis II*, Cairo, 1932, Pl. 24.

[6] H. E. Winlock, *The Treasure of three Egyptian Princesses*, New York, 1948.

[7] PM i. 175, No. 16. [8] *BAR* ii, § 592.

Rekhmirēʿ, whose well-preserved tomb is visited by every tourist to Thebes. He held the office of vizier in the 'Southern City', having his opposite number in the north at the 'Residence', by which Memphis must be meant. No more than a passing allusion can be made to the scenes of foreigners and craftsmen which adorn the walls, but there are pictures which cannot be so lightly dismissed of the officials of many towns from Senmūt, the island of Bigga in the First Cataract, to Asyûṭ in the XIIIth Upper Egyptian nome; these pictures display in most cases the mayor, the district registrar, some scribes, and other minor functionaries, bringing all manner of commodities as dues payable into the bureau of the vizier. One wall is devoted to a flowery eulogy of that great man's office with a brief description of his introduction into the royal presence; but far more important are two long inscriptions repeated *verbatim* in the tombs of several viziers. One of these, noted already in an earlier part of this book, records the speech supposed to have been spoken by the Pharaoh on the day of his chief magistrate's appointment; he is told, for example, that the vizierate is no sweet-tasting undertaking, but one as bitter as gall, and that a petitioner better likes to be allowed to pour out his grievances than that they should be put right. Valuable as is this text psychologically, it is not historically as illuminating as the companion inscription setting forth the manifold duties of the vizier. The only trouble is that we cannot be sure of the date when these evidently much-loved compositions were written; it is not inconceivable that they might even go back to the Middle Kingdom.

Of other outstanding personages known to have flourished in this reign the number cannot be much less than a hundred, many of them possessing fine tombs in the hill of Sheikh ʿAbd el-Ḳurna, where paintings and inscriptions record their multifarious activities. Equal to Rekhmirēʿ in importance was the high-priest of Amen-Rēʿ Menkheperraʿsonb, whose duty towards the great temple of Karnak demanded the accumulation of treasures from all the world; his wall-paintings show Hittite and Syrian princes bringing their tribute of costly vessels, while officials from Coptos offer gold in rings and bags as the contribution of the eastern desert and of Cush; the inscriptions speak of the obelisks and flagstaffs which it was his business to see erected, and there are pictures of carpenters and farmers adding their quota to the god's wealth. It is impossible here to do more than mention one or two other prominent functionaries of the age, nor can as yet a satisfactory synthesis of the whole be presented. The tomb of one Dḥouti who was overseer of the northern countries and a general has not been discovered, but the Louvre has a magnificent gold dish given him by the king, and various objects that belonged to him are in other museums;[1] he is also the hero of a fragmentary tale which bears some resemblance to that of the Forty Thieves.[2] A difficulty which will often be felt is when an official is found engaged in occupations not at all related to his principal functions. For example Minmose, an overseer of works who arranged building constructions in more than a dozen temples, accompanied Tuthmōsis III on expeditions to both Nubia and Syria and collected taxes on his behalf; he was also made overseer of the prophets in the temples where he worked.[3]

For the last twelve years of Tuthmōsis III's reign no expedition to Syria is recorded. Indeed, the Napata retrospect of year 47 has nothing further to report from that direction except annual deliveries of wood dragged to the coast by the princes of the Lebanon, there to be loaded into Egyptian ships. In year 50 the king, returning from Nubia, passed through the First Cataract where, following the example of Senwosre III and Tuthmōsis I, he caused to be cleared a channel which had become blocked with stones.[4] Probably the last phase of his life was spent in planning new buildings and in enjoyment of the vast wealth which he had accumulated. But what was happening meanwhile in the ever troubled north-east? Khatti[5] had been passing through a prolonged spell of internal dissension, and was not yet in a position to extend its power farther than Aleppo, which its king Tudhaliyas II attacked and destroyed at an undetermined date in the middle of the fifteenth century. The main danger to the Egyptian influence at this period came from Mitanni, perhaps mentioned in hieroglyphic texts as early as the reign of Amenōphis I.[6] This powerful kingdom was ruled by a

[1] F. Chabas, *Œuvres diverses*, i. 225 ff. Th. Devéria, *Œuvres diverses*, i. 35 ff.; *Urk.* iv. 999 ff. [2] *JEA* xi. 225 ff. [3] *Urk.* iv. 1441 ff. [4] *BAR* ii, §§ 649–50.
[5] Gurney, p. 26. [6] In the inscription quoted p. 175, n. 3.

dynasty of Aryan stock, who had imposed their dominion on Hurrians from the mountains of Armenia. To what extent the Mitannians ever actually encroached into northern Syria is doubtful; in the hieroglyphic inscriptions the terms Mitanni and Nahrin are synonymous, though the more frequently used name Nahrin strictly refers only to the land beyond the Euphrates. At all events the constant boasts that Nahrin has been trampled under foot leave no doubt as to who the prime instigators of rebellion and unrest in Syria and Palestine were felt to be; and so potent was the threat from Mitanni and, after its overthrow by Suppiluliumas in 1370 B.C., from its Hittite and later its Assyrian successors, that never again for nearly 800 years did an Egyptian army penetrate as far as the Euphrates. This slowly weakening power of Egypt did not, however, deter Tuthmōsis III's son from attempting to emulate the victories of his father.

Amenōphis II (*c.* 1436–1413 B.C.) was the son of the Ḥashepsowemeryetrēʿ already mentioned as Tuthmōsis III's chief wife, and was born at Memphis.[1] At an early age he was engaged in supervising deliveries of wood to the great dockyard of Peru-nūfe near Memphis and at the same time seems to have held the office of *setem*, the high-priest in that northern capital.[2] A great stela[3] unearthed near the great Sphinx gives an exaggeratedly laudatory account of his accomplishments. His muscular strength was extraordinary: we are told that he could shoot at a metal target of one palm's thickness and pierce it in such a way that his arrow would stick out on the other side; unhappily the like had been related of Tuthmōsis III, though with less detail,[4] so that we are not without excuse for scepticism. None the less there are other examples of his athletic prowess too individual to be rejected out of hand. When he was eighteen years of age he was already an expert in all the art of Mont, the god of War. As an oarsman wielding an oar 20 cubits long he was the equal of 200 men, rowing six times as far as they could without stopping. So admirable a horseman was he that his father Tuthmōsis entrusted him with the finest steeds of his stable, and these he trained so skilfully that they could cover long distances

[1] *Urk.* iv. 1366.
[2] *ZÄS* lxvi. 105 ff.; lxviii. 7 ff.
[3] *ANET*, p. 244.
[4] Op. cit., p. 243.

without sweating. A strange inscription from Semna dating from year 23[1] gives an inkling of his character in later life. So far as it can be understood he seems while drinking to have given free expression to his contempt for his foreign enemies, declaring the northerners, including 'the old woman of Arpakh' and the people of Takhsy,[2] to be a useless lot, but he orders his viceroy in Nubia to beware of the people there and of their magicians, and urges him to replace any objectionable chief by some man of humble birth. A typically Egyptian combination of naïveté and boastfulness!

The building activities of Tuthmōsis III were continued energetically by his son. At Karnak so much honour had been done to Amen-Rēʿ that without wholly neglecting the great Theban god Amenōphis II preferred to devote his piety to the provinces. A rock-tablet at Ṭura shows that in year 4 Minmose was still busy in the temples of the Delta.[3] At Amada, an important town in the very centre of Lower Nubia, much remains of the fine temple begun in the previous reign, the local deity Horus of Miʿam being, however, somewhat pushed into the background by the great national gods Rēʿ-Ḥarakhti and Amen-Rēʿ.[4] Under pictures of them seated in a bark as though visiting the place and regaled with wine by the king is a well-preserved stela that was long the principal source of information concerning the latter's achievements. After the inevitable epithets proclaiming his power there comes a recital of the constructions in the temple, these repeated in identical terms in a fragmentary duplicate emanating from the temple of Chnūm at Elephantinē.[5] Then follow some sentences recording an act of barbarity which in the crude moral atmosphere of that warlike age could be regarded as a ground for special pride. The stela, we learn, was erected

after His Majesty had returned from Upper Retjnu and had overthrown all those disaffected towards him, extending the boundaries of Egypt in the first campaign of victory. His Majesty returned joyful of heart to his father Amūn when he had slain with his own club the seven chieftains who had been in the district of Takhsy, they being placed head downwards at the prow of His Majesty's ship of which the name is

[1] *Urk.* iv. 1343–4.
[2] See p. 200.
[3] *Urk.* iv. 1448.
[4] PM vii. 65 ff.
[5] *ANET*, pp. 247–8.

ʿAkheprurēʿ-the-Establisher-of-the-Two-Lands. Then six of these enemies were hanged on the face of the enclosure wall of Thebes, the hands likewise, and the other enemy was shipped up to Nubia and hanged upon the enclosure wall of Napata in order to cause to be seen the victorious might of His Majesty for ever and ever.

The Amada stela is dated in year 3, and the Syrian campaign is there described as the first campaign of victory. This expression has caused puzzlement to scholars because the same words are applied to another great stela of year 7 with which we shall be dealing shortly. Too much has possibly been made of this discrepancy if, as seems not unlikely, the expedition against Takhsy, a district at no great distance from Ḳadesh on the river Orontēs, was the same as that mentioned on the statue of Minmose from Medâmûd,[1] who says that he saw the prowess of His Majesty when he 'plundered thirty towns in the district of Takhsy'; Tuthmōsis III is here ostensibly the king referred to, but perhaps it was really Amenōphis II acting in his father's stead. There is, indeed, some doubtful evidence of a co-regency at the end of Tuthmōsis's reign,[2] though this would contradict the statement in the above-mentioned narrative of the warrior Amenemḥab.

A very fragmentary and defective stela describing Amenōphis II's victories had long been known at Karnak, but was practically useless until in 1942 what is in part a duplicate and is in almost perfect condition was found at Memphis.[3] In spite of considerable differences the two inscriptions supplement one another usefully. A blemish common to both is due to many sentences having been effaced by the partisans of the fanatical king Akhenaten, damage which the pundits employed by Sethōs I, that great restorer of earlier monuments, were unable to make good. The following freely translated excerpts will illustrate one of the liveliest and most informative narratives which Egyptian history has to show.

After the date in year 7 and the inevitable epithets extolling the valour of the king a brief paragraph describes the destruction of a

[1] Above, p. 197, n. 3.

[2] The cartouches of both kings stand side by side, not only in the temple of Amada, but also in Theban tombs 41 and 200. However, the student must be warned against this kind of evidence.

[3] *ANET*, pp. 245–7; see too below, p. 211.

place called Shamash-Edom which was not more than a day's march from Ḳaṭna, an important town 11 miles north-east of Ḥomṣ.[1] This quickly achieved victory left in Egyptian hands a small number of Asiatics and cattle. At this point the narrative proper begins:

His Majesty crossed the Orontēs over water turbulent like the god Rashaph. Then he turned around to look after the rear of his army and saw some Asiatics who had come surreptitiously from the town of Ḳaṭna to attack the king's army. His Majesty was equipped with weapons of warfare and His Majesty pounced upon their back like the flight of a divine falcon, and they gave way, their hearts fainting, each one fallen upon his fellow, including their captain. There was none with His Majesty save himself and his strong right arm. His Majesty slew them with a shot.

Following a brief reference to the king's departure and to the booty taken, the Karnak text continues with a fuller version:

Second month of the Summer season, day 10, turning back southwards. His Majesty proceeded by chariot to the town of Niy, and the Asiatics of this town, men and women, were on their walls adoring His Majesty and showing wonderment at the goodly god.

Twice previously we have referred to Niy as the scene of an elephant hunt. The mention here is valuable as corroborating the view that this place was not on the Euphrates as some had supposed. The next paragraph presents a difficulty inasmuch as what must surely be understood as the town of Ugarit lacks an essential consonant; Ugarit is the present-day Râs esh-Shamra on the coast a little to the north of Laodicea, where Cl. Schaeffer has excavated with great success, among other valuable finds being many clay tablets written in alphabetic cuneiform characters.

Now His Majesty had heard that some of the Asiatics who were in the town of Ukat were seeking to find a way of casting the garrison of His Majesty out of his town and to subvert the face of the prince who was loyal to His Majesty. Then His Majesty became cognisant of it in his heart, and surrounded everyone who defied him in this town and slew them at once. Thus he quelled this town and calmed the entire land.

[1] *Onom.* i, p. 166*.

Some repose was needed at this juncture and after rest in a tent set up in the neighbourhood of Tjalkhi,[1] the king went on to plunder some villages and at others to accept the submission of their headmen. On arrival at Ḳadesh some of the princes together with their children were made to take oaths of loyalty. By way of exhibiting his skill and at the same time manifesting his bonhomie

His Majesty next shot at two targets of copper in their presence on the south side of this town, and they made excursions at Rebi in the forest, and brought back numberless gazelles, foxes, hares, and wild asses.

More serious tasks lay ahead, however, and the Memphis stela recounts the remainder of Amenōphis's first campaign in the following words:

His Majesty proceeded on his chariot to Khashabu,[2] alone and without a companion, and returned thence in a short time bringing sixteen living Maryannu at the side of his chariot, twenty hands at the foreheads of his horses and sixty cattle driven in front of him. Submission was made to His Majesty by this town. Now as His Majesty was going south in the Plain of Sharon,[3] he found a messenger of the prince of Nahrin carrying a clay tablet at his neck, and took him as a living prisoner at the side of his chariot. Then went forth His Majesty with two . . . to Egypt, the Maryannu as a living prisoner on one chariot together with him. Arrival of His Majesty at Memphis with joyful heart like a victorious bull. Amount of this plunder: Maryannu, 550; their wives, 240; Canaanites, 640; children of princes, 232; female children of princes, 323; female musicians of the princes of every land, 270, together with their instruments of silver and gold. Total, 2214. Horses, 820; chariots, 730, together with all their weapons of warfare. Now the god's wife, king's wife, and king's daughter [name lost] saw the victories of His Majesty.

The second campaign, in year 9, was on a smaller scale than the first, the king-led Egyptian army not venturing farther north than the Sea of Galilee. Several of the places named, Apheq, Yeḥem, Socho, and Anaharath, are mentioned in the lists of Tuthmōsis III, in the Old Testament, or in both, and their sites have been identified with some probability. The recital is in much the same vein as

[1] Am. 126. 5, see *Onom.* i. 165*. [2] Am. 174. 4.

[3] Near the coast between Carmel and Joppa; mentioned several times by Isaiah and and in a few other biblical passages.

that of the first campaign, but there are some novel features. The night's rest in the royal tent is again mentioned, but now the god Amūn appears in a dream and promises victory. After an important capture of prisoners and plunder, we read of their being surrounded by two ditches filled with fire, and of the Pharaoh keeping watch over them the whole night through, attended only by his personal servants; this insistence on the personal bravery of the sovereign in the absence of his army is a commonplace of such inscriptions and characteristic of the large element of romance that they contain. A careful analysis by E. Edel of the totals of plunder concluding each campaign has brought to light important details, only a few of which can receive comment here. It now emerges that the list at the end of the Memphite stela embraces the results not solely of the second campaign, but also those of the first; only thus is it possible to explain the inclusion of 15,070 Nagasu prisoners, since these are clearly the Nukhashshe of the cuneiform records, who are known to have occupied the region between Ḥomṣ and Aleppo;[1] the number given is, of course, fantastic, like the figures quoted for the Shōsu or Beduins and for the Khorians who may derive their name, later extended to all Palestinians and Syrians, from the Hurrian invaders from the north. Immediately preceding there is a reference to the ʿApiru, a much-discussed term which we cannot afford to ignore;[2] a few years ago it was confidently asserted that these people were identical with the Hebrews of the Old Testament, but this is now denied by all but a few scholars; it is, however, generally accepted that they are to be equated with the Ḫabiru (better Ḫapiru) of the ʿAmârna tablets, apparently a generic term for 'outcasts' or 'bandits' belonging to no fixed ethnic groups; in Egyptian texts they appear as Asiatic prisoners employed in stone quarries. More agreement has been reached about the term Maryannu mentioned a number of times on our stelae; this Indo-Iranian word indicates the highest rank of fighting men in the towns of Syria, those who were entrusted with chariots and horses of their own.

The Memphis stela terminates with a paragraph worth translating in full:

[1] *Onom.* i, pp. 168* ff.

[2] References, see below, p. 211.

Now when the prince of Nahrin, the prince of Khatti and the prince of Sangar heard of the great victory which I had made, each one vied with his fellow in all manner of presentations from all lands, and they spoke in their hearts to the father of their fathers to pray for peace from His Majesty in return for the giving to them of the breath of life: 'We come with our tribute to thy Palace, O son of Rēʿ Amenōphis, ruler of rulers, raging lion in every country and in this land eternally.'

The interest here lies in the mention of the three great northern powers[1] who might be casting covetous eyes upon the Syrian province; perhaps indeed it was only their mutual rivalries which prevented one or the other of them from seeking to oust the Egyptians from what remained of Tuthmōsis III's Asiatic conquests. In the seventeen or twenty years still left of Amenōphis II's reign there is no hint of further warlike undertakings, and in that of his son Tuthmōsis IV, to whom Manetho, for once trustworthy, assigns nine years, the suppression of a Nubian rebellion in year 8[2] is almost all that is recorded. In this quarter-century so destitute of noteworthy historical information, prominent dignitaries were adorning their tombs at Ḳurna with splendid paintings; such a one, for instance, was Ḳenamūn,[3] Amenōphis's great steward in the Memphite shipbuilding centre of Peru-nūfe; among his duties was to present to the king, on the occasion of the New Year, all the finest products of his workshops; statues, vases, shields, chariots, and furniture of every kind are exhibited on the tomb-walls most delicately drawn and painted. A stela from year 1 of Tuthmōsis IV[4] relates how he, whilst hunting as a stripling in the neighbourhood of the Great Sphinx of Gîza, received in a dream the promise of kingship from Ḥarmakhe (Harmachis), the solar god whom it embodied; in return he was to free the deity from the encumbering sand, and the lost ending must have told how he acquitted himself of this duty. Apart from this fanciful narrative the reign has little to record, though mention must be made of the greatest of all obelisks, 105 feet in height, which now stands in front of the church of St. John Lateran in Rome; this monument had lain neglected at Karnak until Tuthmōsis IV took its erection in hand.[5] The funerary temples

[1] See above, p. 193.
[2] *BAR* ii, §§ 823–9; *Urk.* iv. 1545 ff.
[3] PM i. 123, No. 93.
[4] *BAR* ii, §§ 810–15.
[5] *Urk.* iv. 1548 ff.

INTERIOR OF THE TOMB OF NAKHT
Wall-paintings from western Thebes, Dyn. XVIII

PLATE XII

COLOSSAL STATUES OF AMENŌPHIS III

Western Thebes: the Vocal Memnōn on the right; in the distance the gallery-tombs of Sheikh ʿAbd el-Ḳurna

of both Tuthmōsis[1] and his father[2] occupied their natural places along the fringe of the western desert at Thebes, but of them hardly anything remains. The tomb of Amenōphis II, discovered at Bîbân el-Molûk by V. Loret in 1898 still contains the king's sarcophagus, and in it his mummy, though this had been tampered with and robbed.[3] Five years later the tomb of Tuthmōsis IV[4] was discovered by Howard Carter, likewise with his great sarcophagus, as well as many pieces of the funerary furniture; a mummy purporting to be his was, however, found enclosed in a late coffin in the tomb of Amenōphis II, the body being, according to Elliot Smith, that of an extremely emaciated young man not more than twenty-eight years of age.

With the accession of Amenōphis III (*c.* 1405–1367 B.C.) Dyn. XVIII attained the zenith of its magnificence, though the celebrity of this king is not founded upon any military achievement. Indeed, it is doubtful whether he himself ever took part in a warlike campaign. In his fifth year a rebellion in Nubia had to be suppressed, as we learn from three bombastic records on rocks near the First Cataract;[5] but if this was the same occasion as that much more soberly described on a stela in the British Museum,[6] the Egyptian army was under the command of the often-named viceroy Mermose, and when it is said that 'the strong arm of Amenōphis captured' the enemy, this need not mean that he was present in the flesh. The scene of the victory was the district of Ibhe whence King Merenrēʿ of Dyn. VI had obtained the stone for his pyramid. The number of prisoners taken was small, all told no more than 1052. Nevertheless the Nubian province bears solid testimony to Amenōphis III's greatness; not only did he build stately temples at Sedeinga[7] and Soleb[8] a little distance to the north of the Third Cataract, but his 'living image' actually received a cult in the latter place, as his wife Tiye did at the former.

A new method of commemorating outstanding events of the reign was obtained by the fabrication of large scarabs bearing hiero-

[1] PM ii. 159.
[2] Op. cit. ii. 149.
[3] Op. cit. i. 29, No. 35; Hayes, *RS*, pp. 23–25.
[4] PM i. 30, No. 43; Hayes, op. cit., pp. 25–27.
[5] B*AR* ii, §§ 842–5; *Urk*. iv. 1661 ff.
[6] B*AR* ii, §§ 851–5.
[7] PM vii. 166–7.
[8] Op. cit. 169–72; B*AR* ii, §§ 893–8.

glyphic legends. Hitherto the information which scarabs had to offer was confined to a few short words; now these were expanded into a whole narrative or its equivalent. Five varieties[1] are known, all of them associating with Amenōphis his famous queen Tiye, whose parents are named in two cases; they are the god's father, prophet of Mīn at Akhmîm and overseer of horses Yuia and the chief lady of Amūn's harem Tjuia, their titles being given in the superbly furnished tomb discovered at Bîbân el-Molûk by Theodore M. Davies in 1905;[2] thus were disposed of the earlier theories ascribing to Queen Tiye a foreign origin. A difficulty now arose, however, in the fact that the scarab recording the two days' hunt in which nearly a hundred wild bulls were captured, while mentioning her as queen, is dated as early as year 2; from this it was argued that Amenōphis III could not have been the son of Tuthmōsis IV, since the mummy of the latter found, as we have already said, in the tomb of Amenōphis II, was pronounced to be that of a young man not more than twenty-eight years of age.[3] To this and other similar contentions sufficient answers have now been found.[4] The crowning proof that Amenōphis III was the son of Tuthmōsis IV is given in the great temple which Amenōphis built at Luxor and where the scenes attributing a divine parentage to the monarch are re-enacted in relief; as with Ḥashepsowe at Dêr el-Baḥri, Mutemuia, the mother of Amenōphis, is represented as the consort of the god Amūn, who is said to have 'assumed the form of this husband, King Menkheprurēʿ', that being the Prenomen of Tuthmōsis IV.[5]

The shooting of 102 fierce lions by the king himself over a period of ten years is perhaps more credible than the picture painted upon Tutʿankhamūn's casket (above, pp. 56–57), but of greater interest is the making of a large pleasure lake for Queen Tiye. The scarab recording this gives the measurements as 3,700 by 700 cubits, figures not wholly out of accord with the view that the lake in question is the Birket Habu lying to the south of the great temple of Medînet Habu at Thebes and immediately to the east of Amenōphis's palace site in the so-called Malḳata. The statement that this lake was dug

[1] *BAR* ii, §§ 860 ff.; *Urk.* iv. 1737 ff.
[2] PM i. 30–31 (No. 46).
[3] For this controversy see Vandier, pp. 383–4.
[4] *ZÄS* lxv. 98 ff.
[5] A. Gayet, *Le Temple de Louxor*, Cairo, 1894, Pl. 63, fig. 205.

in 15 days is, however, hard to believe. The palace,[1] or complex of palaces, is of great importance as one of the few royal residences of which considerable portions remain; like all Egyptian buildings made for the living it was constructed almost entirely of brick, but the plastered walls were adorned with lovely painted images of birds, water-plants, and the like.[2] Here too was a festival hall where Amenōphis celebrated his Sed-festivals or Jubilees in his 30th, 34th, and 37th regnal year. The nature of these already-mentioned festivals still remains obscure,[3] though it is evident that they in some way celebrated renewals of the royal power; images of the various provincial gods were brought to the capital where the ceremonies were performed. The Rosetta Stone gives as the Greek equivalent the term 'Thirty-year Festival' and several of the Pharaohs did in fact hold their first Sed-festival in their thirtieth year, but there are inexplicable exceptions.

On what is not quite appropriately known as the Marriage Scarab the names of Tiye and her parents are followed by the words:

> She is the wife of a victorious king whose southern boundary is to Karoy, and his northern to Nahrin.

Karoy[4] may have extended even beyond Napata and was the limit of the viceroy's administrative province. As regards Nahrin the claim here made was perhaps more of an aspiration than a fact. Nevertheless, friendship with Amenōphis was of sufficient importance to the prince of Mitanni to entitle another scarab dated in year 10 to record

> a miracle, brought to His Majesty, the daughter of the prince of Nahrin Sutarna, Kirgipa and persons of her harem, 317 women.

A flood of light has been thrown on the relations of Egypt with Mitanni and the neighbouring countries in this reign and the next by an extraordinary find now to be described. In 1887 a peasant woman gathering the fertilizer known as *sabakh* amid the ruins of

[1] *JNES* x. 35 ff., &c. [2] H. Frankfort, *The Mural Painting*, London, 1929.
[3] The main facts, H. Bonnet, *Reallexikon d. äg. Religionsgeschichte*, Berlin, 1952, pp. 158–60.
[4] T. Säve-Söderbergh, op. cit., Index under Kari.

El-ʿAmârna, a village about 190 miles south of Cairo, chanced upon a large number of clay tablets incised with wedge-shaped characters. Nothing of the kind had ever been seen in Egypt before, and of these strange and apparently worthless objects some were sold for a song, others destroyed, and many more lost. The first antiquaries into whose hands they fell judged them to be forgeries, and it was only after much discussion and the acquisition of specimens by various national museums that they were recognized for what they really were, namely the actual correspondence of Amenōphis III and his successor with the different Asiatic rulers of their time, both great and small.[1] The writing was Babylonian cuneiform, which served as the diplomatic medium of those days. Here the names of the princess and her father appear as Gilukhipa[2] and Shuttarna,[3] while the Pharaoh, whose Prenomen in hieroglyphic we render as Nebmaʿrēʿ, is addressed as Nimmuaria, which was presumably nearer the real pronunciation; the writer is Tushratta, Shuttarna's son, who had acceded to the Mitanni throne after the murder of an elder brother.[4] From one of Tushratta's letters we learn that his grandfather Artatama I had given a daughter in marriage to Tuthmōsis IV, though only after repeated requests.[5] Nothing more is heard about the host of damsels stated on the scarab to have accompanied Gilukhipa to Egypt, but it is clear that substantial gifts from both sides were always a concomitant of these much-desired matrimonial transactions. On the whole Amenōphis III's relations with Tushratta were cordial, but those between him and Kadashman-Enlil I, the King of Babylonia, were less so, the latter complaining that he had been unsuccessful in finding out whether his sister, another lady sent as a bride to Egypt, was alive or dead.[6] In this reign no letters passed between Egypt and Assyria, which had temporarily become a vassal of Mitanni, nor as yet was there any correspondence with the Hittites, though there are letters from Amenōphis to the prince of Arzawa, an Anatolian land even farther afield. At the back of all this epistolary activity two motives stand out conspicuous, the enhancement of personal prestige and the desire for valuable commodities. Babylonia, for example, fur-

[1] See below, p. 211.
[2] Am. 17, 5. 41.
[3] Am. 24, i. 47; 29, 18.
[4] Am. 17, 11–20.
[5] Am. 29, 16–18.
[6] Am. 1, 10–14.

nished horses, lapis lazuli, and other costly materials, while Alasiya, believed to be Cyprus, exchanged copper for gold, of which all these countries supposed Egypt to possess inexhaustible supplies. The frankness with which these traffickings were carried on is amazing. The Asiatic rulers treat with their Egyptian 'brother' on terms of absolute equality, and although the letters never omit the initial greetings demanded by courtesy, there is a complete lack of reticence in the wheedling requests which alternate with accusations of meannesss. On the whole, however, the impression left is that of a diplomacy well aware of the mutual advantages to be gained from a consistently friendly approach. Far different is what the ʿAmârna correspondence has to teach us about the relations of the smaller principalities of northern Syria, but further mention of the violent dissensions which had arisen there must be deferred until their cause in the disastrous policy of Amenōphis III's successor has been laid bare.

At the Egyptian Court there was one man[1] whose outstanding ability obtained full recognition at the time, and later even led to his deification, as in the case of the wise Imḥōtep (pp. 72–73). This was Amenḥotpe, the son of Ḥapu, born to unimportant parents in the Delta town of Athribis, the modern Benha. Although by far the most honoured of Amenōphis III's servants, he never attained any of the highest offices of state. The numerous statues which the king's favour caused to be erected in the temples of Amūn and of Mūt at Karnak all portray him as a 'royal scribe' seated on the ground with an open papyrus on his lap. His main title was that of a 'scribe of goodly young men', a term habitually used to describe the functionaries charged with finding able-bodied recruits for military or other purposes. The inscriptions engraved around the squatting figures are none too explicit in their information, but leave no doubt as to his responsibility for the transport and erection of the two great seated images of Amenōphis III still to be seen near the road leading to the western desert from the Nile opposite Luxor.[2] These had been quarried in the Gebel el-Aḥmar to the north-east of Cairo, the source of the fine reddish crystalline sandstone so much

[1] See below, p. 211. The main inscription, *BAR* ii, §§ 911–20.

[2] One of them is the 'Vocal Memnōn' mentioned above, p. 7; see Pl. xii.

affected in this reign; it was no mean feat to move from the 'Lower Egyptian Hēliopolis' to the 'Upper Egyptian Hēliopolis' a pair of colossi each nearly 70 feet in height. The remains of the huge funerary temple in front of which they stood are now buried beneath the cultivated fields. In return for this and other signal services Amenōphis III rewarded this namesake of his with a stately temple immediately to the west,[1] and from that time forth until the Graeco-Roman age the cult and the memory of Amenḥotpe, the son of Ḥapu, never waned. As he himself tells us, he was eighty years old before he died, and he played a prominent part in the preparations for Amenōphis III's first Sed-festival. Whether he was actually the author of the wise sayings with which he was later credited is doubtful; the few fragments left appear to be of Greek origin.

The first half of Amenōphis III's long reign was an era of prosperity such as Thebes had never previously enjoyed. The most costly products of Nubia and Asia flowed to the Southern City in an uninterrupted stream, to which Crete and even Mycenae seem to have added contributions. Many other dignitaries of the reign are known from fine tombs or statues of their owners or from the sealings of jars that had contained the food, beer, or wine which they contributed to the royal palace.[2] Even if the proud Pharaoh's foremost thought was for the splendour of his own funerary temple and the adjacent palace, he by no means overlooked the claims of the temples in the southern capital. Long inscriptions[3] recount his benefactions at Karnak and at Luxor, and one dedicatory text even furnishes details of the gold and semi-precious stones which he devoted to their adornment;[4] needless to say, the figures given are quite incredible. The wealth of the temple of Amen-Rēʿ must have been enormous, and its high-priest Ptaḥmose was the first to be able to add to his sacerdotal authority that inherent in the rank of vizier.[5] Little could the Theban nobles have been aware of the storm so soon to break over their beloved homes and to work havoc in their most cherished ideals and beliefs.

[1] PM ii. 160.

[2] See the article by Hayes quoted p. 211.

[3] *BAR* ii, §§ 878–92; 899–903; the texts, *Urk.* iv. 1646 ff., 1722 ff.

[4] *Urk.* iv. 1668.

[5] G. Lefebvre, *Grands prêtres*, pp. 99 ff.; also *ZÄS* lxxii. 62–63.

SELECT BIBLIOGRAPHY

Tombs and sarcophagi of the period: W. C. Hayes, *Royal Sarcophagi of the XVIII Dynasty*, Princeton, 1935.

The Ḥashepsowe controversy: K. Sethe, *Das Hatschepsut-Problem*, in *Abh.* Berlin, 1932; W. F. Edgerton, *The Thutmosid Succession*, Chicago, 1933; Hayes, op. cit., p. 3, n. 14; Vandier, pp. 381–3.

Career of Senenmūt: Winlock, *Excavations*, pp. 145–53.

The Annals of Tuthmōsis III: most recent translations, *ANET*, pp. 234 ff.; discussions, H. H. Nelson, *The Battle of Megiddo*, Chicago, 1913; R. O. Faulkner, in *JEA* xxviii. 2 ff.; H. Grapow, *Studien zu den Annalen Thutmosis des Dritten*, in *Abh.* Berlin, 1949.

The Palestinian place-names: J. Simons, *Handbook for the Study of Egyptian Topographical Lists*, Leyden, 1937; M. Noth, *Der Aufbau der Palästinaliste Thutmoses III* in *ZDPV* lxi (1938), 26–65.

Tombs of great Theban contemporaries of Tuthmōsis III: N. de G. Davies, *The Tomb of Rekh-mi-rēʿ at Thebes*, 2 vols., New York, 1943; Nina and Norman de G. Davies, *The Tombs of Menkheperrasonb*, &c., London, 1933.

Asiatic campaigns of Amenōphis II: *Urk.* iv. 1299 ff. E. Edel, *Die Stelen Amenophis II aus Karnak und Memphis*, in *ZDPV* lxix (1953), 98–176. The ʿApiru people: ibid., p. 170; also R. Borger, *ZDPV* lxxiv (1958), 121–3, and T. Säve-Söderbergh in *Orientalia Suecana*, i. 1 ff.

Amenōphis III: W. C. Hayes, *Inscriptions from the Palace of Amenhotep III*, in *JNES* x (1951) 35–40; 82–104; 156–83; 231–42.

The El-ʿAmârna letters: S. A. B. Mercer, *The Tell el-Amarna Tablets*, 2 vols. Toronto, 1939, based on J. A. Knudtzon and O. Weber, *Die El-Amarna Tafeln*, 3 vols., Leipzig, 1915.

Amenḥotpe, son of Ḥapu: W. Helck, *Der Einfluss der Militärführer in der 18. ägyptischen Dynastie*, Leipzig, 1939, pp. 2–13; C. Robichon and A. Varille, *Le temple du scribe royal Amenhotep*, i, Cairo, 1936.

IX

THE RELIGIOUS REVOLUTION AND AFTER

IN some respects the last years of Amenōphis III seem to have followed a normal course. Surrounded by everything that wealth could give he continued to reside in his luxurious palace on the west of Thebes, whence he carried on his correspondence with the Asiatic kings and the lesser chieftains of Palestine. Doubtless Queen Tiye still exerted an important influence upon his counsels. Special favour was shown to a daughter of theirs named Sitamūn, to whom there appears to have been given, with Amenḥotpe son of Ḥapu as its steward, an establishment of her own in the palace area.[1] Since this Sitamūn adds to her title of 'king's daughter' that of 'king's great wife'—there is even a faience knob on which the cartouches of Tiye and herself face one another each preceded by this title—several scholars have maintained that the old king married his own daughter,[2] and this unwelcome conclusion is difficult to resist. At all events he was not averse to replenishing his harem. There he already had a sister of the king of Babylonia, but was clamouring for a daughter as well.[3] Of Gilukhipa nothing more is heard except greetings from her brother Tushratta.[4] Several other letters, however, deal with the negotiations for the Egyptian king's marriage with Tadukhipa, the daughter of the same Mitannian king;[5] in this case Tushratta insists on her becoming Amenōphis's wife and the 'mistress of Egypt' and as an inducement sent with her a splendid assortment of gifts which are enumerated in great detail.[6] The damsel's arrival was long delayed, but meanwhile Tushratta was, by anticipation, proudly proclaiming the Pharaoh as his 'son-in-law'.[7] Perhaps the marriage was never consummated, for by this time Amenōphis III was probably a sick old man. In the hope of bringing about his recovery

[1] *JNES* x. 35–36. [2] *PSBA* xxiv, 246; *Ann. Serv.* xl. 651–7; xlv. 123–4.
[3] Am. 1. 11–14. [4] Am. 17. 5–6; 19. 6. [5] Am. 20. 8–16. [6] Am. 22.
[7] Am. 20. 1–3; 21. 1–6.

Tushratta, adopting an expedient for which there are Egyptian parallels, sent to Thebes an image of the goddess 'Ishtar of Niniveh', praying that she should be treated as hospitably as on a previous occasion and be safely returned to her own country.[1] The ʿAmârna letter recording this is dated in year 36, and it is known from other sources that Amenōphis III lived to complete his thirty-seventh if not his thirty-eighth year.[2] But that was the end and the next letter from Tushratta is addressed to the all-powerful widow Tiye and, recalling the good relations which had persisted between him and her late husband, expresses the hope that those with her son may be ten times as cordial.[3] A fine tomb of normal type had been excavated for Amenōphis III in the western branch of the Bîbân el-Molûk,[4] and there is every reason to think that he was actually buried there. His own sepulchre was not, however, destined to be his final resting-place, for his mummy, showing plain signs of acute suffering from toothache, was found by Loret in the tomb of Amenōphis II, whither it had been transferred by the high-priest of Amūn Pinūdjem three and a half centuries later.[5]

For the transition to the reign of Amenōphis IV the letters from Tushratta are doubtless our best authority. In that to Queen Tiye it is clearly implied that the new king ascended the throne only after his father's death, and the same is asserted even more clearly in a letter to the young ruler from the great Hittite monarch Suppiluliumas.[6] Hence the much canvassed co-regency must be an illusion. A hieratic docket in what was probably the first letter[7] addressed by Tushratta to Napkhuria—this being the cuneiform rendering of Amenōphis IV's Prenomen Neferkheprurēʿ—dates it in year 2, and states that the Court was still in residence in western Thebes. We learn too that Tadukhipa's connubial duties had now been transferred from the father to the son,[8] and it has sometimes been suggested that this Mitannian princess was none other than the beautiful Nefertiti, familiar to the modern world from her wonderfully modelled and painted head in the Berlin Museum.[9]

[1] Am. 23. [2] See above, p. 207. [3] Am. 26. [4] Hayes, *RS*, pp. 27–30.
[5] *Bull. Inst. ég.* 1898, 109, 111; Elliot Smith, *RM*, 46–51.
[6] Am. 41. This letter, however, strangely gives the Pharaoh's name as Ḫuria.
[7] Am. 27. [8] Am. 28. 8; 29. 3. [9] Discussion, Vandier, 384.

Obstacles to this theory are, however, that Nefertiti is known to have had a sister in Egypt,[1] and that Tey, the wife of the elderly officer Ay who ultimately became king, claimed to have been her nurse.[2]

A son of more unlikely an appearance than Amenōphis IV could hardly have been born to altogether normal parents. Though his earliest monuments do not present his features and figure as markedly different from those of any earlier Egyptian prince, the representations of only a few years later (see Pl. XIV) provide us with frankly hideous portraits the general fidelity of which cannot be doubted. The elongated head slopes forward from a long thin neck; the face is narrow, showing a prominent nose, thick lips and a rounded protruding chin; the body with its sunken chest, swelled out stomach, wide thighs, and slender calves, is the reverse of virile. In the sculptured reliefs Akhenaten, as he later preferred to call himself, is often shown lolling effeminately upon a cushioned chair; yet the standing colossi from his peristyle court at Karnak have a look of fanatical determination such as his subsequent history confirmed only too fatally. In order to evaluate justly the religious revolution which he brought into being it is necessary to summarize, if only in a provisional and one-sided way, the main aspects of the traditional worship which he temporarily replaced with a rigid monotheism of his own devising.

The Egyptian religion, as it had already persisted for well over 1,500 years, resulted from the fusion of a large number of originally independent tribal cults. Every town had its own particular deity, sometimes manifested in a material fetish but more often in some animal shape; such were the cat-goddess Bast of Bubastis, the cobra-goddess Edjō of Butō (the modern Kôm el-Farâ'în), the ibis Thōth of Hermopolis Magna (Eg. Khmūn), or Wepwawe (Ophōis) the jackal-god of Lycopolis (Eg. Saūti, modern Asyûṭ). As the pantheon gathered coherence, these animalic divinities were furnished with the bodies and limbs of ordinary mortals and credited with human attributes and activities. Their resulting double nature paved the way for two opposing tendencies. On the one hand the innate Egyptian conservatism, coupled with a keen local patriotism, militated against the suppression of individual differences; the animal

[1] Benremūt, Davies, *Am.* vi, Index, p. 39.

[2] *JNES* xiv. 170–1.

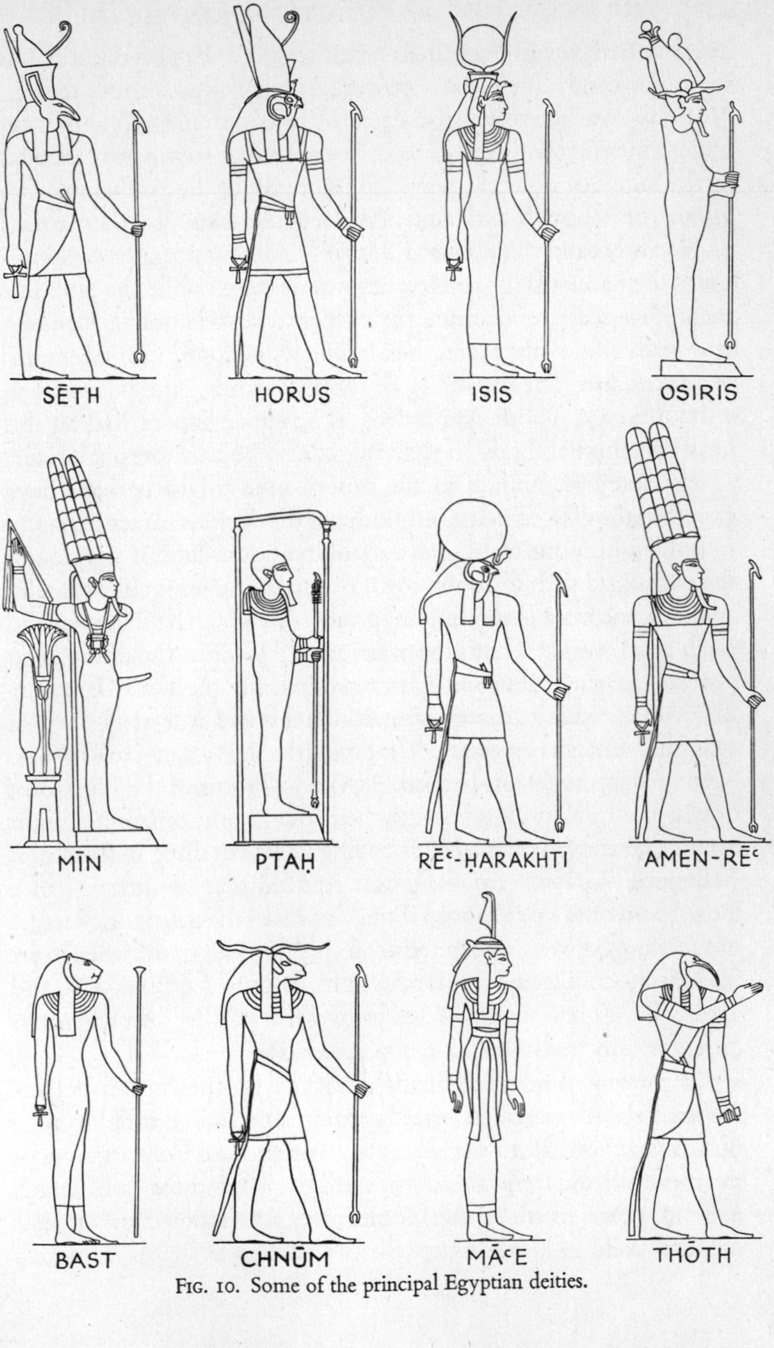

FIG. 10. Some of the principal Egyptian deities.

heads remained and the system never ceased to be polytheistic. On the other hand, there was a powerful urge towards monotheism. Not only was the town-god declared to be unique and almighty, but his identity with the gods of certain other towns was asserted in a number of different ways. Thus Sopdu of the Arabian nome, Ḥemen of Asphynis, and ʿAnti of Antaeopolis were all of them forms of Horus because they shared the same falcon-appearance. Sometimes the name might be the common feature, while the embodiment changed; for example the cow-goddess Ḥatḥōr of Dendera was really none other than the Ḥatḥōr worshipped near Memphis in a sycamore. The instability of form shown by some deities was extraordinary; Thōth was indeed as a rule an ibis or had an ibis head on a human body, but he might also be a cynocephalus ape, or else manifest himself in the moon. One might perhaps have expected the class of deities embodying the various forces of nature to remain immune from such variability, but it did not so remain; the earth-god Gēb took the form of the ram Chnūm at Hypsēlis, and Shu, the male embodiment of the Void which held heaven and earth apart, was at Thinis the warrior-god Onūris. Of all the great powers exerting influence upon terrestrial life the sun is assuredly that which exhibits the greatest constancy and is least in need of changing imagery; yet at Hēliopolis (the Egyptian Ōn) he was envisaged as the falcon-headed Ḥarakhti ('Horus of the Horizon') or else as a human king bearing the name Atum; or else he might even be conceived of as a beetle rolling its ball of dung in front of it (Khopri). Nor was this all; it was realized that the prestige of a local god would be enhanced if the word Rēʿ, the commonest name of the sun-god, were appended as an epithet to his own, whence we find the crocodile-god Sobk of Anasha described as Sobk-Rēʿ, and above all the great Amūn of Thebes was from the Middle Kingdom onwards universally acclaimed as Amen-Rēʿ.

The bewildering multiplicity displayed by the Egyptian Pantheon as elaborated by its priestly exponents could not fail to produce a reaction. Both for everyday parlance and on account of the monotheistic trend there was need for a word for 'sun' which had no religious or anthropomorphic associations, or at least reduced them to a minimum. Such a word was *ỉtn* which we habitually render as 'the Aten' or as 'the sun's disk'. It is often difficult to tell when this term has or has not a religious implication. For example, when the Story of Sinūhe (pp. 130–1) speaks of the death of Ammenemēs I and says

He went aloft to heaven and became united with the disk, the limb of the god being merged in him who made him

it is futile to dispute whether the word *ỉtn* refers to the deity or not. Less ambiguous is the phrase 'lord of all that the disk surrounds', an epithet frequently (and very oddly) applied to 'the living Aten' who was the object of Akhenaten's worship; here the word translated 'disk' obviously refers to the visible celestial body. A careful scrutiny of the inscriptions of the time of Amenōphis III[1] shows a much more widespread use of the term than previously, and it is legitimate to see in this fact an anticipation of the doctrine soon to assume so momentous a character. A small detail of significance is the name 'The Aten gleams' given to the bark in which Queen Tiye disported herself upon the lake dug in her honour (p. 206). An unpublished tomb at Thebes (No. 46) undoubtedly belonging to Amenōphis III's reign gives its owner the title 'Steward in the Mansion of the Aten', and it is difficult to interpret this otherwise than as implying that the Aten already received a cult at Thebes. Evidence of another kind is found on the well-known stela of the same reign inscribed with a long hymn to the sun-god composed by the twin architects Suti and Ḥōr;[2] here the god is addressed as Amūn and as Ḥarakhti and the word *ỉtn* occurs only incidentally, but both content and expression so closely resemble Akhenaten's famous psalm that we cannot but conclude that the revolution was already 'in the air'.

Yet it was only after various initial tentatives that the heretical doctrine received its final shape and that the practical consequences made themselves fully felt. Down to his fifth year[3] Amenōphis IV still used in his Nomen the significant words *'Imn ḥtpw* (Amenḥotpe) which he had inherited from three of his predecessors; the entire Nomen, including at its end an equally significant adjunct,

[1] *ZÄS* lix. 109 ff.

[2] *Bull. Inst. fr.* xli. 25 ff.

[3] Gauthier, *LR* ii. 343–5.

signifies 'Amūn is content, the god ruler of Thebes'. Under this name he is shown worshipping Amen-Rēʿ in the sandstone quarry of Gebel Silsila,[1] the reason being that the inscription beneath deals with buildings to be erected within the precincts of the temple of Karnak, where in fact many later mercilessly destroyed fragments of Akhenaten's chapels have been found. In the said inscription the young king curiously describes himself as 'first prophet of Rēʿ-Ḥarakhti Rejoicing-in-the-Horizon in his name the sunlight (Egyptian "Shu") which is Aten'. The elaborate designation here given to the sun-god is that which subsequently became the first version of the Aten's name, though there divided between two cartouches so as to emphasize the new deity's kingly status.[2] How dependent upon the ancient cult of Hēliopolis this early work was is seen not only from its dedication to Rēʿ-Ḥarakhti, but also in its mention of 'his great obelisk in Karnak', for at Hēliopolis the impressive monolith known as the *benben* or obelisk (p. 85) was as characteristic of the place as was later at Arabian Mecca the black stone known as the Kaaba. So too in year 16[3] the high-priest of the Aten Meryrēʿ still bore the time-honoured Hēliopolitan title 'greatest of seers'. The difficulty of escaping wholly from earlier tradition is one which never ceased to make itself felt, however much it may have been theoretically desired.

The new conception of the sun-god presaged in Rēʿ-Ḥarakhti's extended title was soon to have visual consequences that wrought havoc with long-cherished priestly susceptibilities. For a short time the radical changes about to transform the entire character of Egyptian art could pass practically unnoticed. Rēʿ-Ḥarakhti was still figured as of human shape, but with the head of a falcon surmounted by the solar disk; the young king was still content to be portrayed as of stiff conventional mien.[4] But this conformity with tradition was not destined to last. The royal revolutionary had aesthetic as well as religious ambitions of his own, and quickly imposed new fashions upon the artists of his Court. The winged solar disk of Horus the Beḥdetite which had hitherto presided rigidly over scenes and inscriptions now vanished and was replaced

[1] PM v. 220. [2] *JEA* ix. 168 ff. [3] Petrie, *Tell el Amarna*, Pl. 22. 3.
[4] *ZÄS* lii. 73, fig. 1.

PLATE XIII

THE VIZIER RAʿMOSE OFFERS FLOWERS TO AMEN-RĒʿ

PLATE XIV

SANDSTONE STATUE OF AKHENATEN

From his temple at Karnak. About 13 ft. high

by a golden sun shedding its rays beneficently over king and queen, over the altars at which they officiated, and over the pictures of temple and palace. To discard completely every anthropomorphic association was impossible; the rays had to be shown with hands holding ☥ 𓌀 the symbols for 'life' and for 'dominion' or 'power', and the kingly nature of the visible celestial body was indicated by the uraeus or cobra that hung from the gleaming circle even as it had always adorned the brow of the Pharaoh. Nowhere is the contrast between the old and the new modes of representation better seen than in the fine tomb of the vizier Raʿmose at Thebes. Here sculptured reliefs of great beauty adorn the larger part of the walls, once explicitly dated to the reign of Amenōphis IV who is portrayed in the old conventional manner.[1] Suddenly there comes a change. On the opposite side of the doorway the very same king and his wife Nefertiti are depicted in the new style, leaning over a balcony under the rays of the Aten to bestow necklets of gold upon their chief magistrate;[2] officials of the royal harem and various servants are in attendance, and the appearance of all these persons is as different from what is seen in the rest of the tomb as can well be imagined. An exaggerated liveliness and a visible emotional intent are conspicuous; a bolder sweep of line and backs bowed lower stress the deference owed to the king; and one can hardly be deceived in the impression that the peculiarities of Akhenaten's own body have been consciously imitated in the shapes given to his subjects. A magnificently drawn scene of foreigners follows, as yet untouched by the sculptor's chisel. After this all is blank; the tomb is unfinished and the subsequent history of Raʿmose unknown. Hand in hand with his disappearance went that of the other great dignitaries of his time; attempts have been made to break the silence of the next few years by deductions from the titles found on their statues and in their inscriptions, but the results have been far too speculative. All that we can safely maintain is that the revolutionary cult and its artistic expression, the latter including the appalling colossi already mentioned, were pushed ahead at Karnak, where they cannot have failed to excite the wrath of the Theban priesthood and their antipathy to Akhenaten and all his works.

[1] Davies, *Ramose*, Pl. 29. [2] Op. cit., Pl. 33.

The curtain next rises far away from Thebes and in the sixth year of Akhenaten's reign. El-ʿAmârna, already mentioned in connexion with the cuneiform tablets found there, was the site selected for a startling innovation by the self-willed but highly courageous monarch. Half-way between Cairo and Luxor the eastern mountains recede leaving a crescent-shaped plain about 8 miles long and 3 broad; here there was ample room for a great city, while on the left bank beyond the Nile a much broader expanse afforded scope for the agriculture which a large population would demand. The name chosen by Akhenaten for his new city was Akhetaten 'The Horizon of Aten'. The popularly used modern name Tell el-Amarna wrongly combines that of a modern village El-Till in the north with that of the tribe of the Beni ʿAmrân inhabiting the district, and the more accurate designation El-ʿAmârna is now generally accepted. Excavations begun by Flinders Petrie in 1891 were carried on with only the inevitable interruption caused by the First World War right down to 1937, first by German and then by British archaeologists.[1] A vast number of brick buildings, or rather of their ground-plans, have been unearthed; of stonework but little remained, but there was a great harvest of valuable antiquities, the most sensational finds being the cuneiform tablets stored in what the bricks used in it call 'the Place of Pharaoh's Dispatches'[2] and the wonderfully lifelike statuary discovered in the atelier of the master-sculptor Dḥutmose.[3] It is impossible here to enumerate even a portion of the imposing structures that have been identified, palaces, temples, mansions of the functionaries, a workman's village, and desert altars raised in honour of the Aten. To give an idea of the magnitude of some of these edifices it may be mentioned that the great temple of the Aten had a length of little less than 200 yards.

There are, however, all too many signs of the haste with which the constructions were thrown up; the workmanship everywhere is shoddy, though this is often disguised by the beauty of the wonderfully naturalistic pictures of birds and vegetation painted upon plaster walls and floors. Of the greatest possible value for our knowledge of the life here carried on are the sculptured reliefs in the tombs of officials cut into the sides of the eastern hills; the single-

[1] PM iv. 192 ff. [2] Petrie, op. cit., Pl. 42; *PSBA* xxiii. 219. [3] PM iv. 202–3.

handed recording of these has been the fine achievement of N. de G. Davies who, however, had everywhere to bemoan the vandalism, both ancient and modern, which had destroyed so much. Lastly must be mentioned the family tomb which Akhenaten caused to be prepared 4 miles away in the eastern desert;[1] his prematurely deceased second daughter Meketaten was actually buried there, but apparently neither her parents nor any of her sisters. Concerning Akhenaten's own probable fate more will be said later.

The original finding of the site is recounted by Akhenaten himself on great boundary stelae of which no less than fourteen, several of them completely defaced, have been found backing upon the hill-sides both east and west of the river.[2] There are two versions of the text, a longer and a shorter. The shorter and better preserved tells how on the thirteenth day of the eighth month in year 6 the king, mounted in a golden chariot, fared north from the richly ornamented tent where he had spent the night in order to fix the limits of the projected city of Akhetaten. After sacrificing to the god he drove southward to a spot where the rays of the sun shining upon him indicated that the southernmost boundary ought to be. Here he swore an oath by his father the Aten and by his hope that the queen and their two elder daughters would attain old age, to the effect that he would never pass beyond this boundary and beyond two more on the east bank and three on the west. All the land within that area was to belong to the Aten and should any damage or obliteration befall the stelae demarcating it he vowed that he would make it good. Finally, mention is made of a renewal of the oath in year 8. A far longer inscription on other boundary stelae must be of the same date since it elaborates the same facts, while adding much of interest. Unfortunately, many passages are irretrievably lost. After a reference to his first survey of the place and to the great sacrifice which followed we are told that Akhenaten summoned his courtiers and military commanders and explained to them the wish of the Aten that Akhetaten should be built. He went on to say that no one had known of the site except the Aten himself, and that consequently it was his and his alone. At length the courtiers reply and assure the king that all countries

[1] PM iv. 235–6. [2] Op. cit. iv. 230–2.

will arrive carrying gifts upon their backs to present them to the Aten. Then, after much praise of the god, comes Akhenaten's oath that he will never extend the city's boundaries nor allow his spouse to persuade him to do so. He next enumerates a number of sanctuaries which he will build in Akhetaten, ending with a reference to the above-mentioned family tomb; here he, his wife, and his daughters were to be buried even if they died in some other town. A curious addition states that the Mnevis-bull of Hēliopolis should likewise be buried in the Aten's city, another sign how dependent the new Atenism was upon one of the oldest of Egypt's religious cults.

The inscriptions here summarized throw a flood of light upon the most important action of Akhenaten's career, but raise a number of problems and leave many questions unanswered. The determination to create a new capital at El-ʿAmârna was doubtless prompted by the recognition that the cults of the Aten and of Amen-Rēʿ could no longer be carried on side by side, but we are left in the dark as to the exact form taken by the rupture. This must have been the moment when the young king changed his Nomen Amenḥotpe into Akhenaten, which means 'Serviceable to the Aten'. There are no signs of hostility to his dead father, though he too had borne the name Amenḥotpe; on the contrary, temple-reliefs from Soleb in Nubia,[1] as well as a stela from Hieracōnpolis in Upper Egypt, depict Amenōphis IV in the act of offering to a deified Amenōphis III, rare cases which must belong to a phase immediately preceding the revolution, since the falcon-headed Ḥarakhti on the stela is already equipped with the cartouches and the doctrinal epithets of the Aten. Equally significant of Akhenaten's filial piety are certain inscriptions where his father's Prenomen Nebmaʿrēʿ was left unerased and grotesquely used a second time to replace the offending Nomen.[2] The name Nebmaʿrēʿ was likely to find favour with Akhenaten because of its meaning 'Lord of Truth (*māʿe*) is Rēʿ', for he prided his own self upon the epithet 'Living upon Truth'. It must, however, be observed that *māʿe*, unavoidably translated 'Truth', does not signify a love of reality, though the realistic bias is plain enough in Akhenaten's *art nouveau*; R. Anthes

[1] PM vii. 169–70. [2] *JEA* xliii. 14, n. 8.

has shown that in the ʿAmârna texts *māʿe* always means 'orderly, well-regulated existence,' and has no reference to factual truth at all.[1] As regards Akhenaten's mother Tiye, it is clear that he always remained on the best of terms with her, and she may indeed ultimately have come to live at El-ʿAmârna, where pictures in the tomb of Ḥuya, the steward of her estate, show her dining with her son and daughter-in-law, though whether only on a brief visit or as a permanent resident is uncertain.[2]

The oaths sworn by Akhenaten that he would never enlarge the Aten's territory are a mystery. Do they mean that the dissensions between him and the priesthood of Amen-Rēʿ were at first amicably settled, he being content to live and worship in his own way at a place of his own choosing? At all events there is no hint of civil war, and he even envisages the possibility that his family and himself may be in some other city at the time of their death. The lack of dated inscriptions is a serious hindrance. Papyri from as late as year 5[3] found at Kôm Medînet Ghurâb at the entrance to the Fayyûm still use the name Amenḥotpe and mention Ptaḥ and offerings to other gods and goddesses, but perhaps as yet the Aten heresy had not reached so far north. The rock-inscription of the architect Bek at Aswân proves that at some moment in the reign stone was being quarried there for 'the great and mighty monuments of the king in the house of Aten in Akhetaten',[4] and at Aswân and Wâdy Ḥalfa records of Akhenaten's Nubian viceroy Dḥutmose are found.[5] Also the name *Gm-ỉtn* 'Finding Aten' of the important settlement of Kawa, beyond the Third Cataract, probably testifies to Akhenaten's influence there.[6]

Of the personages upon whom Akhenaten later bestowed fine rock-tombs at El-ʿAmârna only one is known to have followed him from Thebes. This is his butler Parennūfe,[7] part of whose Theban tomb,[8] subsequently abandoned, was adorned with reliefs in the old style, while another part depicted the Aten in true ʿAmârna fashion. The rest of Akhenaten's favourites appear to have been *novi homines*, few of whom ever attained high positions. The

[1] *JAOS* 1952, Supplement. [2] Davies, *Am.* iii, Pl. 4. [3] See above, p. 217, n. 3. [4] *BAR* ii, §§ 973–6. [5] *JEA* vi. 34–35. [6] Säve-Söderbergh, p. 162. [7] Davies, *Am.* vi, Pls. 2–10. [8] *JEA* ix. 133 ff. with Pl. 23.

house of a vizier Nakht[1] was found among the ruins, but it is not known whence he came or how far his jurisdiction extended. The mayor of Akhetaten bore a tell-tale name which being translated means 'Akhenaten created me'.[2] Several were priests and two were overseers of the royal harem; there was also a chief physician. A commander of the army of course there had to be,[3] and a standard-bearer[4] will have been one of his officers. The venerable Ay, of whom much more will be heard later, was superintendent of all the king's horses.[5] A captain of police[6] was required to keep order in the city. Of really exalted station was only the overseer of the treasury.[7] The scenes of life in the city are extraordinarily vivid. How far genuine conviction, and how far self-interest, actuated the members of Akhenaten's entourage cannot be ascertained at this distance of time. He certainly loaded them with golden necklets and provided them with food from his own table. At least one of his officials confesses that he had been raised from humble rank to a position where he hobnobbed with noblemen.[8] There can be no doubt that Akhenaten regarded himself as the apostle of the new faith, and there are several inscriptions in the tombs testifying to the readiness with which his doctrine was listened to, a typical example[9] being

How prosperous is he who hears thy Doctrine of Life, and is sated with beholding thee, and unceasingly his eyes look upon Aten every day.

So too the king himself says to his high-priest Meryrēʿ, as well as to his chamberlain Tutu[10]

Thou art my great servant who hears my Doctrine. Every commission which thou performest my heart is content with it, and I give thee this office in order that thou mayst eat the victuals of Pharaoh thy lord in the House of the Aten.

These brief extracts suffice to show how little the new order had changed the relation between sovereign and subject; indeed the

[1] PM iv. 206. [2] Davies, *Am.* iv, Pl. 37. [3] Op. cit., Pl. 35.
[4] Op. cit., Pl. 39. [5] Op. cit. vi, Pls. 22 ff. [6] Op. cit. iv, Pls. 14 ff.
[7] Op. cit. v, Pl. 15. [8] Sandman, 61. 12–16. [9] Op. cit. 92. 8–9; 60. 6.
[10] Op. cit. 1. 7–9; 80. 17–81. 1.

main difference was the more vocal character of the traditional obsequiousness. No tombs in Egypt are more crowded with inscriptions than those of El-ʿAmârna, invariably belauding the Aten or the king or the benefits bestowed on the tomb-owner; the language is not wholly lacking in beauty, but is undeniably stereotyped in its expression. The great hymn in the tomb of Ay[1] is justly celebrated, and probably rightly ascribed to Akhenaten himself, though differing but little from others in the necropolis. The following is a fairly literal translation:

Thou arisest beauteous in the horizon of heaven, O living Aten, beginner of life when thou didst shine forth in the eastern horizon, and didst fill every land with thy beauty.

Thou art comely, great, sparkling, and high above every land, and thy rays enfold the lands to the limit of all that thou hast made, thou being the sun and thou reachest their limits and subjectest them to thy beloved son.

Being afar off, yet thy rays are upon the earth. Thou art in men's faces, yet thy movements are unseen. When thou settest in the western horizon, the earth is in darkness after the manner of death. The night is passed in the bedchamber, heads covered, no eye can see its fellow. Their belongings are stolen, even though they be under their heads, and they perceive it not. Every lion is come forth from its lair and all snakes bite. Darkness is (the sole) illumination while the earth is in silence, their maker resting in his horizon.

The earth grows bright, when thou hast arisen in the horizon, shining as Aten in the daytime. Thou banishest darkness and bestowest thy rays. The Two Lands are in festival, awakened they stand on their feet, thou hast lifted them up. Their limbs are cleansed, clothes put on, and their hands are upraised in praise at thy glorious appearing. The entire land does its work. All cattle are at peace upon their pastures. Trees and pasture grow green. Birds taking flight from their nest, their wings give praise to thy spirit. All animals frisk upon their feet. All that flyeth or alighteth live when thou arisest for them. Ships fare north and likewise fare south. Every road is opened at thy appearing. The fish in the river leap before thy face. Thy rays are in the Great-Green.[2] Who causest the male fluid to grow in women and who makest the water in mankind; bringing to life the son in the body of his mother; soothing him by

[1] Sandman, 93–96.

[2] The name commonly given to the sea.

the cessation of his tears; nurse (already) in the body, who givest air to cause to live all whom thou makest, and he descendeth from the body to breathe on the day of his birth; thou openest his mouth fully and makest his sustenance. The chick in the egg speaketh in the shell; thou givest him air in it to make him live; thou hast made for him his completion so as to break it, even the egg, and he cometh forth from the egg to speak of his completion, and he walketh upon his two feet when he comes forth from it.

How manifold are thy works. They are mysterious in men's sight. Thou sole god, like to whom there is none other. Thou didst create the earth after thy heart, being alone, even all men, herds and flocks, whatever is upon earth, creatures that walk upon feet, which soar aloft flying with their wings, the countries of Khor[1] and of Cush, and the land of Egypt. Thou settest every man in his place, and makest their sustenance, each one possessing his food, and his term of life counted; tongues made diverse in speech and their characters likewise; their complexions distinguished, for thou hast distinguished country and country.

Thou makest the Nile-flood in the netherworld, and bringest it at thy pleasure to give life to the common folk, even as thou makest them for thyself, the lord of them all who travailest with them; the lord of every land who shinest for them, the Aten of the daytime, great of majesty. All distant lands, thou hast made their life. Thou hast set a Nile-flood in the sky,[2] and it descendeth for them and maketh waves upon the mountains like the Great-Green to drench their fields in their villages. How efficacious are thy plans, thou lord of eternity. A Nile-flood in heaven, it is thy gift to the foreign countries and to the animals of every country which walk upon feet. But the Nile-flood comes forth from the netherworld for the land of Egypt. Thy rays foster every mead. When thou shinest forth, they live and they grow for thee.

Thou makest the seasons in order to prosper all that thou hast made, the winter to cool them, the summer-heat that they may taste of thee. Thou hast made the sky distant to shine in it and to see all that thou hast made, being alone and shining in thy various forms as the living Aten, appearing gloriously and gleaming, being both distant and near. Thou makest millions of forms out of thee alone, towns and villages, fields, roads, and river. Every eye beholds thee in front of it, thou being the disk of the daytime. . . .

There is none other that knoweth thee except thy son Neferkheprurēʿ-waʿenrēʿ. Thou hast caused him to be skilled in thy ways and in thy

[1] Palestine and Syria, see *Onom.* i. 180* ff.

[2] The rain is meant.

strength. The earth comes into being upon thy hand even as thou makest them. Thou hast shone forth and they live. Thou settest and they die. Thou thyself art lifetime and men live by thee. Eyes are in presence of beauty until thou settest. All work is laid aside when thou settest on the right.[1] Rising thou makest prosper . . . for the king, movement is in every leg since thou didst found the earth. Thou raisest them up for thy son who came forth from thy body, the King of Upper and Lower Egypt, living on Truth, the lord of the Two Lands Neferkheprurēʿ-waʿenrēʿ, the son of Rēʿ, living on Truth, lord of glorious appearings Akhenaten great in his duration; with the king's great wife, whom he loves, the lady of the Two Lands, Nefernefruaten-Nefertiti, may she live and flourish for ever and ever.

This colourful hymn, whose striking resemblance to Psalm civ has often been pointed out, embodies nearly the whole of Akhenaten's creed on the positive side, but contains little that had not been said in earlier hymns to the sun-god. The theme is the beneficent power of the sun as a physical force, and the reformer did everything in his power to rid that force of anthropomorphic associations. His deity was the great luminary itself, exerting its beneficent life-giving influence through the rays whose brilliance and warmth none could fail to experience. Such a conception could be maintained visually to a large extent, and no graven image presented the Aten in human shape. Verbally, however, the new faith broke down, since Language by its essential nature describes all happenings in terms of human behaviour. When hymns are addressed to the Aten in the second person, when in a shorter poem of similar tenor he is called 'the mother and father' of all created things,[2] and when Akhenaten himself is treated as a beloved son who had come forth from the Aten's rays, the contradiction is apparent. Atenism was no mere physical theory, but was a genuine monotheism, and it is in the moral courage with which the reformer strove to sweep away the vast accumulations of mythological rubbish inherited from the past that his true greatness lay; a negative greatness, no doubt, but one that has been unjustly denied him. Yet it cannot be gainsaid that Akhenaten's conduct was that best calculated to excite

[1] The Egyptians habitually looked southwards, so that for them 'west' and 'right' were identical.

[2] Davies, *Am.* iv, Pl. 32, Apy 4.

his enemies' ire. In proportion as his power grew, the stronger the ardour with which he persecuted time-honoured tradition. At a given moment he banished the mention of Rēʿ-Ḥarakhti from the Aten's first cartouche or Prenomen (above, p. 218) replacing it by 'Ruler of the Horizon', while in the second cartouche the word Shu, though it had meant no more than 'sunlight', had to be rejected owing to its assonance with the name of the god of the Void.[1] But Akhenaten's destructive zeal did not stop here. The true faith could not be spread without suppression of the countless gods and goddesses hitherto worshipped. Accordingly he dispatched his workmen throughout the entire length of the land to cut out their names wherever they were found engraved or written. Needless to say, the hated Amen-Rēʿ was the chief victim of his iconoclastic rage. But also the simple word for 'mother' being homonymous with the name of the Theban goddess Mūt had to discard the hieroglyph of the vulture and be spelt out with the alphabetic signs for $m+t$. The very word for 'gods' was taboo, and concerning Amenḥotpe, Akhenaten's own earlier Nomen and that of his father, we have already spoken.

There is an incongruity about the reliefs found upon the El-ʿAmârna site which will certainly have disgusted the traditionalists. Akhenaten's own portrait was always very much in the centre of the picture, and the manner in which his cartouches are set side by side with those of the Aten show that he was by no means disinclined to claim a share in his divine father's divinity; indeed, one has sometimes the impression that this share approached complete identity. An indication in this direction is the epithet 'he who is in the Sed-festival' which became a regular concomitant of the god's titulary; for the Sed-festival or Jubilee was essentially a royal celebration, and the implication seems to be that the Aten and his god-like son started simultaneously upon a new phase of their common existence. It is significant also that while Akhenaten prayed to the Aten, his subjects just as often prayed to him. On the other hand, the manner in which he advertised his domesticities assorted ill with such lofty pretensions. He is always accompanied in the scenes by his wife Nefertiti and by several of their daughters, of whom there

[1] *JEA* ix. 168 ff.

A. Akhenaten worships the Aten

B. Akhenaten as family man

LIMESTONE STELAE FROM EL-ʿAMÂRNA

THE TOMB OF TUTʿANKHAMŪN

The Ante-chamber as first seen. The two statues of the king guard the entrance to the burial-chamber, this shut off by a sealed plaster partition. In front the splendid chest with paintings of warfare and hunting. To the left other boxes, chairs, and a ceremonial couch

were ultimately six. On one stela a female infant is seen being kissed by the royal father, while a second babe is being dandled upon the queen's knee (Pl. XV).[1] Whilst entertaining or being entertained by his mother Tiye Akhenaten is depicted gnawing a large cutlet, while Nefertiti deals similarly with a roasted bird.[2] The king's affection for his spouse and later for his son-in-law are shown without any reticence. How different from the dignified deportment of ancient times, when the utmost degree of familiarity exhibited was an arm stiffly stretching around the spouse's waist!

A defect of the Doctrine was its complete lack of ethical teaching. For this the elimination of Osiris was no doubt largely responsible. Not that his myth had ever been deeply spiritual, but it had recounted the triumph of good over evil and had told of wifely devotion and filial piety. The funeral cult still retained much of its outer forms, but these were now robbed of their former meaning.[3] Large scarabs were still inserted in the mummy, but the inscriptions no longer implored the heart to refrain from bearing witness against the deceased when his earthly deeds were weighed in the balance. Ushabti-figures (above, p. 32) were still in vogue, but no longer relieved their owner from the duty of agricultural labour in the netherworld. It seems likely that Akhenaten's dogma never penetrated deeply into the consciousness of the masses. The workmen's village of El-ʿAmârna has brought to light various traces of the older worship, amulets of the dwarf-like god Bes, the sacred eye of Horus and the like. The full extension of the new faith requires further investigation. Memphis certainly had a temple of the Aten,[4] and scattered up and down in the country, though not north of Hēliopolis in the Delta, fragments of Atenist reliefs have been found. With regard to Nubia see above, p. 223.

Akhenaten has sometimes been credited with a desire to found a universal religion. The texts lend but little support to this supposition. It is true that the great poem above translated mentions both Syria and Nubia, but it could hardly fail to be known that the same sun shone upon Egypt and these countries alike, nor that they were irrigated by rain instead of by the Nile inundation. Of propa-

[1] *ZÄS* lii. 78, fig. 9.
[2] Davies, *Am.* iii, Pl. 4.
[3] *ZÄS* lv. 2–4; *JEA* xliii. 19.
[4] PM iii. 220.

gandist effort in the north there is no indication. On the contrary, the king's interests appear to have been almost parochial. In his enthusiasm for the temple services, these celebrated in full sunlight, not as formerly in dark closed-in chapels, he was unwilling to trouble himself with foreign affairs. For the same reason the charge of pacifism brought against him overshoots the mark. It is an often repeated accusation that by his sloth and his hatred of war he threw away the great Egyptian empire built up in Palestine and Syria by Tuthmōsis III. The whole question needs reconsideration in the light of the ever increasing information being gathered about those countries through archaeological and philological research. It may even be doubted whether the much vaunted Egyptian empire ever existed. The defeat of Mitanni by Tuthmōsis I may have brought about an attempt in that direction, but there is no evidence that his success was followed up in the next two reigns. It would be perverse to minimize the splendid achievement of Tuthmōsis III, but this started with the uprising of a vast coalition of petty Palestinian and Syrian chieftains, and even after Mitanni had again been vanquished, thirteen more separate campaigns were needed in order to maintain the Egyptian suzerainty. We may guess, though it is little more than guesswork, that while the seaports were strongly held, military governors were stationed at key-points. At all events the many small city-states among which the entire country was divided will have considered themselves at most as vassals of Pharaoh, to whose protection they looked as the least of several evils. Dissensions among themselves will have prompted them to seek help wherever they could find it, and Egypt was not always judged to be the safest power to which to turn. It is wrong to regard Akhenaten as the sole Pharaoh responsible for the loss of Egyptian prestige. Amenōphis III was at least equally to blame. Several letters addressed to him by Akizzi of Ḳaṭna complain bitterly that his failure to send troops is enabling Aitugama, the ruler of Ḳadesh, to win over several other local princes to the side of the Hittites;[1] and the people of Tunip in another letter,[2] this perhaps to Akhenaten, declare that for twenty years past they had been begging for aid, but that none had come. A very large proportion of

[1] Am. 53. 11 ff.; 54. 26 ff.; 55. 16 ff.

[2] Am. 59. 13 ff.

the ʿAmârna letters[1] is concerned with desperate appeals by Rib-addi, the regent at Byblos, to obtain help against ʿAbdiashirta, who was the king of Amor, at that time the coastal district extending from the level of the Lebanon northwards as far as Aradus; ʿAbdiashirta and after his assassination his sons, and chief among them Aziru, were, in spite of some early pretences, inveterate enemies of Egypt, first allying themselves to those enemies of the Pharaoh known as the Ḫapiru (p. 203) or Sa-gaz 'cut-throats' and later to the Hittites. The long drawn-out story of Ribaddi's attempt to maintain his loyalty to Egypt belongs to the history of Palestine and Syria rather than to that of Egypt and, fascinating as is this drama, it is too complex to be followed up here. But since we shall later have to reckon seriously with the aggressive might of the Hittites, at least a paragraph must now be devoted to their emergence in the north Syrian arena.

The ethnic term Hittites comes to us from the Old Testament, where it is the designation of one of a number of peoples whom the Israelites found inhabiting Palestine when they entered the Promised Land. It is only a slender thread of descent that connects them with the great nation of the Khatti with whom we have now to deal, but in scholarly usage the name Hittites has come to stay, and no attempt will here be made to disown it. Nor can space be devoted to the steps which led through northern Syria to the discovery of the Hittite capital of Khattusas in Anatolia some 95 miles due east of Ankara and only half as much again to the south of the Black Sea. Excavations begun in 1906 by Hugo Winckler brought to light in this mountain fastness near the village of Boghazköy a royal archive comprising about 10,000 cuneiform tablets written in a language which, after prolonged research, proved to belong to the Indo-European family. Happily the content was to a large extent historical in character and provided precise details concerning foreign relations both before and after the period with which we have been concerned in this chapter. An obscure age for which sources of information are wanting was brought to an end at a somewhat uncertain date in the middle of the fifteenth century B.C. by Tudhaliyas II, usually regarded as the founder of the Hittite

[1] Mercer [ii], pp. 836–7.

Empire. It must have been one of his predecessors whose envoys brought presents to Tuthmōsis III as already mentioned (p. 193). However, a new period of Hittite weakness followed, in the course of which Mitanni recovered from its defeat by Egypt and indeed became the dominant power in northern Syria. As such, Mitanni stood in the way of Hittite expansion to the south-east, just as Arzawa stood in its way to the west. To this state of affairs the accession of Suppiluliumas about 1375 B.C. put an end. Suppiluliumas was a great warrior whose long reign, punctuated with successful diplomatic moves, as well as outstanding military triumphs, concluded, after the murder of Tushratta, with the reduction of Mitanni to the condition of a buffer state between himself and the rising might of Assyria. Not long afterwards Mitanni disappeared as a kingdom to be reckoned with, leaving the Hittites as the virtual dictators in the entire region west of the Euphrates; and so they remained throughout the whole of the following century. At the beginning of Suppiluliumas's reign he wrote to the future Akhenaten referring to the death of his father Amenōphis III[1] and reminding him of an unfulfilled promise to send him some statues of gold and silver; apart from one more incomplete letter from the El-ʿAmârna find which may have had Suppiluliumas as its author, direct communications between the Hittites and Egypt appear to have ceased for a while; Suppiluliumas can have had but little use for so supine a correspondent.

For the remainder of Akhenaten's reign documents of historical import are entirely lacking, and we are dependent upon what can be gleaned from the ruins at El-ʿAmârna. The second daughter Meketaten died, and the mourning at her funeral was graphically depicted on the walls of the great royal tomb.[2] At some time or other after year 12 the Queen Nefertiti seems to have fallen into disgrace, unless she too had died; in a particular building named Maruaten to the south of the city her name is constantly erased and replaced by that of the eldest daughter Merytamūn,[3] whose husband Smenkhkarēʿ for a short space succeeded Akhenaten upon the throne. The relationship between this ephemeral king and his

[1] See above, p. 213, n. 6. [2] PM iv. 236. [3] *CoA* i. 155, with n. 3.

father-in-law is mysterious. There is a stela[1] where two kings are shown seated together on most affectionate terms, and though the cartouches contain no hieroglyphs, they must be Akhenaten and Smenkhkarēʿ respectively. Another peculiar fact is that in an alternative form of Smenkhkarēʿ's Nomen he is called Nefernefruaten-beloved of Waʿenrēʿ,[2] the first element in which is the name that had always been borne by Queen Nefertiti, while the second element Waʿenrēʿ is a standing epithet of Akhenaten; thus it looks as though Smenkhkarēʿ had displaced the queen in the king's favour. In the absence of any double datings the hypothesis of a co-regency must remain doubtful. In a tomb at El-ʿAmârna[3] where Akhenaten was shown together with his spouse rewarding the tomb-owner with gold their cartouches were replaced by those of Smenkhkarēʿ and Merytamūn, which may well indicate that the older king had perished before his younger associate left El-ʿAmârna for Thebes. That the latter step was actually taken is attested by a hieratic graffito of his third year at Ḳurna in which one Pwaḥ, a 'scribe of the offerings of Amūn in the Mansion of 'Ankhkheprurēʿ (this the Prenomen of Smenkhkarēʿ) at Thebes' indites a hymn to the ancestral god.[4] Hence it is clear that Akhenaten's son-in-law and former favourite was the first to abandon the Aten heresy. A few rings from El-ʿAmârna and the fragment of a relief from Memphis[5] are among the only other relics of this short reign, apart from the faint possibility that we may actually possess the mummy of the young renegade.

For a considerable time the storm-clouds had been gathering around the unfortunate reformer's person, but we have no exact knowledge as to how his adventurous career terminated. Jar-sealings of year 17 are known, but this will have been the last. There are good grounds for thinking that his hope of burial in the spacious tomb at El-ʿAmârna which he had planned for himself and his family was never fulfilled. The shattered fragments of four red granite sarcophagi found their way from the site to the Cairo Museum,[6] and Pendlebury unearthed parts of Akhenaten's magnificent alabaster Canopic chest,[7] explicitly observing that this had

[1] *JEA* xiv, Pl. 4. [2] Ibid. 5. 10 ff. [3] Davies, *Am.* ii, Pl. 41. [4] *JEA* xiv, pp. 10 ff. [5] PM iii. 220. [6] *Ann. Serv.* xxxi. 102, n. 2. [7] Op. cit. xl. 537 ff.

never been used, as it was quite unstained by the black resinous substance seen in other royal tombs. It is evident that the avenging hand of the traditionalists had here been hard at work. The problem now shifts to Thebes. In 1907 archaeologists employed by the American millionaire Theodore M. Davis chanced upon a much ravaged tomb in the Bîbân el-Molûk which was at first over-hastily acclaimed as that of Queen Tiye.[1] For this there was the excuse that the battered remains of a large gold-covered shrine were found, the inscriptions of which declared that it had been made by Akhenaten for his mother. But there was also a much disfigured and patched-up coffin which contained a mummy, and this mummy the eminent physiologist Elliot Smith pronounced to be that of a man. The prominence of the name of Akhenaten upon the coffin now seemed a clear indication that its occupant had been none other than the heretic king himself, and this remained the accepted opinion until in 1916 Daressy[2] produced evidence that the original owner of the coffin had been a woman whom he believed to have been Queen Tiye, but that it had been later adapted to receive the remains of a king; Daressy felt unable, however, to give credence to the view that the king in question was Akhenaten, his own opinion being that Tutʿankhamūn was the intended occupant. In 1931 Engelbach took up the controversy afresh,[3] and the tomb of Tutʿankhamūn having been discovered in the meantime, the candidate chosen for the ownership of the mummy now became Smenkhkarēʿ. In that view Engelbach was strongly supported by D. E. Derry, who as the result of a careful re-examination of the skull declared that it could not possibly have been that of Akhenaten, but had belonged to a much younger man.[4] The contradictory judgements of two very distinguished physiologists being involved, this aspect of the problem must remain undecided, but as regards the coffin, C. Aldred has produced arguments which go far towards a final solution of the problem. Recalling the splendour of Tutʿankhamūn's funerary equipment with its four coffins, one of solid gold, he maintains that Akhenaten must certainly have made similar arrangements for himself, so that the rather second-rate coffin

[1] *JEA* xliii. 10 ff.
[2] *Bull. Inst. fr.* xii. 151 ff.
[3] *Ann. Serv.* xxxi. 103 ff.
[4] Op. cit. 115 ff.

found in the Theban tomb could not conceivably be one which the heretic king had designed for his own obsequies. Various archaeological features, Aldred continues, confirm that the intended occupant had been a woman, though no positive testimony remains to show which of the ʿAmârna ladies she was. Decisive above all for the fact that this female coffin had been adapted for Akhenaten himself is a bronze uraeus-serpent bearing Aten's name in its later form; no doubt this had been later affixed to the forehead. Equally important as evidence are the four magical bricks found in the tomb placed in their right respective positions;[1] the bricks carry Akhenaten's cartouche, and their presence is explicable only if they were deemed to be performing their proper function of protecting the king against evil spirits. Accordingly it is certain that the persons who arranged the burial believed, rightly or wrongly, that they were burying Akhenaten himself. In our opinion it is a plausible hypothesis that a few of his faithful followers had salvaged from the tomb at El-ʿAmârna as much funerary furniture as they could, and had transported it to Thebes to give some semblance of a decent interment to the master whom they had revered almost as a god. If Derry's verdict were correct, even in this last act of loyalty they would have been mistaken, and it then would become conceivable that Akhenaten's body had been torn to pieces and thrown to the dogs. Of the execration in which he was held not long after his death there is no doubt, and a couple of generations later he was referred to as 'the enemy of Akhetaten'.[2] El-ʿAmârna was forthwith abandoned, never again to be used as a place of residence; hence the importance of its ruins as revealing what an Egyptian capital was like at a definitely fixed moment.

Smenkhkarēʿ's successor was that Tutʿankhamūn whose name will remain for ever famous on account of the sensational discovery of his tomb by Howard Carter in 1922. Since he was little more than eighteen years of age when he died, and yet had reigned for a full eight, he must have been a mere child when he came to the throne. When the unwrapping of the mummy revealed his face, the discoverers were so much struck by its resemblance to that of Akhenaten that they conjectured him to be the latter's son by an

[1] *JEA* xliii. 23.

[2] Gardiner, *Mes*, 23, n. 82; *JEA* xxiv. 124.

unofficial marriage; other scholars believed that they had found evidence of his being a son of Amenōphis III; it is better to admit that nothing is definitely known about his parentage. He may well have owed his kingly title to his wife ʿAnkhesnamūn, the third daughter of Akhenaten and Nefertiti. During her parents' lifetime she had been known as ʿAnkhesenpaten, but like her husband Tutʿankhaten had expelled the reference to the hated sun-god from her name as soon as they turned their backs on El-ʿAmârna. This must have been at the earliest possible moment, since no trace of them has been found on that site except a few scarabs.[1] There are difficulties arising from ʿAnkhesnamūn's age which shall here be stated without any attempt to solve them. In the tomb were found two human foetuses, both probably female, which must surely have been hers, and a slab of stone found at Ashmûnên mentions a small daughter bearing the same name as hers but adding to it the distinguishing epithet 'the child'. On the strength of the presence on the same slab of the cartouche of her father Akhenaten, an incestuous marriage of the two after Tutʿankhamūn's death has been suggested, but quite unjustifiably.[2] Even more tenuous are the grounds on which a union with the aged official Ay has been deduced.[3] It is the conviction of the present writer that the virtue of this beautiful young queen has been unjustly impugned, though as will be seen hereafter, she was by no means averse in her widowhood to the thought of a second marriage, and that with a foreigner.

Tutʿankhamūn appended to his name the epithet 'Ruler of southern Ōn', which means that he regarded Thebes as his principal city. Accordingly the large stela[4] which he caused to be erected near the Third Pylon of the temple of Karnak portrays him making offerings to Amūn and Mūt, though as sovereign of the whole of Egypt he also claimed to be beloved of Atum Ḥarakhti at Hēliopolis, and of Ptaḥ at Memphis. The long inscription is expressed along the usual conventional lines, but there is one passage which evidently corresponds pretty accurately to the historic truth:

When His Majesty arose as king, the temples of the gods and goddesses, beginning from Elephantinē down to the marshes of the Delta

[1] Petrie, *Tell el Amarna*, Pl. 15.
[2] *ZÄS* lxxiv. 104.
[3] *JEA* xviii. 50.
[4] PM ii. 16–17; *JEA* xxv. 8 ff.

had fallen into decay, their shrines had fallen into desolation and become ruins overgrown with weeds, their chapels as though they had never been and their halls serving as footpaths. The land was topsy-turvy and the gods turned their backs on this land. If messengers were sent to Djahi (Syria) to extend the boundaries of Egypt, they had no success. If one humbled oneself to a god to ask a thing from him, he did not come, and if prayer was made to a goddess, likewise she never came. . . . But after many days My Majesty arose upon the seat of his father[1] and ruled over the territories of Horus, the Black Land and the Red Land being under his supervision.

The text goes on to say that whilst the king was in his palace of the House of ʿAkheperkarēʿ (Tuthmōsis I) at Memphis, he took counsel with his heart as to how he might best placate Amūn and the other gods, the fashioning of richly bejewelled statues and the like being regarded as the best way of securing the renewal of their favours. There is no doubt that Tutʿankhamūn and his advisers did their utmost to propitiate angry heaven. For example, at Luxor a vast peristyle hall was superbly decorated by him with reliefs[2] illustrating the great festival of Amen-Rēʿ when the god paid his annual visit to the neighbouring more southerly temple, but his authorship of this splendid achievement was very nearly obliterated by the usurping hand of his successor. There are a few other official buildings of this reign, but none of sufficient interest to be mentioned in the present account. Of outstanding importance, however, is the finely painted Theban tomb of his Nubian viceroy Ḥuy, where the details of his administrative province extending from El-Kâb to Napata are graphically illustrated. Ḥuy was thus in control of the principal gold-bearing area; the El-ʿAmârna letters never tire of regarding Egypt as the land where 'gold is as plentiful as dust'.

A tiny piece of gold-leaf discovered by Theodore Davis's collaborators in a mud-filled chamber in the Bîbân el-Molûk is more revealing than many a more pretentious object.[3] Here is depicted

1 This conventional phrase need not be taken to prove that Tutʿankhamūn was really a son of Akhenaten.

2 W. Wolf, *Das schöne Fest von Opet*, Leipzig, 1931.

3 Th. M. Davis, *The Tombs of Harmhabi and Touatânkhamanu*, London, 1912, p. 128. fig. 4.

Tutʿankhamūn followed by his wife as he stands poised to slay an enemy whom he has grasped by the hair of his head. To the left, shown as a fan-bearer with hand upraised in adoration, is the already often mentioned god's father Ay. It is highly doubtful whether Tutʿankhamūn was ever engaged in any military or semi-military exploit, but this presentation of Ay points to a moment when he was the actual power behind the throne, but claimed no more than that. Another fragment from the same source gives him the title of vizier.[1] Before Tutʿankhamūn died, however, Ay had already assumed kingly titles, or, in other words, posed as a co-regent. As such he is represented in the rough paintings on the walls of Tutʿankhamūn's burial-chamber, where he conducts the youthful king's funerary obsequies.[2]

Until Akhenaten broke the sequence by his departure to El-ʿAmârna every Pharaoh since Tuthmōsis I had made himself a grandiose tomb in the Bîbân el-Molûk, and in the two succeeding dynasties the same course was pursued. But not one of these tombs had escaped the depredations of robbers. The reliefs displaying the mysteries of the netherworld still remained to adorn the walls of the long galleries, and one or two sarcophagi might also be found, perhaps even a despoiled royal mummy. But of all the treasures that the kings had hoped still to possess in the future life hardly a fragment had been left. Only one ruler belonging to this long period was unaccounted for; there was a chance that the tomb of Tutʿankhamūn might have eluded the greed of the marauders. It was with this remote possibility in mind that Howard Carter, working on behalf of the Earl of Carnarvon, had doggedly advocated the continuance of digging which had thus far proved very unlucrative. A last chance having been conceded Fortune proved favourable. A sealed door lying deep and hidden by the debris heaped over it when the tomb of Ramessēs VI was cut out of the hillside pointed the way into a set of four rooms of which the two inner ones were almost intact, whereas the outermost contained furniture hastily rearranged after having been plundered by robbers and the remaining fourth chamber behind it served as a dumping ground for *disjecta membra* which could not be easily mended. The

[1] Op. cit., p. 133. 15. 3. [2] *Ann. Serv.* xxxviii. 641 ff.

tomb was in fact that of Tutʿankhamūn. The contents of the front room surpassed anything that an excavator in Egypt had ever witnessed or dreamt of (Pl. XVI): great couches, chairs, painted and inlaid caskets, alabaster vases, a superb throne, a pile of overturned chariots, to mention only some of the treasures. But we must not linger here to describe the details of this extraordinary find. Suffice it to say that when three months later the plaster partition guarded on both sides by sentinel statues was broken down there was revealed a great gilt and faience shrine ultimately found to contain three more gilt shrines, one inside the other; within these was the huge yellow quartzite sarcophagus serving as receptacle for three magnificent coffins, the innermost of pure gold. Last of all was disclosed the royal mummy with its splendid gold mask and an almost overwhelming wealth of jewels between the wrappings. It is impossible to overestimate the importance of this discovery for archaeology and as a sample of what other Pharaonic burials may have been like, but it must be admitted that its addition to our historical knowledge has been meagre. The age of the young king and the fact that his successor the god's father Ay conducted the funerary ceremonies have already been mentioned; it remains to state that the comparatively humble tomb in which he was laid amid such splendour was clearly not meant for him. The great shrines had been so hastily assembled that they were orientated contrary to the directions painted on them.[1] The quartzite sarcophagus and its granite lid were not mates, and there is much more evidence of the scurry with which Tutʿankhamūn was consigned to what aspired to be his 'house of eternity'. There is no further testimony to tell what part Ay played in all this, but he is known to have reigned into his fourth year,[2] when he was succeeded by a monarch of a very different calibre.

We must not, however, turn our backs upon Ay without mentioning some facts which many historians have ignored, while others have held diametrically opposed views concerning them. There is, at all events, an incontestable affinity between him and that Yuia whom we have seen to have been the father of Queen Tiye and consequently the father-in-law of Amenōphis III (p. 206).

[1] *Ann. Serv.* xl. 136 ff. [2] PM v. 22.

Both prefixed to their name the epithet 'god's father', which in some cases appears to signify little more than a person of advanced age and recognized respectability. Yuia in his tomb at Thebes bore the title 'overseer of horses', while Ay at El-'Amârna is 'overseer of all the horses of His Majesty'. Even more remarkable is the connexion of both with the town of Akhmîm, where Yuia was a prophet of Mīn as well as superintendent of that god's cattle,[1] and where King Ay erected a shrine and left a long inscription.[2] Just as Yuia's wife Tjuia was the mother of Queen Tiye, so Queen Tey, the spouse of King Ay, had previously been the nurse of Queen Nefertiti. Little wonder if, in view of these facts, P. E. Newberry propounded the theory that Yuia and Ay, as well as their wives Tjuia and Tey, were actually identical.[3] It must be understood that the names which, in a purely conventional manner, we render in these divergent ways, offer no real obstacle to this theory; such is the nature of hieroglyphic writing at this period that we cannot be sure if what appears to be written as Yuia may not have been pronounced Ay, and similarly with the names of the wives. Chronologically, however, Newberry's view, which he himself never published, is absolutely impossible; since, moreover, the mummies of both Yuia and Tjuia, evidently very aged people, were discovered in their Theban tomb, it would be necessary to assume that Yuia or Ay, whichever pronunciation we might prefer for him, had before his death been forced to renounce his kingly title, and to revert to the position of a commoner. C. Aldred has made the plausible suggestion[4] that the future monarch Ay was the son of Yuia; this certainly would explain the similarity of their titles and their close connexion with Akhmîm, but is unsupported by any definite evidence. Needless to say, the tomb which Akhenaten had granted to Ay at El-'Amârna was never used. On Ay's return to Thebes and to orthodoxy he caused a sepulchre to be prepared for himself in the western valley of the Bîbân el-Molûk near that of Amenōphis III.[5] It is a small affair, and only one room at the end of the passage approached by a flight of steps is decorated. The religious scenes show a close resemblance to those in Tutʿankhamūn's burial cham-

[1] Th. M. Davis, *The Tomb of Iouiya and Touiyou*, London, 1907, pp. 5, 7.
[2] PM v. 17. [3] *JNES* xiv. 168, n. 2. [4] *JEA* xliii. 30 ff. [5] PM i. 28, No. 23.

ber, but there is a picture of the king fowling in the marshes for which analogies are found only in the tombs of non-royal personages. The rose-coloured granite sarcophagus, later broken to pieces, excited the admiration of the early Egyptologists. Throughout the tomb the cartouches have been erased.

An extraordinary event that dates from the time immediately following the death of Tutʿankhamūn has now to be recorded. This is a cuneiform text[1] quoting a letter addressed to the Hittite king Suppiluliumas by a young widow, who can only have been ʿAnkhesnamūn, though what appears to have been her name has through some error received a distorted form. She explains that she has no son, and begs the Hittite king to send one of his own to marry her and promises that he shall be acknowledged as the Pharaoh. Suppiluliumas is sceptical about the genuineness of this request and dispatches an official to investigate. The widow indignantly protests her *bona fides*, and a young Hittite prince was finally granted, but was murdered on the way. This led to a war against Egypt[2] though nothing is known about it from Egyptian sources.

The accession of Ay's successor Ḥaremḥab offers a reminder that for Dyn. XVIII no mention has been made of Manetho. For good reason, since the names of the sixteen kings given by Africanus and the fourteen recorded by Eusebius appear in an incredibly garbled form, some of them wholly unrecognizable; moreover, the last two are certainly to be identified with Ramessēs II and Merenptaḥ and rightly reappear in Manetho's Dyn. XIX. Ḥaremḥab is named twice, first as Ōros immediately after that Amenōphis famous in connexion with the statue known as the Vocal Memnōn (above, p. 209) and secondly as the Armais whom the Greeks equated with Danaus and around whose person and that of his brother Sethōs was spun a complicated romance. For the sequence of the Dyn. XVIII kings we have not only the evidence of the monuments, but also that of the Abydos and Saḳ âra king-lists, which, understandably ignoring Akhenaten and his three successors as tainted with Atenism, place Ḥaremḥab immediately after Amenōphis III, thus agreeing with the Ōros of Manetho. It is a curious thing that while

[1] Translated *ANET*, p. 319. [2] Op. cit., p. 395. 4.

the Manetho presented by his excerptors betrays much obvious confusion, his lengths of reign in several cases approximate to reality and consequently, though they can never be wholly trusted, nevertheless cannot be wholly ignored. In giving 36 or 38 years to Ōros, Eusebius may have come pretty near to the truth, for we possess a graffito believed to belong to his year 27,[1] and it is clear that when an inscription of the time of Ramessēs II speaks of a law-suit as having taken place in Ḥaremḥab's fifty-ninth year, this includes the twenty-eight or thirty years from the death of Amenōphis III to that of King Ay. Let it be remembered, however, that in these chronological matters we have to content ourselves with mere approximations. The letter of ʿAnkhesnamūn to Suppiluliumas, when compared with that of the Hittite king to Akhenaten at the beginning of his reign, adds some slight confirmation, since if we allow seventeen years to Akhenaten and eight to Tutʿankhamūn, we find that these twenty-five years fall within Suppiluliumas's forty years (1375–1335 B.C.) as calculated or conjectured by scholars in the parallel field of study.

It seems appropriate to regard Ḥaremḥab as belonging neither to Dyn. XVIII nor to Dyn. XIX, but as occupying an isolated position between them. His parents are unknown, and there is no reason to think that royal blood flowed in his veins, though it is possible that it may have done so in the veins of his spouse Mutnodjme. No children of theirs are recorded, so that any kinship with the first ruler of Dyn. XIX cannot be affirmed, and indeed is improbable. There is a fine statue in the Turin Museum[2] portraying husband and wife together, with a long inscription on the plinth where his journey to Thebes to be crowned is recounted after a vaguely expressed preface dealing with his antecedents. Thence we learn that he was a native of the unimportant town of Ḥnēs on the east bank of the Nile some 110 miles from Cairo, and that it was to the favour of the local falcon-god Horus that he owed his advancement. As usual, the language employed to narrate his career is so flowery that only with difficulty can solid historical facts be extracted from it. A passing reference to his being summoned into the royal presence when 'the Palace fell into rage' seems to hint that he faced the

[1] This, however, is doubted, see *CoA* iii. 157–8. [2] *JEA* xxxix. 13 ff. with Pl. i.

wrath of Akhenaten successfully. He tells us that 'he acted as vice-regent of the Two Lands over a period of many years' and the verb here used agrees so well with the substantive in the title 'viceregent (or 'deputy') of the king' found on several monuments that we have reason to think of him as carrying on the government in the north while the heretic king was absorbed in his religious celebrations far away in the south.

The tomb at Saḳḳâra[1] dates from a time when Ḥaremḥab had no thought of occupying a place amid the proud succession of the Pharaohs. Added to his principal rank of 'great commander of the army of the Lord of the Two Lands' are such epithets as 'whom the king chose out of the Two Lands to administer the two regions' and again 'envoy of the king in front of the army to the southern and northern lands'. If the second of these epithets fails to carry conviction in view of the circumstances of the times, still less can we trust a traditional third which represents him as 'accompanying the king in his goings in the southern and northern country'.[2] The wonderful reliefs in the tomb, now scattered among many museums, so exclusively display him as an active military commander that we cannot deny some reality to his implied warlike campaigns, though no sober recital remains to testify to them. Of particular interest is a picture where Ḥaremḥab, loaded with golden necklets, stands before the king—whose image together with that of the queen has not survived—and announces the visit of a number of foreign princes.[3] He then turns to a group of Egyptian officers and officials and reports to them the message of the Pharaoh. From the much-damaged legends appended to this scene the following is excerpted:

And . . . [it has been reported that?] some foreigners who know not (how) they may live are come from (?) . . . their countries are hungry, and they live like the animals of the desert, [and their child]ren(?) . . . the Great of Strength will send his mighty arm in front of [his army? . . . and will] destroy them and plunder their town(s) and cast fire [into] . . . [and] . . . the foreign countries will(?) set others in their places.

This extract is shown exactly as found in the original hieroglyphs;

[1] PM iii. 195–7; *JEA* xxxix. 3 ff.

[2] Gauthier, *LR* ii. 382.

[3] *JEA* xxxix. 5, fig. 1.

nothing could better illustrate the condition of many of the texts upon which the historian of Ancient Egypt has to rely for his knowledge. In the early days of our science it was doubted by many whether the Ḥaremḥab who made this tomb for himself was really, in spite of its exceptional beauty, the future king, but the uraeus-serpent later added to his brow[1] leaves no doubt about the matter.

If, as seems almost certain, the Memphite tomb belongs to the reign of Akhenaten, the duties of Ḥaremḥab at that time will have been mainly military. A fragment now mislaid tells how he was sent as king's envoy to the region of the sun-disk's uprising and returned in triumph; but no details are given. Under Tutʿankhamūn he will have served rather as an administrator; a statue from Memphis and another from Thebes depict him as a royal scribe writing down his sovereign's commands.[2] A funerary procession represented in a tomb-relief shows him taking precedence over the two viziers existing at that time.[3] The Turin statue makes no reference to his relations with Ay, but simply goes on to relate how his god Horus brought him southwards to Thebes where he was crowned by Amūn and received his royal titulary. After this he returned downstream, which presumably means that he had decided to make Memphis his capital. The rest of his life seems to have been devoted to restoring the ruined temples of the gods, renewing their ritual observances, and endowing them with fields and herds. One detail is significant: we are told that the priests whom he appointed were chosen from the pick of the army; clearly Ḥaremḥab never forgot his military upbringing. At the same time he was not ready to tolerate abuses that had arisen through the actions of his soldiery. A sadly defective stela at Karnak[4] described the measures which he took to establish justice throughout the land, but there is hardly a sentence well enough preserved to give a clear idea of the grievances in question. We can at least see that arbitrary exactions had resulted in ordinary citizens being deprived of their boats with their cargoes, or again being beaten and robbed of the valuable hides of their cattle. The penalties imposed were of great severity, the malefactors in the worst cases being docked of

[1] *ZÄS* xxxviii. 47 ff. [2] *JEA* x. 1 ff. [3] *ZÄS* xxxiii, Pl. 1; lx. 56 ff.
[4] PM ii. 62 (65); *Urk.* iv. 2140 ff.

their noses and banished to the fortress-town of Tjel on the Asiatic border, and in the lesser cases punished with a hundred strokes and five open wounds. Were this unique inscription better preserved, much would have been learnt about the reorganization of the country, for example its being kept in order by the division of the army into two main bodies, one in the north and another in the south, each under a separate commander; or again the institution of law-courts in all the great cities, with the priests of the temples and the mayors of towns as the judges; for all of which services those who performed them faithfully were to be suitably rewarded by the king in person.

Building was certainly Ḥaremḥab's main preoccupation during his later years. At Karnak he took the first steps towards the creation of the great Hypostyle Hall, the completion of which was the glorious achievement of Ramessēs II;[1] he also made himself responsible for the Ninth and Tenth Pylons to the south,[2] the former giving him the welcome opportunity of demolishing constructions due to Akhenaten in the earliest stage of his career. The immense avenue of ram-headed sphinxes running from Karnak to Luxor seems also to have been his. At Luxor he usurped from Tutᶜankhamūn the magnificent reliefs which Tutᶜankhamūn had himself usurped or continued from Amenōphis III.[3] Without here attempting to enumerate Ḥaremḥab's various works elsewhere, we must nevertheless mention the attractive speos at the Gebel Silsila[4] where his triumph, real or fictitious, over the Nubians is graphically depicted. On the west bank at Thebes he undertook a vast funerary temple that Ay had begun,[5] but of this no more than the foundations remain. The indefatigable Th. M. Davis financed the excavation in the Bîbân el-Molûk which led to the discovery of Ḥaremḥab's spacious tomb,[6] with its many decorations left unfinished; the magnificent sarcophagus, closely resembling that of Ay, still occupies its appointed place in the burial-chamber.

[1] Seele, *Coregency*, 7 ff.
[2] PM ii. 59 ff.
[3] Op. cit. ii. 102–3.
[4] PM v. 208 ff.; Wreszinski, ii, Pls. 161–2.
[5] Hölscher, *Temples of the Eighteenth Dynasty*, pp. 63 ff.
[6] See above, p. 237, n. 3.

SELECT BIBLIOGRAPHY

J. D. S. Pendlebury, *Tell el-Amarna*, London, 1935, a popular account of the history and the excavations.

N. de G. Davies, *The Rock Tombs of El Amarna*, 6 vols., London, 1903–8. The texts in this fundamental work are more easily quoted from the book by M. Sandman, *Texts from the Time of Akhenaten*, Brussels, 1938.

The excavations of the Egypt Exploration Society at El-ʿAmârna: Various authors, *The City of Akhenaten*, 4 vols., London, 1923–51; in vol. iii, elaborate discussions of the inscriptions by H. W. Fairman.

The supposed co-regency of Amenōphis III and Amenōphis IV: Fairman in *CoA* iii. 152–7.

The Art of El-ʿAmârna: *The Mural Painting of El ʿAmarneh*, ed. H. Frankfort, London, 1929; articles by H. Schäfer in *ZÄS* lii. 73 ff.; lv. 1 ff.; lxx. 1 ff.

The Tomb of Tutʿankhamūn: H. Carter, *The Tomb of Tutankhamen*, 3 vols., London, 1923–33; Penelope Fox, *Tutankhamun's Treasure*, London, 1951.

The coffin of Akhenaten: A. H. Gardiner, *The so-called tomb of Queen Tiye*, in *JEA* xliii. 10 ff., but see also xlv. 10 and other articles ibid. xlvii.

Some recent controversial articles: K. C. Seele, *King Ay and the Close of the ʿAmarna Age* in *JNES* xiv. 168 ff.; C. Aldred, *The End of the El ʿAmarna Period*, in *JEA* xliii. 30 ff.; P. van der Meer, *The Chronological Determination of the Mesopotamian Letters in the El-Amarna Archives*, in *Ex Oriente Lux, Jaarbericht* No. 15. (1957 – 1958) 75 ff.

Ḥaremḥab: K. Pflüger, *Haremhab und die Amarnazeit*, Zwickau, 1936; articles by A. H. Gardiner quoted above, p. 242, n. 2; p. 243, n. 3. The Karnak decree: W. Helck in *ZÄS* lxxx. 109 ff. Nubia: Nina de G. Davies and A. H. Gardiner, *The Tomb of Ḥuy, viceroy of Nubia*, London, 1926.

The Hittites: O. R. Gurney, *The Hittites* (Pelican book), Harmondsworth, 1952.

X

THE RAMESSIDE PERIOD: (I) THE NINETEENTH DYNASTY

AFTER the recovery from the religious revolution Egypt was a changed world. It is not easy to define the exact nature of the changes, since there are many exceptions; yet it is impossible not to notice the marked deterioration of the art, the literature, and indeed the general culture of the people. The language which they wrote approximates more closely to the vernacular and incorporates many foreign words; the copies of ancient texts are incredibly careless, as if the scribes utterly failed to understand their meaning. At Thebes the tombs no longer display the bright and happy scenes of everyday life which characterized Dyn. XVIII, but concentrate rather upon the perils to be faced in the hereafter; the judgement of the heart before Osiris is a favourite theme, and the Book of Gates illustrates the obstacles to be encountered during the nightly journey through the netherworld. The less frequent remains from Memphis show reliefs of only slightly greater elegance. The temples elsewhere depict upon their walls many vivid representations of warfare, but the workmanship is relatively coarse and the explanatory legends are often more adulatory than informative. In spite of all, Egypt still presents an aspect of wonderful grandeur, which the greater abundance of this period's monuments makes better known to the present-day tourist than the far finer products of earlier times.

Two statues found at Karnak in 1913,[1] taken in conjunction with the famous stela of the year 400 discovered at Tanis fifty years earlier (p. 165), prove the founder of the NINETEENTH DYNASTY to have been a man from the north-eastern corner of the Delta whom Ḥaremḥab raised to the exalted rank of vizier. Praʿmesse, as he was called until he dropped the definite article at the beginning of his

[1] *Ann. Serv.* xiv. 29 ff.

name to become the king known to us as Ramessēs I, was of relatively humble origin, his father Sety having been a simple 'captain of troops'. We can well imagine Ḥaremḥab as having wished to choose his main coadjutor from within his own military caste. The statues, practically duplicates of one another, portray Praʿmesse as a royal scribe squatting upon his haunches in the approved manner of his kind. The half-opened papyrus on his lap enumerates the various high offices to which his lord had raised him. Besides the vizierate these include the positions of superintendent of horses, fortress-commander, superintendent of the river-mouths, commander of the army of the Lord of the Two Lands, not to mention several priestly titles. Most significant of all is his claim to have been 'deputy of the King in Upper and Lower Egypt', as Ḥaremḥab had been before him. Praʿmesse was an old man when he ascended the throne. He was not destined to enjoy the royal power for long. Manetho, as quoted by Josephus, allows him only one year and four months of reign, a span not necessarily contradicted by the dating in year 2 on the sole dated monument which we possess, a stela from Wâdy Ḥalfa now in the Louvre.[1] Even this appears to have been erected by his son and successor Sety (Sethōs I), who set up in the same place a stela almost identical in tenor and dated in year 1 of his own reign.[2] These two documents record the establishment at Buhen (Wâdy Ḥalfa) of a temple and new offerings to Mīn-Amūn, for whose cult prophets, lector-priests, and ordinary priests were appointed, together with male and female slaves from 'the captures made by His Majesty'; these last words need not be taken too seriously in view of the shortness of the reign, and indeed peace may at this time have been firmly established in Nubia, where Pesiūr,[3] the King's Son of Cush of Ḥaremḥab's reign, was possibly still in office. Ramessēs I's monuments in other parts are very scanty. A few reliefs bearing his name on and near the Second Pylon at Karnak suggest that he either initiated or acquiesced in the stupendous change there from Ḥaremḥab's open court with a central double line of giant columns like that at Luxor to the great Hypostyle Hall which is among the chief surviving

[1] PM vii. 130; *BAR* iii, §§ 74 ff.
[2] PM vii. 129.
[3] *JEA* vi. 36 ff.

wonders of Pharaonic Egypt (see Pl. XVIII).[1] His own tomb in the Valley of the Tombs of the Kings was planned to rival in size that of his predecessor, and only stopped short, doubtless owing to his death, at the chamber below the second flight of stairs, where his sarcophagus may still be seen.[2] His coffin and mummy suffered a fate not unlike that which befell the mummies of other kings: from his own tomb they were transported first to that of Sethōs I, and thence to the great *cache* at Dêr el-Baḥri.[3]

The great ruler who occupied the throne for the next fifteen or more years was imbued with true affection and loyalty towards his father. But filial piety has its limits, and in the important funerary sanctuary which Sethōs I built for himself at Ḳurna, the northernmost of the line of temples fringing the western desert at Thebes, he could spare only a few rooms to Ramessēs I.[4] At Abydos, however, he appended to his own great temple a small chapel with beautifully painted reliefs[5] and a fine stela in which he extolled the virtues of his progenitor.[6] Yet for all the recognition which Sethōs was prepared to pay his father, he was not averse to regarding himself as the inaugurator of a new period. This he showed by means of the phrase 'Repetition of Births' appended to datings of his first and second regnal years, and by inserting the corresponding epithet in his Two-Ladies name and sometimes in his Horus-name, as had been done by Ammenemēs I at the beginning of Dyn. XII (p. 127). But there may have been an additional reason for this. If the calculations of the astronomical chronologers are sound, a new Sothic period[7] began about 1317 B.C., a very short time before Sethōs I came to the throne. Now the Alexandrian mathematician Theōn, referring to the Sothic period, speaks of it as the era 'from Menophrēs', and this royal name has been interpreted by Struve, followed by Sethe,[8] to be a slightly corrupted form of the epithet *Mry-n-Ptḥ* 'Beloved of Ptaḥ' which normally stands at the beginning of Sethōs's second cartouche. This clever conjecture may or may not be right.

1 PM ii. 16 (25)–(26); Seele, op. cit., §§ 22 ff.
2 *Bull. Inst. fr.* lvi. 189 ff.
3 *JEA* xxxii. 27 ff.
4 PM ii. 146 (xxix).
5 Op. cit. vi. 31–33.
6 *Ann. Serv.* li. 167 ff.; *Rev. d'Ég.* xi. 1 ff.
7 See above, p. 65.
8 *ZÄS* lxiii. 45 ff.; lxvi. 1 ff.

As a stranger from the extreme north and with no royal lineage behind him, Sethōs ran a serious risk of being viewed as an upstart. The gods of the land had by no means completely recovered from the injuries inflicted upon them by the partisans of Akhenaten. Here Sethōs found an opportunity of winning popularity; doubtless it was with this in view that he set about restoring the mutilated inscriptions of his predecessors. But his cleverest move consisted in founding a temple whose magnificence should vie with that of the very greatest fanes of the capital cities. Abydos, the reputed home of Osiris, had always been a favourite site for the building activities of the Pharaohs, but to none of Sethōs's predecessors had it occurred to honour the place on such a scale as he devised. His temple,[1] together with the mysterious cenotaph at the back of it, remains to this day a place of pilgrimage which no enterprising sightseer would willingly miss. The reliefs of the walls, in many cases still retaining the brilliance of their original colours, display a delicacy and a perfection of craftsmanship surprising on the threshold of a period of undisputed decadence. The inherited name of Sety 'the Sethian' attests a devotion to the very god who had been the murderer of the venerated *numen loci*. All the more necessary was it for him to placate Osiris, or rather his powerful priesthood. Despite Sethōs I's lavish expenditure on this great monument the architects whom he employed did not care to give Sēth a place among its divine occupants, and even in their writing of the monarch's name the figure of Osiris  was prudently used in place of the grotesque animalic image 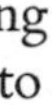 of his mortal enemy. By way of compensation, however, Osiris was not permitted to be exclusively worshipped here at Sēth's expense. The temple was conceived of as a national shrine. Beside Osiris, chapels were set apart for his wife Isis and for his son Horus, these three constituting the age-old triad of Abydos. But neighbouring their chapels are others of equal size and importance dedicated to the three chief gods of the capital cities, to Amūn of Thebes, to Ptaḥ of Memphis, and to Rēʿ-Ḥarakhti of Hēliopolis. Nor was Sethōs I the man to dissociate himself from this august company. It was to his own cult that he caused to be consecrated the seventh and southernmost chapel. To modern minds this action

[1] PM vi. 1 ff.

might well seem intolerably presumptuous, but not so to an Egyptian Pharaoh. Was he not from time immemorial a great god, if not the greatest of all? How should he not possess a cenotaph in the holiest place of the Two Lands? And lastly, we must never forget that early religion universally took for granted the principle *do ut des*. All the gods would have languished, and rightly, had not the Pharaoh's self-interest demanded the steadfast maintenance of their cults.

The foundation or even the re-dedication of a temple was by no means complete when the actual building was ended; priests of different grades had to be appointed, menial servants found to discharge the ordinary duties of maintenance and commissariat, and large tracts of land set apart to supply the revenues required for the upkeep. In return for this, a royal charter was usually issued to define the rights of the sacred establishment and its employees. Passing reference has been made to the decrees from the end of the Old Kingdom which protected the temple of Mīn at Coptos from outside interference. Good fortune has preserved for us the charter or part of the charter granted by Sethōs to his great new sanctuary at Abydos; and this, strange to say, is inscribed on a high rock at Nauri a short distance to the north of the Third Cataract.[1] After a long and poetically worded preamble describing the wealth and beauty of the temple 600 miles away, there follow the specific commands addressed to

> the Vizier, the officials, the courtiers, the courts of judges, the King's Son of Cush, the troop-captains, the superintendents of gold, the mayors and heads of villages of Upper and Lower Egypt, the charioteers, the stable-chiefs, the standard-bearers, every agent of the King's House and every person sent on a mission to Cush.

It must suffice here to mention a few of the ways in which the privileges of the temple staff might be infringed. These men might be seized personally, moved from district to district, commandeered for ploughing or reaping, prevented from fishing or fowling, have their cattle stolen, and so forth. Also any official who did not exact justice from the offenders was himself to be severely punished.

[1] *JEA* xiii. 193 ff.; xxxviii. 24 ff.

Paragraph after paragraph deals with such matters, but it has to be confessed that the entire decree is very carelessly drafted, and leaves the impression rather of artificial legalistic form than of precise legal enactment.

Among the dependants of the Abydos temple mentioned in the Nauri text are the gold-washers who were employed at the mines in the neighbourhood of the Red Sea. Their task was to effect the extraction of the precious metal by washing away the lighter substances in the pulverized stone. The hard lot of the actual miners is described in a passage quoted by Diodorus Siculus (iii. 12–14) from the geographer Agatharchides. It was important that these poor wretches should reach the scene of their labours without perishing on the way. In a long inscription of year 9[1] engraved on the walls of a small temple in the Wâdy Abbâd some 35 miles east of Edfu Sethōs describes the measures he has taken to remedy their situation. A brief extract will illustrate the style and substance of the narration:

> He stopped on the way to take counsel with his heart, and said: How miserable is a road without water! How shall travellers fare? Surely their throats will be parched. What will slake their thirst? The homeland is far away, the desert wide. Woe to him, a man thirsty in the wilderness! Come now, I will take thought for their welfare and make for them the means of preserving them alive, so that they may bless my name in years to come, and that future generations may boast of me for my energy, inasmuch as I am one compassionate and regardful of travellers.

Sethōs then recounts the digging of a well and the founding of a settlement in this locality. Another inscription in the speos warns later rulers and their subjects not to misappropriate the gold which was to be delivered to the Abydos temple, and ends with a curse:

> As to whosoever shall ignore this decree, Osiris will pursue him, and Isis his wife, and Horus his children; and the Great Ones, the lords of the Sacred Land, will make their reckoning with him.

Among her northerly neighbours Egypt's prestige had fallen to a very low level, a situation which Sethōs at once set to work to

[1] *JEA* iv. 241 ff.

repair. The warlike scenes depicted upon the exterior north wall of the great Hypostyle Hall at Karnak[1] combine with conventional illustrations of the king's personal prowess much information of a genuine historical character. These reliefs are no great works of art, despite the prancing steeds of Pharaoh's chariot and the agonized contortions of his victims; but surely unique must be the picture of Sethōs on foot, with two Syrian prisoners tucked under each arm. There are two series of scenes, both converging towards a central doorway near which Amūn stands to welcome the returning conqueror and to witness the doubtless merely symbolic battering to death of the vanquished chieftains; the lesser captives who follow in long lines were destined to become slaves in the workshops of the temple of Karnak. On the eastern side the lowest register shows the military road along which Sethōs's army had to pass before he could reach his main objectives in northern Syria. The starting-point, as with Tuthmōsis III and others, was the fortress of Tjel, the Latin Silē or Sellē,[2] close to the modern El-Ḳanṭara so well known to our own soldiers in the two world wars. Thence the way led across the waterless desert of the Sinai peninsula beyond a small canal now replaced by that of Suez. The reliefs[3] display in correct order the many small fortified stations built to protect the indispensable wells, and these together with a town with lost name which is evidently Raphia, 110 miles from Tjel, constitute the earliest equivalent of a map that the ancient world has to show. Twenty miles further on, described as 'town of Canaan' is the Philistine Gaza a short distance within the Palestine border. Before arriving there Sethōs had been compelled to inflict a great slaughter on the rebellious nomads of the Shōsu who barred the way.[4] It is difficult to say how far the campaign of year 1 extended since the top register on the east half of the wall is lost; but it certainly reached as far as the Lebanon, where the native princes are seen felling the cedars or pines needed for the sacred bark and flagstaffs of the Theban Amūn. What the accompanying hieroglyphic legend describes as 'the ascent which Pharaoh made to destroy the land of Ḳadesh and the land of the Amor' probably belongs to a later year;

[1] Wreszinski, ii, Pls. 34 ff.; *JEA* xxxiii. 34 ff. [2] *JEA* x. 6 ff. [3] Op. cit. vi. 99 ff. [4] B*AR* iii, § 88.

the Ḳadesh here mentioned is naturally the all-important city on the Orontēs, while the land of Amor is the adjacent north Syrian region extending to the Mediterranean coast. Of the two remaining registers in the western half-wall that in the middle records a battle against the Libyans, of whom but little has been heard since the beginning of Dyn. XII. The lowest register shows Sethōs at grips with the Hittites, the strength of whose empire had been steadily growing in the hands of Suppiluliumas's son Mursilis II; naturally the reliefs display Sethōs as the victor. Stelae from Ḳadesh itself[1] and from Tell esh-Shihâb[2] in the Haurân bear Sethōs's name, but are of far less importance than the two inscriptions of his reign found at Beisân, the Beth-shean of the Old Testament, some 15 miles south of the Sea of Galilee and only 4 to the west of the Jordan. Here since the time of Tuthmōsis III a fortress of considerable size had housed the Egyptian garrison, and within its chapel had stood the stelae which told of Sethōs's exploits in the neighbourhood. One of them which is nearly illegible, but has been skilfully deciphered by Grdseloff,[3] deals with the ʿApiru-people discussed above, p. 203. The other, which is well preserved,[4] narrates as follows:

Year 1, third month of Summer, day 2 . . . on this day they came to tell His Majesty that the vile enemy who was in the town of Ḥamath had gathered unto himself many people and had captured the town of Bethshaēl, and had joined with the inhabitants of Peḥel and did not allow the prince of Reḥob to go forth. Thereupon His Majesty sent the first army of Amūn 'Powerful of Bows' to the town of Ḥamath, the first army of Prēʿ 'Manifold of Bravery' to the town of Bethshaēl, and the first army of Sutekh 'Victorious of Bows' to the town of Yenoʿam. Then there happened the space of one day and they were fallen through the might of His Majesty, the King of Upper and Lower Egypt, Menmaʿrēʿ, the Son of Rēʿ, Sety-merenptaḥ, given life.

All the places here named have been identified with some probability, none of them at any great distance from Beisân; the capture of Yenoʿam had been depicted in the Karnak reliefs. No more in the way of commentary is needed than to draw attention to the

[1] PM vii. 392.
[2] Op. cit. vii. 383.
[3] B. Grdseloff, *Études égyptiennes*, ii. Cairo, 1949.
[4] PM vii. 380.

three army corps named after the gods of Thebes, Hēliopolis, and the later Pi-Raʿmesse respectively; these we shall find reappearing in the Ḳadesh campaign of Ramessēs II, and they seem to imply the presence of really strong forces in the Palestinian area. Perhaps in the quarter of a century from the beginning of Dyn. XIX Egypt possessed as much of an Asiatic empire as at any other period in her history. Nevertheless, the main administration probably lay in the hands of the local princes, and apart from the commanders of garrisons the Egyptian officials claimed no more authoritative title than that of 'king's envoy to every foreign country'. In Nubia, on the other hand, real governors were the King's Son of Cush and his two lieutenants, though here too Sethōs had to take military action against a remote tribe in the fourth and eighth years of his reign.[1]

Apart from the temples of Ḳurna and Abydos already mentioned and the work on the great Hypostyle Hall at Karnak Sethōs I's buildings are relatively unimportant. On the other hand, the sepulchre which he caused to be excavated for himself in the Bîbân el-Molûk is the most imposing of the entire necropolis. It is over 300 feet long and decorated from the very entrance with admirably executed and brilliantly coloured reliefs equalling in quality those found in the great monument at Abydos. The fine alabaster sarcophagus is now the treasured possession of the Soane Museum in London. It had early been robbed of its occupant, whose mummy ultimately found its way to the *cache* at Dêr el-Baḥri.[2] Sethōs was a man of only moderate height, but the well-preserved head, with heavy jaw and a wide and strong chin, is cast in a markedly different mould from that of the Dyn. XVIII kings.

If the greatness of an Egyptian Pharaoh be measured by the size and number of the monuments remaining to perpetuate his memory, Sethōs's son and successor Ramessēs II would have to be adjudged the equal, or even the superior, of the proudest pyramid-builders. The great Hypostyle Hall at Karnak is in the main his achievement, and on the west bank at Thebes his funerary temple known as the Ramesseum still retains a large part of its original grandeur. At Abydos[3] his temple stands as a not unworthy second

[1] Säve-Söderbergh, p. 168. [2] PM i. 175. 18. [3] Op. cit. vi. 33 ff.

side by side with that of his father, which he finished. The edifices at Memphis[1] have been largely demolished by later marauders greedy for suitable building stone, but portions of great statues of Ramessēs II attest the former presence of a vast temple of his; moreover, this is referred to in a well-known stela preserved in the Nubian temple of Abu Simbel, where Ramessēs acknowledges the blessings conferred upon him by the Memphite god Ptaḥ.[2] The remains at Tanis will be spoken of later. It is in Nubia, however, that his craze for self-advertisement is most conspicuous. Omitting the names of four important sanctuaries which under any other king could not be passed over in silence, we cannot refrain from voicing our wonder at the amazing temple at Abu Simbel with its four colossal seated statues of Ramessēs fronting the river.[3] Yet in spite of all this monumental ardour, Ramessēs II's stature has undeniably suffered diminution as the result of the last half-century's philological research. Previously the nickname Sese given him in some later literary texts[4] had persuaded Maspero that he was none other than the conqueror Sesōstris so widely celebrated in the classical authors; we now know that this half-mythical personage had arisen from the conflation of two separate kings of Dyn. XII.[5] The less enviable claim to have been the Pharaoh of the Oppression survives in the works of the ablest conservative scholars only in a greatly modified form, while a by no means negligible minority of historians are profoundly sceptical of the entire Exodus story.[6] Lastly Ramessēs II's glamour as a triumphant conqueror has been much dimmed by evidence from the Boghazköy records. None the less the events of his sixty-seven years of reign are better known and present more of interest than those of any other equal span of Egyptian history.

For the beginning of the reign the main source is an inscription of great length known to Egyptologists by the name *Inscription dédicatoire* given to it by G. Maspero, its first translator.[7] This occupies an entire wall in the temple of Sethōs I at Abydos and is in the main a boastful account of Ramessēs's virtue in completing his father's splendid sanctuary. The space devoted to factual narrative

[1] PM iii. 218. [2] Op. cit. vii. 106; *BAR* iii, §§ 394 ff. [3] PM vii. 95 ff. [4] *ZÄS* xli. 53 ff. [5] Above, p. 136. [6] Above, p. 156. [7] *BAR* iii, §§ 259 ff.

is but small, but an important passage describes Ramessēs's promotion in early youth to the position of crown prince and subsequently his association with Sethōs upon the throne:

> The Universal Lord himself[1] magnified me whilst I was a child until I became ruler. He gave me the land whilst I was in the egg, the great ones smelling the earth before my face. Then I was inducted as eldest son to be Hereditary Prince upon the throne of Gēb (the earth-god) and I reported the state of the Two Lands as captain of the infantry and the chariotry. Then when my father appeared in glory before the people, I being a babe in his lap, he said concerning me: 'Crown him as king that I may see his beauty whilst I am alive.' And he called to the chamberlains to fasten the crowns upon my forehead. 'Give him the Great One (the uraeus-serpent) upon his head' said he concerning me whilst he was on earth.

The accuracy of this statement has been impugned, but wrongly, since scenes at Karnak and at Ḳurna confirm Ramessēs's co-regency with his father.[2] Probably, however, he was less young when the co-regency began than this passage suggests, because there is evidence that he accompanied Sethōs on his military campaigns whilst he was still only the heir-apparent, and further because the passage just translated goes on to say that Sethōs equipped him with a female household and a king's harem 'like to the beautiful ones of the palace'; he must have been at least fifteen years old at the time, and in guessing at the length of the co-regency we must remember that Ramessēs had still a reign of little less than seventy years ahead of him, for he undoubtedly counted his first year from his accession after Sethōs's death. The Abydos inscription also gives us some information concerning his first actions after the accession. Like Ḥaremḥab he had come to Thebes to take part in Amūn's great feast of Ope, when the god was carried in state in his ceremonial boat from Karnak to Luxor. The festivities over, he set forth by river to his new Delta capital, stopping at Abydos on the way to do reverence to Osiris Onnōphris and to give orders for the continuation of the work on Sethōs's temple. This visit gave him the opportunity to appoint as new high-priest of Amūn a man who had previously been high-priest of Onūris at Thinis, of Ḥatḥōr at

[1] This is here an epithet of Sethōs I.

[2] Seele, op. cit., pp. 23 ff.

Dendera, and also at some places farther south; this preferment is proudly recounted by Nebunenef, the priest in question, in his tomb at Thebes.[1] Proceeding on his way northwards Ramessēs arrived at 'the strong place Pi-Raʿmesse, Great-of-Victories', thenceforth to be, with Memphis as an alternative, the main royal residence in the north throughout Dyns. XIX and XX.[2] It is agreed that this town, the Biblical Raamses, was situated on the same site as the great Hyksōs stronghold of Avaris (above, p. 164) and that its principal god was Sutekh, as the name of Sēth was by this time mostly pronounced. P. Montet and the present writer have strongly maintained that this was none other than the great city which was later called Djaʿne, Greek Tanis, the Zoan of the Bible. No one who has visited the site or has read about its monuments in books can have failed to be impressed by the multitude of the remains dating from the reign of Ramessēs II. On the other hand, some 11 miles to the south, at Khatʿâna-Ḳantîr, portions of a fine palace of Ramessēs II,[3] adorned with splendid faience tiles, have staked out a rival claim to be the true Pi-Raʿmesse 'the House of Raʿmesse', and among other scholars Labib Habachi has been particularly active and successful in finding stelae and other evidence from the same neighbourhood which might swing the pendulum in that direction.[4] According to this theory the monuments of Ramessēs II at Tanis were transported there by the kings of Dyn. XXI, who are known to have chosen that city as their capital. The debate continues, and cannot be regarded as finally settled either the one way or the other.

A fine stela of year 3 found in the fortress of Kûbân in Lower Nubia records the successful digging of a well in the land of Ikita where gold was to be found in large quantities.[5] The King's Son of Cush confirmed the report that when gold-workers were sent thither only half of them ever arrived, the rest having perished of thirst on the way; he added that the well commissioned by Sethōs I had proved a failure, unlike that in the Wâdy Abbâd mentioned above. Doubtless the supplies of the precious metal from farther north were growing exhausted, whence it became increasingly

[1] *ZÄS* xliv. 30 ff.
[2] *JEA* v. 127 ff.; 179 ff.
[3] PM iv. 9.
[4] *Ann. Serv.* lii. 443 ff.
[5] PM vii. 83; *BAR* iii, §§ 282 ff.

important to utilize the desert road of the Wâdy 'Allâḳi which opened out eastwards from near Kûbân. For our purpose, however, this inscription is mainly of interest as corroborating Ramessēs'l early appointment as crown-prince and his participation in all royas enterprises from his very childhood; we are told that he 'served as captain of the army when he was a boy in his tenth year', not an impossibility in the Orient when understood with the necessary qualification.

At the very beginning of the reign we have the first Egyptian mention of the Sherden,[1] pirates who later undoubtedly gave their name to Sardinia, though at this time they may have been dwelling in a quite different part of the Mediterranean. A stela from Tanis[2] speaks of their having come 'in their war-ships from the midst of the sea, and none were able to stand before them'. There must have been a naval battle somewhere near the river-mouths, for shortly afterwards many captives of their race are seen in the Pharaoh's body-guard, where they are conspicuous by their helmets with horns, their round shields and the great swords with which they are depicted dispatching the Hittite enemies. Little more than a century later many Sherden are found cultivating plots of their own, these doubtless rewards given to them for their military services. But they were not the only foreigners whom Ramessēs II was apt to use in this way; a literary papyrus reflecting the conditions of his reign[3] describes an expeditionary force of 5,000 out of which, besides 520 Sherden, there were thrice that number of Libyans belonging to the tribes of the Ḳeheḳ and Meshwesh, together with 880 Nubians; most of these were doubtless prisoners of war or the children of such, for there is no evidence that mercenaries were employed at this time, as is often erroneously stated.

A great trial of strength between Egypt and the Hittites could not be delayed. Ramessēs was ambitious to repeat his father's successes in northern Syria, and Muwatallis, the grandson of Suppiluliumas, was determined to uphold the many treaties that had been made with the petty princes of that region. The first 'Campaign of Victory', as large-scale Asiatic expeditions were termed in the Egyptian records, took place in year 4, when Ramessēs led his

[1] *Onom.* i. 194* ff. [2] *Kêmi*, x. 63 ff., with Pl. 6. [3] *ANET*, p. 476.

troops along the coast of Palestine as far north as the Nahr el-Kelb ('Dog-river') a few miles beyond Beyrût, where he caused a stela,[1] now illegible except for the date, to be carved facing the sea. To the following year belongs the mighty struggle in which Ramessēs performed a personal feat of arms that he never tired of proclaiming to his subjects on the temple-walls built by him. The story is told in two separate narratives which usefully supplement one another and are illustrated by sculptured reliefs accompanied by verbal explanations. What was at first known to Egyptologists as the Poem of Pentaur is a long and flowery inscription now described simply as the 'Poem', though it is no more of a poem than many another historical record from other reigns; the attribution to Pentaur was dropped when it was recognized that he was merely the scribe responsible for a particular copy preserved in a papyrus shared by the Louvre and the British Museum. The text, often defective in the individual hieroglyphic examples, has been reconstructed from eight duplicates in the temples of Karnak, Luxor, Abydos, and the Ramesseum, while the shorter version known as the 'Report' or the 'Bulletin' has been similarly edited from the same temples, except that it is not found at Karnak but exists in the great sanctuary of Abu Simbel.[2]

Ramessēs and his army crossed the Egyptian frontier at Silē in the spring of his fifth year, and just a month's marching brought him to a commanding height overlooking the stronghold of Ḳadesh from a distance of about 15 miles. Ḳadesh, now Tell Neby Mend, lies in the angle formed by the northward flowing Orontēs and a small tributary entering from the west, and as already stated, its great strategic importance was due to its position near the exit from the high-level valley between the Lebanons called the Biḳâʿ. Along this valley every north-bound army had necessarily to pass if it was wished to avoid the narrow route, intersected by river-mouths, along the Phoenician coast. Ḳadesh had, as we have seen, been captured by Sethōs I, but had since fallen into Hittite hands. This was Ramessēs's obvious objective and the place which gave its name to the great battle about to be fought. The Egyptian army was divided into four divisions of which those bearing the names

[1] PM vii. 385.
[2] *BAR* iii, §§ 298 ff. See too below, p. 279.

of Amūn, Prēʿ, and Sutekh have been encountered on the stela of Sethōs from Beisân (p. 254), while the fourth, named after Ptaḥ of Memphis, appears here for the first time. Ramessēs having passed the night on the afore-mentioned hilltop south of Ḳadesh made an early start next morning, doubtless hoping to have captured the fortress-town before dusk. At the head of the division of Amūn he descended some 600 feet to the ford of the Orontēs just south of Shabtuna, this evidently the modern Ribla. Either before or immediately after crossing the river, two Beduins were brought to him who, on being questioned, declared that they had been with the Hittite king, but that they wished to desert to the Pharaoh; they also stated that the Hittites were still far away in the land of Khaleb (Aleppo) to the north of Tunip. Misled by this information Ramessēs and his body-guard pushed ahead of the rest of the army, and began to set up camp to the north-west of the fortress-city some 6 or 7 miles from the ford. Obviously the wise course would have been to wait until the rest of his army had reached the left bank, so that all could have advanced together. Instead of this Ramessēs placed a distance of some miles between himself and the division of Prēʿ, while the division of Ptaḥ was even farther back; the division of Sutekh was so far away that it could play no part in the battle and is not heard of again. It was not until the king was seated upon his golden throne in his final camping-place that the unwelcome truth dawned upon him. Two captured Hittite scouts betrayed the fact that the entire army of Asiatic confederates lay hidden to the east of Ḳadesh, fully equipped and ready to fight. Clearly something had gone seriously wrong with the Egyptian intelligence service. Hardly had Ramessēs had time to reproach his officers than the enemy were upon him. They had passed round to the south of the town, forded the river, and cut their way through the division of Prēʿ. Thereupon Ramessēs dispatched his vizier to hasten the arrival of the division of Ptaḥ, which as yet had barely disengaged itself from the forest of Robawi, and a message was sent to the royal children to flee behind the palisade of shields surrounding the still unfinished camp and to keep clear of the fight. At this point in the two narratives Ramessēs's desire for self-glorification takes the upper hand, and his personal prowess is dwelt upon at great length. He describes himself as deserted by his whole army and surrounded by the vast host of the Hittites, whose king had collected for his crowning enterprise auxiliaries from so far west as the Ionian coast and from his principal neighbours in Asia Minor. Translation of a part of the 'Poem' will reveal the style in which Ramessēs's feat of arms is there presented.[1]

Then His Majesty arose like his father Mont and took the accoutrements of battle, and girt himself with his corselet; he was like Baʿal in his hour, and the great pair of horses which bore His Majesty, belonging to the great stable of Usimaʿrēʿ-setpenrēʿ, beloved of Amūn, were named Victory-in-Thebes. Then His Majesty started forth at a gallop, and entered into the host of the fallen ones of Khatti, being alone by himself, none other with him. And His Majesty went to look about him, and found surrounding him on his outer side 2500 pairs of horses with all the champions of the fallen ones of Khatti and of the many countries who were with them, from Arzawa, Masa, Pidasa, Keshkesh, Arwen, Kizzuwadna, Khaleb, Ugarit, Ḳadesh, and Luka;[2] they were three men to a pair of horses as a unit, whereas there was no captain with me, no charioteer, no soldier of the army, no shield-bearer; my infantry and chariotry melted away before them, not one of them stood firm to fight with them. Then said His Majesty: What ails thee, my father Amūn? Is it a father's part to ignore his son? Have I done anything without thee, do I not walk and halt at thy bidding? I have not disobeyed any course commanded by thee. How great is the great lord of Egypt to allow foreigners to draw nigh in his path! What careth thy heart, O Amūn, for these Asiatics so vile and ignorant of God? Have I not made for thee very many monuments and filled thy temple with my booty, and built for thee my Mansion of Millions of Years and given thee all my wealth as a permanent possession and presented to thee all lands together to enrich thy offerings, and have caused to be sacrificed to thee tens of thousands of cattle and all manner of sweet-scented herbs? No good deeds have I left undone so as not to perform them in thy sanc-

[1] Kuentz, pp. 237 ff.

[2] The first three names belong to countries to the south-west of Khatti, and so too the last (Luka, the Lycians). The Keshkesh are the Gashgash of the cuneiform tablets, to the north-east. Arwen is unidentified. Kizzuwadna corresponds roughly to Cilicia. Khaleb is Aleppo. For Ugarit see above, p. 201. The Dardany mentioned elsewhere in the 'Poem' are doubtless Homer's Dardanians. For detailed discussions see *Onom.* i. 123* ff.; see too the map Gurney, p. xvi.

tuary, building for thee great pylons and erecting their flagstaffs myself, bringing for thee obelisks from Elephantinē, even I being the stone-carrier, and have led to thee ships on the Great-Green, to carry to thee the produce of the foreign lands. What will men say if even a little thing befall him who bends himself to thy counsel?

There is much more in this strain before it is told how His Majesty routed the foe single-handed, hurling them into the Orontēs. What actually happened? It cannot be doubted that the Egyptian king did display great valour on this momentous occasion, but both the 'Report' and the sculptured scenes suggest that what saved Ramessēs was the arrival, in the nick of time, of the youthful troops that had been mentioned earlier as stationed in the land of Amor; perhaps we should think of them as coming up from the neighbourhood of Tripoli along the road crossed by the Eleutheros river; at all events they attacked the Hittites in the rear and completed their discomfiture. The Egyptian sources mention by name a number of prominent Hittites who were either drowned in the river or trodden underfoot by Ramessēs's horses; among them a brother of the Hittite king, who himself is described as taking no part in the fight, but cowering somewhere in the background. Finally, the 'Poem' reports the arrival of a letter in which the Hittite ruler praises the Pharaoh's valour in the most exaggerated terms and ends with the words 'Better is Peace than War; give us the breath (of life)'.[1] Unhappily the Boghazköy tablets tell a very different tale.[2] On one of these Khattusilis, Muwatallis's brother and successor, recalling the events of earlier years, relates how Ramessēs was conquered and retreated to the land of Aba[3] near Damascus, only to be replaced there by himself as regent. From another tablet we learn that Amor, which had perhaps been subject to the Egyptian power since the time of Sethōs, now fell to Muwatallis, who replaced its king by one of his own choice. However, if the Egyptian reliefs are to be trusted, after the Ḳadesh episode Ramessēs enjoyed a number of military successes. In year 8 he reduced a whole series of Palestinian fortresses including Dapur

[1] Kuentz, p. 319.

[2] References, see below, p. 279.

[3] Ubě of the El-'Amârna tablets, see *Onom.* i. 152*, 181*.

in the land of Amor,[1] though he had also been obliged to storm Ashkelon not far from the Egyptian border.[2] There is also talk of an occasion when in fighting against a Hittite town in the territory of Tunip he had not even troubled to don his corselet.[3] Whatever the exact truth of all these warlike proceedings, everything pointed to the necessity of ending a conflict profitable to neither side, and we shall see that this necessity was fully realized a few years later.

It is one of the great romances of Near Eastern discovery that the treaty concluded in year 21 of Ramessēs II between him and Khattusilis should have come to light in separate copies found in both the Egyptian capital of Thebes and the Hittite capital of Boghazköy, cities 1,000 miles apart on opposite sides of the Mediterranean.[4] The Egyptian version, written in hieroglyphic, can be read on a stela standing upright against a wall in the temple of Karnak.[5] The Hittite version, a little less complete, is given on two clay tablets inscribed in Babylonian cuneiform; it is not an exact duplicate, but to a large extent shows identical clauses and expressions, all the more interesting because they triumphantly confirm the accuracy of the labours of philologists in the two distinct fields of study. An offensive and defensive alliance is concluded between the two monarchs, reaffirming one that had existed in the reign of Suppiluliumas, and this alliance is to hold good in the event of either of the parties' death. Neither is to encroach upon the territory of the other, and each is pledged to render assistance in the case of attack from any other quarter. Provision is made for the extradition of refugees in either direction, but these are not to be treated as criminals on their return. The Egyptian document differs from the Hittite by invoking as witnesses many gods of both countries, and by describing the silver tablets which are to be exchanged; no doubt similar perorations would have been found in the Hittite tablets had these been preserved in their entirety.

It was found politic to cement the friendship between the two great powers of the time in other ways as well, and a lively correspondence sprang up between the two Courts. The Boghazköy fragments include congratulations on the conclusion of the peace

[1] *BAR* iii, §§ 356 ff.; Wreszinski, ii, Pls. 90–91, 107–8. [2] Op. cit. ii, Pl. 58.
[3] *BAR* iii, § 365; *ZÄS* xliv. 36 ff. [4] *JEA* vi. 179 ff. [5] PM ii. 49. 2.

treaty addressed to Khattusilis by Ramessēs's chief wife, Nofretari, by his mother Tuia, and by his son Seṭhikhopshef. At least eighteen letters from Ramessēs himself have survived, though mostly in a poor state of preservation, and a very curious and interesting fact has revealed itself, namely that almost identically worded tablets were sent not only to Khattusilis, but also to Pudukhipa his queen; evidently the Hittite queen played a much more important political role than the Queen of Egypt, influential and prominent though the latter was in all other respects. Much of the letter-writing between the two monarchs turns upon a marriage arranged between Ramessēs and a daughter of Khattusilis. This union actually took place in year 34, when the princess was brought to Egypt and there given the name Maḥornefrurēᶜ or Manefrurēᶜ. The story is told in a great inscription of which copies were exposed to the public view at Karnak, Elephantinē, Abu Simbel, and Amâra, and doubtless in other temples as well.[1] It is difficult to imagine a less complimentary way in which relations with a friendly foreign potentate could be presented. More than half of the hieroglyphic text is devoted to fulsome eulogies of the Pharaoh. When at last the obsequious author embarks upon a narrative of facts, the account which he gives runs roughly as follows: the Syrian princes had been in the habit of sending yearly tribute to the Egyptian king, not even withholding their own children. Only Khatti held aloof, so that Ramessēs found himself compelled to exact compliance by force of arms. Years of dearth ensued for Khatti, until its king decided to make overtures to his victorious enemy.

Thereupon the great king of Khatti wrote seeking to propitiate His Majesty year by year, but never would he listen to them. So then when they saw their land in this state of havoc through the great might of the Lord of the Two Lands, the great king of Khatti spoke to his soldiers and his nobles saying: What means this when our land is desolated, our lord Sutekh being wroth with us, and heaven not giving the water that is our need? It were fitting that we be despoiled of all our possessions, my eldest daughter at the head of them, and that we bring gifts of homage to the good god, so that he may give us peace and we may live.

The carrying out of this decision is described in much detail.

[1] *Ann. Serv.* xxv. 181 ff. Abbreviated version, *Ann. Serv.* xxv. 34 ff.

Stress is laid on the difficulties of the journey and of the many mountains and narrow defiles through which the travellers had to pass. When the Pharaoh, for his part, realized the necessity of sending troops to welcome the princess and her retinue, he feared the rain and the snow usual in Palestine and Syria in time of winter. For this reason he made a great feast for his father the god Sutekh praying him to vouchsafe mild weather, a miracle which actually occurred. The arrival in Egypt was the occasion for great rejoicing, the representatives of both nations eating and drinking together and 'being of one heart like brothers, and there being no rancour of one towards the other'. Happily the Hittite maiden's beauty found favour in Ramessēs's sight, and she was quickly raised to the position of King's Great Wife; if the wonderful statue of her royal husband in the Turin Museum (Pl. XVII) tells the truth they must have been a handsome pair. By a strange chance we have evidence that this alien spouse was sometimes taken to the harem kept by the sovereign at Miwēr, a town at the entrance to the Fayyûm; a scrap of papyrus found by Petrie lists garments and linen belonging to her wardrobe.[1]

Though this foreign alliance was by no means, as we have seen, unique in Egyptian history and may indeed even have been repeated later in the same reign,[2] yet it was long remembered, doubtless on account of the outstanding importance of the contracting parties. A fine stela in the Louvre which was formerly held to narrate a kind of sequel is now recognized as a later fiction intended to enhance the prestige of the Theban god Chons.[3] It tells how the younger sister of Ramessēs II's Hittite queen—here, however, described as the daughter of the king of a remote country called Bakhtan—was possessed by an evil spirit, and how a messenger was dispatched to Egypt to seek medical help. The skilled physician Dḥutemḥab having failed to effect a cure, an image of Chons himself was sent and quickly exorcised the evil spirit. Whether this unhistoric narrative was the product of Ptolemaic times or earlier, its substance is truly Egyptian in character, and recalls the sending of the Ishtar of Nineveh to heal Amenōphis III.

So proud was Ramessēs II of his extensive progeny that it would

[1] *RAD* 23, 23*a*. [2] *BAR* iii, §§ 427–8. [3] Lefebvre, *Romans*, pp. 221 ff.

BLACK GRANITE STATUE OF RAMESSĒS II
Probably from Karnak. Turin Museum

PLATE XVIII

THE HYPOSTYLE HALL AT KARNAK

be wrong to omit all reference to the long enumerations of his sons and daughters to be read on the walls of his temples.[1] At Wâdy es-Sebûaʿ in Lower Nubia over a hundred princes and princesses were named, but the many lacunae make it impossible to compute the exact figure. From several temples it is clear that the eldest son was Amenḥiwenamef, but his mother is unknown and he evidently died early. It will be recalled that Sethōs I provided his youthful co-regent with a large number of concubines, and these will have been responsible for the vast majority of children about whom nothing more is heard. The most highly honoured were naturally those born to Ramessēs II by his successive King's Great Wives. Queen Isinofre was the mother of four who are depicted together with her and her husband.[2] Foremost among them is Raʿmesse, at a given moment the crown prince, but it was his younger brother Merenptaḥ, the thirteenth in the Ramesseum list, who survived to succeed his father. Another son who perhaps never had pretensions to the throne was Khaʿemwīse, the high-priest (*setem*) of Ptaḥ at Memphis; he gained great celebrity as a learned man and magician, and was remembered right down to Graeco-Roman times;[3] it was doubtless in that capacity that he was charged with the organization of his father's earliest Sed-festivals from the first in year 30 down to the fifth in year 42; Ramessēs II lived to celebrate twelve or even thirteen in all. A daughter of Isinofre, who bore the Syrian name of Bintʿanat,[4] is of interest for a special reason: she received the title King's Great Wife during her father's lifetime; we cannot overlook the likelihood that she served at least temporarily as his consort. Even more frequent are the references to Queen Nofretari-mery-en-Mūt,[5] the Naptera of an already mentioned Boghazköy letter; she is familiar to Egyptologists as the owner of a magnificently painted tomb in the Valley of the Queens on the west of Thebes,[6] this henceforth the burial-place of many females of the Ramesside royal family. Ramessēs II himself had a tomb at Bîbân el-Molûk no doubt once as large and fine as that of Sethōs I, but now closed owing to its dangerous condition. The great king's mummy suffered a fate

[1] Petrie, *History*, iii[3]. 35 ff., 82 ff.

[2] Lep. *Denkm.* iii. 174*e*, 175*h*.

[3] Gauthier, *LR* iii. 84 ff.; see too below, p. 279.

[4] Op. cit. iii. 102–3.

[5] Op. cit. iii. 75–7.

[6] PM i. 45, No. 66.

similar to that of so many of his predecessors, finally finding its way to the *cache* at Dêr el-Baḥri;[1] until moved to the mausoleum at Cairo his corpse could still be seen as that of a shrivelled-up old man with a long narrow face, massive jaw, and prominent nose, conspicuous also for his admirably well-preserved teeth.

That for Egypt herself the reign of Ramessēs II was a period of great prosperity cannot be doubted. Monuments of the period, dated and undated, are very numerous,[2] but are mostly memorials of individual persons throwing little or no light upon the state of the country as a whole. The value of recent attempts to construct a coherent picture out of the titles borne by such individuals need not be denied, but the results thus obtained are too speculative to receive more than a passing glance in the present book. To mention here only the highest functionaries of the administrative and the priestly orders respectively, it may be noted that the vizierate was usually in the hands of a single dignitary, though at the outset there was one vizier for Upper Egypt and another for Lower Egypt;[3] the High-priest of Amen-Rēʿ at Thebes certainly retained his pre-eminence in his own sphere, but his office was not yet hereditary, and we have no means of knowing to what extent the wealth of the god's estate had increased or diminished since the religious revolution[4]—two of these pontiffs[5] are interested only to tell us by what steps and at what ages they climbed to the top of the sacerdotal ladder. An exception to such jejune information is found on the walls of a tomb at Saḳḳâra belonging to a no more exalted personage than a scribe of the treasury in the Memphite temple of Ptaḥ.[6] Here are set forth at length the proceedings in a trial in which the matter at stake was the ownership of a tract of land in the neighbourhood of Memphis. This estate, the plaintiff Mose maintained, had been given by King Amōsis as a reward to his ancestor Neshi, a ship's captain. Much litigation arose in subsequent generations. In the time of Ḥaremḥab the Great Court sitting in Hēliopolis and presided over by the Vizier sent a commissioner to

[1] PM i. 175, No. 17.
[2] Petrie, *History*, iii³. 89 ff.
[3] Von Beckerath, *Tanis*, pp. 59 ff.
[4] Lefebvre, *Grands prêtres*, pp. 157 ff.
[5] Bekenkhons, op. cit., pp. 132 ff.; Roma-Roy, pp. 139 ff.
[6] The name Mose here adopted replaces Mes formerly used, see below, p. 280.

the locality where the property was, whereupon a lady named Wernero was appointed to cultivate the land as trustee for her brothers and her sisters. Objection to this arrangement having been raised by a sister named Takharu, a new division was made whereby the estate, hitherto indivisible, was parcelled out between the six heirs. Against this decision Mose's father Ḥuy appealed together with his mother Wernero, but Ḥuy died at this juncture, and when his widow Nubnofre set about cultivating her husband's inheritance she was forcibly ejected by a man named Khaʿy. As a consequence Nubnofre brought an action against Khaʿy before the same high tribunal, but this action, dated to year 18 of Ramessēs II, went against her, and it was only later that Mose, by this time presumably grown to manhood, appealed for the verdict to be reversed. His deposition was immediately followed by that of the defendant Khaʿy, and it is from their combined statements that we learn what had happened. When the Vizier came to examine the title-deeds he could not fail to perceive that there had been forgery on one side or the other. Nubnofre then proposed that a commissioner should be sent with Khaʿy to consult the official records of Pharaoh's treasury and granary at the northern capital of Pi-Raʿmesse. To her dismay her husband's name was not found in the registers which the two, acting in collusion, brought back with them, and accordingly the Vizier, after further inquiry, gave judgement in favour of Khaʿy, who received in consequence 13 arouras of land. To Mose, determined to recover his rights, no alternative was now open but to establish with the help of sworn witnesses the facts of his descent from Neshi and of his father's having cultivated the estate year by year and having paid the taxes on it. The testimony afforded by the men and women cited by him, taken together with the written evidence previously used, no longer left any uncertainty as to the rightness of his cause, and though the end of the hieroglyphic inscription is lost we cannot doubt that the Great Court together with the lesser one at Memphis delivered a final verdict re-establishing Mose in his inheritance. The colourful and vivid story here told, though dealing with only a small estate and relatively unimportant litigants, is so illuminating that it cannot be studied with too great care. One point of importance that emerges is the equality of men and women as regards both proprietorship and competence in the law-courts.

The second half of Ramessēs II's reign seems to have been free from major wars. Khattusilis's son and successor Tudhaliyas IV was too much absorbed with his western frontier and with his religious duties to give rein to any aggressive intentions, and indeed the once so powerful Hittite Empire was already moving towards its decline. However, in keeping the peace with Khatti Egypt was merely exchanging one adversary for another still more formidable; it was no longer a question of Egypt's upholding her sovereignty in a distant province, now her own borders were seriously threatened. It is unnecessary to suppose that Sethōs I's conflict with the Tjeḥnu depicted at Karnak was a very big affair, but it foreshadowed the trouble which was to come from that quarter before long. There is written evidence that the north-west corner of the Delta was protected from Libyan invasion by a chain of fortresses extending along the Mediterranean coast;[1] many stelae of the time of Ramessēs II have come to light near El-ʿAlamein and others even still farther to the west.[2] At Es-Sebûaʿ in Lower Nubia an inscription of year 44 tells of Tjemḥu captives employed in the building of the temple there.[3] It was in the fifth year of Merenptaḥ that the danger came to a head, the ringleader being Maraye, son of Did, the king of that tribe of Libu (Libyans) which here makes its first appearance. Among the allies of his own race were the already mentioned Ḳeheḳ and Meshwesh, but he had also summoned to his aid five 'peoples of the sea',[4] forerunners of the great migratory movement about to descend on Egypt and Palestine from north and west. The names of these confederates are of the utmost interest since, like the Dardanians and Luka (Lycians) who supported the Hittites at the battle of Ḳadesh, they introduce us, or seem to introduce us, to racial groups familiar from the early Hellenic world. The Aḳawashꜣ mentioned here but never again hereafter are as a rule confidently equated with the Achaeans of Mycenaean Greece, but the writing does not quite square with that of the much disputed Ahhiyawā of the Hittite tablets, who at all events have an equal

[1] *BAR* iii, §§ 580. 586. [2] PM vii. 368–9. [3] *Bull. soc. fr. d'Ég.*, No. 6 (1951), Pl. 1. [4] *Onom.* i. 196*.

claim. The Luka appear to have played only a minor part, and occur in the Egyptian records only once again in the name of a slave.[1] To identify the Tursha with the Tyrsēnoi often asserted to be the ancestors of the Etruscans is too tempting to be dismissed out of hand, like the Shekresh or Sheklesh who so irresistibly recall the name of the Sikeloi or Sicilians. The supposition that some of the Tursha and the Sheklesh fought on the side of the Egyptians is certainly due to a mistranslation. Unhappily there are no reliefs to illustrate the appearance of these enemies of Merenptaḥ and the only clue to their identity beyond their names is the indication that whereas the Libu were uncircumcised and were therefore made to suffer the dishonour of having the genitals of their slain piled up for presentation to the king, the Sherden, Sheklesh, Aḳawasha and Tursha, being circumcised as the Egyptians themselves had been from time immemorial, received only the lesser disgrace of their hands being cut off and presented instead. However, this indication complicates the problem rather than the reverse. We may perhaps sum up the probabilities regarding these 'peoples of the sea' by saying that since all their names so readily find affinities in the Hellenic world, some at least of the proposed identifications are likely to be correct, though there is no guarantee that the tribes in question were already located in the places where they ultimately settled down.

The details of Merenptaḥ's great victory over the invaders were recounted in a long inscription carved on a wall of the temple of Karnak,[2] but the topmost blocks of the vertical columns of hieroglyphs having disappeared not enough remains to slake our curiosity; nor is the situation remedied by some equally defective narratives from elsewhere.[3] What we do glean, however, is highly interesting. It was no mere foray in quest of plunder that had been attempted, but permanent settlement in a new home. Maraye and his allies had brought their women and children with them, as well as cattle and a wealth of weapons and utensils which were subsequently captured. Yet it was want that had prompted them to this venture; to quote the actual words of the Karnak text:

[1] *Onom.* i. 128*. [2] PM ii. 49 (6); *BAR* iii, §§ 569 ff.
[3] *Ann. Serv.* xxvii. 19 ff.; *ZÄS* xix. 118.

they spend the day roaming the land and fighting to fill their bellies daily; they have come to the land of Egypt to seek food for their mouths.

Such was the nature of the Libyans as it appeared to Merenptaḥ on hearing of the graver attack that now confronted him. That attack must have come from pretty far west, from Cyrenaica or even beyond, since Maraye's first move was to descend upon and occupy the land of Tjeḥnu. It was not long before they had plundered the frontier fortresses, and some of them had even penetrated to the oasis of Farâfra. The Great River or Canōpic branch of the Nile marked, however, the limit of their advance, and the decisive battle, when it came, seems to have been at an unidentified locality named Pi-yer, doubtless well within the Delta. It is plain that Merenptaḥ himself took no part in the struggle; he must have been already an old man when he came to the throne. Still the victory was naturally credited to him, after he had seen in a dream a great image of the god Ptaḥ who handed him a scimitar saying 'Take hold here and put off the faint heart from thee'. Six hours of fighting sufficed to rout the enemy, the wretched Maraye escaping capture by fleeing homeward at dead of night. The total of Libyans killed exceeded 6,000, not counting many hundreds of the allies, and of prisoners taken there seem to have been more than 9,000. These at least are the figures which emerge from the two damaged sources at our disposal, but of course we must make allowance for the usual exaggeration.

A much more lyrical account of Merenptaḥ's triumph can be read on a great granite stela which he usurped from Amenōphis III and caused to be set up in his own funerary temple on the west of Thebes.[1] If this excellently preserved monument adds but little to our knowledge of the physical facts, yet it bears witness to the relief felt in Egypt at the averting of a terrible danger. That relief finds expression in the grateful epithets accorded to the sovereign:

Sun which has lifted the storm-cloud that had been over Egypt, and which has caused To-meri to see the rays of the disk; remover of a mountain of copper from the necks of the well-born and giving breath to the common folk who were stifled; washing free the heart of Ḥikuptaḥ (Memphis) from its enemies.

[1] PM ii. 159. Latest translation *ANET*, pp. 376–8.

Here are some of the taunts flung at the ill-starred Maraye:

the vile chief of the Libu who fled under cover of night alone without a feather on his head, his feet unshod, his wives seized before his very eyes, the meal for his food taken away, and without water in the water-skin to keep him alive; the faces of his brothers are savage to kill him, his captains fighting one against the other, their camps burnt and made into ashes.

In happy contrast is the state of Egypt herself:

Great joy has come about in Egypt, rejoicing is gone forth in the villages of To-meri. They talk of the victories which Merenptaḥ-ḥotpḥimāʿe has gained in Tjeḥnu-land. How lovable is he the victorious ruler, how exalted is the king among the gods, how fortunate is the commanding lord. Pleasant indeed is it when one sits and chats. One can walk freely upon the road without any fear in the hearts of men.

It would be superfluous to translate further a text which continues tirelessly in this strain, but towards the end there comes a passage that is justly celebrated:

The princes are prostrate and cry 'Mercy!' Not one lifts his head among the Nine Bows. Tjeḥnu-land is destroyed, Khatti at peace, Canaan plundered with every ill, Ashkelon is taken and Gezer seized, Yenoʿam made as though it never had been. Israel is desolated and has no seed, Khor[1] is become a widow[2] for To-meri.

The mention of Israel here is unique in Egyptian writing, and could not fail to be disturbing to scholars who at the time of the discovery in 1896 mostly believed Merenptaḥ to have been the Pharaoh of the Exodus.[3] The explanations now given are very various. Actually the name does not occur again in non-Biblical sources until after the middle of the ninth century B.C., when Mesha King of Moab is said to have fought with Israel.[4] That Merenptaḥ actually did exert some military activity in Palestine is confirmed by the epithet 'reducer of Gezer' which he receives in an inscription at Amada.[5] Otherwise conditions on the north-eastern front appear to have remained peaceful and normal. Extracts from the journal

[1] Palestine and Syria, see above, p. 226, n. 1.
[2] A play on the name Khor.
[3] See above, p. 156, n. 1.
[4] *ANET*, p. 320, confirming 2 Kings iii. 4 ff.
[5] *Rec. trav.* xviii. 159.

of a border official dated in Merenptaḥ's year 3 enumerate the successive sendings of dispatches to different garrison-commanders and other persons, among them the prince of Tyre.[1] This interesting excerpt is found in one of those collections of miscellaneous writings of which a number have survived; they were apparently intended for school use and though hardly to be described as historical documents they throw light on many sides of Egyptian life of the period. Among other passages from a similar source which have been quoted rightly or wrongly as illustrating the sojourn of the Israelites in Egypt is the report of another official who writes as follows:[2]

We have finished allowing the Shōsu (Beduin) tribes of Edom to pass the fortress of Merenptaḥ which is in Tjeku to the pools of Pi-Tūm of Merenptaḥ which are in Tjeku, in order to keep them alive and to keep alive their flocks by the goodness of Pharaoh, the beautiful sun of every land, in Year 8, third epagomenal day, the birthday of Sēth.

The Pi-Tūm here named is obviously the Pithom of Exod. i. 11 and, whatever the exact site, it certainly lay within the Wâdy Ṭumîlât, the fertile depression which runs through the desert separating the Delta from Ismâʿîlîya. Whether Tjeku is the Succoth of the Exodus story is more doubtful, though often accepted so to be.

A literary papyrus probably written in Merenptaḥ's reign contains a composition which is as instructive as it is amusing.[3] This professes to be the reply by a scribe Ḥori to a letter just received from his friend the scribe Amenemope. After elaborate greetings and compliments Ḥori expresses his disappointment and then launches out on a long ironic demonstration of Amenemope's incompetence. The helpers whom he has called to his aid have not improved matters. Various situations are adduced in proof of the criticisms: Amenemope has failed in his tasks of supplying the troops with rations, of building a ramp, of erecting a colossal statue, and so forth. But it is his ignorance of northern Syria which comes in for the severest condemnation. Many well-known places

[1] Caminos, *Misc.*, pp. 108 ff. [2] Op. cit., p. 293.
[3] Latest translation, *ANET*, pp. 475–9.

are named which this pretender to the rank of *maher* has never visited or where some trouble or other has befallen him; he has never reached Beisân or crossed the Jordan; he knows nothing about Byblos or Tyre; his horse has run away and his chariot has been smashed. Even towns as near at hand as Raphia and Gaza are unknown to him. Needless to say, one of the chief reasons for writing this strange work has been to give the author the chance of airing his own knowledge; but historically the text is enlightening inasmuch as there must have been a class of able scribes who had an intimate acquaintance with Palestine and Syria and were accustomed to travel there without mishap.

It is under Ramessēs II at latest that an entirely different source of cultural and historical information begins to assume outstanding importance. Whether or no the Pharaoh now lived at and governed from one or other of the Delta capitals he always aspired to burial in the ancestral necropolis of Thebes, and from the very beginning of his reign a large body of skilled workmen was continuously engaged upon the excavation and decoration of his tomb in the Bîbân el-Molûk. These men and their families formed a special community dwelling in the village of Dêr el-Medîna high up in the desert above the great funerary temple of Amenōphis III and every aspect of their lives and interests is revealed in the writings found either here or in the actual place of their daily work. Papyrus being comparatively rare, expensive and perishable, most of what has survived is inscribed on the scraps of limestone and the potsherds which lay on the ground only asking to be used and which Egyptologists know under the somewhat inappropriate name of 'ostraca'; thousands have been published and thousands more await publication in our museums or in private hands. Besides literary, religious, and magical fragments there are records of barter, payment of wages in corn or copper, hire of donkeys for agricultural purposes, lawsuits, attendances at and absences from work, visits of high officials, model and actual letters, in fact memoranda of every kind. No synthesis can be here attempted, but it was necessary to mention a mass of material through which a restricted, but not insignificant, picture of Ramesside life can be brought before the eyes of the modern reader.

Merenptaḥ was an old man when he died, bald and corpulent. His end may have been thought to be approaching as early as his eighth year, when the preparations for his funeral were being actively pursued; nevertheless, he lingered on for two years more.[1] No doubt he was buried in the granite sarcophagus of which the beautiful lid is still to be seen in his tomb in the Bîbân el-Molûk, but at some later period his mummy was moved to the tomb of Amenōphis II, where Loret discovered it in 1898. With his death we enter upon a series of rather short reigns, the sequence of which has been much debated. The problem is of the kind at once the joy and the torment of Egyptologists. Prominent here again is the question of superimposed cartouches, another royal name being substituted for one that has been chiselled out. Arguments based upon this procedure are, as has been already said, highly precarious; apart from the difficulty of deciding which name lies uppermost, there always remains the possibility that this belonged to the earlier of the two kings, having been restored as the result of some loyalty or animosity which cannot now be fathomed. Here the reader must rest content with a bare statement of what seems the most probable course of events. There is little doubt but that Merenptaḥ was followed by his son Sety-merenptaḥ, mostly known as Sethōs II. Memoranda on ostraca mention both the date of his accession and that of his death, this latter occurring in his sixth year. In the meantime a certain Neferḥōtep, one of the two chief workmen of the necropolis, had been replaced by another named Pnēb, against whom many crimes were alleged by Neferḥōtep's brother Amennakhte in a violently worded indictment preserved in a papyrus in the British Museum.[2] If Amennakhte can be trusted, Pnēb had stolen stone for the embellishment of his own tomb from that of Sethōs II still in course of completion, besides purloining or damaging other property belonging to that monarch. Also he had tried to kill Neferḥōtep in spite of having been educated by him, and after the chief workman had been killed by 'the enemy' had bribed the vizier Praʿemḥab in order to usurp his place. Whatever the truth of these accusations, it is clear that Thebes was going through very troubled times. There are references elsewhere to a 'war' that

[1] Caminos, *Misc.*, p. 303.

[2] P. Salt 124, see *JEA* xv. 243 ff.

had occurred during these years, but it is obscure to what this word alludes, perhaps to no more than internal disturbances and discontent. Neferḥōtep had complained of the attacks upon himself to the vizier Amenmose, presumably a predecessor of Praʿemḥab, whereupon Amenmose had punished Pnēb. This trouble-maker had then brought a plaint before 'Mose', who had deposed the vizier from his office. Evidently this 'Mose' must have been a personage of the most exalted station, and it seems inevitable to identify him with an ephemeral king Amenmesse whose brief reign may have fallen either before or within that of Sethōs II. A tomb belonging to Amenmesse exists in the Bîbân el-Molûk,[1] but it is a relatively poor affair in which most of the decorations have been erased, though enough of the inscriptions remains to furnish us with the name of his mother Takhaʿe, possibly a daughter of Ramessēs II. The monuments of Sethōs II are scanty, the most imposing being a small temple in the forecourt at Karnak, and nothing more is known about the events of his reign. In his well-decorated tomb his cartouches have been erased and later replaced, the erasure being perhaps the handiwork of Amenmesse. Elliot Smith, describing his mummy found in the tomb of Amenōphis II, speaks of him as a young or middle-aged man.

His immediate successor was a son who was at first given the name Raʿmesse-Siptaḥ, but who for some mysterious reason changed it to Merenptaḥ-Siptaḥ before the third year of his reign.[2] He is closely associated in most of his few inscriptions with an important functionary named Bay, who boasts of having been 'the great chancellor of the entire land'. There is good reason for thinking that Bay was a Syrian by birth, possibly one of those court officials who in this age frequently rose to power by the royal favour. In two graffiti he receives the highly significant epithet 'who established the king upon the seat of his father' and it is almost certain that he was in fact the actual 'king-maker'. The epithet in question implies that Siptaḥ was a son of Sethōs II, but it is unknown who was his mother. He was probably a mere boy at the time of his accession since he was still young when he died after a reign of perhaps not more than six years. There now comes upon

[1] PM i. 12, No. 10.

[2] See *JEA* xliv. 12 ff. for all the following.

the scene a remarkable woman of the name of Twosre. Jewellery discovered by Theodore Davis in a nameless *cache* of the Bîbân el-Molûk shows her to have been Sethōs II's principal wife; a silver bracelet depicts her standing before her husband and pouring wine into his outstretched goblet. It is a strange and unprecedented thing that three contemporaries should all have possessed tombs in the Valley of the Tombs of the Kings. The tomb of Bay is small and unadorned, but still its location testifies to the power which he must have exercised. Siptaḥ's tomb, in which his mummy doubtless lay until shifted to that of Amenōphis II, is much more imposing, but the cartouches on its walls have been cut out and later replaced, like those in the tomb of Sethōs II. Twosre's tomb is even more intriguing. Here she bears the title King's Great Wife by virtue of her marriage to Sethōs II, but an isolated scene shows her standing behind Siptaḥ who is offering to the earth-god; Siptaḥ's name has been destroyed and that of Sethōs II substituted for it. Since there are excellent reasons for thinking that Sethōs was the earlier of the two kings, this replacement must have been due to Twosre's later preference to be depicted with the king who had been her actual husband. Subsequently Setnakhte, the founder of Dyn. XX, took possession and possibly destroyed Twosre's mummy, after someone had removed to a place of safety the jewellery above mentioned. The sole hypothesis which seems to account for these complicated facts supposes that when Bay forced the youthful Siptaḥ onto the throne, Twosre was compelled to accept the situation, but still retained sufficient power to insist on having her own tomb in the Valley, an honour previously accorded to only one other royalty of female sex, namely Ḥashepsowe, Tuthmōsis III's aunt. Like Ḥashepsowe, Twosre ultimately assumed the titles of a Pharaoh and possibly reigned alone for a few years. Siptaḥ had caused a small funerary temple to be built for himself to the north of the Ramesseum at Thebes,[1] and here the name of Bay figures with his own on the foundation deposits, a startling fact that goes far towards demonstrating the interpretation here given. Of Twosre only one stray intrusive scarab was found there. Twosre's separate funerary sanctuary to the south of the Ramesseum[2] may have been

[1] PM ii. 149. [2] Op. cit. ii. 159.

begun at the same time or else may be somewhat later. Here she assumed a second cartouche which is also found combined with the first on a plaque said to come from Ḳantîr in the Delta, and there are a few more traces of her reign in the north, and even at the turquoise mines of Sinai.[1] Manetho ends Dyn. XIX with a king Thuōris said to have reigned seven years, and there can be but little doubt that the distorted name and erroneous sex recall the existence of the third woman in Egyptian history who had possessed ability enough to wrest to herself the Double Crown, but whose power had been insufficient to secure the perpetuation of her dynastic line.

SELECT BIBLIOGRAPHY

Ramessēs II's dedicatory inscription in Sethōs I's temple at Abydos: H. Gauthier, *La Grande Inscription dédicatoire d'Abydos*, Cairo, 1912; Id., translation, *ZÄS* xlviii. 52 ff.

The Hittite war of Ramessēs II: J. H. Breasted, *The Battle of Kadesh*, Chicago, 1903, fundamental; the texts, Ch. Kuentz, *La Bataille de Qadech*, Cairo, 1928; A. H. Gardiner, *The Ḳadesh Inscriptions of Ramesses II*, Oxford, 1960; the cuneiform tablets translated by A. Götze, *OLZ* xxxii (1929), 832–8; also *ANET*, p. 319; see too E. Edel in *Zeitschrift für Assyriologie*, xlix. 195 ff.

The treaty of year 21: the most recent translations, Egyptian by J. A. Wilson, in *ANET*, pp. 199–201, Hittite by A. Götze, ibid., pp. 201–3.

The letters of Ramessēs and members of his family to Khattusilis and his queen: E. Edel in *Zeitschrift für Indogermanistik und allgemeine Sprachwissenschaft*, lx. 72 ff. Letters concerning the Hittite marriage, E. Edel in *Jahrbuch für kleinasiatische Forschung*, ii. 262 ff.; and again in *Geschichte und Altes Testament*, pp. 29 ff.

The prince Khaʿemwīse: F. Ll. Griffith, *Stories of the High Priests of Memphis*, Oxford, 1900, pp. 2–5; *Studies presented to F. Ll. Griffith*, London, 1932, pp. 128–34.

The Sed-festivals of Ramessēs II: R. Mond and O. H. Myers, *Temples of Armant*, London, 1940, pp. 143–4.

The High-priests of Amūn: G. Lefebvre, *Histoire des grands prêtres d'Amon de Karnak*, Paris, 1929.

[1] *JEA* xliv. 20.

The lawsuit of Mose: A. H. Gardiner, *The Inscription of Mes*, in *Untersuchungen zur Geschichte und Altertumskunde Ägyptens*, ed. K. Sethe, vol. iv. Leipzig, 1905; see too R. Anthes in *Mitt. Kairo*, ix. 93 ff.

The Libyans: W. Hölscher, *Libyer und Ägypter*, Glückstadt, 1937.

The Peoples of the Sea: G. A. Wainwright in *JEA* xxv. 148–53.

Theban ostraca: main publications by J. Černý, G. Posener, and A. H. Gardiner; brief general account by J. Černý in *Chronique d'Égypte*, No. 12 (1931), 212 ff.

The Karnak temple of Sethōs II: H. Chevrier, *Le Temple reposoir de Séti II*, Cairo, 1940.

The end of Dyn. XIX: A. H. Gardiner, *Only one King Siptaḥ and Twosre not his Wife*, in *JEA* xliv. 14 ff.

XI

THE RAMESSIDE PERIOD: (2) THE TWENTIETH DYNASTY

MANETHO has no more to tell us about Dyn. XX than that it consisted of twelve kings of Diospolis (Thebes), who reigned according to Africanus for 135 years and for 178 according to Eusebius. Nevertheless it was a period of stirring events and at least one mighty Pharaoh. Also a number of lengthy and highly informative writings have survived, the discussion of which will demand considerable space. Meanwhile the enemies of Egypt were drawing ever closer, foreshadowing the humiliations which little over a century later were to reduce her prestige almost to vanishing point. At the outset, however, it seemed that an epoch of exceptional splendour was about to dawn, and a retrospect contrasting this with a largely imaginary period of previous gloom is worth quoting if only to exemplify a standing convention of Pharaonic historical writing.[1]

The land of Egypt was cast adrift, every man a law unto himself, and they had no commander for many years previously until there were other times when the land of Egypt consisted of princes and heads of villages, one man slaying his fellow both high and low. Then another time came after it consisting of empty years, when Arsu a Syrian was with them as prince, and he made the entire land contributory under his sway.

The text goes on to speak of the bloodshed which ensued, and the neglect with which the gods were treated until they restored peace by appointing Setnakhte as king. In this strange passage the glorious achievements of Dyns. XVIII and XIX are ignored and we are transported back to the conditions of pre-Hyksōs times. The sole specific fact recorded is the emergence of a Syrian condottiere who gained mastery over the entire land; the identity of this

[1] P. Harris 75. 2–5, translated *ANET*, p. 260.

foreigner has been much debated, the most interesting suggestion, due to Černý, being that we have here a veiled reference to the 'king-maker' Bay mentioned at the end of the last chapter. But the writer's only purpose here was to extol the new sovereign of Egypt. Little is known about Setnakhte except that he was the father of the great king Ramessēs III and the husband of the latter's mother Tiye-merenēse. There are reasons for thinking that the interval between the end of Dyn. XIX and his accession was quite short, perhaps not more than ten years. He may have reigned less than two years. He usurped the tomb of Twosre and was doubtless buried in it; his coffin was found in the tomb of Amenōphis II,[1] but his mummy has not been discovered.

Whatever the author of the retrospect may have pretended, Ramessēs III was himself very conscious of the greatness of the most celebrated of his predecessors in Dyn. XIX, for he modelled both his Prenomen and his Nomen upon those of Ramessēs II. His early years were fraught with terrible dangers. In the south, it is true, he had little to fear. Nubia had grown into an Egyptian province, and the scenes which have survived of a battle in this direction seem likely to be mere convention borrowed from earlier representations.[2] For the very real and dangerous conflicts which Ramessēs III had to face our knowledge is mainly derived from the inscriptions and reliefs on the walls of his great temple of Medînet Habu, the best preserved and most interesting of all the funerary sanctuaries on the western side of Thebes. This splendid monument, with its gigantic pylons and noble columnar courts, lay within inner and outer enclosures containing, besides the central shrine itself, a whole township of dwellings for the priests and their dependants, as well as a garden and a lake. The outer girdle wall of crude brick, approached by a canal branching off from the Nile, had a height of 59 feet and a thickness of 25 feet, the length from front to back exceeding 300 yards. The centre of the eastern side exhibited a unique feature in a lofty gatehouse built to resemble one of those Syrian fortresses which the Egyptian armies had met with so often in their Asiatic campaigns, but here the purpose was not military, the upper stories serving as a resort where the Pharaoh could dis-

[1] PM i. 29, No. 35.

[2] Säve-Söderbergh, pp. 173 ff.

port himself with the ladies of his harem. The palace proper abutted onto the south side of the temple's first court, with a balcony where the king might appear in order to distribute rewards to such nobles as he wished to honour. The walls of no other temple show scenes of greater interest. Religious subjects of course predominate, but pictures of warfare are also numerous and supplement the written legends in the most valuable fashion, the more so since the latter have a turgidity in which narrative passages almost disappear amid the plethora of adulatory rhetoric.

The long inscription of year 5 first tells of a campaign against the western neighbours of Egypt known generically as the Tjeḥnu.[1] These people were incensed at having had imposed upon them a new ruler of the Pharaoh's choice; the royal wisdom so highly praised in the hieroglyphs had evidently not been appreciated. Colour on some of the sculptured reliefs shows prisoners with red beards, side-locks, and long richly ornamented cloaks. Three tribes are here mentioned, the Libu or Libyans who as we have seen are commemorated in the name still applied to the whole north-eastern part of Africa outside Egypt, the Sped of whom nothing more is known, and the Meshwesh, first mentioned under Amenōphis III,[2] who henceforth play an ever increasingly important part in our historical records; they are commonly thought of as the equivalent of the Maxyĕs located by Herodotus (iv. 191) in the neighbourhood of Tunis.[3] The next threat to Egypt was far more formidable, being nothing less than an attempt on the part of a confederacy of sea-faring northerners to establish themselves in the rich pasture-lands not only of the Delta, but also of Syria and of Palestine. Permanent settlement was their aim, and they brought their women and children with them in wheeled carts drawn by humped oxen.[4] We have seen that an attack of this kind, in which the sea-peoples and the Libyans had been in alliance, had been repelled by Merenptaḥ. Now the Mediterranean war, though almost simultaneous with the Libyan wars of years 5 and 11, is described as a separate event, but was none the less dangerous on that account. The main aggression, dated to year 8, swooped down by land and sea simul-

[1] *Hist. Rec.*, pp. 19 ff.

[2] *JNES* x. 91.

[3] *Onom.* i. 119* ff.

[4] *Med. Habu* [i], Pl. 34.

taneously. The Sherden were once again among the hostile forces, and once again warriors of this race are shown fighting both with and against the Egyptians. The long-since moribund Hittite Empire was swept away, and with it the Anatolian allies who had taken part in the battle of Ḳadesh. Of the enemies who had confronted Merenptaḥ perhaps only the Sheklesh still played a part; a new tribe named the Weshesh are a mere name.[1] Of deep interest alike to Greek scholars and to Orientalists are three new peoples who emerge here for the first time, though it is just possible that the Danu or Danuna, surely the Danaoi of the *Iliad*, may have been mentioned once in the El-ʿAmârna letters.[2] Much more important, however, are the Peleset and the Tjekker, since the incursion of these tribes into Palestine was to some extent successful and permanent. A narrative dating from about a century later describes the Tjekker[3] as sea-pirates occupying the port of Dōr, but nothing more is known of them or of the name they bore. The Peleset,[4] on the other hand, are the Philistines who were later alternately conquerors of and conquered by the Israelites, who gave their name to Palestine and whom our modern parlance still remembers in an unfairly depreciatory way; there was a tradition that they came from Caphtor or Crete, but this may have been only a stage in their migratory wanderings; in the Medînet Habu reliefs both they and the Tjekker have feathered head-dresses and round shields.

The rebuff inflicted upon these aggressive peoples is splendidly depicted in the reliefs, the naval battle in particular being unique among Egyptian representations. The verbal descriptions are sandwiched into a boastful speech addressed by Ramessēs III to his sons and his courtiers; the following extracts omit sentences from which nothing historical is to be learned.[5]

The foreign countries made a plot in their islands. Dislodged and scattered by battle were the lands all at one time, and no land could stand before their arms, beginning with Khatti, Ḳode, Carchemish, Arzawa, and Alasiya. . . . A camp was set up in one place in Amor, and they desolated its people and its land as though they had never come into being. They came, the flame prepared before them, onwards to

[1] *JEA* xxv. 148 ff.
[2] *Onom.* i. 124* ff.; but see Gurney, pp. 42–43.
[3] *Onom.* i. 199* f.
[4] Op. cit. i. 200* ff.
[5] *Hist. Rec.*, pp. 53 ff.

Egypt. Their confederacy consisted of Peleset, Tjekker, Sheklesh, Danu, and Weshesh, united lands, and they laid their hands upon the lands to the entire circuit of the earth, their hearts bent and trustful 'Our plan is accomplished!' But the heart of this god, the lord of the gods, was prepared and ready to ensnare them like birds. . . . I established my boundary in Djahi,[1] prepared in front of them, the local princes, garrison-commanders, and Maryannu.[2] I caused to be prepared the river-mouth like a strong wall with warships, galleys and skiffs. They were completely equipped both fore and aft with brave fighters carrying their weapons and infantry of all the pick of Egypt, being like roaring lions upon the mountains; chariotry with able warriors and all goodly officers whose hands were competent. Their horses quivered in all their limbs, prepared to crush the foreign countries under their hoofs.

Ramessēs then compares himself to Mont, the god of war, and declares himself confident of his ability to rescue his army.

As for those who reached my boundary, their seed is not. Their hearts and their souls are finished unto all eternity. Those who came forward together upon the sea, the full flame was in front of them at the river-mouths, and a stockade of lances surrounded them on the shore.

For the details of the naval defeat we turn rather to the reliefs than to the verbal descriptions, although in the latter the outcome was described in the graphic words[3]

a net was prepared for them to ensnare them, those who entered into the river-mouths being confined and fallen within it, pinioned in their places, butchered and their corpses hacked up.

The artist has managed to combine into a single picture[4] the various phases of the engagement. First we see Egyptian soldiers attacking unperturbedly from the deck of their ship; opposite them in a vessel held fast with grappling irons the enemy is in the utmost confusion, two of them falling into the water, while one looks towards the shore in the hope of mercy from the Pharaoh. Another of their vessels, however, displays them met with a shower of arrows from the land. The Egyptian fleet now turns homeward, taking with it numerous captives helpless and bound; one of them

[1] Palestine and Syria, see *Onom.* i. 145*.

[2] See above, pp. 202–3.

[3] *Hist. Rec.*, p. 42.

[4] Nelson in *JNES* ii. 40 ff. Part here in Fig. 11.

Fig. 11. The Battle against the Peoples of the Sea (part)

seeking to escape is caught by a soldier on the bank. On the way upstream a capsized vessel is encountered, with its entire crew flung into the water. The defeat of the invaders is complete; nine separate ships have sufficed to tell the tale, and there remain to be recounted only the presentation of the prisoners to Amen-Rēʿ and the other details of the triumph.

The external troubles of Egypt were not yet at an end. In year 11 the Libyan peril flared up afresh. On this occasion the enemy is specifically stated to have been the Meshwesh. A circumstantial account[1] of Ramessēs's dealings with these people is given in the closing section of the great papyrus from which the retrospect at the beginning of this chapter was quoted and concerning which much will be said later.

The Libu and Meshwesh were settled in Egypt and had seized the towns of the Western Tract from Ḥikuptaḥ (Memphis) to Ḳeroben,[2] and had reached the Great River[3] on its every side. They it was who had desolated the towns of Xois[4] for many years when they were in Egypt. Behold, I destroyed them, slain at one stroke. I laid low the Meshwesh, Libu, Asbat, Ḳaiḳash, Shaytep, Hasa, and Baḳan, overthrown in their blood and made into heaps. I made them turn back from trampling upon the boundary of Egypt. I took of those whom my sword spared many captives, pinioned like birds before my horses, their women and their children in tens of thousands, and their cattle in number like hundreds of thousands. I settled their leaders in strongholds called by my name. I gave to them troop-commanders and chiefs of tribes, branded and made into slaves stamped with my name, their women and their children treated likewise. I brought their cattle to the House of Amūn, made for him into everlasting herds.

Two great inscriptions at Medînet Habu, both dated in year 11,[5] deal exclusively with the same struggle, but their flowery language, in which many foreign and otherwise unknown words occur, conveys far less information than the passage above quoted. There is only one addition; we learn that Mesher, the Chief of the Meshwesh, was taken prisoner, and that his father Keper appealed for

[1] *BAR* iv, § 405. [2] Thought to be near Abukîr.
[3] The Canopic, most westerly, branch of the Nile.
[4] The modern Sakhâ on the Canopic branch. [5] *Hist. Rec.*, pp. 74 ff., 87 ff.

mercy in vain; this incident is also depicted in the striking scene[1] where are enumerated the hands and phalli of the slain, the captives, the arms taken as booty, and the cattle added to the herds of the Theban god and those otherwise disposed of. The numbers given, though great, are by no means incredible. Another picture[2] shows the Egyptians fighting from two fortresses, a clear indication that they had been on the defensive.

At Medînet Habu there are several scenes of campaigns in Asia which still require consideration. On one wall Ramessēs III is seen attacking two Hittite towns, one of them labelled 'The town of Arzawa';[3] in another scene the town of Tunip is being stormed,[4] and in a third a town of Amor is on the point of surrendering.[5] All these pictures are clearly anachronisms and must have been copied from originals of the reign of Ramessēs II; there is ample evidence that the designers of Medînet Habu borrowed greatly from the neighbouring Ramesseum. Confirmation is given in the papyrus cited above; this has no mention of a Syrian campaign, still less of one against the Hittites. All that is said is that Ramessēs III 'destroyed the Seirites in the tribes of the Shōsu';[6] the Shōsu have been already mentioned as the Beduins of the desert bordering the south of Palestine, and 'the mountain of Seʿīr' named on an obelisk of Ramessēs II[7] is the Edomite mountain referred to in several passages of the Old Testament. It looks as though the defeat of these relatively unimportant tent-dwellers was the utmost which Ramessēs III could achieve after his struggle with the Mediterranean hordes, and this allusion closes for more than two centuries the story of Egypt's strivings to achieve an Asiatic empire.

Although Ramessēs III reigned for full thirty-one years[8] and celebrated a Sed-festival perhaps at the beginning of his thirtieth, there are signs of various internal troubles, particularly towards the end of his life. At one moment the monthly rations due to the workmen engaged on the royal tomb were sadly in arrears, and this led to strikes ended only by the intervention of the vizier To, who was however unable to supply more than half what was actually re-

[1] *Med. Habu* [ii], Pl. 75.
[2] Op. cit. [ii], Pl. 70.
[3] Op. cit. [ii], Pl. 87.
[4] Op. cit. [ii], Pl. 88.
[5] Op. cit. [ii], Pl. 94.
[6] *BAR* iv, § 404.
[7] *Kêmi*, v, Pl. 3.
[8] *BAR* iv, § 182.

quired.[1] Far more serious was a conspiracy which threatened the life of the monarch himself.[2] From early in the reign there had been indications that trouble was likely to arise over the succession. To judge from the latest date recorded at Medînet Habu, that great temple had been completed by year 12, and it is a curious fact that though, as in the Ramesseum, many of the king's sons were there depicted, as well as the queen in a few instances, no names were ever filled in, though space was left for them. And yet it is certain that the son who actually succeeded as Ramessēs IV was already alive, since his mummy, discovered in the tomb of Amenōphis II, was that of a man 'at least fifty years of age and probably more'. Without speculating on this and much further evidence of the kind which complicates the history of all the next reigns, we turn now to the graphic story related in several papyri of which the most important is preserved in the Turin Museum. This magnificent manuscript, written in large hieratic majuscules befitting a state document of the highest importance, suggests that its original home may have been the temple-library at Medînet Habu. Omitting for the moment the long but fragmentary introduction which precedes the main narrative, we now quote the first entry:

The great enemy Paibekkamen who had been major-domo. He was brought on account of his having attached himself to Tiye and the women of the harem. He made common cause with them and proceeded to carry their words outside to their mothers and their brothers and sisters who were there, saying 'Collect people and foment hostility' so as to make rebellion against their lord. And they set him in the presence of the great officials of the Place of Examination and they examined his crimes and found that he had committed them. And his crimes took hold of him, and the officials who examined him caused his punishment to cleave to him.

Twenty-nine of the criminals, classified in five categories, are dealt with in similar manner, besides six wives not individually specified. A curious fact is that a number of the men's names have been deliberately disguised, apparently on account of some over-auspicious word that entered into their composition. Thus a certain

[1] *JNES* x. 137 ff.; *RAD*, pp. 49 ff.

[2] *BAR* iv, §§ 416 ff., see too below, p. 314.

butler—very high court-officials were often butlers in Ramesside times—assuredly did not bear the name Mesedsurēʿ here credited to him; *mesed*- means 'hates' and the real name will have been Mersurēʿ 'Rēʿ loves him'. The harem in which the plot was hatched is termed 'the harem in accompanying', presumably one not stationed in a particular place like those of Memphis and of Miwēr in the Fayyûm, but one which accompanied Ramessēs upon his journeyings. Many harem officials were involved, the overseer and deputy-overseer, two scribes, and six inspectors, besides the wives of the door-keepers. More dangerous than most of those arrested was a troop-commander from Cush; he had been suborned by his sister, one of the harem-women, and had their schemes prospered they might have stirred the whole of Nubia inṭo revolt, especially if assisted by the general Paiis. It is characteristic of the age that among both accused and judges several were foreigners: Baʿalmahar was clearly a Semite, Inini is described as a Libyan, and the name of Peluka proclaims him a Lycian. The more prominent among the guilty were allowed to perish by their own hand; others who were left unharmed 'died of their own accord' possibly from starvation. Cutting off of nose and ears was the fate of four officials who in spite of precise instructions given to them had caroused with women of the harem and with Paiis. Only one man, a standard-bearer, got off with nothing worse than a severe reprimand; this was a person who together with two of the four just mentioned, had found a place among the judges when first appointed. It is strange that so little should be learnt about Tiye, the lady around whom the entire plot centred; also her son Pentawēre, possibly the boy whom the conspirators were planning to place upon the throne, is mentioned only very casually as one of those who 'died of their own accord'.

Further light is thrown upon the conspirators' machinations by the other fragmentary papyri dealing with the case.[1] A former overseer of cattle had induced a learned scribe to write magical spells and to make waxen images which were to be smuggled into the harem, but it is expressly said that the ruse was unsuccessful and that the culprits met with the fate that they deserved. It still remains

[1] *BAR* iv, §§ 454–6.

to discuss the nature of these extraordinary documents. A first step in the right direction was taken by Breasted, who noticed that in one place where Ramessēs III is mentioned he receives the epithet 'the great god' reserved for kings already deceased; he concluded that though Ramessēs had ordered the trial he had been severely wounded and had died before the criminals were brought to trial. Unhappily in Breasted's day our knowledge of Late-Egyptian syntax was not sufficiently advanced to enable him to translate the damaged introduction of the Turin papyrus correctly. It is the merit of de Buck[1] to have seen that instead of the king there giving an order in the present tense, the whole text is a narrative of past events fictitiously put into the mouth of the dead monarch. After enumerating the judges whom he had appointed and quoting the words of his instruction to them, he continues as follows:

> And they went and examined them, and they caused to die by their own hands those whom they caused to die, though I know not whom, and they punished the others also, though I know not whom. But I had charged them very strictly saying 'Take good heed and beware lest punishment be inflicted upon anyone crookedly by an official who is not over him'; thus I spoke to them (the judges) again and again. And as for all that has been done, it is they who have done it; let all that they have done fall upon their heads. For I am exempted and protected everlastingly, being among the righteous kings who are in the presence of Amen-Rēʿ, King of the Gods, and in the presence of Osiris, the Ruler of Eternity.

This passage reads like an apologia on Ramessēs III's part for an excessive severity or even some degree of injustice which had been charged against him. The narrative as presented to us was evidently compiled by command of Ramessēs IV, and it will soon be seen how eager the son was to display his deceased father's reign as an epoch of unclouded beneficence. That Ramessēs III himself ordered the trial cannot be reasonably doubted, but the note of self-exculpation here put into his mouth may well have been the invention of his successor. There is no solid ground for supposing that the conspiracy was either wholly or half successful; the mummy of Ramessēs III found in the *cache* at Dêr el-Baḥri[2] is stated by Maspero to

[1] *JEA* xxiii. 152 ff. [2] PM i. 175–6.

have been that of a man about 65 years of age, and no trace of wounds is reported. Nor is there any reason for dating the plot towards the end of the reign; it may have occurred much earlier. No mention of it is found in the great manuscript now to be described.

Papyrus Harris No. 1, in the possession of the British Museum, is the most magnificent of all Egyptian state archives;[1] it is a document 133 feet long by 16½ inches high containing 117 columns of hieratic writing of an amplitude that could only belong to an original of the utmost importance. The somewhat ambiguous information that has survived with regard to its discovery suggests that it, like the conspiracy papyri, once belonged to the records of the great temple of Medînet Habu. The opening page summarizes the benefactions bestowed by Ramessēs III upon the various divinities of the entire land, and here again he is clearly represented as a dead king speaking in his own person. Next, a fine coloured picture represents the king worshipping before Amen-Rēʿ, Mūt, and Chons, the three principal deities of his Theban capital. In a long narrative passage he then describes in rhetorical, self-laudatory fashion all the buildings, temple equipment, lands, ships, and so forth with which he has endowed the city. This is followed by a lengthy statistical section giving precise figures for the donations received from various sources throughout the entire duration of the reign, first the personnel, cattle, vineyards, fields, ships, towns in Egypt and Syria given by the king himself from his first to his thirty-first year, then the amounts obtained by taxation, and lastly other items received in various ways and for other purposes. This part of the book concludes with a prayer in which Ramessēs III asks that as his reward blessings may be bestowed upon his beloved son Ramessēs IV. There follows, written by a different hand, and obviously furnished by the priesthood of Atum in the north, a Hēliopolitan section composed upon exactly the same lines and ending in exactly the same way; to this succeeds a Memphite section addressed to Ptaḥ and to the associated deities of the third great capital city. The remaining local divinities are dealt with comprehensively in a shorter section of special value as showing what towns were par-

[1] Complete translation and analysis *BAR* iv, §§ 151–412.

ticularly honoured by Ramessēs III, but the list names no place farther south than Coptos. Then comes a summary in which are added up, though not without some errors, all the figures previously given, and we see that the estate of Amen-Rēʿ at Karnak was by far the greatest beneficiary. Even if the Pharaoh more frequently resided in Lower Egypt, Thebes remained the spiritual centre of the kingdom, and its wealth was prodigious.

The great roll ended with that comprehensive survey of past and recent events from which several quotations have been given above.[1] Doubtless belonging to the era of peace which followed upon the early wars of the reign were several expeditions which are graphically described: one to Pwēne[2] whence the returning ships brought back with them much myrrh to be presented to the Pharaoh himself at his downstream capital by the children of that distant land's chieftain; quests for copper[3] to some unlocated mines and for turquoise to the famous site of Serâbîṭ el-Khâdim[4] in the Peninsula of Sinai. Ramessēs III had previously boasted of having refrained from taking from the temples one man in every ten to serve in the army, that having been the custom under earlier kings.[5] He would now have us believe that perfect tranquillity prevailed throughout the entire land:[6]

I caused the woman of Egypt to walk freely wheresoever she would unmolested by others upon the road. I caused to sit idle the soldiers and the chariotry in my time, and the Sherden and the Ḳeheḳ in their villages to lie at night full length without any dread.

Some internal disturbances there may indeed have been, apart from the formidable plot above treated at length. There was trouble in Athribis with a vizier who was removed from his office; it may have been on this occasion that, contrary to previous custom, To was granted the vizierate of both halves of the country.[7] The final retrospect was addressed to all the officials and military officers of the land,[8] and concluded by urging them to show loyal service to the new king Ramessēs IV. Perhaps that was the real purpose of this voluminous composition.

[1] pp. 281 ff. [2] *BAR* iv, § 407. [3] Op. cit., § 408. [4] Op. cit., § 409. [5] Op. cit., § 354. [6] Op. cit., § 410. [7] Op. cit., § 361; O. Berlin 10633. [8] *BAR*, §§ 397 ff.

It is only in passing that reference can be made to the buildings erected by Ramessēs III elsewhere, a small temple at Karnak being particularly well preserved. His huge tomb in the Bîbân el-Molûk differs from others of the period by introducing such secular scenes as that of the royal kitchen; the picture of a harper is specially celebrated. This last of the great Pharaohs was followed by eight kings[1] each of whom bore the illustrious name of Ramessēs, now so firmly associated with the thought of Pharaonic grandeur that even when his descendants had long relinquished any pretensions to the throne certain functionaries of high station still prided themselves upon the title 'king's son of Ramessēs'.[2] That Ramessēs IV was a son of Ramessēs III is clear both from the Harris papyrus and from other evidence, but the insistence with which he introduced into Prenomen and Nomen the goddess of Truth whilst protesting that he had banished iniquity arouses the suspicion that his claim was not substantiated without some difficulty. Of his successors at least two appear to have been his brothers. The reigns of all eight kings except Ramessēs IX and Ramessēs XI were short, so that the total for the dynasty works out at less than the figure given by Manetho. The custom of starting upon a tomb in the Bîbân el-Molûk at the beginning of each reign was consistently adhered to, although not quite all these later Ramessides actually found burial in the places to which they aspired, and in three cases the mummies were subsequently removed for safety's sake to the tomb of Amenōphis II.[3] The general trend of subsequent history suggests that the actual residence of these petty rulers was ever increasingly confined to the Delta, as a result of which the importance and wealth of the high-priest of Amen-Rēʿ at Thebes waxed all the more. Monumental undertakings dwindled perceptibly. Asiatic adventures were at an end, and the latest record at Sinai dates from Ramessēs VI. On the other hand the administration of Nubia continued along the old lines, though we hear less about it. In spite of these gradual fallings off, the annals of the twelfth century before our era are no complete blank. A number of highly interesting inscriptions and papyri have survived, but with subjects as disconnected both

[1] See below in the list of kings, p. 446.
[2] See below, p. 314.
[3] Elliot Smith, *RM*, Index; the coffins, PM i. 29, No. 35.

materially and locally as the items in a modern newspaper. Such as they are, it is indispensable here to characterize them.

The reign of Ramessēs IV lasted no more than six years, and in view of its brevity the tale of his building activities is not inconsiderable; where he did not actually erect, at least he commemorated his existence by hieroglyphic dedications. Two great stelae found at Abydos by Mariette proclaim his exceptional piety and devotion to the gods; their wording is unusual, and may reflect royal authorship. A long inscription of year 3 in the Wâdy Ḥammâmât records a quest for the splendid stone of its famous quarry involving more than 8,000 participants. Already in year 1 he had caused the high-priest[1] of Mont to visit the site,[2] and in year 2 had sent other capable officials and scribes to investigate the possibilities. The inscription of year 3, however, acquaints us with an enterprise on a more grandiose scale.[3] The skilled quarrymen and sculptors sent were only a small proportion of the entire number. The 5,000 soldiers were certainly not needed for any combative purpose, but may perhaps be thought of as employed to haul the huge monuments over the rough desert roads. The real problem of this perplexing inscription is to account for the presence so far from the Nile Valley of many of the foremost dignitaries of the land. At their head was the high-priest[1] of Amen-Rēʿ Raʿmessenakhte; for him we have at least the partial excuse that he combined with his sacerdotal and administrative functions that of 'superintendent of works'; he was responsible in fact for the temples and statues with which the Pharaoh endowed the local gods. But how to account for his being accompanied by two butlers of the king, by the overseer of the treasury, and above all by the two chief taxing-masters, all of these important personages being mentioned by their names? Here as so often in our Egyptian records the valuable information for which we have to be thankful is counterbalanced by enigmas that must be left unresolved.

For another important document of this period we have to direct our eyes as far southward as Elephantinē. An ill-written but comparatively well-preserved papyrus in the Turin Museum recalls in

[1] Literally 'first god's servant'; often rendered 'first prophet', see p. 87, n. 1.

[2] PM vii. 333.

[3] *Bull. Inst. fr.* xlviii. 1 ff.

language resembling and no less virulent than the Salt papyrus (p. 276, n. 2) grave accusations against a number of persons,[1] prominent among whom was a lay-priest of the temple of Chnūm charged with many thefts, acts of bribery, and sacrilege, not to mention the inevitable imputations of copulation with married women. Heinous offences against religion were his misappropriation and sale of sacred Mnēvis calves, his joining in the carrying of the god's statue while three of his ten days of purificatory natron-drinking were still to run, and his heaping of gifts upon the vizier's henchmen to make them arrest his priestly accuser while the latter was only half-way through his month of ritual service. Among facts of interest that we here learn were the vizier's power to appoint the local prophets and the intervention of Pharaoh himself to send his chief treasurer to look into the purloining of garments from the temple treasure-house. More serious, because they must have involved the corruptibility of a number of persons, were the losses of corn suffered by the priesthood of Chnūm. Seven hundred sacks per annum were due from estates in the Delta owned by the temple. A ship's captain who had succeeded another deceased in year 28 of Ramessēs III started upon his defalcations in year 1 of Ramessēs IV and in the course of the next nine years down to 'year 3 of Pharaoh', i.e. of Ramessēs V, had stolen a total of more than 5,000 sacks.

The great Wilbour papyrus in the Brooklyn Museum,[2] dated in year 4 of Ramessēs V, is a genuine official document of unique interest. Its main text records in four consecutive batches covering a few days apiece the measurement and assessment of fields extending from near Crocodilōnpolis (Medînet el-Fayyûm) southwards to a little short of the modern town of El-Minya, a distance of some 90 miles. The fields, of which the localization and the acreage are given in every case, are classified under the heads of the different land-owning institutions, these proving to be the great temples of Thebes, Hēliopolis, and Memphis, then after them a number of smaller temples mainly in the vicinity of the plots owned by them, and lastly various corporate bodies too different and too problematic to be mentioned here. The assessments are reckoned in

[1] See below, p. 314. [2] Ibid.

grain and clearly refer to taxes; they are presented in two distinct categories, according as the owning institutions were themselves liable or as the liability rested upon the actual holders or cultivators of the soil. The latter type of paragraph is the more interesting since it names a multitude of different proprietors or tenants, including whole families, men of Sherden race, and sometimes even slaves; in one single paragraph, for example, we find side by side, dependent upon the temple of Sobk-Rēʿ of Anasha and localized near a place named the Mounds of Roma, plots each of ten arouras occupied by the well-known overseer of the treasury, Khaʿemtir, by a certain priest, by a temple-scribe, another scribe, by three separate soldiers, by a lady, and lastly by a standard-bearer. A second text, on the verso of the same roll, deals exclusively with a kind of land known as *khato*-land of Pharaoh; the area of the fields so described appears to have been constantly varied, and we dimly discern in them properties which for some unspecified reason had reverted to the ownership of Pharaoh and had to be disposed of anew by him. Despite the great efforts that have been devoted to the study of this all-important papyrus, the abbreviated style in which it was written and the fact that the scribes were not concerned to offer explanations to posterity have left its main problems a riddle still to be unravelled.[1] To whom were the taxes paid? How can the orderliness here depicted be reconciled with the Pharaonic indigence which, as we have seen, often left the workmen on the royal tomb short of the rations due to them? These and many similar related questions still await their answers, but there is some ground for thinking that the great temple of Karnak, with the high-priest of Amen-Rēʿ at its head, was the principal beneficiary rather than the Pharaoh; it is at least significant that the Chief Taxing-master Usimaʿrēʿnakhte was a son of the then reigning high-priest Raʿmessenakhte. As a valuable addendum to the Wilbour papyrus we may mention a very well-preserved letter dating from the reign of Ramessēs XI some fifty years later; in this letter[2] the mayor of Elephantinē complains to the Chief Taxing-master of his time that taxes had been unjustifiably exacted from him on two holdings for which he disclaimed all responsibility.

[1] Discussions, *JAOS* lxx. 299 ff.; *Bibl. Or.* xvi. 220 f.

[2] *Rev. d'Ég.* vi. 115–24.

The tomb of Ramessēs IV is of special interest because a plan of it, giving the exact dimensions, is preserved on a papyrus in the Turin Museum.[1] The mummy of Ramessēs V, discovered in the tomb of Amenōphis II, reveals the fact that he died of smallpox.[2] He probably reigned little more than four years, the fourth being the highest date known; his own unfinished tomb in the Bîbân el-Molûk[3] was then annexed by Ramessēs VI, who completed its decoration; from the latter king's reign of seven years only insignificant monuments have survived. There is evidence, however, that even if his usual place of residence was in the Delta, he could still command loyalty in Nubia. There the governor still bore the title of King's Son of Cush, and the present holder of the post Siēse is mentioned together with his sovereign at ʿAmâra between the Second and Third Cataracts.[4] For administrative purposes Nubia had long been divided into the two provinces of Wawaĕ or Lower Nubia, and Cush farther south. Under Ramessēs VI the deputy-governor of Wawaĕ was Pennē, who was also mayor of the important town of Anîba.[5] He describes in his tomb a statue of the king which he caused to be made there, and gives a detailed list of the fields set aside for its upkeep; for these services, to which was added the capture of some rebels in the gold-bearing region of Akati, he was rewarded with two silver bowls for unguent, the King's Son of Cush himself, together with the Overseer of the Treasury, visiting Anîba for the presentation.

Meanwhile the office of high-priest of Amen-Rēʿ at Karnak had become hereditary, and after being held by Nesamūn, a son of Raʿmessenakhte, had passed into the powerful hands of Amenḥotpe, another son. At what exact date Amenḥotpe attained this exalted position is not recorded, but in year 10 of Ramessēs IX we find him arrogating for himself an eminence such as no subject of the Pharaoh had ever previously enjoyed. That a great dignitary should figure in the reliefs of a temple was not altogether unprecedented; under Sethōs II the high-priest Roma, also known as Roy, had caused himself to be depicted at Karnak petitioning the god Amen-Rēʿ for long life and power to hand on his office to his

[1] *JEA* iv. 130 ff. [2] Elliot Smith, *RM*, p. 91. [3] PM i. 9–12, No. 9.
[4] *JEA* xxv. 143. [5] PM vii. 76; *BAR* iv, §§ 474 ff.

descendants. But Amenḥotpe went a step further: Egyptian Art had always made a point of proportioning the size of its human representations to the rank and importance of the persons represented, and now for the first time Amenḥotpe, facing the Pharaoh, is shown as of equal height with him. Admittedly Amenḥotpe is here seen receiving rewards in the time-honoured fashion, but the pretension to something like equality is unmistakable. Also this claim accords with as much as we can ascertain from the facts and from subsequent history. The king might be the undisputed ruler in the north, but in the south the great pontiff at Karnak loomed larger than he.

It belongs to the unequal chances of archaeology that more written evidence should be forthcoming from the last reigns of Dyn. XX than from any other period of Egyptian history. The source is the west bank at Thebes, especially Medînet Habu and the neighbouring village of Dêr el-Medîna. Here vast quantities of papyri, more often fragmentary than complete, were discovered in the earlier part of the nineteenth century and are now scattered among the great collections of Europe, the Turin Museum having secured the lion's share from the digs initiated by Drovetti, the French Consul in Egypt. The picture disclosed by the day-to-day journals of work in the necropolis is one of great unrest. Long stretches of time found the workmen on the royal tomb idle, and there are ominous references,[1] many of them dating from the later years of Ramessēs IX, to the presence at Thebes of foreigners or Libyans or Meshwesh, though we do not know exactly how these ought to be interpreted. Were they real invaders or were they the descendants of captured prisoners who had been incorporated into the Egyptian army and who now felt themselves strong enough to rise in rebellion or at all events to create serious disturbances? These questions must remain unanswered for lack of evidence, but at least it is clear that the effect upon the native population was disastrous. More than once the rations of the workmen were two months overdue. Want and greed combined led inevitably to crime. The royalties and noblemen of former days had been buried with the costliest of their possessions, and the temptation of the living to

[1] *JEA* xii. 257–8; xiv. 68.

despoil the dead was overwhelming. Tomb-robbery had been a common practice from the earliest times, but now, it would appear, this mode of counteracting poverty had become so widespread that energetic steps had to be taken to bring the thieves to justice. By a lucky chance a whole series of well-preserved papyri[1] has survived to throw light on the arrests and the trials which began in year 16 of Ramessēs IX and continued, perhaps with an intermediate lull, a whole generation later. Some account has been already given of two of the most famous of these fascinating documents, namely the Abbott and the Amherst papyri.[1] Both tell their tale in characteristically dramatic fashion, reading more like chapters out of a novel than like sober excerpts from official administrative records. It is in the later batch of which Papyrus Mayer A is the most complete example that we come nearest to the actual procedure followed in the judicial examinations of witnesses. The following is an example:

> There was brought the scribe of the army ʿAnkhefenamūn, son of Ptaḥemḥab. He was examined by beating with the stick, and fetters were placed upon his feet and hands; an oath was administered to him, on pain of mutilation, not to speak falsehood. There was said to him, 'Tell the way in which you went to the places together with your brother'. He said, 'Let a witness be brought to accuse me'. He was examined again, and he said 'I saw nothing'. He was made a prisoner for further examination.

Even those witnesses who were subsequently found innocent and set free had to undergo the ordeal of the bastinado.

These were important state trials, and the judges specially chosen to conduct them were the highest available officials, under Ramessēs IX the vizier Khaʿemwīse, the high-priest of Amen-Rēʿ at Karnak, the *setem*-priest of the Pharaoh's own funerary temple, two important royal butlers, a general in charge of the chariotry, a standard-bearer in the navy, and finally the mayor of Thebes Pesiūr, the sworn enemy of Pwēro, the mayor on the west bank, whom he had tried with very limited success to make responsible for the thefts in the royal tombs. The court presiding over the later

[1] See above, pp. 118, 161 ff., 173.

trials was similarly constituted, but the high-priest is lacking, probably because engaged upon even more important business; here the names of the judges are all changed, this marking the lapse of time between the two sets of events. The Pharaoh, though absent from Thebes, was not indifferent to the crimes committed against the buried treasures of his predecessors; the trials were ordered by him and at least in one case the condemned were imprisoned until the king should decide what their punishment should be.

In the wider historical sense the importance of these happenings at Thebes lies rather in the hints of great political occurrences let drop by the witnesses in making their depositions or otherwise indicated in the papyri of these times. Ramessēs IX, after reigning for seventeen or more years, was succeeded by the tenth of the name, whose highest date is year 3. The long line of Ramesside kings came to an end with Ramessēs XI, whose Prenomen Menmaʿrēʿ-setpenptaḥ recalled the great monarch Sethōs I of two centuries earlier. His first eleven years have left no contemporary dated records, but information written down a decade later leaves no doubt as to the troublous condition of the land. It is probably to the early years of the reign that belongs a momentous event recalled in the testimony of a porter named Ḥowtenūfe:

> The barbarians came and seized Tḥō (the temple of Medînet Habu), while I was looking after some asses belonging to my father. And Peheti, a barbarian, seized me and took me to Ipip, after wrong had been done to Amenḥotpe, who was formerly high-priest of Amūn, for as long as six months. And it so happened that I returned when nine whole months of wrong had been done to Amenḥotpe, and when this portable chest had been misappropriated and set on fire.

Elsewhere mention is made of 'the war of the high-priest' which must surely refer to the same event; the ambitious priest who had been so powerful under Ramessēs IX here met with his nemesis.[1] Chronological considerations make it impossible to link up this conflict with a revolt in which a certain Pinḥasi was the protagonist. In Papyrus Mayer A, a document dating from late in the reign of Ramessēs XI, some of the thieves are stated to have been 'killed

[1] *JEA* xii. 254 ff.

by Pinḥasi', while others perished in the 'war in the Northern District' and we read too of a moment 'when Pinḥasi destroyed Ḥardai', which is the town called Cynōnpolis by the Greeks, the capital of the seventeenth nome of Upper Egypt. The name Pinḥasi is written in such a way as to make it certain that he was an enemy of the loyalists at Thebes, and the absence of any title shows that he was a very well-known personage. He can hardly have been other than the King's Son of Cush who was responsible for the collection of taxes in towns south of Thebes in year 12, and to whom in year 17 a somewhat peremptory order was sent by the king bidding him co-operate with the royal butler Yenes in the fabrication of a piece of furniture needed for the temple of a certain goddess, and in supplying various semi-precious stones required for the workshops of the Residence City. It seems, accordingly, that his rebellion must have been posterior to year 17. There is a possible reference to him in a letter of considerably later date which suggests that he retired to Nubia and carried on his resistance there. But apart from this, nothing more is heard of him, nor are we able to guess anything beyond the fact that he was presumably a native of Anîba in Nubia, where a tomb prepared for him has been found.

It was not until after the defeat of Pinḥasi that his title of King's Son of Cush, together with other offices which went with it, could be annexed by a personage of vastly greater importance. The earlier stages of Ḥriḥōr's career are wrapt in mystery. His parentage is unknown, for he never mentions either father or mother. That his overwhelming power rested upon his tenure of the post of high-priest at Karnak is certain, since his name is almost invariably preceded by the epithet 'First prophet of Amen-Rēʿ, King of the Gods', and we shall soon find him depicted acting in that capacity. It is unlikely that so important a post, commanding as it did the accumulated wealth of centuries, should have been left vacant for long, and it is natural to suppose that Ḥriḥōr was the immediate successor of Amenḥotpe. There is no evidence, however, that he passed through the various priestly grades which normally led up to the high-priesthood, whence it has become fashionable to suppose that originally he, like King Ḥaremḥab before him, had previously been an army officer. It is true that together with the son and grandson who succeeded him, he habitually used the title 'Commander of the Army', or 'Great commander of the army of Upper and Lower Egypt', but those functions may have been dictated merely by the necessities of the times, or have been prompted by his taking over the dignities of Pinḥasi, whose governorship of Nubia he is unlikely ever to have exercised; at some uncertain moment he also laid claim to the title of vizier, though there are grounds for thinking that this post was actually in another's hands. There is one tenuous clue which might account for Ramessēs XI having chosen him to become high-priest. His wife Nodjme, who by reason of her marriage to him would naturally acquire the station of 'great one of the concubines of Amen-Rēʿ' was the daughter of a lady named Ḥrēre, who bore the same title and was consequently in all probability the widow of Amenḥotpe. If so, Ḥriḥōr may have attained his principal honour through marriage, though his own strong character will in any case have played a large part in the appointment.

The development of this great pontiff's ambition may best be seen in the temple at Karnak which Ramessēs III had begun to erect in honour of Chons, the youngest member of the Theban triad.[1] The original founder and his son Ramessēs IV had succeeded in completing no more than the sanctuary and the surrounding inner chambers, nor was it until the reign of Ramessēs XI that the building was continued southwards with a hypostyle hall. In some of the scenes of this hall Ramessēs is shown making offerings to the local gods in the traditional fashion, but in others Ḥriḥōr obtains a predominance never before accorded to a mere subject. It is not entirely unnatural that as high-priest of Amen-Rēʿ he should be depicted censing the on-coming or halted bark of the supreme deity, especially since mention of Ramessēs is made in the words with which Amūn expresses his gratification at the splendid monument bestowed upon the city by the king. However, on four of the eight columns occupying the centre of the hall it is Ḥriḥōr who with unheard-of presumption caused himself to be displayed performing some ritual act before one or other member of the triad, and in two of the three dedicatory inscriptions running along the base of the

[1] PM ii. 75 ff.

walls Ḥriḥōr alone is named as the donor, the king's person being completely ignored. When, possibly only a year or two later, Ḥriḥōr added a forecourt still farther south, we here find him with the royal uraeus upon his brow or even wearing the double crown, though still arrayed in the costume of the high-priest. What is still more significant, he has now, in the absence of any allusion to Ramessēs, assumed the full titulary of a Pharaoh, with a Horus-name of his own and separate cartouches for Prenomen and Nomen: 'Horus Strong-Bull-son-of-Amūn, King of Upper and Lower Egypt, lord of the Two Lands, First-prophet-of-Amūn, bodily son of Rēʿ, Son-of-Amūn-Ḥriḥōr.'

In the face of this evidence it is comprehensible that the older Egyptologists should have interpreted the accession of Ḥriḥōr as the final triumph of the priesthood of Amūn, and should have assumed that he did not claim the throne until natural or unnatural death had removed the last of the legitimate Pharaohs. Gradually, however, fresh testimony has come to light which compels us to reconstruct the facts in a different way. Instead of dates continuing to be expressed, as normally, in terms of the regnal years of the monarch, a mysterious new era named the Repetition-of-Births makes its appearance. When we recall that the usurper Ammenemēs I had adopted the expression *Weḥam-meswe* 'Repeater of Births' as his Horus name (p. 127), and that Sethōs I, very nearly the founder of Dyn. XIX, had appended the same words as here to datings of his first and second years (p. 249), it is obvious that some sort of Renaissance was signified thereby. Fortunately we are able to determine the exact regnal date of this. Papyrus Mayer A in the Liverpool Museum is headed 'Year 1 in the Repetition-of-Births' and enumerates precisely the same thieves as are listed on the *verso* of the already much-discussed Papyrus Abbott, which bears the date 'Year 1, first month of the Inundation season, day 2, corresponding to Year 19'. After much hesitation and discussion it has been realized that this year 19 could only belong to the reign of Ramessēs XI who, however, was known from a stela found at Abydos to have survived until his twenty-seventh year. Now it could hardly be doubted that the Renaissance in question referred to some momentous occurrence or decision in Ḥriḥōr's career, so that this must have fallen at a time when the suzerainty of the last Ramessēs had run only two thirds of its course. The question has been clinched by a relatively recent discovery.[1] A scene and inscription carved upon a wall of the temple of Karnak illustrates one of those oracles which became more and more frequent about this period. A scribe of the storehouse at Karnak had to be appointed, and the name of one Nesamūn had been put forward. The god's approval was indicated by a 'great nod' or downward inclination of the bark of Amen-Rēʿ as it was carried in procession on the shoulders of the priests. The importance of this incident lies in the personality of the high-priest who put the question and in the date at the beginning of the inscription. The date is given as 'Year 7 of the Repetition of Births . . . under Ramessēs XI', accordingly in the twenty-fifth year of that king's reign. The figure of the high-priest is accompanied by the words 'The fan-bearer to the right of the King, the King's Son of Cush, the First prophet of Amen-Rēʿ, King of the Gods, the Commander of the Army, the Prince Payʿonkh'. Now Payʿonkh was Ḥriḥōr's eldest son, and since it is inconceivable that Ḥriḥōr should have relinquished the high-priesthood during his lifetime we cannot but conclude that he died before the seventh year of the Renaissance and at any rate more than a year before his sovereign.

In the light of these circumstances the Theban theocracy founded by Ḥriḥōr assumes a considerably changed aspect. That he united all the powers of the State in his own person and handed them on to his descendants seems clear from the military, judicial, administrative, and sacerdotal titles which he and they bore, but actual assumption of the Double Crown was denied him. So long as Ramessēs XI lived it was he who was referred to as the Pharaoh. Within the precincts of the great temple of Karnak Ḥriḥōr might certainly flaunt a royal titulary, even if he could there find for himself no more imposing a Prenomen than 'First prophet of Amūn'. In the few cases where his name occurs outside Karnak it is never enclosed in a cartouche, nor did he ever venture to employ regnal years of his own.[2] The dating by years of the 'Repetition of Births' probably refers to some favourable turn in the fortunes of the

[1] Nims in *JNES* vii. 157 ff.

[2] Gauthier, *LR* iii. 232 ff.

country, but this did not bring Ramessēs back to Thebes, where his tomb was left incomplete and unoccupied. Concerning Ḥriḥōr's own tomb our records are completely silent and excavations have revealed no trace of him in the Bîbân el-Molûk. His wife Nodjme, who apparently gave him nineteen sons and five daughters, seems to have survived him and more will be heard of her later. A long inscription at Karnak may have cast further light on Ḥriḥōr's life, but is too fragmentary to supply any useful information. The coffins of Sethōs I and Ramessēs II, found in the *cache* at Dêr el-Baḥri, carry dockets stating that in year 6 (clearly of the Renaissance) Ḥriḥōr caused those kings to be buried anew, but obviously not in their final resting-place. A statue at Cairo and a stela in the Leyden Museum are the only remaining records of importance, apart from a papyrus which paints so broad and convincing a picture that the often debated question whether it is genuine history or fiction founded upon fact becomes largely academic; most scholars would probably subscribe to Lefebvre's verdict 'C'est un roman historique'. This fascinating document was bought in Cairo by Golénischeff in 1891 together with two other literary papyri of which one at all events was written by the same hand. It tells the story of the misfortunes of Wenamūn, a Theban sent on a mission to Syria at the very close of Dyn. XX. The narrative is dated in a year 5 which, in the light of what is now known, must belong to the Renaissance explained above. Ḥriḥōr is the high-priest at Karnak, while Tanis is ruled by that Nesbanebded who subsequently became the first king of Manetho's Dyn. XXI. These two great men are on good terms with one another, neither of them as yet claiming the kingship. The real Pharaoh, namely Ramessēs XI, is mentioned only once in a cryptic utterance. In such circumstances Egypt was evidently too weak to command respect abroad, and the conversations of Wenamūn with the princes whom he met afford a revelation of the contemporary world unequalled in the entire literature of the Nearer East. It is for that reason that, departing from our usual habit, we give in the following pages a virtually complete translation.

Year 5, fourth month of the Summer season, day 16; the day on which Wenamūn, the elder of the portal of the estate of Amūn, lord of the Thrones of the Two Lands, set forth to fetch the timber for the great noble bark of Amen-Rēʿ, King of the Gods, which is upon the river and is called Amen-user-ḥē. On the day of my arrival at Tanis, the place where Nesbanebded and Tentamūn are, I gave them the dispatches of Amen-Rēʿ, King of the Gods. And they caused them to be read before them and they said: 'We will surely do as Amen-Rēʿ, King of the Gods, our lord has said.'

I stayed until the fourth month of the Summer season[1] in Tanis. And Nesbanebded and Tentamūn sent me forth with the ship's captain Mengebet, and I went down upon the great sea of Syria in the first month of the Summer season.[1] And I arrived at Dōr, a Tjekker-town[2], and Beder its prince caused to be brought to me 50 loaves, one flagon of wine, and one haunch of an ox. And a man of my ship fled after stealing one vessel of gold worth 5 *deben*, four jars of silver worth 20 *deben*, and a bag of silver, 11 *deben*; total of what he stole, gold 5 *deben*, silver 31 *deben*. And I arose in the morning and went to the place where the prince was and said to him: I have been robbed in your harbour. But you are the prince of this land and you are its controller. Search for my money, for indeed the money belongs to Amen-Rēʿ, King of the Gods, the lord of the lands, it belongs to Nesbanebded, it belongs to Ḥriḥōr my lord and to the other great ones of Egypt; it belongs to you, it belongs to Waret, it belongs to Mekamar, it belongs to Tjikarbaʿal the prince of Byblos.' He said to me: 'Are you in earnest or are you inventing? For indeed I know nothing of this tale that you have told me. If it had been a thief belonging to my land who had gone down into your ship and had stolen your money, I would have replaced it for you from my storehouse, until your thief had been found, whoever he may be. But in fact the thief who robbed you, he is yours, he belongs to your ship. Spend a few days here with me, that I may search for him.'

I stayed nine days moored in his harbour, and then I went before him and said to him: 'Look, you have not found my money.'

There follows a much broken passage the gist of which may be guessed to be as follows. Wenamūn expresses the wish to depart with some ship's captains about to put to sea, but the prince urges him to refrain, suggesting that he should seize goods belonging to the suspected persons until they had gone to search for the thief. Wenamūn, however, prefers to continue his journey and after

[1] The dates as written in the original are irreconcilable. [2] See above, p. 284.

touching at Tyre leaves that port at daybreak. He is soon at Byblos, where Tjikarbaʿal is the prince. There he comes across a ship that contains 30 *deben* of silver, which he annexes saying that the money shall remain with him until those whom he addresses have found the thief.

. . . They departed, and I celebrated in a tent on the shore of the sea in the harbour of Byblos. And I found a hiding place for Amūn-of-the-Road[1] and placed his possessions within it. And the prince of Byblos sent to me saying: 'Remove yourself from my harbour.' And I sent to him saying: 'Where shall I go? . . . If you can find a ship to carry me, let me be taken back to Egypt.' And I spent twenty-nine days in his harbour and he spent time sending to me daily to say: 'Remove yourself from my harbour.'

Now whilst he was offering to his gods, the god seized a young man of his young men and put him in a frenzy and said to him: 'Bring the god up and bring up the envoy who is carrying him. It is Amūn who sent him, it is he who caused him to come.' And the frenzied one was in a frenzy during this night, when I had found a ship with its face set towards Egypt and had loaded all my belongings onto it and was watching for the darkness saying 'When it descends, I will put the god aboard so that no other eye shall see him.' And the harbour-master came to me saying: 'Wait here until tomorrow, so says the prince.' And I said to him: 'Was it not you who spent time coming to me daily saying "Remove yourself from my harbour", and have you not said "Wait here this night" in order to let the ship which I have found depart, and then you will come again and tell me to go?' And he went and told it to the prince. And the prince sent to the captain of the ship saying 'Wait until the morning—so says the prince.'

And when the morning came, he sent and brought me up, while the god was reposing in the tent where he was on the shore of the sea. And I found him seated in his upper chamber with his back against a window, while the waves of the great sea of Syria beat behind his head. And I said to him: 'Amūn be merciful(?).' And he said to me: 'How long until today is it since you came from the place where Amūn is?' And I said to him: 'Five whole months until now.' And he said to me: 'Supposing you are right, where is the dispatch of Amūn which is in your hand, and where is the letter of the First Prophet of Amūn which is in

[1] This was the image of the god which it was thought would ensure the success of Wenamūn's mission. For other instances of travelling statues see pp. 212–13, 266.

your hand?' And I said to him: 'I gave them to Nesbanebded and Tentamūn.' Then he was very angry and said to me: 'Well now, dispatch or letter there is none in your hand, but where is the ship of pinewood which Nesbanebded gave you and where is its Syrian crew? Did he not entrust you to this barbarian ship's captain to cause him to kill you and that they should throw you into the sea? From whom then would the god have been sought for, and you too, from whom would you too have been sought for?' So he said to me. But I said to him: 'Is it not an Egyptian ship and an Egyptian crew which carry Nesbanebded? He has no Syrian crews.' And he said to me: 'Are there not twenty vessels here in my harbour which do business with Nesbanebded, and as for that Sidon, that other place by which you passed, are there not fifty more ships there which do business with Waraktir, and which toil to his house?'

I kept silence at that great moment.

Then he proceeded to say to me: 'On what commission have you come?' And I said to him: 'I have come in quest of the timber for the great noble bark of Amen-Rēʿ, King of the Gods. What your father did and what the father of your father did, you too will do it.' So I said to him. And he said to me: 'They did it in truth. You shall pay me for doing it, and I will do it. Certainly my people performed this commission, but only after Pharaoh had caused to be brought six ships laden with Egyptian goods and they had unloaded them into their storehouses. But you—what have you brought to me myself?' And he caused the daybook rolls of his fathers to be brought and he caused them to be read before me. And they found entered on his roll a thousand *deben* of silver, things of all sorts. And he said to me: 'If the ruler of Egypt had been the possessor of mine own and I too his servant, he would not have caused silver and gold to be brought when he said "Perform the commission of Amūn"; it was no gratuitous gift that they used to make for my father. And as for me too, I myself, I am not your servant, and I am not the servant of him who sent you either. When I cry aloud to the Lebanon,[1] the heaven opens and the timber lies here on the shore of the sea. Give me the sails that you brought to carry your ships which are to bear your timber to Egypt. Give me the ropes that you have brought to lash together the cedars which I am to fell for you in order to make them for you . . . which I am to make for you for the sails of your ships and the yards may be too heavy and may break and you may

[1] Tjikarbaʿal claims that he has only to open his mouth and it will rain logs.

perish in the midst of the sea. Behold, Amūn will give voice in the heaven having placed Sutekh beside himself.[1] True, Amūn fitted out all the lands. He fitted them out after having earlier fitted out the land of Egypt whence you have come. And craftsmanship came forth from it reaching to the place where I am. And learning came forth from it reaching to the place where I am. What then are these foolish journeyings which you have been caused to make?' But I said to him: 'False! No foolish journeyings are these on which I am now engaged. There are no boats on the river which do not belong to Amūn. His is the sea, and his the Lebanon about which you say "It is mine". It is the growing-place for Amen-user-ḥē the lord of all ships. Truly it was Amen-Rēʿ, King of the Gods, who said to Ḥriḥōr my master "Send him", and he caused me to come with this great god. But now see, you have let this great god spend these twenty-nine days moored in your harbour without your knowing. Is he not here, is he not what he was? And you stand chaffering over the Lebanon with Amūn its lord. As for what you say that the former kings caused silver and gold to be brought, if they had possessed Life and Health, they would not have caused the goods to be brought; it was in place of Life and Health that they caused the goods to be brought to your fathers. But Amen-Rēʿ, the King of the Gods, he is the lord of this Life and Health, and he was the lord of your fathers. They passed their lifetime offering to Amūn, and you too, you are the servant of Amūn. If you say "Yes, I will do it" to Amūn, and you complete his commission you will live, will be prosperous, will be in health, and will be good for your entire land and your people. Do not covet aught belonging to Amen-Rēʿ, King of the Gods—truly a lion loves his property. Let your scribe be brought to me that I may send him to Nesbanebded and Tentamūn, the officers whom Amūn has given to the north of his land, and they will cause to be brought to you the wherewithal. I will send him to them saying "Let it be brought until I have gone to the south" and I will cause to be brought to you all your deficit as well.' So I said to him.

And he placed my letter in the hand of his envoy, and put on board the keel, the prow-piece, and the stern-piece, together with four other

[1] Sutekh is here the god of the thunder. The prince's none too clear argument seems to be that Wenamūn having come totally unequipped he may well suffer shipwreck, in which case all that Amūn will do is to thunder. Tjikarbaʿal then admits that Amūn, having originated Art and Science in his own country, had since spread them into all other lands. But Amūn having thus given all that he has to give, there is no point in Wenamūn's present journey.

hewn planks, total 7, and he caused them to be brought to Egypt. And his envoy who had gone to Egypt returned to me in Syria in the first month of the Winter season, Nesbanebded and Tentamūn having sent gold, 4 jars; 1 *kakmen*-vessel; silver, 5 jars; coverlets of royal linen, 10 pieces; fine Upper Egyptian linen, 10 veils; plain mats, 500; ox-hides, 500; ropes, 500; lentils, 20 sacks; fish, 30 baskets. And she[1] sent to me coverlets, fine Upper Egyptian linen, 5 pieces; fine Upper Egyptian linen, 5 veils; lentils, 1 sack, and fish, 5 baskets. And the prince rejoiced, and he fitted out 300 men and 300 oxen, and he placed superintendents in charge of them to cause them to fell the logs. And they felled them and they lay there during the winter. And in the third month of Summer they dragged them to the shore of the sea. And the prince went forth and stood by them, and he sent to me telling me to come. And when I had been brought into his presence, the shadow of his lotus-fan fell upon me. And Penamūn, a butler of his, approached me saying: 'The shadow of Pharaoh your lord has fallen upon you.'[2] And he was angry with him and said 'Leave him alone.' And I was brought into his presence and he proceeded to say to me: 'Look, the commission which my fathers performed formerly, I having performed it—but you have not done for me yourself what your fathers did for mine. Look, the last of your timber has arrived and is in its place. Do according to my will and come and place it on board, for will they not give it to you? Do not come to look at the terrors of the sea, but if you look at the terrors of the sea, look at my own. Assuredly I have not done to you what was done to the envoys of Khaʿemwīse[3] when they passed seventeen years in this land and died on the spot.' And he said to his butler: 'Take him and let him see their tomb where they lie.' But I said to him: 'Do not make me see it. As regards Khaʿemwīse, those envoys whom he sent to you were men, and he himself was a man. But you have not here one of his envoys when you say "Go and look at your companions". Do you not rejoice that you can cause to be made for yourself a stela and that you can say on it: "Amen-Rēʿ, King of the Gods, sent me Amūn-of-the-Road his envoy, together with Wenamūn his human envoy, in quest of the timber for the great noble bark of Amen-Rēʿ, King of the Gods. I felled it and I put it on board and I provided it with my ships and my crews. And I caused

[1] No doubt Tentamūn.

[2] Doubtless an insulting taunt, possibly meaning that Wenamūn and the Pharaoh were alike 'under a cloud'.

[3] Possibly Ramessēs IX, but certainly a king, Wenamūn's counter-argument being that even kings were human, whereas he himself was in the service of a god.

them to reach Egypt so as to beg for me from Amūn fifty years of life over and above my fate." And it would come to pass if after another day an envoy who had knowledge of writing were to come from the land of Egypt and were to read your name upon the stela, you would receive water of the West just like the gods who are there.' And he said to me: 'This is a great testimony of speech that you have said to me.' And I said to him: 'As regards the many things which you have said to me, if I reach the place where the First prophet of Amūn is, and he see your commission, your commission will draw profit unto you.'

And I went off to the shore of the sea to the place where the logs were laid, and I saw eleven ships coming from the sea which belonged to the Tjekker, they saying: 'Imprison him, let no ship of his leave for the land of Egypt.' Thereupon I sat and wept. And the letter-writer of the prince came out to me and said to me: 'What ails you?' And I said to him: 'Do you not see the migrant birds which go down twice to Egypt? Look at them, how they come to the cool waters. Until what arrives am I to be abandoned here? And do you not see those who have come to imprison me again?' And he went and told it to the prince. And the prince began to weep on account of the words that were said to him, they being so painful. And he sent out his letter-writer to me bringing me two flagons of wine and a sheep. And he caused to be brought to me Tentnē, an Egyptian singing-woman whom he had, saying: 'Sing to him, do not let his heart be worried.' And he sent to me saying: 'Eat and drink, and let not your heart be worried. You shall hear tomorrow all that I shall say.' The morrow came and he caused his council to be summoned and he stood among them and said to the Tjekker: 'What mean these journeyings of yours?' And they said to him: 'We have come in pursuit of the fighting vessels which you are sending to Egypt with our adversaries.' And he said to them: 'I cannot imprison the envoy of Amūn within my land. Let me send him away, and you shall go after him to imprison him.' And he loaded me up and sent me thence to the harbour of the sea. And the wind drove me to the land of Alasiya.[1] And the inhabitants of the place came out against me to kill me, but I forced my way through them to the place where Ḥatiba, the female prince of the town was. And I found her as she was going out from her one house and was entering into her other house. And I greeted her, and said to the people who stood around her: 'Is there not one among you who understands the language of Egypt?' And one among them said: 'I

[1] Generally recognized to be Cyprus, see too *Onom.* i. 131*; *ANET*, p. 356, n. 3.

understand it.' And I said to him: 'Tell my mistress: as far as Nē,[1] as the place where Amūn is, I used to hear that injustice is done in every town, but that justice is done in the land of Alasiya. Is then injustice done every day here?' And she said: 'What indeed do you mean by saying it?' And I said to her: 'If the sea is angry and the wind drives me to the land where you are, will you cause me to be received so as to kill me, although I am the envoy of Amūn? Look now, as regards myself they would seek me to the end of time. But as regards this crew of the prince of Byblos whom they seek to kill, will not their master find ten crews of yours and himself too kill them?' And she caused the people to be summoned, and they were made to attend. And she said to me: 'Pass the night. . . .

The rest is lost. Wenamūn must have succeeded in reaching home, otherwise his report could never have been written. We now stand on the threshold of an entirely different Egypt, but before we pass to the consideration of Dyn. XXI mention must be made of an important series of letters discovered early in the nineteenth century and now scattered among many museums and private collections. The excellent edition by J. Černý shows that they are all concerned with the life and doings of a scribe of the royal tomb at Thebes named Dḥutmose and with his son Buteh-amūn, together with their relatives and friends. Much of the contents turns upon domestic affairs, but there are many allusions to current historic events. Ḥriḥōr's son and heir Pay'onkh is now the high-priest of Amen-Rē' and it is certain that he never claimed the kingship. The correspondence seldom mentions him by name, but no doubt it is he who is often alluded to as the 'Commander of the Army'. The close relationship between this exalted personage and Dḥutmose was due to the latter acting as a sort of agent for him at Thebes, while Pay'onkh was engaged on a campaign in the south, apparently against the former King's Son of Cush Pinḥasi (above pp. 301–2). The kinsfolk of Dḥutmose express great anxiety for the safety of Dḥutmose in his journeyings to bring weapons and other supplies to his chief. Almost a dozen letters emanate from Pay'onkh himself, written by his secretaries in a trenchant style. In three almost identical letters to his mother Nodjme, to Dḥutmose, and

[1] An abbreviation of *Nē-rese* 'the Southern City', namely Thebes, wrongly vocalized in the Bible as Nō.

to another official the general instructs them to stop the mouths of two Madjoi-policemen who have spoken indiscreetly by killing them and having them thrown into the river by night. It would be interesting to know the exact reason for so sinister an order, but at least it testifies to the unhappy state of affairs prevailing at this troubled moment in Egyptian history. There are added to the letter addressed to Dḥutmose some words that can hardly be construed otherwise than as a reference to the absentee Ramessēs XI: 'As for Pharaoh, how shall he reach this land? Whose master is Pharaoh still?'

SELECT BIBLIOGRAPHY

The temple of Medînet Habu: complete publication in course of production by the Oriental Institute of Chicago University; of the 9 volumes already issued vols. i and ii (1930, 1932) deal with the historical scenes and inscriptions; translations in W. F. Edgerton and J. A. Wilson, *Historical Records of Ramses III*, Chicago, 1936; the architectural volumes by U. Hölscher.

The harem conspiracy: besides the great Turin papyrus and the Lee and Rollin papyri translated by Breasted and de Buck (above, pp. 289, n 2; 291, n. 1) there are also a fragment at Varzy (*RAD*, p. xviii) and some strange excerpts in an old work by Rifaud, *Bull. Inst. fr.* l. 107 ff.; see too *JEA* xlii. 8, 9.

The great Harris papyrus: see further H. D. Schaedel, *Die Listen des grossen Papyrus Harris*, Glückstadt, 1936.

The successors of Ramessēs III: Seele in O. Firchow, *Ägyptologische Studien*, Berlin, 1955, pp. 296 ff.; Nims in *Bibl. Or.* xiv. 137–8; Černý, in *JEA* xliv. 36 f.

The title King's Son of Ramessēs: Petrie, *Hist.* iii. 242; additions, Roeder in Pauly-Wissowa, *Real-Encycl.* under Ramses, col. 225.

Monuments of Ramessēs IV: L.-A. Christophe, in *Cahiers d'histoire égyptienne*, iii (1950), 47 ff.; W. Helck in *ZÄS* lxxxii. 98 ff. The great Abydos stelae, (1) B*AR* iv, §§ 469–71, (2) *Bull. Inst. fr.* xlv. 155 ff.

The Elephantinē scandal: the text, *RAD*, pp. 73 ff.; translation by T. E. Peet in *JEA* x. 116 ff.; see too S. Sauneron in *Rev. d'Ég.* vii. 53 ff.

The Wilbour papyrus: ed. A. H. Gardiner, 4 vols., Oxford, 1941, 1948–52.

The high-priest of Amen-Rēʿ Amenḥotpe: G. Lefebvre, *Grands prêtres*, pp. 185 ff., 267 ff.; also the same author's *Inscriptions concernant les grands prêtres d'Amon Romê-Roÿ et Amenhotep*, Paris, 1929.

The Tomb-robberies: T. E. Peet, *The Great Tomb-robberies of the Twentieth Egyptian Dynasty*, 2 vols., Oxford, 1930; this includes the Amherst papyrus, later, when completed by a new find (p. 162, n. 4), to become known as *Pap. Léopold II* published by J. Capart and A. H. Gardiner, Brussels, 1939; see too *JEA* xxii. 169 ff. The most important of the later batch of these papyri, T. E. Peet, *The Mayer Papyri A & B*, London, 1920. See too above in the text, p. 300, n. 1.

Pinḥasi: as viceroy in Nubia, *Rec. trav.* xxxix. 219–20; as insurgent, Peet, *Tomb-robberies*, p. 124; later in Nubia, Černý, *Late Ramesside Letters*, Brussels, 1939, pp. 7–8; tomb at Anîba, PM vii. 79.

Ḥriḥōr: Lefebvre, *Grands prêtres*, pp. 205 ff., 272 ff.; in temple of Chons, PM ii. 79–81; wife Nodjme and family, Gauthier, *LR* iii. 236 ff.

The Renaissance: Černý in *JEA* xv. 194 ff.; *ZÄS* lxv. 129–30.

Wenamūn: latest translation, J. A. Wilson in *ANET*, pp. 25–29; the text, A. H. Gardiner, *Late-Egyptian Stories*, pp. 61–76.

The correspondence of the scribes Dḥutmose and Butehamūn: see under Pinḥasi above, the book by Černý. See too A. H. Gardiner, *A Political Crime in Ancient Egypt* in *Journal of Manchester University Egyptian and Oriental Society*, 1912–13, pp. 57–64.

XII

EGYPT UNDER FOREIGN RULE

THROUGHOUT the eleventh and following centuries before our era the essential duality of the land of the Pharaohs found novel and unexpected expression. The initial stage could not have been better characterized than was done by the ill-starred envoy Wenamūn. Egypt was now governed from two separate capitals, Thebes in the south and Tanis in the north; and, strange to say, the relations between the two halves of the country were amicable and co-operative. For the moment the kingship was in abeyance; Wenamūn is insistent in maintaining that everywhere, not in Egypt alone, the overlordship belonged to the Theban god Amūn, earthly monarchs being mere mortals. We have now to show how this situation developed. The absence of a Pharaoh could not be long tolerated, and Nesbanebded quickly asserted his claim. The name means 'He who belongs to the Ram of Djedě'—Djedě being the important town in the centre of the Delta known to the Greeks as Mendēs. Manetho heads his TWENTY-FIRST DYNASTY of seven Tanite kings with Smendēs, a pronunciation of Nesbanebded doubtless not far wide of the mark. As a native of Djedě Smendēs can have had no personal right to the throne, and it seems obvious that, apart from his own vigorous character, he owed his kingship to Tentamūn, whose name tells its own tale and whom Wenamūn always represents as associated with him; clearly she was the link binding Thebes and Tanis so closely together. It is nevertheless odd that Thebes accepted the suzerainty of Tanis so submissively. The sole surviving record of Smendēs's reign is a much damaged inscription on a pillar in a quarry at Gebelên.[1] Here it is related how Smendēs sat in his palace at Memphis excogitating some pious deed that might do him honour. On its being represented to him that a colonnade built by Tuthmōsis III at Luxor was subject to flooding up to the roof, he sent three thousand workmen

[1] *BAR* iv, §§ 627–30.

to hew the sandstone necessary for the repairs. Thus not only had Smendēs moved his official residence to the extreme north of the Delta, but also he found himself free to undertake building operations well to the south of Thebes. Nothing of the kind is attested for his successors, whose remains in Middle and Upper Egypt amount to no more than some mentions in a small temple of Isis at the foot of the Great Pyramid,[1] a chapel of Siamūn at Memphis,[2] and a few unimportant objects found at Abydos.[3] None the less it is certain that they were regarded as the sole legitimate Pharaohs, not only by themselves, but also by posterity. Manetho's enumeration of dynasties never again refers to Thebes, and it appears that nearly all the datings found in the inscriptions there are in terms of the Tanite reigns. To be buried in the Bîbân el-Molûk was no longer an aspiration, and Montet's excavations at Tanis have brought to light in that place the tombs of Psusennēs I and of Amenemope, the second and third monarchs of the dynasty, if the probably ephemeral Neferkarēʿ (p. 47) be ignored. These sepulchres are, however, mean and insignificant structures when compared with the great gallery tombs to the west of Thebes, not to speak of the mighty pyramids of earlier times. Nor is the degeneracy of the new régime more than thinly disguised by the rich jewellery with which Montet's many years of patient digging were rewarded.

At Thebes the pattern of government bequeathed to his descendants by Ḥriḥōr was continued by them with but little change. The high-priesthood was held successively by Payʿonkh, Pinūdjem I, Masaherta, Menkheperrēʿ, and Pinūdjem II, passing from father to son except in the case of Menkheperrēʿ who was preceded by his brother. Together with their sacerdotal title all these pontiffs assumed that of 'Great Commander of the Army' or even 'Great Commander of the Army of the entire land', clearly indicating the unsettled state of the country; the occasional additions of 'Vizier' or 'King's Son of Cush' are probably merely traditional. It cannot be doubted that there were ties of marriage and friendship between the two capitals which made their co-existence natural and perhaps even necessary. The god Amūn having been adopted at Tanis, it might possibly be wrong to deduce Theban birth from the names

[1] PM iii. 5. [2] Op. cit. iii. 225. [3] Op. cit. v. 78, 80.

of the northern Pharaohs Amenemope and Siamūn, but the very unusual Psusennēs, meaning 'The Star which arose in Thebes', cannot be denied significance. Alone among the contemporary high-priests of Amen-Rēᶜ Pinūdjem I definitely asserted his right to be regarded as the Pharaoh, taking to himself a Prenomen as well as a Nomen, but even with him the records bearing his name write it more frequently without a cartouche. Extremely curious is the fact that at Tanis Psusennēs I often uses the epithet 'high-priest of Amen-Rēᶜ',[1] and even once in a very full titulary describes himself as 'great of monuments in Ipet-eswe', i.e. at Karnak.[2]

The part played by women in ancient Egypt had always been great, but at this juncture was greater than ever. The inscriptions are abnormally communicative in the use of such epithets as 'King's Daughter', 'King's Great Wife', but the establishment of flawless genealogies has thus far proved a baffling task, and it has to be admitted that research on this topic is still in its infancy. A perplexing feature of the problem is that the same female name was often borne by several different individuals. The title 'God's Wife of Amūn', of which the first component goes back far into the past, henceforth won an ever increasing political importance, though its exact implications are mysterious. Under Pinūdjem I the Maᶜkarēᶜ who bears this title is depicted as a mere child,[3] though she has often been credited with being his wife; very possibly she was the daughter of Psusennēs I. She is certainly to be distinguished from a later Maᶜkarēᶜ who was a daughter of the Tanite king Psusennēs II[4] and whose rights as an heiress were set forth on a long inscription in the temple of Karnak.[5] This is but one example of the difficulties which cluster round the names of such princesses as Ḥenutowĕ, Isimkheb, and others. Here it need only be added that some of these royal ladies enjoyed no inconsiderable wealth through their tenure of priestly offices. For instance Neskhons, the well-known wife of Pinūdjem II, is described on a coffin bearing her name[6] as

first chief of the concubines of Amen-Rēᶜ, King of the Gods; major-domo of the house of Mūt the great, lady of Ashru; prophetess of

[1] *Psus.*, pp. 16–17. [2] Op. cit., p. 136, fig. 51. [3] *Rec. trav.* xiv. 32.
[4] *BAR* iv, §§ 738–40. [5] PM ii. 54 (16). [6] Daressy, *Cerc.*, p. 112.

Anḥūr-Shu the son of Rēʿ;[1] prophetess of Mīn, Horus, and Isis in Ipu;[2] prophetess of Horus, lord of Djuef;[3] god's mother of Chons the child, first one of Amen-Rēʿ, King of the Gods; and chief of noble ladies,

to which an accompanying column of inscription adds four more local priesthoods. Unhappily the name of Neskhons has been painted over that of Isimkheb to whom, therefore, these titles doubtless properly belong. If the localities mentioned in them are to be taken seriously, it would seem that the Theban influence extended far northwards into Middle Egypt, a fact confirmed at El-Ḥîba[4] by bricks bearing the names of the high-priests Pinūdjem I and Menkheperrēʿ. Of El-Ḥîba we shall hear again in connexion with Dyn. XXII. These complications are typical of the difficulties which attended the unravelling of the problems of Dyn. XXI. Further attempts at elucidation must be left to the future; the material is abundant, but mostly ambiguous. Here we must content ourselves with giving some account of two great discoveries by which the views of the historians have been completely transformed.

In the last quarter of our nineteenth century objects belonging to Dyn. XXI had long been finding their way into the antiquities' market, and their abundance and evident importance made it clear that some of the inhabitants of Ḳurna had lighted upon a tomb or *cache* of an altogether exceptional kind.[5] By 1881 official investigation could no longer be delayed, and G. Maspero, then Director of the Antiquities Service, took the matter energetically in hand. In course of time suspicion narrowed itself down to the ʿAbd er-Rasûl family. All attempts to make the finders divulge the secret failed until the eldest of them, realizing that this was about to be betrayed by one or other of his brothers, resolved to steal a march upon them. Hence the discovery of the wonderful hiding-place of so many of the royal mummies which has been partially described or alluded to in earlier pages of the present work.[6] A deep shaft to the south of the valley of Dêr el-Baḥri led down into a long passage ending in a burial-chamber which had been originally occupied by a half-forgotten queen Inhaʿpy. Coffins, mummies, and other

[1] At Thinis. [2] Akhmîm. [3] A town a little to the north of Asyûṭ.
[4] PM iv. 124. [5] Op. cit. i. 173 ff. [6] pp. 164 etc.

funerary furniture were found piled up in this inconspicuous burial-place, having been brought there after considerable peregrinations by successors of Ḥriḥōr. Almost since the times of their actual burial the mighty kings of Dyns. XVII to XX had been exposed to violation and theft on the part of the rapacious inhabitants of the Theban necropolis, and it was only as a last frantic effort to put an end to such sacrilege that the high-priests of Dyn. XXI intervened. This they could do with greater confidence since the golden ornaments and other precious possessions had long ago disappeared, so that little more than the coffins and corpses remained to be salvaged. However, for the modern world thus to recover the remains of many of the greatest Pharaohs was a sensation till then unequalled in the annals of archaeology; to be able to gaze upon the actual features of such famous warriors as Tuthmōsis III and Sethōs I was a privilege that could be legitimately allowed to the serious historian, though it was for a time denied to the merely curious. Besides the nine kings who were found there were a number of their queens, as well as some princes and lesser personages. Hieratic dockets on certain coffins or mummy wrappings disclosed the dates of the reburials and the authorities responsible for them. More important from the purely historical point of view were the intact coffins of high-priests of Dyn. XXI and their womenfolk, the hieroglyphic inscriptions furnishing no small portion of the material for the discussions contained in Maspero's fundamental monograph on the find. Among the latest burials were those of Pinūdjem II and his already-mentioned spouse Neskhons. After them the *cache* was sealed up in the tenth year of the Tanite king Siamūn,[1] but was reopened once more in the reign of King Shōshenḳ I in order to inter a priest of Amūn named Djedptaḥefʿonkh.[2]

In 1891, just ten years after the discovery above described, the same native of Ḳurna who had divulged the secret of the royal mummies pointed out to E. Grébaut, Maspero's successor as Director of the *Service*, a spot to the north of the temple of Dêr el-Baḥri where a tomb of altogether exceptional importance could be expected. A few blows with a pick revealed a shaft leading to a gallery nearly 80 yards long followed by a rather shorter northerly gallery

[1] *JEA* xxxii. 24 ff. [2] Gauthier, *LR* iii. 307.

at a somewhat lower level. Here G. Daressy, placed in charge of the operations, came upon no less than 153 coffins, 101 of them double and 52 single, together with many boxes of ushabti-figures, Osirian statuettes of which some enclosed papyri, as well as other objects of lesser interest. Near the entrance the coffins were in utter disorder, but farther inwards they were stacked up against the walls in opposite rows leaving a passage-way in the midst. An innermost chamber had been reserved for the family of the high-priest Menkheperrēʿ, but later the galleries were used indiscriminately for members of the priesthood of Amen-Rēʿ. The actual mummy-cases were generally of anthropoid shape covered with polychromatic religious scenes and inscriptions finished off with a yellow varnish; for the historian they had little value except as giving the names and titles of their owners, among whom there were a certain number of women, mainly temple musicians. Of great importance, on the other hand, are the leather braces and pendants found upon the mummies, for they frequently depict the contemporary or an earlier high-priest standing in front of Amūn or another deity; and of perhaps greater interest are the legends often written upon the mummy-cloth, since these usually state the date at which it was made. Here, in a word, we have a primary source for the clarification of this complicated dynasty.

From the end of Dyn. XX onwards the outstanding feature of the Theban administration was its recourse to oracular decisions on all occasions. We have seen how under the high-priest Payʿonkh a temple appointment was effected by this method, the great god Amen-Rēʿ halting his processional bark to nod approval when the right name was presented to him. Later when the inheritance of the princess Maʿkarēʿ was in dispute,[1] it was Amen-Rēʿ, accompanied by the goddess Mūt and the child-god Chọns, the two other members of his triad, who decided the issue. Again, when Menkheperrēʿ became high-priest his first act was to inquire from the supreme god whether certain persons who had been banished to the oasis could now be pardoned and allowed to return to Thebes.[2] To judge by the size of a great inscription[3] engraved on a wall at Karnak the trial of an official for dishonesty which Pinūdjem II was called upon

[1] Above, p. 318. [2] *BAR* iv, §§ 650–8. [3] PM ii. 61 (58); see too below, p. 350.

to initiate must have been one of exceptional importance; in this trial a whole series of questions were addressed to the deity, who seems to have been unwilling to proceed to his yearly ceremonial visit to Luxor until the matter was settled; the first step consisted in placing before him two tablets the one affirming and the other denying that there was a case calling for investigation. In short, so far as our limited material goes, there was no subject demanding the high-priest's personal intervention which was not settled by an oracular response. A lengthy papyrus found in the Dêr el-Baḥri *cache*[1] shows that even the dead could be protected in the same manner; the following are two brief extracts:

> Hath spoken Amen-Rēʿ, King of the Gods, the great mighty god who was the first to come into being: I will deify Neskhons, the daughter of Tḥendḥoūt, in the West, I will deify her in the necropolis; I will cause her to receive water of the West, I will cause her to receive offerings in the necropolis.

And then a little later:

> I will turn the heart of Neskhons, the daughter of Tḥendḥoūt, and she shall not do any evil thing to Pinūdjem, the child of Isimkheb; I will turn her heart, and will not allow her to curtail his life; I will turn her heart, and will not allow her to cause to be done to him anything which is detrimental to the heart of a living man.

These last phrases are the more interesting, since they throw some light on the connubial relations of the now familiar princess Neskhons and her husband the high-priest Pinūdjem. But still more important is the exordium to the same papyrus, which shows how great a change had come over the concept of the supreme Theban deity since the beginning of the Ramesside period. The epithets given to Amen-Rēʿ are more remarkable for what they suppress than for what they disclose. Mythological traits are sternly excluded, and if the solar nature is still explicit in his time-honoured name, all that is now asserted is that 'he causes all mankind to live, and crosses the heaven untiringly' and that 'being an old man he begins the morning as a youth'; a little later we are told quite inconsistently that 'his right eye and his left eye are the sun and

[1] *JEA* xli. 83 ff.

moon'. Great stress is laid upon his essence as the primordial deity from whom every god came into being; his uniqueness and his inscrutable nature are strongly emphasized, use being made of the play of words between his name and the verb-stem *amen* 'to be hidden'. The existence of other deities is ignored rather than denied, and there was no persecution of them as in the Aten period. Indeed, as already noted, his daughter Mūt and the youthful moon-god Chons, both localized in the Karnak area, are inseparable from him in the religious ceremonies, having barks of their own following his in the festival processions. It will be realized that, though in this newly developed concept of Amen-Rēʿ the Theban priesthood came very near to a monotheistic cult, this monotheism was of a markedly different character from that promulgated by the heretic king Akhenaten. It would be interesting could we confidently diagnose the reasons for the over-exaltation of the mighty Theban deity. Had the chaotic conditions of the times brought about an abnormal upsurge of religiosity? Or were the priests anxious to shift from their own heads the responsibility for anything that might get them into trouble? However this may be, the immense prestige of the god served as a useful foil to the Tanite royalty, the factual dominance of which could thus be admitted without over-much self-abasement.

Whereas the sequence and the mutual relationships of the Theban high-priests are firmly established, the like is not true of the Tanite rulers. For the first four we may probably accept Manetho's order of Smendēs, Psusennēs, Nephercherēs, and Amenōphthis, but the Osochōr whom he gives as his fifth name must be suspected of being borrowed from Dyn. XXII, while for the Psinachēs that follows no hieroglyphic equivalent can be suggested. Here, however, must be inserted that Siamūn who sealed up the great Dêr el-Baḥri *cache*, and who is known to have reigned into his seventeenth year.[1] At the end of the dynasty Manetho names a second Psusennēs, and this, as we shall see, is confirmed by the monuments. It has, however, sometimes been supposed that there was yet a third Psusennēs, who would have to be distinguished from Psusennēs II. The chronology of Dyn. XXI is even more debatable

[1] *Rec. trav.* xxx. 87.

than the order of its monarchs. Africanus gives 26 years to Smendēs, 46 to Psusennēs I, and 14 to Psusennēs II, with much shorter periods for the rest, but the early sources are silent for all three reigns. On the other hand a mislaid piece of linen reported by Daressy[1] named according to him a year 49 of Amenemope, but this is extremely improbable, since the tomb at Tanis in which his mummy originally lay is of the humblest description, in no way comparable to that of Psusennēs I, its next-door neighbour.[2] For this stretch of time there are no synchronisms to help, but Manetho's total of 130 years can hardly be lowered without doing violence to the general chronological picture which the experts have deemed to be necessary. That so little is heard of the relations of Egypt to Palestine and the countries beyond was the natural result of her own divided state. Since Assyria as well was fully occupied with her own internal troubles Palestine and Syria had been able to develop small, but nevertheless thriving, kingdoms of their own, Phoenicia, Philistia, Israel, Moab, and Edom, each of which had no more formidable adversaries to contend with than its neighbours in the adjacent areas. Trade and other cultural contacts with the greater powers on the Nile and the Euphrates will have continued to exist, but causes for political friction or military measures will have been sedulously avoided. What little of the kind we hear of is derived from the Old Testament, as we shall soon see.

Not long after 950 B.C. the Pharaonic sway passed into the hands of a family of alien race. Their earliest rulers styled themselves 'chiefs of the Meshwesh', often abbreviated into 'chiefs of the Ma',[3] but sometimes paraphrased as 'chiefs of foreigners'. They were evidently closely akin to those Libyans whom Merenptaḥ and Ramessēs III had repelled with such difficulty. But they are not to be regarded as fresh invaders; the most plausible theory is that they were the descendants of captured prisoners or voluntary settlers who, like the Sherden, had been granted land of their own on condition of their obligation to military service. Be this as it may, they had waxed so numerous and so important that they were able to take over the government with the minimum of friction. Like the Hyksōs before them they were anxious to pose as true-born

[1] Gauthier, *LR* iii. 293. [2] *Psus.*, pp. 173–5. [3] *Onom.* i. 120*.

Egyptians, though retaining on their heads the feather which had always been characteristic of their appearance. But their foreign origin was also betrayed by such barbarous names as Shōshenḳ, Osorkōn, and Takelōt, to mention only those borne by actual kings. These three names were known to Manetho as members of his TWENTY-SECOND DYNASTY, this containing six more kings unnamed and yielding according to Africanus a total of 120 years. Egyptologists, on the other hand, have found it necessary to distinguish no less than five Shōshenḳs, four Osorkōns, and three Takelōts. The entire period is one of great obscurity and we must here, as elsewhere, content ourselves with selecting for description the most outstanding personalities and episodes. By way of generalization it may be said that the character of these later dynasties remained closely similar to that of Dyn. XXI. The main capital was in the north, either at Tanis or at Bubastis, but at Thebes the high-priests still exercised undisputed religious authority, while relations between the two halves of the country continued to vacillate between friendship and enmity. It was an age of rebellions and confusion for which the historian has but scanty sources, in spite of the valuable material forthcoming from a stupendous discovery now to be described.

In 1850 Auguste Mariette, a young man none too well placed to secure his future as an Egyptologist, found the long-sought opportunity in a mission to Cairo to purchase Coptic manuscripts for the French Government. The inevitable delays and obstacles encountered on his arrival had the compensating advantage of making possible a flying visit to the pyramids and tombs of Saḳḳâra. A limestone head emerging from the desert recalled to his mind not only some sphinxes that he had seen at Alexandria, but also a passage of Strabo (xvii. 1. 32) speaking of the sand-covered sphinxes which led to the temple of the Apis. Convinced that he was on the track of the famous Memphite Serapeum, Mariette was quite content to forget about his Coptic commission and, hiring thirty native workmen, set about uncovering the avenue pointing in the direction of some high mounds. The avenue proved to be of great length and months passed before he found himself in a chapel erected by the Pharaoh Nekhtḥareḥbe (Nectanebus II). This, however, was obviously not the goal aimed at, but the interest excited by Mariette's undertaking had caused a large new credit to be voted to him. It was November 1851, more than a year after his leaving France, before Mariette entered the vast subterranean structure where the Apis bulls were buried. Huge sarcophagi had contained the mummies of no less than sixty-four bulls, the earliest dating from the reign of Amenōphis III and the latest extending down to the very threshold of the Christian era. Thousands of stelae and other objects attested the devotion of priests or other worshippers, and many of the inscriptions being dated the great discovery proved to be of inestimable chronological importance. The Apis bull was during its lifetime a sort of emanation of the Memphite god Ptaḥ, but having connexions also with Osiris and the falcon god Ḥarakhti. On its death and replacement by another living animal it was buried with pomp as the Osiris-Apis, a name equating it with the Serapis whom the Ptolemies adopted as their principal divinity. Unhappily the very magnitude of the find proved a disadvantage. The haste with which so many objects had to be removed and shipped to France prevented the proper observations and copies being made, and neither the expert knowledge nor the money needed was available for the full publication of which Mariette dreamed but was never able to undertake. To G. Maspero and É. Chassinat belongs the credit of having done much to remedy this situation,[1] each in his own way, and plans are on foot to make accessible to scholars the vast accumulations still existing in the Louvre, but it cannot be denied that a large part of the scientific value of Mariette's wonderful discovery is irretrievably lost.

Strangely enough not a single inscription of Dyn. XXI was found in the Serapeum, but the material bearing upon Dyn. XXII and others later is all the richer. Prominent among this material is the stela of one Ḥarpson[2] who traces his descent through sixteen generations to a Libyan forebear of unknown date named Buyuwawa. Ḥarpson was alive and flourishing towards the end of the long reign of Shōshenḳ IV and though he himself claims to have been no more than a prophet of Nēith he counted among his ancestors four consecutive kings, each said to be the son of his

[1] PM iii. 205–15. [2] Op. cit. iii. 209; *BAR* iv, §§ 785 ff.

predecessor, the earliest of whom was Shōshenḳ I, the founder of Dyn. XXII and by far the most important member of his clan. He is first heard of in a long inscription found at Abydos[1] whilst he was still no more than 'great chief of the Meshwesh, prince of princes'. His father Nemrat, son of the lady Meḥetemwaskhe—both mentioned by Ḥarpson—had died and Shōshenḳ had appealed to the reigning king to permit the establishment at Abydos of a great funerary cult in his honour. Both the king and 'the great god' (doubtless Amūn) had replied favourably. There can be but little doubt that the Pharaoh in question was the last Psusennēs, it being known that Shōshenḳ's son and successor Osorkōn I took to wife that monarch's daughter Maʿkarēʿ.[2] There is thus a strong probability that the transition from Dyn. XXI to Dyn. XXII passed off peacefully, though a stela from the oasis of Dâkhla[3] dated in Shōshenḳ's fifth year speaks of warfare and turmoil as having prevailed in that remote province. Several sons of the new ruler are known and he seems to have assigned to them such positions as would be most likely to secure the permanence of his régime. The stela of Ḥarpson appears to represent Karʿomaʿ as Shōshenḳ's wife and the mother of Osorkōn I, but she is elsewhere described as an 'Adorer of the God', a title believed to exclude any matrimonial relationship; at all events Osorkōn I was a son of his predecessor. A lengthy inscription discovered at Ihnâsya el-Medîna,[4] the Hēracleopolis so prominent in the First Intermediate Period, is of interest for several reasons. Together with other texts it acquaints us with a second Nemrat who was not only 'head of the entire army' and a 'great chief of foreigners',[5] but also one of those princely persons who were pleased to claim descent from the Ramessides; his mother Penreshnas was herself daughter of a 'great chief of foreign lands'.[6] This Nemrat came to his father Shōshenḳ and reported that the temple of the Hēracleopolitan god Arsaphēs had been bereft of the customary revenue of bulls needed for the many sacrifices to be made in all the months of the year; he himself was ready to contribute no less than sixty bulls, but the towns, villages, and officials of the nome would have to supply the rest;

[1] *JEA* xxvii. 83 ff. [2] *BAR* iv, §§ 738 ff. [3] *JEA* xix. 19 ff.
[4] See below, p. 351. [5] i.e. of Meshwesh Libyans. [6] *Ann. Serv.* xviii. 246–9.

a long list was appended, and the king issued a decree ordering this to be acted upon, incidentally congratulating Nemrat on a beneficence equal to his own. What was the reason for this special favour accorded to Hēracleopolis? No certain answer can be given, but it is significant that most of Ḥarpson's ancestors, both male and female, had held priesthoods in that city, and that nearly 300 years later governors of the Thebaid were apt to be chosen from among its inhabitants. A third Nemrat[1] who was a son of Osorkōn II bore the title 'commander of the army of Ḥa-Ninsu' (Hēracleopolis) and the same designation occurs with Bekenptaḥ, a brother of the high-priest Osorkōn under Shōshenḳ III.[2] Can it be that the Meshwesh who now arose to royal power had previously been settled in that neighbourhood, on the direct route through the oases from their original Libyan home? Manetho speaks of Dyn. XXII as Bubastite and of Dyn. XXIII as Tanite, and there is good evidence connecting their kings with those flourishing towns of the eastern Delta. Nevertheless the suggestion above made deserves serious consideration. A third son of Shōshenḳ I was Iuput, whom he appointed to be high-priest of Amen-Rēᶜ at Karnak, thus breaking with the tradition of heredity previously observed for that post. This was a particularly wise move, bringing that all-important office under the close control of the sovereign, and the same policy seems to have been pursued for several generations to come. That the position was fraught with danger is clear from the retention of the title 'great commander of the army'; the high-priests were not merely priests, they were also military men. The outstanding achievement of Iuput, or perhaps we should rather say of his father, was the erection of an entrance into the precincts of the main temple of Karnak continuing westwards the south wall of the vast Hypostyle Hall. The Bubastite Portal, as it is generally called, was squeezed in between the Second Pylon and a small temple of Ramessēs III standing in the way of a huge first court which Shōshenḳ undoubtedly planned from the start, but which he did not live to accomplish. A rock-inscription at Silsila West[3] records the opening of a new quarry to supply the sandstone for this projected court and pylon; the inscription is dated in Shōshenḳ's

[1] Gauthier, *LR* iii. 345. [2] See below, p. 333. [3] *JEA* xxxviii. 46 ff.

twenty-first year, his last according to Manetho, but it is difficult to believe that the first step, namely, the building of the portal, had not long since been taken. The decoration of its walls illustrates the event to which Shōshenḳ I, the Biblical Shishak, owes a unique celebrity.

A full half-century earlier Joab, in command of King David's forces, had devastated Edom and put its entire male population to the sword. Hadad, a child of the Edomite royal family, had escaped to Egypt and as he grew up found favour with the Pharaoh, who gave him to wife the sister of Tahpenes his queen. Later, Hadad returned to his own country against Pharaoh's will, and became a life-long enemy of Solomon (1 Kings xi. 14 ff.). A somewhat similar incident arose when, after Solomon's death, Jeroboam, an upstart pretender to his throne, fled to Egypt under Shishak (1 Kings xi. 40) only to return later as king of the ten tribes, while Rehoboam, Solomon's son, had to content himself with kingship over Judah. Meanwhile, however, relations between Egypt and the Israelite royal house had drawn closer. To quote the actual words of the Hebrew annalist: 'And Solomon made affinity with Pharaoh king of Egypt, and took Pharaoh's daughter and brought her into the city of David' (1 Kings iii. 1), and again, 'Pharaoh had gone up and taken Gezer, and burnt it with fire, and slain the Canaanites that dwelt in the city, and given it for a portion unto his daughter, Solomon's wife' (1 Kings ix. 16). All these statements read like authentic history, but no confirmation is obtainable from the Egyptian side, and chronological uncertainties, though confined within fairly narrow limits, are sufficient to render it doubtful which particular Pharaohs were in question; also the name Tahpenes is unidentifiable in the hieroglyphs. But we have not long to wait for a genuine synchronism: 'And it came to pass in the fifth year of king Rehoboam, that Shishak king of Egypt came up against Jerusalem; and he took away the treasures of the house of the Lord and the treasures of the king's house; he even took away all' (1 Kings xiv. 25–26). The probable date is about 930 B.C. The chronicler was evidently less troubled by the desecration of the holy city than by the loss of the gold shields made by Solomon, which had to be replaced by others of brass. No mention of either

Gezer or Jerusalem is made in the surviving names accompanying the great scene of the Bubastite Portal. These names are presented in the traditional fashion with which we became acquainted in connexion with the conquests of Tuthmōsis III, namely, attached to the busts of prisoners whom the gigantic figure of Pharaoh leads forward for presentation to his father Amen-Rēʿ. The enumeration is disappointing; of the 150 and more places named only a few are well enough preserved to suggest definite routes and these skirt around the hill-country of Samaria without reaching the centre of the Israelite kingdom; nor is there any hint that they ever touched Judah at all. There are, however, some indications of a raid into Edomite territory. The long-accepted belief that a 'field of Abraham' was to be read in the list is now rejected. However, the discovery at Megiddo[1] of a fragment mentioning Shōshenḳ leaves no doubt as to the reality of his campaign, though it remains wholly obscure whether it was an attempt to revive ancient glories, whether it was designed for the support of Jeroboam, or whether it was a mere plundering raid. That both Shōshenḳ and his successor Osorkōn I renewed the secular friendship of Egypt with the princes of Byblos is confirmed by the presence of statues of them there,[2] probably gifts sent by those Pharaohs themselves.

Little is known about the first Osorkōn and his successor the first Takelōt except that the former reigned at least thirty-six years and the latter possibly as much as twenty-three. The obscurities of Egyptian history now deepen to such an extent that only rarely can a glimpse of the sequence of events be caught. The reason is that the centre of activity had shifted to the Delta, from the wet soil of which only few monuments have been recovered. Thebes, though still full of its own importance, had politically speaking become a backwater. Little beyond self-adulation and barren genealogies is to be gained from the verbose inscriptions on the many statues of Theban worthies emanating from the great find at Karnak alluded to above on p. 54. For the regnal years of the Dyns. XXII and XXIII Pharaohs the Nile levels recorded on the quay in front of the temple[3] are of considerable value. In Middle Egypt not far north of Oxyrhynchos a fortress with a temple in which

[1] PM vii. 381. [2] Op. cit. vii. 388. [3] *ZÄS* xxxiv. 111 ff.

Shōshenḳ I and Osorkōn I had a hand seems to have served as a sort of boundary or barrier between north and south; this already mentioned site of El-Ḥîba had as its divinity the ram-headed 'Amūn-of-the-Crag' also described with the picturesque epithet 'Amūn great-of-roarings'. It is only in the reign of Osorkōn II that a glimmer of light begins to emerge from the darkness. No attempt will here be made to discuss the succession of Theban high-priests all apparently struggling to assert their independence of their liege-lords at Tanis. At Tanis Montet discovered the tomb of Osorkōn II, despoiled of its riches by robbers, side by side with the sarcophagus of a high-priest of Amen-Rēʿ Ḥarnakhti who appears to have been his son. At Bubastis Naville had fifty years earlier unearthed a great granite gateway decorated with invaluable reliefs depicting episodes of the important, but still highly problematic, royal Sed-festival; this had been celebrated in Osorkōn II's twenty-second year, when he took the opportunity of decreeing exclusion from all other services of the harem-women of the temple of Amen-Rēʿ as well as of other temples in his two cities. The brief, but important, inscription[1] ends:

> Lo, His Majesty sought for a great benefaction unto his father Amen-Rēʿ when he proclaimed the first Sed-festival for his son who rests upon his throne, that he might proclaim for him many great ones in Thebes, the lady of the Nine Bows. Said by the King in front of his father Amūn: 'I have exempted Thebes in her height and her breadth, being pure and garnished for her lord, there being no interference with her by the inspectors of the king's house, and her people being exempted for all eternity in the great name of the goodly god.'[2]

This can only be interpreted as an admission of the independence of Thebes, whether as the recognition of a *fait accompli* or because Osorkōn found it politic to make this concession.

After Shōshenḳ I the next four kings had contributed but little to the decoration of the Bubastite Portal at Karnak, and the high-priest Osorkōn, the son of Takelōt II, was not the man to leave unoccupied blank walls offering so clear an invitation. His actions and policy are recorded in no less than seventy-seven immensely tall columns of hieroglyphs disposed in two separate inscriptions.

[1] *Festival Hall*, Pl. 6.

[2] The 'goodly god' is Osorkōn himself.

Though handicapped by gaps in the text no less than by gaps in our philological knowledge, R. Caminos, working upon the copies provided by the Oriental Institute of the University of Chicago, has extracted as much of the historical gist as is humanly possible. Osorkōn's story begins in the eleventh year of his father's reign. He was then living at El-Ḥîba, according to his own account free from any ambition. As governor of Upper Egypt he was soon, however, called upon to quell a rebellion which had broken out at Thebes. On the way thither he halted at Khmūn (Hermopolis Magna), paid homage to its god Thōth, and caused some damaged sanctuaries to be restored. On arrival at the southern capital, he was welcomed with joy by the whole city, and particularly by the priesthood. There he soon restored order, burning with fire the guilty ones who were brought to him. The children of former magnates were reinstalled in their fathers' offices and five decrees were issued benefiting the various temples of Karnak in different ways. To the modern reader some of the good deeds of which Osorkōn speaks must seem extraordinarily trivial, for example, the gift of oil for a great lamp to burn in the sanctuary of Amen-Rēʿ, and the provision of one goose daily to each of two other temples, that of Mont and that of Amenope, making 730 geese in the course of the year. All this was done 'on behalf of the life, the prosperity, and the health' of his father Takelōt. In the recital of year 12, Osorkōn excels himself in his euphuistic exuberance, dragging in all the principal deities of the Pantheon in order to illustrate his wisdom and virtue. Perhaps there was a temporary lull in the antagonism between north and south; it is said that Osorkōn visited Thebes three times in a year, bringing ships laden with festal offerings. But in year 15 there arose new convulsions in which he 'did not weary of fighting in their midst even as Horus following his father; years elapsed in which one preyed upon another unimpeded'. At last, however, he had to admit that he knew no way of healing the state of the land except by conciliation. To this view his followers gladly assented and a great expedition to Thebes was fitted out, numberless ships bringing offerings of all kinds to Amen-Rēʿ. Osorkōn's speech to the god seems to have included reproaches that he had unduly favoured the rebels, but this was not taken amiss, and agreement was easily reached. There follows a brief reference to further trouble when Osorkōn found himself without a friend, but this was overcome by fresh oblations to the deity. The wall of the Bubastite Portal on which the foregoing narrative stands afforded no room for the remainder of Osorkōn's career, and he preferred to devote the considerable space which was left to a long enumeration of the gifts made by him down to King Shōshenḳ III's twenty-ninth year. Nor was this the end of him, for another inscription[1] describes him as high-priest again visiting Thebes together with his brother Bekenptaḥ, after they had overthrown their enemies who stood in their way. By then he must have been well on in his seventies.

The importance of Osorkōn's very lengthy autobiographical text lies less in the personality of its central figure than in the picture which it presents of an Egypt torn by dissension and seeking to maintain the sovereignty of the rulers in the north; this state of affairs may have continued right down to the end of the dynasty. It is desirable to point out how one-sided is the account given by our Osorkōn. He usually presents himself as the high-priest of Amen-Rēʿ, but what reality can be attached to such a title when borne by a prince who often resided at El-Ḥîba and whose visits to Thebes were only occasional? Meanwhile the daily ritual at Karnak would have had to be carried on, and it seems unlikely that there was not always a high-priest in residence, even if he had to retire when faced by superior claims or superior force; this has indeed been conjectured for a certain Ḥarsiēse who appears, like our Osorkōn, to have held the position under Shōshenḳ III.[2] But there had already been another high-priest Ḥarsiēse, successor in that capacity of his father Shōshenḳ, a son of Osorkōn I.[3] Here we encounter one of the principal difficulties confronting study of the period, the recurrence over and over again of the same names in both parts of the country; this applies even to the royal Prenomen, no less than eight kings using that which long before had been employed by Ramessēs IV, namely, Usimaʿrēʿ-setpenamūn.[4] The problems are most baffling, nor can they be tackled with much profit until the

[1] *Rec. trav.* xxii. 55; xxxi. 6; xxxv. 138.
[2] Vandier, pp. 567 f.
[3] Op. cit., pp. 528, 560.
[4] Gauthier, *LR* iii. 430–1.

scattered and fragmentary inscriptions have been collected anew, accurately copied, and properly edited; and even then it is extremely doubtful whether a coherent account will emerge. Meanwhile we must be contented with isolated facts, such for example as Montet's finding at Tanis the remains of Takelōt II lying in a usurped sarcophagus of the Middle Kingdom and accompanied by his canopic jars and ushabti-figures. Towards the end of the dynasty the Serapeum material begins to be of real assistance, the inscriptions mentioning the dates of birth and death of several Apis bulls, together with the length of their lives; hence, for instance, it has been calculated that Shōshenḳ III reigned no less than fifty-two years and was succeeded by a king named Pemay ('The Cat').[1] Throughout the entire dynasty the reigns are unexpectedly long, a fact which appears to contradict our earlier generalization that in Egypt length of reign usually spells a prevailing prosperity. Manetho gives Dyn. XXII only 120 years, but the accepted chronology finds itself compelled to legislate for fully two centuries, namely from 950 to 730 B.C.

Manetho's TWENTY-THIRD DYNASTY consists of only four kings, the third (Psammūs) being unidentifiable and the fourth (Zēt) confined to Africanus and probably an error. At the head of the dynasty is a Petubastis said to have reigned 40 years according to Africanus, but only 25 according to Eusebius; he is mentioned in several of the quay inscriptions at Karnak, one of them of year 23. Serious reasons have been advanced for regarding Dyn. XXIII as contemporaneous with Dyn. XXII, and indeed the second name is given as Osorchō or Osorthōn. Matters are complicated by the existence of another Petubastis who had a different Prenomen[2] and is probably to be recognized in the hero of a late demotic romance of which there are several versions. It remains to be mentioned that there are other obscure kings presumably belonging to this period who cannot be placed; they are probably to be accounted for by the ever increasing segmentation of the land, a fact that will be amply demonstrated in the new phase of Egyptian history about to be described.

The next entries in Manetho as reported by Africanus are brief

[1] *BAR* iv, §§ 771 ff.; 778 ff.

[2] Gauthier, *LR* iii. 397–8.

enough and interesting enough to be quoted *in extenso*: 'TWENTY-FOURTH DYNASTY. Bochchōris of Sais, for 6 (44)[1] years: in his time a lamb spoke . . . 990 years. TWENTY-FIFTH DYNASTY, of three Ethiopian kings (*a*) Sabacōn, who taking Bochchōris captive, burned him alive and reigned for 8 (12) years, (*b*) Sebichōs, his son, 14 (12) years, (*c*) Tarcos, 18 (20) years; total 40 years.' Here at last we are heartened by some resemblance to authentic history, though of course we must disregard the characteristically Manethonian allusion to the lamb which prophesied with a human voice and, as a demotic papyrus tells us, foretold the conquest and enslavement of Egypt by Assyria. It is strange, however, that Manetho makes no mention of the great Sudanese or Cushite warrior Piʿankhy who about 730 B.C. suddenly altered the entire complexion of Egyptian affairs. He was the son of a chieftain or king named Kashta[2] and apparently a brother of the Shabako whom Manetho presents under the name Sabacōn. But to obtain a rough perspective of the new order of things we must look back some 700 years. Already under the Tuthmōsides a flourishing Egyptian town or colony had grown up near the massive rock of the Gebel Barkal, this of no great height, but all the more striking through its isolation in the midst of the plain about a mile from the river.[3] The provincial capital of Napata situated a short distance downstream from the Fourth Cataract at the foot of the 'Holy Mountain', as the Egyptians called it, was sufficiently remote to develop without much danger of interference. Under Tutʿankhamūn it was the limit of the Nubian viceroy's jurisdiction.[4] In Ramesside times remains on the spot and references in the texts are infrequent, and under Dyns. XXI and XXII they are completely absent. Still, we may be sure that Egyptian culture still persisted there in a dormant condition coupled with a passionate devotion to Amen-Rēʿ, the god of the mother-city Thebes. It was probably that devotion which actuated Piʿankhy's sudden incursion into the troubled land of his Libyan adversaries. The great stela[5] recovered from the ruins by Mariette is one of the most illuminating documents that Egyptian history has

[1] The bracketed numbers here and below are those of Eusebius.

[2] *JEA* xxxv. 149.

[3] See the fine drawing *JEA* xxxii, Pl. 11.

[4] *BAR* ii, § 1022.

[5] PM vii. 217; *BAR* iv, §§ 796 ff.

to show, and displays a vivacity of mind, feeling, and expression such as the homeland could no longer produce. The scene at the top already presages the situation reached at the end of the campaign. Amen-Rēʿ, accompanied by the goddess Mūt, occupies the centre of the field, with Piʿankhy standing in front of the god's seated figure. To the right a woman representing the king's wives advances followed by a king Nemrat leading a horse and holding a sistrum. In the foreground below the three kings Osorkōn, Iuwapet, and Peftuʿabast, kiss the ground in front of the conqueror and his deity, and behind the latter five more humbled magnates, two of them mere mayors of towns, but beside them two 'great princes of the Ma', do homage in similar grovelling attitudes. The text of the stela shows that all the Delta and a large part of Middle Egypt had split up into separate principalities, and if the rulers of four of these are described as kings, it is doubtless because they, as their names indicate, belonged to the family of Dyn. XXII, though the connexion is far from clear. Piʿankhy's recital, dated in his twenty-first year, starts by telling how an adventurous Delta prince named Tefnakhte had seized the entire west as far south as Lisht, sailing upstream with a great army; at his approach the headmen of towns and villages had opened their gates and came cringing at his heels like dogs. Then he turned eastwards and after capturing the principal towns on the right bank laid siege to Hēracleopolis, which he surrounded on all sides to prevent anyone from entering or leaving. Grave as was this news, it failed to worry Piʿankhy, who, we are told, 'was in great heart, laughed and his heart was glad'. The officers of his army in Egypt were unable to take the situation so lightly and asked 'Wilt thou keep silent so as to forget Upper Egypt, while Tefnakhte presses forward unhindered?' They further reported that at Ḥwēr near Hermopolis Magna Nemrat had razed the walls of the neighbouring Nefrusy, had cast off his allegiance to his sovereign, and that Tefnakhte had rewarded him with everything that he might chance to find. This was too much for Piʿankhy, and he now wrote to his commanders in Egypt ordering them to beleaguer the entire Hare nome. At the same time he gave strict instructions as to the strategy they were to pursue:[1] they were to let the enemy

[1] *JEA* xxi. 219 ff.

choose his own time for the battle, in their sure knowledge that it was Amūn who had sent them; but also when they came to Thebes they were to purify themselves in the river, to array themselves in clean linen, to rest the bow and loosen the arrow, nor were they to boast of their might, for

without him no brave has strength; he maketh strong the weak, so that many flee before the few, and one man overcometh a thousand.

Encouraged by these lofty sentiments the Nubian contingent set out for Thebes, where they did all that had been commanded them. A vast host sailing south to do battle with them was defeated with great slaughter, ships and men being captured, and many prisoners dispatched to Napata where His Majesty was. Hēracleopolis, however, remained to be recovered, and the stela at this point gives a long list of Tefnakhte's confederates stating the names of the towns of which they were the rulers; as one might expect, King Osorkōn was located at Bubastis, while Tefnakhte himself is now described as 'prophet of Nēith, lady of Sais, and *setem*-priest of Ptaḥ', i.e. as the principal priest at both Sais and Memphis. Again a great slaughter ensued, after which the remnant were pursued and slain in the neighbourhood of Pi-peḳ. But King Nemrat had sailed south to the Hare nome, believing that its capital Hermopolis Magna was at grips with the forces of His Majesty, whereupon the whole of the province was invested on all four sides. Nevertheless the news of minor victories which reached Piʿankhy gave but scanty satisfaction;

Thereupon His Majesty raged like a panther. 'Have they allowed survivors to remain from the armies of Lower Egypt, letting the escaper among them escape to tell the story of his campaign, and not causing them to die so as to destroy the last of them? As I live and as Rēʿ loves me and as my father Amūn favours me I will fare downstream myself and will overturn what he has done and will cause him to desist from fighting for all eternity.'

Piʿankhy goes on to say that he would take part in the New Year's celebrations at Karnak and also those of the feast of Phaōphi when Amūn went in solemn procession to Luxor, and on the very day of the god's return home he promises

I will cause Lower Egypt to taste the taste of my fingers.

Meanwhile the advance troops had overwhelmed Oxyrhynchos 'like a flood of water', had forced their way into El-Ḥîba with the help of a scaling ladder, and had also taken the town of Ḥeboinu, but these successes brought no contentment to Piʿankhy's impatient heart. He, however, had to fulfil his vow of attendance at the Theban festivals before he could take ship to Hermopolis. Arrived there, he mounted his chariot and pitched his tent to the south-west of the town, but before taking part in the siege again addressed a thorough scolding to his soldiers for their indolence. Then

a ramp was made to cover the wall and a machine to raise on high archers shooting and slingers slinging stones so as to kill people among them every day.

Soon Hermopolis began to stink, and the inhabitants flung themselves upon their bellies supplicating the king for mercy, and messengers went in and out bringing gifts of gold and chests full of clothing, whilst the crown on Piʿankhy's head and the uraeus on his brow inspired unceasing awe. Thereupon Nemrat's wife came to supplicate 'the king's wives, the king's harem women, the king's daughters, and the king's sisters' begging them to intercede with 'Horus, lord of the palace, whose power is great and his triumph mighty'. Piʿankhy seems next to reproach Nemrat for his hostile action to which that humbled enemy can make no better reply than to bring a horse for the king and a sistrum for the queen as depicted in the scene at the top of the stela. The pious monarch's first act was to sacrifice to Thōth and the other deities of the place, after which he inspected Nemrat's palace and store-houses and had his womenfolk presented to him, but in the latter he took no pleasure. He was, however, aroused to a pitch of fury on finding the horses of Nemrat's stable in a starving condition, and he upbraided him bitterly. The narrative continues in the same vein with an account of Peftuʿabast's surrender of Hēracleopolis accompanying this with a particularly eloquent speech. El-Lahûn at the entrance to the Fayyûm was the next place to fall, after Piʿankhy had urged its inhabitants not to choose death in preference to life; Tefnakhte's own son was among those allowed to escape without punishment. Meidûm and Lisht followed suit, but Memphis presented a much tougher undertaking, no heed being paid to Piʿankhy's protestation that all he wished to do was to make offerings to its god Ptaḥ, and to his assurance that no one would be killed except such rebels as had blasphemed against God. Night gave Tefnakhte the opportunity of intervening with 8,000 picked warriors, but he departed on horseback in a hurry to rally the Delta princes, whom he thought to win over by promises of the rich supplies to be found in the city. When Piʿankhy reached Memphis in the morning, he found it strongly protected by water reaching up to the walls and by its newly built battlements. Great diversity of counsel existed as to the best way of facing this situation, but Piʿankhy swore an oath that Amūn's help would give him the victory, and this did in fact happen. Mindful as ever of his religious duties, the king purified the entire place with natron and incense and performed all the rites demanded of a monarch. The inhabitants of the surrounding villages fled without its being known where they went, and Iuwapet and other princes came with presents 'to see the beauty of His Majesty'.

Much more space would be required in order even to paraphrase the remaining events of a campaign described with such breadth and with such a wealth of colourful incident, but we must refrain from anything more than a passing reference to Piʿankhy's doings in Hēliopolis, the holiest of all Egypt's cities, and to the assurance given him by Peteēse of Athribis that neither he nor the other princes would conceal any of the things which he might covet, particularly the horses. In the end Tefnakhte himself made a complete submission saying:

> I will not disobey the King's command, I will not reject what His Majesty says, I will not do evil to any prince without thy knowing it, and I will do what the King says.

A last trait must not be omitted since it confirms a statement made by Herodotus (ii. 37) and other classical writers, but none too well authenticated in the native sources. When two princes from the north and two from the south came as representatives of the entire land to do homage to Piʿankhy, only Nemrat was admitted to the palace, since the others had eaten fish and were impure. A trifling detail such as this is a salutary reminder that we are here dealing with a moral and intellectual atmosphere vastly different from our own. Much that Diodorus has to say about the strictly regulated life of a Pharaoh may well be true, even if we have no means of verification. It would be interesting to know the actual author of the vivid story recounted in Piʿankhy's great stela. He was evidently well versed in Middle Egyptian diction, from which various borrowings can be quoted. But behind the verbal expression we cannot fail to discern the fiery temperament of the Nubian ruler, a temperament which had also as ingredients a fanatical piety and a real generosity. His racial antecedents are obscure, the view that he came of Libyan stock resting on very slender evidence. The vigour and individuality shared with him by his successors makes it equally unlikely, however, that they were simple descendants of emigrant Theban priests, as some have supposed; their names are outlandish and non-Egyptian, and fresh blood must have come in from somewhere to give them such energy. It is strange that after the defeat of Tefnakhte Piʿankhy appears to have retired to his home at Napata, leaving hardly a trace of himself in Egypt. He was buried at Kurru[1] in the first true pyramid of a series of tombs going back for six generations.

Tefnakhte seems to have been left to his own devices, and a unique stela in the Athens Museum presents him as king making a donation of land to the goddess Nēith of Sais in his eighth year. Manetho does not mention him, but Diodorus and Plutarch name Tnephachthos as the father of Bochchōris and as an advocate of the simple life. We have already noted what Manetho has to tell about Bochchōris, who for other Greek writers was proverbial as a judge and a lawgiver. Under the name Bekenrinef he appears on a stela from the Serapeum which records the burial of an Apis-bull in his sixth year;[2] that year will have been his last if Manetho is to be trusted.

Meanwhile a new enemy had loomed up in the east. For two centuries past the small kingdoms of Syria and Palestine had been

[1] PM vii. 197. [2] Op. cit. iii. 209.

able to subsist with but little outside interference. But now they found themselves faced with a regenerated, ambitious, and tyrannical Assyria. Tiglath-pileser III (745–727 B.C.) in a series of campaigns in the west ravaged Damascus and deported to Assyria a

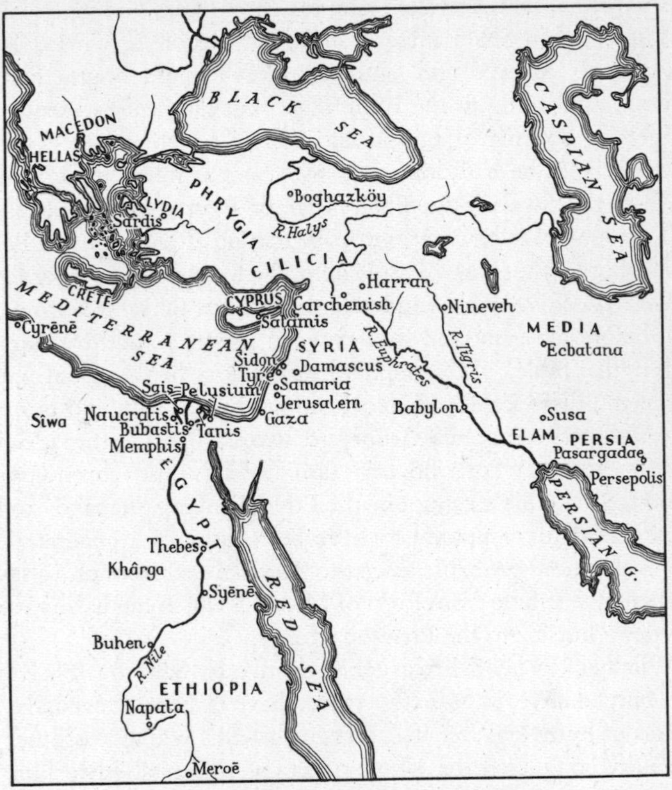

MAP III. The Near East in the First Millenium B.C.

large part of its population;[1] he did also the like to Israel, deposing its king Pekah and replacing him by Hoshea (732 B.C.).[2] For these events and those of the next half-century our sole authorities are the Old Testament and the cuneiform inscriptions, the texts from Egypt never mentioning Assyria, although in the end even Thebes itself was to fall a temporary victim to the far stronger Asiatic

[1] 2 Kings xvi. 9; *ANET*, p. 283.

[2] 2 Kings xv. 29–30; *ANET*, p. 284.

power. Yet it was clearly to Egypt that the petty rulers in Palestine looked for help against the northern invaders. Under Shalmaneser V, Tiglathpileser's short-lived son, Hoshea broke into open rebellion,[1] with the tragic result that Samaria was captured and destroyed, although it held out for three years and only fell in 721 B.C., when Shalmaneser's successor Sargon II 'carried Israel away unto Assyria' and 'shut' Hoshea 'up and bound him in prison'. According to the Biblical account Hoshea 'had sent messengers to So king of Egypt, and offered no present to the king of Assyria, as he had done year by year'. Scholars are agreed to identify this So with the Sib'e, *turtan* of Egypt, whom the annals of Sargon state to have set out from Rapihu (Raphia on the Palestinian border) together with Hanno, the King of Gaza, in order to deliver a decisive battle. Under Tiglath-pileser the same Hanno had fled before his army and 'run away to Egypt',[2] and now Sargon tells us that Sib'e, 'like a shepherd whose flock has been stolen, fled alone and disappeared; Hanno I captured personally and brought him in fetters to my city Ashur; I destroyed Rapihu, tore it down and burned it'.[3] For phonetic and probably also chronological reasons So and Sib'e cannot be the Ethiopian king Shabako, so that these names are supposed to have been those of a general. This seems the more probable since the Assyrian text goes on to say 'I received the tribute from Pir'u of Musru',[4] which can hardly mean anything but 'from the Pharaoh of Egypt'.

Whether Bochchōris was taken captive by Sabacōn (Shabako) and burned alive, as Manetho would have us believe, we have no means of knowing, but it is certain that this younger brother of Piᶜankhy conquered the whole of Egypt, and established himself there as a genuine Egyptian Pharaoh. The texts of Sargon appear to indicate 711 B.C. as the likely date.[5] Shabako reigned at least fourteen years, when he was succeeded by Shebitku (Sebichōs in Manetho), whom we must assume to have held the throne until the accession of Taharḳa (Tarcos) in 689 B.C., this date fixed by Apis stelae. Considering the combined length of these two reigns, it is strange how seldom the names of Shabako and Shebitku are

[1] 2 Kings xvii. 3 ff. [2] *ANET*, p. 283. [3] Op. cit., p. 285.
[4] Op. cit., p. 286. [5] Another opinion is 715 B.C., see *Bull. Inst. fr.* li. 27.

encountered. Apart from the pyramids at Kurru where they were buried[1] and from a horse-cemetery in the same place, their Nubian home has hardly a trace of them to show. There are some indications that Shabako made Memphis his capital,[2] but Thebes also testifies to his building activities; at Karnak and Medînet Habu there are chapels erected by the same king.[3] There was the less need for the Ethiopian monarchs to keep guard over the temple of their revered god Amen-Rēʿ since their political power at the southern capital was otherwise represented. An essential feature of late Egyptian history is the importance gained by the royal princesses who bore the titles of 'God's Wife of Amūn', 'Adorer of the God', or 'Hand of the God'. In earlier days the epithet 'God's Wife' was commonly accorded to the Pharaoh's spouse, and doubtless carried with it a religious significance that remains to be determined. From Dyn. XXI onwards, however, this epithet was transferred to a king's daughter who became the consecrated wife of the Theban god, and to whom human intercourse was strictly forbidden. Such a one appears to have been the earlier Maʿkarēʿ believed to have been the daughter of the Tanite king Psusennēs I; her mummy was found in the Dêr el-Baḥri *cache*, accompanied by that of an infant which suggests that she had died in childbirth after having offended against the rule of chastity imposed on her. It was only at the beginning of the Ethiopian supremacy, however, that the appointment of a God's Wife became a deliberate instrument of policy, and for this to happen the device of adoption had to be brought into play. Thus Kashta, who before Piʿankhy had presumably made himself master of the Thebais, caused his daughter Amonortais I to be adopted by Shepenwepe I, the daughter of the last Osorkōn, and this Amonortais served again as adoptive mother to a second Shepenwepe, the daughter of King Piʿankhy.[4] Such a God's Wife wielded great influence, and was to all intents and purposes the equal of the king her father, not only having great estates and officials of her own, but also being authorized to make offerings to the gods, a right elsewhere reserved for Pharaoh himself; the main limitation to her authority was that it was confined to Thebes,

[1] PM vii. 196–7.
[2] Op. cit. iii. 220, 226.
[3] Op. cit. ii, Index, p. 201.
[4] *Kawa* i. 119–20.

where she lived and died, at the end obtaining a burial-place near the temple of Dêr el-Medîna.

The absence of the names of Shabako and Shebitku from the Assyrian and Hebrew records is no less remarkable than the scarcity of their monuments in the lands over which they extended their sway. It is all the more interesting to find Sabacōs mentioned by Herodotus (ii. 137) as an Ethiopian whose army drove a rival Pharaoh into the fen-country of the Delta; this marks the point at which the Greek historian begins to show some knowledge of the true sequence of events, though his account never liberates itself from that fanciful anecdotal character which was as great a delight to him as it is to us. With the accession of Taharḳa, the brother and successor of Shebitku, our documentation becomes abundant. The excavations of F. Ll. Griffith at Kawa midway between the Third and Fourth Cataracts brought to light no less than five great stelae, for the most part very well preserved, recounting the occurrences of his early years and the donations which he made to the temple in which they were found. Fragmentary duplicates of the most important of these stelae have been found at Matâʿana, at Coptos, and at Tanis, showing that Taharḳa was nothing loath to publicize his fortunes and his achievements. We learn that at the age of twenty he and others of the king's brothers were sent for from Nubia to join Shebitku at Thebes, where he quickly won the latter's special affection. After Shebitku's death he was crowned at Memphis and his first act was to remember the ruinous state of the temple of Kawa as he had seen it on his way to Egypt; his restorations and the multitudinous gifts which he heaped upon the local god Amen-Rēʿ attest the devotion which he continued to feel towards the country of his birth. Of particular interest is the mention of 'wives of the princes of Lower Egypt' and of 'children of the princes of the Tjeḥnu'[1] whom he transported thither as temple-servants, since this seems to imply victories over the mainly Libyan rival princes in the Delta. The sixth year of his reign was for him an *annus mirabilis*, a specially high Nile in Egypt itself and heavy rain in Nubia providing both lands with exceptional harvests and great prosperity; and in that same year he welcomed to Memphis

[1] *Bull. Inst. fr.* li. 28.

his mother Abar whom he had not seen since his departure from Nubia. Characteristically all these hieroglyphic memorials paint a roseate picture; there is no hint of the disasters which Taharḳa had actually to face; and the buildings which he initiated at Karnak and at Medînet Habu prove that in the long-stretched Nile Valley works of peace were still possible even in a period of vital danger from the north-east.

The smouldering hostility of the two great powers flared up afresh under Sennacherib (705–681 B.C.), whose third campaign started with the subjugation of the Phoenician coast-towns. Trouble had, however, arisen farther south: the people of the Philistine city of Ekron had expelled their king Padi on account of his loyalty to Assyria, but Hezekiah of Judah who had received and imprisoned him became afraid and appealed to Egypt for help.[1] A great defeat was inflicted on the Egyptian and Ethiopian forces at Eltekeh, Padi's throne was restored to him, and many towns of Judah were ravaged, though Jerusalem was not taken. To avoid this, Hezekiah submitted to pay a heavy tribute. It has been much disputed whether this was Sennacherib's sole clash with Egypt, but a straightforward reading of 2 Kings xix. 8–35 demands that there was another. It is there recounted that 'Tirhakah, king of Ethiopia', had come out to fight against the Assyrians, but that the angel of the Lord had smitten a vast multitude of them in the night, so that in the morning 'they were all dead corpses'; the next two verses state that Sennacherib thereupon returned to Nineveh and dwelt there until he was assassinated. In the fantastic but amusing account that Herodotus (ii. 141) gives of this abortive attack upon Egypt, the Assyrian retreat after reaching Pelusium was due, not to plague as the Old Testament suggests, but to swarms of mice who ate up the invaders' quivers and bows. Since Taharḳa succeeded Shebitku only in 689 B.C. he cannot well have been the enemy whom Sennacherib defeated at Eltekeh, and short of denying the accuracy of the Biblical story we must suppose that he aimed at following up that victory by a later blow, which, however, circumstances prevented. The enemies will not have met.

It had long become clear that a decision between the equally

[1] *ANET*, pp. 287 f.

pertinacious Assyrian and Ethiopian rulers would have to be reached, but in point of fact there was a third party to the dispute and it was with this that the ultimate victory was destined to lie. As in the time of Piʿankhy Lower Egypt and a part of Middle Egypt had disintegrated into a number of petty princedoms always ready to side with whichever of the two great powers would be the more likely to leave them their independence. One of these was to prevail before long, but for the moment it was Assyria which held the upper hand. Esarhaddon (680–669 B.C.), the son of Sennacherib, continued his father's aggressive policy with even greater success. The Egyptian records are silent, but stelae and tablets inscribed in cuneiform give circumstantial accounts of the campaign in which, after subjugating Syria, he drove Taharḳa reeling back to the south. Here is a shortened excerpt from the best preserved of his inscriptions:[1]

From the town of Ishhupri as far as Memphis, a distance of fifteen days, I fought daily very bloody battles against Tarḳu, king of Egypt and Ethiopia, the one accursed by all the great gods. Five times I hit him with the point of my arrows inflicting wounds, and then I laid siege to Memphis, his royal residence; I destroyed it, tore down its walls, and burnt it down.

After mentioning the booty which he carried off to Assyria he continues:

All Ethiopians I deported from Egypt, leaving not even one to do homage to me. Everywhere in Egypt I appointed new kings, governors, officers, harbour overseers, officials, and administrative personnel.

Soon after setting out for a further campaign Esarhaddon fell ill at Harran and died, enabling Taharḳa to regain Memphis and to occupy it until driven out afresh in Ashurbanipal's first campaign (667 B.C.). The new Assyrian king found that 'the kings, governors, and regents' whom his father had appointed in Egypt had fled and needed to be reinstalled. The famous Rassam cylinder gives an invaluable list of these petty princes,[2] naming all the more important Delta towns besides others farther south such as Hēracleopolis, Hermopolis, and Asyûṭ. Thebes (Ni) was occupied for the first time, but only to be surrendered temporarily:[3]

[1] *ANET*, p. 293. [2] Op. cit., p. 294. [3] Op. cit., p. 295.

The terror of the sacred weapon of Ashur, my lord, overcame Tarḳu where he had taken refuge and he was never heard of again. Afterwards Urdamane, son of Shabako, sat down on the throne of his kingdom. He made Thebes and Hēliopolis his fortresses and assembled his armed might.

The narrative goes on to tell that Urdamane, the name given by the Assyrians to the Ethiopian king Tanuatamūn, reoccupied Memphis, and it was not until Ashurbanipal returned from Nineveh and started upon his second campaign that the Ethiopian abandoned first Memphis and then Thebes and 'fled to Kipkipi'. That was the last of him so far as the cuneiform records are concerned. Ashurbanipal claims to have conquered Thebes completely and to have carried away to Niniveh a vast booty, but that appears to have been his final appearance in Egypt (663 B.C.). Before describing the arrangements which he had made for reducing the Delta to vassalage we must follow up the fortunes of Tanuatamūn so far as any light is thrown upon them in the Egyptian records.

Found at Gebel Barkal at the same time as the great inscription of Piʿankhy is one of the reign of Tanuatamūn known as the Dream Stela.[1] The facts recorded are the same as those of the cuneiform cylinder above quoted, but it would be difficult to find a greater contrast than that of the two presentations: both tell a tale of triumph, but in the one case the victor is Ashurbanipal, in the other Tanuatamūn. The Ethiopian relates how, in the first year of his reign, he saw in a dream two snakes, one on his right hand, the other on his left, and this was interpreted to him in the following words:

Upper Egypt belongs to thee, take to thyself Lower Egypt. The Vulture and Uraeus goddesses have appeared on thy head, and the land is given to thee in its length and breadth, and none shall share with thee.

Then Tanuatamūn 'arose upon the seat of Horus in this year and went forth from the place where he was even as Horus went forth from Chemmis',[2] and proceeded unopposed to Napata where he made a great feast to Amen-Rēʿ. Faring downstream, he did similar

[1] *BAR* iv, §§ 919 ff.

[2] The place amid the Delta swamps where the god Horus passed his infancy.

homage to Chnūm of Elephantinē and to the Amen-Rēʿ of Thebes. On the way to Memphis he was welcomed everywhere with great rejoicing, and on arrival at the northern capital

> the Children of Rebellion came forth to fight with His Majesty, and His Majesty made a great slaughter among them, their number is unknown.

Thus Tanuatamūn took Memphis and made offerings to Ptaḥ and the other gods of the city, after which he sent a command to Napata to build a great portal there in token of his gratitude.

Before commenting upon the story as here told it will be as well to summarize with some extracts the rest of Tanuatamūn's stela. Next we read:

> After this His Majesty fared downstream to fight with the princes of Lower Egypt. Then they entered within their walls, like . . . entering into their holes. Thereupon His Majesty spent many days beside them, and not one of them came forth to fight with him.

So Tanuatamūn returned to Memphis, there to cogitate on his next step. A message then came saying that the princes were ready to wait upon him, and on his asking whether they wished to fight or if they wished to become his servants they assented to the latter course. Thereupon they were admitted to the palace, where the king told them that victory had been promised him by his god Amūn of Napata. In their reply the prince of Pi-Sopd acts as their spokesman, and all undertake to serve him loyally. After being entertained at a banquet they ask to be allowed to return to their towns so as to get on with their agricultural labours. They then disperse and the inscription comes to an abrupt end.

There is probably much truth in both the Assyrian and the Ethiopian accounts, but the way in which they dovetail into one another is not altogether clear. Taharḳa and Tanuatamūn are mentioned together on a building at Thebes, but there is no reason to suppose a co-regency. Of Taharḳa's end all we know is that he returned to Napata and was buried at Nûri,[1] a short distance to the south. Tanuatamūn's successful occupation of Memphis and his reconciliation with the Delta princes preceded Ashurbanipal's thrust southwards to Thebes, but his end was not yet. At Thebes

[1] PM vii. 223.

all through these troublous times a man of great ability managed to retain the practical power side by side with the God's Wife, Shepenwepe II, a sister of Taharḳa. Mentemḥē is first mentioned in the Rassam cylinder of Ashurbanipal, where he figures as 'king of Thebes'. In point of fact he was only the 'fourth prophet of Amūn', though descended from a distinguished priestly family; it is certain that he altogether overshadowed the 'first prophet'. His grandfather bore the title of 'Vizier', while his father Nesptaḥ was merely the 'mayor of Nē' (Thebes).[1] His monuments are numerous, naturally for the most part confined to Thebes, but two short inscriptions from Abydos[2] suggest that his authority may have extended as far north as that city. Of great interest is a long, but unfortunately much-damaged hieroglyphic text occupying the side-walls of a small chamber in the temple of Mūt at Karnak,[3] the back-wall showing a scene of Taharḳa worshipping the goddess and followed by Mentemḥē with his father and his son. This proves that Mentemḥē, for all his power, regarded himself as no more than a faithful subject of the Ethiopian king. None the less the inscription boasts of numerous and varied constructions and repairs such as at other times could only have been ascribed to the Pharaoh: here the sovereign is only indirectly alluded to, and Mentemḥē takes all the credit to himself, no doubt justifiably. The references to the topsy-turvy state of the land are few and obscure, and there is, of course, none to the brief occupation of the southern capital by the Assyrians.

Tanuatamūn kept up the pretence of being the true Pharaoh for several years after Ashurbanipal's hasty raid upon Thebes. A few inscriptions of his have been found there, one of them recording a sale of land in his eighth year.[4] Long before that he will have retired to Napata, ultimately dying there and being buried at Kurru.[5] After a little short of seventy years the Ethiopian venture had come to an end. Apparently all direct contact between the two kingdoms now ceased, though some sort of trade relations will have persisted. The northern boundary of the Napatan kingdom was probably Pnūbs south of the Third Cataract; between there and Aswân may

1 Articles by Legrain in *Rec. trav.* xxxiii ff.
2 PM v. 78.
3 PM ii. 92; *BAR* iv, §§ 901 ff.
4 *Ann. Serv.* vii. 226.
5 PM vii. 196.

have become a sort of no-man's-land inhabited by wild tribes. Henceforth the Ethiopians began to look southwards instead of northwards, establishing a new capital at Meroē within the fork of the Atbara and the Nile; here cattle could be raised and crops grown, and there were also abundant deposits of iron. If there was thus politically a scission between Egypt and Ethiopia, nevertheless the old Pharaonic culture died in the latter country only very slowly; the temples exhibited the same stereotyped scenes in relief; the royal tombs were pyramidal in shape. Several fine stelae written in passably good Middle Egyptian were found together with that of Piʿankhy at Gebel Barkal, one of King Aspelta giving a graphic account of his election as king.[1] Some generations later similar hieroglyphic inscriptions, though still using the Egyptian language, are barbaric to the point of unintelligibility. Meanwhile there had been developed out of the Egyptian hieroglyphs an alphabetic script used for writing the native language, and side by side with this there was developed a linear type of writing corresponding to the native hieroglyphic sign for sign. In the decipherment of these two scripts jointly known as Meroitic, F. Ll. Griffith played the largest part. It does not belong to our task to recount the story of this gradual deterioration, which came to a head with the destruction of Meroē by Aeizanes of Axum about A.D. 350.

SELECT BIBLIOGRAPHY

The great Dêr el-Baḥri *cache*: discovery and general account, G. Maspero, *Les Momies royales de Déir el-Baharî*, Cairo, 1889; the actual mummies, G. Elliot Smith, *The Royal Mummies*, Cairo, 1912; the coffins, G. Daressy, *Cercueils des cachettes royales*, Cairo, 1909; the tomb of Inḥaʿpy, J. Černý in *JEA* xxxii. 24–30.

The tomb of the priests and priestesses of Amūn: bibliography, PM i. 198; complete list of the coffins, their owners, and their contents, *Ann. Serv.* viii. 3 ff.

Characterization of Dyns. XXI and XXII: Ed. Meyer, *Gottesstaat, Militärherrschaft und Ständewesen*, in *Sitzungsberichte* of Berlin Academy, 1928. Trial

[1] PM vii. 217.

of an official by oracle, É. Naville, *Inscription historique de Pinodjem III*, Paris, 1883. The titles 'God's Wife', 'Adorer of the God', M. F. Laming Macadam, *The Temples of Kawa*, Oxford, 1949, i. 119 ff.

Tanis: P. Montet, *La Nécropole royale de Tanis*, i. *Les Constructions et le tombeau d'Osorkon II*, Paris, 1947; ii. *Les Constructions et le tombeau de Psousennēs*, Paris, 1951; iii *Chèchanq* III, 1960; brief summary, Vandier, *Clio*³, pp. 534–7.

Dyn. XXII: the Bubastite Portal, *Reliefs and Inscriptions at Karnak*, iii, Chicago, [1954]; translations and commentaries, R. Caminos, *The Chronicle of Prince Osorkon*, Rome, 1958; É. Naville, *The Festival-Hall of Osorkon II in the Great Temple of Bubastis*, London, 1892. Importance of Hēracleopolis, F. Ll. Griffith, *Catalogue of the Demotic Papyri in the John Rylands Library*, Manchester, 1909, iii. 71 ff.; the stela of Nemrat, son of Shoshenḳ I, P. Tresson in *Mélanges Maspero*, Cairo, 1935–8 [ii], pp. 817 ff.

The Serapeum of Memphis: see above, p. 326, n. 1.

Egypt and Palestine: T. E. Peet, *Egypt and the Old Testament*, Liverpool, 1922; the campaign of Shoshenḳ I, D. M. Noth, *Die Schoschenkliste* in *ZDPV* lx. 277–304.

Ethiopian period: H. von Zeissl, *Äthiopen und Assyrer in Ägypten*, Glückstadt, 1944; excavations by G. Reisner and Dows Dunham, at Kurru, PM vii. 195 ff.; at Gebel Barkal, op. cit. vii. 203 ff.; at Nûri, op. cit. vii. 223 ff.; by F. Ll. Griffith at Kawa, op. cit. vii. 180 ff. Good summary account of the American work, Dows Dunham, *The Egyptian Department and its Excavations*, Boston, 1958, pp. 100 ff.

The Assyrian records: *ANET*, pp. 282 ff.; *Documents from Old Testament Times*, ed. D. Winton Thomas, London, 1958.

Meroē, PM vii. 235 ff.; Dows Dunham, op. cit., pp. 119 ff.

XIII

THE LAST ASSERTIONS OF INDEPENDENCE

AT the close of Ashurbanipal's Egyptian campaign the power of Assyria was at its zenith. He had defeated his foes in all directions, but they were too tenacious of their independence to allow him more than a brief breathing-space. The kingdom of Elam, his hereditary enemy to the east, was the first to give trouble. No sooner was this danger overcome than a new coalition of wider scope came into being, part in which was taken by his own treacherous brother Shamashshumukin, the semi-independent ruler of Babylon. It was clear that Ashurbanipal could retain his hold on the Egyptian Delta only through the loyalty of his own nominees. He was able to leave there only very few Assyrian troops. Esarhaddon had initiated the policy of replacing those princes whom he could not trust by others of his own choice. Among these latter was Nekō of Sais, not improbably a descendant of Piʿankhy's adversary Tefnakhte. But this Nekō had soon rebelled and been carried away together with others captive to Nineveh.[1] Evidently, however, Ashurbanipal had recognized in him a man of ability and enterprise since he showed him mercy, loaded him with fine raiment, jewels, and other riches and

> returned to him Sais as residence where my own father had appointed him king. Nabushezibanni his son I appointed for Athribis, treating him with more friendliness and favour than my own father did.

Manetho makes this Nekō I the third king of his TWENTY-SIXTH SAITE DYNASTY, preceding his name with those of an unidentifiable Stephinatēs and an equally problematic Nechepsōs. There are good historic reasons, however, for taking Manetho's fourth king Psammētichus I as the real founder of the dynasty; the name, for all its outlandish appearance, is an Egyptian one meaning 'the negus-vendor', a designation apparently connected with

[1] *ANET*, p. 295.

Herodotus's story (ii. 151) of his improvisation of a libation bowl out of his helmet.[1] On an Apis stela he follows immediately upon Taharḳa, Tanuatamūn not being alluded to.[2] Most of Egypt was now in the hands of independent princes whose interest it was to combine against the foreigner rather than to indulge in internecine strife. Thus came about, with Psammētichus as its leader, the 'Dodecarchy' which Herodotus (ii. 147) describes in his usual romantic fashion. The Greek historian's statement (ii. 152) that Psammētichus had been a fugitive in Syria from Sabacōs who had killed his father Nekōs is impossible chronologically; when and where Nekō[3] found his death is unknown. There is a possibility that Psammētichus was the son to whom the Assyrian name Nabushezibanni had been given; however, in the account of Ashurbanipal's third campaign contained on the Rassam cylinder he appears with a name very different from both this and the Egyptian form. On the cylinder the circumstance which enabled Psammētichus to free himself from the Assyrian domination is recounted in an altogether trustworthy manner.[4] It is there told that Gyges, the King of Lydia, being attacked by the savage Cimmerian hordes had with Ashurbanipal's help succeeded in repulsing them. But then, as Ashurbanipal writes:

> his messenger, whom he kept sending to me to bring me greetings, he discontinued because he did not heed the word of Ashur the god who created me, but trusted in his own strength and hardened his heart,

the result being that the Cimmerians invaded and overpowered the whole of his land. The same passage states that Gyges

> sent his forces to Tushamilki, King of Egypt, who had thrown over the yoke of my sovereignty.

A distorted reference to the troops sent to Egypt by Gyges may possibly be found in the bronze-clad Ionians and Carians who according to Herodotus (ii. 152) helped Psammētichus to gain the mastery over the other Delta princes. This will presumably have occupied him during the first years of his reign; no monument of his is dated before year 9. In that year he succeeded in extending

[1] F. Ll. Griffith, *Rylands Papyri*, iii. 44, 201.

[2] *BAR* iv, §§ 959–62.

[3] So too hieroglyphic; Assyrian Nikū; the Nechaō of Manetho is inaccurate.

[4] D. D. Luckenbill, *Ancient Records of Assyria*, ii, §§ 784–5.

his influence over the Thebaid by the method employed by other Pharaohs before him. A great stela found at Karnak[1] relates how he sent his eldest daughter Nitōcris to become the 'God's Wife' of Amūn as successor to Shepenwepe II, the sister of Taharḳa. The journey to Thebes is described in detail. The 'Master of Shipping' Samtowetefnakhte was in charge of the vessels; he was at the same time mayor of the Hēracleopolitan nome, and there is evidence that other members of his family also enjoyed this prerogative, which gave them control over all the river traffic upstream; we have seen that Hēracleopolis had acquired special importance in the Libyan period. On arrival at Thebes Nitōcris was received with great rejoicing, in which the reigning God's Wife joined. More important, however, than the opulent feast prepared for her on this occasion were the riches now showered upon her, in seven nomes of Upper Egypt no less than 1,800 arourae of land and in four nomes of the Delta 1,400 more; as a landowner she thus became possessed of some 2,000 acres. But this was not all; the most important priests of Amūn, with the pliant Mentemḥē at their head, provided her with ample rations, to which were added large quantities of bread contributed by the temples of the principal towns. Needless to say, an able chief steward was required to administer such wealth, and Pbes would have been less than human had he refused to avail himself of this opportunity; however, his tomb at Ḳurna[2] and that of Iba,[3] another chief steward of this long reign, are considerably less pretentious than those of several others of the same dynasty who held the like post.

Sixty years later, when Nitōcris was an old woman, the same process renewed itself, and she was forced to accept as her future successor ʿAnkhnasneferibrēʿ, the daughter of Psammētichus II and the owner of a magnificent sarcophagus now in the British Museum. She arrived in Thebes and was received there by her adoptive mother in the first year of her father's reign, and she appears to have had conferred upon her at the same time the dignity of First Prophet of Amūn, a position not accorded to any other 'God's Wife'; but it was not until Nitōcris died in the fourth year of

[1] *BAR* iv, §§ 935 ff. [2] PM i. 165, No. 279. [3] Op. cit. i. 69, No. 36; *Ann. Serv*. v. 94–96.

Apriēs that she attained to the latter even more important post. These facts are related on a stela now in the Cairo Museum,[1] which dwells upon her installation at Karnak and the attendance upon her of the priesthood, but says nothing about the endowments which had figured so largely in the case of Nitōcris.

The history of Egypt now becomes increasingly merged into that of the Middle East and of Greece, and our main authorities besides Herodotus are the cuneiform chronicles, the Jewish historian Josephus, and the Old Testament. It does not fall within the scope of this Introduction to deal with the principal facts more than sketchily, and we shall concentrate rather upon whatever the hieroglyphs have to contribute to the general picture. Nevertheless, it will be unavoidable to outline the broad trend of the development. We may pass rapidly over such conventionally worded inscriptions as that of Ḥōr,[2] the military commander at Hēracleopolis, in the temple of which he erected many buildings. Nor need we dwell at length on the statue of Nesnimu,[3] a prophet of Horus of Edfu, whom Psammētichus I promoted successively to be mayor of eight different towns, some in the Delta and some in Upper Egypt; the significance of this important act remains to be explained. This, however, is the place to expatiate on two related facts, namely the ever-increasing influx of foreigners into the country and the remarkable degree of archaism shown in the art and the religious texts of the period; it is as though the more mixed the blood of the inhabitants became the greater was the nostalgia for the Old Kingdom when the Pharaohs were true-born Egyptians and their monuments displayed a grandeur the decay of which was now all too apparent. It is in the Saite dynasty that the ancient titles of the nobility were revived, that their sculptures and reliefs were deliberately copied from those of the Old Kingdom, and that their tombs were inscribed with extracts from the Pyramid Texts. From this time onward there is a marked increase in Egyptian religiosity. Animal worship was ever more sedulously cultivated, neighbouring provinces and villages actually fighting one another in defence of their own particular preferences. Gifts of land to the temples became very frequent, the king willingly accepting such sacrifices

[1] *Ann. Serv.* v. 84 ff. [2] *BAR* iv, §§ 967 ff. [3] *ZÄS* xliv. 42 ff.

on the part of private owners in order to propitiate the hereditary priesthoods. There can be no doubt but that political considerations played a part in all this, for after all Psammētichus was himself half a Libyan, and the intense nationalism of the Egyptian natives found appeasement in this way. Moreover, Syrians and Jews had poured into the country, the latter forming a colony at Elephantinē where they were even permitted to build a temple to their god Yahu, the Jehovah of our Authorized Version.[1] We must here too refer to the different hereditary classes of the population upon which Herodotus (ii. 164–8) lays so much stress. From Ramesside times Libyans and other Mediterranean peoples had, as we have seen, contributed a substantial part to the armies on which the Egyptian monarchs relied; land had been bestowed upon them in return for their services, and it is not to be wondered at if their capabilities were now directed to agriculture rather than to warfare. There is probably a large element of exaggeration and distortion about the account given by Herodotus of that portion of the population known to the Greeks as *machimoi* 'warriors'. According to him they were exclusively trained for war and forbidden to learn any other craft; also they were settled in different nomes of the Delta, the Hermotybians and the Calasirians in separate districts of their own; the former name has not been identified in the hieroglyphs, but the latter occurs a number of times as a proper name of which *-shīre*, the second half, is the word for 'little'. But even if there was thus a definite section of the people devoted solely to warfare, it cannot be disputed that the Greeks whom Psammētichus deliberately encouraged also played a large part in a situation fraught with both external and internal dangers. In the wake of the troops sent by Gyges there followed Ionian traders only too glad to obtain a permanent foothold in so fertile and wealthy a land. Psammētichus for his part was content to acquire new forces of proven valour to counterbalance the *machimoi* who were always more or less under the control of the local princes of their particular districts. A great advantage which accrued to the Saite king was the skill of the Greek colonists as mariners. Their ships carried Egyptian corn to their fatherland, which paid for it with silver. Apart from military

[1] Bibliography, Kienitz (see p. 382), p. 39, n. 2.

action which, as we shall see, became necessary on the north-east border, garrisons had to be maintained on both the western and the southern fronts; Herodotus (ii. 30) reports such garrisons 'at Daphnae of Pelusium, another towards Libya at Marea', and a third at Elephantinē; and he goes on to say that the last-named, not having been relieved for three years, revolted and deserted to Ethiopia, which at that time enjoyed the reputation of a kind of El Dorado; Psammētichus is stated to have set forth in pursuit of them, but to have been unsuccessful in persuading them to return. We have hieroglyphic authority for a similar revolt and desertion under Apriēs,[1] but on that occasion the superintendent of the southern frontier, Nesḥōr, managed to overpersuade the fugitives.

An Apis stela proves that Psammētichus died after a reign of fifty-four years and was succeeded by his son Nekō II in 610 B.C. The new king was hardly less enterprising than his father, but was less fortunate. His native monuments are not very numerous, and are singularly uninformative. For his achievements at home Herodotus is again the main source. A courageous attempt to link the Nile with the Red Sea by a canal had to be abandoned, but it is almost certain that Phoenician ships sent by him to circumnavigate Africa succeeded in doing so, returning through the Pillars of Hercules in his third year. In order to understand the military undertakings in which Psammētichus and Nekō found themselves involved on their north-eastern front, we must be given a rough idea of what had been happening there since the former's accession. When the victorious Ashurbanipal withdrew his army from Egypt, no serious retaliation from that quarter was to be expected. It appears, however, that Egyptian troops pursued the retreating Assyrians into Philistia as had happened 900 years earlier after the expulsion of the Hyksōs; but Herodotus's account (ii. 157) of a twenty-nine year siege of Ashdod, the longest in history, can hardly be correct as it stands. Far more dangerous for Assyria was an invasion of Scythians who swept through that country and, according to the Greek writer (i. 105), were halted at the Egyptian frontier only by gifts and entreaties on the part of Psammētichus. Even more formidable, however, was the emergence in north-

[1] *BAR* iv, §§ 989-95.

western Iran of the great new empire of the Medes under Phraortēs and his son Cyaxarēs. In 627 B.C. Ashurbanipal died, and a year later, after an Assyrian army had been decisively beaten by the Babylonians always striving to assert their independence, Nabopolassar 'sat on the throne in Babylon'. All attempts on the part of the Assyrians to regain the lost ground were unsuccessful. By 616 B.C. it had become clear to Psammētichus that an alliance between Medians and Babylonians would be more dangerous than the Assyrians had ever been, so he decided to throw in his lot with his former enemies. The decision was unfortunate because in 612 B.C. Niniveh fell and was ravaged and looted with characteristic thoroughness. The Assyrian king Ashur-uballiṭ attempted to carry on the struggle from Harran far to the west, and for the next years the issue remained undecided. From 609 B.C. no further mention is made of this last king of Assyria, and Nekō now took his place as the main adversary of Nabopolassar. When 'Pharaoh-necoh, King of Egypt, went up against' the Babylonians, as we read in the Old Testament, all went well with him at first. King Josiah of Judah made the mistake of intervening at this juncture and was slain at Megiddo by Nekō (2 Kings xxiii. 29–30); a hieroglyphic fragment from Sidon[1] attests the latter's control of the Phoenician coast, made the easier by his possession of a Mediterranean fleet. In 606–605 B.C. the Egyptians captured the strong-point of Kimukhu and defeated the Babylonians at Ḳuramati, both places situated on the Euphrates south of Carchemish.[2] There, according to the Babylonian Chronicle, Nebuchadrezzar, the son of Nabopolassar,

crossed the river to go against the Egyptian army which lay in Carchemish. . . . fought with each other and the Egyptian army withdrew before him. He accomplished their defeat and beat them into non-existence. As for the rest of the Egyptian army which had escaped from the defeat and no weapon had reached them, the Babylonian troops overtook and defeated them in the district of Hamath, so that not a single man escaped to his own country. At that time Nebuchadrezzar conquered the whole area of Khatti-land.[3]

[1] PM vii. 384.

[2] Wiseman, *Chronicles* (see p. 383), pp. 23, 67.

[3] Op. cit., pp. 25, 67–68. At this period the geographical term Khatti included the whole of Syria and Palestine; see above, p. 231.

or, as 2 Kings xxiv. 7 says,

the king of Egypt came not again any more out of his land; for the king of Babylon had taken, from the brook of Egypt unto the river Euphrates, all that pertained to the king of Egypt.

The great battle of Carchemish took place in 605 B.C. and Nabopolassar died a month or two later. After Nebuchadrezzar's speedy return to Babylon to assume the kingship he returned to Syria to carry on his campaign against that country. In 604 B.C. the Babylonians attacked and sacked Ashkelon, an event which may have given rise to an appeal to the Pharaoh for help by a coastal city.[1] We have the authority of the above Old Testament statement for believing that the appeal remained unanswered. Nebuchadrezzar seems never to have given up hope of securing the Egyptian border, since in 601 B.C., according to the same Babylonian Chronicle, he deliberately marched against Egypt, but was driven back with heavy loss and retired to Babylon. This ended direct hostilities between the two countries for several years to come. The defeat of the Babylonians was probably the cause of Jehoiakim's defection and alliance with Egypt despite the warnings of the prophet Jeremiah (xlvi. 14 ff.).

When Nekō II died in 595 B.C. he was succeeded by his son Psammētichus II, whose relatively short reign of six years has frequently been underestimated. In point of fact the number of monuments naming himself or his officials is considerably greater than that of his two predecessors, and a much-discussed expedition to Nubia lends it a special interest. Knowledge of this expedition is mainly derived from the longest of a group of Greek inscriptions carved upon one of the colossi of Ramessēs II at Abu Simbel;[2] in translation this reads:

When King Psammētichus came to Elephantinē, this was written by those who sailed with Psammētichus the son of Theoclēs, and they came beyond Kerkis as far as the river permits. Those who spoke foreign tongues were led by Potasimto, the Egyptians by Amasis.

Both Potasimto and Amasis are known to have lived under Psammētichus II and to have held high military posts. The Nubian

[1] Wiseman, p. 28, n. 5. [2] Kienitz, pp. 41–42.

expedition is recorded also on much-damaged stelae from Tanis and Karnak,[1] the former dating it to year 3 and mentioning a native ruler whose forces had been massacred, while the latter states that Pnūbs was reached. But if it is thus certain that the campaign (or was it a mere foray?) extended farther south than was formerly supposed, it is unlikely that, as has been suggested, this was Psammētichus's answer to an Ethiopian attempt to regain the hold upon Egypt lost after Tanuatamūn's flight from Thebes. Nevertheless, it was in his reign that a marked hostility towards the Ethiopians on the part of the Saites is first noted, the names of Taharḳa and his predecessors being systematically erased from their monuments. An equally problematic event of Psammētichus II's reign is an expedition to Phoenicia mentioned in a later demotic papyrus; this seems to have been a peaceful affair since priests from many temples were summoned to take part.[2]

Meanwhile the situation in the north-east had grown increasingly complicated. In 590 B.C. the aggressive Median king Cyaxarēs became engaged in a fierce war against the neighbouring kingdom of Lydia, ended five years later by a diplomatic marriage between the two families.[3] In these circumstances clearly Nebuchadrezzar could look for no help from his powerful ally. Nevertheless, it was impossible for him to remain inactive when in 589 B.C. Zedekiah of Judah rebelled against him, and at the beginning of the following year he invested the Holy City. In 589 B.C. Psammētichus II died, and was succeeded by his son Apriēs, the Pharaoh Hophra of the Bible (Jer. xliv. 30), who at once set about reversing the peaceful, defensive policy adopted by his predecessors. The prophets Jeremiah and Ezekiel are our main authorities for his intervention in Syria. To meet this attempt to relieve Jerusalem, Nebuchadrezzar broke off the siege,[4] only to renew it later; in 587 B.C. the city fell and was completely destroyed, Zedekiah being taken prisoner at Jericho; the larger portion of the Jewish population was deported to Babylonia, but later some of the remnant, feeling the situation in Judah to be intolerable, fled to Egypt taking the prophet Jeremiah with them (Jer. xliii. 6). The part played by Apriēs in all this

[1] *Bull. Inst. fr.* l. 157 ff. [2] Kienitz, p. 25. [3] Op. cit., p. 26.
[4] Op. cit., p. 28.

is obscure, the Egyptian records being completely silent. At the very beginning of his reign he appears to have sent troops to Palestine in support of the Jews, but then to have withdrawn them; an attack of his army upon Sidon and of his fleet upon Tyre is reported, but at least the first half of the statement does not square with the rest of the evidence; nor perhaps does the second half, since the exiled priest Ezekiel (xxvi. 1 ff.; xxix. 17 ff.) testifies to a siege of Tyre by Nebuchadrezzar lasting thirteen years without his ever succeeding in capturing the island state.[1]

In 570 B.C. Apriēs became embroiled in a new and unhappy adventure; Herodotus here takes up the story. At Cyrēnē, far out on the North-African coast, the Greeks had created a large and thriving colony, the reverse of welcome to the indigenous Libyans. One of the Libyan chieftains, Adicran, turned to Apriēs for protection.[2] The Egyptian army which was sent suffered an overwhelming defeat; for this Apriēs was rightly blamed and in consequence lost his throne. Monuments from his reign of nineteen years are fairly numerous, but his importance as a Pharaoh is altogether overshadowed by that of the usurper who supplanted him.

When Herodotus's account of Amasis[3] (570–526 B.C.) is shorn of its lively and picturesque gossip, what is left is likely to be sound history. He was a man of the people upon whom acceptance of the Double Crown was thrust by opportunity and the indignation of his compatriots. The native Egyptians were unanimous in his support, while the troops loyal to Apriēs were chiefly Greeks, somewhat strangely so since he had recently been fighting against a Greek colony. The civil war that ensued cannot have lasted more than a few months and was confined to the north-western Delta; Herodotus (ii. 169) locates the decisive battle at Mōmemphis, whereas a great red granite stela which narrated the triumph of Amasis placed it at Sekhetmafka near Terâna on the Canōpic branch; it is regrettable that this important stela[4] is almost illegible, having been used as the threshold of a palace at Cairo. Apriēs was taken alive

[1] Kienitz, p. 29, n. 1.
[2] Hdt. iv. 159.
[3] Manetho writes Amōsis, like the first king of Dyn. XVIII; the Egyptian original ʿAḥmōse is the same in both cases.
[4] *Rec. trav.* xxii. 1 ff.

and brought to Sais, which had been his own place of residence and now became that of Amasis. We are told that the victor at first treated his royal prisoner kindly, but later handed him over to the fury of the populace; the stela seems to confirm that he buried him with the honour due to a Pharaoh. A cuneiform fragment in the British Museum ascribes to this same year, the thirty-seventh of Nebuchadrezzar's reign (568–567 B.C.) some sort of military action against Amasis,[1] but it is unlikely that the two powers ever came into conflict with one another either at this time or later, when the great Babylonian monarch was succeeded by three weak kings and then by a fourth, Nabonidus (555–539 B.C.), whose troubles never took him nearer to Egypt than northern Syria and Edom. As a ruler Amasis proved predominantly a man of peace. In the west he made a treaty of alliance with Cyrēnē, and if he brought certain towns on the island of Cyprus into subjection that was his only conquest. Certain it is that dependence upon Greek energy and enterprise became more and more indispensable to him. His own prudence and conciliatory nature made him equally popular with the westerners and won him the well-merited epithet of Philhellene (Hdt. ii. 178). Symptomatic of these good relations were his marriage to Ladicē, a Cyrēnaean lady, his large contribution to the rebuilding of the destroyed temple of Delphi, and his rich gifts to several other Greek temples. His friendship with Polycratēs, the successful but treacherous tyrant of Samos, is the subject of the well-known story of the ring told by Herodotus (iii. 41–43). Nevertheless, something had to be done in order to mitigate the envy of the native Egyptians to whom, after all, his debt was enormous. As merchants settled in the Delta the Greeks were becoming unduly powerful; Amasis checked this development by confining their activities to the great city of Naucratis[2] rediscovered by Petrie a little distance to the south-west of Sais; here the population was exclusively Greek; great temples were built by the different communities of colonists, and Naucratis became the forerunner of Alexandria and, in its own age, of not much inferior importance. Egyptians and Greeks were alike satisfied; this action on the part of Amasis was a political masterpiece. It was doubtless the result of

[1] Wiseman, pp. 94–95. [2] PM iv. 50.

his own sagacity combined, if Herodotus can be believed, with a convivial and light-hearted temperament that he was able to retain his throne for forty-four years, just escaping the catastrophe which only a year later (525 B.C.) was to overtake his country.

The unification of a world torn by unceasing wars was long overdue and was now to be attempted on a grand scale. The initiative came from a most unexpected quarter. Persia, in the original sense of the name, is the land lying along the eastern side of the Persian Gulf and extending far inland, with Persepolis and Pasargadae as its capitals. From this mountainous and in part inhospitable country arose the Aryan family of the Achaemenids from whom the all-conquering Cyrus II (*c.* 558–529 B.C.) sprang. The first kingdom to be overrun was Media, where Astyagēs, the son of Cyaxarēs, was able to put up only slight resistance before being ousted from his capital Ecbatana, midway between Susa and the Caspian. Next was the turn of Lydia. Foreseeing what was to come, its king Croesus had sought alliances with Egypt, Babylonia, and Lacedaemon, but before help from them could arrive, Sardis was captured (546 B.C.) and Lydia ceased to exist as a separate kingdom (Hdt. i. 79 ff.). The cities of the Ionian coast were now at the Persian monarch's mercy; leaving them in the charge of his generals, Cyrus was free to direct his energies elsewhere. Babylon was naturally his next objective, but he was in no hurry to cope with it. Here Nabonidus, the scholar and antiquarian king, was reigning after a ten years' exile at Taima in Arabia, whence he returned in 546 B.C. on the invitation of the subjects with whom he had previously disagreed. In 539 B.C. Babylon was occupied, Cyrus with characteristic wisdom sparing the king's life and relegating him to distant Carmania either as governor or as exile. So far-flung an empire would naturally demand much consolidation, and little is heard of Cyrus's military activities during the next few years. He was well aware, however, that the conquest of Egypt was a necessity, and this task he entrusted to his son Cambysēs. He himself perished in 529 B.C. whilst combating attacks by Turanian hordes on his northern frontier; within thirty years he had arisen from humble beginnings to be the most powerful monarch that the world had thus far ever known.

Difficulties connected with the succession kept Cambysēs fully occupied for the next three years, but the murder of his brother Smerdis left his hands free to proceed with the undertaking bequeathed to him by his father. Phoenicia had submitted voluntarily, providing him with a fleet invaluable for his coming operations. Cyprus abandoned its allegiance to Amasis, who died in 526 B.C., escaping only by a few months the shattering blow which was to befall his son Psammētichus III. The battle of Pelusium (525 B.C.) was fought with great stubbornness, but in the end the Egyptians fled in disorder to Memphis, which surrendered only after a siege of some duration (Hdt. iii. 13). Egypt thus passed into Persian hands, Manetho's TWENTY-SEVENTH DYNASTY. Cambysēs' own reign was to last only three years longer, and each of the further expeditions which he planned proved unsuccessful. A projected attack upon the Carthaginians came to nothing, since the Phoenicians refused to fight against people of their own blood. The far more ambitious campaign against the Ethiopians, in which Cambysēs himself took part, proved a perfect fiasco owing to neglect of proper preparation, while a force sent across the desert to the oasis where Alexander the Great consulted the Oracle of Amūn two centuries later (Sîwa) was overwhelmed by a sandstorm and disappeared. The anger of Cambysēs at these failures was boundless and is said to have brought on an attack of madness; but at least the whole of Egypt had been won. According to Herodotus Cambysēs was a monster of cruelty and impiety, his folly culminating in the killing of the sacred Apis bull; this act is, however, rendered more than improbable by the evidence from the Serapeum, two of these holy animals being recorded for his reign, and the sarcophagus of one of them being said by its inscriptions to have been dedicated by the Persian king himself.[1] It is true that a Jewish document[2] of 407 B.C. speaks of 'the destruction of all temples of the Egyptian gods' in the time of Cambysēs, but by then the king's evil reputation had had plenty of time to spread, and the damage done in that direction may have been confined to the withdrawal of the large official grants of materials that had previously been the custom. We shall see that a less severe view of the conqueror was taken by

[1] Posener (see p. 383), pp. 30 ff. [2] *ANET*, p. 492.

a high official who managed to secure his favour and to retain his important position throughout the following reign. On Cambysēs' return to Asia in 522 B.C. Egypt was left in charge of the satrap Aryandēs who, however, later fell under suspicion of disloyalty and was executed.

Meanwhile the Magian Gaumata had given himself out to be the real Smerdis and had won wide recognition throughout the Persian provinces. Discordant accounts are given of Cambysēs' death, probably on his way home to combat the pretender. The throne now fell to Darius I, the son of Hystaspes and a member of the family of Cyrus. In his long reign of thirty-six years (521–486 B.C.) the Persian Empire was organized with consummate statesmanship, but only comparatively little is known of events in Egypt during this time. His first years were fully occupied in cruelly suppressing revolts and disorders that had followed his slaying of Gaumata, and it was not until 517 B.C. or thereabouts that he was able to visit Egypt. Of real importance, however, as illustrating his interest in the ancient civilization which had now come under his sway is an order sent to the Satrap in his third year bidding him assemble the wisest men among the country's soldiers, priests, and scribes; they were to set forth in writing the complete law of Egypt down to year 44 of Amasis, a task which kept them busy until his own nineteenth year.[1] There is no reason to doubt the authenticity of this royal order, although it is made known to us only in a much later copy on the back of a demotic papyrus of miscellaneous contents; indeed it goes far towards justifying Diodorus's description (i. 95) of Darius as among the greatest of Egypt's law-givers. Equally interesting is the information given by several huge stelae[2] confirming what Herodotus (ii. 158; iv. 39) has to tell about Darius's completion of the canal leading from the Nile to the Red Sea. Nekō II had been compelled to abandon this project, but Darius not only repaired the channel in its entire length, but was also able to dispatch through it twenty-four ships laden with tribute for Persia. The stelae commemorating this were erected at intervals along the banks of the canal; inscribed both in hieroglyphs and in cuneiform they are in deplorable condition, but tell their

[1] See below, p. 383. [2] Posener, pp. 48 ff.

story in unmistakable fashion. That Darius, in governing Egypt, wisely sought to pose as a legitimate Pharaoh continuing the work of his Saite predecessors is shown by a variety of evidence. He alone of the Persian kings undertook building in the temples of the Egyptian gods; the stately and well-preserved temple of Amūn in the oasis of Khârga[1] is almost entirely due to him, and here he, like Cambysēs before him, receives a complete royal titulary. A general whose business it was to summon all the mayors of the country to bring gifts for the embalmment of an Apis bull bore the same name as King Amasis and wrote it in a cartouche, although his stela alludes to the Persian invasion.[2] Similarly Khnemibrēʿ, the superintendent of works in the entire land, whose name is identical with the Prenomen of the same king;[3] his many rock-inscriptions in the Wâdy Ḥammâmât range from the last year of Amasis to the thirtieth of Darius. But the sole hieroglyphic memorial of the entire Persian period which presents a biography of any length is that inscribed on a fine naophorous statue preserved in the Vatican.[4] Its owner Udjeḥarresne had been the commander of sea-faring ships under both Amasis and Psammētichus III, but the narrative of his subsequent career starts with the arrival of the Persians in his native land:

There came to Egypt the great chief of every foreign land Cambysēs, the foreigners of every country being with him. When he had taken possession of this entire land they settled down there in order that he might be the great ruler of Egypt and the great chief of every foreign land. His Majesty commanded me to be chief physician and caused me to be at his side as companion and director of the palace, and I made his titulary in his name of King of Upper and Lower Egypt Mesutirēʿ. And I caused him to know the greatness of Sais which is the seat of Nēith the great, the mother who gave birth to Rēʿ and who was the initiator of birth after there had been no birth.

The thought contained in the last few words is expanded by the mention of the actual temple of Nēith as well as of other shrines in what had been the Saite capital. Then the speaker continues on another part of the statue:

[1] PM vii. 277 ff. [2] Posener, pp. 41 ff. [3] Op. cit., pp. 88 ff.
[4] Op. cit., pp. 1 ff.

I made petition beside His Majesty the King of Upper and Lower Egypt Cambysēs concerning all those foreigners who had settled down in the temple of Nēith, that they should be driven thence and that the temple of Nēith should be in all its splendour as it was aforetime. And His Majesty commanded that all the foreigners who had settled in the temple of Nēith should be driven out and that all their houses and all their superfluities which were in this temple should be thrown down, and that all their own baggage should be carried for them outside the wall of this temple. And His Majesty commanded that the temple of Nēith should be cleansed and all its people placed in it, together with the priesthood of the temple. And His Majesty commanded that the revenues should be given to Nēith the great, the god's mother, and to the great gods who are in Sais as they were aforetime. And His Majesty caused that all their festivals and all their processions should be made as they were made aforetime. And His Majesty did this because I caused His Majesty to know the greatness of Sais—it is the city of all the gods, they resting on their thrones in it eternally.

Udjeḥarresne was naturally concerned only to vaunt his influence with his new master, but there is no reason to doubt that Cambysēs was willing, whenever it suited his interest, to do honour to the gods of Egypt, and the text goes on to relate that he himself came and prostrated himself before the goddess as every king had hitherto done, after which he made her a great banquet. Obviously biased as these passages are, they must be set against the execrations for which Herodotus is responsible. Udjeḥarresne touches only very lightly upon 'the great trouble that had come about in the entire land of Egypt'. There is much more of interest in this unique inscription, but it must suffice here to make brief reference to the House of Life or scriptoria which Darius, himself in Elam, sent Udjeḥarresne to re-establish in Egypt. They were to be staffed 'with persons of rank, not a poor man among them'. Apparently it was only in connexion with the departments concerned with medicine that Udjeḥarresne was thus to be employed, for not only was he a chief physician, but also the text names as the purpose of his scriptoria to 'revive all that are sick'. At all events these sentences illustrate once again the enlightened way in which Darius conceived of his duty as King of Egypt; he was no mere despot avid of power and content to leave the welfare of his dominions in the hands of his satraps.

Of equal interest for the history of these times, though of wholly different character, is a great demotic papyrus discovered at El-Ḥîba and brilliantly deciphered by F. Ll. Griffith. It is a petition probably written in the ninth year of Darius by an elderly temple-scribe named Peteēse. He is complaining of wrongs done to himself and his family in connexion with the prophetship of Amūn of Teudjoi (El-Ḥîba), his native place, and in connexion with the priesthoods of other associated gods, all of which carried with them substantial emoluments. It is an intensely complicated and confused story which Peteēse has to tell, and the events that he narrates go back 150 years, to the fourth year of Psammētichus I. At that time his ancestor of the same name had restored the ruined temple of Amūn on behalf of his cousin, yet another Peteēse, who was the Master of the Shipping resident in Hēracleopolis Magna and the virtual governor of Upper Egypt. As a reward for these services Peteēse I had been accorded all the priesthoods in question. His descendant of four generations later has a lurid tale of murder, imprisonment, and tribulation to recount. His enemies have been various personages who had from time to time succeeded with the help of the highest authorities then in power to deprive the Peteēse family of their rights, and who had been backed up by others described generally as 'the priests'. No attempt can here be made to estimate the historical accuracy of all this, but it cannot be disputed that the world to which the papyrus bears witness was one of widespread graft and corruption. One detail corroborated from an outside source is the mention of that same Master of Shipping whom we found arranging the God's Wife Nitōcris's journey to Thebes (p. 354).

Wise and enlightened as was Darius's rule, his empire was too vast not soon to exhibit signs of fragility. Already in 499 B.C. the Ionian cities were in revolt, and the assistance lent to them by Athens and Eretria made war between Persia and the western Greeks only a matter of time. The resounding defeat of Artaphernēs, Darius's nephew, at Marathon (490 B.C.) could not fail to have serious repercussions throughout the entire Middle East. In 486 B.C.

the Egyptians rose in revolt, and it was only in the second year of Xerxēs, who succeeded his father towards the end of 486 B.C., that the rebellion was finally quelled. Herodotus relates (vii. 7) that the new monarch 'reduced all Egypt to slavery much greater than it had suffered in the reign of Darius'. Needless to say Xerxēs made use of his suzerainty there to further his own ends; before the battle of Salamis (480 B.C.), where he sought to avenge himself upon the Greeks, a large Egyptian fleet was given an important part to play (vii. 89). But for the advantage of the Egyptians themselves Xerxēs did little or nothing. The monuments are almost completely silent. No temples were built and but few Egyptian officials were employed. Throughout these years Upper Egypt appears to have been entirely tranquil, since a Persian who had probably visited the Wâdy Ḥammâmât for the first time in the sixth year of Cambysēs, did so at intervals right down to Xerxēs's twelfth year;[1] he describes himself as governor of Coptos and was very possibly charged with protecting the road to the Red Sea. After him his younger brother made similar visits in the reign of Artaxerxēs and had now added to his Persian name the truly Egyptian one of Djeḥō.

A great change had by this time come over the hitherto more or less uniform civilization of the land of the Pharaohs. As before, the native population carried on their personal business in their own language, employing the highly cursive style of writing which became known to the Greeks as Enchorial or Demotic. But so far as the government was concerned, Egypt was now only the farthest removed province of a great foreign empire. The Persian king and overlord, residing in Susa or in Babylon, left the actual administration in the hand of a local governor known as the 'satrap'. For all bureaucratic purposes the Aramaic language and script were employed. Aramaic was a north-Semitic idiom which, after extending widely to Mesopotamia with the peoples deported thither, doubtless later spread southward with, for example, the exiled Jews whom Cyrus allowed to return to their original home; and in the end this idiom completely replaced Hebrew in Palestine. It must not be imagined that in Egypt the use of Aramaic was confined to the Jews, though that impression might be conveyed by the great and

[1] Posener, pp. 123, 178.

sensational finds of papyri written in that language discovered on the island of Elephantinē just north of the First Cataract. It is true that the persons whose concerns are there displayed in such abundance and variety were all or mainly Jews, but they were members of a frontier garrison and consequently in the service of the Persian régime. The most convincing evidence, however, that Aramaic was the medium in which the Persian administration was carried on is afforded by a batch of letters mostly addressed to his subordinates in Egypt by the satrap Arsamēs who was in power throughout the whole last quarter of the fifth century; these letters, written on leather, doubtless emanate from the satrap's chancery, probably at Memphis; they were purchased from a dealer who either could not or would not reveal the place where they were found.

Little else would be known about Egypt in the fifth century but for the Greek historians, and in them only on account of her relations with the Athenians. Following the disturbances which arose after the murder of Xerxēs and the accession of Artaxerxēs I (465 B.C.) serious trouble sprang up in the north-western Delta. Here a certain Inarōs,[1] the son of Psammētichus—both names are Egyptian, but Thucydides (i. 104) calls him a king of the Libyans—revolted and established his headquarters at the fortress of Marea not far from the later Alexandria. The first clash with the Persians took place at Paprēmis, an uncertainly identified place somewhere in the west; the force under the satrap Achaemenēs, the brother of Xerxēs, was defeated and he was killed; the remnant of his army retreated to Memphis and entrenched themselves there. Inarōs was now in complete possession of the Delta, but apparently made no claim to the kingship. The inevitable relief from Persia was long in coming, but in expectation of it Inarōs called for help upon the Athenians, at that time successfully warring against the Persians in Cyprus. With their aid two-thirds of Memphis or the 'White Wall', as Thucydides correctly termed it, was taken, but the rest held out until the Persian general Megabyzus drove off the besiegers, who in their turn found themselves confined within an island in the marshes called Prosōpitis.[2] It was not until 454 B.C. that Megabyzus gained the upper hand; few of the Athenians escaped and a number of

[1] Kienitz, p. 69, from Thuc. i. 104; Hdt. iii. 12; vii. 7.

[2] Thuc. i. 109.

ships arriving too late to be of assistance were annihilated: Inarōs himself was betrayed into Persian hands and was crucified.[1] This, however, was not quite the end of the revolt. A chieftain named Amyrtaeus—again the name is pure Egyptian—remained undefeated in the extreme western part of the Delta.[1] He once more summoned the Athenians to his support and a number of their ships actually started, but the death in Cyprus of the Greek commander Cimon caused them to turn back.[2] Shortly afterwards peace was declared between Athens and Persia[3] and the interference of the former in Egyptian affairs came to an end (449–448 B.C.).

Excepting the west of the Delta the whole of Egypt was now at peace. Foreigners from all parts were welcome, particularly the Greeks. So widely had the latter extended their commerce that Naucratis could no longer maintain her monopolistic position, and lost her special importance. Herodotus toured Egypt shortly after 450 B.C., and though the undoubtedly fictitious claims that sixth-century philosophers like Thales and Pythagoras derived much of their wisdom from Egypt warn us to be sceptical also in the cases of Democritus of Abdera and Plato, there is little question but that the country would have been open to them. Some xenophobia there doubtless was, possibly once even a petty uprising against the alien rulers, but especially in Upper Egypt it will have required differences of race and religion to fan any unrest into flame. Such a case arose on the island of Elephantinē in 410 B.C. Here the worshippers of Yahu (p. 356) and the priests of the ram-headed god Chnūm lived cheek by jowl. The native priests took advantage of the absence abroad of the satrap Arsamēs to bribe the local commandant Vidaranag, with the result that the Jewish temple was completely razed to the ground. Vidaranag was punished, but for a time the temple remained unbuilt. The Aramaic papyri recounting this matter comprise a petition sent to Bagoas, the governor of Judah, pleading for the rebuilding, and it appears that this was ultimately conceded.[4]

The forty years ending with the death of Darius II in 404 B.C. are a complete blank so far as Egypt is concerned, and it is only amid

[1] Thuc. i. 110. [2] Thuc. i. 112; Hdt. ii. 140; iii. 15.
[3] Kienitz, pp. 72–3; but see too *CAH* v. 469–71. [4] *ANET*, p. 492.

the stirring events attending the accession of Artaxerxēs II that she re-enters upon the Middle Eastern stage. Manetho ends at this point his Dyn. XXVII of Persian rulers, and makes his TWENTY-EIGHTH DYNASTY consist of a single king Amyrtaeus of Sais, presumably a kinsman of the Amyrtaeus who carried on the struggle of Inarōs after the latter's capture by his enemies. The Greek historians make only one doubtful allusion to the new Pharaoh, Diodorus (xiv. 35), who is here responsible, mistakenly calling him 'Psammētichus, a descendant of the (famous) Psammētichus'. The episode in question tells how after the battle of Cynaxa (401 B.C.), where the insurgent prince Cyrus was defeated and killed, his friend the Memphite admiral Tamōs, whom he had appointed governor of Ionia, fled to Egypt to escape the vengeance of Artaxerxēs II's satrap Tissaphernes, taking all his ships with him; but Amyrtaeus, if it was he whom Diodorus referred to as Psammētichus, put Tamōs to death. According to a later Egyptian tradition Amyrtaeus in some way offended against the dictates of Law, with the consequence that his son was not suffered to succeed him. The conviction that earthly prosperity and righteous conduct are inexorably bound up together finds expression in the curious and cryptic papyrus passing under the inexact name 'The Demotic Chronicle'. That is the papyrus from which we learned about Cambysēs' withdrawal of grants to the Egyptian temples (p. 364) and about Darius's command that the laws of the country should be recorded in writing (p. 365); it is, however, the composition on the *recto* with which we have here to deal. This is a strange farrago of calendrical data, festivals, and geographical references which would have no value or meaning for us without the interpretations or prophecies accompanying each item. These are of great historic interest inasmuch as they include two absolutely correct sequences of the kings 'who came after the Medes' (i.e. after the Persians) from Amyrtaeus down to Teōs, the second king of Manetho's Dyn. XXX. The oracular text thus claiming to find a relation of cause and effect between virtuous conduct and successful life on earth is believed to have been a priestly product of the second century B.C. Manetho allots to Amyrtaeus a reign of six years, which is probably correct since the Aramaic papyri from Elephantinē include a promise of the repayment of a debt dating from his fifth year.[1] Apart from a letter from the same source quoting his name in close proximity to that of Nepherites, his immediate successor, there exists no further reference to him, and he has left no monuments. We are in the dark alike as to how he came by his throne and as to how he lost it.

Henceforth down to the conquest by Alexander the Great in 332 B.C. the sole aim of Egypt's foreign policy was to defend her independence against an empire which persisted in regarding her simply as a rebellious province. In this policy Egypt was successful except for a spell of ten years at the very end. A constant obstacle, however, was the rivalry between the different princely families of the Delta. Manetho's TWENTY-NINTH DYNASTY, monuments of which are found as far south as Thebes, hailed from the important town of Mendēs and comprises only four kings together totalling barely twenty years (399–380 B.C.); the first and last kings both have the name Nepheritēs, of which the etymological meaning is 'His great ones are prosperous', but whereas Nepheritēs I reigned for six years, Nepheritēs II ruled for only four months. There is a discrepancy between Manetho's list and that of the Demotic Chronicle which has puzzled some Egyptologists, Manetho placing Achōris, in Egyptian Hakōr or Hagōr, before Psammūthis ('The child of Mūt'), while the papyrus inverts the order; the probable solution is that the first year of both kings was identical, so that either statement is legitimate. Psammūthis, whose sole existing remains are at Karnak, with the name of Achōris cut above his, reigned only one year, whereas Achōris, whose monuments are numerous and found in all parts of Egypt, maintained his position for thirteen. If we have dwelt at some length on these otherwise none too important Pharaohs, it is on account of the aforementioned moral judgements of the Demotic Chronicle, since these certainly reflect authentic history; thus of Achōris it is said that he fulfilled the time of his rule 'because he was generous to the temples', but that he 'was overthrown because he forsook the Law, and showed no care for his brethren'.

For less vague information we are wholly dependent upon the Greek authorities. From Xenophon (*Anab.* i. 4. 5) we learn that

[1] Kraeling, p. 283.

Persia had assembled a mighty army in Phoenicia; this had doubtless been intended for the subjection of Egypt,[1] but the project came to naught on account of Cyrus's dangerous and unsuccessful gamble. As a result the Greek cities of Asia Minor, which had sided with him, found themselves in dire peril. To rescue them Sparta, though deeply in Cyrus's debt, now went to war with his country's still very formidable power (400 B.C.). The struggle lasted for years. In 396 B.C. Sparta sought alliance with Egypt, which was readily granted. Diodorus (xiv. 79) relates that in reply to the Spartan king Agesilaus's request the Egyptian Nephereus, i.e. Nepheritēs I, placed at his disposal 500,000 bushels of corn, and the equipment for 100 triremes. It was stipulated, however, that this handsome subsidy should be fetched by the Spartan fleet, but before it reached Rhodes that island had gone over to the Persians so that their admiral, the Athenian Conon, was able to annex the whole consignment.

Not long afterwards, in 393 B.C., Achōris came to the throne, and the alliance with Sparta having proved unprofitable, he was only too glad to look for assistance elsewhere. This he found through a treaty with Evagoras, the able and ambitious king of Salamis in Cyprus, who had already made himself master of many other towns on the island. Evagoras had been a friend of the admiral Conon, so that collaboration with him carried with it close co-operation with Athens. By this time, however, both Persia and Sparta were tired of war, and in 386 B.C. the Peace of Antalcidas was arranged, by which a free hand in all the Greek cities of Asia was ceded to Persia in exchange for autonomy in all the other Hellenic states.[2] As a consequence Achōris and Evagoras stood alone, and Artaxerxēs was now free to deal with whichever he chose. Egypt was the first to be attacked, but had by this time again become a strong and wealthy country; Chabrias, one of the best generals of the age, left Athens to enter Achōris's service. Little is known about this war except that it dragged on until after 383 B.C. and was referred to contemptuously by the Athenian pamphleteer Isocrates. Evagoras proved a great help, carrying his arms into the enemy's camp and capturing Tyre and other Phoenician

[1] Kienitz, p. 76. [2] Op. cit., p. 84.

towns; later, however, his fortune changed and after losing an important sea-battle he was besieged in his own town Salamis. He had defied the Persians for more than ten years, at the end of which dissensions among their leaders made them ready to accept his submission on honourable terms (380 B.C.).[1] After a considerable time as a faithful vassal of the Persian king he fell victim to a conspiracy. If the Demotic Chronicle can be trusted, misfortune attended Achōris at the last. After the four months' reign of his son Nepheritēs II, the kingship passed into the hands of a general from Sebennytus. Manetho's THIRTIETH DYNASTY consists of three members, the names of the first and third being presented by him in so similar a form (Nectanebēs and Nectanebos) that they are best discarded in favour of the etymologically quite distinct Nekhtnebef and Nekhtḥareḥbe. Of these two, though their relative order has often been disputed, it is now certain that Nekhtnebef was the earlier.[2] The multitude of his monuments[3] might leave the impression of unbroken peace and prosperity; the oldest parts of Philae were built by him; at Edfu he was remembered as the donor of much land to the temple of Horus; a great stela at Ashmunên (Hermopolis Magna)[4] records extensive additions to the temples of the goddess Neḥmetʿaway, of the primeval Ogdoad, and of the twice-great Thōth himself; and a finely inscribed inscription from Naucratis commemorates the imposition of a 10 per cent. duty on imports to that town and on goods manufactured in it, the proceeds to be devoted to the enrichment of the goddess Nēith of Sais. But a very different story emerges from the Greek historians of whom Diodorus (xv. 41–43) is once again the foremost representative. Artaxerxēs II (404–358 B.C.) was still reigning in Persia and as determined as ever that Egypt should be humbled and reduced to her former dependent condition. However, his preparations for the invasion proceeded only very slowly. First he insisted on Athens recalling from Egypt the able Chabrias, who had thereafter to content himself with a military post at home. It was not until 373 B.C. that the great Persian host, led by the satrap Pharnabazus and the commander of his Greek mercenaries Iphicrates, set forth from

[1] Kienitz, pp. 86–87.

[2] Vandier, pp. 624–5; Kienitz, p. 199.

[3] Enumerated op. cit., pp. 199–212.

[4] *Ann. Serv.* lii. 375 ff.

Acre. On reaching Pelusium it was realized that an attack from that quarter was hopeless, but that one or other of the less well-fortified Nile mouths held out better prospects. And so it turned out; the barrier of the Mendēsian branch was breached, and many Egyptians were killed or captured. Against the will of Pharnabazus Iphicrates sought to push on to Memphis, and whilst the antagonism between the two commanders delayed the Persian effort, Nekhtnebef's forces gathered strength and encircled the besieged invaders on all sides. The inundation of the Nile now intervened as a welcome ally; such parts of the Delta as were not a lake became a swamp and the Persians were forced to retreat. For the second time Egypt escaped reoccupation.

The next years were marked by rebellions of the satraps everywhere, in the course of which Nekhtnebef found protection for himself by subsidies of gold to the various combatants. When he died in 363 B.C. he was succeeded by his son Teōs, or Tachōs[1] as some Greek writers call him; Nekhtnebef's father had borne the same name. The time seemed ripe for a direct attack on the Persians.[2] The aged Spartan king Agesilaus arrived in Egypt with 1000 hoplites, where the Athenian Chabrias joined him. In the attack on Phoenicia which ensued (360 B.C.) Teōs insisted on commanding his own Egyptians, and Agesilaus, enraged at the mirth excited by his odd appearance and demeanour, lent his support to the young Nekhtḥareḥbe whom a large party of followers put up as a rival to Teōs. The entire expedition ended in a fiasco. Nekhtḥareḥbe returned to Egypt as Pharaoh, and Teōs fled to Persia, where he lived and died an exile.

Looked at from the Egyptian angle, the reign of Nekhtḥareḥbe (360–343 B.C.) might seem an almost exact replica of that of Nekhtnebef. Both kings ruled for eighteen years and the building activity of both was immense.[3] But meanwhile world-shaking events were preparing. The accession of Artaxerxēs III Ōchus (358 B.C.) put new life into the tottering Persian Empire. Order was restored among the satraps of Asia Minor, but the energy required for the effort precluded the thought of any attack upon Egypt. By 350 B.C., however, Ōchus was ready. No details are

[1] Djeḥo in Egyptian. [2] Diod. xv. 90, 92. [3] Kienitz, pp. 193–212; 214–30.

known, but this war was a complete failure, with the result that revolts against the Persian domination broke out everywhere. Phoenicia and Cyprus were in the forefront of the rebels. Long before this Greek soldiers and Greek commanders were the greatest asset upon which either side could count. But Egypt was the most important objective on account of the gold and the corn which she alone could supply in abundance, and her reconquest was an absolute necessity. First, however, Phoenicia and Palestine had to be dealt with. Sidon was the centre of the revolt and had invited retaliation by a violently destructive blow against the occupying Persians. In their dread of what was to come the Sidonians appealed to Egypt, but Nekhtḥareḥbe contented himself with sending a limited contingent of Greek mercenaries under Mentor of Rhodes. Diodorus (xvi. 40–51) tells the story of the next few years in great detail which can only be summarized here. Ōchus's preparations were on a vast scale, but even before the arrival of very substantial forces from the Greek cities of the mainland and of Asia Minor he was able to inflict horrible punishment upon Sidon, whose treacherous king Tennes conspired with Mentor to deliver up the city, whereupon the inhabitants burned their ships and many of them sought voluntary death in the flames of their own homes.

In the autumn of 343 B.C. the Persian army set forth upon its momentous campaign against Egypt, the Great King himself at its head. Pelusium was the first Egyptian town to be attacked and put up a stiff resistance. Ōchus had, however, planned simultaneous entry into the Delta at three different places, and it was near one of the western Nile mouths that penetration was achieved; the inundation season was at an end so that the disaster of thirty years earlier was no longer to be feared. Misfortune attended the defenders from the start. Sallying forth from the neighbouring fortress the Greek mercenaries under Cleinias of Cos were heavily defeated and he himself was killed. The terror-stricken Nekhtḥareḥbe, instead of standing his ground, retreated to Memphis, which he put in readiness for a siege. But meanwhile Pelusium had been taken, the garrison surrendering under the promise that those who did so would be well treated. A similar assurance was given elsewhere and soon Egyptians and Greeks were vying with one another which of them should be the earliest to avail themselves of this clemency. The third corps under Mentor and Ōchus's close friend and associate Bagoas had also met with success. The capture of Bubastis by the combined forces was an important event, after which the other Delta towns capitulated with all haste. Egypt was now at Ōchus's mercy, and Nekhtḥareḥbe, realizing the situation to be hopeless, gathered together so much of his belongings as he could and departed upstream 'to Ethiopia', after which nothing more is heard of him.

By Ōchus's strategical skill and political sagacity Egypt was a Persian province once more. Diodorus (xvi. 51) may here be quoted:

> Artaxerxēs, after taking over all Egypt and demolishing the walls of the most important cities, by plundering the shrines amassed a vast quantity of silver and gold and carried off the inscribed records from the ancient temples, which later on Bagoas returned to the Egyptian priests on the payment of huge sums. Then when he had lavishly rewarded the Greeks who had accompanied him on the campaign, each according to his deserts, he dismissed them to their native lands; and having installed Pherendates as satrap of Egypt, he returned with his army to Babylon, bearing many possessions and spoils and having won great renown by his successes.

No doubt the hand of the conqueror lay heavy upon the conquered country, and the lamentations of the First Intermediate Period are echoed in the Demotic Chronicle. But there is no reason to believe the later writers who attribute to Ōchus the same sort of sacrileges as had been attributed to Cambysēs; the later Persian monarch was surely too wise for that. Nevertheless, the immense power and prestige which he had brought to his empire was not destined to last long. In 338 B.C. he was poisoned by his intimate Bagoas and his youngest son Arsēs put in his place, only to be murdered by the same hand two years later. Arsēs was then replaced by a collateral Darius III Codomannus, the last of the Achaemenids, who promptly poisoned Bagoas, that masterful villain meeting with a well-deserved fate. With Darius III ended the THIRTY-FIRST DYNASTY which later chronographers added to Manetho's thirty; nominally his reign in Egypt lasted for four years, but before the termination of these the Persian Empire was no more, and the ancient world had started upon an entirely new era.

Theoretically, this book has aimed at basing its presentation of Egyptian history solely upon the native sources, but the last two chapters have demonstrated the impossibility of such an undertaking. Not only has our narrative here been mainly concerned with happenings in the Delta, whence hieroglyphic inscriptions of interest are exceedingly rare, but also the cuneiform inscriptions which have been quoted are always dry annalistic statements of fact, while our Greek testimony, though not eschewing colourful description where that seemed pertinent, has invariably been the work of sober professional historians. Projecting this state of affairs backwards, we can now better appreciate how one-sided our knowledge of the earlier periods must necessarily be. It is true that the age of Persian domination is not wholly lacking in historical information of a sort, but a couple of examples will illustrate the difficulties encountered in our attempts to utilize them. A stela preserved in Naples,[1] but originally found at Pompeii, contains the 'biography' of a Samtowetefnakhte who held important priestly offices in the XVIth nome of Upper Egypt; his name and the prayers which he addresses to Arsaphēs, the ram-headed deity of Hēracleopolis, show him to have belonged to a family mentioned several times already (pp. 354, 368). In the following excerpt he is speaking to his god:

I am thy servant and my heart is loyal to thee. I filled my heart with thee and did not cultivate any town except thy town. I refrained not from exalting it to everyone, my heart seeking after right in thy house both day and night. Thou didst unto me things better than it a million times. Thou enlargedst my steps in the palace, the heart of the goodly god being pleased with what I said. Thou didst raise me out of millions when thou turnedst thy back to Egypt and placedst the love of me in the heart of the Prince of Asia, his courtiers thanking god for me. He made for me the post of overseer of the priests of Sakhme (i.e. as physician) in place of my mother's brother the overseer of the priests of Sakhme for Upper and Lower Egypt Nekhtḥeneb. Thou didst protect

[1] *Bull. Inst. fr.* xxx. 369 ff.

me in the fighting of the Greeks when thou repelledst Asia and they slew millions beside me, and none raised his arm against me. My eyes followed Thy Majesty in my sleep, thou saying to me 'Hie thee to Hēracleopolis, behold I am with thee'. I traversed foreign countries alone and I crossed the sea and feared not, remembering thee. I disobeyed not what thou saidst and I reached Hēracleopolis and not a hair was taken from my head.

This narrative illustrates once again the high repute in which Egyptian physicians were held, but loses half its value because there is no certain indication of its date. Scholars have differed upon this point, Erman arguing in favour of the time of Marathon, whereas Tresson, the last editor, identifies the battle between Greeks and Persians as that won by Alexander at Gaugamela. These are extreme differences, but there are others; between them it is impossible to decide.

Another knotty problem is raised by a certain Khababash who assumed the title of a Pharaoh. An Apis sarcophagus of his second year is known, and the marriage contract of a petty Theban priest is dated in his first year. More interesting, however, is the information about him disclosed by a stela of 311 B.C., when the later Ptolemy I Sōtēr was as yet only the satrap of Egypt. In form this inscription is a eulogy of Ptolemy's great achievements, but its evident purpose was to record his restitution to the priests of Butō of a tract of country which, after having belonged to them from time immemorial, had been taken from them by Xerxēs, who is described as an enemy and malefactor. Khababash, having listened to the priests' plea and having been reminded that the god Horus had expelled Xerxēs and his son from Egypt by way of punishment, granted the petition, as was likewise done later by Ptolemy. There are here two clues to the historical position of Khababash: first he was clearly posterior to Xerxēs, and secondly he is said to have made his decision after having explored the Delta mouths through which the 'Asiatics', i.e. the Persians, might be expected to attack Egypt. There is a third clue in the fact that the abovementioned marriage contract was signed by the same notary as signed another document of 324 B.C. Various theories have been advanced, but all that can be safely said is that Khababash was one of the latest, if not the very latest, of the non-Persian and non-Greek rulers who dared to assume the titulary of a native-born Pharaoh; but his name is quite outlandish.

The great event which settled Egypt's fate and determined the nature of her government for the next three centuries was Alexander the Great's conquest of her in 332 B.C. The rise of Macedon as the dominant power in the world had begun to be reckoned with as a possibility as early as 338 B.C., when the doubtfully Greek Philip II, having crushed all resistance by his defeat of Athens and Thebes at Chaeronea, founded a Hellenic League which was to ally all Greece in subservience to himself. But no one could then have foreseen the glittering victories which, within a decade, had made his young son Alexander the undisputed master of the entire eastern world. It seems likely that Alexander himself was not fully aware of his purpose until he had conquered Asia Minor and driven Darius into flight at the battle of Issus some 15 miles north of the modern Alexandretta (333 B.C.). Even then his first thought was not the pursuit of the Persian monarch, but the subjection of Syria and Egypt. The siege of Tyre was a long and tedious business, but after that difficulty had been overcome, nothing delayed his march until he arrived at Gaza, which resisted desperately. When Egypt was reached in 332 B.C., the Persian satrap surrendered without striking a blow. Alexander hastened upstream to Memphis, sacrificed to the Apis bull, was accepted as Pharaoh, and then returned to the coast. Here on the shore of the Mediterranean near a village named Rhacōtis he traced out the lines of the future great city of Alexandria before starting out on his famous visit to the oracle of Amūn in the oasis of Sîwa. Whether Alexander had at this time any definite thought of his own divinization is uncertain, but that solemn landmark in his life was an inevitable consequence of age-old Egyptian tradition; the Pharaoh was necessarily the son of Amūn and therefore himself a god. Alexander's stay in Egypt was prolonged only sufficiently to enable him to appoint native governors, to make wise provision for the collection of taxes under his financial superintendent Cleomenēs of Naucratis, and to establish a small standing army under his friend Ptolemy. Then he was quickly off to liquidate the Persian Empire and to explore its territories as far as India. His subsequent fate is no concern of this book, however tempting it might be to follow up a career of such unparalleled brilliance. He fell seriously ill after his return to Babylon in 323 B.C. Here he died in Nebuchadrezzar's palace when he was not 33 years old and before he had completed the thirteenth year of his reign.

Naturally the history of Egypt does not end here, and indeed is entering upon a new phase at the present time. But the consecutive sketch which is all that can be offered by us has to be concluded somewhere, and it is best to place our full-stop before the commencement of the long-drawn-out dynasty of the Ptolemies. Under them Egypt was a changed land; the administration was Greek, although to a large extent the native population continued to live its own life, to write in its own language, and to observe its traditional customs. Throughout the Ptolemaic and Roman periods the Greek-speaking and Latin-speaking rulers of the land retained their highly politic pose of genuine Pharaohs, of worshipping the ancient gods of the country, and of conciliating the priesthoods by providing money for the building or extension of the great temples. It might seem ludicrous to dispense here entirely with descriptions of such splendidly preserved monuments as the temples of Edfu and Dendera, to fail to add our voice to the laments over the impending submergence of the Nubian temples in the interests of growing and hungry generations, and to pass over with no more than brief allusions such all-important inscriptions as those of the Rosetta Stone and the Decree of Canopus. But if the youthful critics for whom we chiefly write reproach us with such omissions, we must remind them that we have still a promise to redeem; the prehistory and early dynastic history of Egypt remain to be discussed before we may lay down our pen.

SELECT BIBLIOGRAPHY

For the entire period, F. K. Kienitz, *Die politische Geschichte Ägyptens vom 7. bis zum 4. Jahrhundert vor der Zeitwende*, Berlin, 1953; *Cambridge Ancient History*, vols. iii, iv, vi; H. R. Hall, *The Ancient History of the Near East*, 8th ed., London, 1932.

The Jews in Elephantinē: besides works quoted Kienitz, p. 39, n. 2 see E. G. Kraeling, *The Brooklyn Museum Aramaic Papyri*, New Haven, 1953.

Dyn. XXVI, Chronology: R. A. Parker in *Mitt. Kairo*, xv. 208–12; *JEA* xxxi. 16 ff. Nekō II: the abortive canal to the Red Sea, Hdt. ii. 158; the circumnavigation of Africa, Hdt. iv. 42. Amasis and Apriēs: Hdt. ii. 161–3, 169; history and character of Amasis, Hdt. ii. 172–82.

The rise of Media, Hdt. i. 95 ff. The Babylonian kings Nabopolassar and Nebuchadrezzar, D. J. Wiseman, *Chronicles of Chaldaean Kings*, London, 1956, pp. 5 ff.; Kienitz, pp. 18 ff.

The rise of Persia: *CAH* iv. 1 ff.; Cyrus the Great, legend of birth and upbringing, Hdt. i. 107 ff.; character of the Persians and events of reign, with long digressions, Hdt. i. 131 to end.

Dyn. XXVII, the hieroglyphic inscriptions: edited and translated G. Posener, *La première domination Perse en Égypte*, Cairo, 1936; Cambysēs, *CAH* iv. 15 ff.; Kienitz, pp. 55 ff.; Hdt. iii. 1 ff. The official language used, G. R. Driver, *Aramaic Documents of the Fifth Century* B.C., Oxford, 1957. Darius I, *CAH* iv, ch. 7; codification of Egyptian law, W. Spiegelberg, *Die sogenannte demotische Chronik*, Leipzig, 1914, pp. 30 ff. The Petition of Peteēse: F. Ll. Griffith, *The Demotic Papyri in the John Rylands Library*, Manchester, 1909, vol. iii, pp. 60 ff.; an interpretation, G. A. Wainwright in *Bull. Rylands Libr.* xxviii, no. 1, 1944.

Dyns. XXVIII-XXX. Relations with Persia, from Greek sources, Kienitz, pp. 76–112. Monuments and inscriptions, op. cit. pp. 190–230. The dates elaborately discussed (for the findings see in our text), op. cit., pp. 166–80.

Dyn. XXXI. Artaxerxes III Ōchus conquers Egypt (Second Persian Domination), *CAH* vi, pp. 21–24; 151–4. Papyri and inscriptions, Kienitz, p. 231. The problematic Khababash, op. cit., pp. 185 ff., 232.

Alexander the Great: conquest of Egypt, *CAH* vi, pp. 154–6; 373–9; his successors, E. Bevan, *A History of Egypt under the Ptolemaic Dynasty*, London, 1927.

BOOK III

BACK TO THE BEGINNING

XIV

PREHISTORY

NO more difficult task confronts the historian than to trace the gradual emergence of a civilization, since this necessarily belongs to ages where written documents are either non-existent or very scanty. At the same time no problem is more interesting, and the reader would have just cause for complaint if this book dispensed with any attempt to face it. That, however, such an attempt has been postponed until after a more comprehensive account had been given of the Manethonian dynasties finds partial justification in the history of our science. Some seventy years ago it would have been difficult to point to any Egyptian antiquity demonstrably older than the age of the pyramid-builders, Manetho's Dyn. IV. Palaeolithic implements had indeed already been found, but these differed little from those discovered in Europe and had about them nothing specifically Egyptian. Mēnēs and his immediate successors were known only from the classical writers and the native king-lists; what lay behind Mēnēs was a complete blank. The filling up of this blank began in 1894–5, when Petrie and Quibell, digging at and near Naḳâda in Upper Egypt,[1] came upon vast cemeteries revealing skeletons hunched up on their sides as though in sleep and accompanied by, among other objects, pottery bearing strange geometrical patterns and rude delineations of animals and ships. In the opinion of the puzzled excavators these

[1] W. M. F. Petrie and J. E. Quibell, *Naqada and Ballas*, London, 1896.

remains could not possibly be Egyptian, and evidence that later proved to be mistaken suggested a date in the dark period which followed Dyn. VI. Barely a twelve-month had elapsed, however, before the experienced prehistorian J. de Morgan finally dispelled the illusion of the New Race.[1] Unsystematic soundings on a number of Upper Egyptian sites had brought to light burials and pottery of closely similar kinds, always associated with an abundance of flint implements and an almost complete absence of metal objects. Petrie was quick to acknowledge his mistake, and the subsequent researches of himself and his assistants, together with those of scholars from various other countries, have developed the study of predynastic Egypt into a very flourishing, but at the same time highly complex and problematic, branch of Egyptological science. By a curious chance the very same years were destined to see the first discoveries of monuments of Dyns. I–III, and here again Petrie and Quibell were among the pioneers. Meanwhile the geologists had started upon their probing into the even more distant past, though it was not until considerably later that their investigations joined up ever more closely with those of students whose interests centred solely in the earliest fortunes of the human race. The story, though still presenting one gap of great magnitude, can now be set forth in a reasonably consecutive form.

At a very remote period, possibly fifty million years ago, the whole of what is now Egypt, as well as large parts of North Africa and Arabia, had become submerged beneath the sea. It was within this period, known as the Cretaceous, that the Nubian sandstone and, above it, the earliest limestones and clays were laid down. After a long space land reappeared, but only to be overwhelmed once more by the sea advancing from the north. This long-drawn-out episode ushered in an age of vast duration in which Eocene limestone, called nummulitic from the marine fossils occurring in it, was deposited. There succeeded a stage during which the Red Sea depression was formed and foldings on either side produced the high mountains of the Sinaitic peninsula and of the eastern desert. It was only later, at the end of the Miocene period, that the present-day Nile began to carve out its valley to far below the

[1] *Recherches sur les origines de l'Égypte*, 2 vols., Paris, 1896–7.

existing alluvial floor. The Delta did not exist as yet, its place being occupied by a gulf of the Mediterranean. Towards the close of the following Pliocene period a great movement of elevation set in, preceding which, however, the Nile channel had become almost filled with gravels and sands brought into it by lateral streams and downwash from the sides. Into these accumulations the Nile now started eroding its final channel, successive stages being marked by gravel terraces at ever lower levels. The five highest of these, in course of which the Pliocene passed into the Pleistocene, show no stone implements or other relics of prehistoric man, but the next two reveal rough hand-axes of flint so similar to ones of the last Ice age discovered in Europe that it has become customary to call them by the names Chellean and Acheulean first used in France. The two following terraces show implements of the type now known as Levalloisian.[1] At no great distance below, the present-day flood-level is reached, resting upon an extensive deposit of silt which shows that after erosion had taken place to a great depth a long period of deposition had reversed the river's downward course. The elaborate investigations which Drs. Sandford and Arkell have devoted to these movements throughout the entire length of the country indicate that various Late- and Post-middle Palaeolithic remains must lie embedded in the silt, and highest of all the Late-Palaeolithic flints called Sebilian after a village Sebîl in the neighbourhood of Kôm Ombo. As long ago as the seventies of the last century implements of the Palaeolithic and Neolithic periods had begun to be picked up on the surface of the high desert, but it required the systematic explorations above outlined, coupled with others by Misses Caton Thompson and Gardner in the Fayyûm and the oasis of Khârga, to establish the exact correlation between the various phases of Palaeolithic man and the successive stages in the formation of the Nile Valley. One able and cautious geologist[2] has hazarded the guess that the Sebilian culture may have ended about 8000 B.C., which is about 5,000 years before the beginning of the period with which this book is mainly concerned.

While Europe was still in the grip of the ice, and Neanderthal

[1] Called Mousterian by earlier writers.

[2] J. Ball, *Contributions*, pp. 29, 176.

man eked out a scanty existence as a hunter and searcher after vegetable food, a considerable part of North Africa was kept habitable by continuous rains. Where now there is waterless desert, there was then still a sufficiency of plant and animal food to support human life. What manner of men they were who hunted or grubbed for roots it is hard to say, but a few fossilized bones discovered at Ḳâw el-Kebîr suggest that their possessors may not have differed greatly from the race who inhabited the same parts right down to dynastic times. As the Pleistocene period pushed on towards its end, and the Nile carved its way deeper, narrowing its channel as it went, the increasing desiccation of the highlands drove man and beast ever nearer to the river, where the annual deposition of the rich Nile mud urged to a fuller and more settled agricultural life. And so began that rather more advanced age of man known as the Neolithic.

Prehistorians have found that, whether they looked to Europe, to Africa, or elsewhere in the world, the terms Palaeolithic and Neolithic have served their purpose pretty well. These terms refer to stages of human development, not to dates; for instance some work of the aborigines of Central Australia may be said still to be in the Palaeolithic or Old Stone stage, while the otherwise highly cultured Maoris were, less than two centuries ago, not yet out of the Neolithic Age, that is to say the age of New Stone. By these terms allusion is made to the nature of the implements which their owners used; in the one case to implements of unpolished, and in the other of polished, stone; but the term Neolithic has come to bear a somewhat different sense, or rather to imply the additional qualification of the absence of copper tools, or even the absence of copper for any purpose whatsoever. Now just as we saw the Sebilian (Late Palaeolithic) culture vanishing into the silt accumulated beneath the Nile, so too the Neolithic stage, in the most uncompromising sense of that expression, has become completely withdrawn from our sight. The interval between its beginning and that of the Tasian-Badarian phase with which our story will take up afresh has been reckoned at three thousand years or more, during which time the Nile Valley acquired its present size and something like its present climate, whereas the surrounding desert, as already said, became ever less habitable, leaving Egypt as a sort of vast oasis in which a highly individual civilization was free to evolve its own forms uninterruptedly.

Before proceeding to discuss the earliest Neolithic settlements in Upper Egypt it will be well to mention a few sites, mostly in the northern part of the country, where no trace of the use of metal has been found. The most extensive of these is Merimda-Beni Salâma, on the desert-edge 30 miles to the north-west of Cairo. Here Austrian and Swedish excavations brought to light the remains of a village community that dwelt in reed huts partly sunk below ground-level; their grain was stored close at hand in silos made of baskets of straw coated with clay. Weaving is attested by scraps of cloth and by spindle whorls. Ornaments are few, but there are ivory bangles and beads of bone and shell. The pottery, which like all predynastic ware was fashioned in ignorance of the potter's wheel, is mostly rude and without decoration. It has been regarded as a mark of extreme antiquity that here the dead were buried, not in cemeteries, but between or even within the huts of the living. A minority opinion, however, denies the temporal priority of the Merimdian finds, attributing them to a belated civilization that flourished when metal objects had already become common in Upper Egypt. To this the answer has been given that another northern site showing very similar characters, namely that excavated by Miss Caton Thompson to the north of the Birket Ḳârûn (Fayyûm Neolithic A), lies so high above the lake that to assume a later date for it does not fit in with the other culture-levels observed on the site.

Leaving such debatable matters to the experts, we turn our eyes southward to the stretch of country between Asyûṭ and Akhmîm. Here, at Dêr Tâsa and Badâri on the east bank, G. Brunton excavated cemeteries and village settlements with a claim to antiquity not far short of that of Merimda. The sites lie only a few miles apart and the Tasian finds are so intermingled with the Badarian that it has been doubted whether the two stages are to be distinguished. If Tasian really be a separate stage, it is peculiar only in the total absence of metal and the more primitive appearance of its pottery and other objects. The Badarian pottery exhibits a perfection of workmanship never again equalled in the Nile Valley; its finer ware is extremely thin and shows a rippling that occurs later only very rarely. There are brown and red vessels, both with and without the rippling, which have the blackened tops and insides that are the outstanding characteristic of the stage next following. Rather shallow bowls are the commonest form; rims and handles are very rare. Some ivory spoons and combs seem strangely sophisticated for so remote a period, and of the three nude female figurines found at least two are more shapely than their Amratian successors. A few copper beads and a copper awl suggest the advisability of henceforth substituting for 'Neolithic' the term 'Chalcolithic' (or 'Aeneolithic') as applied to those ages when copper and flint were simultaneously in use. Let it here be noted that flint was retained for ceremonial implements long after copper had become general for tools and weapons; as late as Dyn. XII wooden sickles are still provided with teeth of flint.

An absolute dating of these earliest stages of Egyptian culture was long regarded as out of the question, and is likely to remain so until the validity and utility of the new radio-carbon technique have been demonstrated beyond a peradventure. Meanwhile to Petrie has been due a makeshift substitute which, precarious as it looks to the outside observer, has won almost universal commendation from those who have put it to a practical test. This is his famous system of Sequence Dating.[1] Starting from what appeared to him the indisputable development in wavy-handled pots from true handles to mere ornamental appendages he assigned a S.D. number to each stage, and then worked into the series other types of objects found accompanying such pots; finally from comparison of the S.D. positions of all the contents of any given tomb-group he managed to fix the relative temporal position of this as a whole. Petrie started his S.D. numbers at 30 leaving the lower numbers for possible future discoveries anterior in time; his end-date, S.D. 77, corresponds with the beginning of Dyn. I. The Badarian remains fall outside the range of Petrie's Sequence Dates, and have therefore had allotted to them the numbers S.D. 21–29, which were reserved for some such contingency. At Naḳâda had been found

1 First expounded in his *Diospolis Parva*, London, 1901, pp. 4 ff.

graves of two distinct periods referred to particularly by foreign scholars as Naḳâda I (S.D. 30–39) and Naḳâda II (S.D. 40–62) respectively. For these terms, however, Amratian and Gerzean are now commonly substituted, the former named after El-ʿAmra,[1] a site near Abydos where there occurred no mixture of the two styles of products, and the latter after Gerza[2] for a similar reason. The Amratian period has several remarkable types of pottery peculiar to itself, in addition to the already mentioned black-topped kind, which is the commonest type of all. It used to be thought that the black tops and insides were due to the vessels being inverted at the time of firing, while the top parts owed their red colour to oxidization due to exposure in the fresh air. Experiments appear to have shown, however, that the black-topped effect was reached in two stages, so that the simultaneous existence of a highly burnished all-red pottery need cause no surprise. Very characteristic of Amratian is the style known as 'white cross-lined'. This consists of red polished ware adorned with dull white paint. The often very attractive geometrical patterns are made up of close parallel lines or a sort of network, and are not seldom accompanied by or alternate with the figures of animals, men, and trees. Much rarer are black pots with incised ornamentation picked out with white paint. Vases of stone are also of frequent occurrence, using not only hard varieties like granite and basalt, but also softer kinds like steatite and alabaster. Figurines of earthenware and ivory represent men wearing the penis-sheath and women with some analogous covering; very strange are the ivories, sometimes flat pieces and sometimes tusks, showing men with pointed beards and without any indication of bodies and limbs; some of the women are tattooed, others are steatopygous and frankly hideous. The long-toothed combs have tops imitating birds or animals. Omitting reference to less characteristic objects there remains to be mentioned the rare occurrence of faience; to the beads of copper are now added pins, and one or two instances of the use of gold are already attested.

[1] D. Randall-MacIver and A. C. Mace, *El Amrah and Abydos*, London, 1902; see too PM v. 106–7.

[2] Excavated by G. A. Wainwright, see Petrie, Wainwright, and Mackay, *The Labyrinth, Gerzeh and Mazghuneh*, London, 1912.

With the Gerzean period there comes about a great change, once again most conspicuous in the pottery. The white cross-lined ware is now replaced by a buff variety decorated with red zigzag lines or spirals, or else with many-oared boats each with two cabins and a sort of flagstaff or standard, with or without rows of flamingoes and occasional depictions of men and animals. In the whole history of pottery there is no sort less easily mistaken or more characteristic of a particular period and people. At Hieracōnpolis F. W. Green discovered a tomb with wall-paintings clearly of the same type.[1] The wavy-handled pots to which Petrie attached such importance start in the Amratian period at S.D. 35, but belong mostly to the Gerzean. Stone vessels employ even more showy kinds of material, among them diorite and serpentine. A difference between the Amratian and Gerzean stages is seen in the mace-heads; in the former these are disk-shaped with very sharp edges, in the latter they are pear-shaped; the hieroglyphs 𓌈 and 𓌉 illustrate the difference. A development of great importance is the increased employment of copper, now used for weapons and tools as well as for articles of toilet.

Badarian, Amratian, and Gerzean layers have been found in stratification at Hammâmîya near Badâri, so that there can be no doubt that the terms refer to temporal distinctions. However, the same terms serve also to describe local range. All three stages are exemplified in Lower Nubia and even beyond, though they are apt to lag behind whenever Egypt herself advances into new phases. Apart from Nubia Badarian remains have been found from Hieracōnpolis in the south to Maḥasna north of Abydos, Amratian from Armant to Nag'a ed-Dêr on the east bank opposite Maḥasna. Gerzean has a wider span, since the village of Gerza lies more than 200 miles farther downstream, near Meidûm. It would be unwise to assert a complete uniformity throughout Upper Egypt at any given moment, but no very marked local differences contradict such a supposition. On the other hand, there does appear some reason for contrasting the Upper Egyptian predynastic culture with that of Lower Egypt as represented by Merimda, the Fayyûm, Ma'âdi near Cairo and El-'Omâri near Ḥelwân, more especially

[1] J. E. Quibell and F. W. Green, *Hierakonpolis II*, London, 1902, Pls. 75–79.

since a difference of race is here discernible. It is true that the anthropological evidence from Merimda is not wholly satisfactory, but the experts have felt justified in proclaiming the presence there of a fairly tall people with much greater skull-capacity than that possessed by the southerners.[1] These latter were long-headed—dolichocephalic is the learned term—and below even medium stature, but negroid features are often to be observed. Whatever may be said of the northerners, it is safe to describe the dwellers in Upper Egypt as of essentially African stock, a character always retained despite alien influences brought to bear on them from time to time.

To revert to the temporal aspect of the three stages it is to be regretted that some archaeologists still use expressions like 'the Amratian civilization', 'the Gerzean civilization'—expressions which seem to imply breaks in development as radical as those between Egypt's Roman and Islamic periods. However striking the change from the one stage to the other may appear, the continuity of the evolution as a whole must be affirmed with all emphasis, but without denying that impulses from abroad may have been needed to stimulate every important step forward. To illustrate this continuity two pieces of evidence will here be adduced, the one general and the other special. Throughout the entire period the graves were narrow trenches of oval or rectangular shape in which the bodies were laid on their left side with knees drawn up to near the level of the faces, the head more often to the south than to the north; and together with the dead man were buried his most treasured possessions, as well as the rougher utensils and tools which would enable him to carry on his accustomed life in the hereafter. The inherent unity of these funeral arrangements is not contradicted by the variations introduced from time to time, as when the matting used by the Badarians to line the graves was replaced by wooden boards for sides and roof, an innovation which led on in due course to the sarcophagi of the dynastic age. Burial in the contracted position persisted for the poor many centuries after mummification and interment in sumptuous stone tombs had become the rule for the rich.

Even more eloquent testimony to the cultural continuity is pro-

[1] For Derry's pronouncements see below, p. 399.

vided by the thin flat palettes of stone which were employed for grinding up the malachite used for the adornment or magical protection of the eyes. Such palettes occur already, not only at Dêr Tâsa, but also at Merimda, in both places still of the simplest rectangular or elliptic forms, and not yet of the greenish slate which became customary later. From Amratian times come the earliest examples of the lozenge and ovoid shapes which subsequently obtained so splendid a development. Side by side with these, all sorts of fanciful forms came into fashion, some imitating fish, others turtles, others again quadrupeds like hippopotamus and hartebeest. The palettes with tops having a bird's head symmetrically placed at each corner are of special interest, since such symmetry becomes later one of the clearest indications of Mesopotamian influences. Towards the end of the Gerzean period designs in low relief put in their first appearance, but as yet occupy only a tiny portion of the surface; the designs are emblematic and have defied all attempts at interpretation. Here clearly we have the ancestors of the magnificent sculptured palettes of which only thirteen, including some fragments, have survived.[1] The artistry displayed in these, the reliefs spread over the entire field, and also the size of the largest, suggest that they were votive objects never intended for use. When the first examples came to light, it was even doubted whether they were of Egyptian workmanship at all, but such doubts were laid to rest by the discovery in 1897 of two more specimens in the temple of Hieracōnpolis, one of them the famous palette of Naʿrmer[2] to be discussed later. It now became evident that these commemorative palettes belonged to the very latest predynastic times, if not in some cases to the protodynastic, the most important novelty disclosed by them being scanty, but indubitable, examples of hieroglyphic writing.

Among these fascinating late predynastic palettes the one here illustrated (Pl. XIX)[3] has been chosen, not on account of its artistic superiority—others are more attractive—but because of its clearer signification. The obverse shows seven buttressed rectangles evidently representing conquered townships, into which symbolic creatures hack their way with picks. The hieroglyphs, mostly

[1] PM v. 104 ff., 194. [2] Op. cit. v. 193. [3] Op. cit. v. 105, No. 6.

single, inside the rectangles were evidently intended to convey the names of the places. It has been suggested that the attackers (falcon, lion, scorpion, &c.) should be interpreted as depicting under different aspects one and the same victorious chieftain,[1] but it surely is more probable that they represent distinct provinces warring together as a coalition; note particularly the two bird-standards demolishing the fortress in the lower left-hand corner, which may well represent the later Coptite nome, the fifth of Upper Egypt. On the reverse, oxen, donkeys, and rams are seen walking peacefully towards the right, each species within a separate register of its own, while at the bottom are trees which P. E. Newberry (strongly opposed by L. Keimer)[2] conjectured to be olives; beside the trees is the monogram 𓇳, which Sethe rightly read to mean Tjeḥnu-land,[3] the land of those Libyans known as Tjeḥnyu (p. 35). It requires no great acumen to diagnose the cattle as booty, and the trees as yielding the much-prized Tjeḥnu-oil.

This interpretation appears to be corroborated, though with an important difference, by the nearly perfect object known as the Palette of the Hunt.[4] Here a number of men carrying bows, spears, boomerangs, and lassos are shown coping successfully with the fauna of the desert; two lions have been transfixed with arrows, and an ibex lassoed by the horns; other animals, including an ostrich and a desert hare, are in headlong flight. But the main interest, apart from two cryptic hieroglyphic symbols, resides in the accoutrement of the men. They are bearded like the conquered foes on the Naʿrmer palette (Pls. XXI, XXII), have feathers in their hair,[5] and tails attached to their short skirts. The tails are a feature characteristic of the Pharaohs themselves, and apart from them are known only from representations of conquered Libyan chieftains sculptured on a walls[5] leading up to the pyramid-temple of the Pharaoh Saḥurēʿ of Dyn. V;[6] these same chieftains, who also wear the penis-sheath, have a strange little tuft of hair standing upright above their foreheads which reminds one irresistibly of the 'uraeus'

[1] *ZÄS* lii. 56.
[2] *Bull. Inst. fr.* xxxi. 121 ff.
[3] See above, n. 1.
[4] PM v. 104, No. 3.
[5] The absence of the feather on the palette of Naʿrmer and with the prisoner chieftains about to be mentioned is perhaps a sign of defeat, see the quotation p. 273, top.
[6] L. Borchardt, *Das Grabdenkmal des Königs Saḥurēʿ*, ii, Leipzig, 1913, Pls. 1, 5.

PLATE XIX

THE TJEḤNU PALETTE
Slate, predynastic. Cairo Museum

THE GEBEL EL-ʿARAḲ KNIFE-HANDLE
Ivory, predynastic. Now in the Louvre

(cobra) on the Pharaoh's brow. Can it be that the predynastic kings of Lower Egypt, or of the western Delta, were actually of Libyan stock, and that it was from them that the later rulers of the united Two Lands inherited the tail and the uraeus, those very unexpected items in the royal insignia? But there are other possibilities. Saḥurēʿ's Libyan chieftains might be imitating the Egyptian kings. Or again, the eccentricities of wardrobe above specified may not have been confined either to Libyans or to Lower Egypt, but have been widespread African. The Egyptian word for Nubians, as well as that for soldiers generally, is determined (p. 23) with the figure of a man wearing a feather on his head ([hieroglyph]), and we have above called attention to Amratian figurines from Upper Egypt showing the penis-sheath. Hence all that we are at present entitled to conclude is that as regards equipment, which does not necessarily imply race, there was an affinity between Libyans, Egyptians, and Nubians which confirms our description of the earliest culture of the Nile Valley as essentially African.

The Palette of the Hunt differs from the Cairo fragment naming Tjeḥnu-land inasmuch as its Libyans, if such they be, are happy sportsmen, not defeated foes. H. Ranke[1] has argued for the early date of this palette on the ground that its figures are displayed in a free and somewhat disorderly fashion contrary to the later Egyptian habit of disposing its men and animals upon straight ruled lines, as exemplified in the Cairo fragment and the Naʿrmer palette. There is perhaps more cogency in Ranke's claim of a Delta origin for the palette, partly on the grounds already stated and partly on account of the standards which three of the huntsmen hold in their hands. These seem to represent the symbols for 'west' (𓋀) and for 'east' (𓋁) respectively and that ever ingenious scholar Kurt Sethe[2] had found good evidence for these having originally symbolized the opposite sides of the Delta. But what was intended by the hunting scene as a whole remains obscure, since it is impossible to accept Ranke's daring suggestion that the wild beasts of the Delta had become a menace and that east and west had joined hands to put an end to their depredations.

Mention of the standards on the Palette of the Hunt brings a

[1] In the article quoted PM v. 104, No. 3.

[2] *Nachr. Göttingen*, 1922, 197 ff.

reminder that no explanation of those seen in the ships of the Gerzean pottery has yet been offered. Newberry made a collection of them, and sought to show that most at least were the ensigns of the Delta nomes or provinces. There is but little doubt that they are the equivalent of our own national flags, and that they were intended to signify possession of the ships by this or that local community. But Newberry's attempts at identification[1] were mostly mistaken and we remain in ignorance what particular localities were meant. Much less enigmatic are the corresponding standards on one of our decorative palettes,[2] on which the top is occupied by a 'powerful bull' goring to death a recumbent man of the type above described as 'Libyan'; the bull is the king, whether of Upper or Lower Egypt or of both, since precisely that epithet is constantly applied to the reigning monarch. Below, doubtless attached to the half-destroyed figure of a prisoner, is a rope grasped by hands growing out of five standards of the kind later found as nome-signs, the most easily recognizable of them being the standard of the nome of Akhmîm, the ninth of Upper Egypt, symbol .[3] The intention of the palette is thus evident; it records the massacre or capture of Lower Egyptian or Libyan enemies by an Upper Egyptian chieftain at the head of a combination of several provinces.

Such is the general trend of the palettes with warlike representations, and the remarkable thing about them is that they are all concerned with what is in effect internecine warfare; they show no sign of a clash with eastern invaders, with one possible exception, namely the famous Gebel el-ʿArak knife-handle in the Louvre,[4] an ivory object showing the pursuit of game on one side and a battle on the other (Pl. XX). There, above the scene of the chase, is a cloaked personage standing between two lions which he seems to have tamed. The combatants on the other face—they use weapons no more formidable than sticks—have the same appearance as on the palettes, but below them are two rows of ships separated by slain warriors, and the upper row shows the vertical prows and sterns and even the crescent-crowned poles typical of Mesopota-

[1] *Ann. Arch. and Anthrop. Liverpool*, v. 132 ff.

[2] PM v. 105, No. 4.

[3] See too below, p. 403, Fig. 12, centre.

[4] Op. cit. v. 107.

mian craft of a very early period. The heroic figure posed between two lions in true Sumerian fashion has the garb and head-gear of an early Babylonian divinity. To H. Frankfort, whose researches on these foreign relations admirably supplemented those of others, is due a useful tabulation of the points of connexion between the two civilizations,[1] and he agreed that the Babylonian phase when the similarities were at their height was the so-called Jamdat Nasr period, dated approximately to about the beginning of the Egyptian Dyn. I. Then it was that hieroglyphic writing first emerged in Egypt, though traceable in Mesopotamia somewhat further back. The comparisons are unquestionable, and are such as seem natural growths on Babylonian soil, but alien to the spirit and tradition of Egypt, whence indeed they disappeared after a few centuries. The great recessed tombs of brick (p. 406, Fig. 15 below) belonging to Dyns. I–III have their prototype in Mesopotamia, and so have the cylinder seals whose arrival must be fixed to well before Dyn. I. The composite animals, winged griffins and serpent-necked felines, are non-Egyptian in character and almost confined to the palettes and knife-handles. The entwined necks seen on the Naʿrmer palette and a few other objects are definitely Mesopotamian in conception, though Egyptian in execution, and so are the antithetically arranged groups like the giraffes on another palette and the Gebel el-ʿArak̦ lions.

How is this Mesopotamian influence to be explained historically? Can it be viewed simply as the continuation of a pressure that may have begun as early as Amratian times, only greatly accelerated and magnified? It is not intended to discuss here the very early connexions which E. Baumgartel, among other investigators, finds between the Iranian pottery and those of the contemporary Egyptian predynastic periods. But we do suggest that nothing less than an infiltration into Egypt of Mesopotamian craftsmen can account for the introduction, at the threshold of Dyn. I, of the striking architectural and artistic innovations above outlined. Indirect trade relations are clearly insufficient, while on the other hand actual invasion seems too much to assume. Let us frankly admit our ignorance in these matters, nor let us attempt to adjudicate between

[1] *AJSL* lviii. 355.

those who advocate the line of approach from the Red Sea through the Wâdy Ḥammâmât and the town of Coptos,[1] and those who favour the northerly route from Palestine.[2] But it seems permissible to give it as our opinion that the proved Mesopotamian influence would have amply sufficed to set in motion that rapid progress which created for Egypt a highly individual civilization from the forms of which she thereafter never widely departed.

Reviewing the predynastic period as a whole, we are seriously handicapped by our inability to determine how long it lasted. It was precisely that inability which prompted Petrie to invent his system of Sequence Dating. None the less, both he and others have been unable to refrain from guesses on the subject. The maximum guess is perhaps that of Petrie himself,[3] who placed the Fayyûm remains at 9000 B.C., the Badarian at 7471, and Mēnēs at 4326—we have stated (pp. 62 ff.) our reasons for rejecting the last as impossible. The great excavator G. Reisner[4] ran to the opposite extreme with the estimate of 1,000 years for the predynastic period. The matter is important, since it raises the question as to the kind of life which was possible at the various stages. If heavy rains were still periodic over the desert neighbouring the Nile, then the Neolithic period even as late as the Tasians may have looked to the uplands rather than to the Nile Valley for whatever grain they were able to produce. Then again there is the problem presented by the Valley itself. How long did it take to regulate the effects of the inundation so as to convert a region of jungle and swamps into a land of radiant cornfields? Of one thing we may be certain: we should be seriously deluded if we imagined the aspect of the Valley in the predynastic age to have at all resembled what is to be seen there today. It was doubtless much more like the present Sudanese Upper Nile with its marshy tracts and thick undergrowth of papyrus infested with crocodiles, the haunt of wild creatures of all kinds. As methods of drainage were introduced, arable lands increased, and the

[1] Baumgartel, following Petrie, on p. 44 of her work cited opposite.

[2] Engelbach in *Ann. Serv.* xlii. 201 f.

[3] *The Making of Egypt*, p. 9.

[4] *The Development of the Egyptian Tomb*, Cambridge, Harvard Univ. Press, 1936, p. 343.

swamps receded to near the desert edge. Also the fauna gradually migrated southwards, together with the papyrus and the lotus. We have not the means at our disposal to trace this development step by step.

SELECT BIBLIOGRAPHY

Prehistory: from the vast literature only some of the most comprehensive and the latest works can be quoted: Sir Flinders Petrie's final conclusions, *The Making of Egypt*, London, 1939; E. J. Baumgartel, *The Cultures of Prehistoric Egypt*, revised edition, Oxford, 1955; in French, É. Massoulard, *Préhistoire et Protohistoire d'Égypte*, Paris, 1939; J. Vandier, *Manuel d'archéologie égyptienne*, vol. i, Paris, 1952; C. Bachatly, *Bibliographie de la préhistoire égyptienne (1869–1938)*, Cairo, 1942. Among the assistants of Petrie whose excavations have contributed most to our knowledge special mention must be made of G. Brunton and G. A. Wainwright; German excavators, H. Junker and A. Scharff.

Geology: J. Ball, *Contributions to the Geography of Egypt*, Cairo, 1939, ch. ii; for the terraces see op. cit., ch. iii, and ibid., p. 41 n., for the works by K. S. Sandford and W. J. Arkell; for the investigations by Miss Caton-Thompson and Miss Gardner, see op. cit., pp. 184–6.

Merimda-Beni Salâma: see the reports by H. Junker quoted C. Bachatly, op. cit., pp. 33–34; summary and discussion, Vandier, op. cit. i. 95 ff.; Baumgartel's divergent opinion, see her op. cit., pp. 14 ff.; 120 ff.

Dêr Tâsa: G. Brunton, *Mostagedda and the Tasian Culture*, London, 1937; Vandier, op. cit. i. 167 ff.

Badâri: G. Brunton, *Qau and Badari*, 3 vols., London, 1927–30; Brunton and Caton-Thompson, *The Badarian Civilisation*, London, 1928; Vandier, op. cit. i. 191 ff.

The slate palettes: the earlier types, W. M. F. Petrie, *Prehistoric Egypt Corpus*, London, 1921, Pls. 52–59; the later decorative types, Petrie, *Ceremonial Slate Palettes*, London, 1953.

The physical differences between northerners and southerners: D. E. Derry's findings discussed in Vandier, op. cit. i. 11–13.

XV

MANETHO'S FIRST TWO DYNASTIES. EPILOGUE

THE memorable years which gave Egyptologists their first glimpse of the predynastic period also brought them face to face for the first time with the earliest dynasties. The pioneer in this field was E. Amélineau, a Coptic scholar with no previous experience of excavating. Supported by funds from private sources he started operations at Abydos in 1895, working westwards until he reached a low spur of the desert known as Umm el-Ḳaʿâb 'Mother of Pots' after the innumerable potsherds covering the surface.[1] In this remote spot, a full mile distant from the cultivation, he came upon a cluster of brick pit-tombs which subsequently proved to have belonged to the kings of Dyns. I and II. According to his count they were sixteen in number, and since, so far as he could see, the royal names were all of the Horus-name type (pp. 51–52), while none of them corresponded to the names in Manetho and the king-lists, he naturally concluded that his new kings were those 'Followers of Horus' whom the Turin Canon of Kings gives as the predecessors of Mēnēs and whom Manetho describes as Demigods or Mānēs. Closer study by competent philologists quickly dispelled this error. Amélineau's excavation was badly conducted and badly published, and it was fortunate when in 1899 Flinders Petrie obtained a permit to investigate the site anew. The highly successful results of his work were made accessible with exemplary rapidity in several memoirs published by the Egypt Exploration Fund. The cemetery was found to have been sadly devastated long before Amélineau added to the confusion; the burnt wooden linings of the tombs and the wide scattering of broken fragments were tracked down to Copts of the fifth or sixth century. In spite of these disadvantages Petrie was able, besides planning the tombs, to recover a vast multitude of important objects, including inscribed

[1] PM v. 78 ff.

stone vessels, jar-sealings, ebony and ivory tablets, as well as several superbly carved stelae of imposing size.

Meanwhile scholars in Europe had got to work on the inscriptions found by Amélineau. Griffith in England[1] and Sethe in Germany were among the first to recognize that they were here in the presence of remains of Manetho's Dyns. I and II. An epoch-making article by Sethe (1897)[2] drew special attention to the facts that in some cases the Horus-name of the king was accompanied by another introduced by the title 'King of Upper and Lower Egypt' or by this followed by the Two-Ladies title (above, p. 51) and that it was these secondary names which corresponded to those in the Ramesside king-lists and in Manetho. Naturally these secondary names had undergone some deformation in course of time, but the divergences were not difficult to account for. Thus the Usaphais whom Manetho gives as the fifth king of Dyn. I was traced back to a hieroglyphic group probably to be read as Zemti, while Manetho's sixth king Miebis had as its original an unmistakably written Merpibia. The seventh one, Manetho's Semempsēs, appeared as a priestly figure holding a stick at Umm el-Ḳaʿâb and a sceptre in the Abydos king-list,[3] while the eighth and last king of the dynasty, using Ḳaʿa as his Horus-name and occasionally also as his personal name, was only slightly, and quite comprehensibly, disguised as Ḳebḥ in the Abydos list and the Turin Canon. The historic sequence of these four kings was luckily confirmed by two incised stone vases discovered many years later.[4] This opportunity is taken to note that the transcription of hieroglyphs belonging to the earliest period is a matter of great difficulty, so that names are apt to be rendered very differently by different scholars, as will be apparent from two Horus-names of Dyn. I. That belonging to the fourth king read as Zet by Petrie clearly equates its bearer with the cobra-goddess, whose name probably sounded more like Edjō than like Uadji as advocated by some. On the other hand, if for the fifth king Petrie's Den is here preferred to Sethe's widely accepted Udimu meaning 'the water-pourer', it is because this is highly

[1] In Petrie, *Royal Tombs*, see p. 427.

[2] *ZÄS* xxxv. 1 ff.

[3] *Ann. Serv.* xliv. 284 ff.

[4] C. M. Firth and J. E. Quibell, *The Step Pyramid*, Cairo, 1935, Pls. 88. 1; 105. 3.

speculative and it seemed better to retain their usual values for the two alphabetic signs with which the name is written.

The problems raised by the first four kings of Dyn. I, with Mēnēs at their head, are less easily solved and demand a wider perspective than has sufficed for the last four. It is desirable, therefore, here to interpose some account of some excavations prior to Petrie's decisive discoveries at Abydos. In 1897 Petrie's partner J. E. Quibell had been digging at El-Kâb, an important site on the east bank some distance to the north of Edfu. Here the local goddess was the vulture Nekhbe who shared with the cobra Edjō of Butō in the Delta the honour of providing the Pharaoh with his Two-Ladies title. In view of the great antiquity of that title important finds might have been expected, but Quibell's results were disappointing. All the more exciting, therefore, was the success awaiting him in the following year at Kôm el-Aḥmar almost opposite across the river. This was known to be the ancient Nekhen mentioned in certain Old Kingdom official titles, and the Greek Hieracōnpolis on account of the falcon-god Horus who was the principal deity worshipped there. The great prize was the famous slate palette of Naʿrmer mentioned several times in our last chapter and here depicted in Pls. XXI, XXII. It needed but little acumen to recognize in this object an indisputable link between the late predynastic and the earliest dynastic periods; material, design, and subjects depicted obviously pointed to it as the latest example of the series of palettes now familiar to the reader, and on the other hand the Horus-name Naʿrmer was soon to make its appearance at Umm el-Ḳaʿâb. But before going into further details about Naʿrmer—the reading of the name is not quite certain[1]—there must be some discussion of a still earlier king to whom, for lack of any phonetic equivalent, we must refer as the Scorpion king. Apart from inexplicable mentions on a vessel from Ṭura,[2] on a slip of ivory from Umm el-Ḳaʿâb,[3] and possibly on the palette reproduced above in Pl. XIX, the only remains of him are votive offerings found in the temple of Hieracōnpolis. The most impressive is a large broken mace-head of hard limestone carrying scenes in high relief. The main scene is ceremonial, as on most similar memorials of

[1] *Ann. Serv.* xlix. 217 ff., 547. [2] Junker, *Turah*, p. 7. [3] *RT* ii, Pl. 3. 19.

THE PALETTE OF NAʿRMER, *recto*
Slate, from Hieracōnpolis, Dyn. I. Cairo Museum

PLATE XXII

THE PALETTE OF NAʿRMER, *verso*

See on Plate XXI

Dyn. I, and has as central figure the king wielding a hoe in both hands; he wears a tunic fastened over his left shoulder and the bull's tail, a common attribute of royalty, attached above the girdle; on his head is 𓋑, the crown of Upper Egypt. Of greater historical importance are the representations in the upper register. Here is seen a procession of military standards surmounted by the emblems of various nomes or provinces, among them the belemnite of Mīn and the animal of Sēth; tied to each standard by a rope passing round its neck is a lapwing 𓅚 dead or as good as dead (Fig. 12);

FIG. 12. The provinces capture the Lapwings.

facing in the opposite direction was another procession of standards having bows 𓌒 similarly attached, but only one complete standard is preserved. The general meaning is clear: the Scorpion king claimed victories over the Nine Bows, i.e. the various peoples in and on the borders of Egypt, and also over a later often mentioned part of the Egyptian population known as the Erkhēye or 'Lapwing-folk' and held by many Egyptologists to have been the subjugated inhabitants of the Delta. It is significant, however, that in spite of the widespread victories of which the Scorpion boasts he makes no pretence of having been the king of a united Egypt. That honour was reserved for Naʿrmer, who on one side of his palette wears the white crown 𓋑 of Upper Egypt, while on the other, as well as on a mace-head of almost equal importance, he has assumed the red crown of Lower Egypt 𓋔, apparently the first Egyptian monarch to do so. It is precisely this fact which justifies the belief that Naʿrmer was none other than Mēnēs himself. It is needless to comment at great length on scenes which to a large extent explain themselves, but two features of the palette are too interesting to be passed over in silence. To the right of the figure of Naʿrmer with arm upraised to brain the enemy whom he holds by the forelock is an enigmatic group of emblems combined into a single whole. It is clear that as yet the learned men of the country had not developed the power of writing complete sentences; the most they could do was to exhibit a complex of pictures which the spectator would then translate into words. That the falcon of Horus represents Naʿrmer is evident, and the rope attached to the head of a bearded enemy and held in the falcon's hand needs no commentary. The bolsterlike object from which the prisoner's head protrudes is obviously his native country, and it is now held that the six papyrus plants growing out of it represent Lower Egypt, of which the papyrus was the symbol. Thus the entire complex would mean 'The falcon-god Horus (i.e. Naʿrmer) leads captive the inhabitants of the papyrus-country'. It is perhaps not fantastic to interpret the device occupying the middle of the *verso* as symbolizing the union of the two halves of Egypt; the two long-necked felines appear to be restrained from fighting by a bearded man on each side. Up above, Naʿrmer, as King of Lower Egypt, is seen inspecting the results of his victory; in front of him are the standards of his confederates and there is a ship which appears to have brought him to the place where his decapitated enemies are still lying. Thus this splendidly devised and executed votive palette may reasonably be understood as commemorating the very events upon which rested the fame of Mēnēs as founder of the Pharaonic monarchy.

Nevertheless the identity of Mēnēs remains the subject of scholarly controversy, and it will not be superfluous to review the reasons that have been advanced. Among the jar-sealings discovered at Umm el-Ḳaʿâb there was one in which the signs 𓏠𓈖 *mn* without preceding title were found immediately adjacent to the Horus-name Naʿrmer[1], and this was taken as a proof that Naʿrmer and

[1] Petrie, *Royal Tombs*, ii, Pl. 13. 93. See here Fig. 13.

Mēnēs were identical, and similar reasoning appeared to equate the Horus Djer and the Horus Edjō (Petrie's Zet, the Serpent King) with the kings given as Iti and Ita in the Abydos list. Unfortunately, as both Griffith and Sethe pointed out, a like argument would

FIG. 13. Supposed sealing of Mēnēs (restored).

FIG. 14. Tablet with the name of Mēnēs (restored).

furnish us with two distinct names for the Horus ʿAḥa, neither of them found in the king-lists, and there are other objections of the same kind. Consequently this criterion is worthless, though of course its rejection does not prove Naʿrmer not to have been Mēnēs. Of far greater interest is the ivory tablet here reproduced in Fig. 14.[1] This was found by De Morgan in 1897 in a huge

[1] PM v. 118. Here seen with the later found fragments, *Ann. Serv.* xxxiii, Pls. 1, 2.

recessed tomb at Naḳâda, the scene of Flinders Petrie's earlier prehistoric discoveries. Concerning the nature of this object there is no dispute; it is a label intended to indicate the date and the contents of some vessel or receptacle to which it was to be tied. In the top row to right of the centre is the Horus-name of King

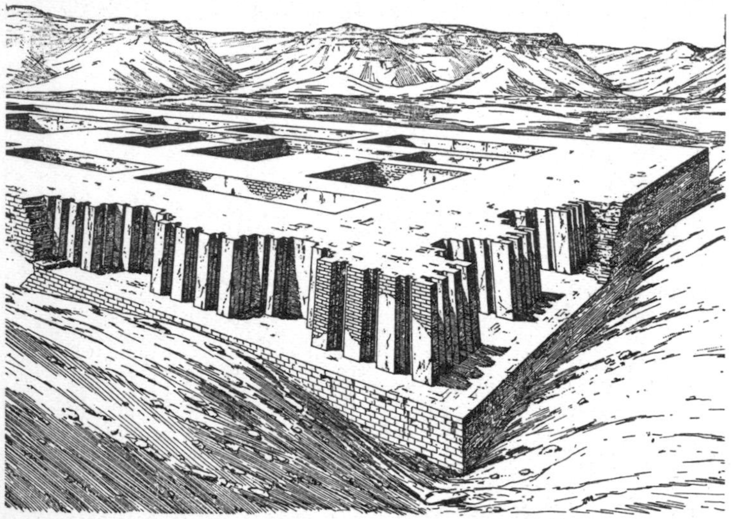

FIG. 15. Recess-panelling in the great tomb of Naḳâda.

ʿAḥa ('The Fighter') occurring also on jar-sealings from the tomb and in various other places; behind the *serekh* (p. 52) is the ship in which the king was doubtless supposed to have been faring; in front is seen a group of hieroglyphs enclosed in a sort of booth or pavilion, and it is upon this group that the divergent opinions of scholars have been concentrated. There can be no question that the vulture and cobra over two basket-like signs constitute the Two-Ladies title which, as has been seen, was often used to introduce the personal names of Dyn. I kings, and it was unreasonable to deny, as several scholars have done, that the hieroglyph beneath is the draughtsboard 𓏠 reading *mn* or that it gives the personal name of Mēnēs. L. Borchardt was the first to recognize the latter obvious fact, but he unfortunately jumped to the conclusion that ʿAḥa and Mēnēs were identical, a view accepted also by Sethe, and it was consequently assumed that the Naḳâda tomb was that of Mēnēs himself. To this interpretation there are two serious objections: in the first place it ignores the boothlike structure within which the name of Mēnēs is written, and in the second place it overlooks the fact that the hieroglyphs of the Two-Ladies title here face towards the right, whereas it was elsewhere the universal rule to make the signs of the Horus-name and the king's personal name face one another. Add to these objections the consideration that this top register ought to commemorate some outstanding event by which the year of the tablet's fabrication could be remembered, and it must be concluded that ʿAḥa is here depicted as visiting some place connected with Mēnēs. Grdseloff,[1] to whom, following a suggestion by Newberry, belonged the credit of having insisted upon these points, ingeniously quoted a passage in the Pyramid Texts where the king is described as erecting the temporary structures needed for a royal funeral, and this may possibly have been the actual ceremony depicted on the tablet. Here, then, although there is no proof that Naʿrmer was Mēnēs, we at least obtain the assurance that Mēnēs was not ʿAḥa, but must have been his predecessor. The choice certainly lies between Naʿrmer and ʿAḥa, whose Horus-names share the peculiarity of showing the falcon in a crouching form and usually as resting on a curved boat-like base, whereas the later kings of Dyn. I depict the falcon as upright and having a straight line at the top of the *serekh*. A further ground for rejecting the identity of ʿAḥa and Mēnēs is that, if they were identical, we should have expected to find ʿAḥa mentioned at Hieracōnpolis, whereas no trace of him has been found there. We can here only allude in passing to a mysterious king Ka whose Horus-name occurs at Umm el-Ḳaʿâb and a few other places, and is written in the archaic way just noted; no one has put forward his name as a candidate in the issue here discussed, and we may safely disregard any such possibility.

The unanimity with which all later authorities proclaim Mēnēs to have been the first of the Pharaohs receives virtual confirmation from the famous 'Palermo Stone' (above, pp. 62–64). The top row of the *recto* gives only the rather fantastically written names of a

[1] *Ann. Serv.* xliv. 279 ff.

number of kings concerning whom the annalist had no further information to offer. It cannot be doubted that the second row began with Mēnēs, though the portion mentioning him is lost; the analogy of the two other kings of Dyn. I recorded in the large Cairo fragment makes it well-nigh certain that both his Horus-name and his personal name would have been found there, presumably accompanied also by the name of his mother. The year-spaces below the heading doubtless attributed to each year of his reign what was considered to be its outstanding event, though for this the chronicler of so remote an age may possibly have had to draw upon his imagination. It would have been interesting to know whether the unification of the Two Lands was explicitly mentioned; that was at all events the momentous achievement which in the eyes of the Egyptians marked the beginning of human history. A remembrance of it is found in the words 'Union of Upper and Lower Egypt; circumambulation of the wall(s)' by which alike on the Palermo Stone and elsewhere the first year of each king was characterized; this evidently referred to the ceremony which legitimized him as descended from the founder of his line. The walls here alluded to will have been those of Memphis, the foundation of which is ascribed to Mēnēs by Herodotus (ii. 99) and with some confusion by Diodorus (i. 50); also the Rosetta Stone, referring to Memphis, speaks of the ceremonies customarily performed there by the king on assuming his high office. Thus the removal of the royal residence from somewhere in the south to this admirably situated position at the apex of the Delta must be viewed as a direct consequence of the establishment of the double kingdom. The other important acts attributed to Mēnēs by Herodotus have been discussed by Sethe with great ingenuity; they are the creation of a great embankment which should protect Memphis from being overwhelmed by the Nile-flood and the building of the temple of Ptaḥ to the south of the fortified walls; confirmation of the latter event is implied by a palette of Dyn. XIX mentioning the Ptaḥ of Mēnēs.[1] Other facts connecting Mēnēs with Memphis cannot be enumerated here.

The importance of that great city in Dyn. I has been strongly

[1] *ZÄS* xxx. 43 ff.

underlined by the excavations conducted at the edge of the western desert some 3 miles farther north. The long row of brick mastabas unearthed by W. B. Emery since 1935 differ from those found at Abydos by Petrie through their greater complexity, and are on an average nearly twice as large. Their structure as disclosed in the plans, as well as the inscribed objects found in them, proclaims them all to belong to Dyn. I, the oldest dating from the reign of ʿAḥa. A rapid development is visible, but leaves the main features unaltered. A great brick rectangle showing the characteristic palace-façade panelling (Fig. 15) on the outer side encloses a number of oblong magazines symmetrically disposed around a twice as large sepulchral chamber which tends to go deeper in course of time, and to be reached by a descending stairway starting at or near the enclosure wall; in the earliest examples there is no connexion whatever between the compartments, so that their contents must have been stored there before the superstructure was added; in the end the compartments disappear and are replaced by a sepulchral chamber of increased size.[1] There are wooden floors and roofs, and there is some use of stone. Sometimes the walls exhibit painted geometrical patterns.

For the historian the point to be emphasized is the homogeneity of the remains in both parts of the country. Architecturally there are indeed certain differences between north and south, the greatest perhaps being the absence of the palace-façade panelling at Abydos, though it is present in the great Naḳâda tomb; in both areas there is much variation between tomb and tomb. In all other archaeological respects the similarity amounts almost to identity, and this applies alike to furniture, stone vessels, tools, and the tablets or labels used for dating; in the jar-sealings the similarity is particularly apparent, the same patterns and the same hieroglyphic combinations recurring at both Memphis and Abydos. No more convincing testimony to the unity of the land could be desired. There is evidence too of identical customs that tend to corroborate the connexion with Mesopotamian culture stressed in the last chapter. Many of the great tombs are surrounded by long lines of small burial chambers adjoining one another, and the contents of these

[1] For plans see Emery, *Great Tombs* (p. 428), i, pp. 2–18; ii, Pls. 1, 2; iii, Pl. 2.

attest the immolation of servants or other living creatures to accompany their lord in the hereafter. In one of Emery's tombs at north Saḳḳâra attributed on slender grounds to a queen Mernēit many adult skeletons were found in the same contracted positions all facing in the same direction; the words of their discoverer are well worth quoting:[1]

> No trace of violence was noted on the anatomical remains, and the position of the skeletons in no case suggested any movement after burial. It would therefore appear probable that when these people were buried they were already dead and there is no evidence of their having been buried alive. The absence of any marks of violence suggests that they were killed by poison prior to burial.

Emery goes on to say that some of the objects found in these intact tombs suggest definite professions, and he instances the presence of model boats in one case and in another that of a copper chisel contained in an alabaster vase. At Abydos the corresponding subsidiary graves contain rough stelae giving personal names sometimes accompanied by hieroglyphs indicating sex, condition, or the like; many of the occupants were women, some of them captives of war; several dwarfs occur and also a few dogs; a title often found on cylinder seals seems to show that some of the buried were above the rank of menials, and in one case[2] for which there is a still more remarkable counterpart among Emery's finds[3]—both date from the reign of King Ḳaʿa—an imposing stela bears titles clearly belonging to a personage of much distinction.

In view of such information about people who at best were subordinates it is tantalizing that certain knowledge concerning those in whose honour their lives were sacrificed is denied us in every case. There is not one of the central sepulchral chambers in the great mastabas but is bereft of its original occupant, leaving us only with jar-sealings, scratchings on jars, and the like as basis for our conjectures. Of profound interest as Emery's revelations have been, they have also proved most unsettling. The discoveries at Abydos had convinced scholars that they were there in possession of the actual burial-places of the earliest Pharaohs, and confirmation seemed forthcoming from Manetho's statement that Dyns. I

[1] Op. cit. ii. 142. [2] Petrie, *Royal Tombs*, i, Pl. 30. [3] Emery, op. cit. iii, Pl. 39.

and II were of Thinite origin, for the Egyptian town of Tjēne was in the near neighbourhood of Abydos. But now the greater size and magnificence of the Memphite tombs raised the suspicion that these were the true royal tombs of the period, and the matter was still further complicated by the existence of other not less important isolated mastabas of the same period at Ṭarkhân, some miles to the south of Lisht, at Gîza, and farther north at Abu Roâsh. Could these really only be the tombs of fine noblemen outdoing in splendour the sovereigns of whom they were the vassals? Such was the inevitable first impression given by an immense 'palace-façade mastaba' at north Saḳḳâra with which the series of discoveries opened. This was attributed by Emery to a provincial administrator named Ḥemaka on the strength of many jar-sealings there found. But the Horus Den, the fifth king of Dyn. I, was also prominent upon the jar-sealings, which mention too a 'seal-bearer of the King of Lower Egypt' with a name compounded with that of the goddess Nēith. Now Ḥemaka is again found in conjunction with King Den at Abydos; of his importance there is no shadow of a doubt, but it may here be said once and for all that jar-sealings are well-nigh useless as evidence for the ownership of a tomb, though if they give, as they often do, the name of a king they are good evidence for the date. By way of illustration we may recall the tomb at Naḳâda where the tablet of Mēnēs was found (pp. 405 f.); this tomb is only a trifle smaller than that ascribed to Ḥemaka, but three times larger than the largest of the supposed royal tombs at Abydos. The tomb at Abydos which Petrie doubtingly attributed to King ʿAḥa is an insignificant single chamber which can hardly have been his. At Naḳâda sealings of the Horus ʿAḥa are numerous, the *serekh* sometimes standing alone, but sometimes accompanied by the hieroglyphs for *ḥt* and sometimes by three identical birds; since these birds occur alone on several stone jars it has been suggested that they gave the name of the noble who owned the tomb. But there are two more plausible candidates for the ownership, firstly ʿAḥa himself and secondly a queen Nēit Ḥetepu. The name of the queen is written in a most interesting way, the element Ḥetepu enclosed in a *serekh* surmounted by the crossed arrows which were the archaic way of writing the name of Nēith, the goddess of the Lower Egyptian city of Sais (Fig. 16). The analogy with the Pharaonic Horus title is complete, and when we find both at Abydos and at Saḳḳâra the name of another queen or princess Merneīt, as well as the element *-nēit* at Abydos in the names of some of the sacrificed slave-women, it is a plausible conjecture that diplomatic marriages were arranged between royal ladies from Sais and the conquering king from Upper Egypt; and doubtless the queen-to-be was accompanied by other women as concubines. It is, accordingly, by no means improbable that the Naḳâda tomb was that of ʿAḥa's spouse, though why she should have been buried in this remote spot is inexplicable. The supposition that the tomb was that of ʿAḥa himself, as was at first imagined when ʿAḥa was thought to be Mēnēs, has been rendered most unlikely by Emery's discovery at Saḳḳâra of a vast mastaba in which the sealings almost all showed the name of the Horus ʿAḥa either alone or accompanied by the above-mentioned signs for *ḥt* or else by hieroglyphs appearing to read 'son of Isis', though it would be surprising if the consort of the god Osiris were really named at so early a date. Thus there seems considerable likelihood that the Saḳḳâra tomb is really that of ʿAḥa. The facts concerning the three tombs which have been claimed as his burial-place have been discussed at length merely to serve as an example of the difficulties with which their excavators have confronted us. Emery's highly successful digs have brought to light no less than fourteen great palace-façade mastabas extended in a line along the edge of the escarpment, and in all of them jar-sealings of the Dyn. I kings have disclosed the approximative dates; apart from Naʿrmer only Semempsēs is missing, and the large Cairo fragment of the Palermo Stone shows that he reigned no more than nine years. Emery is convinced that he has discovered the actual tombs of the other six kings of the dynasty from ʿAḥa onwards, and since we have reason to believe that Mēnēs moved from the south to make Memphis his capital his hypothesis is highly probable. But Djer is mentioned in two tombs and Den

Fig. 16. *Serekh* of Queen Ḥetepu.

in four or even five, while the great tomb known as Gîza V[1] has almost as good a claim as Saḳḳâra No. 3504 to have belonged to Edjō the Serpent King. Two of the tombs are perhaps rightly thought to have been those of queens, and it is possible after all that the tomb ascribed to Ḥemaka may have really been his, and the same possibility arises with regard to a magnate named Sabu under ʿAndjyeb[2], though not to the prince Merka under Ḳaʿa.[3] In none of the fourteen tombs is there absolute certainty. Also there are still scholars who maintain that Abydos was the authentic royal cemetery, and they can point as proofs to the magnificent stone stelae which stood in front of the great burial chambers and among which that of the Serpent King in the Louvre is the finest. The Egyptians of much later date may themselves have believed that their earliest kings were here buried, for they placed in the Abydene tomb of Djer a huge sarcophagus representing the god Osiris, the prototype of all dead Pharaohs.[4] Emery's belief, for which there is much to be said, is that the tombs at Abydos are cenotaphs due to the theory that the Pharaoh ought to possess separate tombs as King of Upper and King of Lower Egypt respectively. That an Egyptian king could erect for himself two huge pyramids, and those even in the same neighbourhood, was seen in the case of Śnofru (p. 78), and for written testimony to the existence of cenotaphs the reader may be reminded of what is stated about Queen Tetisheri on p. 172. Among the sceptics who doubt Emery's contention H. Kees is the most eminent, and in a review[5] he has gone some distance towards demolishing as evidence in its favour the criterion of size, and shows that no argument can be drawn from the presence or absence of subsidiary graves of sacrificed subordinates; also he lays stress on the existence on other sites of tombs identical with those at Saḳḳâra in structure and contents. At one moment the astonishing discovery on ledges around the Saḳḳâra tombs of bulls' heads modelled in clay, but fitted with actual bulls' horns, might conceivably have been guessed to indicate royal tombs, but of the three examples thus far laid bare two

[1] Petrie, *Gizeh and Rifeh*, London, 1907, pp. 2 ff.
[2] Petrie, *Royal Tombs*, i. 27. 64.
[3] Above, p. 410, n. 3.
[4] PM v. 79.
[5] *OLZ*, 1957, pp. 12–20; also 1959, pp. 566–70.

appear to have belonged to queens, while there is no evidence that the third belonged to a king. We cannot leave the topic of Emery's great finds without referring to the exquisite beauty of many of the objects found; the craftsmanship and artistic design of the stone vessels excel everything that was achieved later. An extraordinary and unexplained fact about all the tombs both at Saḳḳâra and at Abydos is that in every case they had been wilfully destroyed by fire, whereas the same is not true of the tombs of Dyn. II.

The events chosen as means of dating both on the tablets or labels and on the Palermo Stone are mostly of a religious character. Every second year saw the occurrence of a 'Following of the Horus' which, whether as an actual Royal Progress by river or as a merely reminiscent ceremony, certainly recalled those historic voyages in which the king proceeded northwards to bring about the unification of the Two Lands, as depicted on the palette of Naᶜrmer; there the king is shown already wearing the crown of Lower Egypt, while the military standards which accompany him are the equivalents of the gods of the various nomes allied with him; a later misinterpretation of these 'Followers of Horus' was mentioned above, p. 400. Another totally unexpected kind of event which was evidently regarded by the earliest Pharaohs as of sufficient importance to serve as name of a year was the fashioning of some great cult-image; this was expressed by such terms as 'Birth of Anubis', 'Birth of Mīn', the word for 'birth' being the consequence of the belief that the statues became really alive after the ceremony of 'Opening the Mouth' had been performed over them. The inauguration or visiting of certain buildings seems to have loomed equally large in the eyes of those responsible for finding names for the years. It is only rarely that warlike achievements are mentioned. Under King Djer the large Cairo fragment of the Palermo Stone mentioned a 'Smiting of Setje', a geographic expression which we must render approximatively as 'Asia', and under a later monarch we read of a 'Smiting of the Iuntyu'[1], an equally vague designation of the peoples living to the north-east of the Delta. An exceptionally fine tablet formerly in the MacGregor collection[2] represents King Den in the act of massacring an Asiatic who is shown as inhabiting

[1] Pal. *recto* 3. 2.   [2] *ZÄS* xxxv. 7.

the sandy desert presumably of Sinai; the accompanying hieroglyphs present no difficulties of interpretation, reading clearly 'First time of smiting the Easterners'. Perhaps even more interesting than this reference to what may have been no more than a border incident is this evidence of the rapid development of hieroglyphic expression. Before the end of Dyn. I it will have become possible to convey the gist of whole sentences by sequences of separate signs, a signal advance upon the stage represented by the palette of Naʿrmer.

Manetho's SECOND DYNASTY of nine kings from Thinis presents even more intractable problems than its predecessor. Four of the Manethonian names are recognizable, despite grave distortion, in the Ramesside king-lists, though it needed a demonstration of great acumen to show how Manetho's Tlas originated in a king Weneg known only from fragments of bowls stored in the underground galleries of the Step Pyramid. The king-lists enumerate eleven kings in place of Manetho's nine, but of these only four find confirmation in the monuments. The order of the first five kings is established with certainty, but the existing remains ignore Boēthos and Kaiechōs and offer us in their stead a Ḥotepśekhemui and a Nebrēʿ. The former name is interesting, for it signifies 'The Two Powers are pacified' and we shall soon find evidence that this expression implies recovery from a precedent condition of turmoil or anarchy; the reason for the transition from Dyn. I to Dyn. II can thus be divined. Though Boēthos is unknown to the contemporary hieroglyphs, the form Bedjau in which the king-lists introduce it to us is found on an Old Kingdom writing-board in front of five well-known kings of Dyns. IV and V.[1] With the third king of Dyn. II we reach a sequence of three kings, namely Binōthris, Tlas, and Sethenēs, where the monuments, the king-lists, and Manetho are in agreement, for Binōthris is evidently the extended equivalent of the hieroglyphic name which to the eye appears to read Nūtjeren, though scholars have argued in favour of the transcriptions Ninūtjer or Neterimu; concerning Tlas we have already spoken, and Sethenēs is undoubtedly the Send to whom we shall return later, a most curious name since it means 'the Afraid'. Chapter and verse for these first five members of Dyn. II will be found below

[1] *ZÄS* xlviii. 113.

on pp. 431–32. It may here, however, be added that Ninūtjer presides over the fourth line of the Palermo Stone in such a way as to show that he reigned not much less than thirty years.

With the one exception of Nebka the remaining six names in the king-lists are a mystery, since not a trace of their bearers has been found elsewhere. Neferkarēʿ, Manetho's Nephercherēs, may indeed be fictitious, since the reference to the sun-god Rēʿ in its termination seems to point to later times, and there were in fact

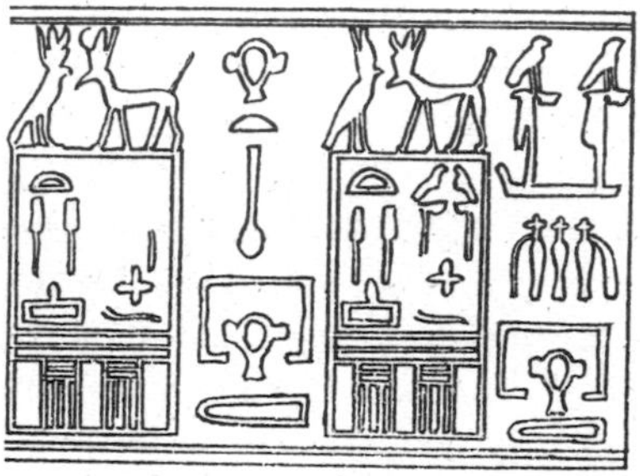

Fig. 17. *Serekh* of King Khaʿśekhemui.

monarchs so called in Dyns. VI, VIII, and XXI. Nor need there be any perplexity about ʿAka which appears to be the correct reading in the Turin Canon, an isolated occurrence possibly the result of corruption of some kind. On the other hand Neferkaseker, Ḥudjefa, and Beby of the Ramesside tradition cannot be dismissed quite so easily, the more so since the Canon attributes to them reigns of substantial length. It can only be supposed that they were real occupants of the throne whose claims to recognition were deemed by Manetho and his forerunners to be superior to those of certain Pharaohs from the south completely ignored by them. To those Pharaohs, four at most and possibly only two, we now turn. At Umm el-Ḳaʿâb Petrie excavated at opposite ends of the protodynastic cemetery a small tomb belonging to a king Peribśen and an exceptionally elongated one belonging to a king Khaʿśekhemui. The *serekh* of the former monarch showed the extraordinary feature of being surmounted by the Sēth-animal 𓃩 instead of the usual falcon 𓅃 of Horus, while the *serekh* of Khaʿśekhemui exhibited the Sēth-animal and the Horus-falcon face to face, each wearing the double crown of Upper and Lower Egypt (Fig. 17). Explanations which have already been given, as well as the analogy of Queen Nēit Ḥetepu commented upon p. 411, leave no doubt as to the meaning of this procedure, and this is borne out by the name Khaʿśekhemui itself and by the addition Nebuiḥotpimef which follows as part of the name. In translation the entire combination runs 'The Two Powers are arisen, the Two Lords are at peace in him'. In other words, King Khaʿśekhemui now embodies in himself the two gods between whom hostility had arisen through Peribśen's repudiation of his traditional ancestor in favour of that deity's arch-enemy. Clearly great disturbances lie at the back of these revolutionary moves, but it is impossible to diagnose their nature. In the distant past Horus had been particularly associated with the Delta, while the cult of Sēth was localized near Naḳâda (Ombos) in Upper Egypt. Yet it seems impossible to interpret the facts as a struggle between the Two Lands in which Peribśen had to content himself with being the ruler of Upper Egypt. Had there been such a contest between north and south would not Peribśen have asserted his pretension to be the embodiment of Horus all the more vigorously? A further complication is that on certain sealings of Peribśen the Sēth-like animal is given the name Ash[1], and this is known to have belonged to the Libyan counterpart of the Ombite. It was hinted above that this cluster of kings might involve only two instead of four and we must now follow up that possibility. In the tomb of Peribśen there were found jar-sealings of a Horus Śekhemyeb, and it was at first supposed that Śekhemyeb was the Horus-name of Peribśen himself, though such a supposition was contradicted by the presence of Sēth on the *serekh* in most of the sealings, as well as on the two fine granite stelae which had stood in front of the tomb-chamber. A subsequent dig a little distance away brought to light a king Śekhemyeb Perenmāʿe who now was understood to be a predecessor of Peribśen; later the same full name was found on fragments from the Step Pyramid. There is much likelihood in Grdseloff's guess[2] that Śekhemyeb Perenmāʿe was merely the name of Peribśen before he abandoned his allegiance to

[1] Or Sha, see Borchardt, *Saḥurēʿ*, p. 74; also *JEA* xiv. 220 ff.

[2] *Ann. Serv.* xliv. 295.

Horus in order to become the fervent worshipper of Sēth. More difficult is the question of the Horus Khaʿśekhem whose monuments are confined to Hieracōnpolis. They consist of a broken stela, two great stone bowls, and two seated statues of limestone and slate respectively; the slate statue is the more complete, but half the face is broken away, whence the features are better seen on that of limestone now in Oxford; the pose, the style, and the workmanship are such as would have been impossible at the beginning of Dyn. II and go far towards corroborating the position of this king towards its conclusion. The bases of both statues are decorated with roughly engraved figures of slain enemies in every conceivable attitude of torment, and their number is given as 47,209. The stela reveals who these enemies were, for a bearded head carrying a feather is attached to the same bolsterlike oval as is seen on the palette of Naʿrmer, clearly indicating Libyan foes. The design scratched on the bowls shows the vulture-goddess Nekhbe of El-Kâb presenting to Khaʿśekhem the symbol for the unification of the Two Lands, while her hinder claw rests upon a circular cartouche enclosing the signs for Besh; this Besh is more likely to be Khaʿśekhem's personal name than the name of a conquered country or chieftain. The right side of the design is occupied by the hieroglyph for 'year' accompanied by the words 'of fighting and smiting the northerners'. On all these objects the white crown of Upper Egypt is worn. But to return to our problem: what was the relation of Khaʿśekhem of Hieracōnpolis to Peribśen on the one hand and to Khaʿśekhemui on the other? The hypothesis at present most in favour is that Khaʿśekhem was the immediate successor of Peribśen, whose name does not occur at Hieracōnpolis, and that he won back the Delta and was followed by Khaʿśekhemui. But would this latter king, if preceded by a worshipper of Horus, have recalled in his name the former dissension between Horus and Sēth? The possibility that the Horus Khaʿśekhem and the Horus-Sēth Khaʿśekhemui were one and the same person cannot be ruled out, such a conjecture assuming that he had preferred the latter form of his name while the conflict with Peribśen was still fresh in his mind, but it is a serious objection that Khaʿśekhemui has monuments of his own at Hieracōnpolis distinct from those of Khaʿ-

śekhem, the principal one being the great pink granite jamb of a gateway[1] bearing on the back the scene of an episode in some important foundation ceremony. An objection to regarding Khaʿśekhem as a separate king intervening between Khaʿśekhemui and Djośer, the founder of Dyn. III, is that a sealing found in Khaʿśekhemui's tomb at Abydos[2] names a queen Ḥepenmāʿe as 'mother of the king's children' and that this same Ḥepenmāʿe is named as 'mother of the King of Upper and Lower Egypt' on a sealing in the great tomb of Bêt Khallâf near Abydos where Djośer's prominence even prompted the guess that he might be the owner.[3] It has been consequently supposed[4] that Khaʿśekhemui and Ḥepenmāʿe were the actual parents of Djośer; the conjecture is tempting, but if correct one is left wondering why there should have been a change of dynasty at this point. Before leaving the subject of Khaʿśekhemui it must be mentioned that the making of a copper statue of his is recorded in the fifth line of the Palermo Stone;[5] also that a breccia fragment with his name was discovered at Byblos.[6]

As has here more than once been pointed out, little importance can be attached to small objects found in distant parts, but there is some solid evidence of dealings, friendly or otherwise, between these later kings of Dyn. II and the north. Not only do there exist sealings giving Peribśen the epithet 'conqueror of foreign lands', but there are also grounds for thinking that it was he who introduced the cult of Sēth into the north-eastern Delta.[7] Concerning the fragmentary stela of Khaʿśekhem from Hieracōnpolis[8] we have already spoken; conflict with a Libyan enemy is there clearly indicated. Nothing more definite, however, can be learned about the events of this troubled period. That its kings did not fall into immediate disrepute is evident from the inscriptions of some mastabas at Saḳḳâra which presumably belong to Dyn. IV. In one of them a certain Sheri declares himself to have been 'overseer of the priests of Peribśen in the necropolis, in the house of Śend, and in all his places'.[9] More problematic are some broken pieces from

[1] *JEA* xx. 183–4; *Hierakonpolis*, i, Pl. 2. [2] *RT* ii, Pl. 24, No. 210.
[3] J. Garstang, *Mahâsna and Bêt Khallâf*, London, 1902, Pl. 10, No. 7.
[4] Sethe in op. cit., n. 3 above, pp. 22–23. [5] *JEA* i. 233–5. [6] PM vii. 390.
[7] *Ann. Serv.* xliv. 295–8. [8] *Hierakonpolis*, ii, Pl. 58. [9] *Ann. Serv.* xliv. 294.

the tomb of a prophet of that King Nebka whom the Turin Canon and the Abydos king-list place immediately before Djośer;[1] this king is named also in the story of the Magicians referred to above, p. 84, where, however, it seems to be implied that his reign fell between those of kings Djośer and Śnofru. From what has been already said Nebka could not have been the predecessor of Djośer unless he were a successful rival of Khaʿśekhemui; the nineteen years assigned to him remain a problem. In the footnotes to the list of kings below may be read the fantastic occurrences attributed to the kings of Dyn. II by Manetho; it need hardly be repeated that those occurrences are drawn from the fictional literature which was evidently one of the Egyptian historian's main sources of inspiration.

Manetho's totals of 253 years for Dyn. I and 302 for Dyn. II of course cannot be trusted, and we must again stress the improbable nature of the 450 years which the Palermo Stone seemed to demand for the two dynasties combined. But however long or short the period, it sufficed to imprint upon the civilization of Ancient Egypt the peculiar stamp which thenceforth distinguished her remains so markedly from those of the neighbouring countries. The splendid efforts of Petrie and a highly skilled body of later excavators have enabled scholars to observe step by step the material developments which transformed a semi-barbarous culture into one of great refinement and prodigious power, but in the absence until Dyn. V of adequate written evidence the corresponding intellectual and religious developments have remained hidden. When at last the Pyramid Texts and other such material reveal something of the Egyptian mind, many survivals of past history are found embedded therein, and the question then arises as to how far we can disentangle out of the confused and complex data the various stages which made of Egypt what she had by this time become. But before discussing some of the views that have been expressed on this subject it will be well to recall what the Egyptians themselves had to say about their remote past.

No explicit statement dates from earlier than Ramesside times, when the Turin Canon (p. 48) furnishes us with an account in

[1] *Äg. Inschriften aus den kön. Museen zu Berlin*, i, Leipzig, 1913, p. 30.

substantial agreement with that of Manetho. In both authorities the oldest kings belong to the Great Ennead, that family of nine deities which the Pyramid Texts (§ 1064) definitely associate with the theology of Hēliopolis. For that reason the list ought to have begun with the sun-god Rēʿ-Atum, but in Manetho, which is here alone preserved, Hēphaestos, i.e. Ptaḥ of Memphis, is placed before Hēlios, suggesting that this particular version was compiled in Dyn. VI, the kings of which came from that city. After Agathodaemōn (the air-god Shu), lost in the Canon, there follow in agreement therewith Cronos (the earth-god Gēb), then Osiris, then Typhōn (Sēth) the murderer of Osiris, and then Horus his father's avenger. In both sources the goddesses Tephēnis, Nut, Isis, and Nephthys are omitted on account of their feminine sex, but in earlier traditions the Great Ennead included them as the consorts of four of the males, though not attributing to them reigns of their own. Concerning these purely mythical rulers no more need be said at present. They are succeeded in Manetho by a number of monarchs described as Demigods and as Dead Ones (Greek νέκυες, Latin Mānēs), the human Mēnēs then following at the head of Dyn. I. The Turin Canon, which had already placed a 'Horus of the Gods' immediately after Sēth, names a second Horus at the end of the divine dynasty, and apparently a third a little farther down. After this a number of broken lines conclude with the already mentioned 'Followers of Horus', these qualified as 'exalted spirits', the immediate predecessors of Mēnēs. Now Sethe had rightly diagnosed the Shemsu-Ḥōr ('Followers of Horus') as the kings of Hieracōnpolis and of Butō respectively,[1] but by an oversight he omitted the most decisive proof of his contention. This, as Griffith pointed out orally to the present writer, occurs in a hieroglyphic papyrus of Roman date which undoubtedly incorporates a mass of traditional lore familiar to the learned of the age of Cheops;[2] here we find side by side two entries reading (1) 'Souls of Pe (Butō, see below, p. 422), Followers of Horus as Kings of Lower Egypt', and (2) 'Souls of Nekhen (Hieracōnpolis, see ibid.), Followers of Horus as Kings of Upper Egypt'. It would be impossible to find any more precise

[1] *Beiträge*, pp. 3 ff.; see above, p. 70, n. 1.
[2] *Two Hieroglyphic Papyri* (Egypt Exploration Fund), London, 1889, Pl. 9, fragm. 10.

reminder of that concluding phase of predynastic history which, starting out from Hieracōnpolis, ended with the conquest of Lower Egypt by Mēnēs and with the unification of the Two Lands. In the papyrus just quoted the word for 'King of Upper Egypt' (*nswt*) is written quite normally with the reed 𓇓, and the word for 'King of Lower Egypt' (*bity*) with the bee 𓆤. It falls into line with the undoubted triumph of Mēnēs that in the *insibya*-title of the Pharaohs 𓇓𓆤𓏏𓏏 (p. 51) the reed should have priority in the hieroglyphic writing, just as in the *nebty*-title of the royal titulary 𓅒𓎟𓆗𓎟 (ibid.) the vulture-goddess of El-Kâb has priority over the Lower Egyptian cobra-goddess Edjō of Butō. Odd as it may seem to readers unacquainted with old Egyptian habits, such graphic precedence must be understood as having a real historic significance. Lastly, if anyone should still doubt the reality of a predynastic line of rulers in Butō he must surely be convinced by the isolated mention in the Pyramid Texts (§ 1488) of the 'Kings of Lower Egypt (*bitiw*) who are in Pe' (Butō), and by the fact that it was Upper Egypt, not Lower Egypt, which gave to the language its generic word 𓇓𓏏𓈖 *nswt* for 'king'.

All these facts together corroborate and amplify what was deduced from Quibell's discoveries at Hieracōnpolis: the separate kingdoms of Nekhen and Pe were undoubted realities, as was also their unification by Mēnēs. There remain, however, difficulties not to be lightly brushed aside. J. A. Wilson has pointed out[1] how unsuitable both Hieracōnpolis and Butō were to become permanent royal residences, the former town lying in an arid and infertile tract near the extreme limit of Upper Egypt, while the latter town was situated almost like an island amid the watery fens of the north-western Delta; Wilson's suggestion is that both may have become holy cities and possibly places of pilgrimage. A much more daring hypothesis which has obtained some popularity of late must be resolutely combated. This hypothesis maintains that all the talk about the Two Lands, the contrasting of Upper and Lower Egypt, the antithesis of the Two Ladies, and other expressions of the kind, are no more than fiction due to a supposedly deep-rooted penchant of the Egyptian mind in favour of opposing dualistic

[1] *JNES* xiv. 210 ff.

conceptions. It is not necessary to deny the ancient people's fondness for contrasted phrases like 'heaven and earth', 'man and woman', 'Black Land and Red Land' (p. 27), but to dismiss as simple chimeras all statements relating to the two kingdoms is to fly in the face of common sense. A less fantastic, but still wrong-headed, variant of the same contention[1] is based upon the assumedly water-logged condition of the Delta in the centuries before Mēnēs. It is true that before the construction of dykes and other such irrigational measures the growth of important towns there must have been difficult and restricted. Nevertheless, the possibility of a very considerable Lower Egyptian kingdom is easily proved. Particularly the western side of the Delta had important cities as early as Dyn. I; the temple of Nēith of Sais is depicted on a tablet of ʿAḥa,[2] and another of the reign of Djer[3] shows a building at Dep, one of the two mounds constituting the town of Butō. A relief in the Step Pyramid of Djośer[4] records some ceremony in connexion with Lētopolis (Ausîm) only a few miles to the north-west of Cairo. The multitude of captured cattle seen on a slate palette implies a large population of owners. The many Delta nomes administered by the wealthy nobleman Metjen towards the end of Dyn. III[5] evidently had a long history behind them. Osiris as the 'lord of Djedu' (Busiris in the middle of the Delta) is perhaps not named much earlier than Dyn. VI, but that famous religious centre is mentioned together with the similarly named Djedĕ (Mendēs) in the Pyramid Texts (§ 288), and we cannot expect to be in possession of the earliest testimony to their existence. An attempt to show that Hēliopolis cannot have been the capital of a prehistoric kingdom is hardly likely to find many converts, even if the assertion that such a kingdom actually existed rests on a somewhat precarious basis. Lastly, the writing of the *insibya*-title with two separate words for 'king' and of the *nebty*-title with two locally contrasted goddesses need not be construed as showing that the two kingdoms were of equal extent and importance; all that can be taken as certain is the simultaneous existence of both.

[1] See below, p. 428.
[2] *RT* ii, Pl. 3A, 5.
[3] Schott, *Hieroglyphen*, in *Abhandlungen* of the Mainz Academy, 1950, Pl. 7, fig. 15.
[4] *JEA* xxx, Pl. 3, fig. 3.
[5] *BAR* i, §§ 172–4.

Scepticism is better justified with regard to several yet earlier periods, not merely a single one, which a famous book by Kurt Sethe sought to deduce from the religious texts. His elaborate arguments are set forth with a logic and a clarity which cannot but command admiration. Nevertheless, his colleagues have almost unanimously felt that the story which he presents, when taken in its entirety, is too good to be true. On the other hand, the assertion by H. Kees, in an equally learned work, that no historical conclusions can safely be drawn for times farther back than that of the Hieracōnpolite and Butite kingdoms, is certainly wide of the mark. The myth of Osiris, the main lines of which need not be repeated, is too remarkable and occurs in too many divergent forms not to contain a considerable element of historic truth, though we must be on our guard against over-speculative reconstruction of details. Of the three chief actors involved the one whose nature and origin are least open to dispute is the god Sēth, whom the Greeks identified with their Typhōn on account of his turbulent character. It is needless here to discuss his strange appearance , which is not that of any extant animal. That he was the local god of Ombos (hieroglyphic ) opposite Ḳûs in the fifth Upper Egyptian nome is revealed by his constant epithet 'the Ombite, lord of Upper Egypt', this being found as early as the Pyramid Texts (§ 204). Now Ombos is only 2 or 3 miles distant from Naḳâda where Petrie found his immense prehistoric cemeteries, and it seems natural to associate the conflict between Horus and Sēth with the time when so flourishing a civilization was at its height. The falcon-god Horus presents greater problems. When his image is juxtaposed to that of Sēth in the writing, or when they are both depicted face to face in human form, it seems inevitable to regard him as the representative of Lower Egypt. In this connexion, however, Sethe has been shown to be for once wrong in his facts. For no better reason than that the name of the modern town of Damanhûr between Alexandria and Cairo means etymologically 'the town of Horus' he assumed this to be the falcon-god's birthplace, an assumption which involved localizing there a place called Beḥde often mentioned in conjunction with Horus in the same way as Ombos was with Sēth. It has now, however, been established[1] that Beḥde was situated at Tell Balamûn, an obscure settlement regarded by the Egyptians as the northernmost of their towns, while another tradition named Chemmis, another place in the marshes, as the home of Horus's childhood. Now the one circumstance in the Osirian story whose historicity cannot be doubted is the defeat of Sēth by Horus, which when translated into non-religious terms signifies the conquest of a strong power in the south by a still stronger power from the north. The victory of Horus is commemorated by the placing of his image above the *serekh* at the beginning of the royal titulary, and by the use of the hieroglyph 𓅆 as determinative (p. 23) of the name of any male deity whatsoever. It is also significant that the name of Horus precedes when such expressions as 'the mounds of Horus' and 'the mounds of Sēth' are found in parallelism, or when the falcon of Horus and the Sēth-animal serve as ideograms of the word *nebwy* 'the Two Lords'. These orthographic peculiarities are the exact reverse of what was seen to be the custom with the *nebty*- and *insibya*-titles of the Dyn. I kings. It is thus apparent that the developed titulary incorporates reminders of two distinct periods of predynastic history and that the earlier of them was the period of Horus's triumph over Sēth, or in other words that of Lower Egypt's penetration into Upper Egypt.

That the conflict was a fierce one is suggested by the legend that Sēth deprived Horus of an eye, but that Horus retaliated by inflicting a still graver injury. However, the upshot was that Horus took the place of Sēth, absorbing into himself the personality of his enemy. This is clearly indicated by a passage in the Pyramid Texts (§§ 141 ff.), and still more significantly by the queen's title 'She who sees Horus and Sēth' found already in the tomb of Djer; that early date rules out the suggestion which has been hesitantly made that the contest between the two gods originated historically in the facts above related concerning Peribśen and Khaʿśekhemui. If we accept as a hardly deniable reality the overwhelming of Upper Egypt by a northern power whose ruler identified himself with Horus, a necessary consequence will have been some sort of predynastic fusion of the Two Lands, and it is a fact not to be mini-

[1] *JEA* xxx. 23 ff.

mized that after a sequence of at least ten Lower Egyptian kings in the top row of the Palermo Stone, the largest of the Cairo fragments recorded six or more kings wearing the Double Crown. It is doubtful whether Sethe would have recognized in this observation of Breasted's the Hēliopolitan supremacy which he believed to have followed upon the triumph of the falcon-god and in the course of which he supposed the doctrine of the Great Ennead to have been evolved; but at least he would not have found there any contradiction of his own euhemeristic reconstruction. It will be noted that the doctrine of the Great Ennead implicitly contains the whole of the Osirian myth, to which we must now return, since as yet next to nothing has here been said about Osiris himself. Sethe assumed Osiris to have been an ancient king upon whose tragic death the entire legend hinged. Nothing could be less certain.[1] It must be left to writers on Egyptian religion to debate the origin of a god of whom not a trace has been found before the time of the Pyramid Texts. In the myth he plays a quite subsidiary part, serving merely to accentuate the wickedness of the defeated Sēth and the virtue of Horus, his son and avenger. Not until classical times are any beneficent deeds or warlike exploits ascribed to him as a living monarch; everywhere he is a dead king, or king and judge of the dead. Alternatively and doubtless more primitively he is presented to us as the vegetation which perishes in the flood-water mysteriously issuing from himself and which is renewed in the coming year. Thus for historical purposes nothing can be retained out of the Osirian myth beyond the dim recollection of a struggle in which Lower Egypt prevailed over Upper Egypt. Whether this can in any way be connected with the Mesopotamian influence which we have regarded as a certainty is a question that must be left outstanding, but it is relevant to bear in mind a difference of race which appears to be a well-established fact. No one has had better opportunity than Dr. D. E. Derry to examine the skulls and other physical evidence from the two parts of the country, and he has asserted with all emphasis that 'another race in addition to that represented by the remains found in all reliably dated Predynastic graves occupied Egypt in Early Dynastic times'.[2]

[1] *JEA* xlvi. 104. [2] Op. cit. 80 ff.

We approach the end of our speculations, but in a few last words we must revert to Sethe's theory of a Hēliopolitan period in which all the cardinal doctrines of the Egyptian religion were evolved. That theory cannot be refuted with certainty, but there is much to be said for Kees's opposing view that the early Manethonian dynasties were the main breeding-time for the theological developments revealed in the Pyramid Texts. The gifted people who were responsible for the great achievements recorded earlier in this chapter will not have been wholly remiss in matters of the intellect and the imagination. But in this contention we re-enter the field of unverifiable conjecture, and the reader will not be sorry to quit a region where a solid foothold of evidence is so lamentably absent.

Looking back upon the contents of this book the writer is keenly aware how short a distance he has been able to penetrate into the heart of his subject. He would fain have painted a comprehensive picture of the world's greatest early civilization, but space and time have forbidden. Hence little has been told about Ancient Egypt's art and craftsmanship, the noblest of her achievements, little too about her religion, as alluring as a will-o'-the-wisp by reason of its mystery and even in spite of its absurdity. Nor has it been found possible to discourse upon mummies and mummification, those sidelines of Egyptian culture which make the most appeal to the museum-visiting public. Gratitude to the excavators and scholars who have unveiled so much of the past has dictated much of our exposition; the book has been almost as much about Egyptologists as about Egyptology. But this has not been unintentional; we frankly admit our aim to have been propaganda, and our ambition will not have been satisfied unless we succeed in winning at least one fresh recruit to our fascinating field of research.

SELECT BIBLIOGRAPHY

Umm el-Ḳa'âb: E. Amélineau, *Les Nouvelles fouilles d'Abydos*, 4 vols., Paris, 1899–1905; W. M. F. Petrie, *Royal Tombs of the Earliest Dynasties*, 2 vols., London, 1900–1; *Abydos*, i, ii, iii, London, 1902–4.

Kôm el-Aḥmar: J. E. Quibell and F. W. Green, *Hierakonpolis*, 2 vols., London, 1900–2.

Naḳâda: the royal tomb, J. de Morgan, *Recherches sur les origines de l'Égypte*, Paris, 1897, [ii], ch. 4.

Saḳḳâra: W. B. Emery, *The Tomb of Hemaka*, Cairo, 1938; *Ḥor-Aḥa*, Cairo, 1939; *Great Tombs of the First Dynasty*, 3 vols., i, Cairo, 1949; ii, London, 1954; iii, London, 1958.

The philological aspects: K. Sethe, *Beiträge zur ältesten Geschichte Ägyptens*, Leipzig, 1905, in *Untersuchungen zur Geschichte und Altertumskunde Ägyptens*, iii.

Dyn. II: elaborate discussion, Vandier, op. cit., 3rd. ed., pp. 163 ff.

Denial of a separate kingdom of Butō in predynastic times: H. Frankfort, *Kingship and the Gods*, Chicago, 1948, pp. 19 ff.; denial of an earlier Hēliopolitan kingdom, E. J. Baumgartel, *The Cultures of Prehistoric Egypt*, revised edition, Oxford, 1955, pp. 3 ff.

Hypotheses concerning predynastic history: K. Sethe, *Urgeschichte und älteste Religion der Ägypter*, Leipzig, 1930; contradictory view, H. Kees, *Der Götterglaube im Alten Ägypten*, Leipzig, 1941.

A good account of the complex facts relating to Osiris in H. Bonnet, *Reallexikon der ägyptischen Religionsgeschichte*, Berlin, 1952, pp. 568 ff.

APPENDIX

THE KINGS OF EGYPT FROM MANETHO, THE KING-LISTS, AND THE MONUMENTS

NAMES of kings used by other Egyptologists are added in round brackets.

Under the heading MANETHO the version of Africanus is indicated by A, that of Eusebius by E.

Under the heading KING-LISTS A stands for the Abydos list, S for the Saḳḳâra list, T for the Turin Canon, and P for the Palermo Stone; the accompanying numerals give the place in the list; om. = omits. In T only the years are noted, the months and days being omitted as a rule.

PREDYNASTIC KINGS (*not in Manetho*)

P, *recto*, top register; 7 names completely, 2 only partly preserved, all wearing the crown  of Lower Egypt; traces of more determinatives at each end; the main Cairo fragment has lost all names, but of the 10 determinatives 6 wear the double crown  of United Egypt.[1]

The Scorpion king, see above, p. 402.

Ka, see above, p. 407.

EARLY DYNASTIC PERIOD

FIRST DYNASTY

MANETHO 'eight kings of Thinis'.[1] Conjectural dates, from 3100±150 B.C.

Manetho	*King-lists*
(1) Mēnēs,[2] A 62 yrs., E 60 yrs.	Meni, A 1; S om.; T 2. 11
(2) Athōthis,[3] A 57 yrs., E 27 yrs.	Teti, A 2; S om.; T om. Iti, A 3; S om.; T 2. 12; P Itit. Ita, A 4; S om.; T 2. 15(?)
(3) Kenkenēs, A 31 yrs., E 39 yrs.	
(4) Uenephēs,[4] A 23 yrs., E 42 yrs.	
(5) Usaphais, AE 20 yrs.	Zemti(?), A 5; S om.; T 2. 16
(6) Miebis, AE 26 yrs.	Merbiape, A 6; Merbiapen, S 1; T 2. 17
(7) Semempsēs,[5] AE 18 yrs.	Priestly figure, A 7, P; S om.; Semsem, T 2. 18
	Ḳebḥ, A 8; S 2; T 2. 19
(8) A Biēnechēs / E Ubienthēs } 26 yrs.	A om.; Biunūtje S 3; T 2. 20
Total: A 253 yrs.; E 252 yrs.	

On the MONUMENTS the following kings correspond to those of the King-lists above; as explained in the text, p. 400, the Horus-name was generally used, though sometimes accompanied or replaced by the title 'King of Upper and Lower Egypt' (the *Insibya*-title, abbrev. I) and/or by the Two-Ladies title (*Nebty*-title, abbrev. N). There are difficulties of identification only about the first four names and particularly that of Mēnēs.

Horus-name	*Insibya- and/or Nebty-names*	*Name in the King-lists*
Naʿrmer	Men, N	Meni
ʿAḥa	—	Teti
Djer (Zer), P	Itit, P	Iti
Edjō (Zet, Uadji)	Iterti(?),[6] N	Ita
Den (Udimu)	Zemti(?), I	Zemti(?)
ʿAndjyeb (Enezib)	Merpibia, I	Merbiape
—(?), P[7]	Priestly figure, N, IN	Semsem
Ḳaʿa[8]	Ḳaʿa, N, IN or Śen, N	Ḳebḥ

[1] Manetho uses the adjective Thinite; the corresponding Thinis is not found in Greek, but is demanded by the Egyptian original. Near Girga N. of Abydos.

[2] A, 'he was carried off by a hippopotamus and perished'.

[3] A, 'he built the palace at Memphis; his anatomical works are extant, for he was a physician'.

[4] A, 'a great famine seized Egypt; he raised the pyramids near Kōkōmē'.

[5] A, 'in his reign a very great calamity befell Egypt'.

[6] *JEA* xliv. 38. [7] Not Śekhemkhe, see p. 74. [8] *Ann. Serv.* xliv. 281, Fig. 28.

SECOND DYNASTY

MANETHO 'nine kings of Thinis'.

Manetho	*King-lists*	*Reigns in Turin Canon*
(1) Boēthos,[1] A 38 yrs.	Bedjau, A 9; ST om.	
(2) Kaiechōs,[2] A 39 yrs.	Kakau, A 10; S 4; T 2. 21	lost
(3) Binōthris,[3] A 47 yrs.	Banūtjeren, A 11; S 5; T 2. 22	,,
(4) Tlas, A 17 yrs.	Wadjnas,[4] A 12; S 6; [T 2. 23]	,,
(5) Sethenēs, A 41 yrs.	Sendi, A 13; S 7; T 2. 24	,,
(6) Chairēs, A 17 yrs.		
	ʿAka, T 2. 25; AS om.	
(7) Nephercherēs,[5] A 25 yrs.	Neferkarēʿ, S 8; AT om.	
(8) Sesōchris,[6] AE 48 yrs.	Neferkaseker, S 9; T 3. 1; A om.	8 yrs.
	Ḥudjefa, S 10; T 3. 2; A om.	11 yrs.
	Beby, S 11; Bebty, T 3. 3; Djadjay, A 14	27 yrs.
	Nebka,[7] A 15; T 3. 4; S om.	19 yrs.
(9) Chenerēs, 30 yrs.		

Total: A 302 yrs.; E 297 yrs.

(10) Manetho adds as No. 1 of Dyn. III a Necherōphēs[8] with 28 yrs., whose authenticity seems extremely doubtful.

[1] A, 'in his reign a chasm opened at Bubastus and many perished'.

[2] A, 'in his reign the bulls, Apis at Memphis and Mnevis at Hēliopolis, and the Mendesian goat, were worshipped as gods'.

[3] A, 'in his reign it was decided that women might hold the kingly office'.

[4] See above, p. 415 and below, p. 432, n. 5.

[5] A, 'in his reign, the story goes, the Nile flowed mixed with honey eleven days'.

[6] A, 'his height was 5 cubits, 3 palms'.

[7] See above, pp. 419–20.

[8] A, 'in his reign the Libyans revolted against Egypt, and when the moon waxed unexpectedly they surrendered in terror'.

(Continuation of Dyn. II on p. 432)

SECOND DYNASTY (*cont.*)

The MONUMENTS mention, apart from Nebka at the end of the dynasty, only Nos. (3), (4), and (5) of the Manethonian tradition, and replace its Nos. (1) and (2) by other kings of whom the position is definitely fixed.

Horus-name	*Insibya- and Nebty-names*	*Names in the King-lists*
Ḥotepśekhemui[1] [2]	Ḥotep,[2] IN	
Nebrēʿ *or* Raʿneb?[1] [3]	Nubnūfer,[3] I	
Ninūtjer *or* Nūtjeren;[1] P. *recto* 4.	Ninūtjer[4] *or* Nūtjeren, IN	= Banūtjeren
	Weneg,[5] I, IN	= Wadjnas
	Śend, I[6]	= Sendi

The next six kings of the king-lists are not mentioned on any contemporary monuments, where they are replaced by the following:

Horus-name	*Insibya- and Nebty-name*
(*a*) Śekhemyeb-Perenmāʿe[7]	Śekhemyeb-Perenmāʿe, IN[8]
Seth-name	
(*b*) Peribśen(i)[9]	Peribśen(i), I[10]
Horus- and Sēth-name	
(*c*) Khaʿśekhemui-Nebuiḥotpimef[11]	Khaʿśekhemui-Nebuiḥotpimef, IN[12]
Horus-name	
(*d*) Khaʿśekhem[13]	

See the text for the probability that (*a*) was merely the earlier name of (*b*) and the possibility that (*c*) was the earlier name of (*d*).

[1] These three together on the Cairo statue, L. Borchardt, *Statuen*, Berlin 1911, Nr. 1.

[2] Both together, *Ann. Serv.* iii. 187. Separately, Ḥotepśekhemui, *RT* ii. 8. 8–10; Ḥotep, *Ann. Serv.* xxviii, Pl. 2. 1.

[3] Nebrēʿ, *Ann. Serv.* iii. 188. Nubnūfer, op. cit. xxviii, Pl. 2. 7, 8. Identity uncertain.

[4] Position after Nebrēʿ, see *RT* ii, Pl. 8. 12.

[5] *Ann. Serv.* xliv. 288–91.

[6] Ibid. 292–4.

[7] Petrie, *Abydos III*, Pl. 9. 3; also without Perenmāʿe, *RT* ii, Pl. 21. 164 ff.

[8] *Ann. Serv.* xxviii, Pl. 2. 2, 3.

[9] *RT* ii, Pls. 21, 22.

[10] *RT* ii, Pl. 22. 190.

[11] *RT* ii, Pl. 23. 191–200; omitting Nebuiḥotpimef, Pl. 24.

[12] *RT* ii, Pl. 23. 201.

[13] Quibell, *Hierakonpolis*, i, Pls. 36–40; the stela, op. cit. ii, Pl. 58.

OLD KINGDOM

THIRD DYNASTY

MANETHO 'nine kings of Memphis'. Conjectural date from 2700 B.C.

Manetho	*King-lists*	*Reigns in Turin Canon*
(1) Necherōphēs,[1] 28 yrs.		
(2) Tosorthros,[2] 29 yrs. =	... Djośer-za, A 16; Djośer, S 12; Djośer-it(?), T 3. 5[3]	19 yrs.
	Teti, A 17; Djośer-teti, S 13; Djośer-ty, T 3. 6	6 yrs.
	Sedjes, A 18; Nebkarēʿ, S 14; ... [djefa?], T 3. 7	6 yrs.
(3) Tureis, 7 yrs.		
(4) Mesōchris, 17 yrs.		
(5) Sōuphis, 16 yrs.		
(6) Tosertasis, 19 yrs.		
(7) Achēs, 42 yrs.		
(8) Sēphuris, 30 yrs.		
(9) Kerpherēs, 26 yrs.		
Total: 214 yrs.		
	Neferkarēʿ, A 19; ST om.	
	Ḥuny, S 15; A om.; Ḥu ..., T 3. 8	24 yrs.

Of the kings named above the MONUMENTS know only the first (Djośer, Horus-name Netjrikhe) and the last (Ḥuny, Horus-name unknown). See the text (pp. 74–75) for three others whose Horus-names are Śekhemkhe, Khaʿba, and Zanakht.

[1] Transferred back to Dyn. II to leave Djośer as first of Dyn. III as in T.

[2] A, '⟨under whom was Imuthēs⟩, he reckoned ⟨with⟩ the Egyptians as Asclēpios on account of his medical skill and who invented building with hewn stone; he also devoted attention to writing'.

[3] Introduced by a rubric.

FOURTH DYNASTY

MANETHO 'eight kings of Memphis belonging to a different line'. Under the heading 'King-lists' H signifies a sequence of five kings of this dynasty recorded in a rock-inscription, perhaps of Dyn. XII, discovered in the Wâdy Ḥammâmât.[1] Conjectural date of Dyn. IV, from 2620 B.C.

Manetho	*King-lists*	*Herodotus*	*Turin Canon*
(1) Sōris, 29 yrs.	= Śnofru, A 20; S 16; T 3. 9		24 yrs.
(2) Sūphis,[2] 63 yrs.	= Khufwey [for Khnomkhufwey], A 21; S 17; T [3. 10]; H 1	Cheops	23 yrs.
	Ra‘djedef, A 22; S 18; T [3. 11]; H 2		8 yrs.
(3) Sūphis, 66 yrs.	= Ra‘kha‘ef[3] or Kha‘frē‘, A 23; S 19; T 3. 12; H 3	Chephrēn	lost
	Ḥardjedef,[4] AS om.; H 4; [T 3. 13?]		lost
	Ra‘baef,[4] AST om.; H 5		om.
(4) Mencherēs, 63 yrs.	= Menkaurē‘, A 24; S 20; T [3. 14?]	Mycerīnus	18 yrs.[5]
(5) Ratoisēs, 25 yrs.	A om.; S had 4, now destroyed; T [3. 15?]		4 yrs.
(6) Bicheris, 22 yrs.	A om.; S had 4, now destroyed; T [3. 16?]		2 yrs.
(7) Sebercherēs, 7 yrs.	A om.; S had 4, now destroyed		
	Shepśeśkaf,[6] A 25; S om.; T om.?		
(8) Thampthis, 9 yrs.			
Total: 277 yrs.			

On the MONUMENTS the Horus-name henceforth becomes of much less importance than the Nomen, which is regularly written in a cartouche and is often found as a component in the names of kinsmen or courtiers. Only the following kings are represented:

Horus-name	*Nomen*	*Herodotus*
Nebmā‘e	Śnofru	
Medjdu[7]	Khufwey	Cheops
Kheper[8]	Ra‘djedef	
Useryeb	Kha‘frē‘	Chephrēn
Kakhe[9]	Menkaurē‘	Mycerīnus
Shepśeśkhe[10]	Shepśeśkaf	

[1] *Bull. Soc. fr. d'Ég.*, No. 16 (1954), pp. 41 ff.

[2] A, 'he reared the greatest pyramid, which Herodotus says was made by Cheops; Sūphis had a contempt for the gods and he composed the Sacred Book, which I acquired in Egypt as being of great value'.

[3] See above, pp. 80–1.

[4] Known only as princes, not as kings, in later literature.

[5] Tentatively assigned to Mycerinus; possibly 28 yrs., not 18.

[6] Precedes Uśerkaf, first king of Dyn. V, in the tomb cited p. 89, n. 2.

[7] Or Medjuro as *Nebty*-name, *Wb.* ii. 192. 11.

[8] Gauthier, *LR* i. 84.

[9] *Ann. Serv.* xlv. 53.

[10] *Urk.* i. 160, corrected.

FIFTH DYNASTY

MANETHO 'eight[1] kings from Elephantinē'. Eusebius confuses this dynasty with Dyn. VI. Conjectural date, from 2480 B.C.

Manetho		*King-lists*	*Turin Canon*
(1) Usercherēs, 28 yrs.	=	Uśerkaf, A 26; S 25; T 3. 17?	7 yrs.
(2) Sephrēs, 13 yrs.	=	Śaḥurēᶜ, A 27; S 26; T [3. 18]	12 yrs.
(3) Nephercherēs, 20 yrs.	=	Kakai, A 28; Neferirkarēᶜ, S 27; T [3. 19]	lost
(4) Sisirēs, 7 yrs.	=	Shepśeśkarēᶜ, S 28; A om.; T [3. 20]	7 yrs.
(5) Cherēs, 20 yrs.	?=	Raᶜneferef, A 29; Khaᶜneferrēᶜ, S 29; T [3. 21]	$x+1$ yrs.
(6) Rathurēs, 44 yrs.	?=	Niuśerrēᶜ, A 30; S om.; T [3. 22]	11 yrs.
(7) Mencherēs, 9 yrs.	=	Menkauḥōr, A 31; S 30; T 3. 23	8 yrs.
(8) Tancherēs, 44 yrs.	=	Djedkarēᶜ, A 32; Maᶜkarēᶜ? S 31; Djed, T 3. 24	28 yrs.[2]
(9) Onnos, 33 yrs.	=	Uniś, A 33; S 32; T 3. 25	30 yrs.
Total: 248 yrs.		T3. 26 'Total. Kings from Meniti(?) to [Uniś]'	lost

On the MONUMENTS some of these kings use a name compounded with that of the sun-god Rēᶜ, the precursor of the later Prenomen; this is enclosed in a cartouche. The personal name or Nomen is less often used.

Horus-name	*Rēᶜ-name*	*Nomen*
Irmāᶜe	none	Uśerkaf
Nebkhaᶜu	Śaḥurēᶜ	none
Uśerkhaᶜu	Neferirkarēᶜ	Kakai
?	[Shepśeśkarēᶜ][3]	Izi?[4]
Neferkhaᶜu	none	Raᶜneferef
Setibtowě	Niuśerrēᶜ	Iny
Menkhaᶜu	none	Menkauḥōr[5]
Djedkhaᶜu	Djedkarēᶜ	Izozi
Wadjtowě	none	Uniś

[1] He enumerates nine.

[2] One of the papyri mentioned on p. 87 speaks of Djedkarēᶜ's 'sixteenth time', i.e. presumably year 32.

[3] Only a scarab is known, Gauthier *LR* i. 119.

[4] *ZÄS* l. 3. [5] Variant Ḥorikau, *ZÄS* xlii. 8.

SIXTH DYNASTY

MANETHO 'six kings of Memphis'. Conjectural date from 2340 B.C.

Manetho		*King-lists*	*Turin Canon*
(1) Othoēs,[1] 30 yrs.	=	Teti, A 34; S 33; T [4. 1]	lost
		Uśerkarēᶜ, A 35; S om.; T [4. 2]	lost
(2) Phios, 53 yrs.	=	Piopi, S 34; Meryrēᶜ, A 36; T [4. 3]	20 yrs.
(3) Methusuphis, 7 yrs.	=	Merenrēᶜ, A 37; S 35; T [4. 4]	44? yrs.
(4) Phiōps, 99 yrs.[2]	=	Neferkarēᶜ, A 38; S 36; T [4. 5]	90 [+x] yrs.
(5) Menthesuphis,[3] 1 yr.	=	Merenrēᶜ-ᶜAntyemzaef A 39; T [4. 6]	1 yr.
(6) Nitōcris, 12[4] yrs.	=	Nitoḳerty, T 4. 7 (or 4. 8?); A?	?
Total: 203 yrs.		T4, 14. '[Total]. Kings [from Teti to.....]	181 yrs.

The first five of these kings are known from the MONUMENTS, with the following names:

Horus-name	*Rēᶜ-name*	*Nomen*
Sḥeteptowĕ	none	Teti
	Uśerkarēᶜ[5]	none
Merytowĕ	Neferzaḥōr,[6] later Meryrēᶜ	Piopi (Pepi I)
ᶜAnkhkhaᶜu	Merenrēᶜ	ᶜAntyemzaef
Netjerkhaᶜu	Neferkarēᶜ	Piopi (Pepi II)

After Nitoḳerty the Turin Canon had five kings before the total concluding Dyn. VI is reached, but only the first three names are preserved, and only the last four lengths of reign, as follows:

Prenomen	*Nomen*	*Turin Canon*	
lost	Neferka, child . . .	T 4. 9	lost
lost	Nūfe	T 4. 10	2 yrs. 1 m. 1 d.
Ḳakarēᶜ[7]	Ibi[7]	T 4. 11	4 yrs. 2 ms.
lost	lost	T 4. 12	2 yrs. 1 m. 1 d.
lost	lost	T 4. 13	1 yr. 0 m. ½ d.(?)

The successors of Merenrēᶜ-ᶜAntyemzaef in the Abydos list cannot be certainly equated with any of the above, and are treated below under Dyn. VIII. Two unplaced kings Ity and Imḥōtep[8] are named in the Wâdy Ḥammâmât, and were possibly contemporary with Dyn. VI.

[1] A, 'he was murdered by his bodyguard'.
[2] A, 'began to reign at the age of six and continued to a hundred'.
[3] Manetho read the falcon in the boat (ᶜAnty?) wrongly as Mont.
[4] A, E, 'the noblest and loveliest of the women of her time, of fair complexion, who raised the third pyramid'. For possible Prenomen see p. 437, n. 2.
[5] Two cylinder seals, Hayes, *Scepter*, i, p. 125.
[6] *ZÄS* xliv. 129; lix. 71; Vandier, p. 232.
[7] Ruined pyramid at Saḳḳâra, see Vandier, p. 234.
[8] Op. cit., pp. 233 f.

SEVENTH DYNASTY

MANETHO 'seventy kings of Memphis, who reigned for 70 days', A.

This dynasty appears to be wholly spurious.

FIRST INTERMEDIATE PERIOD

EIGHTH DYNASTY

MANETHO 'twenty-seven kings of Memphis, who reigned for 146 years'. So A; E has five kings and 100 years. No names are mentioned.

See above, pp. 102, 108, for the eighteen successors of Piopi II named by their Prenomens and Nomens in the Abydos list; the footnotes here mention any inscriptions or objects which have been found attesting their existence.

A 39, Merenrēᶜ-ᶜAntyemzaf.[1] A 40, Netjerkarēᶜ. A 41, Menkarēᶜ.[2] A 42, Neferkarēᶜ. A 43, Neferkarēᶜ-Neby. A 44, Djedkarēᶜ-Shemaᶜ. A 45, Neferkarēᶜ-Khendu.[3] A 46, Merenḥōr. A 47, Sneferka.[4] A 48, Nikarēᶜ.[4] A 49, Neferkarēᶜ-Tereru.[5] A 50, Neferkaḥōr. A 51, Neferkarēᶜ-Pepysonb. A 52, Sneferka-ᶜAnu. A 53, Ḳa?kaurēᶜ.[6] A 54, Neferkaurēᶜ. A 55, Neferkauḥōr.[7] A 56, Neferirkarēᶜ.

An unplaced king mentioned in a Coptos decree has the Prenomen Wadjkarēᶜ;[8] two Horus-names from the same source, probably the predecessor and successor of A 55 respectively, Khaᶜ[bau] and Demedjibtowĕ.[9]

NINTH DYNASTY

MANETHO, A, E, 'nineteen kings of Hēracleopolis, who reigned for 409 years.[10] Achthoēs, the first of these, terrible beyond all before him, wrought evil things for those in all Egypt, but afterwards he fell a victim to madness and was destroyed by a crocodile'.

1 See already under Dyn. VI.

2 According to Newberry perhaps the Prenomen of Nitōcris, *JEA* xxix. 51 ff.

3 On a barbaric cylinder, *JEA* xii. 92, fig. 6.

4 These together on a gold plaque, Brit. Mus. 8444.

5 On a seal or scarab, Petrie, *Scarabs and Cylinders*, Pl. 10. 7, 10.

6 Perhaps Prenomen of Ibi, see Dyn. VI, under T 4. 11.

7 In decrees found at Coptos, *JEA* xxxii. 5, 6, j. to q.; Horus-name Netjribau.

8 *Urk.* i. 306. 13. 9 *JEA* xxxii. 21–23. 10 E, 4 kings and 100 years.

TENTH DYNASTY

MANETHO 'nineteen kings of Hēracleopolis, who reigned for 185 years'.

Dyns. IX and X are here taken together; they are totally disregarded by the Abydos and Saḳḳâra king-lists, but the Turin Canon once named eighteen kings; see too the total in 5.10. Of these the name of the third is Neferkarēʿ (4. 20) and Akhtoy is only the fourth (4. 21); then follow five, all damaged and unidentifiable. A fragment (No. 48) repeating Neferkarēʿ and Akhtoy cannot belong to column 5, where it has been wrongly placed.

The MONUMENTS add but little to the three kings named Akhtoy and to the Merykarēʿ[1] discussed in the text, pp. 112 ff.

MIDDLE KINGDOM

ELEVENTH DYNASTY

MANETHO 'sixteen kings of Diospolis (Thebes) who reigned for 43 years; after whom Ammenemēs, 16 years'.

The Turin Canon gave six names headed by a rubric (5. 11), but only the last two are preserved; the Abydos and Saḳḳâra lists admit only these two kings. Utilizing also the Karnak list and the MONUMENTS the sequence may be established as follows:[2]

Horus-name	*Prenomen*	*Nomen*	*King-lists*	*Turin Canon*
		[Inyōtef][3]	T [5. 12]	lost
Sehertowĕ	none	Inyōtef (I)	T [5. 13]	lost
Waḥʿankh	none	Inyōtef (II)	T [5. 14]	49 yrs.
Nakhtnebtepnūfe	none	Inyōtef (III)	T [5. 15]	8 (or 18?) yrs.
Sʿankhibtowĕ / Nebḥedje / Samtowĕ [4]	Nebḥepetrēʿ[5]	Menthotpe (I)	T 5. 16; A 57; S 37	51 yrs.
Sʿankhtowef	Sʿankhkarēʿ	Menthotpe (II)	T 5. 17; A 58; S 38	12 yrs.
Nebtowĕ	Nebtowerēʿ	Menthotpe (III)	TAS om.	om.

The Turin Canon gives Dyn. XI a total of 143 yrs.; dating back from 1991 B.C. for Ammenemēs I this gives 2134 B.C. for the beginning of the dynasty.

[1] See too Gauthier, *LR* i. 209 f.

[2] *Mitt. Kairo*, xiv. 42 ff.

[3] Only a hereditary prince; the Antef of older Egyptologists.

[4] Apparently three distinct Horus-names for consecutive stages of Menthotpe I's reign. The Mentuhotep of older Egyptologists.

[5] For the changed spelling in the final stage of the reign see p. 120.

TWELFTH DYNASTY

MANETHO 'seven kings of Diospolis'; for Ammenemēs I see under Dyn. XI. T 5. 19 has as heading: '[Kings .... of the] Residence It-towĕ'.

	Manetho		*King-lists*	*Turin Canon*
	Ammenemēs, 16 yrs.	=	Sḥetepibrēʿ, A 59; S 39; T 5. 20	[2]9 yrs.
(1)	Sesonchosis,[1] 46 yrs.	=	Kheperkarēʿ, A 60; S 40; T 5. 21	45 yrs.
(2)	Ammanemēs,[2] 38 yrs.	=	Nubkaurēʿ, A 61; S 41; T [5. 22]	10+ (or 30+?)
(3)	Sesōstris,[3] 48 yrs.	=	Khaʿkheperrēʿ, A 62; S 42; T [5. 23]	19 yrs.
			Khaʿkaurēʿ, A 63; S 43; T [5. 24]	30[+x]
(4)	Lacharēs,[4] 8 yrs.	=	Nemaʿrēʿ, A 64; S 44; T [5. 25]	40[+x]
(5)	Amerēs, 8 yrs.			
(6)	Ammenemēs, 8 yrs.	=	Maʿkherurēʿ, A 65; S 45; T 6. 1	9 yrs. 3 ms. 27 ds.
(7)	Scemiophris,[5] 4 yrs.	=	Sebekkarēʿ, A om.; S 46; Sebeknofrurēʿ, T 6. 2	3 yrs. 10 ms. 24 ds.

Total: A 160 yrs.; E 245 yrs.

T 6. 3 concludes thus: 'Total, kings of the Resid[ence It-towĕ[, 8 [kings] make 213 yrs. 1 m. 16 ds.' A 65 and S 46 are followed immediately by Nebpeḥtirēʿ, i.e. Amōsis I of Dyn. XVIII.

The MONUMENTS show co-regencies for the first three reigns, and there are indications of successive co-regencies also for Ammenemēs III and IV, as well as for Ammenemēs III and the female king Sebeknofru.[6]

	Horus-name	*Prenomen and Nomen*	*Highest date*	*Co-regency begins yr.*	*Probable dates* B.C.[7]
(1)	Weḥammeswe	Sḥetepibrēʿ Amenemḥē (I)	30	21	1991–1962
(2)	ʿAnkhmeswe	Kheperkarēʿ Senwosre (I)	44	43	1971–1928
(3)	Ḥekenemmāʿe	Nubkaurēʿ Amenemḥē (II)	35	32	1929–1895
(4)	Seshemutowĕ	Khaʿkheperrēʿ Senwosre (II)	6		1897–1877
(5)	Netjerkhepru	Khaʿkaurēʿ Senwosre (III)	33		1878–1843
(6)	ʿAbau	Nemaʿrēʿ Amenemḥē (III)	45	(43?)	1842–1797
(7)	Kheperkhepru	Maʿkherurēʿ Amenemḥē (IV)	6		1798–1790
(8)	Meretrēʿ	Sebekkarēʿ Sebeknofru	—		1789–1786

It will be seen that the figures given by the monuments are in close agreement with those of the Turin Canon.

[1] A, E, 'son of Ammanemēs'. [2] A, E, 'he was murdered by his own eunuchs'.

[3] A, E, 'in nine years he subdued the whole of Asia, and Europe as far as Thrace, everywhere raising memorials of the condition of the peoples, engraving on the stelae the parts of men for those who were noble, and the parts of women for those who were ignoble, so as to be esteemed by the Egyptians as first after Osiris'.

[4] Elsewhere the name is given in a number of different forms, Labarēs coming closest to the hieroglyphic writing, see Waddell, p. 224, n. 1. Manetho comments 'he built the labyrinth in the Arsinoite nome as a tomb for himself'.

[5] A, 'his (i.e. No. 6's) sister'. [6] See above, p. 141.

[7] Parker, p. 69. See too Edgerton in *JNES*, i. 307 ff.

SECOND INTERMEDIATE PERIOD

MANETHO's Dyns. XIII–XVII see pp. 147 ff.; no names are offered except for the Hyksōs rulers. A and S ignore the period altogether. K gives a number of names, but in disorderly sequence. The kings of the Turin Canon (T) are here enumerated complete, with additional names from elsewhere in square brackets [ ]; an asterisk ★ denotes those known also from monuments or other objects; the lengths of reigns are those of T, where preserved.

6. 5 ⟨Sekhem⟩rēʿ-khutowĕ [Amenemḥē-Sebekḥotpe],[1] K★ [he made in] kingship, 2 yrs. 3 ms. 24 ds.
6. 6 Sekhemkarēʿ A[menemḥē-sonbe]f?★...........Unoccupied, 6 yrs.
6. 7 Rēʿ?-[A]menemḥē★?[2]......3 yrs.
6. 8 Sḥetepibrēʿ★?[3].....1 [yr.] (Another of this name 6. 12)
6. 9 Afnai
6. 10 Sʿankhibrēʿ [Ameny-Inyōtef-Amenemḥē]★, K (Another of this name 8. 18)
6. 11 Smenkarēʿ
6. 12 Sḥetepibrēʿ[3] (Another of this name 6. 8)
6. 13 Swadjkarēʿ (Another of this name 8. 6)
6. 14 Nedjemibrēʿ
6. 15 Rēʿ?-Sebek[ḥot]pe (I?), son of Nen(?)...., 2 [yrs.]
6. 16 Ren[so]nb, he made 4 months.
6. 17 Auibrēʿ....7 [ms.?] (Another of this name 8. 12)
6. 18 Sedjefakarēʿ [Kay-Amenemḥē]★....yrs.
6. 19 Sekhemrēʿ-khutowĕ-Sebekḥotpe (II?) [Wegef], K?★....yrs.
6. 20 Woser[ka]rēʿ-Khendjer,★....yrs.
6. 21 [Smenkh]karēʿ the General★
6. 22 ....ka[rēʿ] Inyōtef★?
6. 23 ....ib?sēt
6. 24 Sekhemka?rēʿ[4]-Sebekḥotpe (III?),★ 3 yrs. 2 [ms.]....
6. 25 Khaʿ[sekhem]rēʿ-Neferḥōtep, son of Ḥaʿonkhef, K★, 11 yrs. 1 m. ....
6. 26 Rēʿ?-Siḥatḥōr,........3 [ms.?]
6. 27 Khaʿneferrēʿ-Sebekḥotpe (IV?), K★
7. 1 Khaʿḥōteprēʿ [Sebekḥotpe V?], 4 yrs. 8 ms. 29 ds.
7. 2 Waḥibrēʿ-Iaʿyeb,★ 10 yrs. 8 ms. 28 ds.
7. 3 Merneferrēʿ,★ he made in king[ship] 23 yrs. 8 ms. 18 ds.
7. 4 Merḥōteprēʿ [Inai], K★, 2 yrs. 2 ms. 9 ds.
7. 5 Sʿankhrēʿenswadjtu, 3 yrs. 2 ms......[ds].
7. 6 Mersekhemrēʿ-Ind, K, 3 yrs. 1 m. 1 d.
7. 7 Swadjkarēʿ-Ḥōri, 5 yrs. 8 [ms.?]

[1] Discussion, Vandier, pp. 322–3. [2] Op. cit., pp. 323–4. [3] Op. cit., p. 325.
[4] Perhaps to be emended to the well-known Sekhemrēʿ-swadjtowĕ.

7. 8 Merka[w?]rēʿ-Sebek[ḥotpe],* K, 2 yrs. 4[ms.?]
7. 9 . . . . 11 [ms.?]
7. 10 . . . . 3 [ms.?]
7. 11–12 lost
7. 13 . . . . . mose
7. 14 Rēʿ. . . . māʿe Ibi*
7. 15 Rēʿ. . . . . . weben Ḥor. . . .
7. 16 Rēʿ. . . . . . ka
7. 17–21 lost
7. 22 Merkheperrēʿ
7. 23 Merka[rēʿ]
7. 24–27 lost
8. 1 Neḥasy* . . . yrs. . . . . 3 [ms.?]
8. 2 Khaʿtyrēʿ . . . . [yrs.] 3 [ms.?]
8. 3 Nebfaurēʿ, 1 yr. 5 ms. 15 ds.
8. 4 Sḥebrēʿ, he made in kingship, 3 yrs. . . . . . ms. 1 d.
8. 5 Merdjefarēʿ, 3 yrs. . . . . . .
8. 6 Swadjkarēʿ, 1 yr. . . . . (Another of this name 6. 13)
8. 7 Nebdjefarēʿ, 1 yr. . . . . .
8. 8 Webenrēʿ, . . . [1?] yr. . . . . .
8. 9 . . . ., 1 yr. 1 m., ...
8. 10 . . . . [djefa?rēʿ], 4 yrs.
8. 11 . . . . [we]ben[rēʿ], 3 [yrs.]
8. 12 Auibrēʿ. . . . . . (Another of this name 6. 17) [Unoccupi]ed, 18 ds.
8. 13 Heribrēʿ. 29
8. 14 Nebsenrēʿ. . . . . . . 5 [ms.] 20 ds. Unoccupied, ...
8. 15 . . . . . . rēʿ. . . . . . . 21 [ds.?]
8. 16 Skheperenrēʿ, 2 yrs. 1 [d.?]
8. 17 Djedkherurēʿ, 2 yrs. 5[ds.?]
8. 18 Sʿankhibrēʿ. . . . . . 19 [ds.] (Another of this name 6. 10)
8. 19 Nefertemrēʿ. . . . . 18 [ds.]
8. 20 Sekhem. . . . . rēʿ, he made [in king]ship, ... months
8. 21 Kakemurēʿ. . . . . . yrs. . . . . .
8. 22 Neferibrēʿ* . . . . . yrs. . . . .
8. 23 Ya. . . . . yrs.
8. 24 Khaʿ. . . . rēʿ. . . . . .
8. 25 ʿAakarēʿ. . . . .
8. 26 Smen. . . rēʿ. . . . . .
8. 27 Djed. . . . rēʿ. . . . . .
Four or five names lost

The fragments now arranged as columns 9 and 10 contain mostly broken names, but also some, particularly 9. 17–22 and 10. 1–11, which are obviously fantastic and do not belong to real kings. Among the real kings are the following: 9. 7 Snefer[ka?]rēʿ, K; 9. 8 Men.....rēʿ; 9. 9 Djed.....rēʿ; 9. 14 Ink....; 9. 15 Ineb?...; 9. 16 Ip....; 9. 29....ka[rēʿ?] Nebennati; 9. 30 .....ka[rēʿ?] Bebnem. Tentatively placed in col. 10 is the important fragment relating to the Hyksōs:

10. 20 [Chieftain of a foreign country], Khamudy[1]

10. 21 [Total, chieftains of] a foreign country, 6, they made 108 yrs.[2]

What is now mounted as col. 11 consists of two pieces, the lower giving little more than the lengths of five reigns, namely 2, 2, 4, 3 and 3 yrs. In the upper part of the column the following can be read:

11. 1 Sekhem..rēʿ 3 yrs.
11. 2 Sekhem..rēʿ 16 yrs.
11. 3 Sekhems..rēʿ 1 yr.
11. 4 Swadj[en?]rēʿ 1 yr.
11. 5 Nebiri⟨er⟩au*[3] 2(?)9 yrs.
11. 6 Nebitau .....
11. 7 Smen..rēʿ ..yrs.
11. 8 Seweser..rēʿ 12 yrs. Unoccupied....days
11. 9 Sekhemrē-shedwīse ....yrs.
Five names lost
11. 15[Total], 5 kings......
11. 16 Woser...rēʿ
11. 17 Woser...

For the Hyksōs rulers see opposite and above, pp. 149–50, 155–72.

Kings assigned to Dyn. XVII because (*a*) coffins or other objects have been found at Thebes, (*b*) named in the Inspection under Ramessēs IX, or (*c*) possibly identifiable with names in the Turin Canon. The sequence is uncertain except in Nos. 9–11, who immediately preceded Dyn. XVIII. Objects naming them, Vandier, pp. 318–21, discussions, op. cit., pp. 296–7, 328–33.

1. Sekhemrēʿ-waḥkhaʿ Raʿḥotpe, *c* = T. 11. 1?
2. Sekhemrēʿ-wadjkhaʿu Sebekemsaf, *c* = T 11. 2?
3. Sekhemrēʿ-smentowě Djeḥūty, *a*; *c* = T. 11. 3?
4. Swadjenrēʿ Nebirierau, *a*; *c* = T 11. 5
5. Nubkheperrēʿ Inyōtef, *a*; *b*
6. Sekhemrēʿ-wepmāʿe Inyōtef-ʿo, *a*; *b*
7. Sekhemrēʿ-herḥimāʿe Inyōtef, *a*
8. Sekhemrēʿ-shedtowe Sebekemsaf, *a*; *b*; *c* = T 11. 9?
9. Senakhtenrēʿ? Taʿo, *a*; *b*
10. Seḳenenrēʿ Taʿo, *a*; *b*
11. Wadjkheperrēʿ Kamose, *a*; *b*

For other kings of the Second Intermediate Period see the authorities quoted above, p. 175.

[1] Not in a cartouche.

[2] The 100 certain, the 8 less so.

[3] See p. 161 for a stela where this king's Prenomen is Swadjenrēʿ, as in 11. 4.

THE HYKSŌS RULERS

Africanus describes MANETHO's Dyn. XV as consisting of 'six foreign from Phoenicia, who seized Memphis; who also founded a town in the Sethroite nome, from which as a base they subdued Egypt.' He then names the six kings in slightly different form and order from Josephus (above, p. 156), namely: (1) Saitēs, 19 yrs.; (2) Bnōn, 44 yrs.; (3) Pachnan, 61 yrs.; (4) Staan, 50 yrs.; (5) Archlēs, 49 yrs.; (6) Aphōphis, 61 yrs.

Apart from T (p. 442, top) the KING-LISTS make no mention, but the Memphite list of priests (pp. 50, 160) gives an ʿAḳen (? = ʿAḳenenrēʿ) next after Ibi (? = T 7. 14), then after five priesthoods a Sharek, and lastly an Apōp immediately before Amāsis of Dyn. XVIII.

The MONUMENTS show only four names of importance:

Prenomen and Nomen	
ʿAḳenenrēʿ Apōpi	No dates
Nebkhepeshrēʿ Apōp	"
Seweserenrēʿ Khayan	"
ʿAweserrēʿ Apōpi	sole date 33 yrs.

NEW KINGDOM

EIGHTEENTH DYNASTY

Name used in this book	*Prenomen and Nomen*	*Highest date*	*Conjectural dates* B.C.
Amōsis	Nebpeḥtirēʿ ʿAḥmose	22	1575–1550
Amenōphis I	Djeserkarēʿ Amenḥotpe	21[1]	1550–1528
Tuthmōsis I	ʿAkheperkarēʿ Dḥutmose	4(or 9?)	1528–1510
Tuthmōsis II	ʿAkheperenrēʿ Dḥutmose	18[2]	1510–1490
Ḥashepsowe	Maʿkarēʿ Ḥashepsowe	20	1490–1468[3]
Tuthmōsis III	Menkheperrēʿ Dḥutmose	54	1490[4]–1436
Amenōphis II	ʿAkheprurēʿ Amenḥotpe	23[5]	1436–1413
Tuthmōsis IV	Menkheprurēʿ Dḥutmose	8[6]	1413–1405
Amenōphis III	Nebmaʿrēʿ Amenḥotpe	37	1405–1367
Amenōphis IV / Akhenaten	Neferkheprurēʿ-waʿenrēʿ Amenḥotpe / Akhenaten	17	1367–1350
Smenkhkarēʿ	ʿAnkhkheprurēʿ Smenkhkarēʿ Nefernefruaten-merwaʿenrēʿ	3	1350–1347
Tutʿankhaten / Tutʿankhamūn	Nebkheprurēʿ Tutʿankhaten / Tutʿankhamūn	9	1347–1339
Ay	Kheperkheprurēʿ Itnūte-Ay	4	1339–1335
Ḥaremḥab[7]	Djeserkheprurēʿ Ḥaremḥab	27?[8]	1335–1308?

[1] Above, p. 175, n. 3.

[2] *Ann. Serv.* i. 99.

[3] About 22 years as senior co-regent of Tuthmōsis III.

[4] Parker in *JNES* xvi. 42.

[5] *Urk.* iv. 1343.

[6] Op. cit. iv. 1545.

[7] Intermediate between Dyns. XVIII–XIX.

[8] See p. 242, n. 1.

EIGHTEENTH DYNASTY (*cont.*)

MANETHO: J = Josephus; A = Africanus; E = Eusebius.

A, 'Diospolites, 16 kings'; E, 'Diospolites, 14 kings'.

J, Tethmōsis,[1] who drove the Shepherds out of Egypt, 25 yrs. 4 ms.; A, Amōs, length of reign not given; E, Amōsis, 25 yrs.

J, His son Chebrōn, 13 yrs.; A, Chebrōs, 13 yrs.; E, Chebrōn, 13 yrs.

J, Amenōphis,[2] 20 yrs. 7 ms.; A, Amenōphthis, 24 (21) yrs.; E, Ammenōphis, 21 yrs.

J, His sister Amessis,[3] 21 yrs. 9 ms.; A, Amensis, 22 yrs.; E omits

J, Her son Mēphrēs, 12 yrs. 9 ms.; A, Misaphris, 13 yrs.; E, Miphrēs, 12 yrs.

J, His son Mēphramuthōsis,[4] 25 yrs. 10 ms.; A, E, Misphragmuthōsis,[5] 26 yrs.

J, His son Thmōsis,[6] 9 yrs. 8 ms.; A, E, Tuthmōsis, 9 yrs.

J, His son Amenōphis,[7] 30 yrs. 10 ms.; A, E, Amenōphis, 31 yrs.[8]

J, His son Ōros,[9] 36 yrs. 5 ms.; A, Ōros, 37 yrs.; E, Ōros, 36 or 38 yrs.

There follow four names doubtless representing predecessors of Ōros (= Ḥaremḥab), who then reappears with the expanded name Harmais:

J, His daughter Acenchērēs, 12 yrs. 1 m.; A, Acherrēs, 32 yrs.; E, Achenchersēs, [12 yrs.]

J, Her brother Rathōtis, 9 yrs.; A, Rathōs, 6 yrs.; E omits

J, His son Acenchērēs, 12 yrs. 5 ms.; A, Chebrēs, 12 yrs.; E, Acherrēs, 8 yrs.

J, His son Acenchērēs II, 12 yrs. 3 ms.; A, Acherrēs, 12 yrs.; E, Cherrēs, 15 yrs.

J, His son Harmais,[9] 4 yrs. 1 m.; A, Armesis, 5 yrs.; E, Armais, 5 yrs.

Manetho as reported by J concludes his Dyn. XVIII with four successors of Harmais (= Ḥaremḥab) whom he ought to have placed in Dyn. XIX, where they will be named. As already noted on p. 156 J's excerpts from Manetho were introduced to support the latter's belief that the biblical account of the Exodus and the expulsion of the Hyksōs under Tethmōsis refer to one and the same historic event, a view rejected in Rowley's book, p. 130, n. 2. Admittedly the lengthy excerpts in question embody also several popular stories of the most fantastic description explicitly recognized as such by the Jewish historian.

1 By corruption for Amōsis. 2 Amenōphis I. 3 Ḥashepsowe?
4 Tuthmōsis III. 5 'In his reign the flood of Deucaliōn's time occurred', A.
6 Tuthmōsis IV. 7 Amenōphis III.
8 'Reputed to be Memnōn and a speaking statue', A, E. 9 Ḥaremḥab.

NINETEENTH DYNASTY

Name used in this book	*Prenomen and Nomen*	*Highest year-date*	*Conjectural dates* B.C.
Ramessēs I	Menpeḥtirēʿ Raʿmesse	2	1308
Sethōs I	Menmaʿrēʿ Sety-merenptaḥ	11[1]	1309–1291
Ramessēs II	Usimaʿrēʿ-setpenrēʿ Raʿmesse-miamūn	67	1290[2]–1224
Merenptaḥ[3]	Binerēʿ-meramūn Merenptaḥ-ḥotpḥimāʿe	10	1224–1214
Sethōs II	Usikheprurēʿ-setpenrēʿ Sety-merenptaḥ	6	1214–1208
Amenmesse[4]	Menmirēʿ-setpenrēʿ Amenmesse-ḥeḳawise	—	—
Siptaḥ	Sekhaʿenrēʿ-setpenrēʿ Raʿmesse-siptaḥ	(1)	(1208)
Siptaḥ (later)[5]	Akhenrēʿ-setpenrēʿ Merenptaḥ-siptaḥ	6	1208–1202
Twosre	Sitrēʿ-meryamūn Twosre-seteptenmūt	8?	1202–1194?

The female Pharaoh Twosre was followed by a kingless period of short duration.

DYN. XVIII (CONTINUED) AND DYN. XIX IN MANETHO: J = Josephus; A = Africanus; E = Eusebius.

After Harmais (see opposite) there follow, in AE at end of Dyn XVIII:

J, His son Ramessēs,[6] 1 yr. 4 ms.; A, Ramessēs, 1 yr.; E omits

J, His son Harmessēs Miamūn,[7] 66 yrs. 2 ms.; A omits; E, Ramessēs, 68 yrs.

J, His son Amenōphis,[8] 19 yrs. 6 ms.; A, Amenōphath, 19 yrs.; E, Ammenōphis, 40 yrs.

J, His son Sethōs,[9] 'also called Ramessēs, whose power lay in chariotry and fleet', [10 yrs.]; A, E omit

Manethō's Dyn. XIX begins here; A, Diospolites, 7 (6) kings; E, Diospolites, 5 kings.

A, Sethōs,[10] 51 yrs.; E, Sethōs, 55 yrs.

A, Rapsacēs,[7] 61 yrs.; E, Rampsēs, 66 yrs.

A, Ammenephthēs,[8] 20 yrs.; E, Ammenephthis, 40 yrs.

A, Ramessēs,[11] 60 yrs.; E omits

A, Ammenemnēs,[12] 5 yrs.; E, Ammenemēs, 26 yrs.

A, E, Thuōris,[13] (described as a king), 7 yrs.

[1] Stela from Gebel Barkal, *ZÄS* lxix. 74. [2] Parker in *JNES* xvi. 43.
[3] Often given as Meneptah, see below under Manetho; also *OLZ* vi. 224.
[4] Very brief, before or in the reign of Sethōs II. [5] *JEA* xliv. 12 ff.
[6] Ramessēs I. [7] Ramessēs II. [8] Merenptaḥ. [9] Sethōs II. [10] Sethōs I.
[11] Sethōs II, see above, n. 9; some confusion with Ramessēs II. [12] Amenmesse?
[13] Queen Twosre: 'who in Homer is called Polybus, husband of Alcandra and in whose time Troy was taken'; the traditional date for this last event is 1183 B.C.

TWENTIETH DYNASTY

Name used in this book	*Prenomen and Nomen*	*Highest year-date*	*Conjectural dates* B.C.
Setnakhte	Usikhaʿurēʿ-meramūn-setpenrēʿ Setnakhte-mererrēʿ-meramūn	2	1184–1182
Ramessēs III	Usimaʿrēʿ-meramūn Raʿmesse-ḥeḳaōn	32	1182[1]–1151
Ramessēs IV	Ḥeḳamaʿrēʿ[2]-setpenamūn Raʿmesse-ḥeḳamāʿe-meramūn	6	1151–1145
Ramessēs V	Usimaʿrēʿ-sekheperenrēʿ Raʿmesse-Amenḥikhopshef-meramūn	4	1145–1141
Ramessēs VI	Nebmaʿrēʿ-meramūn Raʿmesse-Amenḥikhopshef-nūteḥeḳaōn	7[3]	1141–1134
Ramessēs VII[4]	Usimaʿrēʿ-meramūn-setpenrēʿ Raʿmesse-itamūn-nūteḥeḳaōn	—[5]	1134
Ramessēs VIII[4]	Usimaʿrēʿ-akhenamūn Raʿmesse-Setḥikhopshef-meramūn	—	1134
Ramessēs IX	Neferkarēʿ-setpenrēʿ Raʿmesse-khaʿemwīse-mereramūn	17	1134–1117
Ramessēs X	Khepermaʿrēʿ-setpenrēʿ Raʿmesse-Amenḥikhopshef-meramūn	3	1117–1114
Ramessēs XI	Menmaʿrēʿ-setpenptaḥ Raʿmesse-khaʿemwīse-mereramūn-nūteḥeḳaōn	27	1114–1087

In year 19 of Ramessēs XI began the brief era called 'Repetition of Births', within which Ḥriḥōr, the high-priest of Amen-Rēʿ at Karnak, temporarily arrogated to himself the kingship.

DYN. XX IN MANETHO. Diospolites, 12 kings: A, 'they reigned 135 yrs.'; E, 'they reigned 178 yrs.' No names are given.

[1] Ed. Meyer and others, 1200 B.C.; Rowton, *JEA* xxxiv. 72 places the accession as late as 1170 B.C.

[2] Usimaʿrēʿ- at the beginning of the reign.

[3] Varille, *Karnak* i, Pl. 68 with p. 22.

[4] The order possibly to be interchanged, *Bibl. Or.* xiv. 138.

[5] Doubtful, see *JEA* xi. 72 ff.; xiv. 60.

LATE DYNASTIC PERIOD

TWENTY-FIRST DYNASTY

Conjectural dates, 1087–945 B.C.

MANETHO, here the principal source, names seven kings from Tanis:

Africanus	*Prenomen and Nomen*
Smendēs, 26 yrs.	Ḥedjkheperrēʿ-setpenrēʿ Nesbanebded-meramūn
Psusennēs [I], 46 yrs.[1]	ʿAkheperrēʿ-setpenamūn Psibkhaʿemnē-meramūn
Nephercherēs, 4 yrs.	Neferkarēʿ-ḥeḳawīse[2] Amenemnisu(?)-meramūn
Amenōphthis, 9 yrs.	Usimaʿrē-setpenamūn Amenemope-meramūn
Osochōr, 6 yrs.	unidentified
Psinachēs, 9 yrs.	unidentified
Psusennēs [II], 14 yrs.[3]	Titkheprurēʿ-setpenrēʿ[4] Psibkhaʿemnē-meramūn.

Total as given by Manetho 130 years, but A adds up to 114. To this dynasty doubtless belonged King Siamūn whose names are

Nūtekheperrēʿ-setpenamūn Siamūn-meramūn; highest year-date 17.[5]

For the contemporary high-priests of Amen-Rēʿ at Karnak see above, p. 317, and Gauthier, *LR* iii. 229–85. The dates accompanying them appear to belong to the Tanite kings, but one date of year 48 certainly belongs to the high-priest Menkheper.[6]

[1] So A; E, 41 yrs.
[2] See above, p. 317, but also *Ann. Serv*. xlvii. 207–11.
[3] E, 35 yrs.
[4] Gauthier, *LR* iii. 301, but there assigned to a third Psusennēs.
[5] Op. cit. iii. 294 ff.
[6] Op. cit. iii. 265.

TWENTY-SECOND DYNASTY

Conjectural dates, 945–730 B.C.

MANETHO according to Africanus: Dyn. XXII 'nine kings of Bubastus, (1) Sesōnchis, 21 yrs.; (2) Osorthōn, 15 yrs.; (3, 4, 5) three others, 25 yrs.; (6) Takelōthis, 13 yrs.; (7, 8, 9) three others, 42 yrs.; total, 120 yrs.' Eusebius gives (1) as Sesōnchōsis, then omits (3, 4, 5) and (7, 8, 9), leaving Takelōthis as third and last of the dynasty.

Corresponding to the above on the MONUMENTS:

Name used in this book	*Prenomen and Nomen*	*Highest regnal year*
Shōshenḳ[1] I	(1) Hedjkheperrēʿ-setpenrēʿ Shōshenḳ-meramūn	21
Osorkōn I	(2) Sekhemkheperrēʿ-setpenrēʿ Osorkōn-meramūn	36
Takelōt I	(3) Usimaʿrēʿ Takelōt	7? 23?[2]
Osorkōn II	(4) Usimaʿrēʿ-setpenamūn Osorkōn-meramūn	29
Takelōt II	(5) Hedjkheperrēʿ-setpenrēʿ Takelōt-siēse-meramūn	25[3]
Shōshenḳ III	(6) Usimaʿrēʿ-setpenamūn Shōshenḳ-sibast-meramūn	39
Pemay	(7) Usimaʿrēʿ-setpenamūn Pemay-meramūn	6
Shōshenḳ IV	(8) ʿAkheperrēʿ Shōshenḳ	37

The order of (1)–(4) is confirmed by the stela of Ḥarpson (p. 326), but after Osorkōn I Montet inserts a hitherto unknown

Ḥeḳakheperrēʿ-setpenrēʿ Shōshenḳ-meramūn

whose silver coffin and mummy he found at Tanis.[4] Provisionally this king may be reckoned as Shōshenḳ II in place of the very problematic king previously so numbered[5]—unless indeed he is actually Shōshenḳ I. Takelōt II (5) was the son of Osorkōn II and Shōshenḳ III certainly the successor of Takelōt II. For Shōshenk III's reign of 52 years see above, p. 334.

For the chronology of Dyns. XXII–XXV see Ed. Meyer, *Geschichte des Altertums*², ii. 56 ff.

[1] Thus vocalized in Assyrian rather than Sheshonḳ; the Old Testament gives Shishak wrongly, 1 Kings xiv. 25.

[2] But see Gauthier, *LR* iii. 333, n. 3.

[3] Co-regent with Osorkōn II from the latter's year 23, see B*AR* iv, § 697.

[4] Montet, *Osorkōn II*, p. 11; *Psu.*, pp. 37 ff.

[5] Gauthier, *LR* iii. 350.

TWENTY-THIRD DYNASTY

Conjectural dates, 817?–730 B.C.

MANETHO according to Africanus: 'four kings of Tanis, (1) Petubatēs,[1] 40 yrs.; (2) Osorchō,[2] 8 yrs.; (3) Psammūs, 10 yrs.; Zēt, 31 yrs.; total, 89 yrs.' Eusebius omits Zēt, and gives (1) Petubastis, 25 yrs.; (2) Osorthōn, 9 yrs.; (3) Psammūs, 10 yrs.

The quay inscriptions at Karnak record various dates of King Petubastis, year 23 being the highest; the Prenomen and Nomen are:

Usimaʿrēʿ-setpenamūn Pedubast-meramūn.

The other kings mentioned by Manetho have not been certainly identified in the hieroglyphs. Vandier, *Clio*³, 567 ff., varying slightly the contentions of Ed. Meyer, proposed to place the accession of Petubastis in 817 B.C., which assumes a long overlap with Dyn. XXII. In the interval before the incursion of Piʿankhy (730 B.C.) five kings with short reigns are placed, including two Osorkōns; the quay inscription of year 16 of Petubast makes it contemporary with year 2 of a king Iuputi, whose name recalls that of Iuwapet on the Piʿankhy stela, p. 336.

TWENTY-FOURTH DYNASTY

Conjectural dates, 720–715 B.C.

MANETHO, as above, p. 335, consists only of Bochchōris of Sais, whose father was Technactis according to Plutarch, *De Iside*, ch. 8, and Tnephachthos according to Diodorus I, 45. Reigned 6 yrs. (A), 44 yrs. (E).

Corresponding on the MONUMENTS are:

Shepsesrēʿ Tefnakhte[3]	Sole date, yr. 8
Waḥkarēʿ Bekenrinef[4]	Sole date, yr. 6

See further under Dyn. XXV.

[1] A, 'in his reign the Olympic festival was first celebrated'; the date would then be 776–775 B.C.

[2] A, E, 'the Egyptians call him Hēraclēs'.

[3] Gauthier, *LR* iii. 409.

[4] Op. cit. 410.

TWENTY-FIFTH DYNASTY

MANETHO, 'three Ethiopian kings': (1) Sabacōn,[1] reigned A 8 yrs., E 12 yrs.; (2) Sebichōs, A 14 yrs., E 12 yrs.; (3) Tarcos, A 18 yrs., E Taracos, 20 yrs.

The entire family of six is given below, but the first ruler of all Egypt was Shabako; for the relationships see *JEA* xxxv. 141 ff.

Name used in this book	*Manetho*	*Prenomen and Nomen*	*Highest year-date*	*Conjectural dates* B.C.
(1) Kashta father of (2) and (3)	—	Kashta	—	—
(2) Piʿankhy father of (4) and (5)	—	Usimaʿrēʿ Sneferrēʿ } [2]	21	751–730
[Here intervened Tefnakhte and Bochchōris of Dyn. XXIV, overlapping with (2) and (3) respectively.]				
(3) Shabako brother of (2)	Sabacōn	Neferkarēʿ Waḥibrēʿ } [2] Shabako	15	716–695
(4) Shebitku brother of (5)	Sebichōs	Djedkaurēʿ Menkheperrēʿ } [2] Shebitku	3	695–690
(5) Taharḳa son of (2)	Tarcos	Khunefertēmrēʿ Taharḳa	26	689–664[3]
(6) Tanuatamūn[4] son of (4)	—	Bakarēʿ Tanuatamūn	8	664–656

From about 668 B.C. Taharḳa's rule will have alternated at Memphis with that of Nekō of Sais favoured by the Assyrian kings Esarhaddon and Ashurbanipal.[5]

[1] A, E, 'who taking Bochchōris captive burned him alive'.
[2] For the successive Prenomens see *ZÄS* lxvi. 95–96.
[3] These two dates are certain. [4] Assyrian Urdamane. [5] *ANET*, pp. 294, 297.

TWENTY-SIXTH DYNASTY

MANETHO, 'nine kings of Sais'.

Name used in this book	*Africanus*	*Eusebius*	*Herodotus (ii. 157 ff.) yrs. of reign*
—	—	(1) Ammeris the Ethiopian, 12 yrs.	
—	(1) Stephinatēs, 7 yrs.	(2) Stephinathis, 7 yrs.	
—	(2) Nechepsōs, 6 yrs.	(3) Nechepsōs, 6 yrs.	
Nekō I	(3) Nechaō, 8 yrs.	(4) Nechaō, 8 yrs.	
Psammētichus I	(4) Psammētichos, 54 yrs.	(5) Psammētichos, 45 yrs.	54 yrs.
Nekō II	(5) Nechaō II,[1] 6 yrs.	(6) Nechaō II, 6 yrs.	16 yrs.
Psammētichus II	(6) Psammūthis II, 6 yrs.	(7) Psammūthis II, also called Psammētichos, 17 yrs.	6 yrs.
Apriēs	(7) Uaphris, 19 yrs.[2]	(8) Uaphris, 25 yrs.	25 yrs.
Amasis	(8) Amōsis, 44 yrs.	(9) Amōsis, 42 yrs.	44 yrs.
Psammētichus III	(9) Psammecheritēs, 6 ms.	omits	6 ms.
	Total: 150 yrs. 6 ms.	Total: 163 yrs.	

To the above correspond on the MONUMENTS:

Name used in this book	*Nomen and Prenomen*	*Length of reign from Apis stelae, &c.*	*Dates B.C.*[3]
Nekō I	—	—	—
Psammētichus I	Waḥibrēʿ Psamtek	54	664–610
Nekō II	Weḥemibrēʿ Nekō	15	610–595
Psammētichus II	Neferibrēʿ Psamtek	6	595–589
Apriēs	Ḥaʿaʿibrēʿ Waḥibrēʿ	19	589–570
Amasis	Khnemibrēʿ ʿAḥmose-si-Nēit	44	570–526
Psammētichus III	ʿAnkhkaenrēʿ Psamtek	1	520–525
		Total: 139 yrs.	

[1] A, E, 'he took Jerusalem, and led King Iōachaz captive into Egypt'.

[2] A, E, 'the remnant of the Jews fled to him, when Jerusalem was captured by the Assyrians'.

[3] Parker in *Mitt. Kairo*, xv. 212.

TWENTY-SEVENTH DYNASTY

MANETHO 'eight Persian kings'. Those whose names are found written in Egyptian hieroglyphs are marked with an asterisk.

Africanus	*Eusebius*	*Dates* B.C.
(1) *Cambysēs,[1] 6 yrs.	(1) Cambysēs,[1] 3 yrs.	525–522
	(2) Magi, 7 ms.	
(2) *Darius, s. of Hystaspēs, 36 yrs.	(3) Darius, 36 yrs.	521–486
(3) *Xerxēs the Great, 21 yrs.	(4) Xerxēs, s. of Darius, 21 yrs.	486–466
(4) Artabanos,[2] 7 ms.		
(5) *Artaxerxēs, 41 yrs.	(5) Artaxerxēs Longhand, 40 yrs.	465–424
(6) Xerxēs, 2 ms.	(6) Xerxēs II, 2 ms.	
(7) Sogdianos, 7 ms.	(7) Sogdianos, 7 ms.	
(8) Darius, s. of Xerxēs, 19 yrs.	(8) Darius, s. of Xerxēs, 19 yrs.	424–404
Total: 124 yrs. 4 ms.	Total: 120 yrs. 4 ms.	

Artaxerxēs I never visited Egypt. Nor did Darius II, who seems, however, to have commissioned some building in the temple of Hībis in the Oasis of Khârga.[3] For Artaxerxes II (404–358 B.C.) see pp. 372, 375.

TWENTY-EIGHTH DYNASTY

MANETHO 'Amyrteos (Euseb. -taios) of Sais, 6 yrs.' Date 404–399 B.C. There are no hieroglyphic mentions, but this king is found in both demotic and Aramaic papyri;[4] Greek equivalent Amonortais.

TWENTY-NINTH DYNASTY

MANETHO 'four kings of Mendēs'. Those found on monuments are marked with an asterisk.

Africanus and Eusebius	*Prenomen and Nomen*	*Highest year-date*	*Dates* B.C.
(1) Nepheritēs, 6 yrs.	*(1) — Nefʿaurud	4	399–393
(3)[5] Psammūthis, 1 yr.	*(2) Usirēʿ-setpenptaḥ Pshenmūt	—	[393]
(2) Achōris, 13 yrs.	*(3) Khnemmaʿerēʿ-setpenkhnūm Hakōr	6	393–380
(4) Nepheritēs [II], 4 ms.	(4) — Nefʿaurud (demotic only)	—	—
[(5) Muthis, 1 yr.] Eusebius only and probably never reigned		—	—
Total 20 (21) yrs.			

[1] A, E, 'in the fifth year of his kingship over the Persians became king of Egypt'.
[2] A courtier and murderer of Xerxēs, son of Darius.
[3] Kienitz, p. 73, n. 8. [4] See above, pp. 372–3.
[5] Manetho places Achōris before Psammūthis, see p. 373.

THIRTIETH DYNASTY

MANETHO 'three kings of Sebennytus'.

Name used in this book	*Africanus*	*Prenomen and Nomen*	*Highest year-date*	*Dates* B.C.
Nekhtnebef	Nectanebēs, 18 yrs.	Kheperkarēʿ Nekhtnebef	16	380[1]–363
Teōs or Takhōs	Teōs, 2 yrs.	Irmāʿenrēʿ Djeḥo-setpenanḥūr	—	362–361
Nekhtḥareḥbe	Nectanebos, 18 yrs.	Snedjemibrēʿ-setpenanḥūr Nekhtḥareḥbe	18	360–343
	Total: 38 yrs.			

THIRTY-FIRST DYNASTY

'Three Persian kings.' This dynasty has been added to the genuine Manetho by some later chronographer. The text of Eusebius here given is rather fuller than that of Africanus (A):

'1. Ōchus in the twentieth year of his kingship over the Persians ruled over Egypt 6 years (A 2 yrs.)
2. After whom, Arsēs son of Ōchus, 4 years (A 3 yrs.)
3. After whom, Darius [III], 6 years (A 4 yrs.); whom Alexander of Macedon suppressed.'

Ōchus Artaxerxēs III succeeded his father Artaxerxēs II in 358 B.C., and conquered Egypt in 343 B.C.[2] After Ōchus's murder in 338 B.C. he was succeeded by his youngest son Arsēs, who was himself murdered in 336 B.C. Arsēs was followed by Darius III Codomannus in 335 B.C.[3] Alexander reached Egypt in person at the end of 332 B.C.[4]

[1] Kienitz, pp. 173–5. [2] Loc. cit. [3] Op. cit., p. 110. [4] Op. cit., p. 112.

ADDENDA

P. 26. Instead of the cumbrous Berlin *Wörterbuch* English-speaking students may now be recommended R. O. Faulkner's *Concise Dictionary of Middle Egyptian*, Oxford, 1962.

P. 98. Professor Emery's latest excavations at Buhen (Wâdy Ḥalfa) have revealed the existence there of a copper-working settlement dating from the early Old Kingdom; the names of various kings of Dyns. IV, V were found. The importance of this unexpected discovery is undeniable, but it would be premature to draw far-reaching conclusions.

P. 235. Recently published vases in the Metropolitan Museum of Art and the British Museum name a lady Kyia who is described as 'great beloved wife of' King Akhenaten; see *JEA* xlvii. 29–30. This is the first explicit evidence that the heretic king possessed in addition to his officially recognized queen Nefertiti a concubine who was presumably one of many; for the various wives of Tuthmosis III see p. 195, and for those of Sethos I and Ramessēs II see p. 257.

INDEX

512321